THE WAITING USURPER

A.M. Vivian

Waiting Usurper by A.M. Vivian
Copyright © 2019 A Head

ISBN:978-1-9162168-0-8
Cover designer: Fiona Jayde Media

Published by Walter's Writing Emporium
www.walterswritingemporium.com

E.V.thank you

PART I: KINDLING

Chapter One

THE FLAMES HAD SHOWN ME EVERYTHING exactly as it is now. The dead tangled in heaps across the desolate valley, no longer writhing, no longer screaming, no longer bleeding. Their dried blood like rust splattered over the mud. Despite this knowledge, I still watched the battle unfold. I had to. I had to be a witness for my unborn baby.

From the abandoned cliffs, I saw the shield wall break as bewildered villagers faced enemies charging on horses. Enemies with cloaks billowing like the wings of battle birds. The first smell of fear had seeped into the night. A scramble of sounds followed: swords scraping, axes thudding, arrows hissing, weapons finding their mark, and cries, once arrogant and proud, became full of regret. The echoes have stopped now, and the silence has an ominous presence. For years, we've been fighting our neighbours, the Aralltirs. Pieces of this land have been lost, regained, lost. Again and again and again. And this time, King Onnachild has sacrificed his son, my love, for nothing. I was a child when this conflict started but even then I knew it was a waste of men. Yet the King sleeps with his hopes of victory, just as the villagers do. In that, they are still the same.

I creep from my hiding place though there is no need to; the survivors ran and the dead don't care. One hand covers my nose against the stench of shit, blood, and mud, and the other holds my woollen skirts up from the surrounding carnage as I head towards where my love waits for me. I'll cradle him through one last sunrise; it's my right. He should clasp a lock of my hair in his clenched fist as castle wives do their husbands'. I'll make a crown for him using the trampled grass, and it will rival the daisy one I made him in happier times.

A breeze chills my ankles and bare feet as I step over broken swords, shattered arrows, crushed limbs. When a splinter stabs my toe, I sit on the stump of the Legacy Yew to pull it out. The wind whips my dark hair across my face with the punishment I deserve; I should have made him stay, told him what the fire showed me. He wouldn't have believed me, though. Aelius would have said he couldn't die: he was a king's son.

He did die. First, he fell onto his knees, then his hands, then his face. Even as he dragged himself through the mud, he still wouldn't have believed he could die. I howled his name only for it to be lost in the cacophony of war. Love was not welcome here. How I wished I'd been kinder and not teased him, not made him grin and show his dimple so often the mark remained. I should have given him lines and hard angles so he'd have the face of a warrior. He was too beautiful and too indulged for fighting.

Ravens and eagles circle above the valley, whispering for their spoils of war. I rise; I must reach him before the birds do. And so it is back amongst the dead I go. There's no time to pause and close their eyes. All I can do for them is murmur prayers to gods they no longer believe in. Smoke from smouldering fires mixes with the mist of souls escaping to a better place, where kings don't rule. My breath, a white puff in the morning chill, joins them. To my left, there's movement. Someone's alive. He grabs my foot as I lift it to take another step. His voice is a gurgle. I try to shake him off but he lunges for my skirt, causing me to stumble and almost fall onto a dead horse. I yell at him. I yell an Aegnian curse, kick at him. It makes no difference. He tugs harder. His bloody fingers dig into my thigh. He keeps gurgling words I don't understand as he tries to raise himself up on me. A dagger protrudes from his shoulder, knocking against my hip. Using both hands, I yank it out and I stab him. I stab him for my unborn son. I stab him for all the people his kind killed. And then, when he grabs me no more, I walk on.

My love, my Aelius, is on the outskirts of the battle, alone and special even in death. He's face down, arms splayed as if the ground is his mother. My sob startles me, reminding me I'm alive. I dash over to him, drop onto the frozen ground and gather him up.

There's so little dawn left.

'Stay, stay,' I plead onto his frozen cheek though I know he's gone already; he always was so impatient. 'I'm here. Aelius, it's Niah.' His pale skin is as smooth as a catkin. There's a blue tinge to his lips, and his nose is broken. Mud smudges from him onto me as if I'll be going into battle. Perhaps I will. His promises return: I'd be free of fear, of hunger, of the threats from villagers who said I used the tricks of the Aegni women to entice him. They never realised love is simpler than that.

'Don't forget me.' I press my forehead to his. 'Don't forget how you'd sneak into my hut.' On his skin he'd carry the aroma of castle life: spices and sandalwood. Away from his father's influence, he'd unlace his tunic and take off his boots to be like me. Lying across my lap, he'd twirl my long hair around his ring finger. His blue eyes, as trusting as a baby's, would close and his blond lashes would flutter while I lavished him with kisses, making him giggle until his eyes watered. His eyes will never water again, and his mouth will never make another sound.

I create a fire using wood from arrows and bows, and throw my herbs into its centre: wormwood, sage, fennel, and dried yew berries to call the Aegni women. My ancestors' figures are twisting smoke, denser than the morning mist. Their green eyes are florid dots. I beg them: *Please. Please take Aelius with you; keep him for me so when I die he'll be there waiting. Please. Don't let him go to Onnachild's god.* My tears anoint him.

The horizon stretches red and gold. I can't hold back the sun. My throat hurts as I sing the death song. It's not the perfect tune the official mourners will sing at his funeral. Mine is the song of a real mourner, a real lover, and it's the one he deserves. The village shall know. His father shall know about me and my baby. And I shall have my promises.

'Onnachild will pay for what he's done to you, this land, the Aegni women. For what he's taken from me. I promise that. And I will ... my Aelius, I promise you, I will love you forever.' I place these words on his lips, and with blood, he seals my vows.

Chapter Two

'YOU MUST EAT,' NESSIA SAYS. Her bones creak as she bends to place a wooden bowl beside me on the earthen floor of our hut.

'Yes,' I say and nod, though I must fast for seven days as was customary before Onnachild imposed his new god. My stomach growls. The pain of hunger gives me something else to focus on as I lie on the floor, watching for changes of light across the thatched roof. My love's boots and sword, rescued from the battlefield, rest against the wall, waiting for him to return. Inside the castle, people will be lining up to view his death face, to weep over him. Someone will have cleaned him and changed his clothes. The soot I used to bring him into the Adfyr faith will be gone from his cheeks. He'll look so young.

I don't want to think of him like that, still and stiff. Instead, I picture the undulations of his body, remembering how they'd entice me to grab him, smell him, kiss him. Demanding, he called me, though his grin showed he enjoyed it.

When night comes, Nessia takes away the bowl and throws the contents into the gnarly thicket that separates us from the villagers.

'You must eat,' Nessia says as another dawn arrives. 'For the baby, so he'll grow strong.'

'Yes,' I say. But I want to say no. No, to everything. It doesn't feel like there's a baby inside me. It's as though Aelius never came here, never held me, never teased me. Nothing is real, not even time though the creeping chill of night comes day after day, and winter wants to settle in.

Nessia's calloused hand strokes my cheek. 'I know.'

But she doesn't. She continues: she rises with the sun, she brushes the floor, she poaches, she cooks. Sometimes, when leaves crunch under someone's feet, I catch her cocking her ear towards the door. She expects him to appear like I do. How I fooled you, he'd say, standing in the doorway waiting for adoration.

He doesn't come back.

If only I could call him into the smoke and see his face again. If only I could call my ancestors, but I can't as they must help escort him to his new land, and I don't want him to be unsafe.

'You must eat,' Nessia says.

'Yes,' I say. I yearn to be embraced, to be pulled into arms that will block out everything: the morning sun, the cold, my hunger. I want Aelius to do it. Nessia tries but her arms are too thin and the aged skin yields too much to my grip. She smells of the village. Her greying hair is lank against my face and doesn't tickle.

'A man has been asking about you. A castle man. Stunning he was, like someone went into my dreams and made him.' She smiles, waiting for me to show interest.

I don't.

At night I cry at another day passing without Aelius. Each day makes it more permanent: he isn't coming back. He really isn't coming back. Hunger makes me weak. It brings fitful dreams that are more real than morning is with its sparse bird songs and rustling of villagers heading out to work Onnachild's fields.

'You must eat,' Nessia says.

'Yes,' I say.

She wraps her arms around me, and I rest against her bosom. She cries, and I'm grateful for her tears because mine have dried, as if my eyes are clogged up with mud from the battlefield. When I shiver, she tucks the blanket around my shoulders, but it's not the cold affecting me. It's the dead. They whisper their tales of Onnachild's offences: invasion, famine, murder. The Aegni women visit in these late hours to remind me where I come from: a race of female rulers gifted this land and fire by the gods. Their eyes, green and upturned like mine, flash with the sparks of that first fire, and their dark skin has a burnished red hue. They tell me to be strong, that fate is harsh and never liked by its children. I don't want to see my grandmother and the First Queen. It isn't right that they come when I want Aelius.

'You must eat,' Nessia says, but there's no command left in her voice.

'Yes,' I say because language has deserted me. Even the language my grandmother taught me, the language of the Aegni, has gone. This loss debases me because it makes me like the villagers.

I hear them gossiping as they return from the fields.

'Maybe she won't be so stuck up now,' they say.

'Who'd have her now?'

'Not me,' the men say.

I don't care. I was never meant for a feeble village man.

'You must eat,' Nessia says.

'No,' I say.

The word makes her pause, and she smiles at me. I don't understand why. She pats my head. 'How long left?'

'He's been gone forever.'

She counts on her fingers and then holds up six.

'One left,' I mumble. Surely, I've forgotten how to chew, how to swallow, and my stomach will rebel at the indignation of being forced to continue living. Nessia sits beside me. I nestle against her for comfort and warmth.

'Onnachild's erected a statue of Aelius,' she tells me.

'Where?'

'In the square. The likeness is amazing, everyone says so.'

I struggle to my feet. My head spins. My eyelids flutter.

'Wait until morning,' she says.

I can't wait.

In the statue's shadow is a village girl, hunched over and sobbing. She must have been placed there by the villagers in deference to Onnachild. She stops and swivels to face me. Her expression is one of pity, spiteful pity: I brought this on myself. She takes in my matted hair, my stained dress, and the dirty woollen blanket wrapped around me. I mutter my grandmother's words for strength and the carried sound scares the girl, as I predicted it would. Frantically, she searches around: there's no one but me. She scrambles up and runs away.

Alone now, I step closer to the statue. The gold doesn't catch the winter moonlight the same way my prince's hair did. It looks majestic, a future self he'll never be. The face should be grinning, cheeks plump and dimpled, but instead he's challenging the clouds. I lower myself onto my knees to touch the gold feet. They're hard and flat. The statue has no smell: not of meat cooked in its own fat, not of castle flowers, and not that scent I found in his armpit, behind his knee, and under his hair. It's not him and I can't mourn to a statue. I call out his name to feel it on my lips. My mouth tastes of his blood: copper and bitter.

'If you come back,' I whisper onto the toes, 'I'll be better, kinder. I will. I won't pester you to make me your wife, won't take pleasure from annoying you, even though it makes you look so beautiful ... and I won't call you beautiful again, I won't. I'll call you handsome. If you don't come back ...' I gulp, wrap my arms around the gold ankles. 'I will stop loving you ... I will. I'll make myself forget you, your face, your voice and it will be your own fault and ... to spite you, I will. Aelius ... just come back.'

'He should be begging for your forgiveness, leaving you in this cesspit,' a man says. The voice has a clipped castle accent and my body spasms with unrealistic hope. 'Now, do get up from the dirt.'

'No one tells me what to do.'

'Glad to hear it.'

Chapter Three

AS I TURN TOWARDS THE VOICE, a svelte man, draped in castle finery, steps out from the darkness and into a fuzz of moonlight. He's another statue, one chiselled from silver, because his features are too perfect, too evenly matched, and his white skin is too sleek. He saunters towards me, his blond hair swishing around his slim shoulders. Up close, he's even more arresting. His lips look swollen, almost too large for his angular face. Their down-turned shape and his narrow eyes give him a haughty air as he poses before me.

'Who are you?' I ask.

'Vill Hartnell.' He bows and then presents his hand, palm down like I'm an animal. It's cluttered with silver rings of different shapes and sizes. The nails are clipped, neat, and clean. It isn't the hand of a warrior or a man used to hard work.

'And I should know who that is?'

'Aelius ...' He addresses the statue, shaking his head and tutting. 'You never mentioned me? Well, I suppose you did have more interesting things to occupy your time.'

'You were close to him?'

'You could say I was his adviser, his friend. I assisted him on his nightly jaunts to you.' He wafts out his cloak and draws it up to stop it touching the dirt as he crouches beside me. Moonlight glints across the brooch clasping the edges of his cloak together under his pointy chin. It's a gold hawk: Onnachild's bird. I shuffle back, searching for the quickest escape route.

'Don't be scared,' he says.

'I'm not scared.'

'Of course not. I forget you aren't like the weak castle women, are you, Niah?' He leans closer. 'I'm well aware of who your grandmother was. Who you are.' His self-satisfied smile implies that he's expecting my guard to lower from that confession, but he'll have to wait through many dawns for that. 'We can't talk here.'

'You think I don't know that? I'm not going anywhere with you, though.'

'Wise. Here, perhaps this will persuade you.' He lifts a chunky silver chain out from under his embroidered tunic and leaves it dangling. The

9

green pendant bumps against his chest. He watches it. 'My father's. Go on, take it.'

When I don't move, his fingers fiddle to release the chain from around his long neck. He holds it out towards me, an end wrapped around each forefinger. I reach, tentatively, for the pendant. It's too worn for me to tell if the Aegnian word for fire is there but I can sense my ancestors' presence radiating from it. It's the same charge as in the Legacy Yew. 'A council seal,' he says.

'I know what it is. Why do you have it?'

'It was my father's.'

'You said that. I don't mean that. I mean ... Adfyrism was stamped out. The Aegni women are dead. Onnachild would have you killed for wearing this.'

'And yet I'm still alive.' He puts the necklace back on and then smooths his blond hair. With a flourish, he offers his hand again. 'And you are still alive. There's so much to tell you. But not here.'

Reluctantly, I stand, though I avoid touching him. He mumbles to himself, but then his charming smile returns. 'The church yard?' he suggests.

I nod. As we walk across the village square, his steps shorten and his pace slows to match mine. I'm unsteady on my feet, still weak from hunger, and I find myself leaning on him. We slip in and out of the round shadows the huts make, careful to avoid the mulch tossed out into the narrow passageways.

'What's wrong with these people?' he snaps when he almost slides into a fresh pile steaming in the winter chill. I stifle my amusement as he blocks his nostrils against the stench of it and tuts. A rat, disturbed by the toe of Vill's boots, scurries past and disappears into the shell of the old inn. Bursting from it is the drunken rambling of men huddled around a noxious fire. At traitor's row, Vill ducks to the left but his shoulder still knocks the decomposing feet of a castle man hanging from a hook. The carrion birds have plucked the face raw.

'Lianev.' Vill bows as if they're meeting in the castle hallways. 'Didn't I tell you to be careful when speaking out against Onnachild, even if it was your mine he lost?'

The volume of the drunkards' mumblings rises as though they're answering Vill.

'There are more castle people displeased with Onnachild. Followers too.' His whisper is almost drowned out by the noise of the drunkards.

'Followers?' I stop, forcing him to a standstill. 'Followers?'

His smug smile returns, and he's nodding.

'By the gods, Followers?' My laugh is bitter and short. 'Where were they when my mother starved to death? When Onnachild hanged my grandmother? When the children threw stones at me and tried to drown me?' My fingers run over the dent in my forehead. 'Pledging fealty to Onnachild to save their own hides, that's where they were. So don't talk to me about Followers.'

'I'm glad to see anger in your eyes—reminds me so much of the False Queen's when Onnachild hanged her.' His cold hand cups my chin and tilts my head towards the firelight splaying from the inn.

'Don't.' I jerk away.

'Forgive me. It's just been so long since I've seen eyes like yours.' He saunters off towards the church, his boots scuffing up frost and dirt. I stare up at the castle man, hanging, his belly split and skin turning a black-green. If I want to learn more about the castle then I have no choice but to follow Vill. Whether I'll believe him is a different matter.

He's waiting for me at the graveyard's imposing gates, lounging against them as he plays with his rings. The dance of his white fingers is mesmerising. He glances up at me. 'Ready?'

I nod but don't step forwards. I've not been here since Onnachild's man tried to force me to convert, and the memory of Arnoson's biting hands and grisly smile has me shuddering. The yew tree is a forlorn sight with its boughs stretched low and long, searching for the companions who stood with it before the church was built for Onnachild's second queen.

The click from the gates opening makes me jump.

'After you,' Vill says.

Hitching my blanket up over my shoulders, I step into the grounds. The path is uneven and broken, showing nature asserting its greater authority over Onnachild's god, and that makes me smile.

'Don't you wish we could return to the way things were before Onnachild invaded?' Vill looks back at the church, his nose rumpled and his lips pursed. Its shadow spikes towards rows and rows of gravestones, patchy with lichen and bird droppings. 'I want to bring those days back.'

'And how are you going to do that?' I ask.

'With you.'

My laugh comes out as a snort. Vill's lips pinch together again and he twists the ring on his index finger around. 'If I may.' He smiles but I'm not sure if it's real because his eyes don't crinkle at the edges.

I nod. He ushers me further into the graveyard, stopping by Arnoson's headstone.

'You're the last Aegni woman. The last of the first rulers.' He draws me around to face him, takes both my hands in his. The white of his skin glows compared to the brown of mine. 'You're too young to remember, but your grandmother must have told you about the Golden Years when the Aegni women ruled. Food was plentiful. The land was abundant and lush. The Aralltir were our allies.' He doesn't look much older than me, though, and so I don't trust his recollections. 'No? How about before Onnachild married that second queen, the True Queen as we're meant to call her. Before ... ' With a flick of his wrist, he gestures towards the church. 'Shut your eyes. Go on. That memory must be inside you.'

12

But it's too painful to remember when my grandmother was alive and so my eyes remain open. His sparkle like jewels. The pale-blue irises are almost violet in the moonlight.

'The bouquet of meadows, yew forests, overripe fruit returning to the earth because there was too much for us to pick and we were too full. Fields so plentiful and plush they waved for our attention. The sun warming your face. And colours, do you remember the colours that used to be here? The flowers? I do. Don't you want those things back?' he asks.

'I want to live.'

'Is this living? Here? Hunger? Fear of what the villagers might do to you? Fear you're going to starve like your mother did? I know the villagers chase you from the fields. I know you have no land of your own anymore. Within the castle walls are all the things Aelius promised you. Finery you can't imagine: velvets, silks, lace. All the hare you can eat—venison, pork, and boar too.'

I snatch back my hands. 'They're the dreams of a child.'

'Not dreams. With the support of the right people—'

'Why now?'

'That's a fair question, I suppose.' He brushes a leaf off the arch of the headstone and then perches against it. His slim legs stretch out and cross at the ankles. He taps the space beside him.

I cross my arms and shake my head.

'What? This man doesn't deserve your respect, does he? Arnoson Martison.' One of his elegant fingers trails over the name. '*Keeper of the new faith.* It should read traitor, murderer. What do you care for the bones of a traitor?'

'Nothing.' My feet rub over the gritty mud, and I can't help picturing my grandmother's dirty soles swaying as Arnoson hanged her for refusing to denounce Adfyrism. I, too, am swaying and there's nothing to steady myself with, nothing but the headstone. It's slimy beneath my palm.

'I appreciate it may be sudden to you, but I have been working in the background. I was relying on you, as Aelius's wife, as his queen to persuade Aelius to restore Adfyrism. The old tales enthralled him. You enthralled him, I made sure of that. But with him ... shall we say ... gone ... he can't make you queen. And so we need to ... exploit certain situations. The merchants are tired of these costly wars and continually loaning money on the promise of victory. Yet we have no victories. The castle men are sick of being ruled by a tyrant. The King is weak, and a weak king is easy to deceive.'

'He's weak?'

Vill nods and smiles, seeming to take my question is a sign of agreement. 'Insensible with grief, crying for all he has lost. He's even called back his first son, suddenly remembering he has one. Well, back that son may be, but loved he isn't.'

I spit on my palm and then wipe it clean on my dress. 'Aelius didn't have a brother.'

'You don't remember Raen? Who his mother is? That adulterous False Queen. Please don't look at me like that; I only say what they call her in the castle, and you'll have to endure much more than that once you join me there.' His gaze lowers to my belly. 'You can earn the King's trust by giving him something no one else can: a piece of his son.'

I pull my blanket tighter around me. 'I'm not giving Onnachild anything.' I glare up at the sky, the clouds jagged and grey like the cliffs we used to own before Onnachild lost them to Aralltir. 'He's taken enough of mine.'

'A travesty and I fully intend to make it up to you, if you will let me. Please understand, we've had problems of our own. Why do you think Onnachild continues with these battles? It isn't just pride.' He moves closer, so close that his cloak brushes my wrist. The lining is the softest fur. I grip my blanket to stop my fingers reaching for another touch.

'There are more of us in Aralltir. They're waiting for you: the last Aegni woman returned to the castle, ready to restore peace, prosperity, and Adfyrism. I'm waiting for you. For you to say yes. Say yes and I'll take you to the castle. Say yes, and I'll convince the merchants to support us, the Followers to return. Together we can overthrow Onnachild. Say yes and I will help you become queen.' His lips quirk. 'Queen Niah. How does that sound?'

His tone is lulling and the words are tempting with the punch of the Q, the elongated vowels, and my name so much more enchanting when spoken with a castle accent. His smile shows teeth as white as the jewels I always dreamt of wearing. The combination almost convinces me that I could, that I should. I force my attention away from him, and out beyond the church to the forgotten graves where I scattered my grandmother's ashes, where she scattered the First Queen's ashes. That False Queen, as Vill called her, was Aegnian like I am and she went into the castle. She went in as Onnachild's bride, a gift to bind native and invader, and Onnachild murdered her so he could marry his foreign whore. I imagine my son disturbing the dust to find a trace of me once Onnachild has killed me too.

A breeze carries the perfume of the castle from Vill to me, and I shiver.

'I saw you on the battlefield,' he says.

'You were there?'

'I couldn't save Aelius. But I can save you … if you say yes.'

But I have survived without his help, without the castle, and I have done this by remaining hidden from Onnachild. Vill grips my shoulders. 'You owe it to Aelius. You owe it to your child.' His voice rises. 'You owe it to your ancestors.'

'I owe it to my child to live.'

'What about revenge then? Do it for revenge.'

How familiar that emotion is, like an often-patched blanket covering all hurts and pains. I think back to the day the final pieces were stitched together. Villagers dragged my grandmother from our hut. Her feet scrabbled in the mud. Her dress rode up. Men, women, children shouted, laughed, clapped as Arnoson carried out Onnachild's orders. Nessia and I hid in the bushes. The prickles had dug into my arm, making my skin itch.

I scratch my arm, and as I do, fear swells from my guts as strong as it was that day. Nessia had to hold me back, clasping her hand over my mouth to stop me from screaming curses at them. Later, she cut my grandmother down, staggering when the body dropped into her arms. All I've wanted since that moment was to make Onnachild pay—the desire is stronger than any other emotion, even love. 'The villagers won't accept me.'

'We'll make them.' Vill's fingertips dig into my shoulder. 'Say yes.'

Yet as I keep staring at the forgotten graves, I can't. The promises I made on the battlefield return and have me bristling at my cowardice. But it was easy to make such vows when I held Aelius, when it seemed I'd already crossed into the land of the dead. My hand curves around my belly, heavy with new life. I have something, someone, to live for: my son. Besides, Vill told me there are Followers of Adfyrism. I could go to Aralltir and live there, live without fear. That is if I believe him. Do I?

I shake my head. 'No.'

'You'll change your mind.'

I watch him saunter off and in the moonlight he looks like a memorial come to life.

Chapter Four

THE VILLAGERS HAVE GATHERED by the statue for the funeral procession: stunted children with snotty noses and chapped lips, women with sleeves black as burnt fields, and men bent from defeat. The groans of hungry bellies add an underlying dirge to their chatter. Nessia and I huddle together, our dresses still damp from her trying to dye them last night. The wool hasn't fully taken the colour and so they're as patchy as the winter sky.

'You've some nerve coming here, you hedge-born heathen,' a woman snarls at me, yanking her gangly daughter away.

'You not dead yet?' a stringy man snipes. His wife kicks me in the shin with her bare and muddy foot. A laugh turns into a hacking cough. Their gaunt son jostles me and Nessia, pushing us to the edge of the gathering. 'Here. Here's another one of them fire-fuckers,' he calls out.

I hiss my grandmother's words at him. His face blanches, and he barges his way into the thick of the crowd to hide. I straighten my shoulders, lift my chin, and focus on the procession. At the front is Aelius's coffin, his momentary chance to lead at last. The surface has been buffed and shined to show off the golden threads in the laburnum. Surely, it's far too small to contain his body? The white horses bearing his weight are eager to move, churning up dust and dirtying their legs as they fidget. Onnachild is next, proud and corpulent on a black stallion. He's bulked out in dark fur the same colour as his hair and eyes. He doesn't appear weak or overcome by grief as he stares out, ignoring the villagers' awe-filled gapes. I'm glad I didn't believe Vill.

'A real ruler wouldn't keep sending men to their death,' Nessia moans.

Onnachild is flanked by two grey men who are as watchful and thin as starved wolves. The castle people are behind, each one blond and white-skinned. The weak sun tries to glint off them and the jewels displayed against black clothes, but the people don't need its help to dazzle. Vill is amongst them, poised and perfect. He turns his head left, right, and left again, searching the crowd until he spots me. There's no recognition in his face when our eyes meet. Hopefully, that's a sign he won't seek me out and

17

try to change my mind.

'That him?' Nessia asks. It's not Vill she's pointing at though; it's the man next to him. One who is stockier and taller than the castle men surrounding him. Compared to them he's an ancient oak in a forest of saplings. His colours are vivid against their paleness: honey-coloured skin, dark hair with mahogany tones loose around his broad shoulders, and eyes a deep brown. He doesn't belong with the castle people, bred for beauty and dancing, but down here with us who toil and feel the mud between our toes.

'Raen,' Nessia mumbles in my ear.

'Must be.'

The young women are whispering, appreciatively, about the size of his thighs encased in breeches instead of baggy hose like the village men wear. His hair sweeps across his wide shoulders as he surveys the square, the people gathered, and then raises his head to peer up at the statue. What he sees makes him frown. The wind blows a lock of hair over his face but he doesn't brush it away.

At the command of the wolfish men, the procession moves and, like an afterthought, the villagers tag along. Together, Nessia and I struggle through the crowd, pushing and ducking to get nearer to Aelius. The village men have a desire for revenge set in the lines of their faces, forgetting the fear that made them run.

Sons grumble insults: 'Thieving cross-eyed limp-dicked pig-riding Aralltirs.'

Shuffling footsteps are in time with the steady boom of the castle drums but they have none of the power. The village women clutch at their clothes as they groan death songs that are drowned out by the crisp voices of the official mourners. Nessia sings along with tears in her eyes. I've already sung my song.

The procession leads us to the church where it's as misty as the battlefield was, giving the place a nightmarish echo. The air is thick and damp, carrying a sickly blend of decaying leaves and out-of-season flowers. As I enter the gates, Nessia's fingers slip from mine.

Fresh humps dot the graveyard like the shells of beetles. The castle people are dismounting their horses and merging into a blur of black and white. I elbow my way through them, startled when they tut because I feel as insubstantial as a spirit. I'm not sure I'm even breathing. Deeper I go amongst the shafts of light and shadow their bodies create, pushing against their satin, their furs, their silk, until ... until ...

Before me is a gaping hole in the ground, a headstone new and pale. My stomach lurches and my heart hurts as I read Aelius's name, the date of his birth, and the date of his death. But he doesn't belong there, not in the mud, not in the dark. He's as golden as the sun. A wailing cuts through the harmony of the mourners' song.

It's me. I try to stop but I can't. Onto my knees I fall. Onto the mud, churned up by horses just as the battlefield was. A woman gasps. The taste of Aelius's blood is in my mouth. Rain starts, thin, quick drops. The sky has darkened and thunder rumbles as though it's competing with me. I can't stop my body from heaving as I claw at the mud, needing to clasp something solid, but it oozes through my fingers. Snot and tears mix with the rain on my face. I'm gasping, head turned skywards as if I can call him back.

'For the love of God, help her.' Has the voice come from the earth? It's deep enough, gruff like it's made of stones. Lightning brightens the sky; the gods are angry because Aelius's body should be given to them in fire. An arm goes around my waist and sweeps me up into the air. My legs kick out. I must stay close to the earth, to where my love is going. Another arm reaches around me, and I'm pulled under the shelter of the last yew, the branches scraping across my skin.

The man holding me curses when his back jolts against the trunk and

19

he almost drops me. He sits and settles me in his lap like I'm a child, then he takes off his cloak and covers my head with it to keep me dry. 'Shhh ... shhh ... shhh.' The sound mimics the whisper of a tree. He rocks me. He strokes my back with sweeps as languid as those shhhs. His scent is soothing: fresh sap, autumn forests, and castle life. I take deep gulps of it as I cling to him; he's solid and broad, everything the mud wasn't. Warmth emanates from him like a well-established hearth fire. I yawn onto his chest.

He hums a song my grandmother used to sing, one I've not heard since childhood, and it piques my curiosity so I ease the cloak off my head. Rain drops onto my forehead as I lean back and its chill tingles. His arms tense to bear my weight but his eyes remain fixed over my head, staring off into the distance as though he's lost in a daydream. Under his left eye is a scar shaped like a drop of rain and I almost try brushing it away. His gaze lowers, first to my hand hovering near his cheek and then to meet mine. Raen.

His parents have left their marks in the colours of his eyes: conker brown with three green dots in both. The same green as mine. The same green as his mother's, only the colour shouldn't pass from mother to son. I crane my neck up, lean in to take a better look. He seems as bewildered as I am, with his forehead furrowing as he hunches closer. The shape of his eyes is so similar to Aelius's, but that is the only similarity because Raen's lashes are darker and thicker, the eyebrows heavier, and his eyes deeper set. There's pain in them, an uncertainty. He blinks and his emotions vanish.

'What's your name?' His accent is strange: a hint of the village, the castle, and somewhere else, somewhere I can't place.

'Niah.'

'Ah, so you're Niah. It makes sense now.' He shifts beneath me. 'I'm sure your little display will have been noted.'

'Display?'

He shoves me from his lap and I bump onto the damp ground, dragging his cloak with me.

'Yes, display.'

'I love him.'

'Of course you do. They all do. Look at them there.' He points towards the castle people but his scowl remains fixed on me. 'And now, they must pretend to love me. You know who I am?'

I nod, words lost at his sudden change from kindness to disgust.

'Good. With the way things have turned out I bet Onnachild's glad he didn't kill me, but I doubt you'd agree. It would make things easier for you if I was dead, wouldn't it?' The green in his eyes is vibrant. His breath is hot on my nose. 'Well, I'm back, the second-best son ... the forgotten son ... the disowned son, take your pick. I won't be those things for long. Trust me, I mean to have everything that was Aelius's.'

'He promised it to me,' I manage to spit out.

'I'm sure he did, but it wasn't his to promise.' Then he's standing, looming over me. A sardonic smile is on his face. 'Don't worry, I'll leave you something for your pains.' He chucks his purse at me.

'I don't care about coins,' I say, though I know I'll snatch up that purse the moment he's gone.

'We'll see. It's a hard life for a dead prince's whore, even if she is with child.'

Whore. The word prickles like a thistle in the foot, and I go to defend myself, throw his cloak back at him, only he seems to want that reaction, and so instead I stifle it, swallow his insult. After all, it's no different to those the villagers throw my way. Inwardly though, I curse him in both the languages I know.

As he marches away, I hear a village man warn him, 'You want to be careful of that one, suck your soul out she will.'

Chapter Five

THE PASSAGE OF TIME CAN BE MEASURED by the changes to my body: belly and breasts swelling, my face rounding, and my irises which Nessia says have gone as dark as damp moss. Little else has changed and I'm impatient for it to. Every morning I linger by the battlefield and stare out at Aralltir, my arms cradling my heavy belly. I rock back and forth on my heels with the winter wind as it howls AE-LI-US, AE-LI-US through the valley. The sun shines yellower over Aralltir, and I imagine another woman there, standing as I do, expecting me. She resembles my mother, though I'm not sure I really remember my mother's face. Her hair was lighter than mine and her eyes more hazel than green, I think. The cold wind numbs my cheeks and makes my nose run but I don't turn away. *We'll find safety there*, I tell my baby. I repeat this to Nessia when she returns, a poached hare draped over her shoulder.

'What are you most looking forward to?' I ask her. 'When we get to Aralltir?'

'Seeing the sea again, watching the ships come in with tasty things to eat.' She butts my shoulder with hers. 'Getting fat. So many things. Watching you become the artisan you wanted to be when you were a little girl.'

I smile as I remember carving disjointed shapes into my grandmother's chairs and table and trunk. They were meant to be phoenixes, the gods, Aegnian letters over-spilling with berries. 'We can keep bees again?' I ask.

'We can keep bees if that's what you want.' She settles the hare over my shoulder and then plods off to scavenge for wood.

While she's occupied, I wander to the jagged shadow of the castle and stare up at it. The black towers jab into the grey clouds, which never move or change shape. I wear Aelius's boots and the ground beneath the soles is crisp with frost. My toes wiggle to find the dents his left. I gather Raen's cloak under my chin with one hand. The pin of the hawk brooch digs into my neck. My other hand brushes up the soft fur lining, and I can't help daydreaming about being in the castle. The spirits I might see. Aelius. My stomach rumbles as I imagine the food Vill mentioned.

My dreams are haunted by his face, even more like chiselled silver, and in them I say yes to him. The ancient forests have returned and I'm encircled by yews, our gift from the gods. My dress is green velvet as lush as a summer meadow, though it smells of decay and the taste of it coats my back teeth. Around me are mirrors. Reflected in one I see myself, lean and hungry, eyes weary and narrowed. In another, I'm the First Queen, mature and stately with an expression that gives nothing away. In another, I'm my grandmother, hair streaked with grey and eyes lacklustre. Another, I'm my mother, the image faded as if water has tarnished the mirror. Every morning when I wake, I grab Nessia and make her tell me my name.

'Do you think he'll return? Vill, I mean,' I ask her when she comes to lead me home.

'What does it matter if he does?' She smiles at me. 'We're going to Aralltir once the baby's born, aren't we?'

'Do you think I was right to say no?'

'It wasn't an easy decision.'

'That's not an answer.'

She tips some logs from her arms into mine. Bark catches in the cloak's material and releases an intoxicating earthy scent. 'I don't know what answer to give. I wish I did.'

'I thought Aelius would be able to keep us safe.' I whisper the words towards the wood because speaking them seems a betrayal. 'But he's gone, and I can't help thinking ... I can't help thinking he was right. Raen.'

'It's always a hard life here.'

'But will it be easier in Aralltir? They might have the same land laws, the same hatred of the Aegni.'

'They might.'

'You think I should have said yes?'

'I didn't say that.'

She turns me around and we trudge home, my gaze drifting over my shoulder to the castle.

This dream is different. In it I'm becoming part of the forest, twisting with the creeping vines up trunks, across boughs, delving deep into the ground with the roots where it's warm and moist. Red berries burst against my cheeks. My scent is one of sensual excitement and it mixes so erotically with the forest's own musk.

When I wake the perfume is there in the crook of my arm, and I breathe deeply to take it into my body, that sensation of comfort, of calm. Beside me, Nessia stirs and her bones creak. My son fidgets, making me groan. She reaches around, stained fingers fanned, and tests my belly. 'It'll be today. Gods willing.'

'And then we can leave.'

She nods. 'And then we can leave. But, I've been thinking ...'

'Go on.'

'Why didn't your grandmother tell us? Why not mention the Followers and ... why didn't she leave?'

'You don't believe Vill?'

'Do you?'

'I want to.'

She nods again as she removes her hands. 'We'll leave if that's what you wish.'

I nestle into the blanket and cloak where it's still warm and the aroma of my dream has mixed with the hint of castle in the fur lining. Nessia starts the day, throwing together pottage and then placing the pan over the fire in the centre of our hut. A stabbing pain comes, once, deep between my hips. I moan.

'How long will it take before he's born?' I ask once the pain has passed.

'Baby will be here as soon as he's ready, no sooner, no later; it's the way they assert their authority.' Nessia returns to comfort me with a pat of my head. 'Your own birth was easy and quick. All your ancestors had good birthing hips.'

'That was twenty-odd years ago—how can you remember that?'

'That's what happens as you get older; the past is easier to remember than yesterday.'

'Yesterday was the past, too.'

'True.' Her lips quirk. 'Here.' She gestures towards some reeds she has brushed into a corner. 'It will collect the birthing liquid.'

I nod, push aside the blanket and cloak, and use the wall to leverage myself up. Nessia guides me to the reeds and eases me onto them before removing the pan of pottage and adding one of water. The odour of food is sickening this morning and I turn my head when she offers me some.

'It may be a long day,' she warns, but I notice she doesn't eat either. The pan remains there, emitting a tangy steam. She opens the door and leans out to check the weather. 'The sky is the same blue as Aelius's eyes. It's a good omen.'

'Let me see.' I struggle up, desperate to see something like him. It's a relief to be off those scratchy reeds. Nessia holds the door open for me and I duck under her arm.

'You're right,' I say. The sun has risen early, and it reflects off his statue, creating patches of light across the village that show his approval. 'I hope our child has eyes the exact same shade.' My hand caresses my belly as I speak to my son. 'I can't wait to see what you look like.' At the sound of my voice, he causes a deep spasm, and I crouch there until the pain passes.

Nessia squeezes my shoulder then she returns to the fire, throwing a

25

bundle of white sage into it to chase away evil spirits. The scent fills the hut, calming, and making me yawn. I whisper my love's name so low only my unborn child and I can hear it. Soon, there'll be a part of Aelius alive again; the thought helps me to bear the pain.

'Are the spasms getting nearer?' Nessia asks.

'Yes.' I rest my cheek against the door, enjoying the air cooling my skin. Even my palms are sweating. My thoughts drift to the mothers who never got to hold their baby, terrifying me with all the things that could go wrong: baby the wrong way, baby malformed, bright-yellow skin, pale-blue skin. Tears come. Nessia rushes to my side. I grab her rough hand. 'What if something's wrong?'

'Baby will be fine.' She strokes my hair from my clammy forehead, tucks it behind my ears and down the neck of my nightdress. 'He's meant to be born, and you're meant to survive. It's fate. Why else did Aelius come to you, love you, if not to give you a child? So dry your tears.' She dabs my cheeks with her sleeve. 'The gods wouldn't have it any other way. Your ancestors won't let it. Today is a happy day.' She kisses my cheek. 'Do you remember the chant?'

I nod and recite it like a good girl as she leads me to the reeds. The words match the pulse of pain spreading to my lower back, into my thighs. I concentrate on the twitching of my belly, counting between the spasms, counting how long they last. There's a strange popping sensation inside, my eyes widen, and liquid trickles down my leg. It's less than I expected but it doesn't seem to faze Nessia, who looks up from beside the fire and smiles at the straw-coloured stain on my nightdress. 'Baby will be on his way.'

My son can't wait; I can't wait. My skin is tighter. My belly is heavier. The urge to bear down is growing and I fidget there, scattering the reeds across the floor. I kneel, struggle onto all fours, the tip of a reed digs into my palm, and pant. It feels good to pant. In more prosperous times, I saw animals give birth: cows, pigs, and even a horse. They were quick. They made it look easy.

I stand. I waddle. I sit. Kneel. Crouch. Nothing helps the pain. Nessia takes up the chant as she washes her hands and then me. She lifts my nightdress and checks me again. 'Not long now.'

It's impossible to remain quiet, but I don't care if the whole village hears me. I mew and growl. *Please.* I plead to the gods, to my ancestors, to my love. *Give me the strength.* Aelius's scent wafts throughout the hut, and my grandmother's features appear in the fire's smoke. My head rises. My lungs open. I take a deep breath before pushing, pushing down long and hard. Once. Twice against the pain between my hips, between my thighs. Does my child mean to split me in two? My face screws up with the effort. I expect to hear a rip. This is my punishment. My punishment for catching a prince, for thinking I could birth a future king. The spasms don't get easier to bear. My legs tremble. My head lolls against Nessia's chest. She dabs at my forehead with a warm, wet cloth as she hums songs from my childhood. I moan at her, push her away when she tries to check the progress of my baby.

I want to see my son.

'Push. Push,' she urges.

I do. I do.

His head slides out, then his shoulders, slowly; he's commanding all the time in the world. Then, at last, he's fully out, and I'm breathless from the effort. Nessia holds him and she's laughing. I laugh too.

'You've done it.'

'We've done it.'

He doesn't join in with our noise. My heart drops. I feel sick. *Please.* Nessia doesn't look worried. The fire crackles. A goldfinch sings; isn't it too soon for him to be back?

My son cries, finally, and it's the most beautiful sound I've ever heard, more beautiful than any bird song, more beautiful than Aelius whispering my name. Nessia wraps a thin fur around my son and places him on my chest. He's far too small, too delicate for me to keep safe from the villagers, from Onnachild, from hunger. His face is scrunched up with indignation at the world he finds himself in—maybe it's the smell of the pottage— and that makes me chuckle as I run a finger over his damp, red skin. It will fade to pink and there will be no trace of the village. His eyes are a cloudy blue, unfocused, and he has a thin patch of wet hair that will be blond when it dries.

'Niah ...' Nessia crouches beside me.

I don't like the hesitation in her voice. My baby's face shows no sign of disfavour. He has ten chubby toes and ten chubby fingers, and his grip is strong. Already his lips are pursing for my nipple. 'What? What is it? What's wrong?'

She lifts a corner of the fur. 'He is a she.'

'Is that all? It's perfect. A girl. A queen. It'll go from me to her as it did in the Golden Years when the Aegni ruled. As it should.'

Nessia's index finger tickles over my baby's cheek. 'But we'll not be here.'

Chapter Six

SOMEONE HAS LAID PURPLE AND GOLD FLOWERS on Aelius's grave, flowers so bright and luscious they must have come from the castle. Their perfume is delicate in the still night. Bound against my chest is my daughter, and clutched under my arm is a bundle of birch wood which Nessia and I saved for this occasion. I drop the twigs onto his grave, and then caress the mound, imagining it is his chest beneath my palm and that the slight shift of mud is his twitching response.

'Are you ready to see your daughter?' I say onto his headstone.

It's difficult to coax a fire in this dampness. It starts as a flickering flame that teases and toys with me, darting up and then shrinking. I'd chastise it for threatening to go out only I'm too happy. Keeping my daughter pressed to my breast, I murmur my ancestors' words into the flames. With me is a bag of ground herbs: lemon balm, yew berries, rosemary, and wormwood. I put a small clump of the herbs into my baby's tiny hand, close mine around hers, and together we trickle them into the fire. It consumes the offering with a joyful crackle. Blue and green licks curl together as the smoke sweetens.

'Now wish for your father, wish really hard and he'll come for you.'

I picture him lying on my floor with his hair splayed out like shavings of gold. A waft of smoke tickles my cheek; he's here. My heart speeds, swells. I crane my neck. Above us, next to the half-moon, smoke is collecting and darkening to create his features. The oval outline of his face ripples and stretches. I want to reach out, clutch at the intangible smoke, and grab a piece to keep with me always. Instead I hug our daughter, my living, breathing part of him. Smoke splutters from his mouth when he tries to talk. I lean closer to the fire but only hear the wood burning. The image contracts into a ball. It spins, getting denser and darker.

'Aelius!' I scrub away my tears with the edge of my cloak but more come. They're ruining my vision. 'By the gods, Niah, concentrate. Concentrate.' I inhale deeply, pulling in the smoke, and holding it until my chest hurts. Then I exhale through pursed lips. My daughter tugs the ends of my hair. 'Please.' My voice trembles. 'Please.' The ball is still spinning, spinning, spewing out wisps as it tries. 'Trying isn't good enough. Try harder. Please. It's our daughter's naming day. She wants to see you.' The dead can't be called with guilt, I know this, but I keep pressing him. 'Aelius, I need to see you. I miss you. You can't let us down.'

Desperately, I blow on the fire, lob more wood, more herbs at it until the flame is almost smothered. *Please. Please.*

'Don't cry.' My grandmother's voice comes from between the fire's crackles.

'Then make him come. Make him. I miss him. I want him. Help. Please? Can't you?'

A great plume of smoke spurts out from the fire, blocking the moon. It thins, curves, bulges, ripples until his features emerge: each blond eyelash, the dimple in his cheek, his eyes full of sky. He's grinning, proud of himself, as he looks down at us. He puffs out smoke and our daughter tries to catch it, but she's too late and so he puffs more. The balls turn in the drizzle, taking on the glint of falling stars. They settle on my face, damp as a kiss from an open mouth. My daughter's blanket collects beads.

Then he's gone.

'What happened to me?' His voice comes from the fire. A gold spark leaps out, dies on the wet mud of his grave.

'You—'

'But ... But ... I don't understand. I remember ...' The pitch of his voice rises, almost breaks. 'Everything white, the sky, the ground blinding like when someone holds a candle too close to my face. I shouldn't have been scared ... but I was. I wanted you. And I saw myself, and I was ... muddy ... blood ... and you, you were there.'

'I will always—'

'And we have a daughter? I don't understand the future. I don't understand now. I was meant to be king, wasn't I?'

'Yes, my love. Yes, you were meant to be king.'

'But I'm not. She'll have it, the throne. Make sure, to you and then her. My daughter. You promise. You will, I know you will.'

'How?' The fire crackles but gives no answer. 'Whatever you want. Please, just tell me how.' I lean closer. My breath worries the flames.

Nothing.

'How?'

No answer. No voice. No smoke.

'Aelius, tell me, how?'

Still, there's no answer. My daughter and I are alone in the graveyard, alone amongst the dead. I could kick the fire for not doing my bidding, for leaving him still afraid. I grab those garish flowers and smash them against his headstone, sending petals flying, splitting stems. Our daughter cries.

'Calm. Calm,' my grandmother says, though she doesn't appear. The fire is dying, losing its battle against the thickening drizzle. 'Think of your daughter.'

Ashamed, I free my breast, and my daughter feeds.

'What name have you given her?' my grandmother asks.

'Ammi.' My voice sounds thick and sulky. 'For you.'

'He tells me he likes it.'

'He does?'

One last plume bursts from the fire and within it comes the First Queen, her cheekbones high grey traces and her chin a soft curve. The crown she wears sheds soot, which breaks when it reaches the ground.

'Why is she here?' I ask. 'I want Aelius.'

'She's come to see,' my grandmother says.

Then both women are gone, and the flames die so there's nothing but a pile of white and black that reminds me of the castle people gathered here when Aelius was buried. I press my cheek against his headstone and sob.

A bird calls out, heralding a new day. Its sound draws my attention out of the graveyard and to the mountains beyond, welcoming with the dawning sun between their edges. Beyond them is a safe, comfortable life if Vill is right and Followers are there. I should have asked my grandmother.

Villagers are leaving their homes, gathering together with grumbles, to start their walk out for another day of toil in Onnachild's fields. I frown as

I pull my cloak over my head and tuck it around Ammi. Hopefully, we'll pass for a shadow as we slip out from the graveyard. It's only the ache in my heart that tells me I'm not.

Children are not so easy to fool though, and they halt, stare at us, even as their parents try to chivvy them along. 'Oh, it's just Niah,' a boy huffs.

A mother pushes her child behind her, but the dirty face tilts out to keep watch.

'Just like her mother,' a woman says as she scrutinises me and clutches her murky rags to her bony chest. Her cheeks are red and chapped from the wind-chill in the fields.

'They always are,' another says.

'Show us the bastard.'

'A bastard of a bastard will never bring us any luck.'

They swarm together, a clump of brown and grey, their voices low—they're plotting. Every creak, twitch, scuffle goes right through me. My legs shake. I should run but I'm frozen to the spot, a child again.

'Is it really the Prince's?' a small girl asks as she tiptoes from the huddle. Her mother yanks her back.

'Don't be simple; what would a prince be doing with Niah?'

'I saw him.'

The mad hag approaches me, broom still in her hand and pale dust on her skin from her never-ending task of sweeping the path to her hut. I tense my legs to stop the shaking and force my gaze to meet hers. A balding man lumbers over, dragging his wasted leg behind him. 'My wife'll never forgive me if I don't get a peep.'

'Does it have the mark of lust?' The woman's breath smells of decaying teeth. I flinch away when she tries to hook a finger under Ammi's covering, and my arms tighten around my baby. Ammi sleeps on, peaceful and oblivious for now.

'It's simple. It doesn't wake. Look, simple like its mother,' the man shouts to the villagers behind him.

The crowd edge nearer. Their words come back: *run, run heathen bastard. Run, run as fast as you can.* My mouth fills with the taste of stagnant river and my sweat is as cold. I will not retreat. We belong here, Ammi and I. The villagers can't hear how fast my heart is pounding. *Please, protect me*, I pray to the gods. *I can fight one villager but not all of them.*

'Do right by the child,' the hag says. 'Give her to us. We'll save her from you.'

'Never.'

'Then don't expect our kindness anymore.'

Over her shoulder, I spot Nessia rushing to save me. Aelius's sword reflecting the dawn light as she drags it behind her. Seeing her gives me the courage to square my shoulders and draw up to my full height. 'Kindness? You've tried to drown me, stone me. You tried to burn down my hut with me in it. I'm not even allowed to work in the fields. So tell me, when have I ever had your kindness?'

She shakes her head implying I'm the mad one, when everyone knows she's never been the same since she lost her son. 'We tried to keep you from them fire beasts, hasn't worked has it. You get that child in the true religion before evil gets in it as it has you.' She leans closer, swishing her broom over my feet. The bristles scratch my toes but I will not move. I will not. 'And keep your castle men away. We don't want them here with their prying.'

Ammi wakes with a scream. Startled, the pair jump back and scurry to the others.

'You wait,' I yell. 'You wait until I'm riding through this village on my fine horse in the King's procession.' Whether they can hear me over Ammi, I don't know.

Nessia's beside me, out of breath, Aelius's sword between us. Her hazel eyes are as defiant and challenging as mine must be. The crowd is bored though, turning to start their trudge towards the fields, and the hag goes back to sweeping her path. I rock Ammi, stroking her cheeks to calm her. They're the same colour as my love's were: a rose blush. Gazing up at me, she's as trusting and as sure of her fate as he was.

'The castle is where Ammi belongs.' I glare at the misshapen silhouettes of the villagers. 'She should be in silks and velvets. And we should be ruling over all of them. We shouldn't be running scared or, worse, ashamed. The Aegni settled this land and I'm Aegnian. It's hers. It's mine. And so is that castle. Tonight, I will walk right up there, knock on that wall, and demand my place, her place. Tonight.'

'We're not going to Aralltir, then?'

'My grandmother never ran.'

Nessia pats my shoulder. 'No, she didn't.'

Chapter Seven

STRAPPED TO MY BACK and creating a hump under my cloak is a parcel made up of food, water, and the coins Raen threw at me. My toes twitch in Aelius's boots, eager to start this journey, but my knees are soft with trepidation. The incline of the mountain is steeper than I thought now I'm standing at its base and staring up. There are no stars or moon visible tonight, so the castle is the only adornment to the sky. It's an ugly one with its barbed black towers.

'Be sensible, Niah, you're still too weak from the birth,' Nessia says, but there's pride in her voice. 'Vill will come back.'

'How long will that take? No.' I take one step; my grandmother always said every journey starts with one step. Another. And I'm on my way.

Grass and nettles have reclaimed the old path, thinning it to the width of a single foot, but I dare not use the other path created by the castle people in case I meet one. Bracken bends beneath my boots, bounces back. My pace is slow because my body is still sore and unsure of itself after the birth. Several times I have to pause, steady myself with a hand against a bush.

The wind carries the howls of the dead, taking me to days I'd rather forget. When I close my eyes and cover my ears against them, I'm in my memories. My right temple pressed against my grandmother's knee. My arms wrapped around her legs. The First Queen hanging from a tree like a larvae, froth oozing from her mouth, her face purple. Onnachild was on his black stallion. His nostrils flaring and his lips pulled into a tight smile as he watched his wife die. Gagging, I rub my eyes and force myself to look at the castle. First, get there. Get inside and then I'll worry.

My calves ache, each step a strain as the muscle stretches. My grandmother's words return to me: *nothing easy is worth having.* She's right. It becomes harder to anticipate the rocks and dips on the path and so I jolt, stumble. I slip and my hands are too slow to brace my fall so I land on my cheek. The dried mud is gritty and powdery in my mouth, reminding me of my childhood, and I curse the villagers for their tormenting. If only Aelius was here, taking me up on his horse as he always said he would.

My stomach rumbles. My right calf cramps. I sit in the castle's shadow and rest against the side of the mountain to catch my breath. My body isn't going to stop me, not even when my breasts start leaking. Sweat stings my eyes and plasters my hair to my cheeks and neck. I take a sip of water. My feet are throbbing inside the boots so I tug them off, wiggle my toes. This is just a rest, just a short rest before I start again.

I'm dreaming. I know this because I can see my face but it's not mine, though it has my eyes, though our skin is the same earthy colour. I'm a bride, riding to the castle on a white mare, my veil floating out behind me—it doesn't want to go. I'm not sure I do either, but that doesn't matter because my father is behind me, my uncle behind him, and my new husband is at the front. He always gets what he wants—these kinds of men always do.

A shudder wakes me. For courage, I grab my cloak and squash it to my nose. The hawk clasp is cold against my lips. I look down at the village, at the statue. It looks lonely towering above the squat huts. Poor Aelius. There's no time to waste so I jam the boots onto my feet, wincing at the burst blisters on my heels. My limbs are sore and my back stiff, and as I force myself up, I groan. One step. Another. Another. Another as I follow the turn of the old path. What waits for me in the castle? I think of the things Vill promised: velvet and silk and lace, and boar, pork, venison, and those spicy herbs that lingered on my love's skin. My mouth waters. If only Aelius was still there.

My steps shorten as I get nearer the castle. It's wider and taller than it appeared to be when I stood in the shadow it made across the village. The spiked turrets are a series of jagged layers resembling unfurled thistle heads. A thick black wall stretches around it, built by Onnachild to keep out the villagers. I estimate how many more steps it'll take for me to be face to face with that wall: less than 200. I count them off—197, 196, 195.

Eventually, ten, nine, eight, seven, six. I smile, relieved. Then fear follows, slowing me again. Five. Four. Three. Two. One.

My palm presses against the wall. It's slimy, alive with a black moss that shines like wet slate. Its stench reminds me of the battlefield: blood, death, and decay. I rub the sweat from my forehead as I lean back to survey it. It's so ugly, so vast, that my breath catches in awe. My palm runs over stones, hastily and carelessly piled on top of each other, as I search for a way through. There's a small door, iron studs clustered across it like pimples ready to burst. I knock with the heel of my hand. There's no answer. I kick it several times; I've not come this far to be ignored.

'Anyone,' I shout. 'Anyone.'

There's no response.

'By the gods,' I moan, and try again, banging and kicking and yelling.

'What! What!' a man shouts from above me.

I stand back, peer up. He's stood on the wall in armour, sword drawn.

'Woman,' he shouts.

'Woman,' another man answers.

'Wait,' I shout when the man vanishes. *What now?* I slump against the wall and stare down towards the village, a sprawl of dark shadow. The thought of walking back makes me want to cry, but instead I kick the wall and curse.

Then, I hear bolts being drawn, and I straighten up as, finally, the door opens. A thickset man stands there, and to his left is a shorter man. Both have their swords pointing at me. I raise my hands, step back into a puddle.

'What is your business here?' the first man asks.

'No trouble. No trouble at all, I assure you.'

'A woman is always trouble,' the other says, though he lowers his sword.

'I've come to see Vill Hartnell,' I say.

They snigger.

'Plenty of women want to see Vill Hartnell,' the first says to the second.

'Can you get him for me?' I ask. 'Or tell me where I can find him?'

'He'll never come for a dirty village wench.'

'He'll come for me. Tell him it's Niah. I have business with Vill Hartnell.'

'But will he have business with you?' the first says.

'You aren't his type, love.' The other starts to close the door.

'Wait. Wait.' I scrabble in my parcel, a lump of bread drops to the

37

ground. 'Here.' I offer them Raen's coins. The first man leans forwards, picks one up and examines it, then gives it to his colleague, who checks it and nods.

'Well,' the second says. 'Who are we to stand between a master and his pleasure? Enter. And I'll go find our friend, Vill Hartnell.'

The first man snatches the remaining coins before turning sideways to make space for me. I step over the threshold into the wall. The door is shut behind me.

Inside is as dark, damp, and airless as a grave must be. I reach out to feel my way, but the stone is like moist bone, and it makes me cower. The stink of unwashed men, stale breath, and fear gets into my mouth. I want to scratch through the wall, sprint back to the village, and never return. It was foolish to come here; I'm not brave. *Stay calm. Stay calm.*

Light ekes in when another door is opened. I rush towards it, out into the castle grounds with a trip and a lurch. I can breathe again. The air has the tang of spring. By the gods, how I'd forgotten spring. The grounds are celestial: lush grass stretches out in strips of contrasting shades, neat white paths glow in the night, trees have their boughs cropped and trained into circles. I take off my boots to rest my feet on the grass. It's cool and pleasantly damp against my hot and sore soles. I rub them over and over it, sighing at the sensation. It makes the guard laugh.

As I stare up at the castle, my mouth gapes. This is the part built by the first people, the Aegni, and it's exactly how my grandmother described it: the sandstone a creamy yellow, the towers as curved as a woman's hip and at the top they splay like a marigold welcoming in the sun. It's appealing and inviting from this side, the side the village doesn't see.

'Makes you proud, don't it,' he says. 'King's built on it. Had better stone shipped in from his homeland.'

I snort.

'Made it more nice inside, too,' he says, ignoring me. 'And added the glass windows on the other side. And this wall here ...' He pats it. 'This wall he built after the False Queen ... after all that business.'

'I know,' I grumble.

'Ah, we have Vill.' He rushes off to his colleague.

I stand, shake out my dress, and try to smooth my knotty hair as I wait for them to reach me. My legs and arms are itching and throbbing; the nettles must have got me.

'This girl says she has business with you.' There's a touch of disbelief in the guard's tone.

'She does, and I thank you both.' Vill tosses coins to the guards. 'You can return to your posts.'

They bow and disappear into the wall.

'Well, well, well.' Vill crosses his arms. He's immaculate in a tunic of blue and silver that makes him resemble a frozen lake. His blond hair has been brushed and tied at his nape with a blue ribbon as satiny as his hair. As his gaze sweeps up from my swollen toes, I stop scratching and pull my cloak around me to hide the stains my leaking breasts have made. Rather than appearing disgusted by how filthy I am, a smile spreads his plump lips. 'I recognise that cloak. Raen'll want it back.'

'He can keep it once I get in there.' I point at the castle.

'Indeed.' He pivots on his heels and saunters off. A slight flick of his wrist tells me I'm to follow. I scoop up my boots, hugging them close.

We walk in silence, keeping the older part of the castle to our right. Its last curve is broken, stones halved to allow Onnachild's addition to attach itself as black knot does to a tree. On we go, passing a large and peaked window slightly higher than my head. Candlelight flickers from it. Music drifts out. I pause, wanting to peek in and see the castle people dancing, see where Aelius sat, see the trays of food. Will it be as magnificent as I imagined?

Vill whistles at me. I give the window one more lingering glance before chasing after him. When the ground dips, I stumble and drop a boot. We seem to be heading towards a river. Under pine trees we go, the moonlight and branches making shadowy patterns over us. I brush the trunks as we weave between them. Vill slows. 'Spectacular isn't it?' He glances over his shoulder at me. 'This was Aelius's favourite place.'

I can see why. Meadow flowers grow into clusters of blue and yellow. I pick one, and rub its silky petal against my nose as I imagine Aelius sat against a tree trunk, listening to the calming song of the leaves and the river. The sun dappling through the canopy would make the blond hairs on his arm twinkle. We could have rested here together if only ... Vill stops.

'So.' He perches on a low-hanging branch, his long legs crossed at the ankle and his hands clasped around his knees. 'What made you believe you could traipse up here, looking like that, and just demand to be let in?'

'I got tired of waiting.'

'Patience is a virtue you might have to learn.'

'You said you were a Follower and would help.'

'I did, and I am, and if I remember correctly you said no. What has changed your mind? You have changed your mind, haven't you? No, don't answer that last question. Your being here is proof.'

'Did I have a choice?' I sink onto the ground, tired.

'There are always choices; yours just aren't so appealing. Neither are the villagers'. But you, you have a chance, and your child has a chance to live the life you were both meant to.' He smiles. 'I knew you wouldn't let us down, and I won't let you down. The King is already aware that there might be a child; his advisers have tried to dissuade him of this but now ... well, here you are.'

'She'll be safe in the castle?'

'She's the last living piece of his beloved son, she'll be safe. You on the other hand ... I can't guarantee anything, but you have courage and, I presume under that dirt, beauty, and, of course, now you have my assistance.'

He crouches beside me, takes my hand and raises it to his lips. The light kiss he places tickles. 'I can't do anything without your agreement.' His stare is intense with those piercing blue irises.

All I need is to say one word, one word to start changing everything. He leans closer. His grip tightens. What else can I whisper but yes?

PART II: FLINT

Chapter Eight

'THE SERVANTS' ENTRANCE. I'm sure you understand.' Vill opens a plain wooden door. Stepping into the kitchen, I'm overwhelmed by noises, by smells, by wet heat. People are yelling over boiling pans. The smells of cooking meat, spicy herbs that make my eyes water, and the musty undertone of sweat are carried in the steam.

Servants rush in and out of the kitchen, their arms laden with piles of trays, and their brown, shining foreheads peeking over the top. Vill glides through their erratic bustling but I have to sidestep, duck, and weave to avoid feet, shoulders, and elbows. My bare feet stick to the tacky floor. 'Where are we going?' I shout to Vill.

'Somewhere you'll be safe.'

We exit through a larger door, into the castle proper where the hallway is spacious, empty, and peaceful, in direct contrast to the cramped kitchen. Night and day seem to be close companions here, nestling together between these sandstone walls. The wall-mounted torches are a hundred summer suns dotted down the hallways, and moonlight shines in through long windows. The high ceiling curves into a sequence of arches in both directions, and where the points meet is a pattern replicating a bouquet. I twist, turn, then rise onto my tiptoes to get a better look. As I stagger back, my palms connect with the wall, which feels as rough as a peanut shell. There's the lingering scent of incense: the same sweet aroma Aelius carried on his clothes. I take a big breath of it, hold it, and as I sigh it out, my shoulders lower and my lips lift into a grin. 'I'm here, finally.'

'Shush.' Vill nudges me to walk. 'We can't tarry.' He takes a torch from its sconce, waving it as we walk down the hallway, a series of beige rugs underfoot. The weave is better quality than my dress and so I pull my cloak tighter around me to hide the thin material. When the rugs stop, the floor changes from stone to something black and slick that adds a trill echo to the tap of Vill's shoes. The white walls are as sleek and glossy as a castle stallion. A shudder shimmies up my spine, making me hunch, so I suspect we've entered the newer part of the castle: Onnachild's part. I hug Aelius's boots closer and dip my head, my hair slipping forwards and bringing the smell of dried sweat and village. I hum the neglected Aegnian songs for courage as we hurry through.

'I remember that song,' Vill says, but he doesn't join in.

We turn left into a hall lined with portraits in gold frames. I slow to search for similarities to Aelius in their eyes, the curve of their chin, their hair, perhaps find the hint of a dimple. Most of the figures are blond, an insipid blond and not golden like my love, but a few are dark brown like Onnachild.

There's my Aelius. I stop, mouth his name and lean closer to the painting. My index finger traces the laburnum leaves carved into the frame as gently as it did the freckles on his shoulder. His pose is not one I recognise: a condescending lift of his chin and his chest puffed out as though he's holding in a breath. His sleeves are decorated with gold hawks and are so elaborate they make him appear broader than he was, and his head, in comparison, is too small. It's him, and yet it's not him. The eyes are the right cornflower blue but his lips are too pink against skin painted too smoothly; I can't see or feel evidence of the painter's brush. His curls are elegant swirls glowing like the sun is behind him.

'So beautiful,' I whisper. To Vill, I say, 'I'll have this for my walls.'

'I will make sure of it.' He tugs my elbow to get me moving again.

There's a portrait of Onnachild on a black stallion, the muscles of both exaggerated against the greys and blues of a moody sky while he brandishes a sword at a coming storm. His crown adds brightness to the otherwise dark painting. Vill grabs the corner of my cloak and drags me on. We pass squares where the walls are a deeper hue, showing where portraits have been removed. Once we've left that hall, I realise neither the First Queen nor Raen had a likeness hanging.

We turn left again and walk up a staircase which turns and twists. Tucked off from this one is another set of three steps, narrower and worn in the centre, leading to a bowed door of dark wood. Vill struggles with a key in the lock and then passes me the torch so he can push his shoulder against the door. He grunts as he kicks it, the sound so surprising coming from his womanly lips and perfect face. Finally, the door opens, and out rushes the smell of dust, of mould, tainting the fresher, floral air in the hallway. Chilling air surges against me and flutters the torch. 'It's only for tonight. I can do no better at such short notice,' he says briskly, as though he expects me to complain.

But I enter silently and shiver in the round and dank room. Thin slits in the wall don't let in much light, and the ceiling is so high I can't see the top.

'At least no one will come here.' He takes the torch from me. 'And tomorrow I'll send someone over, clean you up.' He licks his finger and rubs my chin. 'Leave it to me to make you beautiful and then you'll be ready to meet the King.'

'I don't need to be beautiful. I need to be powerful.'

His lips quirk. 'Of course, but here, one so often begets the other. Try to sleep tonight. If things go to plan, you'll have a busy day tomorrow.'

I don't ask for details because I'm reluctant to hear Onnachild's name in this room, in this darkness, in case it conjures him up. Instead, I nod. 'Will you leave me the torch?'

'People might see the light.'

He bangs the door shut behind him and I'm alone. I've never been alone before, and it's strange how much smaller it makes me feel. The dark is as thick and ominous as the sky in Onnachild's portrait, the silence a presence that doesn't want me here, and so I stand still, breathing shallowly to keep me hidden, safe. This room is draughtier than my home, and the chill has got into my bones already. I tell myself it is only the cold making me shiver and not the stories of Onnachild's anger returning, being blown in on the draught: him rolling around the floor, pulling straw from his mattress and stuffing it into his mouth because a castle man dared to say no; him slapping a man for being late to the Second Queen's funeral and that same man appearing at traitor's gate; him hacking down the Legacy Yew and ripping up the treaty signed there because the Aegni refused to let him cast aside his first wife.

I try humming to distract myself and to pretend Nessia is here but my voice is higher than hers and doesn't have the same rattle. She'd say that I've faced worse, but I'm not sure if she'd be right. Forcing myself to be brave, I extend my arms out and make my way across the stone floor towards a dark square jutting from the far curve of the wall. My knees bang into it. I lean over and as I test its shape, straw digs into my palm. It's a bed, small enough to accommodate women as they were years ago. The mattress is lumpy and unyielding even when I lie on it and fidget. I hug Aelius's boots to my chest and draw up my legs, telling myself I'm too exhausted, not nervous, to explore the rest of the room.

'I've done it,' I say aloud to feel less alone. Here I am, and I have rescued myself, but the bed smells of women left to sweat and rot, women who should have known better, and I can't help wondering whether they were Aegnian too.

A key scratching in the lock jolts me awake. My body is so stiff curses burst out of me when I move. Vill enters the room and steps into a sliver of sunlight which rebounds off his jewellery, sending white and purple flickers around the room.

'By the gods, it's freezing.' He wraps his arms around his lithe body, today dressed in lilac with white tree blossom embroidered across the front. 'I hope our ancestors will forgive me for leaving you in here. You must forgive me. Today will make it up to you, I'm sure. I've called for a bath and managed to sneak away a Maiden to help you. I've never been so grateful for a disobedient one.'

A short girl wearing a dress the colour of waves and summer skies, and an elaborate headdress made of a gold band, golden rods, and dangling shells, drags in a wooden tub lined with white linen.

'Get it filled and wash her,' he says to the Maiden. 'I'll return later with some food,' he tells me. Then he saunters out, leaving the door unlocked.

The girl peeps up. 'I'll be back.' She bows and shuffles out backwards, the shells on her headdress tinkling.

With the morning sun adding lines of light to the room, I can make out a simple fireplace against one curved wall. It appears not to have been used in a while judging by the ashes and half-consumed wood piled up inside it. I scoop up handfuls of the ash and make a grey pile next to me until it's cleared. Once it is, I rearrange the wood, grab my flint from my pack, and coax a fire into life. The glow is an instant comfort in this dank room, and its warmth helps ease out the crick in my neck.

The Maiden doesn't knock before reappearing with a bucket and this makes me jump away from the fire, hiding my hand in my sleeves. I rub my index finger over the sharp edge of the flint as two young boys, also carrying buckets, follow her. She points at the tub and they tip water into it. Steam swirls up and trails off towards the slit windows, as it wafts past I smell primroses. The boys leave as silently as they came in. Another two boys enter with buckets. The girl remains standing off to the side with her head down and hands clasped in front of her. Two more boys enter, or perhaps it is the first ones returning because none of them look up and so they're indistinguishable with their identical brown clothes, village coloured skin, and brown hair closely cropped. They don't acknowledge me, not even when I purposefully get in their way. Another set of boys appear, empty buckets, and the tub is almost full. Once we're alone, the girl lifts her head and grins, showing a gap between her front teeth.

She's young, maybe no older than eleven, and it is with a childlike curiosity that she stares at me. Her blue eyes are so round they remind me of a doll my grandmother made for me from linen and wool, and her lashes resemble the bristles of a brush in colour and thickness. She has a pointy chin which exaggerates the largeness of her eyes and the plumpness of her cheeks, still bunched up in a grin. Her tiny white hand reaches for my cloak. I step back, getting ready to push her away.

'I'm to help you get ready.' Her voice rises at the end so I'm not sure if it's a question or a statement.

'I can undress myself.' I untie my cloak. She watches me fold it up and set it on the bed. I fumble with the lacing on my dress. Once it's undone, I yank my dress over my head, whip it round to cover my nakedness, and then lift my left leg over the side of the tub and into the water. The heat stings my foot. I gasp, almost drop my dress as I retract my foot, but the cold floor also stings when I put my foot down so I raise it again and leave it there, hovering and dripping water.

47

The Maiden giggles. 'Sorry, Mistress. Sorry. It wasn't my intention. I didn't mean any offence. It was your face ... it looked. Well, I'm sorry.' She curtsies, her skirts pooling around her feet, and gestures for my dress. I step back into the water, bracing myself against the heat. Slowly, I lower, bringing my dress with me.

'I can wash that for you,' she says.

My dress billows out and up. I clamp it between my knees.

'Are you from the village?' She kneels beside the tub.

I nod.

'I thought so, only women here, they like ordering me about and moaning ... the water's too hot, the water's too cold, there isn't enough water ... on and on. Did you not have baths in the village? Oh, I don't mean offence just ... never mind.' She plunges her hand into the tub, scoops up my left arm, and then rubs soap over my skin. It leaves a white gritty trail, but it smells pleasant.

'What is the village like?' she asks.

'Cold and dirty.'

'That's what I heard. We aren't allowed to go there. We aren't allowed to do very much.' Her heavy sigh implies this is the worst thing in the world. 'Why are you here?'

'You don't need to know that.'

'Dunk your head and I'll wash your hair,' she says. 'Will you tell me tomorrow if you're still here? If not, well, I'm good at finding things out.'

I don't want to slide under the water, don't want to feel its pull as it surges over my face to find its way into my nose, my mouth. I grip the sides of the tub.

'It's only water.' Her fingers make surging circles in the tub.

I chide myself, close my eyes, and take a deep breath. My knees peek out of the water and into the cold when I slide down, my grip tightening on the rim. My hair floats, drifts, and sways around me so slowly I feel I'm in a dream. It's a pleasant sensation but, sweet smelling as this water is, it is still water and has its urge to suffocate. I surface, gasping for breath, and splashing water out over the Maiden.

'... that is why I'm not allowed in the Great Hall tonight,' she says, unperturbed by her wet dress.

'What?'

'They caught me eavesdropping when I should have been praying. In my defence, King Onnachild does have a very boomy voice, and if he's in the room next to me, it can be very hard to not get distracted.' She lathers up my hair with the soap and rubs her fingers through it to my scalp. 'Relax. Close your eyes and lean back.'

I do but I don't like it; it's unnerving how exposed my throat is to her, how the tub digs into my neck.

'Under.' She presses on my shoulders.

I slide down again, not letting the water touch my face this time. She fans my hair out, sloshes more water over it as her right hand makes an arch across my forehead. Several times she does this and each time I hold my breath, shut my eyes, grip onto the tub.

'How are we getting on?' It's Vill.

'What are you doing here?' I cry, slipping and splashing more water onto the Maiden as I draw up my knees.

'Don't make a fuss,' he says. 'You've nothing I haven't seen before.'

'She won't give me her dress,' the Maiden says.

'Who cares about that old rag? Throw it away. I've brought new clothes with me and good news. Niah, I've managed to convince the King to see you.'

'Today?' I peer over my shoulder at him. Draped across his outstretched arms is a black dress, and in his hands is a pair of leather shoes with a slight heel.

'Yes, today. And his two advisers, Aesc and Ascelin.' Vill sits on the bed, frowns, and rises again. 'After you're bathed and dressed, the Maiden can escort you.'

'Well, that's exciting,' she says, trying to get my other arm.

I repress a shiver. 'Is it?'

'What is it if it isn't exciting?' Vill asks.

'It's Onnachild.' Each syllable is a stone being dropped into my belly.

'You'll be absolutely fine. We'll make you appear the perfect picture of sweetness and innocence. As long as you remember not to speak to him or look at him until he gives you permission—'

'That's ridiculous. What kind of man can't look a woman in the eye?'

'It might very well be ridiculous but he's the King, so do you think you can try, please, to be a little less surly than you are now? Smile.' He draws one in the air. 'I want you to think simple, think pliable. He appreciates that in a woman. You can do that, can't you?'

I nod but my scowl remains.

'Excellent.' He bows and turns to leave the room.

'Wait,' I shout.

He pauses at the door.

'What about Ammi?'

'Soon.'

'And food? You said you'd bring food.'

'After you've met Onnachild.' And then he leaves us.

'Soon,' I mumble, giving up my struggle with the Maiden and letting her finish cleaning my arm. When she soaps my face, it gets up my nose where it burns and makes me sneeze. She splashes water at me, rinsing off the layer of white, and then gestures for my dress again. I shake my head and point at the soap. She passes it over and I finish washing under the cover of my dress.

'I thought the bath would wash away that brown,' she says, 'turns out it isn't mud but your skin.'

'Not every woman is like the Second Queen.'

'The True Queen you must say.' She crosses herself.

I bite back my thoughts on that, instructing the Maiden to turn around instead so I can get out of the tub. 'To dry yourself,' she explains as she picks up a thin piece of linen from the bed.

I drop my dress and lunge for that linen. Wrapping it around my body, I go to inspect the dress Vill has spread out over the bed. It's weighty, and when I press it up against my body, the skirt continues a long way past my feet. Although I had fancied bright colours, I'm grateful Vill has taken my mourning into consideration and brought a black one.

'I'm surprised he didn't get you something more fashionable,' the Maiden says. 'Vill always makes such a point of looking his best, and he knows all the fashions. He must know no one wears dresses with such a high neckline anymore.'

'Perhaps he means to hide as much of my skin as possible.' Despite her criticism, I still think the dress is exquisite with its thick material and there's a pattern I can touch but not see in this light. It could be feathers or leaves. What does worry me are the two contraptions standing stiff and ominous by the door. They make me think of bridles forced onto wives who gossip against their husbands, though these things are too big for my face, for anyone's face. The Maiden says I'm to wear them and picks up the smaller one. It's tubular with a flat triangular piece at the front that looks like it's been made from a melted sword. I back away. The Maiden titters, hiding her mouth behind the contraption as she fiddles with the tube until it opens and white ribbons dangle.

'It goes around here, like this.' She puts it against her body. 'Everyone wears them, well, everyone except the False Queen when she was here so I hear, but ...'

'Why?'

'Why didn't she? Or why do people? Either way, I don't know. It makes women look better I suppose, at least I think it makes women look better. Come, I'll show you, and I won't do it too tight. I doubt you'll need me to anyway, your waist is a lot smaller than most of the women here; I guess it must be that village food.'

She steps towards me with that thing still held close to her. It doesn't seem so monstrous now, and the ribbons, when I reach for them, are silky and smooth. If this is what I must wear to help Ammi, then I will.

I let the Maiden fit the contraption around my torso. As she pulls on the ribbons it constricts around me, almost cutting my breasts in half as they bulge up. At least it will hide any milk stains should my breasts leak. Next is the larger contraption: a series of circles getting smaller and smaller until they come to a band of white ribbon. I step into it when she tells me to, let her lift it up and then tie it around my waist. She tugs the dress over me, over these implements, and then fusses with ties, hooks, material.

'Will I do?' I ask, struggling to inhale with the cage constricting my ribs.

She steps back to check her work. 'I think the King will see an elegant castle-bred woman and not a dirty villager.'

I smile even though I disagree; after all, nothing can hide my skin. She runs to the bed, jumps onto it, and then beckons me over. Her fingers brush through my wet hair, the touch so soothing my eyes close and I'm lulled into childish daydreams of dancing, of dresses, of jewels, and feasts that last until dawn. I fluff up the foamy lace on my sleeves to check it is real.

'I'm done.' She slaps two thick and shining plaits over my shoulders, the ends resting, damp, on my breasts.

I slip my feet into the shoes Vill left, wincing as they graze over the burst blisters on my heels. The shoes are tight, digging into my feet and pinching my toes, but the Maiden's grin is so infectious I tap my toes like a child playing horses with two shells. She giggles and claps to the rhythm.

'I suppose we better go.' Her words bring me back to reality, back to Onnachild, and my elation is gone as quick as a spooked bird.

The Maiden holds in the sides of my dress so I can pass through the door frame and down the narrow staircase. It's difficult to walk because the cage digs into my belly and the skirt lunges from side to side, taking me with it. I misjudge distances, causing the skirt to bash and bounce off the sandstone walls, several times my ankles threaten to twist. My pace is frustratingly slow as I hobble and wince and curse each step in these tight shoes. Thankfully, the hallways are deserted so only the Maiden sees my clumsy attempt at being graceful.

We halt before a sturdy wooden door covered in carvings of ears and eyes. 'It'll be in there,' the Maiden says. 'The Judging Room.'

The Judging Room ... where the Aegni ruler and her council would sit. I press my right cheek and ear against the orange-tinged door hoping their past discussions on laws, village disagreements, and plans for feast days remain captured within the wood like the sea in seashells. My skirt tilts up but I don't care, not even when the Maiden laughs and tries to hold it down. I breathe in the woody smell as my fingers run over the intricate carvings. How is it that I'm here? How is it that I'm touching the same door my ancestors did? But now ... I move back ... Now it's Onnachild behind that door, on the throne.

I square my shoulders. 'Should I knock?'

'Knock? No, don't be silly. He'll open the door when he's ready for you.' She curtsies and then she dashes off with her skirt gathered in one hand and the other holding her headdress steady.

I try to mimic the Maiden's pose with my hands clasped together in front, head bowed, and lips hinting at a smile. It looked calm and composed when she did it, but I'm not. My mouth is dry, my stomach is churning, and I can't even feel my legs. I try breathing deeply to slow my pounding heart but the cage cuts off each breath and makes the pounding worse.

'He's just a man,' I whisper in my ancestors' language. The words don't help when I'm picturing his smile as he watched his first queen die. I push that image away but what comes in its place is him in that moody painting ready to fight the storm with all the arrogant certainty of a conqueror. The high neckline of my dress presses into my throat, and not even tugging it releases the pressure. The lace around my wrists itches and my dress is getting heavier, pulling on my hips. Relaxing my jaw and shoulders makes me tremble and so I tense them again.

The tapping of my foot echoes and despite how annoying the sound is I can't seem to stop. If I could be myself I'd barge in, but I can't be myself. Vill said I must appear docile, contrite, stupid. I scratch my wrists. The hallway is getting hotter, making me sweat; I'll not resemble a pristine castle woman for much longer.

The door opens.

I duck my head to hide the irritation in my eyes, eyes that will remind Onnachild of the women he killed.

Chapter Nine

I CAN'T RESIST A QUICK LOOK. The two wolf-like men from the funeral block the door. Their clothes are a stormy grey and as pleated as their grey faces. They're mirror images of each other even down to the disdain in their eyes and the hint of suppressed cruelty in their thin lips. The only difference is that one has a scroll tucked under his arm and ink on his fingers. They peer down their flat noses at me as they part to let me enter.

My steps are tentative at first, the clatter of my shoes too loud, and I struggle to keep my focus on the flagstone floor instead of gawking at every detail in this ancient room, built by the first Aegni ruler. It smells faintly of sage, yew trees, and fires as if she has not quite left. My smile becomes real. The stone and mortar walls are crude, rough looking, and dirty in this room which must be the oldest in the castle. There's no fire lit and the winter sun hasn't warmed the room, so my breath comes out in faint puffs that show how shallow and rapid it is.

I head to the large yew table in the centre of the room. Around it are ten chairs, one for each council member. Sunlight enters the room through an arched window and bathes the surface of the table, brightening the orange in the wood and making the browns richer. The edge is crinkled and seems to billow and ripple in the moving light like the sleeves of a dress caught on the wind and, when I get nearer, a faint charge radiates from the table. It tingles my fingers, urging me to press them into the dents and pits left by my ancestors, get the aeons-old dirt under my nails and gather strength from them, but I feel Onnachild's scrutiny as keenly as the field mouse feels the hawk overhead. I take a sidestep so my arm can at least brush against the chairs.

'Hurry up,' a twin moans. His voice is crisp with no accent to betray his roots. The other adviser seizes my left arm, drags me along to position me into a patch of sunshine which highlights the stains on the floor. The pattern on my dress, I can now see, is dark-purple feathers.

'King Onnachild, may I present Niah,' Vill says.

'So you are the child's mother.' Onnachild's voice is thunderous as if he not only faced the storm in his painting but ate it.

Intimidated by that boom, I'm only able to nod and curtsy. My heart pounds too loudly, and fear rises and swells like uncooked dough in my stomach. The advisers position themselves on his left. Their shoes are small and plain grey, a trail of parchment skims the floor between them. Vill is on the other side, a shaft of sunlight making the buckles on his shoes twinkle. Onnachild's feet are hidden by the thick legs of the table.

'And it is Aelius's?' he asks.

I nod again.

'I have seen the child,' Vill says, 'and I swear when I looked into her eyes it was like I was looking into his.'

I can't allow my fear to mute me. After all, Onnachild is only a man, and he doesn't belong here: I do. 'If you would allow me to bring her here, you'll see for yourself.'

'You do not speak to the King until you're spoken to,' a twin says.

'What is its name?' Onnachild asks Vill.

'Grace, for Aelius's mother, for the True Queen.'

I clench my jaw to stop from shouting out that her name is Ammi: Ammi for my grandmother, not Grace, not named for that queen, never that queen.

'She'll be as enchanting as Queen Grace,' Vill says.

'May I speak?' I ask, risking a quick glance.

Onnachild nods.

'I loved him, Your Highness. There was no one else. How could there have been anyone else? He was everything.'

'Will anyone testify to this?' a twin asks.

'The villagers, ask any of them. They saw him come to my hut at night, and they saw him leave when the sun came up.'

Onnachild huffs. 'You think a villager's word means anything?'

'Can anyone in the castle confirm this?' a twin asks.

I wait for Vill to speak up, to say what he told me: how he helped Aelius sneak out to meet me, that he knows Aelius loved me. I glare at his feet, but they don't move and he doesn't speak.

'Well?' a twin snaps.

'I don't know anyone in the castle,' I say. 'I've never been to the castle. How would I know anyone in the castle?'

Vill taps his foot and I force that simpering smile back even though it hurts my cheeks.

'Hartnell informs me you are the girl from the funeral,' Onnachild says.

'Yes, and I cried like you must wish to cry, like you would cry if you were not a king. I couldn't bear this grief if it was not for my child and I come to—'

'You talk too much. You presume more.'

'If I may?' Vill asks.

'Go on,' Onnachild answers.

'She thinks they were in love and to be betrothed.'

Onnachild laughs. 'The things these village girls will believe.'

Vill joins in. I dig my nails into my palms to stop myself scowling at the condescending tone of Onnachild's laughter and stare at the grain of the table. Aelius meant it. He wasn't capable of lying: he wasn't his father. The twins are snorting. 'I won't need to be writing this,' one says, and the parchment is snatched up, creating a chill draught. I hear the scuff of it being wound into itself, and then the thud when it's thrown onto the table.

'Come here.' Onnachild clicks his fingers. 'I want to see you.'

I take two steps but keep my gaze on the floor because my anger will surely be brightening the green in my eyes, and I need to be docile, innocent, stupid. My lips want to curl, the words are like unripe fruit. Onnachild's stocky fingers and hairy knuckles advance towards me. With great effort, I hold steady as they dig into my jaw, yank my face towards the blinding sunlight. As the glare fades our eyes lock.

His are a dark brown, almost black, and they give nothing away. 'Didn't we eradicate all those damned Aegnians?' he says.

A twin stoops, pushes his flat nose near mine. 'I agree she certainly has a look of them.' He straightens and steps back.

'More than a look.' Onnachild releases me and wipes his hand on his sleeve.

'I don't understand.' My lie comes out stuttered and hesitant.

'Of course you don't.' There's a slight upward lilt in Onnachild's voice, suggesting he's mildly amused.

'Niah was born after their time. Her mother captured and dealt with at the border.' Vill's a better liar than I am; his voice steady and emotionless. 'She wasn't raised in Adfyrism. I did check. I would not risk—'

'They cannot harm me.'

'Absolutely. I mean, I wouldn't risk offending you.'

Onnachild grunts and his nostrils flare. I can't stop staring at him, the noble bear as the villagers used to call him, and it's easy to see why he was given this nickname. He's bristly: hair coarse, abundant, and dark brown. The grey in his thick beard makes him look like he's been chewing stones. Pockmarks and scars are scattered over his cheeks and forehead, proving he's met and defeated many blades and illnesses, the evidence collected and worn like castle women wear gems. His nose, large and wide, has been broken repeatedly. As he stares at me, his protruding brow lowers until his bushy eyebrows create a shadow. Like his wall, he's ugly and imposing, yet awe-inspiring because of it. It's impossible to believe my beautiful, slender Aelius came from this beast. Layers and layers of black furs bulk out Onnachild's thickset frame so he spreads, like mould, over and out the throne. The throne.

My gaze rises from his head, only halfway up the throne's high back, to the two phoenixes perching either side with their wings outstretched. My breath catches; it's more spectacular than I ever imagined. Are those eyes glass or real emeralds? The throne and the birds are one expertly crafted piece, buffed and smoothed to bring out the grain of the yew, which twists up like flames reaching to the gods. My fingers twitch to touch it. Onnachild leans forwards. 'Are you coveting my throne?'

'I don't want the throne.' My voice is quieter than I wanted but at least it's steady. I stare down at my hands, darker than any castle woman's, as dark as the women who used to sit on that throne. My legs are trembling again, and this time the hem of my skirt is doing the same.

'No? Then what do you want?'

I close my eyes for a moment to force my memories back to the battlefield, and my loss becomes as heavy as a sodden clod of peat in my chest. 'Aelius back.' My voice breaks and my shoulders drop. 'I miss him so much, Your Highness.' I take a shallow breath. 'I'd have the sound of him walking to my door. I'd have him smiling at me, giggling at a silly private matter.' When I peep up at Onnachild, his lips are down-turned and twitching, a pang of sympathy for the grieving old bear is as startling and painful as stepping on a shard of glass. 'You can't give me what I want. But perhaps my daughter can help lessen some of your grief as she has mine.'

'You would give me the child?'

'No, no, not give. Share.'

'Ah.' He wipes his mouth as though the sadness displayed there was nothing more than a piece of dropped food. 'So with the child comes the mother, is that what you are hinting at?'

'Is that not nature's way?'

The twins huff. 'It is not our way,' one says.

'Never try to bargain with a king,' Onnachild says. 'They take and do not have to give.'

'I don't come to bargain my daughter with a king. I'm no fool. You could take my child, I know that, whether or not I offer to share her, but I was raised to believe in a benevolent king, a king who understands our suffering and ... so here I am, appealing to you as one parent to another and not—'

'Your Highness.' Vill steps forwards, blocking the sun. 'I think I might be to blame for this assumption; I might have suggested she'd be rewarded in order to entice her here. I know how you hate causing a fuss and as you yourself said, these village girls tend to be—'

Onnachild grunts. My eyes dart to Vill, fury and confusion must be tense on my face. He just tilts his head and smiles, such a blank smile I'm even more confused. I spot the flutter of his right index finger, lifting probably to bid me to keep quiet. My heart is pounding again, and I can feel sweat beading at my armpits, my forehead, the nape of my neck.

'I must admit I had an ulterior motive,' Vill continues. 'I thought you might find her heritage ... useful.'

'Useful?' Onnachild barks out the word but he shuffles around to look at Vill as if interested.

'We all know how animalistic these Aegni women are. Well, like animals, I believe they can be taught.' Vill's fingers toy with the chain around his neck, his thumb and forefinger gliding over the silver. Is he trying to remind me of the seal? He can't be wearing it now, surely? I close my mouth and lower my gaze, letting my shoulders sink with the weight of his insults, and hope these are only roles we're playing to fool a king. 'It'd certainly be an entertaining wager, don't you think? An Aegni raised as a villager, who would believe such a wild mongrel could pass for a respectful castle woman? Such a bet would be one way to increase the castle funds. Rumour has it that Cantor is itching for a chance to part with some more money. Don't you think she already looks the part?'

'How do we know she will suit castle life?' one twin asks. 'How do we know she will behave?'

The other snatches up the scroll from the table and slaps it against himself, drawing my attention up to him. His grey eyes narrow and his lips pinch together as he scrutinises me. 'Losing would cost us money and—'

'When have you ever known me to fail?' Vill toys with the end of his sleeve, fluffing up the pleats of material.

'Nothing is certain, not even you, Hartnell.' The amusement in Onnachild's voice smooths out the gruffness.

Vill sidles up to the throne and clutches the peak of a phoenix's wing as he bends lower and closer to Onnachild's grizzly face. 'If she fails, then there are ways of dealing with that problem.'

Onnachild nods, slowly, lips creeping up into a smirk, one as chilling as when he watched his First Queen hang. Is he picturing me in the noose? My mouth dries, becoming as sticky as day-old pottage. He could order my death with little more than a lift of his eyebrow. The twins shuffle closer to him and lower their voices to keep their words between the four men. There's the odd grunt from Onnachild and a 'hmm' from Vill. I swallow hard and lean towards the table, my elbow feeling the charge from the wood. This is my chance, and I can't waste it.

'Can I speak?' I ask but don't wait for a response. 'I'll do whatever you ask of me. I'm willing to learn, to change. I would try my hardest if that would give me and my daughter a better life, the life Aelius wanted for her. I won't embarrass her or you, Your Highness.'

'Shame you didn't think of that before opening your legs.'

I meet Onnachild's eyes again, those black spaces shadowed by his eyebrows. Let him see my anger, to the dogs with being meek and mild after all the insults I've had to bear in this place of my ancestors, deferring to a foreign invader who doesn't deserve to sit on that throne. Seeing my anger seems to please him though, his lips quirking up on one side and a faint chuckle escaping. He settles back, scratches his beard and then says, 'I'll see the child first, and then I will consider what I shall take and what, if anything, I'll share.'

Somehow, I manage to curtsy though my legs are shaking and the dress is heavy. 'Thank you.' I go to kiss his knuckles like a good little subject, but he moves his hand and dismisses me with a wave.

As soon as I'm in the hallway, a stream of curse words bursts out, directed at Onnachild and Vill but also at myself for being so subservient. I want to kick my shoes at the door but there's a tinkle and the Maiden from earlier appears, telling me she's to take me back to the round room.

In the middle of the room is a silver tray with a bowl on it. The tub has gone. My wet footprints lead to the bed where the cloak is still neatly folded and Aelius's boots are tucked under, only the heels showing. My dress isn't there.

The Maiden locks the door behind us, looking sheepish as she does so. I'm too hungry to worry about that. Fighting my skirt, I rush to the food and slide onto my knees. Within the bowl is hot stew seasoned with unfamiliar herbs, the sauce thin and oniony. Beside it is a chunk of bread, lighter than village bread and warm. I dunk it in the stew, watch it soak up the sauce and darken in colour, then thrust it into my mouth. There's wine in it, and the strange herbs leave a slight burn. I fish out a lump of pork with the bread. The meat falls apart on my tongue. How long has it been since I've had pork? I close my eyes to savour the sensations and tastes.

'I'm glad you're here,' the Maiden says as she undoes my plaits. 'It makes things so much more interesting, although since the Prince died a lot of strange things have been happening. I like the change, it was so boring before, all I did was pray and practise. There's another prince, moody thing he is too, although Symphony—she's another Maiden—she said he was handsome. I'm not too sure.'

She continues chattering away about the other Maidens, and so my thoughts drift back to the Judging Room. I try to remember what I said to Onnachild, whether I said everything I needed to, whether I let my grandmother down. My cheeks burn with shame from my attempt to kiss his hairy knuckles. I grimace and spit onto the floor. When I've finished the stew and bread, I wipe my lips and fingers on my sleeve and burp. The Maiden giggles behind her hand.

'What do I do now?' I tug at my dress to let out another burp.

'You should sleep.'

'Sleep? I've not been awake long. What do the castle women do?' I get to my feet, kick off my shoes, and roll my shoulders to release the remaining tension from facing Onnachild.

'Castle women sleep a lot, it passes the time, and the nights here are so long, dancing, drinking, eating, and there are songs. I play those, well with the other Maidens, but you know what I mean. You might be called to those later. You might be here a while, this room I mean, because the King doesn't make his mind up quickly.'

But Onnachild has always been rash and impulsive. He hasn't changed; people are what they've always been. I keep these thoughts to myself and start pacing the room, stepping into slices of sunlight not quite warm. Scratched into the walls are letters; I search amongst them for the First Queen's name: Iansa. 'What do you do?'

'Pray.'

I huff and nod.

'For the castle people,' she says, proudly. 'Because they can't do it for themselves anymore.'

'Why?' I turn to face her and notice she's kicked off her shoes too, blue ones with white soles.

'They don't want to.'

'Typical.' Since there's nothing else to do, I lie on the bed. My skirt pops up and I have to batter it down so I can keep watch of the door opposite.

'You look so different,' the Maiden says. 'You're not just from the village, are you? You were ... Is the child the Prince's?'

'Of course she is. How do you know about that?'

She shrugs and grins, showing the gap in her teeth. 'If only Prince Aelius could see you like this, a castle woman from the fairy tales. He was such a lovely prince, wasn't he? The True Prince we have to call him now that the other one is back.' She shunts herself across the floor until she bumps against the bed, and then she stretches her legs out before her, toes flexing up and down. 'It's a shame that death comes, isn't it?'

'Yes.'

'But life comes too.' She darts up onto her knees, takes my hand in hers. 'I can't wait to meet Grace; she'll bring life back and fun. She'll make Onnachild happy again. Perhaps I'll get to play with her.'

'Her name is Ammi.'

She frowns. 'If Onnachild wants her to be called Grace, then she must be called Grace.'

She's right. I must forget my daughter had another name, a lineage. And if Onnachild agrees to let me stay, I'll have to forget my upbringing, my grandmother, my language, and the gods. No, not forget. I'll pretend, play as a child does. My worries must be evident on my face because the Maiden pats my hand and says, 'It'll be all right. Things always are.'

'Maybe they are in the castle, but they never were in the village.'

There's the scratching of the key in the lock. I roll onto my side, push myself up. The Maiden jumps into a curtsy. It's Vill and with him is Nessia, her face grimy with dried sweat, and her eyes full of mirth. She calls my name. I call hers, struggling off the bed. We bound across the room, lunge into each other's arms. My hug is so tight she groans in my ear. How reassuring it is to rest my chin on her shoulder, to smell home, to feel her beside me again.

'Has it really only been two days?' She squeezes me.

'Should I arrange a bath?' the Maiden asks.

Vill leaves, closing and then locking the door. Nessia and I release each other, but our fingers lace together. 'Ammi?' I ask. 'She's well?'

'She's well.' Nessia's smile deepens her wrinkles, darker than normal because of the dirt on her face. 'Onnachild's guards came to get us.' She laughs. 'Imagine them in their battle dress, just to get an old woman and a babe.'

'Did the villagers see?'

She nods. 'The guards came before dawn, making such a noise that everyone came to their door. At least they gave me enough warning so I could hide Aelius's sword.'

'Excuse me.' The Maiden taps Nessia and grins. 'Who are you? A servant?'

'I am not a servant.'

'Neither am I. Well, I serve the royal family, but ... I'm a Maiden.' She curtsies. 'I'm Melody. What's your name?'

Nessia tells Melody her name and then her attention returns to me. 'Can she be trusted?'

Before I can answer, Melody interjects. 'I can. I can be trusted with many things. I may talk a lot but never about important things, and Vill sent me here, didn't he? Vill trusted me with you.' She looks like she might cry. 'The servants have been talking, asking me questions about you, but I didn't tell them anything and not just because I don't know anything.'

'We'll see,' Nessia mumbles.

Melody gives me an imploring look. As much as I'd like to, I can't say anything different. Not yet. 'She's been ordered to help me, I think,' I inform Nessia.

'Fancy that.' Her thumb and forefinger take up a pinch of my skirt and rub the material. 'You're going up in the world. Thank the gods for Vill.'

'Everyone loves Vill,' Melody butts in. 'I can tell you lots about Vill.'

'You must be tired.' I usher Nessia towards the bed. 'Did they make you walk up?'

Melody follows us, her feet pattering on the floor.

'I got to ride a horse. Me on a horse.' She lowers onto the bed, her bones creaking and her laugh rasping. 'It's been years since I've been on a horse, I can't even remember the last time.' She shakes her head and laughs again, the rasp turning into a cough so I unfold the cloak and tuck it around her. She clutches it under her chin and clears her throat. 'But what has been happening here? Tell me, have you met Onnachild yet?'

I drop beside her onto the lumpy bed, my feet dangle, my head bangs against the wall, and my heart is heavy again with the worry I've let my grandmother down. Why did I try kissing his knuckles?

'I'll take that as a yes.' Her arm goes around my shoulder. 'It couldn't have been all bad. Ammi is here. You have a fancy dress and a full belly. Good things will start happening, you mark my words.'

I nod but her smile doesn't fill me with the confidence it's meant to.

Chapter Ten

'TELL ME I'M NOT DREAMING,' Nessia says as we stand in what Vill calls my dayroom. It's welcoming and cosy with the dark wood-panelled walls and the blazing fire but still I'm on edge. For three days, Nessia and I were locked in that round room, pondering whether we should add our names to those scratched into the walls to prove we existed, and I don't know what has led to this sudden change of circumstance. Or whether I should trust it.

Vill ignored my questions when he hurried us through the hallways but I try pressing him again. 'Has Onnachild decided then?'

'Not officially, and there are certain caveats, but they can be discussed later. For now, explore. Enjoy.' He presents his hand to me, probably expecting me to kiss it in gratitude; I'll wait until I've heard the terms first.

Nessia rushes towards the fire, exclaiming, 'You could fit at least three village huts in here.'

The room has recently been cleaned, the dust motes dancing in the candlelight are evidence of this and the burning incense does not completely mask the odour of neglect. 'Whose room was this?' I drift towards the wood panelling.

'We aren't allowed to talk about that time in the King's life,' Melody says from where she stands by a circular table, a dirty cloth draped over her forearm.

The First Queen's. That explains the feathers and flames carved into the wood. 'Is this meant to be a threat? Do as he says or—'

'More of a reminder, I would suspect,' Vill says. 'Does that matter? It's yours now.'

For how long? Crossing the room, I brush the backs of the four leather chairs arranged around the fire, three neatly poised and one at an odd angle, hoping to feel the First Queen's presence. There's nothing; she's long gone. Nessia jogs past me towards a door on the left. Melody gives chase, leaving the room with a giggle.

'Come.' Vill catches up my arm and leads me into the bedchamber. The red walls and a roaring fire create an opulence that surpasses all my dreams and my mouth drops open. Quickly, I feign indifference again.

'Niah, look.' Nessia's opening trunks and tossing out dresses in greens, reds, oranges. They hit the floor like a flock of dying birds. A bed, high off the ground and plump with pillows and furs, dominates the room. Hung from a wooden frame around it are swaths of red and orange material, gathered and tied to thick wooden poles. Vill gives me a push towards it. Nessia dives onto the bed and the mattress bunches up around her. 'Oh, it's so soft,' she cries out. 'What is it?'

'Hay and feathers,' Melody says.

'Feathers?' Nessia butts her head against it, laughing.

I push the mattress to check how plump and soft it is, and the faint perfume of lavender and sage wafts out making me yawn. The fur coverings, dyed a deep red, change shade when I brush up the pelt.

'You've not noticed; I'm disappointed.' Vill coughs and, when he has my attention, points to the wall under the bed's pelmet. There's my love's portrait. 'As promised.'

'Aelius.' I struggle onto the bed, Nessia tumbling against my legs. Steadying myself with a hand on the wall, I rise onto my tiptoes to be face to face with his image. 'I'm here. I made it.' I kiss his flat lips.

Melody giggles. 'It's not alive.'

'I know that.' I trace the oval of his face. 'And Ammi? When will she join us?'

'Grace, and she'll come with time,' Vill says.

I sink beside Nessia. 'Time? How much time?' The bed moulds itself to my shape, tempting me to give in to sleep, to dreams, to comfort. I slide off it.

'Is Niah to have a new name too?' Nessia asks.

'Not a new name, but a new history and a new future,' he says.

'Like me,' Melody says, as she folds the dresses Nessia sprawled across the floor. 'It's not so bad.'

I make my way to a door off to the right of the bed, drawn by an oddity in the grain.

'She's right,' Vill says. 'It's not so bad or difficult to keep.'

'I don't need to be someone else.' I pull on the door handle. It's locked. 'And neither does Ammi.'

'I think you'll enjoy playing the part. Now come away from that door.'

'What's behind it? Why is it locked?'

'Storage? I don't know. Listen. I spun quite a convincing tale if I do say so myself. Niah, can I have your attention?'

I turn towards him and lean against the door, my fingers still toying with the panels.

'As I was saying ... I've been preparing the castle for my poor nervous cousin, held captive by an overbearing guardian, one so cruel and heartless

I had to rescue you.' His palm rests on his heart and his head tilts. Only his smirk ruins his pose of affected sympathy. 'You led a very sheltered life: never seeing a formal gathering let alone attending one, and never meeting a man who is not your relation. That should explain any shortcomings.'

Nessia laughs which seems to please Vill because he starts preening, puffing out his silver sleeves.

'No one will believe we're cousins.' I try the door again.

'No? Don't you think we both possess excellent bone structure, a haughtiness to our bearing? I'm more refined, that's all.'

'You look like you're made of silver. I'm more mud.' As my hand glides over the wood, a splinter catches in my palm, and I realise the oddity is a hole, not a stain.

'Once you're kept like a real castle woman, that will fade, and there are creams and lotions; soon we'll have you as pale as everyone here.'

'I don't want to be pale.' I squat and peer in the hole but I can't see anything. 'And I don't want to pretend to be someone else. Why can't I be who I am?'

'The wager rests on you proving you can—'

'Be tamed? Be trained, like a dog? What was it you called me?' I whirl around. 'A wild mongrel?'

'Niah, please, we've been over this. I've explained why I had to use such regrettable language. You must learn to have thicker skin. You need a story to explain your sudden appearance, give you a fighting chance against the castle's pre-existing prejudices, should the wager be taken up. As I said, nothing has been officially agreed as yet but Onnachild does love a gamble, and he loves money. Cantor's opinion of both the Aegni and villagers is just low enough for ...' He dismisses the rest of his sentence with a flicker of his fingers. 'Details, things for me to worry about. What you need to concern yourself with is learning to walk.'

'I know how to walk.'

'Trust me, you do not know how to walk. There's nothing in your stamping that is elegant or seductive. Your skirts should sway like flowers in a spring breeze, and not trees crashing in a storm.'

'I can walk.' My attention wanders to my love's portrait and memories of him reaching for my bare bottom as I sashayed across my hut, teasing him with coy glances over my shoulder.

'Then I'll be pleased to be proved wrong,' Vill says. 'Before that, we must eat and drink, I fear this may be a long night. Melody, will you do the honours?'

She jumps to her feet and straightens her headdress before leaving. The dresses remain folded on the floor, and I pause to stroke them on my way across the room to a dressing table set under a series of windows. Thick dust covers its surface and I write *Niah*, big and bold, in it. The chair wobbles when I sit down. I lean towards the mottled mirror and the reflection of my scowl.

'Ammi is well?' I ask.

'Grace. She's well.' Vill's reflection is a silver blur as he ambles across the room. 'Let me tell you how pleased the King is with young Grace; he almost cried when he first held her. The child, in turn, seemed to understand her role better than any castle man because she cooed so cutely at him. I swear I could almost hear his heart breaking. And the advisers, well, they turned an even greyer shade of grey if such a thing is possible. Already, Onnachild's threatening to name Grace as successor unless Raen does as he's told.'

'When will I see her?'

'Soon.'

'Stop saying soon. When?'

'Niah, please, come on, stop worrying,' Nessia says. 'Ammi is with Onnachild, her grandfather. If he intended to harm her or us, he wouldn't have given us this room.'

'That means nothing. Nothing is safe with him.' I spin around. 'Do you forget the funeral so quickly? What was it you said then? Something about—'

'That was a long time ago.'

'Not that long ago,' I mutter under my breath as I turn back to the mirror. Using my sleeve, I buff the dressing table with all the reverence the First Queen should have been shown.

Vill's hand settles on my shoulder, white on the black fabric. 'We'll make everything as it should be.'

'When?'

'All you need to worry about at this stage is convincing Onnachild you can fool the castle people into believing you're one of them and win him this bet. Let me worry about everything else.'

I huff and dodge from his touch. Melody's return with a tray of food stops me pressing him further. Instead, we drag the chairs from the dayroom into the bedchamber where we arrange them around the fire. Vill watches as I eat. He insists I slow down and complains when I thump my chest to dislodge a piece of bread caught by the cage. Eat with your mouth closed, he tells me. Take smaller bites, he tells me. Chew more, he tells me. On and on he waffles until all the pleasure has gone from eating. Nessia drops breadcrumbs and splashes of wine onto the stone floor even though she's trying to follow his instructions too.

As I lick pork juice from my fingers and wrist, Vill tells me that my skirts should not show any ankle when I walk, I must breathe shallowly, I must keep my head lowered, hands clasped in front, shoulders down, chest out, and my steps must be small, toe to heel with a sweep like I'm stroking a lover's skin.

'Are you listening?' Vill clicks his fingers to get my attention.

'Yes.'

'Then walk.'

I'm doing this for Ammi, I remind myself, and so I don't argue that I've not finished eating, but stand and walk towards the window.

'You weren't listening, were you? Chin tilted down, shoulders back and down, I said. Do it again. Nessia, how do you cope with this?'

Wisely, she remains silent. I turn and repeat my journey to the fire, imagining the floor is Aelius's arm and my toes are raising each golden hair.

'Almost. Again.' Vill shushes me away.

I do. At the window, I pivot and walk back again.

'Niah, please remember to appear more docile, simper. Try. You're not even trying. And certainly, don't flash those eyes at me when you disagree.'

Nessia picks up a chunk of bread. 'She can't help that. If you wait for her to tame them, we'll all end up dying in here.'

'Back to the window,' Vill says.

I turn again and do as he says. It's getting easier and I'm sure I'm getting better because my skirt doesn't bob with as much velocity, only Vill doesn't seem to agree as he lets out a long sigh. I skulk off to the chair at the dresser. My defeated expression greets me.

'Maybe a bit of spirit is what the castle needs,' he says. I watch his reflection as he refills his goblet and then takes a big glug. His smile returns. 'Your beauty was enough to entice a prince and it will entice the castle, and an enticed castle will overlook many shortcomings. There's much you need to learn: deportment, elocution, protocol, dancing, dressing. Perhaps you'll excel in one of those.'

'And will I learn their words, to read them?'

'Eventually, I imagine, yes, once you've mastered everything else, and convinced Onnachild you can cast off your village upbringing. I don't see why not.'

'Another thing being withheld.'

'Another thing?'

'Yes, another thing, like Ammi.'

'Why do you want to learn that anyway?' Melody asks and then giggles awkwardly. 'Get someone to read to you, it's not as captivating when you know the tricks the poets use.'

'Because if you can read people can't lie to you.' I make sure to meet Vill's gaze in the mirror. It's pleasing how the surface ruins the perfection of his skin.

'Forgive her,' Nessia says to Vill, and then she chides me. 'Listen to him. He's saying be patient and here you are behaving like a spoilt child.'

'My dear Nessia, thank you but there's no need to defend me,' he says. 'It's a good thing she's impatient, it will make her learn quicker, and once she has learnt enough, we'll meet with Onnachild again, and I'm sure, soon after that, Grace will come. So, Niah, relax. Smile. Enjoy your room. Enjoy your lessons, and I promise, soon you'll gain his trust and favour.' He takes another sip of wine before getting to his feet. 'I must leave, join the others in the Great Hall, and continue preparing them for your arrival. Wish me luck.'

'Good luck,' Melody says as he bows to us one by one.

Nessia toasts him with a chunk of bread and a bulging smile.

'Wait. Are we going to be locked in?' I ask.

'If you wish to lock yourself in, then there's a key in one of those drawers. I won't be locking you in but, and this is a big but, so do pay attention, the King doesn't want you to be seen. Not yet. Not until he says you're ready to be, so I ask you not to leave these rooms without me. I trust you can agree to that?'

I do but my gaze is already drifting to the window, and the need to be outside is crawling under my skin like fleas climb over villagers.

Chapter Eleven

IT'S STILL DARK and the bed is soft, the furs heavy and warm, so I ignore Melody calling for me and hope she'll go away. She's whistling and the shells on her headdress are clanking. My face screws up against the change in light and temperature when she draws back the drapes surrounding the bed, and I press closer to Nessia. Melody jabs me between my shoulders. 'Time to pray.'

I roll over, squinting and grimacing at the candle she's holding. 'Pray?' I spit out the word, reminded of Arnoson and his self-important smile. Melody's startled. Nessia's hand reaches around and tugs at my nightdress, a sign for me to calm down. I suppress my anger with forceful breaths. 'Sorry. It isn't your fault ... it's ... I don't like mornings.'

'Neither do I,' Melody mumbles. 'But Lark never lets us sleep in.'

'Not even villagers get up at this hour.' Nessia grabs at the fur and drags it over her head.

'That's because they don't worship Him properly. That's why they're poor and hungry.'

'Is that what Onnachild told you?' With a big sigh, I sit up.

'No. God did.'

I stifle the urge to share my thoughts on that because she still looks hurt, with her eyes downcast and her pout exaggerated by shadow. Instead, I try to sound playful and coax her out of her mood. 'Can't we just pretend we prayed?'

'But ...' Her forehead wrinkles, and she scratches her nose, bringing the candle dangerously close to her face and so I take it from her. 'I'm to be your spiritual adviser, teach you all about God and praying and ... things like that ... It's what I do. I'm a Maiden.'

'It could be our secret.'

A mischievous grin breaks out and she giggles. 'I suppose it could. I like secrets. I have a secret. If I share mine, will you tell me why you don't want to pray?'

'Maybe.'

This response appears to be good enough for her because she climbs onto the bed, kicking off her shoes. Her knees dig into my shins as she clambers over me, almost knocking the candle from my grip. 'First, I'll tell you why it's a secret. I am a Maiden and I know you're villagers and don't know what that means but here it's very prestigious. We represent God's angels and bless the King with protection and God's grace and other things, too, which I forget. Anyway, we're foundlings, presented to the King and from that moment we become born. But ...'

She shimmies her way between Nessia and me, all elbows and cold feet. 'I'm not a foundling. I have a mother and a father somewhere, and I was stolen from them. It was night and I still remember the cloth over my head, and it was dark. It was a stranger come for shelter, he said, and before the morning he stole me.' She pulls out the fur and punches her fist into it to mimic being put in a sack. She tussles with herself, creating a draught that makes Nessia grumble. 'And I cried, and I cried until he threatened to whip me. A few times he dropped me, on purpose I'm sure, and I got such a sore head from that and the crying. He told me I was going to the King, but I didn't know Onnachild's name then, or the name of this land. I remember all that; even though I'm not supposed to, I do. I don't tell anyone because that would mean the King is missing a Maiden. Lark might have them make me a servant.' She shudders and pokes out her tongue.

Nessia shuffles up into a sitting position. 'That's not a very good secret.'

'It is and now Niah has to tell me why she won't pray.'

'Fair is fair I suppose,' I say.

She wiggles like an excited puppy, bashing my elbow and causing wax to dribble onto my hand. She peels it off, rubbing it between her forefinger and thumb.

'I don't believe in your god.'

Her mouth gapes, she drops the blob of wax, and her eyes widen as they dart from me to Nessia and back. 'Are you teasing? What do you believe in then? There's only ... Are you a heathen? I've never met a heathen.'

'We're not heathens,' Nessia states firmly.

'See this?' I wave the candle, creating fuzzy traces in front of Melody. 'This is proof my gods are real. They gave us this. What would life be without fire?'

'You worship the fire? But that's where bad things come from. Demons. Evil.' She doesn't look scared but rather curious as her palm hovers near the flame. 'Disease and—'

'According to Onnachild.'

'No, according to God. Lark says He speaks through Onnachild ... so ...' She looks to Nessia.

'According to Onnachild,' Nessia says. 'Does the flame feel evil?'

Melody scratches her nose again, leaving a red mark. 'It's pretty.' She crosses herself, peeping over her shoulder although the only thing behind her is the headboard.

'Have you heard of Adfyrism?' I whisper the word out of habit.

Melody says yes, but shakes her head, and the movement sends her headdress slipping over an eye, adding to her bemused appearance. 'No, wait, I do remember. In my early lessons, something about ... It led us into the Great Famine, cursed our battles, made that False Queen bad or lustful or—'

'Lies. All lies. Don't believe anything that comes out of Onnachild's mouth,' I say. 'I bet you didn't learn how he used to follow Adfyrism when he thought he'd get something out of it.'

'But ...' Her mouth remains open, letting out a puff of breath to clear the way for speech, and her eyebrows rise, only for her mouth to close again. I wait for her to formulate her question. Her brow furrows, her lips purse, and she stares into the flame again.

When no question comes Nessia asks, 'Can we go back to sleep now?'

Melody takes off her headdress and hands it to Nessia who drops it over the side of the bed, the shells clattering like a titter of magpies. 'Can I wake you if I have a question?' Melody asks.

'No.' Nessia snuggles into the mattress. 'Ask Niah.'

Melody peers across at me. I nod. After blowing out the candle, I lean out the bed to place it on the floor, and then I shunt down to find the indentation I left on the pillow. Melody fidgets until her feet press on mine and her cheek rests on my chest. 'I can still come here if we aren't praying, yes?'

Her blonde hair and unguarded expression remind me of Ammi so I put my arm around her, hug her close, and say yes. She lets out a contented whistle.

As Vill ushers me from my rooms to my first lesson, I keep caressing the luscious green velvet of my dress, one from the trunk so it has a slight musty smell but underneath that is a hint of sage and lavender. Stitched around the hem and the bell-shaped sleeves are flowers, the silver thread grubby in places, and I enjoy watching them glittering in the morning light as I sashay through the hallways. Pretending I'm heading to an important meeting in the Judging Room, I lift my chin to copy the pose in Aelius's portrait.

'How's my walk?' I ask Vill, the village tones of my voice magnified by the sandstone hallway.

He gives me a quick, assessing glance but does not answer my question. 'You're cheerful this morning.'

'I'm looking forward to learning, making progress.'

Vill puts his finger to his lips to silence me despite the hallways being empty and quiet, only a few servants are pattering around. 'Come on.' He drags me forwards by my arm.

We halt before an oak door stained a deep brown and divided into four panels containing rising swirls that could be flames. Above them, in an arched panel and outlined by dirt, is a faded phoenix with the faintest tint of orange in its majestic head.

'The library.' Vill pushes on the door.

I step inside. The room is darker than the hallway, dominated by the floor to ceiling bookcases, some of which are empty. Candelabras, rising from the floor and tables, and a fire provide most of the light, although there's a shield-shaped patch of faint sunlight on the floor to my left. My ancestors' presence is strong here despite Onnachild having burnt all the Aegnian books. Every single one, religious, historical, even the annual accounts, went up in a pyre in the square. The smoke was so thick and black it covered the village for weeks, found its way onto washing, down throats and up noses. In between crying about how they'd been cursed, the villagers complained of black snot and black spit.

I follow the bookcases around the edge of the room, looking at the titles I don't understand but presume are written in Onnachild's language. The empty shelves must have been polished this morning because there's no dust and the wood gleams, which somehow makes those gaps sadder.

The rustle of material and the creak of leather draw my attention to the centre of the room where a voluptuous woman in black is rising from a chair. 'This is your teacher,' Vill says. 'Mantona.'

She moves like a castle woman, her turn fluid and slow, but she doesn't look like one; her hair isn't blonde and her eyes don't appear to be blue. There are thick blurs of grey through her dark-brown hair, giving the impression that someone with sooty fingers brushed and bundled her hair at her nape. Her gown is low cut and dotted with tear-shaped onyx, although her vast bosom is the only adornment needed. She nods at me, and the birds hanging from her silver earrings seem to be trying to fly away.

I nod in reply and then return to the books, running a finger over the spines. Some are cracked leather. Some are new and hard. One book has a copper bear embossed on the conker-brown leather. My forefinger tips it out from the others. 'What is this book?'

'Later.' Vill takes it from me and puts it onto another shelf. 'Don't be rude. Come meet your teacher.'

I lean against the bookcase and watch her walk towards me, her skirt swishing with a mesmerising rhythm that captures the flickering of the candlelight, and her steps make no sound. Now I understand Vill's complaints about my walk.

'It's a pleasure to meet you.' Despite the clipped castle accent, her voice has a lusciousness that calls to mind sultanas soaked in brandy. She holds out her hand. I take it. It's as warm and plump as my bed but the skin is thin and fragile. It's blotchy: mostly white on the flat back, the knuckles and joints are darker, freckle colour, and there are dashes of red. She leans in, her weight bearing down on my hand and her bosom pressing against my arm. Staring up at her, I notice white powder has settled into the creases on her face and her eyes are hazel. She's scrutinising me intensely, and it makes me want to pull away. 'A real pleasure.' She lets go of my hand and strokes my velvet sleeves. 'Is she wearing—'

'Yes.' Vill sounds irritated. 'I know. I'm working on it. And you need to work on everything else.' He admires the cluster of rings on his fingers, twisting the bands so the gems are central. 'You do realise how important this is? In order for there to be a wager the King must be pleased.'

'When have I ever not pleased the King?' Mantona asks.

'Do I need to answer that?' Vill fixes her with his pale eyes.

They start arguing and so I leave them to it, drifting to the bookcases.

The one next to the window has a burgundy tint from where the sun catches it. With my left palm pressed against the bookcase, I step into the sunshine and look out the window, already wishing my lessons over so I could be out there amongst nature and breathing the crisp air. The lawn is clipped and level, no stones stray from the white paths, and the trees are green and thick with leaves so perfect and lush they could have been made of silk and sown on. A solitary figure disturbs the painting-like effect. I can tell it's Raen from his honey-brown skin and hair the same colour as the bookshelf.

'You can leave us.' Mantona's terse voice brings me back to the room.

'Are we going to look at the books now?' I ask.

'Too much faith in the written word,' Vill mumbles as he leaves.

Raen ambles past the window, close enough for me to see the petals of the white flower he twirls between his fingers. Once he's cleared the window, he pauses, tucks his hair behind his ears, and seems to contemplate something.

'Vill said you're easily distracted,' Mantona says.

'He likes to lecture me.'

'It's in your best interest.'

Raen backs up, stops, and then looks me up and down. Does he recognise me from the funeral or is it the dress? He frowns and steps nearer. My fingers rub against the dirty silver embroidery and I feel, somehow, to blame for the stitching being ruined in this way. I try to copy his disdain as I give his dark-green tunic, black breeches, and boots the once over, but I can't have perfected it because his lips start to lift.

Mantona calls my name. I peep over my shoulder, see she's coming to join me, so I go back to glaring at Raen with the intensity of a cat trying to scare off a rival. He glances at Mantona, his eyes narrowing and his brow lowering. When his gaze returns to me, he's shaking his head and a smile has tilted up one side of his lips. Her skirts knock against mine. 'You met Raen at the funeral.'

'I know.'

Then he's marching away, his shoulders hunched. The white flower is left, crushed, on the path. I huff and push his earlier insult out of my mind. He'll regret it. When I am queen. Reminded of my reason for being here, I stomp to the bookshelf where the book with the bear emblem is, grab the book and open it. The writing is full of spiky and sharp letters that resemble daggers or thorns.

'What does this say?' I thrust the open book towards Mantona.

She takes it, closes it. Her index finger caresses the copper bear as she speaks. 'History. The rise of the noble bear.'

'I want to read this.' I jab at the book. 'This one and all those books. All the history, where he came from, his myths, his legends, about his homeland. All of it.'

She laughs. 'Some of these books will be very boring; they're little more than castle accounts of who owes what and to whom.'

'I don't care. I want to know everything.'

She nods. 'I wouldn't expect anything less. And you will, but first things first, we need to ensure you stay in the castle. Hopefully, the promise of learning to read will keep you focused and interested.'

'It will.'

She disregards the book, shoving it on top of a row of books, and so I don't believe her. Instead, I make a note of where it is—second bookcase from the window, third shelf up, above the thin books covered in black leather and embossed with suns.

'Then we better get on with it,' Mantona says.

I let her lead me to the fire where she shows me how to sit on the floor without my skirt tipping up and exposing my legs. Her dress splays around her, resembling a black puddle, and I'm reminded of the burnt books. I cross my ankles and begin lowering, only for my legs to give out, making me drop and sprawl.

'Let's hope we're more successful with sharpening up that lazy village accent.' There's a touch of amusement in her voice which stops me from being embarrassed. 'Repeat: my name is Niah.'

I do, slowly, and with great concentration to try to clip my village drawl. She grimaces as she points her ear towards me. I brace myself for her criticism but she simply repeats the phrase and gestures for me to try again.

On and on, the same phrase, her modelling how my mouth should move, where my tongue should be. My throat hurts and the words rasp, yet nothing in her expression hints at whether I'm getting better or worse.

'Try closing your eyes,' she says. 'Imagine Aelius saying it.'

'How do you know?' I ask. 'Did Vill tell you? Aelius? Were you close to him?'

She ignores my questions, gesturing for me to speak again. Her instructions don't help; imagining Aelius's voice makes mine trail with longing and adds a breathiness that doesn't belong in a castle accent.

'Don't get disheartened,' Mantona says. 'It'll take more than a day for you to become a castle lady. There will be things you'll find easier than others.' She rearranges my skirt. The firelight adds a moving sheen and I can't help playing with the lay of the fabric. 'What are your talents?'

'Nothing.'

'Everyone has a talent. What did you do in the village?'

'Try to survive. Try to avoid the villagers. We didn't have time for ... talents.'

'There must be something, something you enjoyed doing as a child.'

'Engraving, carving. I wanted to make things.'

'Perhaps embroidery will be to your liking then. We can try that tomorrow, depending on how far we get today.'

'I'd rather learn to read.'

She nods but doesn't answer, implying my request is being dismissed. I stop playing with my dress, settle my hands on my lap. Her gaze lowers to them, and she smiles. 'What is in those books must be treated like the word of a god because here Onnachild is one. He has power over life and death.' Her voice has changed, the tone less seductive and the pitch slightly higher—perhaps I'm only now meeting the real her—and when she looks up, there's something similar to sadness in her hazel eyes. 'Vill was right though: don't put too much trust in the written word. Letters can lie too.'

The door opens, and Vill's there telling me the dressmakers are ready for me. Behind him, peering over the peaked shoulder of his tunic, is one of the advisers. 'How is she doing?' Vill asks Mantona as he shuts the door. While they discuss my progress and potential dress styles, I slink off to the bookshelf and steal the book with the bear emblem. I'll get Melody to teach me if Mantona won't.

Chapter Twelve

MY KNEES DISTURB THE MUD packed around Aelius's grave like it's a blanket and he's a child. 'Hello, my love,' I whisper into the night. My fingers follow the letters of his name as they did when he wrote it in the dirt to show me how it looked. After sneaking a few lessons from Melody these past weeks, I'm able to understand the other words on his headstone: *from God you came and to God you have returned.* But Aelius is not with Onnachild's God, and he doesn't wait for his father. He waits for me.

I stretch out, splay my bare toes into the mud, and rest my head against his stone. Weeds tickle my ankles as the wind blows through them. Without the cages restricting me, I'm able to inhale fully and draw in the earthy scent of mud, the village stench, the smell of rain lingering. It's refreshing to be away from the floral perfume of the castle, and I'd take the stars over a million jewels. Who am I to try to forget the feeling of wind on my face, the ground beneath my bare feet?

For too long I've been trapped in that castle, moving only from my rooms to the library and seeing only the same four people. My legs and arms ache from dancing, my cheeks hurt from perfecting the simpering smile Mantona models, and my thoughts come with a clipped castle accent. Yet still, I've not seen or received word on my daughter.

Tonight, though, I am free. The thought makes me smile. Tonight I need only be Niah from the Aegni, village-raised. And I will see Aelius, be close to his body. I make a fire and trickle my herbs into it. The flames are timid at first, growing more playful as they scurry over each other, and the smoke wiggles along the ground. 'Are you there?'

The breeze carries a hint of his scent as it plays with my hair. I can feel his presence watching, and so I lie over his grave. 'I have your portrait on the wall above my bed. You look so pompous in it, and those sleeves are ridiculous.' I laugh. 'It should have you smiling, your dimple on display. That's how I picture you.' My fingers trail across the mud as though they're running through his curls. 'I'm sorry I've not visited or called you through the smoke, but Onnachild doesn't want me to leave my rooms, and it's too risky to call you in the castle in case he finds out. Those advisers are always watching me. I'm surprised I managed to sneak away tonight.'

The fire crackles but the smoke billowing from it takes no form. Is Aelius punishing me?

'It's been too long, I know. Please let me see you, by the gods, I miss you. It's so hard, you not being there with me. I keep expecting you to jump out from behind a door and surprise me, tell me this is some stupid joke. Perhaps you wouldn't recognise me, though. They're trying to turn me into a castle woman. They have me in these big, fancy dresses that stick out like ... like upside down bowls.'

A twig cracks. A bird flaps from the church roof but there's no response from the fire. 'They're changing me so much, Aelius, so much, and I wonder ... what you would think of me.' I hunch closer to the flames. 'Am I still pretty?' I hold my breath to listen better and close my eyes.

'Prettier.' The word is so quiet it could be a trick of the wind. The hairs on my arms rise. Leaves shuffle. Warmth rolls closer and with it comes the fragrance of castle life, of my love after being bathed in forests. He's returned for me, he must have. My breath catches in my throat, and my heart stutters. Touch comes; it comes to my neck, light as a drift of smoke. The air is charged, coaxing a sigh from my lips, lips already pursing for kisses, kisses that must surely come, and they do. Gentle at first, a brush, tentative as I imagine a spirit must be. His lips move with mine, the pressure increasing, mirroring my longing. When they part, the taste is familiar yet exotic too, speaking of places I've been and places I may never go.

I give myself over to my body, letting only sensations matter: breath tickling, teeth nipping, the rub of stubble. My love always had such smooth cheeks. I won't think about that. Not now. It must be Aelius. It has to be Aelius. A pulse pumps under my lips when I kiss his neck, a heart adds its sound to the night.

'Open your eyes.' The voice is gruff, familiar, but not Aelius. 'Look at—'

'Don't talk.' My eyelids flutter, but I don't want to see who he really is, and so I clench them; they must stay shut. If they open, this moment will be broken. His kisses will stop waking up my skin. *Feel*, my body says. *Feel, and don't think.* I need the glide of skin against skin, the textures, the heat, how it yields. For tonight this man can be Aelius if I

85

want him to be.

Yanking my dress off over my head, I gasp at the shock of chill air. A low chuckle tickles my nipple and a mouth draws it into wet heat, enticing me closer to the thrill, my back arching. My body throbs like frozen hands plunged into scalding water, and it remembers how to live. More, I need more. I guide his hand down my stomach, down between my legs, and I press it there. He cups me, the warmth of his palm spreading until all of me flushes like sunburn. This is what it is to be alive.

'More,' I plead.

A finger starts circling, his touch so confident, so slow, suggesting he's certain I can hold on all night, but it's been so long, too long, and already I'm trembling. My love has returned. I need to feel him inside me, once again, us, united. I unlace him and take his manhood in my hand. It's pulsing with life. Ha! We have outwitted death.

'Now,' I demand. 'Please now.' My hands scrabble to lift his tunic, skimming over muscles that are larger than I remember, a brush of hair that wasn't there before. *Don't think about these differences. It is my love. For one night he can be here, returned.* I pull him down with me, weight, heaviness, solidness above me. The mud below is shifting, releasing more of its scent. I breathe it in. I breathe him in: castles and forests and home. And my body welcomes him in. His groan is so low it could have come from the depths of the earth. Too low. It doesn't matter. I'm alive, and this man on me is alive, eager, and inside. I could laugh at the bliss of it. How the sensations are like sparks from a fire breaking free.

With each thrust and tease of retreat, I cling on, legs wrapped around his waist as I chase and call for more. My head bashes against his stone, but how can he be dead when he's here, inside me, his sweat on my lips, his muscles moving under my hands? I lick his taste from his shoulder: it's wood smoke, it's castle herbs. He tastes different. I won't think of that, not when my body needs this. No more stone. No more gold. No more portraits. *Just follow and let the thrills swell.* I do. I will. I am alive. He is alive. I call out to hear my pleasure, to call for more. It has me writhing, grabbing his long hair. My lips demand a kiss, demand his mouth to open and take in the sound of my release as it pulses around him, teasing out his. I eat his groan, and I take in the pump of his satisfaction. His body slumps onto mine. It's too tall. It's too heavy.

He is not my love.

Of course he isn't. I knew that.

The fire has gone out. I'm nothing more than a stupid village girl naked on a grave; I can't bring the dead back to life. My legs shake. I can't speak, not even to say please as I push at the man's shoulder, which only moments ago was so tempting to my lips. His taste is on them still and nothing of Aelius is in it. How could my body betray me like this? The man's seed spills out and dampens my thighs as he eases off of me. I roll over, covering my face so I can't see him. If I ignore him, perhaps it will be easier to pretend this never happened. But he kisses my back, tries to curl his body around mine. I shudder and shuffle away. I hear his sharp intake of breath. Then he speaks: 'I'd say that was a pleasant surprise, but I'd be lying about the surprise part.'

Raen. I stiffen. Even my heart seems to pause. By the gods, why was it him? Anyone but him. Better he believes me a brazen whore than see me sob with shame at the trick I've played on myself, and so I say, 'You can go, now.'

'I can, can I? How kind. You're done with me, then?'

'Yes, I'm done with you.' My voice is terse. 'Thank you.'

'Thank you?' He scoffs.

Why won't he just shut up and leave?

'Before I go, perhaps you wouldn't mind answering a question for me. They say one prince is as good as another.' His voice is too loud in the quiet graveyard. The tones of castle and village and the place he was banished to grate across my bare skin. 'Now you've used us both, what do you think?'

But I can't allow myself to think; if I think I'll cry. He's not making any moves to leave and so I unfurl my body, force my shoulders back and down as my lessons have taught me. The proud angle of my chin is all Niah from the Aegni. With as much dignity as I can muster, I dress and prepare to beg forgiveness from Aelius's portrait.

Chapter Thirteen

IT'S THERE THE MOMENT I AWAKE: the odour of sex, mud, and forests. I thought I'd left it behind in the village river when I scrubbed myself clean and sobbed but no, I brought it with me.

Nessia's leaning on her side and staring down at me. 'Where did you go last night?' There's a crease across her cheek and I focus on that to stop my mind returning to the damp mud, the coldness of stone, the softness of flesh.

'Nowhere. I was here.'

'What's wrong?'

'Nothing.' My fingers travel to the mark on my neck left by his teeth. I tug a lock of hair over it. 'I didn't sleep well, that's all.'

'Where did you go?'

'Nessia, I'm tired. Please.'

The door opens, saving me from her questions, and Melody drags in a tub. A procession of servant boys carries in buckets of water. The floral-scented steam is too sweet this morning. I roll onto my other side, away from Nessia's inquisitive eyes. Her hand touches my shoulder, probably to encourage me to speak; instead, it makes me shudder and shuffle further away. I can't bear to tell her I've ruined everything. I've let her down.

'Did you see Aelius?' she asks.

One prince is as good as another. My cheeks heat as Raen's words repeat. 'No.'

'You can't see the dead,' Melody says. 'They're dead and that is that. Until you die too and go to God's home.'

'That might be what they've told you,' Nessia snaps at Melody but her frustration must be due to my evasiveness.

Not now, I want to say. The words to describe last night can't be spoken here, not with Aelius looking at me, his expression cold, and not out of protocol, but because he knows. Spirits don't forgive. What if he came into the fire, saw me and Raen? I hide under the furs, only to find the stench of my mistakes there waiting, and so I'm relieved when Nessia peels back the cover, though her frown has me wondering whether she can smell it too.

'Can you really see the dead?' Melody asks. 'Are there any in this room? Over there? There? You know this was the False Queen's room, don't you? Can you see her at the dressing table composing a letter, maybe to her husband, the King, begging for forgiveness? Do the dead talk to you? Can you have a conversation with them like we're having?'

'Sometimes,' I mumble.

'I guess they don't come if they don't want to. Just because someone is dead doesn't make them obedient, does it,' she says.

Nessia rolls me over, tries to fix my eyes with hers but I stare up at the canopy. 'You went to his grave, didn't you? Even though Vill said not to leave these rooms without Onnachild's permission? Niah—'

'Please.' I want her to be quiet. I want to forget.

'There was no comfort there?' Her tone softens.

'I won't be going again.'

'Ready,' Melody calls.

I get out of bed and once I'm standing, Melody picks a twig out of my hair. It's the same colour as Raen's eyes and has three dots of green moss on it. I bash it from her hands and grind it under my bare feet as I walk to the tub. A bath will get rid of him better than a village river did. It will coat me in flowers, make me sweet again.

'By God, what has happened to ...' Melody gasps.

I've not been quick enough between undressing and plunging into the tub, and so she must have noticed the grazes on my back. 'Are servants meant to comment on their mistress's flesh?' I sink into the water to cover the marks. They sting and make me hiss: I deserve this. Nessia clambers from the bed, landing with a dull thud and a groan. She bends me forwards and lifts my hair so she can see for herself.

'Please, Nessia,' I whimper. 'Later.' When Melody isn't here. Later when I understand it.

She releases my hair. I look over my shoulder at her and she nods.

'What happened? What's that on your neck?' Melody asks. 'Where did it happen? If you don't tell me, I'll find out.'

'You will not. If I wanted you to know, I'd tell you. I do not. Some secrets are none of your business.' I slide under the water to muffle her voice.

'What if it isn't meant to be a secret? Some things shouldn't be.'

Nessia takes the cloth from Melody and sends her off to get my dress ready. Once we're alone, I rise and let Nessia help me wash. Her touch is comforting and gentle; it's more care than I deserve after my actions in the graveyard, and it brings tears to my eyes. I dash them away with the back of my hands, hands that touched another. Water splashes as I plunge them into the tub. 'I did something bad, so bad,' I whisper. 'I'm everything they say I am.'

She scoots in front of me and cups my cheeks, the sleeves of her nightdress trailing in the water. 'A mistake is a mistake. Now out you get or you'll be late for your lessons.'

I nod, glad to follow her instructions and give myself to her as she wraps me up like a child in swaddling. She smells unfamiliar. She smells of castle life, soap, and dust. Melody comes over to help me dress, a sullen expression on her face.

'I'm not a servant.' She sounds sulky.

'No, you're not. Sorry,' I say, watching Nessia climb into the bath and wondering whether I should stop her. A leaf is floating on the surface, small and spiky. Where did that come from?

Melody puts the cage around me and yanks on it. I welcome the pain of it digging into my torso, the rub of it against the grazes. Maybe the only way I can be respectable is to be contained in this manner: blood cut off and my back forced straight. My mourning dress feels dishonest and knowing it was the First Queen's reminds me of Raen. Melody guides me to the dressing table, but I avoid my reflection as she works on my hair. The brush of her fingers against my neck makes me flinch and tense. She rummages through a drawer, eventually pulling out emerald earrings and a long line of diamonds which she weaves through my hair.

'Lovely.' She leans back to admire her work.

I don't feel lovely and so I don't return her smile.

'Vill's coming today. I'm sure he'll have good news,' she says.

'Ammi!' I grab Melody's wrist. 'He's bringing Ammi?' My stomach tenses with hope.

'I don't think so. They're looking for nursemaids.'

I let go. 'She doesn't need a nursemaid. She needs her mother. I need her.' But I don't deserve her, not after last night. If Onnachild found out … is my guilt evident on my face? I lean closer to the mirror to check. What I see is emotionless, docile, wholesome, clean, and the irony is not lost on me. My fingers graze the mark his teeth left, expecting to find it still warm. His touch was so precise, so confident, how could it have aroused my body like the eager grabbing of my love?

'Every royal child needs a nursemaid. I bet even Raen had one,' Melody says.

The mention of his name has me pushing away from the dressing table. Pacing, I notice that my walk has changed, but that realisation doesn't make me smile. Nessia, now out of the bath and wearing a simple brown dress, stops me with a strong hand against my shoulder. The urge to bite my nails is strong, only they might taste of Raen, so I clasp them behind me. The gesture makes the cage dig deeper into my bosom.

Vill doesn't knock before entering my bedchamber and his sudden arrival makes me jump. He's dressed in white and would look frozen if it wasn't for the colour in his plump lips.

'You should knock,' I moan.

My surliness doesn't seem to affect his mood as he keeps posing there in the doorway and asks, 'How are we this fine morning?'

'Melody says there's good news,' I say.

'There is indeed good news. The King has requested your presence.'

Onnachild knows. Raen must have told him. I reach around, grab Nessia's hand. I'm being sent back to the village. Or worse.

Chapter Fourteen

'WALK,' ONNACHILD ROARS from the other end of the Judging Room.

Don't think of last night, I tell myself. *Don't think of the First Queen, even if you are wearing her dress.*

'You can do this,' Nessia whispers.

Forcing everything but my training from my mind, I picture Mantona and mimic her walk: small and light steps, hips leading the sway of my skirt, hands together and resting against my stomach. Neither the advisers nor Vill are here, and Nessia is clomping beside me, which should make it easier to face Onnachild but it doesn't. The natural light arches around him in blue and grey tones, and his shadow looms across the floor, a black presence claiming the space as his domain. His smell, meat and decadence, overpowers. I wish I could see his expression, discern whether this old bear is ready to play or kill.

We halt before him, Nessia fumbling into a curtsy. I settle into the pose Mantona had me practise in the mirror: my chin slightly dipped and tilted to one side. With a subtle shake of my head, my hair covers the tell-tale mark on my neck. My eyes flicker up to try to gauge Onnachild's intention, but his expression is blank. Clustered together on the table in front of him are four golden goblets decorated with hawks and knobbly with white gems. Are they for a celebration, sealing an agreement, or to wash away the distaste of dealing with me?

'You. Who are you?' With a curt nod, he gestures towards Nessia.

Her voice is loud and steady as she says her name.

'From the village too?'

'Yes.'

'So now there are two of you. Why am I not surprised? You would do well to remember what I say and ensure it is adhered to fully.'

Nessia nods and stumbles out of her curtsy, reaching for me to help her stabilise herself.

'You,' he barks at me. 'Turn.'

I do as he directs. Once. Twice. Three times. My shoulders are back and down, my neck long, and my head remains tilted as he inspects me from the bottom of my skirt up. It reminds me of being plunged into the village river but I manage to suppress my shiver. He remains impenetrable and gloomy with his dark hair and eyes, tight mouth, and the splatters of grey in his beard. The sound of him scratching it prickles my spine but again, I manage to suppress a shiver and that gives me courage. It seems

I've been trained well; now, if I can keep my words clipped and not slip into my village drawl perhaps ... if he doesn't know about last night. He can't know, can he?

'Stop,' he says.

I do. Nessia curtsies again, but he ignores her and keeps his appraising stare on me. 'Black doesn't suit you.'

A Maiden appears, pours wine into a goblet. He takes a sip and sloshes it around his mouth before waving her away. She leaves the jug of wine. He doesn't pour any for me or Nessia, so if he is celebrating it isn't something we're partaking in.

'I have seen the child.' Onnachild puts the goblet on the table. 'And I have heard from your teacher.'

Concentrating hard to keep my words clipped and precise, I speak slowly. 'All good, I hope.' I widen my smile.

He doesn't smile back.

'Will my daughter be joining us?' I ask, unable to use her new name.

'No.'

'I would like to see her.'

'She will not be coming.'

'When can I see her? How is she? We've received no word of her.'

'Quiet.' A growl comes into his deep voice. 'She is under my care. That is all you need to know.'

'You should be kinder to our guest,' Raen says from behind me.

My stomach spasms.

'Why is it you are always where you aren't wanted?' Onnachild says, speaking my thoughts. His nails tap on the throne, filling the room with the sound of his irritation. Nessia's turning around, elbowing me to do the same. I don't want to but I can't help myself. Is Raen here to tell Onnachild? To gloat? Hopefully, his expression will forewarn me.

He's lounging against the open door, the eyes and ears carved on it

94

around him and mocking me: all-seeing, all-knowing. The simple cut of his tunic accentuates the curve of his shoulder, reminding me of the press of it against my lips.

'I don't suppose you remember me, do you?' he says, ignoring his father's cutting remark. 'I gave you some coins.'

'I remember.'

'It seems you've spent them wisely.' His stare is like Onnachild's, critical and trying to intimidate, but it heats my skin as if it's trickling embers. I squeeze my hands so they don't glide to the mark his teeth left on my neck, the mark his eyes are lingering on. Despite my cheeks burning, I refuse to look away and show I'm ashamed of my actions. No, I will pretend it never happened.

'If you are coming in, then come in,' Onnachild bawls.

Raen nods and closes the door, so leisurely I get the impression he's purposefully trying to annoy his father. It almost makes me laugh. He saunters by me, close enough to make my skirt sway and for me to get a nose full of his scent. I gulp away the taste of him. His fingers trail along the table's surface as lightly as they did my belly. My legs start shaking again. I will deny it, whatever he says about last night.

'Why have we called Niah here today?' Raen smirks over his shoulder at me. His words imply he hasn't told Onnachild. Yet. But that smirk ... I'm not sure what that is hinting at. I gulp again and hope Onnachild is so distracted by Raen he doesn't notice my pose is losing its softness.

'*We* have not called her,' Onnachild says. '*I* have called her.'

'Is she not allowed to sit?' Raen pulls out a chair and then plonks himself down, resting his elbows on the table.

Onnachild sighs. 'Fine. Sit.'

Nessia rushes to pull out a chair for me, one opposite Raen. He slouches in his seat as I sit and ram my back up against the chair's spindles to stop myself hunching. My hands rest on my lap, but my palms are itching to rub against the underside of the yew table. Nessia bumps onto the seat next to me and pats my trembling knee. Raen helps himself to wine but doesn't take a sip. Instead, his fingers run up and down the stem of his goblet. They're long and thick, his knuckles like the nodes on a tree. I can't ... I force myself to focus on the table, follow the dents and scratches my ancestors left across the grain.

'The child is his,' Onnachild says.

'Did we ever doubt that?' Raen answers before I can.

'Village girls are not known for their faithfulness.'

I try not to bristle, digging my nails, neatened by Mantona, into my palms to remind me to hold my simpleton expression. Nessia elbows me and nods towards Raen, who is glaring at his goblet, surely souring the wine, as though it, and not Onnachild, insulted his mother. I peep across at Onnachild; his lips are twitching into a smile as he watches his son.

'She will stay,' he says.

'Is that all it takes to be raised to castle life?' Raen's tone is mocking, but the sentiment hasn't reached his face. 'We best keep such knowledge from the other village women; I don't think I'd be able to fend off their advances.'

Their eyes lock, each man seeming to challenge the other to blink and back down first. My gaze flits from one to the other. Onnachild's countenance resembles his portrait daring the storm, arrogant, powerful, and ready to conquer, and Raen's returning that intensity. It's obvious they have more important things than my indiscretion to concern themselves with; their hatred for each other is as palpable as smoke from burning fields. That hatred makes them more alike, both broad and big-boned, square-faced, and with thick eyebrows lowered and shadowing their dark eyes. Raen's jaw pulses, and I'm sure beneath his beard Onnachild's is doing the same.

'Thank you. We're grateful, Your Highness.' Nessia breaks the tension.

Onnachild keeps staring at Raen. 'Perhaps you should wait before giving your thanks. You have not heard my terms.'

'Please, Your Highness.' I make my voice as sweet as possible, wishing it could replicate that seductive richness Mantona's has. 'But when will I see my child? I didn't give her to you.'

'You are a villager; what is yours is already mine. You will be informed if, and when, I decide you can see her.'

'Of course.' The words hurt my throat.

'You must be kinder,' Raen says. 'Look at me for an example of what happens when a child is denied its mother.' He finally takes a sip of his wine, breaking eye contact with his father but I don't sense that Onnachild has won or a stalemate has been agreed. 'Grace should be here. We are, after all, all that's left of the family.'

'There is still time,' Onnachild mumbles. He shifts in the throne, partially blocking Raen as he addresses me. 'Your teacher informs me you cannot dance, cannot play music, or sew. I have no idea what could have drawn my son to you.'

'Oh, I don't know,' Raen says. 'Village women can be quite charming when they want to be, surely you remember that?'

If he was nearer, I'd kick him but there's no chance of making contact with his shin, so instead, I curl my toes in my shoes and do my best to stop my half-smile becoming a sneer.

'You know we do not talk of that,' Onnachild says.

'You might not but I do.'

'I do not talk of that, and while you are under my roof neither will you.' He bangs his fist on the arm of the throne. Nessia jumps. My gaze darts up to Onnachild's red and tense face. Out of the corner of my eye, I spot Raen smiling, hinting that he intended to anger his father. Onnachild takes a deep breath, flaring out his nostrils. 'Hartnell is convinced that you can pass for a castle woman and Cantor is biting, so I'm inclined to let you stay. You will have a modest salary for clothes; I have no wish to see you in that other village girl's dresses. I will not have people gossip, and I do not wish to be reminded of my mistakes.'

'Then I can hardly see why I'm here,' Raen says.

'We need a prince in the castle, even if it is you.'

The comment makes Raen's jaw twitch, the only sign he heard it. My lips quirk: Raen got the answer to his question. No, one prince is not as good as another. I recall the circumstances that prompted the question, and I'm not so smug.

'As I was saying.' Onnachild heaves at the furs around him, bringing more up onto his shoulders. 'You will remember your place and remember that I grant you said place. And I can revoke my kind offer. You are to earn your keep, as the servants do. Do not forget this.'

I pinch my wrist to stop myself from shouting that he is not kind, and I am not like a servant. He's the interloper in this room, on that throne. I notice Raen tilt his head and slide forwards in his chair. Can he see the anger flashing in my eyes? I take as deep a breath as the cage will allow and get my emotions under control before speaking. 'I'm in your debt, and I hope to remain in your favour.' The words grate more because Raen's watching, judging me.

'And you should,' Onnachild says. 'You will be pretty and pleasing to the eye. I will not have ugly things in my castle, but I will not have you enticing my men and corrupting them with your filthy, licentious village ways. You do as I say, you stay. You get to see your child. I'm keeping this simple so your village brain will understand, so there can be no excuse. Understand?'

I nod and keep my attention on the bulges of his nose, trying to work out how many times it's been broken, but still, I blush at his words because I'm reminded of what I did last night, what it proved. My flush seems to please Onnachild so he must be taking it as a sign of feigned virginal innocence instead of guilt.

'I have no interest in any man. I wouldn't betray Aelius.' It amazes me how steady my voice is. How I can push away thoughts of last night, despite a shaft of sunlight moving and lighting up Raen's skin. It's almost the same shade as the sapwood rippling through the centre of the table. His scent is getting more potent, too: forests, autumn, castle.

'Not for a man with good legs and pleasing eyes?' Raen taunts.

'I would not do so willingly.'

'You will not do so at all.' Onnachild's fingernails tap the throne, drawing my attention to his bristly knuckles. The shame from trying to kiss them is heavy and sickly, but I welcome it replacing the shame from last night which has a different, strange, fluttering quality to it. 'If you stay long enough, and marriage becomes a concern, then I will decide when and to whom, and you will do so willingly. And you ...' He jabs a thick finger towards Nessia. 'You will make sure she doesn't forget her teachings and descend into that base village nature. I don't know what or who you are; I don't care. Here you will be her servant. I'm not providing one. You can have that Maiden, when the castle doesn't need her, to ensure you do not stray from the True God.'

'Thank you, Your Highness. You are most kind.' Nessia nods and bows to him. The best I can manage is not letting my smile falter.

'If you do not obey me, then—'

'I don't think you need to specify,' Raen interrupts. 'We know what happens to village women who forget their place.'

'I told you.' Onnachild smacks the throne again. 'If I have to tell you again ...'

Raen sups his wine. His eyes are sparkling; whether it's caused by the sunlight on him or amusement I can't decide. Nessia nudges me to look at Onnachild. His nostrils are flaring again, his cheeks cranberry red. 'Don't forget I can still send you back. And you.' He points at me. 'I act against my own experiences with your kind. You might look the part, you might even sound the part, but I'm still reminded of the expression "you can't polish a shit", so know this, one slip, one bad word, and you will regret it. My people will be watching you and one indiscretion will be enough.' His finger lifts. 'One.'

'And the child? When I came in Niah was asking when she could see her daughter.'

'When I deem it fit was my answer, and that is still my answer.'

An adviser appears like a suddenly thrown spear. He bends to whisper in Onnachild's ear, and as he does so his grey eyes fix on Raen and his top lip curls. Onnachild nods several times, mutters something I can't hear. While they're distracted, I place my hands on the table, fingers seeking the marks from my ancestors. The charge from the yew is a hot tickle. Onnachild stands and gathers his furs around him, flinging them over his shoulders and disturbing the line of sunshine. 'This meeting is over.'

'Is this anything I need to be aware of?' Raen rises.

The adviser tuts, implying he thinks Raen's an idiot.

'This is *royal* business,' Onnachild says.

I listen to the two men stomp across the room, their whispers a bluster behind them, but my gaze remains on Raen. 'That told me, didn't it.' His voice is emotionless but the green dots in his eyes blaze. 'And you too.' His hands slide across the table as he pushes out his chair. The tips touch mine. Jolt back. The door bangs shut. I let out a breath I didn't realise I was holding, and Nessia slumps and sighs.

As Raen passes me, he bends close and whispers in my ear, 'What do you suppose Onnachild would do if he knew about last night?'

Chapter Fifteen

NOISE BURSTS THROUGH THE OPEN DOOR to the great hall: chatter, music, giggles, guffaws. At last I'm going to see what Aelius saw, see where he sat. I'm going to dance, to laugh, to play. It would be like stepping into a dream if I wasn't so aware of Onnachild's threat. Tonight is my first real test amongst castle women.

'Are you going in?' an adviser asks me.

'Or are you going to stand there all night?' the other says.

Their stares make me feel like I'm still in village rags and not a new dress made especially for me. Vill designed the off-the-shoulder sleeves fluffed out with feathers and the gems clustered on the bodice, and he chose the scarlet fabric. I try not to fuss with the low neckline that exposes more bosom than I'm used to.

'Is this the welcome all new guests can expect?' Vill sidles up to me. His squeeze of my arm is reassuring and so I straighten out my shoulders.

'Forgive us, we forget Niah is kin of yours,' one says, sarcastically.

'It's not for me to forgive but God and Niah.'

'I forgive you,' I say as haughtily as I can.

As Vill and I enter the Great Hall, I try to copy his pose of indifference but it's difficult to do so when the room is more dazzling than I'd imagined. Light is everywhere: diffused, pin-dotted, white, yellow, orange, waving, shimmering. It rebounds off jewellery, off knives, off goblets, off long and arched windows. The scent of beeswax candles, the scent of my childhood, mixes with a thousand different flowery perfumes. Tables make a horseshoe shape around the hall, and there is a larger table at the top of the room that isn't joined. Everyone around the horseshoe is blond, dressed in spring colours, and pale-skinned. Vill's wearing pastel shades of blue and lilac that make his eyes look like glass. I glance at my scarlet dress and my bare arms.

101

'Why did you make me wear this?' I hiss. 'I stand out.'

'You're meant to.' He pats my hand. 'Don't let them intimidate you. We shall take the castle's breath away.'

People call to Vill as we move around a table, and he pauses, flashes his smile at them as he introduces me. The men watch my chest rise and fall. No one contradicts him when he says we're cousins, though afterwards I hear the women gossiping. We pass men prettier than the wives beside them, women spilling out of ornate dresses, men with bellies that protrude like hills. Vill points out the merchants at the far end of the horseshoe, their wealth displayed in the jewelled bracelets layered up their arms.

'Should I go and charm them?' I ask.

A group of them are scrutinising me as if I'm a good to be sold, and judging by the curve of their top lips, they can't think me worth much.

He nods a greeting in their direction. 'Leave them to me.'

It takes me a moment to recognise Mantona because her hair is blonde and not the grey-streaked brown it normally is, and her purple dress adds a blue tinge to the skin across her chest. Her gaze sweeps up and down my dress. 'Very nice.'

'I hope I don't disappoint you.' I sit beside her.

'You won't.' She pours me a goblet of wine. 'I won't let you.'

'You're so lucky to have Vill as your cousin,' the young woman on my other side says. Her blue eyes follow him as he saunters away.

'He has been a good cousin.' I speak carefully so my village accent doesn't slip out.

She sighs wistfully. 'You owe him your life.'

'I do.'

The old man next to her taps her bony arm and chastises her in a low voice. I watch Vill greeting the women on the opposite side of the room, making them fluster and fuss. Everyone else looks bored. Some men slouch in their seats and click for servants to bring more wine. Their wives sit with their arms crossed, sour expressions on their faces.

'Don't stare,' Mantona says.

I nod and lower my head, but only for a moment, I can't help it; I must see. Hung from the walls are intricate tapestries with bright coloured birds: hawks, goldfinches, and a bird I don't know the name of but must have been the Second Queen's emblem. The True Queen, I correct myself. Two glass doors, etched with suns, lead out into the gardens. Higher up, above the doors and the tapestries, wooden beams sprout into arches and brackets, creating a design more intricate than a honeycomb or a spider's web. They lead my eye down the room to the top table.

'That was Prince Aelius's place.' Mantona points at a simple chair made of laburnum. It's below a tapestry depicting winged figures scattering stars, the yellow thread the same colour as his hair. A place has been set as if he'll be joining us, if only he would. How surprised he'd be to see me here. I smile, picturing him there in a tunic decorated with goldfinches and daisies.

Next to his empty seat is Raen. He's slumped down, arms crossed, and a surly expression directed at his goblet. He looks coarse and out of place compared to Vill, who sits on his other side. My gaze darts to the tapestry above him when his head rises. It depicts Onnachild's God, the form surrounded by stitching representing sun rays. Below this figure are faceless, brown shapes which must represent the villagers. I start to frown but manage to catch myself.

'He certainly inherited his mother's looks,' Mantona says. 'It does my heart good to see them back in the castle.'

I'm distracted by the sound of the door closing and the advisers shuffling to the far-left corner of the room. They watch me. I duck my head.

'Don't worry about them,' she says. 'Their appearance is worse than their bite. They came over with Onnachild on his first campaign but I don't know what their names were then. You can tell them apart because Aesc has ink-stained fingers and Ascelin has the bigger nose. They were there at the breaking of the Legacy Treaty but—' She holds her hand up as the background chatter is fading. 'I'll tell you later. The King is coming. Stand when he enters.'

I nod. The only noise comes from the crackling fires. Both advisers slink behind the top table and draw back a red curtain, showing us Onnachild at the bottom of a narrow staircase. His walk has a lumbering quality, like one of his stocky legs is shorter than the other. The servants rush to pull out his chair for him. He glances at Raen then the empty chair before easing into his own. The castle people sit and noise returns.

Mantona talks to the barrel-shaped man on her right and so doesn't continue her story. Servants are flooding into the room, silver trays balanced in their hands and along their arms. They scurry around tables, never bumping into each other, dodging when a castle person's arm shoots out. The trays are placed in front of us: trays with thick sauces that drip onto the table, trays of goose, pork, quail meat, bread as white as doves, vegetables that glisten like jewels. The array of smells and the multitude of choices are overwhelming so I take a sip of my wine, savouring the tones of honey, cinnamon, and ginger.

Mantona dishes out a selection of the foods onto my plate, filling it. 'Eat up. You'll need your strength to survive this castle.'

As I eat, she keeps peeking at me and smiling to herself. I'm too nervous about making a mess of the table or dripping sauce down my dress to enjoy the food. *Take small bites, chew slowly*, I remind myself. Black pepper burns my nose but I stifle the sneeze. Beside me, the young woman chews noisily and bashes me with her elbow while she rips apart the pork on her plate.

'Are you enjoying yourself?' Mantona asks.

'I think ...' I swallow. 'It's a bit daunting.'

'You're doing well.'

Men push themselves away from the table to let their bellies hump up. One undoes his belt, and it hangs like a flattened snake. There are a few low, rumbling burps. None of the plates or trays I see is empty, mine included. It looks like I've hardly eaten yet my belly is pushing against my cage and I'm starting to feel sleepy. I apologise to my gods, in silence, for such waste. As the servants remove the trays, people grab for one last piece of meat, one last piece of bread, even though they look overfull and in pain when they chew.

Mantona leans close, her bosom resting on my arm. 'Now the dancing will start. A time to make alliances, to share secrets, to flirt and catch husbands.'

'Onnachild will not allow that.'

'Nonsense. He's an old romantic at heart, and before you reach that a big ball of lewdness.' Her laugh makes her breasts shake.

'How do you know that?'

She can't hear me because she's rising from her seat and then she's off with the man who was sat beside her. Other people are moving too: women and men couple up and make their way to the central space, older men group together and head towards the doors, the Maidens line up behind Onnachild with their instruments. I spot Melody amongst them even though they're all dressed the same. She's the shortest, and she's grinning at me whereas the others look solemn. Her head lowers when she's nudged by the Maiden next to her. One of them sings. Her voice is clear and strong even when she reaches the high notes which tingle down my spine. I sigh, my gaze lingering on Aelius's vacant chair. If only he was here to experience this with me, hold me for my first dance, giggle when I misstepped.

My view is blocked by Vill and Raen standing in front of me and instantly I'm reminded of what I did. As Raen tucks a lock of hair behind his ear, a waft of his scent drifts over: forests, castle, autumn. I block my nose with the side of my hand.

'My cousin, Niah,' Vill says to Raen. They both seem amused and on the verge of laughter. Has Raen told Vill about the graveyard?

'We've met before,' I say. 'We don't need to meet again.'

'Several times in fact, but never have you looked so beguiling.' Raen's dark eyes linger on my chest, squashed and squished up by the cage. I fight the urge to pull the bodice up, hunching instead. He notices, and his lips quirk, so I square my shoulders, thrust my bosom out to show him I won't be intimidated.

'I'm not sure whether it would be bad manners to ask you to dance since my father said you can't dance, but ...' He holds out his hand for mine. His palm is square, the lines deep, and the pads slightly calloused. How could my body have enjoyed its touch when it is so different to the slim and soft hand of my love? 'Would you like to prove him wrong?'

'With you?'

'Well, I'm here, asking.' He thrusts his hand at me, a challenge. 'I promise to make concessions.'

I don't see that I have a choice, what with the advisers watching me, and so I take his hand.

Chapter Sixteen

'READY?' RAEN ASKS, moving before I can answer. He's probably expecting to catch me off guard, but it doesn't work: my feet follow. My right hand hovers, avoiding his shoulder, the shoulder I've kissed, tasted. I crane my neck, keep my head back, and peer around him. Vill's asking a woman with blonde curls and an insolent expression to dance. Why didn't he ask me, instead of letting Raen? The music tickles through the thin soles of my shoes, and I focus on that rather than the warmth of Raen's palm against mine. His other hand is on my waist, keeping me at a distance as if he's concerned I will dirty his clothes. When I glare up at him, his jaw is tense and his mouth down-turned.

'Why have you asked me to dance?' I ask. 'You clearly don't want to.'

'Perhaps to annoy you. Perhaps to annoy Onnachild.'

'Then why not just tell him about ...' I wince at my stupidity for alluding to the graveyard and then wish I hadn't because the movement draws his gaze down to mine. His eyes narrow and his forehead wrinkles. The hand on my waist tightens then loosens as his gaze darts up over my head again.

'I should, shouldn't I? See I had a bet with myself about you, and I'm pleased to find I was right. You say you loved my half-brother, but I ask myself is love really that convenient? Can there be love when one is starving and the other overfed? How can it be love when you were so eager last night?'

'I made a mistake. You tricked me.'

'I did? How did I do that? I seem to remember it was you who pulled off my tunic, guided my hand—'

'Shut up.' My face burns; his chuckle doesn't help. I kick his shin, stumbling when my foot catches in my skirt. It's so satisfying I'd do it again only he seems unaffected, continuing to stare over me and match the rhythm of the song.

'Onnachild would say it was your nature, your village blood.'

'How can you say such things when your own mother—'

'I won't speak about her. Weren't you listening to Onnachild?' His mocking tone implies that obeying his father is the last thing he'll ever do.

'I remember though, remember her looking majestic as he hanged her.'

'I won't talk about her.' His jaw twitches, and it pleases me to see him affected. 'It's not that easy to forget though is it?' His hold on me tightens as his head turns towards Onnachild. 'Everywhere there are mementoes of Aelius and his mother: the Maidens, the sickly women with their fake hair, the false piety. But you, me, we're memories the King would rather forget. I hope our very presence haunts him.' He lowers his eyes to meet mine. The green dots are wider, bleeding into the surrounding brown. 'You'd do well to tame your ambition, forget your Aegnian ways. When you remember my mother, remember the old gods didn't save her, remember what Onnachild did to her, and be careful.'

'Why do you care?'

'Why do I care?' He leans back, stops dancing and seems confused that I should ask. 'Maybe I don't.' He gathers me up and easily finds the beat of the song. It's such a slow beat I'm not sure why I'm finding it hard to breathe. It must be the cage.

'Or maybe,' he says, 'I'm hoping it'll happen again.'

'It won't, because, to answer your question ... One prince is not as good as another.'

'Why? Because I'm not handsome enough? Not blond enough? Refined enough? Gold enough? Are you already blinded by so much gold?'

'No.'

'Coins are man-made, you know.'

'I know.'

Ignoring him, I watch the pastel-coloured skirts of the castle women fan and spin like flower petals cast into a summer breeze. The patter of their feet on the floor, the rocking of my cage against my legs, and the candlelight are as lulling as a child's song. They call me to relax but I'm here in Raen's arms, tense, and trying to stop my palm from settling on his shoulder, my cheek from resting against his chest. His scent seems a part of this magic, too. I'm sure if I closed my eyes I'd find myself in a forest, dancing amongst a whirl of fire-coloured leaves. How much of this song is left?

'That was clever to get yourself with child.' His harsh tone jolts me back into the room.

'A woman doesn't just get with child.'

'I do know how it works, and it's worked out very favourably for you, hasn't it? Such a perfect copy of her father, she is.'

'You've seen her?' I rise onto my tiptoes, try to meet his eyes so he can't lie but he keeps staring over my head. 'Is she well?'

'I've seen her, blonde and blue-eyed like royalty must be. Not dark and muddy like us.' He chuckles, the sound resembles the rumble of a wagon over stones and it jars just the same.

'I don't know what you find funny.'

'If I don't laugh, then I might ...' His jaw twitches again and his hand leaves my waist to touch, briefly, the scar by his left eye. 'If you don't want the throne then why are you here, Niah?' It's unnerving to hear a village twang in the way he says my name and I almost misstep.

'Because I should be,' I say.

His hand returns to my waist with a light brush, before settling. The touch has us both looking away. My attention is drawn to Aelius's empty place at the top table.

'Onnachild would never have allowed you two to marry, you realise that don't you? Aelius was to marry another foreign princess, breed more feeble children with her.'

'Aelius would have made him.'

'Please. He wouldn't have made anyone do anything. He was a boy, and not just any boy but the King's.' Raen swings me around with such a deft flick of his arm that I lose my centre and grip his shoulder to steady myself. He shrugs off the touch, but it's too late, my palm remembers and throbs like nettles have stung it. I try to shake off the sensation, only it moves up my arm, and the mark his mouth left on my neck warms. I'd rub it but I don't want him to notice and be reminded. My hand returns to hovering above his shoulder, and I force myself to stare at the silver embroidery decorating his black tunic, follow the pattern across his chest. It looks like frosted ivy around a burnt tree.

'To answer your earlier question,' he says. 'Maybe I'm counting on Onnachild seeing your true colours eventually, and then I won't have your fate on my conscience.'

'My true colours?'

He nods and his hair brushes across my knuckles. I bat it away.

'I've had a lesson in being the underdog,' he says. 'Of wanting that throne, so I recognise that ambition in another. A pretty dress, good food, and a room in the castle won't be enough for you. You'll want the whole castle and the throne. Don't think I'll just give it to you.'

'It is not yours to give.'

'Not yet,' he murmurs in my ear. His breath tickles, reminds, awakens. I misstep, bump into him and his hands tighten. He must feel my palm getting sweaty.

'Not ever.'

He chuckles. 'Spoken like a true underdog. Well, be assured, should you manage to keep fooling Onnachild, there'll be a place here for you when I'm king.'

'What if I am queen?'

'That will never happen.' His expression, as he looks down, is soft, playful, and so this seems like a game. I almost smile.

'But—'

'But if you are ...' He lowers his head until we're almost cheek to cheek. He must feel the heat coming off me when he pulls me closer. 'Then I will have died. Unless, of course, Onnachild banishes me again. Yes, I had that talk too, pretty much word for word. What was it he said? One mistake. Not two, but one. Don't forget. One mistake.' His gruff voice and scowl as he waves a finger in front of my nose is such a perfect imitation of Onnachild that I laugh. It feels good to laugh. His smile brightens up his face, makes him almost boyish, and the green in his eyes sparkles like wet moss. He ducks his head, not in a bow to me, but more like he's trying to hide something behind his dark hair. The music stops and my laughter is too loud in the momentary silence before another song begins.

'Now excuse me, I must dance with someone else and try to convince them I'm everything that my wonderful half-brother was.'

I watch him approach Vill and the woman in yellow. Her fingers linger towards Vill as she curtsies to Raen and smiles at him. Vill spots me and swaggers over to my side. I wonder if he's aware of the woman's lecherous gaze following him as Raen draws her into his arms, much closer than he held me.

'Would you care to dance with someone more pleasing?' Vill's hand is out and ready. 'I've been told I'm an exquisite dancer. Think of it as an apology for leaving you with Raen.' He nods towards the man. 'I hope you made a pleasing impression on him.'

I take Vill's hand, the chill of it refreshing after the heat of Raen's. 'He's already made up his mind about me.'

'Then change it. No one is immune to charm. We need him on our side.'

He leads us to the edge of the crowd, probably wanting to show off and have all eyes on him. His movements are so fluid when we dance I'm like a bird soaring through the sky as we pass Mantona partnered by a man whose head only reaches her bosom. She's watching Raen as his tunic tightens, loosens, and tightens across his broad shoulders. The woman dancing with him looks smaller than she did when she partnered Vill.

'Who cares what he thinks?' I say.

'Other women seem to.'

'Then they don't deserve to have sight. He's far too muddy looking, far too wide, like a bull, and there's nothing pleasing in his face, just hardness and bitterness, and that scar, well, it shows how disagreeable he is. Women only want him because he's a prince.'

'But he has not been owned or claimed as such yet,' Vill whispers.

'He may not be?'

'You've read my mind. I'm sure you understand the ramifications for us and Grace—' he holds up his hand to stop me correcting him '—should Raen start pleasing Onnachild.'

'Annoying him will give me great pleasure.'

'You misunderstand me. I'm suggesting much more than that.' The salacious look on his pale face is enough of a hint, so I purposefully misstep and land on his right foot.

Chapter Seventeen

'IT'S IMPERATIVE YOU MAKE SOME VALUABLE FRIENDS if we are to get you that throne,' Vill says. 'So I want that to be your focus rather than, necessarily, pleasing Onnachild and winning his bet. With the right allies, success will be assured in both our ventures.'

The women are watching us from their huddle inside the Sunning Room, a dome-shaped protrusion made of glass. It's an ugly building even with the ripples of spring sunshine across it. A few of the curious faces are familiar from the Great Hall but their hair isn't blonde or white now; instead, it's mousy brown, auburn, black, copper.

'Vill, do you have any news on Ammi?' I ask.

'Grace. Stop scowling, you need to be pleasant.'

'You didn't answer my question.'

He's turning the silver doorknob, which is half-moon shaped, and opening the door. The heat that comes out is thick and damp, bringing with it the odour of stale sweat and sickly sweet flowers. The women move to keep us in their eyeline like cats pretending they're not hunting.

'Don't worry.' He leads me into the room.

'I'm not.'

'Niah, your eyes always betray you. Remember, one day these women will be your subjects, all of them, and they'll have to beg and curtsy to you.' When he laughs the women glare at me. I smile but it feels like I'm baring my teeth in warning.

The further in we go the stronger the smell gets and the denser the heat. As Vill passes them, the women sigh and preen like birds splashing in water. A slim woman with hair almost as dark as my own steps in front of him and stops him by placing her palm flat on his stomach. There's nothing else of the village in her delicate features; the eyes she fixes on me are a deep sapphire and her skin is the same pale pink as her ruffled dress.

'My darling, Nilola.' Vill takes her hand to his lips. 'What a pleasure to see you. When did you return to the castle?'

'Just this morning, but I've been looking for you.' She stares at him with such hunger I'm surprised he doesn't blush. 'Everywhere.'

'Instead, I've found you and again I say, what a pleasure. The castle is not nearly as entertaining with you gone.'

She licks her lips so they shine. 'And you will visit me later?'

'Nilola.' Another woman stamps her foot. I recognise her as the woman who danced with Vill and Raen yesterday. She isn't wearing her wig and her auburn hair is fuzzing around her handsome features. 'How dare you hog Vill all to yourself. Let him sit so he can entertain everyone.' She plants herself beside him, her arm taking possession of his.

I step forwards, into the role I must play. 'Vill has been rude.' I give a slight smile. 'He's not introduced me to his friends as he said he would.'

Both women turn their attention to me. The auburn-haired one crosses her arms under her broad chest and leans back so her stare can take in all of me. Her disdain is an expression I'm well used to: the curling upper lip, the rumpled nose, and narrowed eyes.

'Please do excuse me, Niah. I was so overcome by the sight of these gems I clear forgot my reason for seeking them out.' He drapes an arm across their shoulders. 'Ladies, allow me to present Niah. She's a dear friend to me and the King.'

'The long-lost cousin,' the handsome woman says.

'Yes, my dear, dear cousin as you noted. She's new to the castle and I thought to myself, who would be the best people to help her shake off the restrictions my uncle placed on her? Why Nilola and Beshanie are just the people, with their wicked ways and ready smiles. And now, here you are. God has answered my prayer.' How easy he finds it to lie and how they lap it up, beaming at him.

'I'm not so wicked.' Nilola's eyes suggest otherwise.

'Quiet your mouth,' Beshanie snaps. To us, she smiles again. 'Where are my manners?' Her voice is softer. 'Please, Vill, Niah, come join us.' She directs us to four white chairs and shoos away the women already sitting there. Gingerly, I follow Beshanie's lead and sit. Vill perches on the edge of a seat.

'How do we find you today?' Beshanie asks him. She taps his knee then her fingers curl around it. What at first seemed to be an absentminded gesture becomes a caressing stroke. I can't help watching, open-mouthed, as it crawls up his thigh, for not even a village girl on midsummer night would be so brazen.

'Better for seeing you both.' He covers her hand, stops it moving higher. 'I'm glad to have a reason to visit you today and avoid the hunting. You know how much I hate hunting.'

'Yes. Niah, you called her, has come to the castle.' Beshanie turns her attention to me, her smile drooping. 'I saw you in the Great Hall yesterday. You were in red.'

'I was.'

'My uncle, as you've heard, was not a kind man to my cousin, keeping her away from everyone.' Vill touches his chest as his head tilts and he glances at me with sympathy. 'She needs some companions.'

'I don't know what company we can be for her, as silly as we are.'

'Beshanie, that's exactly why I've brought her to you. You girls have always been able to cheer me from one of my low moods.'

She leans forwards, showing off the dip between her breasts. Her fingers dig into his thigh. Nilola's pout increases and she plays with the ends of her hair.

'Do you have designs on her?' Beshanie asks.

'Goodness no. We've seen each other in swaddling.'

She settles back onto her seat and her fingers loosen. 'Forgive me.' She smiles slyly at me as if I should care that he doesn't favour me.

Another woman yells for Vill from across the room, waving her arms about and exposing dark patches on the underarm of her dress.

'Don't go to her,' Beshanie says.

'You should feel sorry for her.' He caresses her hand. 'She'll not marry as well as you will, Besh.'

'I'm too kind.'

'That you are, and that's why I know I can trust you with Niah.' He nods at each one of us before removing Beshanie's hand, kissing it, and lowering it onto her lap. Then he rises, as graceful as water over a pebble, and leaves me alone with them. Women sway and bob towards him as he moves through the crowd. Nilola's pout vanishes. She leans over and whispers in Beshanie's ear. They snigger.

'He's very popular,' I say.

'Where did you say you were from?' Beshanie asks.

Nilola's staring at my dark hands clasped in my lap. 'You aren't from here are you?'

115

'No, I lived with my uncle.'

'They have a lot of sun there, do they?' Beshanie's gaze also lowers to my hands, her lips quirking at her joke. 'When did you arrive?'

'A few nights ago.'

'You're friends with the King, Vill said.'

'He exaggerates.'

'Aren't you a bit old for your first presentation?' Nilola asks.

'She wasn't presented, though. I wonder why that could be,' Beshanie says. 'Do you know why that was?'

'I don't know the castle rules; should I have been?'

They pretend to try hiding their laughter: Nilola looking over her shoulder and Beshanie coughing. I search for Vill, praying he'll come back and rescue me, but he's leaning over that woman as she rubs his puffed sleeves.

'There's much here to please you, dancing, feasting, and flirting. I think the King wishes to be cheered up. You know his son died?' Nilola curls a lock of her dark hair around her index finger.

'Yes. I see the King is in mourning.'

Beshanie's eyes fix on me, watching, waiting for her moment to pounce. I remain steady, shoulders back and down, and that stupid half-smile on my face.

'There's another prince too,' Nilola says. 'Not as handsome as Aelius was. Aelius was ...' She flutters her hand at her cheeks. 'Almost as handsome as Vill, though he didn't have the same charm Vill has.'

Hearing Aelius's name said in her little girl whine makes my smile falter. Beshanie must view this as her chance because she slides forwards in her seat. 'I heard he had a whore.' Her eyes are full of spite. 'A dirty village whore. She threw herself at him, naked. And well, everyone knows what men are like.'

They laugh so loudly that other women glance over. It pains me to stop my lips from turning into a sneer. One day, I remind myself, they will regret their words. Nilola pinches and pushes down on my shoulder as she thrusts her face at me. 'They say he snuck off to her at night. I suppose at night she wouldn't have been so ugly.'

They might be as malicious as village girls, but these women can't chase me with stones, can't drown me, and so I keep smiling as I sink my nails into Nilola's hand and pluck it off from my shoulder. She stares at her hand then at me, shocked I've drawn blood. As I stand, as I walk away, I keep my attention on them so they know I'm not running away, not backing down, not intimidated.

Vill must have noticed what happened because he's at the door the moment I am. His cheeks are flushed and there's a sweaty print on his tunic. 'Where do you think you're going?' he asks, but he still opens the door.

The air outside has a chill in it and it cools my skin but not my anger. 'Vile. Vile. Vile girls.'

Nilola's still staring at the back of her hand. Beshanie's laughing at her. The other women have their sweaty faces turned towards Vill like wolves to the moon. 'Shush,' he hisses, ushering me away and into the gardens. The paths crunch and scatter beneath my stomping feet; the sound is satisfying. He's quiet beside me. I can feel his disappointment. What else did he expect me to do? A small bird ambles across the path as if its yellow wings are for decoration only. Vill stops at a white bench that faces a fountain where golden hawks and stone women throw water up and out for the breeze to play with.

'There's much they can do to help you.' He pivots to face me. 'Beshanie and Nilola are the indulged daughters of rich men, influential men.'

'I doubt they'll be helping me. Vile.' I brush spray from the fountain off the bench to avoid his gaze. 'They said Aelius was sneaking out to see an ugly village whore.'

'Is that all? They're merely repeating a rumour about someone in the village. They don't know it's you.'

'Oh, they knew.' My fingers slide through the holes in the bench's latticework. The underneath is rough with rust. It smells like blood. 'Vill ... do you think I'm ... Why do you think I took Aelius as my lover?'

'For your ancestors. Why else?'

'Then you think the same as them.' I make a move to walk away, but he stops me by grabbing my elbow and tries to get me to meet his eyes. I stare at the sweaty print on his tunic instead.

'Why does anyone fall in love? Someone has something the other wants, is that not correct? It might be beauty, generosity of spirit, anything. In your case, it was the throne.'

'It wasn't like that.'

'No? So you're not ambitious? You don't want right restored, your ancestors avenged?'

'You know I do.'

'Exactly.' He taps the bench to get my attention.

I ignore him and flick off a flake of paint. It lands white-side up on the path and is lost in the brightness. 'Raen said the same thing,' I mumble.

'Then he's smarter than I thought. Forget the rumour. What does it matter? Women like Beshanie and Nilola will admire you for it. Men will be intrigued by it.'

'I don't want them to be.'

'You want to pretend it never happened?'

'You know I don't want to forget Aelius. I love him. Why does no one believe me?' I kick at the gravel, spreading it from its neat line and into the grass. 'I want him here, alive, with me, without me. The way things were. Anywhere, anyhow if it means he's not dead.'

Vill's sigh is so deep and long that I peer up at him. His features have softened and the spray from the fountain has made his skin iridescent. 'But he is.'

He sits on the bench and draws me down beside him. 'I wish situations were different, but Niah, my poor Niah, they aren't. And he isn't coming back. This is your life now. People will gossip about many things and decide many things between themselves. You have no money. You have no family they know of. Did you think they would just accept you?'

'No, of course not.'

'I suspect you did.' He puts his arm around me. 'Now, see, look at me, they all think I'm in their pocket, their man, and yet I give nothing but charming, empty words. I wasn't grieved when Nilola left the castle; I didn't even notice. I say I was because it will make her eager to do my bidding on the off-chance that I might decide to pleasure her.' Beads of water have settled on his blond hair—even the fountain wants to give him jewels. 'If you wish to remain in this castle, advance, then you must work with me. I can flirt with the women. I can appeal to the men's resentment, logic, their greed, in some cases their sense of injustice, but you need to charm the castle, too. Be more flamboyant, interesting, appealing than the old bear. Make friends with the women. Flirt with the men. Raen. Lust is a powerful thing.'

'No, I won't do it.'

He doesn't need to know about the graveyard because it won't happen again. I try to duck my head away from him and his disgusting words but he's quicker, taking my face between his cool hands. Hopefully, he interprets the burn of my cheeks as anger and not shame.

'Do you think I enjoy debasing myself like that? Presenting myself as little more than a peacock strutting about on display? I'm an intelligent man and sometimes that means using what the gods have blessed me with, but this ...' He gestures to his perfect face. 'This alone is nothing. I observe and listen, and I become what others want to see. That is what you need to learn, that is your real lesson, not those superficial things that

Mantona teaches you. Who cares about embroidery? Be who the King wants you to be. Be whoever the castle people want you to be, and then at night, when you're alone, be yourself.'

'And you? Who do you want me to be, Vill?'

'Queen.' He elongates the word. His eyes are shining like droplets from the fountain. 'I can help you achieve this, introduce you to the right people, even repair the damage done today, but Niah, you have to be ready to play, entice them, captivate them, make them feel special. Learn what motivates them: sex, riches, power, food. It's always one of those. A few well-chosen words, a promise here, a gift there. Get the right people on your side and you'll find the rest of the castle will follow just like they follow changes in style. And then, when you are queen, won't it have been worth it?'

'What about you?'

'Me?' He removes his hands from my face.

'What do you want?'

'From you?'

I nod.

'Why this little finger here could do with a big, bright emerald.' He wiggles it in the air.

Chapter Eighteen

I WAKE WITH A START like someone has pinched me. My surroundings are disorientating: the thick velvet drapes, the soft bed, and the heat. Am I still in a dream? One with princes, princesses, white horses, and feasts that last for days, a bird stuffed in a bird in a bird. My belly hurts from eating too much, and my head is muffled from too much wine. At least Nessia is beside me, snoring. She never snored in the village. I should be tired from dancing in the Great Hall earlier, but my limbs are restless and twitchy, expectant.

There's a cry, one that sounds like it's been going for a while. My breasts start leaking. I search the room, breath held, for the source, but find only shades of grey, of black. There's another cry. It's Ammi. Can she really be so close? Onnachild said he'd decide when I could see her, hold her, so he must be testing me by putting her so near. Not testing, punishing. She cries and cries, the sound mixing with the hooting of the owls outside the window as though she's being carried away by them. The noise is as constant as a winter wind, and it chills my bones the same. I glance at Nessia still sleeping. Why doesn't the crying wake her too?

Ammi's face will be red, snot- and tear-marked. Maybe she's been crying for so long her eyes are dry. Her podgy hands will be in balls. Her chubby legs will be kicking. Maybe she's freezing from having kicked away her furs. Her nursemaid is inept to let her wail on like this. She's crying for me. She's crying to reject all this. Ammi needs her mother, and instead, here I am wrapped up in luxury, breathing in the perfume of incense and flowers rather than her scent. I can't ignore her. To the gods with Onnachild; she's more important than his warning, than a throne, than a promise. I slip out of bed and grab a fur off it. We'll leave here. I'll find a place for us to be together. The world is bigger than the village and the castle. I leave my room, take a torch from the wall, and chase after her sound.

'I'm coming. I'm coming,' I whisper into the empty hallways.

As I pass the Great Hall, the Maidens' singing almost overpowers Ammi's high-pitched wail. A few men are joining in with the Maidens and their sloppy baritones jar. The odour of food and ale lingers and turns my stomach. On and on I rush. From the old sections of the castle to the new sections to the old sections, almost tricking me into thinking I've not moved. Ammi keeps crying, louder and louder, so I must be getting nearer. The fur slides off my shoulders. Draughts flutter the torch and get through my nightdress, making me shiver. Turning a corner, I spot the Judging Room door opening. There's nowhere for me to hide, and it's too late to run away so I sidle up against the wall. Hopefully, whoever is coming out won't notice me.

It's Raen. Of course, it is.

He plants himself before me. 'Who are you off to meet?'

I yank my fur up, clasp it tight against my milk-stained nightdress. 'Not a man, if that's what you're thinking.'

'Good because, otherwise, I'd have to tell Onnachild.'

'I don't care what you do or don't tell Onnachild.' I care only for Ammi. If I could hold her ... whisper in her ear ... sing her a song ... if only for tonight. 'Get out of my way. It's bad enough I have to be polite to you in the Great Hall without having to ... Move.'

He doesn't so I push past him, the torch coming dangerously close to his face.

'Disfiguring me won't help.'

I speed on even though my shins are hurting. My heart's beating so hard I feel it in my stomach, my legs, my face. If I don't get to Ammi soon ... Raen's steps are slow and heavy as he strides beside me.

'Why are you following me?' I ask.

'I want to see what you're up to.'

I shake my head. There isn't time to argue with him. The crying stops. *Why has it stopped? How will I find her now?* I spin around. Hallways lead off left, right, and they all look the same, all lead into darkness. Though this part of the castle is warm, I'm shaking.

'What's going on?' Raen hunches down in front of me. The light of the torch picks out the green in his irises. 'What's worth risking Onnachild's wrath for?'

'Shut up.' I cock my ear, hold my breath. There's the sound of him breathing and the crackle from the torch. Nothing else. *Do I go left? Right?* I step forwards, knocking into him and the contact startles me. He steadies me with a hand on my shoulder and takes the torch with his other hand, holds it out so we're half in shadow, half in light. He's seen Ammi, he told me. The other night, he said he'd seen her. A child needs its mother, he told Onnachild. 'Will you help me?' I plead. 'Ammi ... Grace. Down that way ... she was crying for me.'

'Onnachild has her. You can't just walk to her room. The nursemaid will inform him. The guards will inform him. Do you not realise that?'

My heart is breaking again when I thought there was nothing left of it to break; Ammi can cry for me and I can't go to her. I slump against the wall. I close my eyes.

'Why did you bring her here? Surely you knew Onnachild would take her?'

'It won't be forever.' Just until I'm queen. But how long will that take? Months? Years? If only Raen hadn't been called back to the castle, then it would be easier, quicker.

'It'll be for as long as he wants.'

I open my eyes, and there Raen is: healthy, dark, strong, and frowning. His words sink in, and I realise I've exchanged Ammi for my place here. That was the deal laid out in the Judging Room, the deal I accepted; please Onnachild, win him this bet and I'll get to stay, see Ammi. When will the result be decided though? When will I know if I have fooled everyone into believing I am like them and not village raised. No one has told me that. It will be quicker than waiting until I'm queen, won't it? My head aches, competing with my heart.

'Niah, you need to go back.'

I nod, unsure whether he means to the village or my new rooms. Anywhere will do. Anywhere but here in my nightdress talking to a man, and not just any man, but Raen. He touches my arm, nudges me to get me moving, but my feet are stuck.

'She was crying. Ammi,' I say.

'I heard nothing.'

'I did.'

'It was the spirits. The castle is full of them.'

Why is he scowling?

'No, it was her,' I say. 'She was crying and ...'

'You went to find her?'

'Why is that so strange? I'm her mother.' As I look at Raen, I'm reminded how he was sent away, punished for his mother's perceived infidelity and replaced by his half-brother. How can I trust Onnachild with my daughter when he couldn't even love his own son? I've made a mistake. Another one.

'If it makes you feel better Grace is being well cared for.'

I nod but it doesn't make me feel better.

'All babies cry sometimes,' he says.

I push myself from the wall and turn reluctantly back the way I came, pausing in case there's another cry. There isn't one. Raen doesn't follow. He leaves me to the dark, to find my own way, and I'm grateful for that. My disobedience is another secret he has against me. How many more will I give away?

Chapter Nineteen

SITTING IN THE CASTLE GROUNDS, practising my embroidery, I feel closer to Aelius because, like me, he loved being outdoors with the sun on his skin. It's easy to picture him drinking and playing ball with the castle men, his tunic dampening with sweat. Nessia watches them throw and kick the ball, a twinkle brightening her hazel eyes.

I'd prefer to be practising my reading but Vill said the men wouldn't find it attractive, which makes me hate embroidery even more. Still, at least I'm not him, stuck in that stifling Sunning Room, trying to explain away my behaviour. I'm far too tired after my sleepless night to deal with those vile women.

When the men howl and yell at each other, Melody tuts. 'If the True Queen was still alive, they wouldn't be doing that.'

They're fascinating to me though, more so than recreating the shape of a flower in hessian. I search for similarities to Aelius in their mannerisms, their faces, their bodies trying to make a patchwork of him from them. A group of men give up and splay out on the grass, and I picture Aelius amongst them, face glistening, hair darkened and stuck to his forehead. I can almost smell his fresh sweat.

'That's a man in need of some feminine care.' Nessia points her needle towards Raen who's pacing the grounds—probably measuring how much land there is.

'You might take it back if he sat with you for a while,' Melody says.

He crouches down by the men, thighs bulging, and drinks from one of their flagons. A man with a thick ginger beard, stretched out on the lawn, waves at a pair of women walking past. They flicker sly glances over their shoulders at him. Raen chuckles so loudly the sound must reach the matrons sharing gossip at the wall's furthest edge.

Melody puts down her embroidery and shuffles closer. 'He was passed over, you know, for the younger son, and sent away from the castle when his mother died.'

'Was murdered you mean,' I grumble as my needle stabs my thumb. 'What else do you know about him? Is he liked by the castle people?'

'Why are you asking? Do you have a fancy for him? I wouldn't, if I were you. There are lots more men that are a lot more agreeable.'

'Melody, I don't have designs on anyone. I've recently lost my love, and it's insulting for you to suggest I would.'

'Sorry,' she mumbles. 'I just don't understand why you're interested in him, that's all. Some girls say he's handsome.' She rumples her nose.

'You don't agree?' Nessia asks.

Melody shakes her head so vigorously that her headdress slips over one eye.

I can't deny there is something about him that is handsome, especially when he smiles as he's doing now. Amongst the sloping and undefined chins of the castle men, the hard angle of his jaw makes him imposing. The sun shining on his hair, long and loose, brings out flecks of mahogany. There's nothing in him to add to my patchwork of Aelius. 'I don't care what the women think.'

Melody straightens her headdress, and a bird responds to the tinkling shells. 'When that happened, him getting dismissed, some say it was because ...' She checks around before continuing. 'Because he was a disagreeable child and not fit to be a king, and there was some madness about him, like all the villagers have. But you don't ...' She frowns. 'Anyway, some say it wasn't right he was so close to his mother, following her around, getting under her feet so much that he'd almost trip her up. Unnatural. They normally don't allow that here— children with their mothers.'

'The First Queen lost so many babies.' Nessia glances over at Raen.

'And didn't Onnachild punish us for it,' I mumble, remembering the tale of his rage when he destroyed the Legacy Yew. I stab the hessian.

'That must be why then,' Melody says to Nessia. 'Children, especially princes, are given millions of nurses and tutors to teach them about war and ... and things like that, ruling. That's what happened to Aelius but I don't think he was very good at it, learning, was he? Sorry, I shouldn't have said that, should I? Oh, I shouldn't even call him by his name. It's the True Prince, isn't it? Oh, I can't remember what's right, not now the first one has returned. It's so confusing.'

She scratches her nose with her needle. 'I don't think the King likes him very much, Raen, I mean. He called him back for the funeral because the kingdom needs a prince, but Raen doesn't have the right training. He doesn't know how to rule or anything. The King requested to see him and they had a meeting, three whole days in the Judging Room. Three whole days and nights too, I think. None of us Maidens were allowed in to serve, but I could hear them arguing. Raen's voice is almost as loud as Onnachild's. He's good at shouting, if nothing else. The advisers had to wait on them and they moaned about it for days and weeks when they'd go to the kitchen. I thought it was quite funny.' Her impish smile shows the gap between her teeth.

'Sounds like our meeting with them.' Nessia doesn't smile but seems sad, and I'm not able to question this because Melody continues her gossip.

'The King came out looking more depressed than when he went in and they say he was mumbling to himself like he'd gone mad, mumbling how God had taken the wrong son. And after, he stayed in his rooms like a sulking woman.'

I laugh at Onnachild being described in such a way. Melody looks puzzled until she realises what I'm laughing at and then she joins in. Nessia shakes her head.

'Like a sulking woman, a great big, fat sulking woman.' Melody's head tilts back and her headdress falls off, stopping her laughter.

'What do you think of Raen?' Nessia asks me, her expression so mischievous that I regret telling her about the graveyard.

I yank my thread and ignore her question.

Thankfully, Melody thinks it was directed to her and answers. 'He's not been here long, but ... I find him bad-tempered and sullen.'

'So would I be if my father only remembered me once his favoured child died,' Nessia says.

'He should be grateful to be here at all.' Melody jams her headdress back on and her ears stick out. 'It's only because of the King's kindness that he's allowed. He could have been left in Saddle House.'

The men interrupt us with their screams and howls as they throw themselves at each other, a mass of arms, legs, and hair. Their ball rolls away, forgotten. Raen chuckles but doesn't join in and no one attempts to wrestle him down.

'If it was up to me, I'd have left him there,' Melody says.

'Do you know what Saddle House was like?' I ask.

'Nice enough, I guess.' She pokes her ears behind the band of her headdress. 'It belonged to the False Queen's family supposedly, before she was declared a traitor and the King did what he did. Did they really go elsewhere during winter? Do you remember?'

'Yes,' Nessia says. 'Before Onnachild made war with everyone, they did. Niah's father was a travelling trader.'

'What did he sell? Where did he go?'

'You were talking about Saddle House,' I remind her.

'Yes, yes I was, wasn't I? Saddle House was somewhere else. I don't know where. Anyway, I suppose where doesn't matter, does it? I think it must have been very isolated because he didn't bring many people to the castle with him. I could try and persuade one of them to speak to me; I'm good at that. They're pleasant enough but fiercely loyal to him, which seems a bit strange, don't you think? But they're men and, I guess, men and women have different ideas of what's right. Me, I liked the True Prince. He was always so kind. He'd smile at you and seem grateful for any task you performed for him. He was so pretty too.'

'Yes, he was.' I sigh, remembering how his grin would add a dimple to his cheek.

'Not like this new one. Whenever I'm around him I feel nervous that

I'm going to drop something and be shouted at for it.'

Raen turns his head our way, sheltering his eyes from the bright sun with his arm. Nessia smiles, raising her hand to wave at him.

'What do you think you're doing?' I hiss through clenched teeth.

'I'm calling him over.'

'Have you been talking to Vill, because I'm not—'

'Shush, he's coming.' Melody slaps my skirt with her hessian.

She's right. There's a swagger to his walk, exaggerated by the flagon dangling from his hand and knocking against his hip. I pray he'll walk by as I give my full attention to my embroidery, pulling at the tangled threads which only tighten more. He doesn't walk by. He stops before us, his long shadow darkening my hessian and hands. 'Hasn't your tutor taught you it is bad manners to stare at men in such a brazen fashion?'

'I wasn't,' I moan.

'I was,' Nessia says.

'We're sewing.' Melody holds up her hessian to show him.

He peers over at my attempt, chuckles at its holey stitches following their own randomised pattern and looking nothing like a flower. I cover it with my arm.

'Care to join us?' Nessia pats the grass beside her. Melody pulls a face, expressing my own feelings on the matter. 'Perhaps you could help Niah with her threads.'

He glances at the men, languid and out of breath from their tumbling, at the matrons huddled in a dark group by the wall, at the land dipping away, and then shrugs before sitting between Nessia and I. He stretches his legs out, flexing his feet and making his calf muscles bulge. I try to unpick my last few stitches.

'Cider?' he asks, raising the flagon and gesturing for a Maiden to come over from where they're practising their singing in the shade of an oak tree. One trots over to do his bidding.

'It's too early for cider,' I say.

'I can't think of a better way to waste time. Besides, I think drinking and keeping me entertained might be a task better suited to you than sewing.' He takes my hessian and tosses it onto the grass before us. I should be angry at his insolence but instead, I'm pleased to be saved from the frustration of pricking my fingers further.

'Goblets, please,' he says to the Maiden standing above us.

She glares at Melody, as if demanding her to go but Melody ignores it and holds her sewing up for inspection, so the Maiden nods and leaves us.

'The sun is surprisingly hot for early spring.' Raen tilts his face up to it.

Why is he being so polite and formal?

'Yes, it is.' Nessia's trying to mimic the castle accent and tucking stray strands of her greying hair behind her ears. 'Normally, it would be raining, continually.' She smiles at him and I don't understand that either.

He kicks off his shoes. One lands on my skirt. I shake it off.

'Now this is relaxing.' He lowers onto his back and closes his eyes. His lashes are long, dark, and thick like a woman's. 'Why aren't you with the others in the Sunning Room?'

'I prefer my own company,' I say.

'They're not very nice,' Melody says.

'Not to us outsiders.' A sardonic smile stretches his lips. 'Although I'm sure if you got the throne they'd soon start being nice to you.'

'I intend to make them beg.'

'Me too.' He chuckles. 'Us men were wondering which of us took your fancy. I can make a few recommendations if you wish.'

'I'll not marry.'

'I wasn't talking about marriage.'

'None of them is good enough for Niah,' Melody snaps, then she ducks her head seemingly embarrassed at her outburst.

'Why? They're all rich and well-bred men,' he says.

'I'm still in mourning,' I say, even though I'm dressed in vibrant yellow.

'And how long do you intend to mourn for?'

'Forever.'

'That long. You'll be very boring then and not make any of those influential friends you need.'

'Then I shall be very boring and friendless.'

'I'm told you're used to that state.'

'As are you, so I've heard.'

'Ah, yes. What else have you heard about me?' He opens one eye, peeps at me just as Melody jabs her elbow into my ribs. He notices and chuckles. 'So this is who has been answering your questions, and their opinion of me can't be that favourable if they wish you not to repeat it, or ...' He opens the other eye, rolls onto his side. 'Maybe it's the opposite and their opinion of me is very favourable, and that's what's making them blush.'

'Don't tease her,' I say.

Nessia's laughing, and I glare at her for encouraging him. She shrugs and continues with her embroidery.

'Perhaps you can explain why I interest you.' His fingers play with a blade of grass as he stares up at me.

'I'm interested in everyone.'

'You could just ask me about myself. Isn't that what normally happens?'

'You're not easy to talk to.'

'Is that something else you heard or something you decided by yourself?'

'I don't need anyone else to tell me you're disagreeable and lack manners.'

'Then why call me over?'

'I didn't, it was Nessia.' I point to her.

She's barely controlling her raspy laughter as she bites down on her lip. The line of her sewing has veered to the left. He chuckles. The sound is deep and earthy, and it's almost a pleasant sound. I reach for my hessian, tempted to throw it at him. The Maiden arrives with three goblets. 'There are four of us.' I gesture to our group.

'We Maidens are not allowed to drink cider or wine or ale or any other intoxicating thing. God does not allow this. We must lead by example in these wicked times.' Melody directs her speech towards Raen seeming to need his approval or praise.

'I'm glad to hear you know your lessons,' he says.

She smiles, not noticing his sarcasm, and takes the goblets from the other Maiden, who leaves to re-join the group under the tree. 'I must inspire modesty, piety, and moderation in all things, the True Queen said.' Her eager face remains focused on Raen as she pours us all a drink and hands them out. Nessia rests her hessian in her lap to hold the goblet in both hands. She savours the cider, sloshing it around her mouth, and then licking her lips after.

'She wouldn't be happy with how things are now.' Melody frowns.

Raen nods in mock deference.

'The hypocrisy, considering the woman stole another's husband,' I mumble into my goblet.

'That's Aelius's mother you're talking about,' Raen says, but his lips quirk and almost smile. 'He wouldn't like you saying that.'

'It's true.'

'Thank God she never met you then, the heathen who took her son.'

'Heathen? What are you implying?'

'I'm not implying anything. I've been asking people about you, too. It's impressive, the information villagers are willing to exchange for food. They told me about your ties to the old religion, about your grandmother. I know the villagers shunned you even before you took up with my half-brother, and I know you refused to convert to the new religion.'

'Plenty of village girls used to follow Adfyrism, it means nothing. I denied the old ways, just like they did. My grandmother was killed for worshipping those gods; I wouldn't be so stupid as to keep worshipping them.'

'Not to admit it, anyway.' Raen rises onto his elbow. 'I was told that when Aelius died, you followed the old ways. You fasted for seven days and you called him.'

'The villagers told you that, did they? And you believed them?'

'I saw the fire and herbs at the graveyard.'

My face flushes as I remember: the mud beneath my back, his shoulder against my lips, my body alive again. I grind my goblet into the ground to keep it steady. The grass tickles my fingers like a damp kiss and I let go. The goblet tips over. 'What were you doing there?' Why did I ask when I want to forget all about it?

Raen leans over me to right the goblet, bringing his scent and his warmth closer. 'Deflect my question with one of your own, nicely done,' he says. 'All right, to answer you, I was looking for something.'

'And did you find it?' Nessia's voice is a gentle lull.

'That doesn't matter.' He seems to be staring beyond the castle walls, perhaps even beyond this land, a longing quality in his eyes, then he takes a sip of wine and that emotion vanishes. 'I've answered your question so now you have to answer mine. Why were you there?'

'I wanted to be close to Aelius,' I say. 'It's that simple.'

'That doesn't answer my question. As I said, I saw the fire. You were going to call him which makes me think he's with the old gods and not the new one. Not his mother's god.'

'She doesn't deserve him. She was the heathen, and she helped kill your mother,' I snap.

Melody gasps, crosses herself. Even Nessia's looking annoyed. I've said too much, I realise that, but it felt good to say it, to see Raen's jaw twitch and have him break eye contact with me.

'It's all right.' He stares into his goblet. 'I know what she's trying to do. She wants to know what I think of that queen, whether my feelings will keep me from my father and the throne. Niah, your motives are too easy to read and you must be cleverer than that. Your Maiden here worries that I'll run to the King and tell tales on you, and I could. I think he'd like to hear ill of you.'

'You won't tell him.'

'No. I won't tell him.' His gaze returns to me, those green dots in his irises as lush as the surrounding grass. 'As for the question you seem to be hinting at, well, I don't blame her. She was a young girl, younger than us, and God knows we're still making ... what did you call it? A mistake?'

It's obvious why he's chosen that word, even without that mocking tone, and yet I can't stop from flushing.

'She was just a pawn for her father and brothers, used as my mother was, as everyone here is. You'll soon find this out. Now, please can we stop talking about such macabre things? It's a nice day, and the sun is out. Let's talk about more pleasant matters, surely you can be pleasant?'

'I don't know what topics would interest you.'

'Niah has never been one for pleasantries.' Nessia helps herself to more cider.

'I see. It must be the village in us.' They both laugh. I scowl at Nessia but it doesn't stop her. He lies back down on the grass with his hands behind his head as if we haven't been arguing. 'You knew what to talk about to my half-brother.' The sleeves of his tunic ride up, showing off his honey-coloured skin, which is lighter on the underside of his arm.

'I can't talk to you about such things.'

'And so, I can guess what you talked about: plots and silly wives' tales.' He winks at Nessia. She giggles like a girl. I don't understand what has come over her today.

'Oh, plots and wives' tales.' Melody shuffles closer to us.

I pick up my embroidery, start yanking out the stitches. 'No. We spoke of love, of dreams.'

Melody sighs.

'I bet you did,' Raen says. 'Tell me about them then, the dreams my wonderful half-brother was going to make come true.' He closes his eyes.

'You say you wish to talk nicely and yet you try to engage me in another topic that will create conflict.'

'He was such a sweet boy.' Nessia speaks over me. 'He would bring me treats from the castle, and once he even brought me a new cloak when he heard me complaining at how ragged mine was.' She's tearful. Sometimes I forget she must have her own grief, too. I reach across Raen to touch her knee.

His eyes open at the brush of my sleeve across his mid-drift. His stomach tenses. A line appears between his eyebrows. I dart back.

'I saw him once,' he says. 'I looked at him in his swaddling, that pale face, round blue eyes like his mother and I knew ... I remember vividly that feeling ... feeling that something bad was going to happen to me.'

'You must wish for someone to listen to your story.' Sympathy deepens the wrinkles around Nessia's mouth and eyes.

'My version must be the official version.' He smiles at her, a smile that seems forced and tight. 'And we're all aware of how much that can hide. Although Niah's is a very tall story. I can't see anyone even attempting to control her, and Vill in the role of rescuer ... he'd only lift a sword to check his reflection.'

'Vill has been good to us,' Melody shouts over our laughter.

'It's true,' I say.

'I see Vill has another fan,' Raen says to Melody.

'Vill is a lovely man and so polite,' she says. 'He's lovely to everyone and I don't think ... You should not talk about him like that, not when you are so mean and moody, and ... Vill is worth a million of you and he's our friend and he was the True Prince's friend ... Niah, tell him.' She throws her embroidery away, crosses her arms. 'I like Vill, that's all. He's nice and I don't think it's right to laugh at him.'

'Vill would be the first person to agree with me,' Raen says. 'As for me, well yes, people have said many disparaging things about me, and I'm sure they'll come up with new insults. Not that they'll say them to my face, of course. Doesn't matter, I've endured worse things than being called names.'

'Like what?' Melody asks.

'I think if I told you it would be treason,' he teases.

'Why?' Her eyes are wide and she's pursing her lips, ready to be taken into his confidence. Her anger is clearly forgotten.

'Isn't it treason to talk against the King?'

'Only if he hears.'

'How do I know Niah won't inform him?'

'Oh, she wouldn't. She can keep a secret. You can, can't you, Niah?'

'But we already have so many secrets between us; I don't want to burden her with another.' His gaze settles on my chest, but I refuse to rise to his bait and continue with my stitches instead.

'Oh, what, what?' Melody grips Raen's arm in one hand and mine in the other. 'Tell me. Please.'

'You mean she hasn't?'

'Raen,' Nessia warns.

'There's nothing to say.' I bat away Melody's hand. 'I've forgotten.'

'Already? I'm wounded. Shame, I rather enjoyed myself.' His eyes are alive with possibilities and there's something so captivating about those green dots vivid against the dark brown. I can't stop staring into them, even though my face is burning. If only Nessia hadn't asked him to sit with us. If only he'd leave.

'I'll ask Vill. Yes, if you don't tell me, then I'll ask Vill,' Melody says.

'Vill will know. He knows everything.'

'Not everything.' Raen's smug expression must be the same one he had that night in the graveyard. I stab my needle through the hessian, missing the curved line of the other stitches, and yank my thread so roughly the needle flies off into the grass.

'I thought we were friends, and so that means you're not meant to keep things from me,' Melody says.

'Leave it,' Nessia tells her.

'I seem to have gotten you into trouble.' Raen holds out my needle, so small and silver between his large fingers.

'And you wonder why people think you're disagreeable,' I say.

'I never said that.' He tosses the needle onto my lap when I don't take it. 'I know why people think I'm disagreeable and most of the time they're right. After all those years in isolation, having someone to annoy is a godsend.' He chuckles.

I wish he'd stop laughing and being so pleased with himself. 'Ammi,' I say to placate Melody. 'I tried to see Ammi last night.'

Nessia tuts. 'Really, Niah? After what Onnachild said.'

He lies down and starts humming as if Melody is not sulking, as if Nessia isn't disappointed, as if I'm not scowling at him. It's a song from my childhood and my scowl eases despite my best efforts to remain annoyed with him. He turns his head towards me, and his smile is uncertain—no, not uncertain but confused. He stops humming. Nessia picks up the tune and Melody tries to join in. The smell of lavender toasting in a fire comes to me and makes my shoulders droop as I sigh out my tension. I wonder if he can smell it, too, because his eyelashes flutter as though he's fighting sleep.

He looks so peaceful when he finally gives in: lips parted, chest rising and falling in a slow, steady rhythm. Does he see his mother in his dreams? Nessia leans across, hand out towards Raen's dark hair to soothe him, but she stops herself and gives him a sad smile instead.

Chapter Twenty

MELODY IS LATE to our morning reading session, and so I'm out of bed, dressed and with only my hair needing her help. She looks tired and her fingers are clumsy, jabbing my head with pins and snagging my hair in the brush while I practise reading aloud. When I stop and wince, she doesn't notice.

'What's wrong with you?' Nessia nudges Melody away and takes over.

'I've been serving the King and his advisers all night because Cadence was sick. I don't think she was really sick, I think she ... that doesn't matter. All because they wanted to talk about battles. Could it not have waited till morning?'

'Battle?' The word makes my stomach turn over. Not another. Not so soon.

Nessia pats my shoulder. I stare at her in the dressing table mirror. She has the same expression she had at the funeral: disgust and anger.

'The King says he wants revenge and the advisers say it should be so. They were looking at the big ledgers, the ones with the figures in them, and hammering at the page with their skinny fingers, and the King stomped his fist, shook them up. He said he didn't care for figures. He said we fight now.'

'And they agreed? Vill? Raen?' I grip the dressing table.

'Raen said we should wait, that the Aralltirs will be expecting us, that they'll be ready for us. But the King is king, and he was angry and all red in the face. He was trembling he was so angry. Then I was called away by Lark. I think she knew I was listening too much. But they agreed because he is king and so we shall go into battle again.'

'Again?' I close the book and shunt it away. 'Every year more men go to their deaths and we gain nothing. Nothing. We're lucky the Aralltirs don't push their advantage and take all our land.'

'But don't you want revenge?' Melody holds her headdress and tries to stop the cheerful tinkling of the shells. 'You know, for what they did.'

'Onnachild should never have let Aelius fight.' I turn away from my blanched face in the mirror, from the accusation that I should have tried harder to make my love stay. The taste of his blood comes back to my mouth, bitter and coppery. As I push away from the dressing table, Nessia's hand drops from my shoulder. Outside, the sky has deepened to a battle-axe grey and rain is hammering on the window. Winter has returned, or maybe it's death coming to the castle already. I search for the village amongst the view but its sprawl is hidden by the rain. It's calling to me though, it's in my skin, it's in my blood, just as Aelius is.

'It wasn't the Aralltirs who killed him,' I wipe my lips, 'but a greedy king. There should never have been a battle. Before Onnachild we lived in peace, but no, he has to be greedy, he has to—'

The knock at my door makes Melody gasp and drop her headdress. I look over at Nessia, now slumped on the bed and rubbing her temples. 'Get the door,' she says.

Melody nods, running off and jamming her headdress on.

It's only Vill, calm and composed in emerald green. 'I presume from your expression that you've been informed.' He makes his way straight to the fire, palms out. 'It's so damn cold in that room.'

'Yes, we've heard.' I pace, trying to outwalk my fear and guilt, outwalk the image of Aelius falling and falling and calling, outwalk the odour of blood and piss and shit, and the sound of those horses, of weapons clashing, of men wailing and grunting. I bite the skin around my nails until my fingers are sore and they look like village hands again. My index finger runs over the scars and calluses my old life gave them. 'We have to stop it.'

Melody puts another log in the fire. 'We'll be safe. War won't touch us.'

'It touches everyone,' I say, 'and everything.'

Nessia's by my side. 'Stop pacing.' Her arm around my waist draws me to her comfort.

I ease into it but then I see Aelius's fall into the mud: the slowed drop, the distortion of his lips when he cried from pain and shock. Lips that had only days earlier been giggling, and now I can't remember how his giggle sounded. I focus on the fire, trying to dislodge that image. The fire's heart is red, dark as blood.

'Will the King sacrifice another son?' Nessia's words draw my attention to her. She's staring up at Aelius's portrait and my gaze follows hers. He's so arrogant in it and that arrogance led to his death, that and his father's actions. I climb onto the bed, stare at his flat face. *Stupid man, leaving me and Ammi so you could play at being a warrior.*

'Raen'll go to avenge his brother.' Melody sounds proud.

'He doesn't care for his half-brother,' I say.

'Raen has agreed,' Vill says.

'Then Onnachild will lose another son.' I turn away from Aelius and stagger across the bed as if it has turned to mud.

'And that is exactly what we should hope for.'

The fire crackles like it is angry and an ember pops from it, making Melody jump and clutch her chest. Nessia rushes to attend to it. I cling to the bedpost, my fingers curled around the thick wood. 'It isn't right.'

'What is and isn't right is immaterial. This is a throne we're talking about here. Neither Raen nor Onnachild is just going to gift it to you,' Vill says. 'With Raen gone, it will make decisions a lot easier for a lot of people.'

An image of Raen dead comes. The red tones in his hair are not from the sun picking out the colour but are streaks of blood, and his shoulder has been ground flat by horses' hooves. And worst of all are his irises, the green in them fading as grass does in a drought. 'I can't.'

'Then what do you propose we do?'

'Stop it, I've already said.'

'I presumed you weren't being serious. Why on earth would we want to stop it?' Vill asks.

'Because people will die, Vill. Villagers will die.'

'Think about it, Niah. Another battle will reduce the coffers some more, require more borrowing. The merchants will pretend to be happy to support the battle, but trust me they won't be. Eventually, they will want payment, which we know Onnachild can't provide. And the castle men who pay others to fight in their place, they won't be happy to keep spending either. Battles are costly, especially when you keep losing. And with Raen dead ... who else will there be for them to support?' He gestures at me with a flourish and a nod of his head.

As I flinch from his distasteful words, my eyes are drawn to the book on the dressing table. How I wish I couldn't read its title: *The Rise of the Great and Noble Bear*. 'I won't have my rule built on death, on blood like Onnachild's was, I can't ...'

'If there was a choice, I'd also prefer not to rely on bloodshed. There's no art to violence. It's the tool of stupid people who lack the wits for diplomacy and manipulation, but needs must, and when an opportunity like this drops into our laps, we'd be foolish to intervene.'

'If I allow villagers to go to their death, then I don't deserve the throne; I'll be no better than Onnachild.' I lunge for the book, slam it onto its face so I can't see the title anymore, but still I turn my back to it.

'Why are you concerning yourself with the villagers?' He takes off a gold ring and rubs at the flesh where it had been. 'After everything they've done to you and your ancestors? If you ask me, they've brought this on themselves.'

'Protect the villagers, protect the land, isn't that the role of an Aegnian queen?' I pace towards the bed. 'There must be other people who think the same as I do, find them. People in Aralltir. The merchants ... you just said ...'

Vill pivots towards me, still rubbing his finger. The flames have added colour to his cheeks, but other than that his face is perfectly blank. 'To plot against Onnachild in this matter would be treason, and we know how that is dealt with. Now, I don't know about you, but I have no desire to die like that. If you don't care for yourself or me, perhaps you need reminding what the King has of yours.'

'Ammi.' I rest my head against the bedpost, inhale the faint fragrance of wood and sage.

'Grace.'

'I am thinking of her.' My lips brush the bedpost. 'Of course, I want more for her than seeing her mother murdered. But ...' I appeal to Nessia hunched up by the fire. 'The horses, the food, the dresses, the throne— none of it will matter if there is no village, no people. How could she forgive me if I don't stop this?'

Nessia looks over her shoulder at me, her brow furrowed. There's soot across her cheek, and that smudge reminds me of home. She'll understand. She must. 'Vill's right,' she mumbles, though it appears to pain her to agree with him. 'We can't risk going against Onnachild and losing her for the villagers. They wouldn't do the same for you.'

'Let's not lie to ourselves: I've already lost Ammi.'

'Must you be so defeatist?' Vill says. 'Your efforts have been noticed by Onnachild, and I'm certain he'll grant permission for you to see her soon.'

If I do as Onnachild says. If I don't try to stop the battle. But I can't let myself get swayed by these potentials, and so I keep my focus on Nessia and that smudge on her cheek. 'Didn't we always say we were better than the villagers? Better than Onnachild? Words mean nothing if we don't prove it.'

'We must leave him to it.' Her attention returns to the fire.

'Listen to her, Niah, if you won't listen to me,' Vill says.

There has to be a way. There has to be something. I sink onto the bed, curl my legs up and clutch them to my chest. If I go against Onnachild ... I shudder as if he's already walking over my ashes. Yet ... Yet, I can't wish for more village deaths, for Raen's death. 'I can't think in this place.' I rub my tired eyes.

The room feels too small, too full of the presence of the First—dead— Queen, as though her spirit is sitting at her dressing table, brushing her hair, hair the same colour as Raen's. Raen. Didn't Melody say something about him standing up to Onnachild? He's not afraid, not like Vill. If he wants to be king, if he has the qualities needed to be a king, he'll understand that we need to protect the villagers. It was the first rule of our ancestors. His mother must have told him that, and he must feel the obligation in his Aegnian blood. If I have to march him down to the village, show him how defeated it already is, then I will.

I grab my cloak from the dressing table chair.

'Where are you going?' Vill asks.

'Raen.'

'He won't go against his father,' Nessia says.

'He will,' I say, remembering how much he enjoyed annoying his father in the Judging Room.

'Let her go,' Vill says as I run from my room.

If seeing the village doesn't move Raen, then perhaps knowing we risk losing more land, more subjects, will make him speak out. I careen around a corner. A group of matrons, dour in black, stop talking to stare at me. Can they see my fear? It's hammering loud enough in my chest for them to hear it. They'd understand, wouldn't they? These women know death, its effects. They wouldn't care about villagers, though; that much is evident in the way they turn their noses up at me. It's hard to nod and smile at them but I try. It's even harder to slow my quick strides into dainty steps. The effort makes my feet hurt.

'Lemon is such an unforgiving colour on dark skin, don't you think?' Beshanie says to her servant as I pass them.

Let her say what she wants; there are more important things than colours. 'Have you seen Raen?'

'Have I seen Raen?' She looks up at the ceiling, pats her lips with her fingers. 'Have I seen Raen?'

'He's in the garden, by the river,' the servant says.

Beshanie clips the servant around the head. 'It was a rhetorical question.'

I bow to them both and rush on, out to the lawns. The rain is cold and hard. The sky is the same patchy grey as my funeral dress was. *No more death, no more, please.* I have to try. I scan the grounds; there's no one. And so I run, run as fast as my legs will carry me, as fast as my lungs will allow. The cage bashes against my ankles so I yank it up. The wind thrashes rain at my legs and face but I press on, sliding across grass, getting stones in my shoes.

I find Raen taking shelter under an apple tree and watching the rain hit the river. He leans out from the tree's cover when I stop with a skid and a yell.

'What are you doing here? People will talk,' he says, but there's no teasing quality to his voice. He's slightly dishevelled and drawn, his hair darkened and kinked by the rain.

I heave to catch my breath, push it down past the stupid cage. The chill of the air stings my throat. I bend double. My hands flail around my back, but I can't get under my cloak to the ties of my dress and the effort frustrates me further. I'm tempted to rip the expensive fabric. Raen goes behind me, yanks on the lacing making it tighten but then it loosens enough for me to take a big gasp. I bat his hands away.

'I was trying to help—can't you think of anything else?' There's something off in his tone.

I glare over my shoulder at him. His eyes are tired, the green dots muted. 'War,' I splutter.

'Yes, war.' He retreats under the tree.

'Don't you care?' I follow him, a drop of rain slides down my neck and makes me shudder.

'You disapprove?'

'People will die.'

'Yes, that tends to happen.'

'Villagers, our people, will die.'

'Are you finally admitting they're my people, too?'

'Don't play stupid games with me, not now. Tell me what you're going to do to stop it.'

'There's nothing I can do.' He bends, picks up a stick. It's damp and mould spotted; surely that green reminds him of his mother's eyes, stirs that Aegnian part within him.

'You must have some influence. He's your father.'

He peers sideways at me through his hair. 'Do you think that carries any weight with him? And for your information, I still haven't been acknowledged as his son.'

'Does that not bother you?'

'I find that I'm used to it.' He pulls bark off the stick in thick strips, and they drop onto his boots, curling like locks of hair. The scent of sap mixes with the rain. It smells of life. 'Onnachild's half mad with grief, everyone can see it. To deny him this battle is to deny his true son and stand against the true bloodline.'

'But you stood up to him, in the Judging Room. No one else did.'

'Did your informer not tell you it made no difference?'

'But, you have to do it. You're the only one who can stop him. You must try.'

'That's very flattering of you.' He sighs, and his shoulders slump—his tunic has turned to armour. 'But it would appear that neither of us has any influence over the King.'

'So you will go to fight?'

He throws the stick into the river, watches it twirl in the current. 'He was my half-brother.'

'You will go, then.'

'How can I not?'

I grab his hands, hands that are gritty and damp from the bark. At first, he struggles against the touch, trying to shake me off, but I hold on, tugging him with all my weight, until he gives in and lowers so we're face to face. If the moss won't remind him, if the wet grass doesn't remind him, then hopefully my eyes will.

'I can't let the villagers go out and face defeat alone,' he says.

'Then you'll die too.'

'Then I'll die, and there'll be no one left to stand in your way, think of that instead.' He's smiling but it doesn't reach his eyes.

'Don't be flippant. I've seen it. I've seen death and battle, you haven't. I saw the villagers trundle out there like death was already weighing them down. They're so small and weak from years of hunger. They didn't stand a chance. Raen, I saw it. I saw them. I felt it. The terror. The hope that death will at least be quick. Please listen to me. I saw men, faces contorting in ways you can't imagine. Men unmanned, pissing themselves like children, screaming like women giving birth but all they gave birth to was their own death ... and blood ... limbs ...'

His hands slide from mine. 'You saw him die?'

'Yes. I saw him die.' Tears sting. My heart hurts with memories. I rest

146

my forehead against Raen's and stare down at the grass. Beautiful, alive grass, not trampled and not darkened by blood. 'He ... I ... He cried out like a child wanting his mother, and I couldn't go to him, couldn't do anything. He was so scared and alone and cold, so cold ... and ... Even in death, he looked shocked and ...' I sniff back my tears. 'To die like that ... I wouldn't wish it on anyone.'

He draws me into his warmth, strokes my back. 'You couldn't have done anything.'

'Maybe not.' I lift my gaze to meet his, hope my tears might move him. He frowns. His hand pauses. Perhaps I'm getting through to him. 'But we can do something now. We could prevent more death. If we worked together ...'

'And have you stab me in the back afterwards?' He wipes away my tears so gently that his harsh words are shocking. 'These might have worked on my half-brother but they don't work on me.'

'Nothing would work on you.' I push him away. 'You have no heart. Your mother would be ashamed. Don't worry; nothing I do will implicate you.'

Defeated, I slink off to my rooms, a grass stain on the hem of my dress and my shoes caked in mud. Tomorrow, if it stops raining, I'll ask my ancestors for advice. Right now, all I want to do is to sleep and forget everything.

Chapter Twenty-One

'NIAH! NIAH!' Vill's yelling startles Nessia awake.

'Ignore him.' I roll over in bed.

'They want you,' he shouts.

I hear him bang into something in the dayroom, and then he opens my bedchamber door with a dramatic sweep and another bang. He stands there, slouching against the door frame. His lips are sloppy, swollen, and red-tinged from drinking wine. A chunk of his blond hair curves under his chin. 'Raen's calling for you.'

'Let him.' I pull the furs over my head.

'Why?' Nessia asks.

'Maybe if Niah had been in the Great Hall she'd know,' Vill says.

I couldn't bear it though; the thought of seeing meat cut into pieces like the men on the battlefield made me nauseous. My intention had been to sleep, only every dream took me back to that valley, full of death and noise, and so I just lay there, my heart as sore as a rotten tooth I couldn't stop my tongue prodding.

'Shall I tell them she's coming or help get her ready?' Melody asks.

'Get her ready. He can wait and the waiting will make her arrival sweeter,' Vill says. 'Don't be too long though. They're very drunk.'

'I didn't say I'd go. I'm tired and my head hurts.'

Nessia shuffles closer and whispers. 'Go, Raen might have changed his mind about the battle.'

'I doubt it,' I mumble.

'What are you whispering about?' Melody pulls back the furs.

'Nothing that concerns you,' I say.

'Ignore her; she's in a bad mood.' Nessia tries to drag me with her as she gets out of bed. I slap her away but Melody joins in, so they're pulling a leg each and I slide off the bed, onto the floor. Vill giggles at me sprawled there while Nessia tries to yank me up by my arms.

'Don't bruise her. Raen doesn't like his women black and blue.' He winks at Nessia. Have they been talking? Has she told him about the graveyard? It makes me more determined not to go.

'I don't care what Raen likes or doesn't.'

'You should.' Vill staggers into my room, towards the trunk. 'Get the green velvet. It will suit your eyes; they shine like stars when you sulk.'

Melody nods and rummages through the trunk. Nessia pours a goblet of wine and thrusts it at me so quickly that it slops over my hand and onto my nightdress. She whispers in my ear, 'Go. Make him choose your side; drunk men are much easier to convince.'

'I'll need more than that.' I drain the goblet in one swift movement.

'Good, so you will go,' Vill says as Nessia refills the goblet.

'To talk about the battle, nothing more.'

'Of course, of course,' Vill says. To Melody, he says, 'She'll wear her hair down but lace the diamonds through it.'

They dress me with rough tugs and pulls as Vill constantly refills my wine, his head turned to preserve my modesty. I drink, one, two, three, until it warms my limbs and dulls my feelings. Melody pinches my cheeks so they flush.

'Be careful with the wine,' Nessia warns. 'Remember you haven't eaten.'

It's a little late for that, I think as I burp.

Vill and Melody hurry me out of my rooms and down the hallways so fast I almost trip. We don't stop at the Great Hall, where the noise is raucous, but dart by and continue to the Judging Room. We pause so I can catch my breath and put on my shoes. Vill fusses with my hair while instructing me to be nice, to smile, to act demure. I'm only half listening, as I wonder how I can get a drunk Raen to do my bidding.

Vill enters the room first, dragging me in behind him. His voice booms and is slurred when he announces me. The room is murky, lit by candles dotted along the table. Smoke obscures it further, making the five men nothing more than blurred shapes, Raen the tallest and widest. I'm already bristling and I haven't even spoken to him yet. This will be harder than I anticipated.

'Ah, she comes, from her bedchamber, comes to grace us with her presence.' Raen's voice is lazy from too much drink and it enhances his village accent.

I slip from Vill and head over to where Raen sits sideways on the throne, his legs slung over one of its arms.

'Someone get her a drink,' Raen shouts.

'Why did you call me here?' I ask.

'Why did you come?'

A servant appears with a small pink bottle, hazy white light refracts across its delicate surface. Vill rests his elbows on a phoenix and observes me with his usual bored expression.

'We're drinking spirits tonight,' Raen says. 'Your favourite kind.' He laughs and the others copy though they can't understand his meaning. 'Sit here with us.' He pats the arm of the throne. 'Tonight, I'm willing to share this with you. Tonight only. Come. Drink that down.'

I gulp the thick spirit straight from the bottle, feel it burn my throat and cling to my back teeth. It's a sensation I'm familiar with, reminding me of the drinks my grandfather made and used for bartering before he was cast out. There's a woody taste hidden in the spirit, a very village taste.

'Where is this from?' I ask.

'It's a present,' Vill says. 'A present from a potential wife.' Is he emphasising the words for my benefit or because he's drunk?

'Did your Maiden not tell you?' Raen asks. 'Yes, a beautiful well-bred princess has expressed interest in my hand, my land, and my throne.' He kicks his heel against it. 'There are lots of beautiful women suddenly noticing my eligibility ... I feel just like a girl must when she's first presented at the castle. Tell us, were you presented?'

'You know I wasn't.'

'She was sat with the King's old mistress,' a man with a ginger beard says. The other men laugh and their lusty stares disgust me. I glare at Vill, wanting to know why he never told me. He shrugs and keeps on laughing.

'In light of Perkin's observation,' Raen swings his legs around and leans forwards, 'tell us, what are you really?'

Aegnian first, villager second but he knows this, so I cross my arms and let my appearance speak for itself. It isn't enough for him, though, and he continues goading me. 'Poor innocent or conniving whore?'

'He doesn't mean to offend,' a man says, his accent neither castle nor village.

'I'm sure he meant to offend. But let us ignore him. Tell me your name. There are so few well-mannered men here that I'd be pleased to make your acquaintance.' I keep my gaze on Raen who can't stop chuckling.

'Gavin.' A short man steps nearer. His hair is white, white as the smoke coming from a pipe being passed around.

'I know what she is,' Perkin says.

'Wait.' Raen holds up his hand. 'Let her tell us.'

I look to Vill for help, but he's smirking and stroking the tip of the phoenix's wing. It's Gavin who speaks up, even though he's little more than a boy compared to these men. 'Don't tease.'

'She doesn't need protecting,' Raen says. 'She could kill a man and have him beg for more, but you're right, we've forgotten our manners and the introductions. Here is Perkin, Martus, Gavin, who I note you already introduced yourself to and who happens to be the bringer of our gifts, and the brother of the interested party. All these men are marriageable. Tell me, which do you choose?'

'None of them. You know that.'

'Not even Gavin here? Wait until you hear what he's worth. Gavin, tell her your title and she'll be interested. We could even marry her off and be done with it.'

'I don't care for marriage or for titles.'

'But he's a prince,' he says. 'You like princes, don't you?'

Raen chuckles and the other men copy him, all except Gavin, who smiles awkwardly at me. I straighten my back and harden my features; I've faced coarser, crueller laughter than this. 'I'll have none and none will have me. I was promised to a man, and I shall continue to love that man and no one else.' My voice is strong and steady. The clipped castle accent gone.

Raen's hand flails towards his companions. 'Oh, hush, hush. Listen to this, listen, my friends. I like this tale of love and honour. Tell them how a poor, simple girl won the heart of a prince. Show them some pretty tears.'

'The only tears I'd cry for you would be due to the smoke in this room.'

'You don't cry that I could be married?'

'Why would I?'

'Not even if I told you that with the Princess comes the promise of more men, money for swords, for—'

'The only person I feel sorry for is the poor girl.' I slam the bottle onto the table.

Raen smiles.

'She's told us nothing,' Perkin grumbles.

'Yes, I'd forgotten my previous question. Well remembered.' Raen's fingers rest on his bottom lip.

'Niah,' I say. 'Vill's cousin.' I lean closer to him. 'Now tell us what you are.'

'Many things.' His voice is low as if we're the only people in the room.

I force out a laugh, loud and hard in his face. 'Ah, he's afraid to tell us. But we don't need you to, we know who you are. You're the least favourite son, cast aside for a younger brother, and only returned because that son was buried.' I watch for his jaw to twitch but it doesn't.

His lips turn up into a tight smile. 'And buried he is with the heart of many a poor village girl.'

'Poor village girl I may be, but I've never chased after another's possession. What is mine, I've always owned completely.' My gaze drifts from Raen to the throne, the green eyes of the phoenixes alive in the candlelight.

'I don't recall having to chase. Wasn't it you—'

'She talks in riddles,' Martus says. 'She bores me.' He snatches the pipe from Perkin and inhales so deeply it makes him cough, snot trickling from his wonky nose.

'She doesn't bore me,' Raen says. 'She amuses me.' He pushes the bottle across the table towards me. I sweep it up, swig from it, hoping he'll blame my flush on the spirit. I slam the bottle down when I'm done. His smirk shows I've not fooled him.

'I know a better riddle,' Perkin says. 'I'm a strange creature, for I satisfy women. I grow very tall, erect in bed—'

'This is not respectful,' Gavin says.

'I'll be forced to take her away if you continue,' Vill threatens, although nothing in his languid posture suggests he'll follow through with it.

'Let's talk of nicer things,' Gavin says.

'Like my potential betrothal?' Raen asks.

'I was talking of nice things,' Perkin grumbles. 'It's an onion.'

Vill's suddenly animated, clapping and calling out, 'Music, let us have music.'

From the upper-left corner of the room, figures appear.

'Something loud and happy,' Perkin shouts out. The players start a jaunty tune.

'I want a song of remembrance.' Raen picks a goblet up from the table and a servant refills it. The music changes, slowing, and the notes trill higher. The hairs on my arms rise as if a spirit is blowing on them. Raen's arm, too, is goosebumped. His expression is so strange I can't read it. There's a distance in his eyes suggesting he's lost in another time, a time when castle and village used to celebrate the gods' days together and this song would drift over spring twilights. It was never played as sadly as this, though; it was played fast and proud.

'This song darkens the mood,' Martus moans.

'It's a song from my mother's time,' Raen says. 'And we shall listen to it.'

'I know another riddle,' Martus says.

He and Perkin huddle together, arms around each other. Gavin frowns at the floor and shakes his head, his white hair a blur. Vill's fingers are tapping on the throne, the candlelight darting across his many rings.

'Dance with me,' Raen says.

'No. I don't think—'

'I want to talk to you.' He stumbles to his feet, clinging to the throne to steady himself. 'Where has your courage gone? Just one dance. Have more spirit if it will help you tolerate me.' He grabs the bottle from the table and shoves it at me.

'It helps everyone tolerate you.' I drink a big glug.

'Don't be cruel.' He takes the bottle from me and places it on the table. Then he grabs my elbow and guides me into the darkness from where the men's voices are faint and their figures are only shadows.

'Why are you trying to embarrass me?' I ask.

'I'm not trying to embarrass you.' He sounds serious but his smile is playful as he guides my hands to his neck. 'There.' His arms go around my waist. His touch is not light as in the castle style.

'This is not proper.'

'They can't see,' he whispers in my ear, sending a thrill down my spine. My body remembers. The spirit has made me weak. I step back but he doesn't let go, his fingers fan out to catch me. 'Please.' There's such longing in his voice, his village-accented voice, that I can't say no. Perhaps I don't want to be alone either. Our cheeks brush as I nod.

'Thank you.' He straightens up, rests his chin on my head.

What does a dance matter? Our swaying from side to side is hardly dancing; it's more like being lulled to sleep. His strong body presses against mine as I remember better times: my grandmother alive, the swell of her pink cheeks when she laughed; the ribbons of the midsummer pole wafting as children danced beneath them. Underneath the fragrance of spirit and wine, I can smell Raen: his scent of castle living, his scent of village past. Everything, everyone, seems so far away, held off by the smoke and darkness so there's only us, isolated from the present and the future. I lean back to look up at him. His eyes are closed and a faint smile is on his lips, and the sight tempts me to ask about his memories, his mother. I'm scared of words, though, of how they might break this drifting off to more pleasant times and so instead, I lace my fingers around his neck to touch his warm skin. His pulse against my wrist beats faster than the song, and his hair tickles my bare arm like the leaves of a weeping willow.

The song starts again, seamlessly, with only the lyrics to show this. 'Why weren't you in the Great Hall?' His baritone adds texture to the song.

The embroidery of his tunic is soft against my cheek as I nuzzle into it, feeling the muscle beneath. 'Is that why you called me here?'

'No.'

My lips relax, and I sigh as tiredness seeps through my body, edged with something that tingles my skin same as a hot bath does. He's the only thing keeping me up and moving: my legs follow his, my feet mirror his, and my waist moves with his hands.

'Were you at Aelius's grave?' he asks.

When I mumble no, my lips brush his tunic.

'You have to forget the dead to live now, isn't that what they say?'

'I won't. I can't.'

'Neither can I.' He pulls me closer. His voice sounds so rough it must be hurting his throat. 'How can I forget my mother when her presence is everywhere? Here. Waiting around the corner. The other side of the door.' His hand lifts from my waist and wafts towards the door, moving cold air.

I press closer to his warmth. 'I see her running down the hallways, laughing as she used to when we played hide and seek. Her voice ...' His hand is back on my waist, a caress from his fingers. 'Speak to me in that language you people have.'

'I can't.'

'Why not?' He pulls away and I stumble. 'Didn't you speak to him in those words? Isn't that how you seduced him?'

I blink away the haze from my eyes, the haze that almost tricked me again. The song is thrumming through my body that is all. 'Get me more spirits.' I raise my voice so the other men will hear my demand.

'Don't bring them here.' He takes hold of my arm. 'They don't understand. You understand though, don't you?'

I'm drawn to the scar on his cheek, curious as to how it got there. Was it worn into his skin through sleepless, motherless nights as a child? But he's Raen, a man who'd prefer to send villagers to their death than risk his place in the castle and so I don't need to know anything else.

'I understand loss.' I stand firm and pull myself up to my full height. 'I understand death and battles and the things I love being used in an old man's game. There's too much I understand, and for that, I deserve my drink.'

'Niah, I'll get it. Later. I need to talk about her.'

'I can't listen to you.'

'You can and you will,' but it isn't a command and that makes what he says worse. I'd rather him threaten me. He turns my hand palm up and with his index finger, he traces over the bumps and dips of it, trying to read the truth of me. It sends sparks across my skin like flint struck against flint.

The song begins again, disorientating me. I want it to be played happily again. I want it played loud and not like this whisper from spirits. Raen leaves me standing alone, perhaps to get me that drink I thought I wanted but don't now; I'm already too giddy. I don't know where to rest my hands, and the men's laughter makes me feel suddenly small and lonely. Raen's chuckle booms over them. How is he so changeable? The boisterous clunking of goblets mixes with the music. I close my eyes, and I'm young again and in our small village garden, twirling to my grandmother's strange poetry, the language Raen wants to hear. The sun is warming my skin, as warm as it used to be in those days when the summer air would hold the perfume of morning showers. And within that scent is the scent of Raen, captured on my skin, my dress.

'Stop the music,' I shout, opening my eyes.

It does stop. The men stop. I stop. Even the candle flames seem to stop. Everything is still, and the stillness feels so close to death it's as if we've summoned it up with our longing for the past. I stifle a sob.

'Niah?' There's concern in Raen's voice, and that is even more disorientating. He clicks his fingers and a different song is played, one without memories, then he reappears in the dark with me when I don't want him to. I snatch his goblet from him and drink it dry, tipping my head back. When it's empty, I press it against my hot forehead. He gathers up my hair with one hand, wafts it to bring coolness to my neck. Our eyes meet. He seems bemused, and I don't know if it's because of what he sees or because he's as surprised by his tender gesture as I am. His mouth opens to speak but no words come. I hold my breath waiting, wondering.

His other hand rises, the back of his index finger skims over my face, clumsily, like he's checking my features: the high curve of my cheekbones, the upward tilt of my eyes, the arch of my eyebrows and then my lips, top, bottom, testing the plumpness of them. They part to taste the woody spirit on his skin. My hands fall limp by my side, drop the goblet.

'I forget why I wanted you here,' he says, frowning. 'What did I want to say? You seem real, amongst all this fakery, perhaps that was it.'

'You're talking nonsense.' I slip away from him, bang up against the door and clutch the handle.

'I always talk nonsense.' His hand reaches towards me but hesitates, shakes there between us. 'Kiss me.' His eyes are pleading, the brown bottomless, the green dots blurred.

'No.'

'You did before. You seemed to like it.'

'I thought you were someone else.' I stare over his shoulder as I try to remain cold to him, try not to respond to the heat coming off his fingers as they get nearer, nearer, and it's not only my collarbone that is warming, it's my neck, my ears, my hands, my knees, places I don't want to think about.

'Him?'

I don't answer, just start opening the door.

'I can give you everything he could.' Raen looks sober with his jaw tight and twitching. There's a challenge in his eyes. Is he wanting me to say no? If so, then why are his fingers following a vein up the inside of my arm? He wants to see me tremble, that must be it. I don't want to give him that satisfaction, but I can't stop myself.

'I'll never love you.' There's even a tremble in my voice.

'Simple, naïve little Niah. I'm not asking you to love me. I'm asking you to bed me, and I'll remember it when I'm king.'

'You'll never get to be king.' I bash his hand away, swear at him in Aegnian: the only words he'll ever hear in it.

'If you're going to curse me at least do it in a language I understand.' The teasing lilt of his voice suggests that I've given him exactly what he wanted this whole time.

Chapter Twenty-Two

THE KING'S MEN, high on black stallions and glinting silver, are in front of my love's statue. Scraggy villagers stare up at them, open-mouthed and confused by the change to their routine. I duck behind my ransacked hut, and pull my hood up over my head, ignoring the useless things scattered around my feet.

'Though we live in the castle and you live in the village, we share the common language, the common religion, and the common traditions. This is our land. This is your land. When we have prospered, you have prospered. When you have gone hungry, we have gone hungry.' Raen's exaggerating his village twang but still his voice is commanding and has me stepping closer. It's only my hand clinging to the half-charred post of my hut that stops me from joining the mass. He has the look of an ancient warrior, composed and imposing as his thighs grip his horse to keep it steady. The light rebounding from Aelius's statue adds an otherworldly sheen to Raen's honey-coloured skin and dark hair, making him even more magnificent by colluding with him. No wonder the villagers are awestruck.

'In our suffering, we are one.' He stares up at the statue. 'Who has not lost a son, a brother, a father? They have taken our men. They have taken our land, but they have not taken our pride.' His baritone is a rumble through the earth. 'These are words, and words alone will not give us back our land, our men; I know this. We need action. Not words. Join us. With God on our side, the True God, we shall be victorious. We will take back our land.' Raen makes a snatching gesture.

'Aye, aye,' a man shouts. Villagers stamp their feet, bash the ends of their tools onto the ground making dull thuds. Some shake their fists. Slurs are shouted like they're blessings: 'Pig-fucking sons of whores', 'beady-eyed tricksters', 'dirty, lying hedge-dwellers.' The stallions dance, ready. Raen holds up a hand and silence returns. Not even the birds dare make a noise. I rest my head against my hut, gripping the post tighter.

'We were great people,' Raen shouts. 'We are still great people. We will show them we fear no pain, fear no challenge, fear no death. We will fight for our brothers, our fathers, our sons and,' he raises his sword, 'for our honour.'

The roar of the villagers is deafening: women, men, children shouting, screaming, hollering, stamping—even babies wail. Fools. All of them are fools, blinded by fancy words and silver. What is pride compared to life? Can they not see these castle men have never had to endure even an hour of hunger? As Raen dismounts his stallion, the villagers surge towards him. They touch his cloak, his armour. A woman tries to touch his hair. I can't hear what he says to her, but it makes her flush and fidget in response. He's smiling, relaxed, and he even chuckles as if they didn't help kill his mother. The excitement is palpable, charging the air like an advancing fire, and it gets to that village part of me, makes my heart thump in my ears as loud as horses storming into battle. I push away from my hut wall; I didn't come here for this.

By the time I've collected the herbs and flowers I need, the sun is setting and spreading its colours across the sky. It'll be dark by the time I return to the castle, and I might miss another night of dining in the Great Hall. Vill won't be happy about that, and Onnachild and the advisers will surely notice, but I can't think of that now. Someone must do something to save these foolish men from themselves. Hopefully, my ancestors will tell me what that should be.

I head to the forgotten graves where their ashes are part of the earth, where I will be alone and undisturbed. The village children used to call the spiky bushes here dead women's fingers, and the wind, they said, spoke for the evil spirits when it howled over the barren expanse. It's howling now as it plays with trophies of hair and cloth caught on the bushes; children must still dare each other to come here as they did in my youth.

Hunched over, cloak billowing around him like the wings of a mythical bird, is Raen. He's kneeling and his head is drooped, but there's no mistaking the impression his body makes against the desolate horizon. How has he managed to find his mother's resting place when only I know where my grandmother scattered her ashes? The wind picks up, pushing at my skirt, at my hair, and I stagger a few steps before I'm able to brace myself against it. I gather up my hair, tuck it down the back of my cloak, and take one, quiet step towards a low bush so I can crouch behind it to observe him. His hands are clasped together, pressed to his chest. His lips move but I can't hear him. He bends from the waist towards the ground, forehead almost in the dust. He rights himself. The wind wafts up his hair, then lowers it carefully onto his shoulders.

'Are you spying on me?' His voice sounds strained.

I'd prefer to stay here, wait for him to leave, but I don't want him to think I'm intimidated and so I step out from behind the bush. He doesn't move as I walk towards him; his stare remains on the horizon. Tears are sliding down his cheeks and he makes no attempt to hide them from me. I've never seen a man cry before and the sight takes my breath away, more so than seeing him on that stallion, because somehow his power is enhanced by this vulnerability. It's mesmerising. It's like snow in the middle of the night, untouched by man or animal. Even the wind's howl quietens to a whisper. I kneel beside him. His lashes are spiked together. His eyes are red-tinged, and his lips are puffed pink. The scar on his cheek is blotchy. I rest my hand on his knee. He glances at the touch but doesn't move away.

'You're weeping?' My voice is little more than a breath.

'And I shall weep more for a good mother and a good wife.' On his lap is a wooden flower, crudely made with the edges still rough.

161

'She was much loved.'

'And much hated.'

'That too at the end. They all were.'

The wind blows a lock of hair across his forehead, and when he dashes it away a smudge of dust is left on his skin. I go to wipe it off but he grabs my wrist. A tear has settled into the pit of his scar—it's found its home.

'What are you doing here?' he asks.

'My ancestors ... I need them.'

He lets go of me. 'I need her too.' He grimaces and shakes his hair off his face. I catch it, smooth it back. It's sleeker than I expected it to be. 'No one speaks of her anymore.'

'Nessia and I do.'

He picks the wooden flower up from his lap and rolls it between his palms. A shard, the same colour as his skin, splinters into his thumb. 'Leave it,' he says when I go to pick it out. He sniffs back his tears. 'Last night ...' His eyes finally meet mine and the edges crease, briefly, with a weak smile. 'I should apologise. This ... this is what I needed, why I asked for you. I wanted to talk about her.'

'We can't, not in the castle.'

'I know, but not talking about her doesn't make what happened go away. Instead ...' His gaze lowers back to the wooden flower. 'I watched them come for her, those same people who were looking at me with love and respect today like it had never happened, like I wouldn't remember, but I do. How could I ever forget? Isolation gives you plenty of time to brood on these things, to feed hatred, and now ...' His fingers caress the flower, running up the stem, over the edges of rough petals. The tenderness of those large fingers is captivating. 'At every turn, I've failed her. I saw them break down the door and drag her out, and I did nothing to stop them. She made me promise I'd stay hidden, but I should have tried.' His lashes are wet with new tears. 'And now, here I am, sitting at his table, eating his food, smiling at him, agreeing with him, breathing the same air as him though it makes me sick to my stomach. I am not his man. I'm doing it for her, not myself, and yet, it looks ... You're right; she would be ashamed of me.'

'I shouldn't have said that.'

'And I shouldn't have come here.' He stands and the flower tumbles to the dust.

'No, wait.' I grab the edge of his cloak. He stares at me, his hair blowing around him, the green in his irises blurred from tears. His lips are pouting. Pain lines his forehead. 'You were a child.'

'I'm a man now.'

But in his eyes, I see only the child he was: scared, alone, and confused. Feelings I recognise, feelings I know as well as I know this dust beneath my knees. 'She understands. She does.'

'I came here for her forgiveness, but all there is here is ...' He stares out to the horizon, seeming to search beyond it.

'Wait.'

He shakes his head and peels my fingers off his cloak. His lips wobble hinting that new tears are readying themselves. I can't bear it, and I don't know why. I jump up, grab his shoulders and try to push him down. Anything is better than seeing him like this; I'd rather he act as he did last night than this. I can do something. I shouldn't. Nessia would tell me I'm mad, perhaps I am, but in this moment I see the village in him. The little boy who lost his mother. And the little girl who lost her grandmother responds. 'Raen.'

He's startled at the sound of his name. I rise onto my tiptoes, press my cheek against his wet one to keep the words between us even though there's no one else here.

'I can call her.'

The eyes he lowers to me are bright with hope and tears. My body throbs with the dangerous anticipation of showing him this, and it spurs me to brush away his tears. I think I feel a tremble from him, but it might be the breeze against my skin. 'Get me some wood.'

He nods, stumbles off. His figure is dark against the setting sun as he gathers wood, a figure searching but never finding what he's really looking for. He's humming though, and a bird is responding to him. I sort through the herbs bunched up in my cloak. Luckily, there were some dried yew berries left in my hut. I couldn't find Aelius's sword, though; some villager must have stolen it along with my bowls and pan.

When Raen returns, we huddle together to create a brace against the wind. His thigh presses into mine. His shoulder knocks mine and together we hunch forwards over the bundle of twigs. The intensity of his stare makes me nervous, and I almost drop the flint on my first attempt. Am I right to show him this? This ability that Onnachild tried to ban, had my ancestors killed because of ... mine and Raen's. I peer sideways at him, at his nose red-tipped by the cold, at his lips pressed together, and his eyebrows lowered. How can I disappoint him and retract my offer now? His hand rests on my knee, a wide hand with dust striped across the knuckles and mud under his nails. A village hand. I take a deep breath and put Onnachild out of my mind.

The fire is quick and eager, so I must have its blessing. The flames light up his features, picking out a shine on his bottom lip and enhancing the depth of his scar. He's trying to control his breathing as he must have done that day he hid from the villagers. I scatter the herbs into the flames. Raen watching the shape of the Aegnian words on my mouth as I call to the ancestors feels as intimate as a kiss and my face flushes. I drop some herbs into his open palm, careful not to touch him.

'Throw them,' I say, using Onnachild's language. 'When she comes, she'll speak through you, not through your ears, you won't hear her there, but you'll feel her words.' I almost pat his chest to show him where he'll feel them. 'And she'll know what you say. Like thoughts.'

He nods and does as I said. The fire gobbles up the herbs and spurts smoke out. I blow into the flames, coaxing out the dead with the breath of the living. Mumbling so he can't hear, I say my final words and hope his mother will appear. Features start to form in the smoke balls. Upturned eyes are drawn out. Their attention is on me, though. Lips, full like Raen's, try to speak to me. *No*, I tell her, *for Raen, please, bring him some comfort.* A big burst of smoke, thick as a storm cloud, hangs in the sky, blocking out the faint and early moon. I turn away. *Speak to Raen, I can wait.*

Flames warm my back. Raen's leg warms mine. I lean into him, rest my cheek against his shoulder. I can feel it moving, hear his breath catching. He chuckles, and it's such a lovely sound that I close my eyes to savour it. His mother's presence flows through me with the heat of the fire, the chill of the wind—and something else, something deeper inside, has my heart beating frantically. A warning? I lift my head, glance behind me. The fire has gone out. The cold has returned. The wind has stopped. All around is darker. When I look up at the sky, the red and orange streaks have gone and only deep blue remains. It's silent except for the sound of my and Raen's breath, matching. The world seems to have stopped.

'I saw her.' He sounds wonder-struck. 'My mother.' He chuckles. 'I saw my mother. Niah, I saw my mother.'

I shuffle around to face him. 'What did she say?'

'Say?' He's staring at me as though he's never seen me before. 'Nothing.' He brushes a lock of hair off my face, tucks it behind my ear, and his fingers linger. 'Niah ...' There's surprise and admiration in the way he says my name. His irises are greener as if his mother has strengthened her claim on him.

I hug him as I should have done when I first found him crying. When our chests touch, I focus on the remains of the fire and not how close my mouth is to the pulse in his throat. The perfume of our ancestors is around us mixing with his scent: earthy, intoxicating, home. *Do not breathe it in*, I tell myself. It's too late, though, and this hug, this comfort I wanted to give, is being charged like the air around a flame. His body is fuel for it. My palms on his shoulder blades take it in. My cheek against his neck takes it in. The sensations thrum through me: breasts, belly, lower. I want to sigh. I want to get away. I want to press myself closer and take him into my body as if I don't know that fire burns.

He places a finger under my chin, tilts my head up. His expression is confusing, something like wonderment is there, and something like bemusement. His eyelids lower, those drenched lashes are dark spikes. He eases nearer, nearer. I hold my breath, unable to move away. He kisses me once, barely touching. Is he scared to? My eyes close and everything is more overwhelming: his presence, the echoing touch from his lips, his scent. His breath tickles, sending a tremble down my spine. We're trapped in this moment: his arm squashed between us, his finger on my chin, lips near but not touching while the last kiss, and the potential for more, lingers, in that space between. My sigh is one long, jagged exhaled breath, and I feel his shoulders quiver under my palms.

A crackle from the fire brings me back to myself, and I push away from him, away from the heat radiating off him. My hands itch. I pull my cloak around me, scratch my palms, and kick out the embers as I pretend I'm unaffected. 'We'll be late,' I say.

Chapter Twenty-Three

I WISH WE HAD BEEN TOO LATE returning to the castle so I could avoid sitting in the Great Hall. Raen's gawping at me from the top table, and between him and the advisers watching from their corner, I feel as exposed as a hare in an open field. The fire's scent is still on me, even though Nessia speedily changed my dress. I slide down in my seat, trying to hide from Raen, the advisers, and all this talk of battles. The men's voices are loud with arrogance and excitement. The Maidens' songs are triumphant as if we've won already. Vill's drawing shapes across the table, lining up goblets and flagons and pretending they're men. Onnachild claps and haws. I can't prevent my frustration narrowing my eyes and furrowing my brow, despite Mantona's constant prompting to remember my lessons.

'It's good to see the King happy again,' she says.

I huff and take a gulp of wine to drown my thoughts and feelings.

'Though it'll kill him if Raen dies. He may not admit it, not even to himself, but it will kill him.' The sadness in her voice draws my attention from Raen to her. She's focused on Onnachild and in her eyes, I recognise love and admiration. It reminds me of Perkin's words: the King's mistress.

'Is it true?' I shuffle closer to her, lower my voice. 'What they say about you and Onnachild? You were ... you loved him and he loved you?'

She smiles, shyly. 'Didn't I tell you nothing Vill ever does is a coincidence?'

I try to ignore the implication but my gaze is drifting back towards Raen. His fingers rest on his lips. Is he thinking of our kiss? Mine rise to do the same, but I stop them in time and reach for my goblet instead. I force myself to refocus. 'If you love Onnachild ... if you've any influence then help me stop this battle.'

'That was a long time ago. People change.'

Raen's rising from the top table, his arms extended as he pushes himself up. He tries to pass a huddle of men but they tug him into embraces, tap his chest, slap him on the back. He smiles at them, nods, appears good-humoured but it's fake, something is off in his smile, in the way he holds himself.

'Back then, the King gave me this, he said I was a warrior woman and deserved some armour,' Mantona says.

'What?' I turn to face her.

She's staring at her raised left hand, the skin wrinkled and so thin her blue veins are visible. She takes off a long, silver ring decorated with a solitary green gem and rests it in her palm. 'I was brave once, perhaps I still am somewhere. I made my choice, and it was not a happy one, and still to this day, I wonder ... Love, it makes us do stupid things and guilt makes us do even stupider things. Remember that.' She places the ring on the table before her. 'Once, I was trusted to keep something hidden from him. I did. I hid it in the most obvious place. People never think to check the most obvious place. It might help, but I can't. Please, Niah, understand my reasons. It may be stupidity or vanity or ... but ...'

'What?' I whisper, aware of Raen getting closer.

'She asked me to hide it and I did. The First Queen.' She hisses the forbidden title through clenched teeth. 'It's in the library.'

I can't ask more questions because Raen has stopped in front of us. He's not looking at me, though; he's scowling at the ring. He picks it up, tries to slide it down his little finger but it catches on his knuckle. The green gem glows against his skin.

'It's yours,' Mantona says to him.

His index finger brushes over the gem. Then in one swift gesture, the ring is gone and his hand is held out for mine. He's pensive, unsmiling, as he leads me out amongst the dancing couples: an old man and a young woman who must be related because they have the same jutting chins, two girls in lilac who've given up waiting to be asked and are partnering each other, and Vill with Nilola.

Our first dance step has me bumping into Raen. Whether it's because of the wine, his nearness, or because we've joined the dance mid-song, I don't know. He nods out the beats to me before starting again, and he keeps tapping them out onto my hip.

'What were you saying to that woman?' he asks once we've settled into the rhythm. 'She's not to be trusted. That ring was my mother's.'

I peek up, my gaze lingering on his lips, the bottom one bigger than the top. How have I not noticed that before?

'Niah, are you listening?' He squeezes me. There's a pleasing tingle through my waist. It's the wine, finally working. 'She won't help you. Why do you look so guilty? You asked her, didn't you? My mother was right, you do need protecting.'

'You said she didn't speak to you.'

He shrugs.

'What else did she say?'

His eyes sparkle with teasing and the green dots are radiant like a coppersmith's fire. No trace of his tears remains. The softness in his expression as he stares down at me, has to go, has to stop. It's making my hands sweat. It has my heart in my throat. His silence is even more infuriating.

'Did she tell you to stop this battle?' I ask.

'I'm not going to tell you what she said, so stop asking.'

'Did she tell you to kiss me?'

Rather than irritating him as I hoped it would, my question makes him smile. 'No, that I did for myself.'

As I try to squirm from his hold, Nilola's skirt bashes into mine and sends it bobbing.

'My mistake.' Vill's smile makes it obvious that he's lying. 'I should lead better.'

The advisers are heading onto the dance floor so I nod and accept Vill's apology. Raen draws me back into the dance, and Vill sweeps Nilola away. I watch them swirl and dip, and try to catch Vill's glance so I can assess what he overheard, but he remains focused on Nilola, joking and making her laugh. Raen squeezes my waist. 'Niah.'

'What?' I snap.

'I want to offer you my friendship and protection.' He chuckles, so he must realise how ridiculous this sounds.

'Why?'

'Why are you so suspicious?'

'Have you forgotten what's between us?' I lean back to see if he's still teasing. He looks at me and that unreadable expression is there again just as it was before he kissed me. I lower my head in case he means to do so again. The dip of his neck has flushed and I can't help wondering whether the colour goes further down. He takes a deep breath and sighs it out. The flush fades.

'No,' he says, and for a moment I've forgotten what we were talking about. 'But it doesn't look like Onnachild's going to die any time soon and so why not be friends? Two outsiders together.'

I stare at the top table where Onnachild's deep in conversation with Gavin, clasping his back and drawing him closer. Gavin is an early-flowering snowdrop in the paws of that grisly old bear. Aelius's chair has been pushed aside to make room, his knife taken up by Onnachild and waved around like a sword. I dip my head to hide my scowl.

Raen squeezes me again. 'Well?'

He can't really want an answer. After last night, the kiss, the graveyard ... he can't be serious, can he? I dare not peep in case that strange expression is still on his face. As I think of those moments shame floods through me. It was only his tears that made me show him his mother, that's all, and now he's bewitched, confused by that. Nothing has changed, he must understand that. I'll make him. I shake my head, but I'm not sure if he's noticed.

'Let me repay the kindness you showed me today.' His voice is soft and so it seems to belong more to the crying man than this one dancing with me.

'That was not kindness.'

'It was the kindest thing anyone has done for me.'

'Then you can't have seen much kindness in your life.'

'Neither have you.'

'Did your mother tell you that?'

'She didn't need to. Stop being so prickly.' He rubs my arms, leaving a warm tingle. 'I'm trying to offer you my friendship and protection.'

I shake off the sensation. 'And why should I accept? I still remember how you threw coins at me. How you called me a whore. How ...' I pause to get my emotions under control as the advisers are creeping close.

'Maybe I misjudged you.'

I huff. 'Nothing has changed.'

'Everything has changed.'

The music ends so abruptly it has me confused, and my hands hang by my sides when we step apart. He cups my elbow with his palm. Mud is still under his nails.

'We can't talk here. Tomorrow. Meet me in the gardens by the fountain, midday when the servants bring around food. I promise to not be inappropriate.' His gaze lowers to my lips. 'Unless, of course, you want me to be.'

My face heats. The advisers are watching so I curtsy and thank him for the dance in a manner far too formal, far too cold.

'How about if I apologise profusely for my behaviour the other night and promise to never speak, or think, of such things again?' He sounds serious but there's a twinkle in his eyes that I can't trust and so I don't answer. 'Well, I'll be there.' He bows. 'I hope to see you.'

Nilola steps between us, her gaze coyly on the floor, even as she thrusts her hands at Raen. With a swish of her skirts, she's off spinning with him, flashing me an expression of smug contentment as she presses herself to him, closer than I'd ever dare.

'It wouldn't be to your advantage to let him see you're jealous,' Vill whispers in my ear.

'I'm not jealous. I'm amazed at her brazenness. Besides, I don't want to dance anymore.'

He follows me back to the table. I sink into my seat and pour myself more wine.

'Why are you so sulky tonight?' Vill asks as he sits beside me. 'Everything's going perfectly.'

'It's not going perfectly.' I push away the wine. My thoughts are swimming enough, and I need to figure out whether Raen's being genuine and what his motivation is. My fingers play with my lips until I realise Vill's watching me, and then I pick at a dried blob of food on the table. Nothing makes sense. Raen says he wants to be friends but last night ... Outsiders, Raen called us. Is that why he made that offer? But then why ... Perhaps Vill can help me make sense of it; he's meant to be my adviser, and he understands castle life better than I do. 'Last night, Raen asked me to bed him.'

'Excuse me? Did I hear correctly?'

'Nothing. He said nothing.' I shouldn't have told Vill—it's the wine making me loose-lipped.

'Ha. He makes it too easy, far too easy. Give him what he wants.'

'Vill.'

'What? It's nothing more than what half these women have done to ensnare their husbands or indeed other women's husbands.' Vill waves a finger in front of my eyes, the garnet from a ring making a red trail, but it's not this he wants me to look at and his finger tilts, directing my gaze to Nilola and Raen. 'If you don't, Nilola will.'

Raen's wide hands are spread around her tiny waist. She's giggling, hiding her head against his chest. He's smiling and playing up to it. Nothing of the vulnerable man I saw today is in the confident way he dances, back straight and rigid. This is the man who's lusty and would bed any pretty woman, just like his father.

'You could have him right in the palm of your hand.' Vill eases me closer with a light tug. 'Think what he'd be willing to do for you. He might even defy Onnachild in relation to this battle. Is that not what you desire?' He helps himself to my wine.

Raen's body moves so gracefully as he dances, surprisingly so considering how muscular he is, and I can't stop remembering how his back moved under my palms when he was atop me. I rest my forehead on my hands to steady my thoughts, to cool my skin. 'I'm tired. I'm ... I'm confused.'

Vill taps my knuckles with the goblet and my fingers open to accept it. 'It's so simple.'

'Is it?' I stare at my love's empty chair, waiting for him as if he'd only stepped out to talk battle tactics with these people who knew him in a way that I didn't and will never get the chance to now. Why do I want to prevent a battle that seeks to avenge his death? I take several sips of wine though they make me nauseous. Vill blocks my vision with his perfect face.

'Aelius would understand. He'd forgive you if it keeps Raen from the throne.'

But Vill doesn't know the dead as I do. When I nod, it's only to shut him up.

'Then I shall go and disturb Nilola and Raen.' He stands.

His words shouldn't please me but they do. It doesn't mean I'll meet with Raen tomorrow. It doesn't mean I'll accept his offer of friendship. My eyes close and I picture Aelius: his blond curls a muddle around his face and his lithe body shining with sweat from our lovemaking.

As my fingers play with the water in the fountain, all I can think about is

Raen's tears, and it makes me want to run away even more. I would too, only Vill said it was either this or sit with the other women in the Sunning Room. My reflection catches my eye and I scowl at it. Vill chose my low-cut dress and the silver daisies threaded through my loose hair; he said I looked alluring. I don't want to look alluring. I disturb my reflection in the water.

'It's good to see you.' Raen's voice startles me as if I've been caught out. He seems uneasy too, curling the same lock of hair behind his ear several times. Is he regretting this as much as I am? 'I was convinced you wouldn't come.'

So was I. I glance back at the castle, at the protruding Sunning Room. 'What do you want?'

He chuckles, dismissing my curtness. 'What's wrong with us spending a lovely afternoon together if we're to be friends?'

'I didn't accept your friendship.'

'Or reject it.' He sits on the side of the fountain, legs crossed. Water spots his shoulder. 'I want to show you something.'

'I'd rather you stopped the battle to show your gratitude.'

'This isn't about showing my gratitude, and can you stop talking about the battle for one day? You're worse than Onnachild.' He's smiling, though.

He jolts up from the fountain—probably because water has gone down his back—and I almost laugh at him until he holds out his tunic and shakes it, flashing his toned stomach. This is a bad idea. He strides off in the direction of the wall encircling the castle grounds; he must have come to his senses. I let out a sigh of relief. He stops, turns to me. 'Are you coming then?'

I rise, shake the water from my fingers, and then head towards Raen. He waits for me to catch up, a smile—that seems genuine—on his face, and then we walk on, side by side, in silence. We don't pause to marvel at the trumpet-like flowers blooming early. The bees buzz at us when we don't move out of their way. We leave the white path, stepping onto grass neatly trimmed into lines of differing shades, and then on to where grass spurts out in thick and shining blades. It brushes against my skirt, and I enjoy watching it ripple in my wake.

When we stop, it's at a pile of charred stones and flint, far away from the castle. Raen crouches to pick up a flint. 'These used to be part of a wall that encased my mother's garden and there ...' He points towards another black pile. 'That must have been the wooden door. It was plain with a simple lock, sometimes in the morning there'd be snails climbing up it. She'd pick them off and place them on the grass to keep them safe. The key was on a piece of leather around her neck; it'd dangle out when she'd bend to pick me up. Hit me on the nose.' He chuckles and rubs his nose. 'It was a village garden, vegetables and herbs. I thought it was so much more beautiful than all the flowers Onnachild liked. It was her sanctuary from the castle, from Onnachild.' He stands up, sniffs the flint, and I wonder what it smells of. When he walks towards the next pile, I follow.

'Can you feel her in it?' He hands the flint to me.

I close my hand around it. It's warm from the sun and him, and the rough corners dig into my palm: comfort and pain. And fear. 'It's just a stone.' I throw it away.

He looks, longingly, at where it's landed but doesn't go after it. Instead, he picks up another one and tosses it from one hand to the other. 'I was allowed to play in the mud: dry, wet. It didn't matter. She'd laugh when I tried to eat it. My mouth would be all gritty and there'd be streaks down my chin and cheek. I loved going to that garden, being alone with her. I loved it because I didn't have to learn the things Onnachild thought a prince should. Instead, I could watch the worms and ladybirds. I found them fascinating. See, I wasn't always so disagreeable.' He smiles then bolts off.

I kick off my shoes and chase after him, my skirt pulled high. The air around my calves and the cool grass beneath my feet are exhilarating, making me leap and whoop. I'm skipping when I finally catch up with him by a patch of thistles. He's chuckling at me and the sound is so joyful, so infectious that I'm laughing too. A silver daisy slips out of my hair. He bends down to pick it up.

'Leave it,' I say. 'It might grow a silver tree, and then we can leave here and not have to worry about crowns and thrones and battles.'

'I like the sound of that.' He stares up at me. His cheeks are flushed from running, laughing, and sunshine. The green in his dark eyes is vibrant. He thrusts his hand into the mud, scoops it up and then watches it tumble between his fingers with all the joy of a small boy. 'This used to be full of lavender. All around here was green and purple. I think I can still smell it.' He scoops up more mud and smells it, closing his eyes.

I smack his hand up. I can't help it; village mischief has overtaken me. The mud goes into his hair, up his nose, some sticks to his eyelashes. I tug at my cage to let out my laughter. He's chuckling again, that deep belly sound which is so appealing I don't notice him scoop up more mud until he's thrown it at me. It gets into my open mouth, down the dip between my breasts.

'I don't care,' I shout, dancing on the spot like it's cooling rain I've been washed in. 'I'm a villager.' My laughter stops; I'm not a villager anymore, and this dress, this cage, never lets me forget it. I let go of my skirt.

He takes my hand before I can brush the mud from my face and leads me to a scorched square of earth. He sits amongst shredded pieces of wood, pats the ground beside him. I settle down on a large, flat stone instead. He stares at my dirty feet, which are peeping out from the bottom of my dress, and smiles. It's a sad one that doesn't reach his eyes.

'She was the most beautiful thing here.' He tilts his head back like he's expecting to see her appear in the sky again, and if I could, perhaps I would make it so. 'They said she met men here,' I'd hear them whispering it around the castle. As they ate her food, they called her names. One time they tried to catch her out, waiting outside the walls for us and when they saw her flushed cheeks, and her dirty hands and knees, they took that as proof.' He gazes down at my hands and strokes mud from my knuckles before pulling them into his lap. Our shoulders bump together. 'When they heard her talk about cabbages and dandelions they laughed, said she was lying. She didn't think Onnachild would believe them; why would she? But he was already making promises to that woman, your love's mother.' His jaw twitches. 'The True Queen.' He pushes away my hands, draws his knees up and wraps his arms around them. 'They tore it down. The night after they watched her hang. Still, no one believed her, not even when they got through and saw the cabbages and the dandelions gone to seed. And now it's gone.' He lets out a deep breath, one so long it's as if he's held onto it through his years of exile.

I rub the small of his back as Nessia used to do for me when I was a child and needing comfort. 'And later that year Onnachild built a wall around the castle to keep the villagers out.'

He nods and leans back into my touch. I increase the size of the circles: stroking up to where his shoulder blades stick out, across to the swell of his ribcage, down to his waist. His tunic gathers up against my palm, exposing the honey-coloured skin on his lower back to the sun. He tenses as my fingertips glide over his hips.

'Why did you bring me here?' I ask.

He shrugs. 'To make sure it's still as I thought?'

'The garden? But—'

'I don't know.' He stretches around to still my touch and peers over his shoulder at me. The sun picks out the mahogany tones of his hair. 'Did you ever have a garden?'

'I think my mother might have had one before she died.'

'How did she die?'

'Starvation.'

'I'm sorry.' He's shuffling around, reaching out to touch my face, sympathy lining his. I veer away from it, almost tip off the stone.

'I barely remember her.'

He doesn't accept my flippant dismissal, and I'm strangely grateful for that. His hand settles on my knee, encasing it in his palm and his fingers settle in the dip behind.

'We kept bees.' I don't know why I'm sharing this with him but I can't seem to stop. 'At least my grandmother did until the villagers came and ...' I gesture to the charred square, to the mounds of seared bricks and flints. 'I told the village children that the bees came back to life at night and because they were already dead, they could sting you and sting you until you dropped dead in a ball of pus.'

'Mean.' He chuckles, and the sound makes me smile.

'Serves them right, and it kept them away.'

'They teased you?'

'No, they didn't tease me. They used to try and kill me. Here.' I gather my hair back from my forehead. 'Can you see?'

He shuffles around, leans forwards, and with both hands on my knees, pushes himself up. I fumble for the dent in my forehead, point to it. Closer he comes, his hair tickling the exposed mound of my bosom. He smells of the mud and a hint of lavender.

'It's very faint,' he says.

'Thanks to Nessia. Come here, feel it.' I take his forefinger and guide it over and across. The touch sends tingles down my neck. He snatches back his hand.

'They did that?' He runs his finger over it again, slower this time. It looks like he's holding his breath.

'Yes, they chased me, and when I fell over they threw stones at me.'

'Poor Niah.' He kisses the dent, quickly, before turning away from me again.

He shunts forwards and then lies on his back with his arms behind his head as if I imagined the kiss. I can feel it though, along with the lingering warmth from his hands on my knees. They've left a stain on my white skirt. His chest and stomach rise and fall, the movement becoming slower and slower. The silence between us is filled with blackbirds chirping and magpies calling for their mate. The sun brightens and fades as it fights through the clouds, and the changing light plays across his features like moods. My bottom starts to go numb, and so I move from the stone, settle beside him. His head turns, and he smiles at me. I wish I could see his eyes but the sun is making him squint.

'She did speak to me.' He rolls onto his side, props himself up on an elbow. His other hand holds back his hair.

'What did she say?'

'She told me not to tell you.'

'She'll tell me if I ask her.'

He chuckles and releases his hair to catch my hand. He raises it to his lips and brushes a kiss over the knuckles. A piece of mud remains on his lips and his tongue darts out to lick it away. 'Will you tell me why you called her for me?'

'I felt sorry for you.'

'Me?'

'I did. I don't now,' I tease.

'Perhaps I should cry again?' He smiles, and his face is so unguarded, trusting, that I can't stop my finger tracing the outline of his scar as I wonder what else he'll share with me.

'How?'

'Onnachild,' is all he says. The catch in his voice warns me not to press further so I don't. He retreats, lying down again, and scowls at the sun, so I settle too into the languid heat, my shoulder against his and my head touching his, pretending I can find out his secrets that way.

Chapter Twenty-Four

'YOU LEFT ME THERE,' Raen says as we dance together in the Great Hall. I can't tell from his expression if he's teasing or genuinely hurt. 'I hadn't finished talking.'

'You were asleep.'

'I woke up.'

'I'd hope so.'

'Really?'

I huff in response and he chuckles, drawing the advisers' glares our way.

'I'd rather not have told you here, but since you've left me no other option ...' He pauses and spins me around as he scans the room. The advisers become a blur of grey. Onnachild's a mass of fur and fury, with his red face and battle words louder than the music. 'You must promise to keep control of your emotions.'

'I can control myself.'

As Vill and Beshanie dance by us, Vill and Raen nod at each other. Their mischievous grins make me nervous. 'Just say it.'

'Wait.' Raen leads me away from the advisers, dipping and sliding so quickly that I almost lose my footing. 'Remember I promised to repay your kindness?' he says once we're on the outskirts of the dancing couples and the advisers are lost amongst the coloured dresses and candlelight. 'And don't you dare mention the battle again.'

'I wasn't going to.'

'Good. Now answer this: what do you want more than anything in the world?'

Ammi. I stop. My skirt hits my ankles. 'Don't tease me.' My heart speeds, thumps. I almost believe. I want to.

'I thought you said you could control your emotions?' He gathers me up, twirls me round and round until I'm breathless. I focus on him, his smile, the joy in his face. My heart believes him. My vision mists up with unshed tears and he becomes hazy. He wouldn't be so cruel as to lie, would he?

'People will soon start leaving the Great Hall. See how tired they are, especially Onnachild.' Raen nods towards the top table where Onnachild's still bleating and banging away. He doesn't seem tired to me. 'He'll be the first to leave, and when he does, so will I. Wait one song and then follow. I'll meet you in the hallway.'

'Don't trick me, please, Raen.'

'I wouldn't. Aren't we friends?'

'Are we?'

'Yes, now shush or the advisers will realise something's up.'

'Really?' I can't contain my smile. 'Really? I'm going to see—'

'Do I need to try and kiss you so you look surly again?'

I hide my face. He chuckles and his chest bumps against my smile. The song is too jubilant, skipping and jumping, and the Maidens' voices soar into a chorus that takes my heart with it. How can I even try to hide my happiness? Raen squeezes me. 'He's leaving now.'

I nod and step away, keeping my head bowed so the advisers, who have slunk towards Onnachild's chair, can't see. Nilola grabs Raen into a dance before he can leave. He doesn't bother hiding his frustration. Gavin asks me to dance, and I'm too excited and distracted to refuse. I let him talk on and on, nodding and smiling when he pauses. I'm going to see Ammi. As long as Raen isn't lying. Could he be lying? He's scowling despite Nilola caressing his neck, and that Raen, the scowling one, would lie to me. The song ends and he slips from her grip without a word. Any moment now I'll find out whether he's telling the truth. It makes me nauseous.

I curtsy to Gavin, make my excuses, and head back to the table to wait out this song. My fingers tap out of time to the beat, which seems to have been purposefully slowed to torture me. The couples are merely swaying, looking like they're being rocked by a breeze rather than dancing. Beshanie's pushing her way through them, perhaps looking for Vill. He isn't there. The advisers move towards her, shooing her away from the dancers. I pour myself a drink for something to do, to fill the time, but I don't drink it because I want a clear head when I see my daughter. I need to be able to note each and every subtle change since we were last together. It was a whole season ago now. A whole season and four days. But before this day finishes, before the moon goes, I'll be with her. Will she still recognise me?

The song must end soon. My feet fidget under the table, kicking the legs.

'Are you all right?' Mantona sits beside me. 'Have you found it?' She looks worried.

'Found what?'

'Nothing, never mind.' Her face relaxes. 'Have you seen Vill? I need to speak with him.'

I shake my head.

'It's unlike him to retire early,' she says, scanning the room.

It doesn't matter. I don't care because the song has ended and another has started, seamlessly, pretending it's the same song, but I know and so I dart up. Mantona doesn't seem suspicious when I excuse myself. *Try to remain calm, try to glide and not stomp from the Great Hall*, I tell myself. Beshanie and Nilola are teasing Perkin by tugging on his beard. Only the advisers watch me as I push the door open. *Please*, I whisper up to the gods, *don't let him be lying.*

Raen's where he said he'd be, leaning against the wall. He's winding a piece of black material round and round his hands. I'm faint with anticipation. He closes the door behind me, and in his eyes is a hint of naughtiness—we're in this together, disobeying Onnachild. I can hardly breathe.

'You can't see where I'm taking you.' He lifts the black cloth. 'If you know where she is, what will stop you from running back there?'

'I can control myself,' I mumble even though I know he's right, and when he places the fabric against my eyes, I don't protest.

'Hold onto my arm and I'll guide you there.' His voice sounds richer, more textured, with the castle and the village jostling against the accent he picked up during exile. His forearm is as sturdy and wide as an oak beneath my hand. My fingers touch his wrist where his pulse is beating as fast as my heart.

I reach out to touch a wall instead. 'You'll guide me into walls.'

'Maybe I will if you don't show more gratitude.' Firmly, he grabs my hand and plonks it back onto his arm. 'This might be the only time I ever get to control you.'

One small step we take. Another. I scrape his heel with my foot. He makes no sound. Another step. Another. He speeds up, too quickly, so I pinch him. He slows again.

'Round the corner, we go now, three steps, left,' he says. 'Left, left, left.' His voice rises as I bump into a wall. 'This is your left.' He pats the hand on his arm.

'I know that.'

'Five steps straight forwards, I presume you can count.'

'Of course I can count.'

I crash into something and my skirt bounces. 'I'll be black and blue tomorrow.'

'Stop moaning. You're going to see your daughter.'

My heart jumps. *Please don't let him be lying. Please,* I keep repeating as we continue walking. Our steps fall into the same rhythm, tapping against the stone floor, padding against the rugs. The castle is noisy with the stones contracting in the early spring air and the wood easing off its burden for the night. We're getting nearer, I can tell; the perfume of the village, of my home is getting stronger. I squeeze Raen's arm tighter and tighter. Why would he help me? Why would he lie? His steps slow but I can't move fast enough and so we fall out of time. Twice, our hips bang. Then suddenly he stops, pats my hand.

'We're here.' His voice has a rumble of excitement and it adds to my own.

I hear a door open, feel the warmth from the room, smell lavender. He leads me over the threshold.

Once inside, our fingers fight to undo the knot of the blindfold. There's her cot made of laburnum. It's too good to be true and so I turn to Raen, seeking confirmation. He encourages me with a nod. Tears are already falling when I rush to her. I lean over her cot and cover my mouth with my hand to stop my sob from waking her. I don't know where to look first. My daughter. My precious daughter. Aelius's. Her rosebud mouth is pursed. Her closed eyelids are the faintest pink and rimmed with golden lashes. Are her irises still blue like his or green like mine? Her arms and podgy fists are resting on a white fur. They clench and unclench. Her hair is the same colour as her father's and settles in fat curls as his did. Her nose has the same rounded tip as his. Is this what he looked like as a baby?

Raen's elbow knocks mine.

'Isn't she beautiful?' I whisper. 'Just like her father.' I rise onto my tiptoes, strain forwards to reach a lock of her hair, to see if it feels as luxurious as Aelius's.

'Don't wake her.'

Her lips move, mimicking nursing. Carefully, I move a curl from her forehead. Her skin is as smooth as a flower petal. She stirs. An arm flails. I'm unable to resist running my finger over the dimples in her fist. Her hand opens and she grabs me. Her grip is tight. She's well fed. She's no sickly village baby; she has a future, and I have given her that. Nothing will hurt her as long as I obey Onnachild.

I can't risk being sent away from her; I must see her become a child, a woman, see how those chubby cheeks thin out, see whether her curls drop as her hair lengthens. Will she be tall and lean like Aelius or curvy like me? My little piece of him gifted to me by the gods. Perhaps she'll be as self-assured as he was. If I have to give myself up, give my gods up to abide by Onnachild's rules, and charm every person in this castle, I will. For her, for my precious little Ammi.

Raen's arm nudges me. 'The nursemaid will be back soon.'

I nod but don't move. I whisper to her in Aegnian, not caring that Raen can hear. 'We'll be together again, I promise, soon, and when we are, I'll tell you the most wonderful stories about your father and where you came from. I love you.'

'We have to go.' He gently pulls me.

He's right. Though it pains me to do so, I ease my finger from her grasp and lower onto my toes.

'Sorry,' he says as he puts the blindfold back over my eyes. At least it will soak up my tears and he won't see them. I'm not sure if they're happy or sad tears. I'm not sure if we're friends or just even.

Chapter Twenty-Five

FOR AMMI, I FORCE MYSELF to the Sunning Room. The women's chatter fades as I enter, but without Vill, I don't hold their interest for long. At least the room isn't as humid as it was on my first visit. The rain, pattering on the glass roof, is helping to keep it cool. It takes all my concentration to not show my true feelings as I make my way to where Nilola and Beshanie sit. What seemed a good idea last night no longer does when they lift their faces towards me, disdain rumpling their noses and curling their lips.

'To what do we owe this visit?' Nilola's voice is too sweet to be genuine.

'Don't you prefer burning your skin?' Beshanie says with open hostility, and I think I prefer it to Nilola's falseness.

'I've been keeping myself to myself. And that may have been a mistake.' I sit and spread out my skirt to show I've no intention of leaving. 'You may have the wrong idea about me.'

'We have exactly the right idea about you,' Beshanie says, 'whatever you might have charmed Vill into saying.' She shifts her purple skirt away, making me think she intends to get up and leave.

'Gossip is just gossip,' I say. 'Although, it does make me sound much more exciting than I really am.' I force myself to laugh.

Beshanie crosses her arms and her fingers tap her forearms. 'Raen, Vill, the True Prince. Don't deny anything. We know. The servants whisper and they whisper pretty loudly if you give them enough coins.'

I should back down from her challenging stare, dip my head in deference, and even try to blush, but I can't bear to appear so weak. 'And lie prettily if they think it will get them even more.'

'They don't lie.'

'Then you don't know servants as well as you think you do,' I say. 'When do they have time to amass such interesting gossip? Why go to such trouble when they can just lie and still be rewarded?'

'Especially your servants,' Nilola says to Beshanie. 'Why only last week they told you that Cathonia had bedded Martus when everyone knows Martus has a problem ...' She wiggles her little finger in the air.

'They're not wrong about her.' Beshanie jabs a plump thumb in my direction. 'Look at her skin, look at how dark it is. If that doesn't show village—'

'It's true, I have some village ancestry.'

Beshanie nods at Nilola as if to say, *see I told you so.* Nilola dramatically shifts her skirt from mine. Another woman glances at me and then shuffles further away. I must keep calm. What did I decide last night? What words did I pick to make my lie seem a truth? I wish I could rub my temples to ease out the tension that's stopping me from thinking, but Beshanie's scrutinising me like a warrior waiting for his opponent to leave his ribs unprotected. I squeeze my finger tight like Ammi did last night, and it helps me focus. 'My mother was born there, but she was sent away, after the ... the False Queen,' I whisper the name as Melody does.

Beshanie's eyes narrow. Nilola's lips twitch into a smile. Both edge closer.

'My grandfather, he was terrified of her becoming a fallen woman, you know, because of her village blood.' It's amazing how exhilarating, how easy it is to lie. 'Vill made me promise not to tell anyone about my heritage. I didn't think it would matter in these times; after all, isn't Prince Raen half village blood?' Why did I mention his name? An image of his honey-coloured skin comes to mind. I can't think of that now. My cheeks are flushing. 'But Vill made me promise, so I did. Please don't tell anyone. Don't tell Vill, he'd be so angry. I can trust you though, can't I? Vill did vouch for you.'

'Vill is very rarely wrong.' Nilola's smile has changed, taken on an air of compassion; she believes me or at least wants me to think she does. Beshanie licks her teeth as if my tale has left a bad taste on them.

The line I had rehearsed last night comes back, and I say it with the same quiver I had practised. 'I must confess I was a little intimidated by you both.'

187

'You should be,' Beshanie says.

Nilola fusses with a loose curl of her dark hair. 'You were scared of us?'

'How could I not be? Vill spoke so highly of you and wanted us to be great friends and—'

'Vill spoke highly of us?' Beshanie asks.

'Always,' I say, 'especially you, Beshanie. Please understand how difficult it's been for me when he's held you both in such high esteem. He's always praising your beauty and your wit. How can I be of any interest to you?'

They swivel away from me towards each other, creating a barrier with their skirts and their shoulders. Nilola's are pointy like a snow-capped mountain in her silver and white gown, and Beshanie's are a not-quite-ripe plum. Have I gone too far or not far enough? They hold their hands up and whisper behind them. It's just whispering yet I feel myself bristle at their rudeness. I'm too tired for this. Like a petulant child, I want to tell them I don't care for their friendship and flounce from the room. For Ammi, I'll stay here, charm, flatter, lie until they accept me.

A woman with a large chin and dead eyes stares me up and down. I glare at her. She goes back to pretending she's interested in a conversation about edging on dresses. I fight back a sigh. I could be in my rooms reading, laughing with Melody, talking to Nessia about things that matter. About the battle. No, I decided not to talk about that, not to think about that. I stare up at the rain sliding off the roof and can't help wishing I was out there, being cleansed, being chilled by it. I squeeze my finger.

'We accept your apology,' Beshanie says.

I fake a smile despite her condescending tone.

'A friend of Raen's and Vill's is a friend of ours.' Nilola's petite features are pretty when she smiles and bats her lashes at me. Beshanie still has the appearance of a man ready to fight, her handsome features taut.

'We should drink to seal our new friendship,' she says, gesturing for a servant.

'So tell me,' Nilola asks. 'Does Raen speak of me?'

'I don't know Raen that well.' My eyes are drawn to outside, to where the fountain is nothing more than a tiny blur in the rain, and I'm reminded of what he has shared with me: his tears which were smaller than the raindrops, and his mother's destroyed garden. I force my attention back to Nilola who's sitting forwards in her seat. 'He wouldn't talk to me about things like that. But I've noticed how he looks at you.'

She wiggles with pleasure and tugs at her hair again.

'He's going to get married,' Beshanie says.

'Nothing has been agreed yet,' Nilola snaps.

'He wouldn't marry you, anyway.'

Nilola shrugs.

'And you?' Beshanie asks me. That assessing stare is back. Did she notice my body tense when she mentioned marriage?

'Me?' I press a hand to my chest to remind myself to stay calm. It doesn't matter that with Raen's princess comes men, money. Comes death. Let them have their folly and let me have my daughter.

'There must be a man that catches your eye,' Beshanie says.

The servant arrives with a tray containing small clay cups and a large lidded jug. She pours pale liquid dotted with herbs into the cups and then passes them to us. Steam wafts out the scent of chamomile. Nilola blows across her drink. 'Now we're friends you must tell us.'

I blurt out the first name I can think of, 'Gavin.'

'A little high for you,' Beshanie says.

'There's nothing wrong with aiming high,' Nilola says.

'There's aiming high and then there's staring at the moon. Do you know it's his sister Raen might marry?'

'I did not,' I lie.

'Perhaps Raen will put in a good word with him for you.'

'I doubt it. Raen dislikes me.' I'm not sure whether this is a lie or not—another thing that kept me awake last night. I sip my drink. It burns my tongue.

'You dance with him,' Nilola says.

'Vill makes him.' The cup is warming my hands, warming them like Raen's skin did when I comforted him. I put my cup on the floor. 'Gavin, well, he's nothing more than a dream, but is it wrong to dream?'

'And such dreams Nilola has.' Beshanie smirks. 'What was it you told me? About Raen stood there, naked, in all his glory and what is it he says to you? What was it you told me?'

I force myself to focus on Nilola and her red cheeks to banish the image Beshanie has created. The cup in Nilola's lap wobbles, hinting that she's considering whether to throw it at Beshanie.

'They're just dreams,' I say to defend Nilola.

She frowns at me. 'What do you care? Do you have a fancy for Raen?'

'No. No, of course not, he's too ... he doesn't please me.' That's one thing I'm certain of.

'Not like Gavin,' Beshanie says.

I smile, timidly, already regretting using his name because there's something working behind Beshanie's eyes, a slyness creeping in. We stare at each other, and I'm sure she doesn't believe anything I've said.

The advisers look shocked when Nilola yells out my name as I enter the Great Hall. She gestures for me to join her and Beshanie at their side of the table. It's worth the embarrassment of so many castle eyes drawn to me if it peeves the advisers. I smile at them as I pass and they nod back, though it seems to pain them. I check their fingers for ink and try to remember which is which.

Nilola and Beshanie stand when I arrive at the empty seat between them and I get the impression it's to show off their golden dresses covered with intricate patterns and gems. Beshanie's hair is natural tonight, giving her the appearance of a flame. Nilola has her fake blonde hair clipped up with gems the same blue as her eyes. She has a cutesy smile for me. 'We can't have you sit with the King's old mistress, not now we're friends. People talk.'

'I hear Vill picks your wardrobe,' Beshanie says as we sit.

'I know nothing about your fashions.'

'He normally has excellent taste.' Beshanie stares down her nose at the plain and inferior fabric of my bodice. Did Vill know they were going to invite me over when he selected my dress?

'What do they wear in your country?' Nilola asks.

'Simple dresses, not these cages,' I say without thinking.

'"Cages", how quaint,' Nilola says.

'I guess if you'd been in one since you were a girl you'd appreciate it,' Beshanie says.

'My mother told me the queen-we-don't-mention didn't like to wear "a cage",' Nilola says. 'They had to force her into one and whenever she was alone, she'd take it off and let her bosoms hang freely. I heard they were like cows' udders by the time they ... you know. But I shouldn't pass on such gossip, Raen wouldn't like it.' She smiles again, sweetly, too sweetly. I copy it. 'We've been thinking about what you said, and we thought it very admirable of you to apologise to us, and we toyed with whether we should apologise too.' She looks over at Beshanie who's playing with her earring as she eyes up Vill at the top table. 'Then we thought it's best to forget it and never mention it again. So let's just pretend it never happened.'

'That's very kind of you.'

Nilola nods. Beshanie pours wine and thrusts the goblet at me. 'It's much nicer than the rubbish the merchants drink or indeed the villagers. I'm told theirs tastes of piss.'

I take a small sip. 'It certainly is better than anything from my uncle's cellar.'

'We always have the best. Our fathers wouldn't have it any other way,' Nilola says, helping herself to more.

Onnachild enters and everyone stands. He glances at the empty chair beside his own. Previously when he's done so it's been with longing, tonight he's squaring his shoulders and thrusting out his chest. When he sits, he motions for Vill to draw closer. Raen angles his chair towards his father and Onnachild doesn't shoo him away.

'Isn't Raen handsome in black,' Nilola says. 'And concentrating like that ...' She lets out a long sigh that's almost a whistle. 'I bet that's how he'd look when—'

'Nilola!' Beshanie snaps.

Nilola shrugs. Beshanie snatches a chunk of bread from a servant, complains at the shape of it and then throws it back at him. He tries to catch it, misses, and so it falls to the floor as she sniggers at his fumbling. He stares at me briefly, long enough for me to catch a glimmer of recognition, and I recognise him, too. There's no mistaking the bulbous tip of his nose and the narrowness of his eyes: he's the son of that hag who threatened Ammi. But he's dead. He scurries away, red-faced and awkward. How many other servants are from the village? It should please me to have them serving me but it doesn't, and I don't know why.

'Raen's looking this way,' Nilola gasps. 'Don't look.'

He is indeed staring at us, his head cocked to one side as though he's asking me a question. I ignore that and focus on the servants darting about with trays of meat, searching for other village faces and lost children. A few raise their heads, sneaking glances at me—perhaps the hag's boy has told them who I am. I don't want the bread anymore. In fact, I don't want anything.

'Has he done something different with his hair?' Nilola asks, slapping

192

me with a piece of pork that leaves a greasy mark on my arm. 'Does it seem different to you?'

I feign interest to appease her; it looks the same to me. The boy appears behind Raen. I move forwards in my seat to get a better view.

'Stop looking,' Nilola says. 'He'll know we're talking about him.'

A tray of sausages is placed on the table before me. The servant darts off before I can see their face.

'What do you think they're talking about?' Nilola asks me.

'Battles.'

Beshanie turns at the sound of my voice, a sour expression marring her handsome features.

'It's all they talk about,' I say. 'It's so boring.'

She doesn't seem convinced by my words but at least she goes back to attacking the meat on her plate.

'I'd love to see Raen in battle,' Nilola says. 'Swinging a blade, masterful. Arms and legs straining.'

She wouldn't say that if she'd seen what I've seen, and I picture him like that: unmanned and skin blue-tinged. Her stare is so lusty and possessive that Raen must surely feel it, yet he's staying focused on Onnachild who's gesticulating wildly. I search for the servant, to double-check he is the hag's boy. If I'm right he's not a boy any longer; he's a few years older than me. Yet that servant was as short and skinny as a child. Am I seeing spirits?

'Do you think they'll dance later?' Nilola asks.

I turn my attention back to her. 'I hope so,' I lie.

She seems placated and starts picking and poking at the food on her plate with the same expression as an old man facing a mountain. She takes the smallest of mouthfuls and chews slowly like a cow. Between each mouthful, she takes a sip of wine. Her eyes keep flitting to Raen, and I find myself copying her. Luckily, he's preoccupied with watching the servants. His fixed smile is at odds with his lowered brow. I wonder if he's thinking back to the village, to his lies: *we have gone hungry*. I push away my plate.

'Not eating?' Beshanie asks. There's a red wine tinge to her lips.

I shake my head. That village boy is staring at me from behind Raen and I can sense his disapproval. I pull at the bodice of my dress, worth more than everything I owned in the village. It doesn't seem right that I'm in it. My eyes meet Raen's and he sits up, swivels around in his seat and faces the village boy.

'Not everyone can eat like you and still retain their figure.' Nilola's castle accent reminds me I'm not Niah from the village, not anymore, despite what that servant's eyes accuse me of.

Beshanie snatches the bread off my plate. 'It all goes to my bosom.'

'Have more wine.' Nilola reaches over to fill my goblet and then her own. She takes a noisy gulp. 'He keeps looking at me.' She swells out her chest.

Beshanie lifts her head and stares his way.

'Don't look,' Nilola says.

'He is indeed,' I say. *Forget that village boy*, I tell myself, *play the part you need to*. His fate is not my concern. He might not even be the hag's boy and what does it matter if he is. 'You are especially lovely in that dress.'

'Yes, I mean, thank you. By God, I can hardly eat out of excitement. Do you think he will try and kiss me tonight, Niah?'

'It's hard to ever judge anything Raen will do.' My skin is flushing from the wine. I should eat something, and so I tear at a piece of bread. Its whiteness is highlighted against my fingers. We never had bread like this in the village. I put it back onto the tray.

'Maybe Gavin will ask to dance with you tonight,' Nilola says.

Beshanie laughs. 'Maybe he will.'

'Please, don't tease me.' I try to sound girlish and gleeful but it just sounds flat.

'He isn't a Vill though, is he,' Beshanie says, playing with her earring. I watch it bob back and forth, and can't stop trying to guess its value: a hut, a year's food, a pig?

Raen's attention is back our way again, I sense it before Nilola squeals and makes me jump. Her voice is rising in pitch, the words coming quicker and quicker making it harder to follow what she's saying, something to do with Raen. Beshanie responds curtly. I keep smiling and nodding, pretending I am deferring to their better opinion. Their jewels catch glimpses of the candlelight and glint like crude copies of stars. My gems do the same, the amber stone on my ring resembling a fire trying to escape its confines. The band is too small, digging into my finger. It refuses to budge when I try to remove it.

Trays are taken away, the food on them mashed up and resembling the mud pies Nessia and I used to make when I was a child. There's so much waste. I remember my mother, not her face, not her touch, but the absence of her, of waking up the morning after she'd died to find her scent lingering, but not her body, and my grandmother had a pinched expression.

'Raen's finished eating.' Nilola elbows me. 'He must be dancing soon. He must. Niah, if he dances with you, since we are friends now, you must tell him how nice I'm being to you.'

I nod and force my features into an expression of simple boredom. Raen's watching the servants carrying the trays and a scowl has darkened his features. I want to go to him, ask whether he sees how unfair this is. He's been to the village so he must care, and if he does, then I won't need to. Why does it even matter to me? My fingers search for the scar on my forehead. Let Raen save them, and I can stay with Ammi. When I picture her, though, she's in a mammoth ball of silk and lace, her father's eyes lost in gluttonous cheeks.

My stomach groans, but it's a mockery of real hunger: shallow and noisy. Onnachild pushes out his chair. His belly is as round and solid as a hill, and he laughs carefree, like a man who hasn't killed hundreds and hundreds of people, and isn't planning on sending more to their deaths. Must I really sit here and do nothing?

'Raen's getting up,' Nilola squeals in my ear. 'He's coming down here.' She pulls a lock of fake hair over her face and flashes her teeth at Beshanie for inspection.

I excuse myself from the table on the pretence of needing some air. They don't hear me anyway; Nilola's too busy getting ready for Raen, and Beshanie has given her attention to a servant carrying a tray of wobbling puddings. *Be careful,* Nessia had warned me last night when I explained my plan and I didn't understand, fully, what I should be careful of. I do now. Be careful not to get lost in the facade.

A few men are making their way out into the garden, talking animatedly about the battle. Stuck amongst their mass, I've no choice but to listen to them spout tactics which I know won't work. Soon, they say. Victory, another says. One holds the door open for me though he doesn't pause in his conversation to acknowledge my thanks. I slip through and try to find a space to be alone, only everywhere has been claimed by the men. Some are pretending to fight, with one brandishing his cutting knife like it's a sword and almost falling with the motion. Men squeeze up to each other even though they're yelling. I'm tempted to move further out, out to where the lights from the Great Hall don't reach, but I'm aware of the advisers standing by the doors and surveying the group.

The moon is out tonight. When I stare up at it I feel so small, so insignificant. *Please don't be angry with me*, I pray to the gods, *I have to choose Ammi.* Their disappointment feels as heavy as a stormy sky. I receive no response from them; perhaps they no longer recognise me.

Again, I search for my scar. This time I fail. How can I not find it? It's unnerving, as if even my bones are being remade in this place. Smoke from men's pipes wafts my way. There's no comfort in that scent tonight, and it doesn't appease the men either as they start arguing—perhaps that man with the knife got his wish and managed to hurt someone. They have no idea what battles are like; they pay others to fight, to die for them. I know, I saw, and there's a reason for that; there's always a reason for anything the gods do.

'I was hoping to find you.' Gavin makes me jump. 'I didn't mean to shock you.' He sounds so genuinely concerned that I put on my fake smile and curtsy low to him. How easy it is for me to fall back into this person Onnachild wants me to be.

'A pleasant surprise.' My voice sounds like Nilola's.

'I've been wanting to ask you to dance,' he says to the ground beneath my feet.

'You have?'

He nods. Through his thin, white hair I can see his scalp blushing. His hands dangle at his sides, fingers twitching. He was not this nervous yesterday.

'It would be my pleasure,' I say.

He lifts his right arm. It's shaking and doesn't stop when I place my hand on it. *This is a game*, I remind myself, *play it.* Yet it doesn't feel fun. As I stare into the Great Hall, at the women and men whirling around together, I've never wanted my grandmother more. She'd know what to do, who I should be. As we walk to join the dancers, I feel myself getting lost amongst them, their flowery scent, their pastel dresses, the light flickering over their pale skin and blond wigs. The only way to feel like myself is to find Vill and Raen, people who know my heritage, my ancestors.

Vill's dancing with a small girl in a sky-blue dress with a white bow at the waist. Raen's partnered with Nilola, her head resting on his chest. He smiles at me. I don't smile back. Gavin bows. His touch on my waist is so light it could be a flower petting me as I walk by.

'I hope I dance well,' he says. 'Better than I did yesterday.'

Was it only yesterday I was dancing with him and he was chatting away? I should have paid more attention, asked more questions about his sister, figured out a way to stop her coming and bringing her men, her money.

'You will dance well enough,' I say. 'Should you make any mistakes, well, I won't notice because these steps are new to me too.'

'Thank you. You're kind. I knew you were kind when I first met you.' His blush is piglet pink, and it makes his eyebrows whiter. 'Raen should not have said those things. I should not have let him.'

I hold my hand up to show he doesn't need to revisit that night, but as we twirl, I'm searching for Raen, wanting him to tell me again all those things about myself that I must not forget. Instead, my eyes meet the eyes of an adviser.

'I shouldn't have mentioned it,' Gavin says. 'I know I said I wouldn't last night but ... I've made you sad. Sorry.'

'I'm not sad,' I say, though my voice does sound sad.

'It's just, well, it still bothers me. I don't know what to tell my sister about Raen. She asks me and I say nothing. I fear she'll want to marry him no matter what I say.'

'She's in love with him?'

'She's in love with this land. She will not be impressed when she sees it, though. It isn't what we were told.'

If I can stop her coming ... and so I give Gavin a smile that I hope is dazzling. It does make him blush again. 'Oh?'

'This is going horribly. I didn't want to ... I've offended you.' He tilts his head towards the ceiling, lips moving silently. His hand on my waist is shaking again. 'What is wrong with me tonight?'

'It's not what I imagined either.' It's a relief to speak the truth.

'No?'

I shake my head. As we turn, I notice Beshanie watching us from her place at the table. There's cruel pleasure on her face and now I understand why Gavin's so nervous tonight: she's told him I'm interested in him. I should be angry, but her trick has given me the chance I need to get more information. 'What were you and your sister expecting?'

'My sister is a great admirer of the True Queen, how she came here, spread the religion to save the people. Yet ...' He peers around at the dancing couples, at the matrons shoving food into their puckered mouths. 'They are not ... This is not what I wanted to talk to you about.' His step falters. It makes him grimace.

'Please, don't worry,' I say. 'It's very comforting to hear my views expressed so clearly and passionately.'

'It is?'

'And if your sister is as wise as you are then she'll see the truth for herself.'

'But she will see it as her purpose to restore decorum,' he says, solemnly. Then brighter he says, 'You think I'm wise?'

I duck my head to imply the boldness of my compliment has embarrassed me. His hands settle a little heavier on me and his steps are less hesitant too. All this lying is coming so easily to me I'm almost proud of myself, though it's such a strange thing to value.

When the music stops and we part, Gavin is unable to make eye contact, staring over my shoulder instead as he stands there, the tip of his shoe making circles across the floor. A new song starts.

'Would you like to sit with me?' I ask since he's made no move to either dance or walk away.

He nods and follows me back to the table. He pulls out a chair for me, waits for me to settle my skirt, and then sits beside me.

'Wine?' he asks.

I nod. 'Thank you.'

He spills some on the table as he fills my goblet. It's almost endearing. 'You're so different from my sister.' He grins, and finally his gaze meets mine, perhaps emboldened now he doesn't have to concentrate on the dance steps. There's something so innocent in his eyes, so trusting, that I'm reminded of Aelius's and for a moment my heart hurts. Gavin's are a paler blue though, and his lashes are bright white. 'I wonder whether she'll take to the castle as you have.'

My attention drifts to the top table, to my love's empty chair and the place still set for him. Onnachild has his elbow in the plate as his index finger prods the table. I stare at the tapestry, at the stars tipping down, to remind myself of the colour of Aelius's hair. 'I'm not so sure I've taken to the castle.'

Gavin places his limp hand on mine. It's slightly clammy. 'You're too modest. Beshanie and Nilola were singing your praises to me.' He's awkward again, snatching back his hand and hiding it up his long sleeve.

'What did they say?'

He glances at me, briefly, as though I have scolded him. 'I don't know how to say it ... this is not how ... I don't know your customs. How things should be.' He gulps. He takes a breath. His face is crimson. 'They said you've set your heart on me.'

'Oh.'

'I don't know what to say to woo you.' He peeps up at me through his lashes.

I smile, too stunned to do anything else. Why didn't I say Perkin had taken my fancy? Anyone. Someone who would laugh it off. Gavin's far too young, too inexperienced to have such a joke played on him. I have caused this. Nilola and Beshanie are standing in a corner, resplendent in their gold dresses, watching, laughing, and I can't tell whether it is me they intended to humiliate or Gavin. Raen breaks my view of them, dancing by with his partner who is talking away and waving her hands near his face. He's peering at me over the top of her head.

Gavin prods my little finger with his. Is he trying to encourage me to speak? His pale eyes are so earnest and a faint frown makes him look timid. If only I were someone different, I want to tell him. I open my mouth to speak. Close it again when his frown deepens. If I were myself then he wouldn't even be entertaining this, and that realisation makes me want to say something cruel, hurt him for being fooled by pretence, but he's as much a tool in this castle as I am and his eyes are too similar to Aelius's for me to hurt him.

'They shouldn't have told you,' I say, softly. 'We can't be anything but friends. My guardian, if he found out, he'd call me back.'

'Maybe I can change your guardian's mind?'

I shake my head and force my lips into a half-smile that is meant to imply sadness, regret.

'I can try though, can't I?'

'No.' The word sounds harsher than I intended. 'Please, it'd make him angry.'

'Then I shall not mention it again. We'll just be good friends, and I will wait for your guardian to die.'

I laugh; I can't help myself. Oh, how different everything would be if Onnachild was dead. Gavin blushes and splutters.

'That was ... that ...' He crosses himself.

'You should go dance with an eligible woman.'

'I don't want to.' He sounds sulky, exactly as Aelius would when he'd tell me not to call him beautiful. Gavin leaves me, though, and I make sure to send him on his way with an expression containing enough longing to ease his pride but steely enough to stop his pursuit.

Nilola rushes straight to him, smiling, playing with her hair and dragging him into a dance so she can get the gossip. Raen excuses himself from his partner even though she's mid-conversation. She looks startled and slightly offended, sloping off towards the merchants' end of the table. Raen is striding towards me, picking up a goblet on his way. I can't cope with him right now, not after Gavin. Everything is too confusing, and I'm done with playing a part. I want to hide under the table, rest my forehead on the stone floor.

It's not him that sits next to me, though, but Vill. He drops down with a heavy sigh. His hair is dull and there are faint blue bulges under his eyes. This is the most imperfect I've seen him, and I don't know whether I like it or not. 'You look tired,' I say.

He picks up a goblet and checks his reflection in it, grimacing at what he sees. 'That I am. Dancing, eating, entertaining, and then summoned to the Judging Room at ridiculous hours by the King.' He runs his hand over his face as if trying to ease his skin back to perfection. 'All seems well with you. I must say Gavin was a nice touch.'

'A nice touch?'

'Yes, that's what I said.'

'That was Beshanie and Nilola ... gossiping, meddling.'

'Marvellous. I knew they could be relied upon to cause mayhem. Still, the cause is irrelevant.' He smooths back his hair. 'What does matter is whether Raen is jealous or not.'

'I don't want him to be jealous.'

'You should.'

'I know what you think. I'm not doing it.'

'Don't pretend to be so ... I'm too exhausted for it. I know about the graveyard.'

My heart lurches and my face flushes. 'What? How?'

'Raen told me. Who else would? Did he say he'd keep it secret? Oh,

202

Niah, surely you aren't as naïve as all that, are you?'

I search for Raen. He's back at the top table, matching Onnachild drink for drink as they dash them back, and then slam their goblets on the table. A servant flits between them, unseen, unacknowledged. Onnachild's animated as he talks to Raen, almost jumping out of his seat as he bangs the arms of his chair. Raen's pushing things across the table, a jug, a knife, a small silver bowl. He seems to be egging his father on with incessant nods. Louder and louder, Onnachild's voice booms, and Raen's chuckling gives it more depth. Their noise fills the hall and makes a few dancers stumble.

'We're friends though,' I say. 'He took me to see Ammi.'

'He's tricking you. Tricking you into complacency. He wants you to think he's your friend. He isn't. Raen's found out about this bet, and he's bet against you. He doesn't think you can pass as a castle lady. Think about it—why else did he ask you to bed him? Take you to see Ammi? If not to prove you can't obey Onnachild. Who knows what would've happened if I hadn't kept the nursemaid distracted. And how do you think I did so?' He pulls his chair closer, rests his elbow on mine. 'He isn't going to be kind to you or Ammi if he becomes King, despite what he says. Why would he? Look at him.'

Onnachild is swaying and staggering into Raen, who's helping to steady his father even though he must be as drunk. They're laughing, joking, and knocking over things on the table. They're the same: decadent and full of arrogance.

'Onnachild's bet,' I say. 'When and how does it get decided?'

Vill wafts away my question. 'Onnachild and Cantor are too busy with this battle to settle such details. What we need to be focusing on is Raen. If he's already told me about the graveyard what will stop him from spouting off to Onnachild or Cantor when the moment serves him and then ... dear, naïve little Niah, where will you be? Make it so he'd prefer to keep your secrets than win a bet. I can manipulate Raen to visit your rooms tonight. But the rest is up to you. You know the saying: you can lead the horse to water but ...'

I picture Raen, pathetic, prostrate, bound and begging at my feet as I sit on the throne, as I command my advisers to punish him for deceiving me, for telling Vill. It doesn't calm my anger, but it does make me nod. Although the water Raen's going to be drinking tonight won't be sweet and seductive like Vill wants—no, it'll be scolding and sour.

Chapter Twenty-Six

'This isn't right. People shouldn't be visiting this late at night,' Melody says as she opens my door. 'Go away.'

'Is that any way to talk to your better?' Raen's voice is thick and slurred.

'No, Your Highness. Please, Your Highness.'

I peer around the side of my chair at him slouching in the doorway. He's dishevelled like he's just woken up, and there's a wine stain on his rumpled tunic. 'I'm Your Highness now?' he says. 'Have I missed a proclamation?'

'No, well, I don't think so. I don't know what you are now. I don't know.' She curtsies to him, tilting her head so low that her headdress falls off and clangs to the floor.

'About time.' I don't even attempt to hide my irritation from my voice. 'Leave us.'

'This isn't the right protocol; a woman shouldn't be in her rooms with a man at night.' Melody appeals to Nessia who is hunched up by the fire with one of Onnachild's books. 'What would Vill say?'

I know exactly what Vill would say, but I keep that to myself. Nessia groans as she gets up. Then she links her arm through Melody's and drags her from the room. The door closing makes Raen's shoulders twitch. He smiles at me, a sloppy one that only lifts the left side of his lips.

'You're lucky I'm still awake,' I say.

'Am I late? Vill didn't mention a time limit. That explains—' His eyes move to my nightdress, pulled over my crossed legs, and then to my hair loose around my shoulders. 'You look so young,' he says, 'and enticing like that.'

'You look tired and drunk.'

'This castle doesn't agree with me.' Something grabs his attention and, like a dog on guard, he tilts his head.

'You told Vill,' I say. 'Why?'

'What did I tell Vill?' His gaze sweeps around the room, making him sway.

'You know very well. Don't make me say it.'

'Ah? Is this that thing we aren't meant to mention?'

'Well?'

'No.'

'Liar.'

'If I did, then I don't remember.'

'Liar.'

He shakes his head, but the gesture looks more like he has something in his ear than a response to my accusation. His forehead remains crumpled and his eyebrows are still low. 'What would it matter if I did? Vill's your man, isn't he? He's the one who sent me to your rooms. Although you're not turning out to be ... this isn't the welcome I was expecting.' He seems distracted because he staggers over to the panelled wall. His palms thump onto the wood, and he presses his ear to it as though listening for something. His eyes close, and his fingers flit over the engraved feathers and flames. 'Nothing here has changed.' He inhales deeply. Is he searching for his mother's scent?

Despite the pained look on his face, I can't let him get away with what he's done. He doesn't deserve my pity, my friendship, and I was a fool to give it to him. 'I'll never trust you again.'

'You never trusted me before,' he says. 'I didn't come for that anyway.'

'Then why did you come here?'

'I wanted to see my mother's rooms.' His hand trails behind him, sliding over the wall, as he heads towards my bedchamber.

'Raen,' I warn him but he carries on, his walk a drunken lumber like his father's, and I'm reminded of Onnachild's threat. 'You shouldn't be here.'

'No? These are my mother's rooms. This is precisely where I should be. It's you who shouldn't be here.' He ducks into my bedchamber.

I rush in after him.

'I wondered where that went.' He's glowering at Aelius's portrait. Then he's drawn to the locked door near the bed, staggering to it. He crouches so he's eye level with the hole. 'That's where I hid.' Frantically, he tries to open the door, yanking, slapping, shouting.

'Raen!'

He stops. His forehead smacks onto the wood. His ribcage swells and contracts rapidly like he's trying to catch his breath. I tiptoe over to him, my steps a light patter.

'I can't stop thinking of her.' His voice catches. 'I can't sleep for thinking of her. When I close my eyes, I see her ... hanging.' He jolts when my hand rests on the small of his back before he sighs and slumps against the door.

'You should go,' I say.

'Why? So I can lie in bed, ruminating. So I can ... Tell me ...' He turns his face towards me, the darkness of the room adding depth to the strain across his forehead, to his scar. 'Do you sleep peacefully?'

'Yes.'

'Now who's the liar?' His eyes narrow. 'You can't sleep either.'

'How I sleep is none of your concern. You need to leave.'

'So you can go back to your dreams of my half-brother?'

'Don't,' I say, though there's a part of me that wants him to rile me up again so I can shout at him, make him leave, stop stroking him.

His eyes challenge me. He pushes away from the door, almost knocking into me. There's such control to his movements as he bends to face me that I question whether he's really drunk and suspect his behaviour might be nothing more than a ploy to get my sympathy.

'Why can't you sleep?' he asks. 'Because you betrayed him? You'll betray him a thousand times more before you die.' His words tickle my lips, send a shiver down my spine. My body's drawn to the heat of him, my thin nightdress no protection. Where has my anger gone when I need it? He told Vill, I remind myself, but it doesn't help. Instead, it reminds me of what he told Vill, of his shoulder against my lips. Would it taste different now it's wine warmed? My hand comes up to push him away only it doesn't, not even when he steps closer. It slides over his shoulder, covering the silver leaves on his tunic. My fingers dig in. Our toes touch: mine bare and his in cool leather. If I were to purse my lips, ours would touch.

'Help me sleep,' he mumbles. 'Please, Niah, I'm so tired. I thought the wine would help, it hasn't. Sit beside me, talk to me in her language.'

'I ...' I shake my head.

'Why not? Can you not control yourself around me, is that it? I can control myself around you. Don't be scared of me.'

'I'm not scared of you,' I say, though my heart is beating as if I am.

'Good.' He walks around me.

I cross my arms over my chest, pin my hands under my arms, safe. My body is cold, yearning for his warmth again. The fire will do just as well.

'If you find it so difficult, then ...'

I turn around. He's sat on the bed, rolling a fur into a fat sausage. He places it down the middle of the bed, his gaze going, briefly, to Aelius's portrait. 'Tell me how to make bread, curse at me, anything in that language.' He shuffles up the bed, rests his head on his arms, waiting. His face is directly under the gaze of my love; Aelius's is delicate and pale with smooth brush strokes whereas Raen's is dark, square jawed, and textured. A stone compared to a flower. His fake smile is goading me. If I don't join him, he'll think he's won, that I can't trust myself to lie beside him, that I lust after him. I don't. My body is lonely, that's all. It's lonely and wanting comfort, comfort that could come from anyone. I have mastery over it so I step nearer.

He makes no movement. I take another step. His eyes shut. There's a deep line between his thick eyebrows. His dark hair is spread out, knotty from nightmares, and there's a dusting of stubble across his chin and cheeks. His arms are crossed over his chest in the pose of the dead. It's too much to see him like this, as he will be on the battlefield if he insists on fighting. I crouch to check his breathing, to rid myself of this foolish dread heavy in my stomach. His breath is steady and long. His lips twitch, again, and again, and then he's smirking. He opens one eye. He pats the bed.

I climb up, sit beside him cross-legged. His skin is darker in the shadows from the bed's canopy, and it makes him seem more villager than castle prince. The green in his opened eye is somehow brighter though there's no light to make it so. 'You have a look of her,' I say. 'A look of the village despite ...' Despite who his father is, despite his arrogance, despite the castle way about him, I almost say; yet as I peer down at his face none of those things are there. 'You don't have that sickly fineness like everyone else, like one strong rain storm would dissolve them.'

'Is that a compliment?'

I can't help smiling. 'I prefer the refined castle fashion.'

'Like Gavin.'

'He's certainly more pleasing to my eye than you are.'

'You're not interested in Gavin.'

'No?'

'No. You are in love with my half-brother.' His eyelid is struggling to stay open. 'Don't use Gavin. He can't help you with whatever you're planning.'

'He told me his sister wants to be like the True Queen.'

His eyes flutter open. 'Every woman wants to be like the True Queen.'

'Why are you entertaining this proposal? Don't you want the old ways back?'

'There's no going back, only forward.' He yawns. 'For the castle, me, you.' His voice is getting deeper as sleep calls him, and the changing tone is lulling, coaxing me. 'Maybe a different forward, but a forward.'

He's not going to leave my bed, that much is evident, and I'm tired too. He's right: I've not been sleeping. It's not nightmares plaguing me, though, but worries concerning Ammi, Onnachild, and him. More specifically, what we've done together. I need to prove to myself, to Aelius, that I have control and my body won't betray him again. Sleeping here will be fine; our bodies are separated by the rolled-up fur, and Aelius's portrait is keeping watch.

When I lie down, my hair almost touches Raen's. His is a shade lighter than mine and streaks run through it like the circles in a tree. I squash my hands against the fur to stop them exploring those colours. He yawns again. 'Talk to me,' he murmurs.

'I remember ...' I roll onto my side. His face settles into a serene expression, lines gone and his jaw slack. 'My grandmother had such admiration for your mother. Iansa.'

His lips move and I wonder if he's repeating his mother's name.

I continue, 'My grandmother knew Iansa when she was a little girl.

Shrewd, inquisitive, stunning, Grandmother said she was. Back then, everyone used to come together for the big celebrations. Feasting, dancing, music.'

'Would you have danced with me?'

'No.'

He smiles.

'My grandmother told me everyone knew Iansa'd catch Onnachild's eye, not because she was beautiful but because she was sharper than any blade. Do you think she loved him?'

'Niah, why are you so obsessed with love? Love has no place here.' He struggles to open one tired eye. 'What difference would it make, anyway? Would it make it better or worse, what he did?' His face is stern again, the lines returned, and both eyes are open, red-rimmed, and staring at the canopy above us.

'I saw her once.' I don't know why I'm telling him this, perhaps to ease out those lines in his forehead. 'I touched her dress, trying to get her attention so I could give her the flowers my grandmother had picked for her. That dress reminded me of spiderwebs in the morning dew, it had that same shimmer. I left a handprint on it. She didn't shout at me, though, or wipe it away. She stopped, smiled as she took the flowers. I felt important, special. Sometimes ...' I take a deep breath. 'I wonder, well, I think I dreamt it ... how things used to be.'

His breathing has slowed. His eyes have shut, his dark lashes creating thick crescents. His jaw has relaxed, and his lips have parted. There's nothing dangerous about him when he's asleep, so I settle down and close my eyes.

In my dreams, his mother is waiting for me. She's calling my name as she runs through a forest thick with yews. Her dark hair streams behind her, a banner of flames, mahogany, and ebony. As I chase her a phoenix breaks through the canopy, lighting up the sky with the colours of a sunrise. I trip on my long castle dress, tumble. The ground catches me, yields to me as the wind skims across my skin. Her gentle chuckle carries like a bird song. The sun heats my body and the earth beneath me. Flowers, trees, and grasses fill the air with their perfume, and mixed in, drifting from the village, is the smell of a pheasant being cooked. I'm not alone. My lips rest against soft skin, the pulse there beating with mine. Our bodies touch as we breathe in the same breath, one full of summer, full of home. It's ebbing away, fading, a dream that refuses to keep me in its comfort.

My eyes open to harsh, real sun streaming in through the window. I blink. Raen's legs are entwined with mine, the fur having unrolled and flattened beneath us during our sleep. My arm is across his chest, rising and falling with his breathing. My shin is nudged against his crotch, held there by the weight of his hand. My knee has gathered up his tunic, and the skin of his belly is warm and smooth like a sun-heated pebble. The rhythm of his breath is as soothing as a bedtime song. Sleep is so seductive after its absence and, perhaps, if I'm still enough it'll welcome me back.

Raen's lashes are fluttering and his eyes are moving under the lids. I wonder whether his dream is similar to mine because there's a faint smile on his face. Will it stop him from going to battle, from marrying a foreign princess who wants to follow the second queen's, the True Queen's, example? His eyes open as if sensing my curiosity and wanting to keep his dreams secret. I smile, shyly. His eyes are shining like conkers washed in rain. My breathing speeds.

This moment isn't real. He isn't real despite the heaviness of his leg on mine, the tickle of hair against my thigh. Nothing is real, so it doesn't matter what I do. It doesn't matter that I press my lips to his, that I tease open his mouth with the tip of my tongue, that I add pressure, that I lean over him. Aelius's portrait catches the corner of my eye. That was real. That was love. This is ... is lust ... loneliness. A dream casting its spell. I jerk away, so suddenly that when he makes a move for me it's only the fur he holds.

Out of bed and shivering in the cold, I stare up at the portrait. It's that body, those lips I want, but no matter how hard I try, I can't remember how they felt. Is this my punishment? His spirit should be haunting me forever, but it's Raen's voice, rumbling and full of sleep, trying to draw me back. It's his body which has left a trembling impression on mine.

The door opens and there, grinning, are Melody and Nessia. My face feels hot, too hot, and my nightdress feels too thin under Raen's stare. I cross my hands over my breasts, squash them down to hide the peaks betraying my lust. 'Get him out.'

Melody titters and no one moves. I repeat myself, shouting this time.

'She's bossy in the morning, isn't she?' Raen teases, sliding out of bed. He seems refreshed, his dishevelled state suggesting play rather than nightmares. We've done nothing, I remind myself. I've done nothing. But I did, once. Once was enough. Is that why the gods are taking away my body's memory of Aelius: the texture of his hair, the pressure of his weight on me, the smell of his sweat, dripping and then drying us together?

'It's still early,' Nessia says to Raen. 'Only a few servants are about.'

Melody's trying to hide her laughter. I glare at her. 'If you dare tell anyone ...'

'I wouldn't,' she manages to say.

'Stop being mean to her.' Raen brushes and shakes out his hair with his fingers. The sun highlights the red tones. 'It's not her fault.'

'No, it's yours.'

'If it makes you feel better, then yes, it's my fault.'

He leaves the room, giving me one lingering backwards glance as his finger trails over his bottom lip. Last night was another trick, and I was foolish to not realise it.

Chapter Twenty-Seven

MY LEGS ACHE AND MY FEET BURN from pacing through the village all day, searching for traces of the Aelius I knew. The villagers have reduced my home to ash, and so when I went there, I couldn't picture us together, him giggling in front of the fire, and I couldn't hear that sound. The statue had nothing of him in it. I went to the graveyard, stood at the gates, unable to move as the wrong memories returned: Vill's face so enchanting in the moonlight, Raen and I. At the battlefield, I found only a group of Aralltirs clearing the valley, their wagons containing black mounds and the odour of rotting flesh. No echoes of Aelius. They chased me away, and so I ran to the forgotten graves, hoping to find peace. I was wrong.

Raen's wooden flower is still here. I stick it into the ground where his mother's ashes have made themselves part of the dirt. He's the only thing I can think about: his hands twisting it, tracing it, and his crying, and the following joy made more poignant by those drenched lashes. Spring refuses to come to this place, but the chilled wind left by its absence suits my mood better. Night is darkening the sky. At the castle, people will be starting to dance. My stomach grumbles from lack of food, and my head throbs with half-formed thoughts.

I start a fire and throw my herbs on it to call Aelius into the smoke. This is what I should have done instead of showing Raen his mother, letting him distract me with those tears, with his tricks. No more. I push my hood from my face, shake out my hair, and concentrate as the smoke grows.

'Why are you here?' the First Queen asks.

It is not her I want to see, bold and vivid in the smoke. Her features are a reminder of Raen: that mahogany hair, the top lip defined with two sharp peaks and the bigger bottom lip.

'I want Aelius. I need Aelius.'

'He won't come.'

'I need him. I need … Aelius, I'm lost.'

'You are not lost.'

'I am. I don't … Make Aelius come.'

'He will not.'

'Why? Aelius?' I search the sky, looking for anything like him, a patch of sky the same blue as his eyes. 'Then my grandmother, give me her. I want her. I don't want you.'

'And yet it is me you have called.'

She is as I saw her on the day I recounted to Raen while we lay in bed, and I remember the feel of his legs between mine, the ridges of his stomach against my bare knee. I shake my head; that's not why I'm here.

'I don't know what to do,' I mumble, and the confession brings some relief.

'You do.'

'You're not being helpful.'

Her laughter adds brown puffs to the horizon, puffs the shade of Raen's eyes.

'Stop it.' I reach up, dash them away. 'Why did you talk to him? What did you tell him?'

'You wanted me to talk to him.'

'But he doesn't follow our religion. He's not—'

'Such a spoilt child, you are. Is that why you called me here? To chastise me?'

'Of course not. What did you say to him? Did you tell him to stop the battle? Did you tell him to disobey Onnachild? You must tell me that at least, please. If you hate the villagers and want them to die—'

'I do not blame them. I blame Onnachild, just as you do.'

'Then tell me how to protect them.'

'I tell you again: you know what to do.'

'If I knew, I wouldn't be here, would I?'

'I thought you came because you wanted to call Aelius?'

'I did. I do. You're so like ...' I can't say it, and I can't look at her anymore with her frustratingly enigmatic smile like her son's, so I concentrate on the fire. The flames are figures dancing in circles, happy villagers.

'Mantona told you; perhaps you were not listening,' she says. 'Perhaps you were distracted. Niah, you are so easily distracted.' She vanishes, leaving a blank sky, one far too vast for me to not be frightened by it, to not feel powerless. Surely, this isn't what my ancestors wish to leave me with? I run through the last time I spoke to Mantona: the ring, dancing with Raen, seeing Ammi. What am I meant to find in those memories?

'Please,' I yell. 'Please.' I'm up on my feet, spinning around, staring at the empty sky. 'I don't know. Tell me. Just tell me.' My voice is hoarse. I sink to my knees, dizzy. Tears drop onto my hands.

'A book.' A flash of light makes me look up and there her face rises high, blanched, stretched, and deathly. There are moving things where her eyes should be, things dropping and dripping but dissipating before they reach the ground. 'Mantona told you. Listen. Pay attention. An Aegnian book. The library. In there you'll find something ... in the book ... something that will help with all your problems.'

'Stop the battle? Take the throne? Which? What should I do?'

'Be careful, I was surprised. I didn't have time. Be more careful than I was, and be quick.'

Then she's gone. The light from the fire is gone. The warmth is gone. My limbs are heavy, and the cold is prickling my skin where my tears fell. Yet, my mind is alive with possibility. A book saved by Mantona, somehow, from being burnt with the others in the village square. I remember my grandmother hugging me as the flames grew. After, she had tapped my chest and told me they were in there. I cried that night, certain it was the greatest loss I could ever experience. How naïve I was. But now ... I rise to my feet, shake the dirt from my skirt. Now, I can have something of my ancestors. I'll be able to see the words of my language, touch them, trace the curves, say them aloud and feel my ancestors speaking to me. I can own something they created. Not alone. I'm not alone.

My speed makes me clumsy and my horse skittish as we race to the wall, to the castle. Eagerness makes me dismissive of the guards, of the servants. My footsteps are noisy as I run through the castle to the library where I've had many of my lessons, where I've practised dancing, where I've listened to lies read from a book containing pictures of women who looked nothing like me. All this time, in that room, were words in my language, waiting for me. How did I not realise? Because I was too focused on becoming what Onnachild wanted me to be.

I grab both door handles, yank. They rattle, locked against me. They've not been locked before. I push against the door with my shoulder. It doesn't budge.

'Tomorrow,' I say with my hands flat on the wooden door.

'Tomorrow,' I tell myself as I trudge through the hallways.

When I enter my room, Melody springs up from the floor by the fire. Her cheeks are bright pink. 'Sorry,' she says.

'Sorry for what?'

Her gaze directs me to a chair, to a pair of long legs stretched out and pointing towards the fire. 'I told him I didn't know where you were, that he couldn't wait; I did.'

'I didn't listen.' Raen leans forwards and turns towards me. 'Where have you been?' He stares at my skirt gathered into a fat knot, exposing my muddy shoes and scuffed knees. 'No need to tell me. What were you doing there?'

He looks peeved, so I ignore his question and head off towards my bedroom to change, gesturing for Melody to follow. I hear Raen get up, the chair scraping against the floor, and when I look over my shoulder, he's there behind me. 'Have you been talking to my mother? Aelius?'

'I'm tired,' I say, though I realise sleep will be elusive tonight. 'Go back to your own rooms. Why are you even here?'

'I had a nightmare.'

Melody titters. Obviously, she doesn't appreciate how lingering nightmares can be. After last night I've learnt not to take anything he says at face value, so I continue on my way to my bedchamber with more speed to my steps.

When I try to close the door behind me, he holds it open. His breath tickles my neck. I raise my shoulders up against it as I keep struggling with the door. Nessia is stirred from her slumber by the noise of our tussle, and she sits up in bed, blinking and grimacing.

'Oh.' She pushes back the covers.

'You stay there. I'll be joining you as soon as ...' I glare at Raen, hoping he'll take the hint. He doesn't.

'Let Nessia sleep,' he says. 'Come sit by the fire with me.' He tugs on my arm, once, twice, again when I don't answer him. 'I'll not outstay my welcome, just, talk with me ... Nothing more.' He crosses his heart with his index finger, as if that makes any difference.

'Then it's settled.' Nessia lies down and pulls the fur over her head.

I stomp past him. Since I won't be able to sleep tonight, I might as well sit with him; it will make time pass quicker if nothing else. My stomach rumbles to remind me I've not eaten but I dare not send Melody out for food because that will leave me and Raen alone. She rushes to fill two goblets with wine, and when Raen and I sit in opposite chairs in front of the fire, she hands them to us and then settles on the floor.

'Have you been avoiding me today?' He takes a sip of wine and the silver shine from the goblet highlights the whites of his eyes. 'There's no need to be embarrassed.'

'Why would I be?'

'You tell me.'

I stare into the fire. The imprint of the dancing figures from earlier has remained in my eyes and they come into these castle flames, only their movements are less joyful, less free. It makes me sigh.

'What can you see?' Raen asks.

'Nothing.' I kick off my shoes, draw my feet and legs up onto the seat, and then settle my skirt over them. I take a big gulp of my wine. 'When are the library doors unlocked?'

My question makes Raen frown.

'They're never locked,' Melody says. 'In case someone needs guidance in the night.'

'They were locked tonight.'

'They shouldn't be.'

'What did you want from the library at this time of night?' Raen asks.

'Niah's obsessed with learning to read.' Melody leans back on her hands and wiggles her bare toes at the fire. 'I told her not to bother. Raen, you can tell her a story, can't you?'

'Perhaps I do owe you a story. I haven't slept as well as I did last night for a long time.'

I huff in response.

'Oh good, can I hear it too?' Melody turns her face up towards him, one side illuminated by the fire. 'We like stories about princes and princesses.'

'I'm sure you do.'

'I don't want a story,' I say.

Raen sips his wine and stares into the flames. His jaw is clenched and the firelight picks out the twitch in it. 'Why did you go down there?'

'Because I wanted to.'

'Niah?' He spins around in his chair, elbows on his knees, face thrust forwards, and the frustration on it stuns me into silence. He sighs deeply and slowly with great control as he scrutinises my face. 'My nightmare ...' he says sternly.

I wait for him to continue but he doesn't. Does he think I should understand its contents, its meaning from his eyes alone? 'It was just a nightmare,' I mumble.

He shakes his head. 'Then why do I have this dread, this ... that you're doing something stupid and here you are ...' He gestures at my muddy skirts with his goblet.

'Why should you care, anyway? If I—'

'I don't know.'

Vill bursts into my rooms. 'There you are,' he says, banging the door shut. 'Oh. This is a surprise. Raen.' He nods at Raen who nods back. 'I'll go.'

Raen stands. 'No. I'll go.' He drains his goblet before putting it down on the floor. His gaze remains on me, pleading with me, but I don't know what he wants. Why does he think I would?

'Don't leave on my account.' Vill backs away.

Nevertheless, Raen does leave, and as the door closes my shoulders drop, tension easing. I slide my legs out from under me and start massaging my sore feet.

'I wasn't expecting to see him here.' Vill stares at the closed door. 'Not after the Great Hall.'

'Why? What happened?'

'If you were there you'd know, and though I should be angry, it seems your absence enticed Raen to your rooms, so instead, I say, well done.' He sits in Raen's vacated chair.

'I thought it was good news.' Melody looks up at Vill for approval.

'It's not good news for us,' he says. 'Princess Eldini is coming to meet Raen.'

And with her, men, money, weapons—he doesn't need to tell me this. My shoulders hunch up. 'Why didn't you say anything?' I ask Melody.

'Raen was here, and he didn't look ... He had a nightmare,' she says to Vill. 'And I thought it might upset him if I mentioned it because he can't want to marry her, can he? I mean, last night—'

'Melody.' I interrupt, but it's too late.

'Oh?' Vill's interest is piqued.

'I did try to hint to him ... that story ... about princes and princess. He's not good at taking a hint.'

'So last night ...' Vill gestures for me to elaborate. 'Did he drink the proverbial water?'

I go to sip my wine to avoid Vill's question and intense stare but my goblet is empty. He takes it from me and holds it out towards Melody. 'And one for me.'

I slide backwards in my seat, rearrange my skirt although it doesn't need rearranging. He stops my fidgeting with a hand cluttered with red and orange gems. 'I have to say he looked very much at home here.'

'I have a new plan.'

He cocks his head to one side. 'Go on.'

'Do you know anything about an Aegnian book being in the library? The First Queen told me about one.'

'A book?' He considers this, tapping his plump lips with his fingers. 'My understanding was that Onnachild burnt them all.'

'Apparently not.'

'What are you expecting to find in it?'

'I'm not sure. She didn't say exactly, something to stop the battle, perhaps.'

'Niah, Niah, Niah.' He twists the ring on his index finger. 'Can you please think beyond this battle? Do I really need to explain myself again?'

'But Vill, listen, what if there's more in the book? What if—'

'What if? What if.' He shakes his head. 'This is what will be ... Raen still your rival, still pleasing Onnachild more and more every day. The Princess Eldini still arrives, still marries Raen, still gets with child and then ... then.' He flicks out his fingers one by one. The knock of his rings against each other has an ominous quality. 'We won't just be going up against Raen, but a foreign power. That is what will be if you continue on this course of action. I fail to see how stopping this battle helps us.'

'So you want to rely on Raen dying in this battle? I won't. Think Vill, if there was nothing in that book that could help, why would the First Queen even mention—' I stop because Melody has returned with the full goblets.

'Point noted.' He rubs his plump lips and stares at the fire. 'If it matters so much to you, Melody will look for it. She won't tell anyone. Will you, Melody?'

'No.' She wiggles with pleasure and awkwardly adjusts her hold on the goblets as he smiles at her. 'Look for what?'

'We need you to steal a book.'

'I'm not a thief.' She blushes. 'I just borrow things, and I always replace them afterwards. I do not steal. Do you think God will punish me for it?' Her bottom lip trembles. 'I'm a rubbish Maiden, but I should never have been one, so it isn't my fault, really. It's what happens when you steal children and don't use real orphans.'

Vill blinks slowly at her, inclines his head, and she seems reassured by this because her lips stop trembling and her big eyes widen. 'A book? What kind of book? Niah, is that why you went to the library? Vill, did you know it was locked tonight?'

He shakes his head.

'The King wouldn't want me to have this book,' I say, 'so you can't tell anyone, not even Raen.'

'Cross my heart and hope to die. Promise. I haven't said anything about you to anyone else, not even Beshanie when she offered me a gold bangle.' Her glance drifts to Vill. 'Is it a heathen book?'

'No, it's not a heathen book.' It's a struggle to keep my voice soft. 'It was written by my people. In my language.'

She nods even though she still looks confused.

'Onnachild has told me I have to forget my past, like you had to forget yours. But we can't forget, can we? We shouldn't.'

'I still know Melody isn't my real name even if I don't remember what my real name is.'

'Wouldn't you want to have something of your parents', if you could?'

She nods. 'But how will I—'

'Good girl.' Vill holds up his hand to quieten her. 'Now, if we can return to our original problem, our bigger concern. Raen. I'm willing to humour this book business but you must ...' He glances sideways at Melody standing there, waiting for instructions. He takes the goblets from her and gestures for her to sit. As he hands one to me, he says, 'You can't hide. People have been asking for you. Raen has been asking for you. Your absence in the Great Hall didn't go unnoticed by the advisers either. If they pry too much ... again, I need not explain myself, do I? I presume you've been where you shouldn't have.' He draws my attention to my muddy shoes on the floor.

'You're right. I'll be more careful.'

'Good.' He sits back in his chair. 'And we'll continue with our original plan. You seduce Raen, gain his loyalty and trust, and I'll keep chipping away at the merchants and Onnachild.'

No, I won't, because tomorrow I'll have the book and it will tell me what to do, and its advice will not involve betraying Aelius. I smile as I watch the flames.

Chapter Twenty-Eight

'POOR RAEN,' Nilola says.

The mention of his name draws my attention back to her and the Sunning Room, away from thoughts of the book, Melody, and the library. 'Why poor Raen?' I ask.

She points to him outside where he's bending to pluck a green rose. He smells it before tucking it behind his ear. He looks drained and there's a lonely air about him. Should I have made him tell me his nightmare? Another trick, no doubt.

'His little mousy princess is on her way,' Nilola says.

Beshanie tuts. 'Mousy doesn't cover it.'

'You haven't seen her. I have. I saw her portrait. Perkin showed me.'

'Vill showed me,' Beshanie says.

Nilola gestures for us to gather closer and then checks no one else is listening before she continues. 'She's little more than a child, a pious, dull child. No wonder Raen looks so crestfallen.'

'Maybe he'll refuse to marry her?' I ask. Perhaps whatever is in the book will make him. Why hasn't Melody come to get me yet? She must have it by now, and here I am sweating and daydreaming as the women gossip and the servants patter about with drinks and fans.

'He should,' Beshanie says. 'If I were a man, I would. Thing looks like she'd break after one good tumble.'

'You know who else is walking around with a face like a rain cloud?' Nilola smirks at Beshanie, seeming to want her permission before continuing. Beshanie sucks on her teeth and that seems enough for Nilola. Her sweaty arm rests on mine and she continues, 'Guess what I heard today.'

Beshanie looks bored.

'Go on,' I say.

223

'I heard Gavin requested an audience with the King, and do you know what for?'

I shake my head.

'Well, you should.' She pauses for effect, waiting to catch Beshanie's interest. 'It seems Gavin is more taken with you than we thought. Word is that he intends to petition the King to force your guardian to consider a betrothal to him. Isn't that something?' She leans back and scrutinises my face. 'You might be a queen after all.'

Don't be tempting the men, Onnachild had threatened. If you're to marry, it will be a man of my choosing, he had said. Or I'll be gone. Away from Ammi. Or worse, like the First Queen.

'You've gone pale,' Beshanie says. 'This should make you happy.' There's a sly smile on her face.

'If my guardian finds out, I'll be sent away.' Why wasn't I crueller to Gavin? It was his eyes, those innocent eyes, so similar to Aelius's, but they are not Aelius's, and now here I am ... I can't leave Ammi. 'The King will never allow it.'

'I wouldn't be so sure of that,' Beshanie says. 'The King needs Gavin's money and men.'

I force myself to smile though it feels nothing like a smile and I'm sure Beshanie notices. Something distracts Nilola, making her shriek and stand so speedily that her skirt knocks mine and Beshanie's. The movement ripples around the room, colours blurring as women and girls rearrange their dresses and wipe the sweat from their faces. 'Raen's coming,' Nilola gasps, plunging her hand down the front of her dress and rearranging her breasts.

A waft of cool air enters the room as Raen opens the door. It's quickly oppressed by the heat. Beshanie grabs Nilola's skirt and yanks her down. She whispers something in Nilola's ear which makes her shoulders bristle. As I watch Raen close the door, Vill's words replay in my mind: *seduce him*. Distasteful little words. As if Aelius, as if loyalty, as if love don't matter. None of these women would have any hesitation in following Vill's plan and mating with Raen. They're already panting as he manoeuvres through the room. His very presence seems to be making the walls throb and ripple, and I feel dizzy. I wave the hot air around me; it makes no difference.

Nilola bites her lips to make them redder. She's not ashamed to stand, to press her breasts against Raen's arm as she offers him her cheek for a kiss. He seems amused by her display although he aims for the air beside her face. Blues, browns, and purples are under his eyes, and the green rose has already wilted and lost a petal. Nilola's hand lingers on his arm while she shouts at a servant to bring a chair over. I sense he's expecting me to rise and offer my cheek to him so I take a sip of my tepid tea.

'What has brought you to us, here,' Nilola purrs, 'today.'

'I thought I should do my bit to keep our castle women entertained since Vill is busy.'

'Where is he?' Beshanie asks. 'He said he'd come see me.' She offers her cheek to Raen, and he bends to give another air-kiss.

'With the King. It seems his opinion is more valid than mine.'

Nilola laughs like he's told a joke. 'Not to us,' she says. 'Never to me.' Her desperation disgusts me, yet how would I be any better if I did what Vill suggests?

'You're kind,' Raen mumbles, uncommitted to the flirtation. 'We missed you in the Great Hall yesterday,' he says to me.

'I've been ill,' I say as blankly as I can when my mind is occupied with Gavin, Onnachild, Ammi, Melody, and my book. Again, I try wafting the air to bring relief. I must appear ill as Nilola turns sideways and blocks her nose by pressing it against Raen's arm. Her hand strays over his chest. Beshanie stands and roughly guides him into a chair, making Nilola huff. I'm done with this display, with Raen's pleasure at being manhandled; he beams at them as though they're doing him the greatest service in the world. Any sympathy I had because of his nightmare vanishes.

A hushed murmur from the women draws my attention, but not Nilola's or Beshanie's as they continue fawning over Raen. It's Vill opening the door. He leaves it open and a slight breeze trickles over as he cuts his way through the huddles of women and girls trying to catch his eye. The easy grace has gone from his walk; instead, his steps are heavy, speedy, and he seems to be struggling to maintain his usual bored expression.

'Am I no longer your favourite?' he asks Beshanie when he stands before her. There's no play or music to his voice, although he manages to flash his perfect smile at her.

She chuckles and flips back a lock of frizzled auburn hair. 'How could you ever doubt me?'

He bends towards her and kisses her cheek. As he makes an exaggerated motion to breathe in her perfume, his nose brushes her neck, and she laughs loud enough to draw everyone's attention to it. One hand lingers about his waist.

'I can't stay, much as I wish to.' Vill straightens up. 'The King wants to see you,' he says to me.

'The King?' My hand darts to my throat. Already?

'It must be because of Gavin.' Nilola winks at me.

By the gods, must I wish this is the least of it? What if he's discovered Melody? Then I'm gone. The book is gone. Ammi. I look to Vill for reassurance. He's pretending to admire one of his rings as he flicks it from his left hand to his right, but the rapid movement hints at something else, something I don't want to know.

'What have you done to young Gavin?' Raen asks.

'Me? Nothing.' I grip the arms of my chair: thin, spindly things. It's Raen's sturdy arm I want.

'He believes himself in love with you,' he says.

Vill's ring hits the ground, and the sound makes me jump. Women are quick to lift their skirts and shriek with excitement when he sinks to the floor to search for it. Beshanie lifts hers above her podgy knees.

'I don't see why he should,' I snap. 'I've only spoken to him twice.'

'Three times,' Raen says.

'We can't keep the King waiting.' Vill abandons the search for his ring, disappointing the surrounding women. Beshanie lowers her skirts. I can't move; my legs have forgotten how to work, and I'm sure my mouth has gaped open.

'He's not in the mood to be kept waiting,' Vill says.

'I ...' I push myself up, keeping hold of the back of my chair. My eyes search for comfort in Raen's but he won't meet my gaze, fussing with his hair instead. He's told Onnachild. The graveyard, calling his mother ... they would be enough to have me sent away, away from Ammi. The advisers, perhaps they saw me, had me followed down to the village ... Or Melody, she's told someone ... everything, and now the book is in Onnachild's battered paws.

I'd ask Vill for a hint, but my mouth is too dry. He grabs my arm. His hand is freezing and damp. Then it relaxes—he must have realised how tight his hold was. Raen's beside me. He can't have told Onnachild, not if he's so close, not if he's whispering, 'Don't worry, I'll come too.'

I reach for him, but stop myself, before our fingers touch, because Nilola's watching. Beshanie's gossiping grates against my skin.

I'm going. For one reason or another, I'm going. Vill leads the way through the Sunning Room, his shoulders back, his hands clasped behind him, and not checking whether I follow. Raen gives my shoulder a gentle nudge to get me moving. He's too calm. No, he's pretending to be calm; his jaw is twitching and he's fighting against his brow lowering. His eyes search my face for an answer. No, they linger because he knows I'm going. This is the dread he spoke of yesterday. There's nothing else to do but

227

copy Vill's pose of elegant indifference as I pass by these inquisitive, white castle faces. Raen's plodding steps are echoes of mine.

Chapter Twenty-Nine

VILL KNOCKS ON THE JUDGING ROOM DOOR. Raen doesn't wait for a response, barrelling in and knocking into the advisers on the other side. They're an unreadable column of grey. Vill follows Raen towards the throne and Onnachild, leaving me alone in the doorway. My legs are shaking. My bladder threatens to betray me, and I can't stop picturing my grandmother swaying, the soles of her dirty feet.

'Go in.' An adviser pushes me. I stumble.

'You're scaring her,' Raen says from beside the throne. He's leaning on it, showing no reverence to either it or his father.

'Good,' Onnachild growls. With the sun behind him, he's a dark bulk as ominous as a storm cloud. Raen's scowl is just as intimidating. I gulp as I try to settle into my pose of deference: gaze lowered, steps steady and graceful. Everything I've done that Onnachild would disapprove of flits through my mind: calling my ancestors, seeing Ammi, Raen. That last thought heats my face and I hope Onnachild doesn't notice.

Passing Vill, I peep at him for reassurance but his arms are crossed, his chin held by his index finger and thumb. He's letting his emotions show and the anger there makes the angles of his face glacial. His large lips are pushed out in a pout. He refuses to meet my eyes, shifting his weight to his other foot instead.

'Hurry up,' Onnachild bellows.

I pray silently to the gods, to my ancestors as I speed up. If I could get my heart under control, if I could take one full breath, then I could face whatever this is with the same dignity the First Queen had when they marched her to the noose. A quick brush of my knuckles against the yew table gives me the strength I need to face my punishment as Niah from the Aegni, village-raised, and not this weak castle-thing Onnachild wants me to be. I lift my gaze from the floor and drop the simpering half-smile.

Onnachild raises one bristly, black eyebrow and his lips quirk suggesting he's looking forward to this, whatever this is going to be. The advisers are gathered on the opposite side of Onnachild to Raen. The twin with ink on his fingers picks up a scroll from the table, and I'm reminded of Mantona's tip for telling them apart—so this one is Aesc. He flicks the scroll to make it unwind and then starts scratching away on it with a quill. The noise brings a throbbing to Raen's jaw. His chest is thrust up and out, straining against his tunic. His presence dominates his father, his shadow longer and bulkier across the table. It weakens my knees. 'Is someone going to explain what this is about?' he asks.

'A kingdom runs on protocol, on rules,' Ascelin says.

'My rules.' Onnachild's voice is so terse my stomach lurches.

'Why has Niah been brought here?' Raen asks.

'That is none of your business. Did we ask for his attendance?'

Aesc scans through the long scroll. 'No.'

'Do you know why you are here?' Onnachild asks me, lurching forwards.

I stare at the throne, at a phoenix's jewelled eye almost hidden by Raen's wide hand. 'No.'

'Have you broken so many of my rules?'

'No.' I slip off one of my shoes, the action hidden by my long skirt, so my bare foot connects with the stones my ancestors walked on, the stones my ancestors laid. I won't be removed from it; it will not let me go. The contact stops the tremors in my legs and cools me. 'I've done nothing wrong.'

'You have disobeyed me, and now you lie to me.' His voice rumbles like it is thunder caught between the Judging Room walls. 'Answer me.'

'I don't know what you refer to.'

'I gave you strict, simple rules that even a village half-wit could understand. And you disobeyed me. You do not disobey your king.'

'Your Highness,' Vill says in a voice I've not heard before, one flat and lower than normal. 'Is this not a matter for me to deal with? You have far more important things to concern yourself with. We still need to liaise with Cantor to finalise the terms of his contribution to this battle.'

'And now you distract me from—' Onnachild stops himself when Ascelin subtly touches his shoulder. He takes a deep breath, expanding his barrel chest and causing his furs to slip down his arm. 'You visited Grace. Don't deny it.'

'I don't deny it.' My eyes dart to Raen. Vill was right: I shouldn't trust Raen. What else has he told Onnachild? 'She's my daughter.'

'She is not yours. She is mine.'

Raen drums his fingers on the back of the throne. Whether it's out of boredom or a desire to draw attention to himself, I can't tell. Either way, it seems to be irritating Onnachild, and he grunts over his shoulder at Raen, who doesn't stop.

'I took Niah to see Grace,' Raen says.

Aesc pauses his scribbling.

'Don't lie for her,' Onnachild snaps. 'The mongrel wouldn't do the same for you.'

'Ask your spies.' Raen matches Onnachild's tone. 'Go on, ask them who led Niah there.'

Onnachild waves Raen's words away, feigning indifference though his nostrils are flaring. 'Do you remember what I said would happen if you disobeyed me?'

I'm too dazed by Raen defending me to answer.

'It was my doing,' he says, 'so if anyone should be sent away it should be me, but you can't do that, can you? Because if you do then we all know what will happen, or rather, what will not happen.'

'That does not mean a goddamn thing.'

'Who are you to talk to the King in this way?' Ascelin says.

'His son.'

'That is debatable,' Onnachild says.

Raen grimaces briefly, before his jaw is hard and tense again. His knuckles bulge as if he's using all his strength and willpower to stop them from moving from the throne.

'I decide when she is fit to see Grace, not you,' Onnachild says.

'Do you not have a heart? Do you not remember what it's like to love someone? To miss someone?' The disgust in Raen's voice startles the advisers. 'I forget, you aren't capable of love.'

Onnachild smacks the table. 'You will not speak to me like this.' His face is reddening, almost crimson, making his irises darker, the white in his beard brighter. Raen's gone too far. The advisers are too stunned to intervene. Vill's trying not to smile, and Onnachild continues to puff up and out, expanding, rising like he's gathering in more storm clouds. The green in Raen's eyes is flashing with hatred as he glowers at the back of his father's head, and it makes me want to step back.

Onnachild starts to rise, spitting, baring his teeth, and yanking up his furs but Raen is exerting contradictory pressure on the throne and so all Onnachild can do is rattle it, making the feet batter and clang on the stone floor. He's cursing, such a guttural sound as he's stuck half up and half down. Aesc drops his scroll. Raen's sneer contains a hint of joy and I realise this is not about me; it's not me he's defending. This show of defiance and strength is for the little boy who couldn't stand up to his father.

I force myself to step closer, unable to watch anymore. Vill tries to dissuade me by widening his eyes but I'm picturing Raen, small and scared, hiding behind the locked door in my bedchamber. Here in the Judging Room, he might be stronger than Onnachild, he might be taller, maybe even angrier, but his father still holds all the power. His father is king. There are better ways to get revenge. Men like Onnachild must be charmed, deferred to, and then stabbed in the back. If Raen wasn't so riled, he'd realise this.

'Your son.' I make my voice sweet and high-pitched, trying to mimic Nilola's. 'He was trying to do what he thought was right. He's learnt how to be just from you, and he wanted to show you that.'

Onnachild gives up his fight with the throne, dropping down into it, and the awful clattering stops. Raen's sneer darts to me, the heat searing, but I don't look away or change tactic. Instead, I focus on my sad memories: my grandmother dying, my first night without Aelius. Tears are what is needed, a show of weakness and vulnerability to sate Onnachild's desire for dominance. Vill slyly nods at me as I dab my eyes. 'Please, don't let me come between father and son. It is my fault. I should have refused his kind offer.'

'Don't flatter him. I know exactly why he did it. He's learnt to be deceitful from his mother, damn that woman.'

'You already have,' Raen snaps, punching the throne.

Onnachild's brow lowers and a cruel smile spreads. He's won this time, as he won in the past, but Raen's standing there, almost crackling with fury, and one day the son will win. It makes my sweaty foot slip across the stone floor.

'Niah is staying,' Raen says through clenched teeth.

'You are not king yet. You remember that. I am king.'

'She will stay here as long as Grace is here.'

'She will stay here until I say otherwise,' Onnachild says. 'I don't have time for this. Get Cantor,' he yells at the advisers. 'And not a word about this to him. Any of you.'

They nod and shuffle away. Vill picks up the scroll, pulls out a chair and sits, hiding his mouth in his hands. I suspect he's smiling behind them.

'You, go.' Onnachild jabs his thumb at Raen and then the door.

But Raen stomps around the table, yanks out a chair, and smacks it against the floor before plonking himself down, elbows on the table.

'Are you still here?' Onnachild shouts at me.

I jam my foot in my shoe, and back away, bowing. They're arguing again the moment I leave the room with only the village twang distinguishing Raen's voice from Onnachild's.

I may be safe in my rooms, but still my hands are trembling as I drink wine like it's water. Even my lips are trembling. It's not Onnachild that has unsettled me, it's seeing Raen so like his father. Nessia shuffles behind me as I pace from door to window, from sunlight to firelight, trying to release Raen's hatred from my body. 'I don't understand,' I mumble to myself, rubbing at the tension in my forehead.

'What don't you understand?' Nessia asks. Her face has filled out and it suits her, makes her look younger, and I'm sure her bones are creaking less. The dress she wears is a simple brown shift but it's new, the material thick and it flatters her growing shape. The only thing that stands between her and hunger seems to be Raen, but I can't put my faith in that kind of man. Yet, he defended me. No, it was not about me. Just how did Onnachild cause that scar?

'I've been foolish.' I glug my wine until there's nothing left in the goblet. As I pace over to a chair, my foot connects with Nessia's discarded book and sends it sliding into the wall. Melody squeals at the bang, presses her fist into her mouth. She's huddled up by the fire, headdress squashed between her thighs and her knees.

I rest against the chair, spot one of Raen's hairs caught and left across the top of it. 'Onnachild only knew about me seeing Ammi,' I say, picking up the hair.

'That's good,' Nessia says.

'Is it?' Melody asks.

'It's enough to send me back, us back, and yet ...' I wind the hair round and round my finger. It digs in. My thumb runs over the indentation it has made, over the skin bulging around it. 'I'm not confused about that.' I pace to the table and refill my goblet. 'How did Onnachild know?'

'Do you know how he knew?' Nessia asks Melody.

She shakes her head.

'Raen?' I ask. 'It would make sense for him to tell Onnachild and see me sent away ... only, he could have told Onnachild—' I stop myself as my face heats. Will I never be free of that guilt? I shouldn't be. 'He has kept my other secrets. Why?'

A burst of laughter from Melody distracts me.

'Melody.' Nessia's warning tone suggests they've spoken about this before, about me.

'What are you laughing at?'

'He loves you.' Melody's voice is muffled by her fist.

'Stop being ridiculous.' Her words make my face and neck burn, and the sensation sends me to the window for chilling air. Opening it, I find the air is motionless and spring-warmed. It smells of trees, of cut grass, and doesn't stop me thinking of Raen. His anger still vibrates through my body, and I'm reminded of the sharp crack of thunder after lightning has struck a tree. His defending me begins to make sense. Didn't he say he was dancing with me, that first night in the Great Hall, to annoy Onnachild? Taking me to Ammi, offering friendship, showing me the garden, they are all part of that same game. A game that will leave me as little more than carrion for two bears to fight over. 'Perhaps we'd be better in the village.'

'I will come too,' Melody cries. 'I don't like Lark, and I don't like the

Maidens, and I won't like this new, stupid princess, and I don't like my stupid headdress.' It clanks to the floor, and the sound goes right through me, reminding me of freezing village nights.

'Stop being so childish,' Nessia says. 'Both of you. You will stay. Ammi will stay. We will stay. Raen has kept your secrets. He'll continue to keep your secrets.'

'Will he?' I peer over my shoulder at her. 'You didn't see how overcome he was with anger. How like Onnachild he was, all reason gone. If we ... I displease him then ... then I don't ... he'll be as cruel as his father.' I gulp down wine as I go back to staring across the lawns to the dotted remains of his mother's garden. How could I have been fooled by that?

'I don't believe it,' Nessia assures me. Her hand, less chapped than it used to be, settles on my shoulder.

'It's even more important I get that book.'

'It wasn't there,' Melody says.

'What?' I spin around, bumping Nessia. I must have heard wrong. 'Not there?'

'No, I mean yes. It wasn't there, and I searched, behind books too, and there was nothing there like Mantona described. Nothing.'

I shouldn't have sent her; I should have gone myself. Tonight, later, I'll go, and if I'm caught, well, will Raen fight my corner again?

Chapter Thirty

I'M TOO FULL OF WINE to answer Nilola and Beshanie when they question me about what happened in the Judging Room. At least the wine has flushed my cheeks, helping me appear embarrassed and contrite as the advisers are not letting me out of their sight, shifting across the Great Hall with every twitch I make.

'Poor, lovelorn Gavin.' Nilola nods to where he sits next to Raen, who looks furious and agitated with his feet tapping beneath the table. 'It must have been a no.'

'Are you going to be sent back?' Beshanie asks me.

'I'm to stay.'

'Good.' Her words seem genuine because she pours me more wine and then places chunks of meat on my plate. The gesture makes me smile, and I force myself to eat in order to clear my head.

'What's wrong with Raen?' Nilola asks. 'He doesn't look like he'll be dancing tonight and there's so little time before that princess arrives.'

'As if you have a chance,' Beshanie scoffs.

'Why not?'

They start arguing and I drift out again. The laughter, the excited chatter, the violent words coming from across the room as the men talk of battles have my thoughts muddled. Onnachild sits in his place like nothing has happened, and he continues to command the room, the servants, and the music. He's laughing, clapping away while Raen broods. When Vill rises, Onnachild calls him over and whispers in his ear. Vill nods, smiling, but says little in response. His appearance, same as Onnachild's, suggests nothing untoward happened today. His blond hair is smoothed back, a shine arching across the top, and his white tunic, embroidered with gold hawks, is pristine. Only Raen and I appear affected, with him crossing his arms over his chest and glaring at his full plate while Gavin chatters to him.

'Niah, what's wrong with you?' Beshanie asks. 'Are you still sick?'

Nilola covers her mouth with her lace sleeve. 'If you are, you should go.'

'That would ruin all the fun,' Beshanie says. 'Here comes Vill, and he isn't happy. It looks like he might have words for you.'

Vill does look annoyed. He's curt when he asks me to dance, not holding out his hand, yet when we're together and lost amongst the colourful dresses and pale faces, he smiles. 'I wish you could have remained.' He keeps his voice low. 'It was spectacular. I've witnessed nothing like it ... and the words they used, well, let's just say Raen's village side was in full effect. Truth be told, I wouldn't have been surprised if punches were thrown. If only they had been, to hit a king is treason even if he is your father. Raen will be banished again within the week, Eldini or no Eldini, if relations continue like this. We could not have planned it better.'

'We? You did nothing.'

'Calm that anger.' He turns me away from the top table and further into the crowd. 'I'm hurt. Do you not believe that everything I do is to advance your cause? I wish you wouldn't doubt me. I knew you weren't in danger.'

'You knew nothing of the sort.'

'Niah, I play my part perfectly at all times, and because of that, I'm privy to all manner of information that others aren't. That Raen isn't. And so I know that scene was all bark and no bite. Onnachild can't afford to get rid of you. To do so would mean abandoning the bet and with this upcoming battle, he needs all the money he can—'

'What does that mean or matter? When has he ever been rational? Look what happened with the First Queen and you want—'

'Shush. Have you forgotten where you are? Lower your voice; do you want the advisers to hear? As I was saying, I know Raen has no idea how low the coffers are and how desperate Onnachild is for money, so he wouldn't realise it was all bark. The scene provided us with the perfect opportunity to see whether he'd come to your defence. Now we know he will, and we can progress from there.'

'What if he hadn't?'

'Please, I could have talked Onnachild out of any rash decision. Can we move on from that?' He waves away my protestation. 'And focus on the outcome. One that we can use to our advantage. Raen's been in a foul mood ever since: belligerent, threatening to refuse Eldini.'

'Really?' No Eldini means no battle, no death.

'I thought that would cheer you up, but please, take that smile off your face. I'm meant to be scolding you.' He's smiling too though. 'Let Raen sulk alone for a while and then later you can ...' Vill leans closer and whispers, 'I'll send a note, telling you where his rooms are.'

'But you said he's going to be ban—'

'I said it's possible if things keep on as they are. If we can keep pushing him. He's gone against his father once for you; imagine what else he'd do if you encouraged his feelings. Refuse Eldini, as I said he's already threatening to. You could get him to refuse to fight, stop the battle. The more he annoys his father the further away he gets from being claimed and named as successor. If he's banished again, the problem goes away, and all without us having to count on the battle to take him out. Isn't that what you want?'

It makes me feel guilty, and I'm not sure why. I glance around Vill's slim shoulder at the top table. Raen's not there. I search for him but can't see his dark hair amongst the blond wigs. Nilola is dancing with a stout man far too old for her, and Beshanie has found a skinny man puffed out with orange sleeves.

'You don't seem happy?' Vill says. 'No, it's right you look downcast. Onnachild has told me to threaten you, send you off to your rooms as punishment. Although he was so livid with Raen, I'm surprised he was able to remember your transgressions.'

Vill spins me, and the room blurs into streaks of yellow and gold, the coloured dresses whirl, and the advisers become hazy lines of grey. The wine sloshes in my belly. Only Vill's voice is clear as he says, 'Go to him, thank him, soothe his anger.'

I break away and stop, my head spinning. A short woman with a tall partner glares at me when they bump into us. I lean closer to Vill. 'I will leave, but not to go to him. I need to get the book.'

'We sent Melody.' He leads me from the dance floor, with a sly glance at Onnachild.

'She couldn't find it.'

'She really is useless. Leave the book, forget about it. Raen's more important. Now, I want you to look tearful and ashamed. You did it so magnificently in the Judging Room.' His fingers dig into my arm. Over his shoulder, I notice the advisers gathering together. Their smiles are cracks in their faces.

'Dash out,' Vill says. 'Cause a bit of a scene, not enough to be disgraceful but enough to draw Onnachild's attention and convince him that you've been suitably chastised.' For good measure, he pinches my arm and steps on my foot. It doesn't make me gasp as he probably intended but fuels my determination to get that book and prove him wrong.

I hurry from the room with my head down to ensure the rage in my eyes is hidden. There better be something in this book to free me from the manipulations of these men. I'll stop this battle, and then I'll deal with them.

Candles have been lit in the library as if I'm expected. I lean out of the room to check behind me once more. Left, right, to be sure the advisers haven't followed me. The hallway is empty and quiet. An owl hoots as though to hurry me, but the anticipation of touching an Aegnian book is so sweet, so exciting I want to savour it. Soon, I'll touch those words written by my ancestors, and it will seem like they're here, living again and whispering in my ears. I close the door behind me.

Ornate candelabras are dotted around the room on tables, on bookcases, and on the floor. They reach up and out like branches, creating the illusion of a silver forest tipped with fireflies and glow-worms. I take a deep breath of the familiar perfume: leather, dust, beeswax ... and Raen.

'It's not here,' he says from the darkness.

'What are you doing here?'

'I could ask you the same thing, but I think I know the answer to that.' He rises from a leather chair. 'I'd have thought after today, after almost being sent back, that you'd stop all this,' he says. 'And yet ...' His fingers trail along the back of the chair, and there's something in that languid movement which makes my face heat. He keeps moving closer, slow and steady, stalking me. Candlelight draws attention to his chin, the tip of his nose, the curve of his lips. 'It's not here. Not anymore.'

'You don't know what I want.'

'You're in the library, so I'm presuming you want a book?' He lowers into a slight squat, pausing when our eyes meet. I brace myself to see anger but there's none, there's only tiredness. 'Or more specifically, my mother's book.'

'How?'

He doesn't answer, and that silence tells me everything.

'She told you?'

He nods.

'Why would she tell you? You can't even read it.'

'I can admire the pictures.'

'You have it?'

He nods.

I can't stop staring into his eyes; the green is the same hue as the clipped lawns, and the brown shines like the bookcases. 'Did you have the doors locked yesterday?'

His lips twitch, trying to stop a smile, and they give me my answer.

'Can I see it?'

He unfurls to his full height. 'No. Now come on.' He gestures towards the door.

I slap away his hand. 'Give it to me. It's Aegnian. It's mine.'

'And mine.' He grips my arms and I think he intends to shake me, only he suddenly lets go and chuckles. 'Listen to us, bickering like children, when it's Onnachild's. Everything in this castle is Onnachild's.'

I try a new tactic, smiling and speaking sweetly. 'If you gave it to me, I could teach you how to read it. Teach you the Aegnian language.'

'And what else would you do with it?' Back down he bends, drawing my face between his hands like I'm a child that needs scolding. 'Something that would draw his attention to it. And then what would he do? Burn it, and then neither of us will have our memories, and you. You.' He butts my nose with his. 'If you're lucky, you'll end up back in the village, back in that hovel to starve and be used by God knows who, and believe it or not but I don't want that.'

'Why?' I whisper, scared of the answer. 'Why did you, today ... against Onnachild?'

He lets go of me, rises in one swift movement, and heads towards a table with an array of candles on it. I almost follow until he blows one out, then another. Footsteps go past outside, hurried footsteps, and we both cock our heads at the sound, waiting for them to fade away.

'Why?' I ask again.

'Because.' His voice is gravelly. He clears his throat. 'Because he hates it, because you're Aegnian like my mother and I want him reminded of her. Does it matter why?' He sighs. 'Just stop playing, Niah.'

'I can't. In that book, she told me, there's something that can stop the battle. Did she tell you the same? You can't use whatever is in there. I can. Please, give it to me.'

His fingers play with the lumps of dried wax around a candle. A piece drops off into the darkness below the table. 'People have always hated each other,' he says. 'Killed each other. There has always been death. There will

241

always be death. You can't make it go away.' His voice is low, lush, tinged with some quality of a night sky.

'Does that mean I shouldn't try? If you don't care about them, then think of yourself. You wouldn't need to go into battle. You wouldn't die.'

As he crosses the room, advancing towards me, light and darkness play over his features: highlighting his lower lip, hiding his lower lip, his scar, enhancing the line of his jaw, an eye here and staring at me, then gone into shadow. The blaze when his eyes reappear in the light has me holding my breath. The branches of the candelabras seem to be offering the candles to him as gifts, the flames drawn to his form and pulsing in the wake of each step he takes. They make him part of this magical forest of flames; the green dots in his irises picked out and turned into fireflies, his face burnished and sculpted like a wooden figurine, and his shadow exaggerated so he's more giant than man. My hand rises to steady my racing heart. When he stops in front of me, he's so close I feel the warmth coming off him, smell the forest on him.

'Do you think I'm scared of dying?' he asks.

'I don't want you to die.'

His expression says he doesn't believe me. I don't believe me. His fingers trace over my lips perhaps to feel whether the words were true.

'Please, don't go to battle.' My voice shakes. The wine, the candlelight, hunger makes me clutch his shoulder to steady myself. My palm itches to touch his scar.

'Don't go to battle either,' he whispers in my ear. His hair tickles my shoulder.

'Then help me.'

He leans back. I watch him gulp, follow the movement of it down his throat to the dip at the bottom, then lower my eyes go, down to his broad chest, the shape of his muscles hinted at by the shadows and light. The rise and fall of his chest speeds as if responding to the speed of mine.

'I'm trying,' he says.

'Why? Did she tell you to?'

'Maybe.' His gaze traces across my face like a caress, and I want to close my eyes against that intensity but I'm transfixed by the green dots in his and the darkness surrounding them. 'Maybe not.' His breath is on my lips. His face is lowering, tilting. I rise onto my tiptoes. My hand slides to his neck, under his hair, and I feel him tense.

'Are you going to kiss me for it?' he asks.

Not for the book, but yes, yes, I want to kiss him, taste him again. My lips are already pursed and tingling with anticipation.

His hands around my waist pull me in closer. 'More?' His voice is a seductive murmur.

'More?'

He nods. 'Do I need to get specific?'

His opinion of me hasn't changed, that much is obvious. I snatch back my hot hand, shake my head to get out whatever strangeness has got into it. He doesn't care for the book, only that I want it. We are not friends. We will not be friends. He chuckles to himself like something has been proved. But what has been proved? Nothing. Once again, I can push him away, can leave him.

Chapter Thirty-One

A HAND'S ON MY BARE ARM. A golden hand. The fingers are fused together. My skin, my bones are no match for precious metal; one wrong move and it will crush me. Eyes stare down at me but they're blank, smooth gold, and I can't see anything in them; they're like the eyes of the dead. I'm yanked off my bed, dragged across the floor. My nightdress rides up past my waist. The whole castle can see me, struggling, bouncing off walls. I don't want to go with him. I don't want to go back. Not with him. I can't speak to say I don't want to go back. Its ears are fused with gold, anyway. It lurches, each heavy step rumbling through the stone floors, worrying the walls. They squeal and squeal like a pig going to slaughter. My ears hurt. My arm hurts. My chest hurts. Laughter. I hear laughter. Beshanie and Nilola are watching and clapping.

The statue doesn't slow. It doesn't pause. A bloody trail smears behind me, but no one will follow it to take me home. *Please, by all the gods, can I go home?* The portraits watch, trapped by frames and paint. They wear the same eerie smile.

Out into the night the statue drags me. It's so dark I can't see. Darker than night. Darker than black. There are no stars. There is no moon. The air is damp. Why won't it let me go? Why won't it leave me here on this mountain? It's because I have its blood in me; I have its dreams in my head. I always knew it would come. I'm sobbing. I'm ashamed to be sobbing but I can't stop. It gathers my ankles into one hand. The crown of my head bangs against the mountain as the statue lurches on and on, down and down to the village. My hair catches in gorse bushes and twigs rip my skin. The thump of my body against the ground has the rhythm of a lover's heart. I'm turning to gold: my ankles, my calves, my knees.

We're in the village, engulfed by the smell of shit and rotting food and it makes me gag. Village mud sticks to me, claiming me again. There's grit in my eyes, in my mouth. The thud of its feet reverberates through the ground, through me. Stones churn up my back, bringing burning as sure as fire does. We're in the graveyard. With the last will of my life, I'm yelling, wailing, searching for something to grab onto. I reach for headstones, but they crumble in my hands. Wind is whipping through the yew tree, lifting the branches and slapping them down against the ground, again and again. My sweat is freezing, is acrid. *Please, not this. Not this. I want to live. I want to live.* The grave is opening, gaping like a hungry mouth. *Not yet. Not yet, please not yet.* The ground is making way for me. The statue shakes me up into the air. My thoughts fall out as coins, tarnished and clipped. It giggles.

There are bones in that grave. There are maggots fat from feasting and glistening. They squirm, slip over each other. I can't recognise anything of Aelius in those bones. He's not there anymore. *Please. I'm still alive. I'm not ready.* A slap. A slap with no sting. I try to open my eyes. I try to free myself.

'Niah. Niah, wake up.' A voice with a hint of castle, with a hint of village. Another slap.

I gasp, dragging in air, and there's the scent of forests, of castle, of autumn. My eyes open. I'm in my rooms. My hands rush to my chest, to the painful beating there. I'm so grateful for the arms wrapped around me, arms that have give, arms that ease me closer to warmth. A curved hand with open fingers smooths my damp hair off my face. I don't understand why Raen is here, seated on my bed, but that doesn't matter. Nothing does as I settle my cheek against his chest. The slow, steady rhythm of his heart is trying to lead mine to a calmer beat.

'It's only a nightmare,' he says.

'It was so ...'

'It wasn't real, you're here with me. I won't let anything bad happen.' His voice is quiet and gentle.

'What if it already has? What if the bad thing is ...' I can't say him, not when he's being so tender, not when it might make him leave me to more nightmares. I clutch his waist tighter. He squeezes me in response.

When I look up, my gaze is drawn beyond him to Aelius's portrait. There's nothing like love in its blank stare. I reprimand it: *you're not here, you let your arrogance, your stupid, pompous arrogance, lead you to death, and I don't want to face this night alone.*

I draw back the furs to invite Raen in. Perhaps he doesn't want to be alone either because he doesn't hesitate in getting under them. He lifts his arm to let me nestle against him and I do. 'What do you dream?' I ask.

'Me? I can't remember.'

I peep up. He's frowning, a faraway look in his eyes. 'And that makes them worse. But I wake in a panic and that ... that ...' He stares down at me. His intense gaze brings comfort as I feel he's seeking a truth about me that no one else has ever gone searching for. 'It stops me from sleeping. I wake worrying about you. Tonight, I knew ... Ever since you called my mother.'

I slide my fingers between his. He smiles wanly, perhaps distracted by his nightmares. Hopefully, we can keep them away tonight, and so I close my eyes again.

Vill's flicking one of his many rings from his index finger to thumb, pretending to admire it and trying to suppress his obvious anger. The ring reflects dashes of morning sunlight onto the floor of my room. The dashes are pale yellow, almost gold, almost the same colour as that nightmare hand. 'You didn't go to Raen's rooms,' he says.

I move in front of the window to block the sunlight and stop it reflecting off his ring. The sun's rays warm the back of my neck like Raen's touch did last night while he caressed and eased out the tension left from my nightmare. I could tell Vill that, but I'm too confused by Raen's appearance, by his tenderness coming so soon after his insults in the library. How did he know I was having a nightmare, and where was Nessia? She was with me in bed when I woke up this morning, and he had gone.

'He has the book,' I say to distract Vill and myself.

'He has the book? Of course, he has the book.' Vill shakes his head. 'And do you know where it will be? In his rooms.'

'Why not ask him for it?' Melody says as she polishes the shells on her headdress. 'He'd let you have it. He's good like that.'

'Must you always be so stupid?' Vill says.

Melody flushes. 'I'm not stupid,' she mumbles.

'He wasn't talking to you.' I glare at him for upsetting her, my arms crossed and my lips tight with determination to not tell him anything. Seeing him so riled is pleasing. There's a mottled colour coming to his cheeks, and his hair has escaped the neat bow at his nape.

'Oh, for pity's sake,' Vill moans as he jams his ring down his finger and flops into a chair. 'Why do you continually refuse to listen to me? If you had, Raen would have already rejected Eldini, and she would not have embarked on her journey to the castle.'

'Aren't you my Follower? You do what I say, not the other way round.'

'Follow you to the noose I will at this rate.' Then he turns to Nessia. 'Is she always like this?'

She doesn't answer but her grin is so cheeky it reminds me of the time we lied to my grandmother about stealing apples from Onnachild's orchards. As she passes by me, heading into my bedchamber, she whispers, 'Put him out of his misery.'

'What was that?' Vill demands.

I tighten the cross of my arms and ignore his inquisitive stare, looking at the mantelpiece instead where his map to Raen's room is scrunched into a tight ball. Nessia is right. 'He was here, last night,' I say. 'Raen.'

'Then why didn't you inform me, instead of letting me go on? Niah, you really will be the death of me.'

'Not like you think. Not like that. How many times must I tell you? I'm not doing that.'

'Answer me this,' he says. 'Just how long do you imagine you can keep a man like Raen interested without bedding him? He has needs and Nilola sniffing around him like a bitch in heat. And Gavin, what did you believe that would accomplish? Yes, by all means, use him to make Raen jealous, but by the gods, are you aware he went to the King to ask for your hand? Did you consider the outcome if Onnachild consented? All our hard work undone. You banished to some miserable country where they don't even have sunshine.'

'Our hard work?' I huff. 'You've not managed much so far, have you? I haven't got my daughter. The other Followers haven't appeared. I haven't heard whether any merchants are going to support me. And I haven't even been told when this stupid bet will be decided.'

'Things are progressing.'

'Progressing?' I glare at him. 'How? When? Specifics, Vill.'

'Patience.' His skin is mottling again. 'Am I supposed to neglect my castle duties because you're here? Do you not think Onnachild might notice, ask questions, if I did? Between his demands and pressing your cause ... I'm positive I've aged ten years.' He rubs his sharp jawline, then his neck. 'I'm working on the merchants, Raen, the Aralltirs and what are you doing? You won't even ... Didn't we discuss this yesterday?'

'Discussed but not agreed. I said no. I said I'd get the book.'

'What if it turns out to be nothing more than her account of the castle funds?'

'There will be something there. She told me. I trust her.'

'And how do you intend to get it?' Vill flings his arms out, clipping the chair. 'If you mate with Raen, he'll give it to you. And refuse Princess Eldini. And stop the battle. What more do you want?'

'You've changed your tune, you wanted the battle. You wanted Raen killed in it.'

'It was an option before Princess Eldini was on her way.' Vill takes a deep breath. Those shafts of golden light have returned, moving across the floor as he toys with his ring. 'The battle only benefits us if the merchants are forced to pay for it. With enough support, Onnachild might actually win, which would be an absolute travesty for us. If you don't do it, I'll be forced to call the Followers and lay siege to this castle, and only the gods know if their number is great enough to be effective, or if they'll be true to us anymore?'

'Wait. What's changed? Isn't that what we were going to do? You said there were thousands waiting in Aralltir to help. You said you were going to call them back.'

'But if the battle happens, how many of them will die? How can I get the trust of the Followers and the Aralltirs if they discover you'd rather sacrifice their friends' bodies, brothers' bodies, sons' bodies in battle rather than loan out your own? Do you think the First Queen wanted to mate with Onnachild? Of course she didn't—she did her duty and put her people first.'

'And look what happened to her.' I turn away from his pale, accusatory eyes, and stare out the window where the white clouds stretch, their edges dissipating to faint blue. The grounds are a lush green and the flowers colourful dots alongside the white paths glowing with sunshine. Meandering amongst these colours is Raen. He looks lost even though this will all be his one day. His, if I don't act.

Images of the future fill the silence: broken bodies and bloody fields; Raen old, angry, drunk and presiding over a wasted country; his masses of children with less village and less Aegnian in their blood; and my Ammi bloated and mean-spirited.

I turn back into the room, rest against the chilled window and watch as Vill gets up and pours himself some wine. His rings clink, continuously, against the goblet until his features settle into his usual bored expression and his skin has that perfectly even tone again. 'All I want, Niah, is what you want. I presume you still want the throne? Grace? To restore the Aegnian line? That is what we're working for, isn't it?'

I nod.

'Then why are we fighting each other?' He offers me a goblet of wine.

'You're worse than Onnachild for stubbornness.' He's smiling, though, like it's a compliment.

I take the goblet, pressing my fingertips into the hard, unyielding metal, but don't drink. My head hasn't cleared from last night and the aroma of the wine churns my stomach. Nessia returns from my bedchamber, one of my dresses draped over her arm and her sewing bag hanging from her wrist. 'Niah, how about ...' Her voice is low and soft, testing me before speaking plainly.

I don't have the patience for it. 'Yes, just say it.'

'Why not do as Vill says?' she asks, calmly, as she settles into a chair. 'Niah, sweetheart, I love Aelius too but he's dead, gone. He's not coming back.'

'Why does everyone keep reminding me? Do you think I've forgotten? Forgotten his touch, his voice, his smile?' I poke myself in my chest, hard, right where my heart should be. I want to hurt it because I am indeed forgetting these things. Wine spills over my hand.

'Lust is not love.'

'They're not separate.' How can she not understand? None of them do. Melody's playing with the stitching on her shoe and trying to pretend she's not here. Nessia's inspecting the hem of the dress across her lap as if her words are inconsequential but they've caused a lewd smile to spread Vill's plump lips.

'Nothing happened,' I shout at him. He starts smoothing his hair back, sparks of golden sunlight flashing off his rings. 'The body doesn't belong to one person and the heart to another.' I grimace at how whiny my voice sounds.

'Nonsense,' he says.

'Your body belongs to you and it's yours to do with what you want.' Nessia shakes out the dress.

'I gave it to Aelius. It is his.'

'The way you're going it will be rotting with his in no time,' Vill mumbles.

I shudder at the memory of my dream and drink some wine to send it away, only when I take a sip the taste of Aelius's blood returns. It's been so long since I've been reminded of his body, how it was once alive, breathing, pulsing. The steps crossing the floor towards me mimic the tap of his boots on the floor of my hut, as muffled, as light.

Vill's hand on my arm startles me; it's as cold as the statue's was. 'You don't have to love Raen, though if he thinks you do so much the better. Keep your heart safe. Keep your heart pining for death and reunion with Aelius if that's what you truly desire. Keep that part of yourself inside but bury it.' He leaves me, returning to his seat. The sun burns away the coldness he left on my arm.

Raen's question reverberate through me: *are you going to kiss me for it?* How close I was to kissing him, but not for the book, no, for other reasons. And perhaps those reasons are worse. I move towards the curtains, out of the warmth and into the shadows, keeping my back to Vill so he can't read all this confusion in my eyes.

But I didn't kiss Raen. I mastered those reasons. In the gardens below, he steps into the shade of a tree as if he's trying to hide from me. He leans against it, his body long and large and darker than the shade. My palm strokes my neck.

'What is more important to you?' Vill asks. 'The throne or your virtue?'

'Aelius would forgive you,' Nessia says.

'Why are you taking his side?' I ask.

'I'm not taking anyone's side. I don't want you to be lonely. It's such a long life when you're lonely. Besides, I know you better than you know yourself, and you want him.'

I spin around, ready to confront her. My words won't come out, and she continues sewing as though she's said nothing. And there's Vill smirking at me like he's backed me into a corner. But there's a better way to get that book. I smile. If Raen is out there in the grounds, then he's not in his rooms and if he isn't in his rooms ... Grabbing Vill's map from the mantelpiece on my way, I rush out my room. I'll steal the book. It's what Niah from the village would do.

Chapter Thirty-Two

VILL WILL REGRET GIVING ME DIRECTIONS to Raen's room once I have the Aegnian book and he's proved wrong. The thought brings a smile. I must be in the most recently built section of the castle because the stone walls are gleaming white and the air is as crisp as an apple. The windows have coloured glass and, through them, the sunlight projects coloured squares onto the white marble floor. I leap from one green square to another, playing a child's game all the way to Raen's door.

His room is so bright it's like stepping into a summer cloud, and it takes a moment for my eyes to adjust. Everything is white except for one pale-blue wall opposite the window. White furs tempt me to slip off my shoes so I can rub my toes over them as I head to the window. The stitching on the white curtains is exquisite, gold thread embroidered into intricate patterns of flowers and grasses. Propped up against the wall is a portrait of a girl. I kneel down for a better look. There's an awkwardness to her pose that suggests she's facing womanhood and she isn't quite sure she wants it. Her forehead is high and wide, and her skin is so pale it seems an omission by the painter rather than a true representation or an artistic choice. On her head, hiding her hair, is an arched contraption, and that is where colour is concentrated, the gold and jewels on it drowning out her features. Around her neck, suspended from a chain of pearls, is a small E.

So this is Eldini, the princess on her way. Poor thing to already be receiving so little reverence from her potential husband. Beshanie and Nilola are right: she looks like a timid mouse. I'll not need to turn Raen away from her, and there will be no children from that marriage.

I scan my surroundings for a place where Raen might have hidden the book. In one corner is a laburnum table with two drawers that have goldfinches for handles and a single scuffed goblet on top. Up close, the goblet is missing a gem, leaving an etched snail without a home, and it looks out of place on the elegantly made table. The bird handles fit neatly into my palms as I ease the drawers open. The book isn't there. I head towards an ornate fireplace made of a white material I don't recognise. Beside the fire is a solitary laburnum chair and on the floor next to the comfy chair is an empty jug. I can imagine Raen sitting there, touching the words he can't read, but the book isn't there.

Turning around, I see a door carved with round suns and triangular rays. Raen's bedchamber. I pause before it, tracing the recurring pattern, and my fingertips tingle. He'd keep the book in there where it might help him sleep. I push the door. Inside smells so strongly of him it's like being pressed against his neck. I rush to open the window and let that fragrance out. From here the village is a brown splodge, too far away, too insignificant amongst the barren fields. Beyond that is Aralltir, green and dotted with white shapes that resemble gems on a velvet bodice. Taking a big breath of the untainted air, I move from the window.

Raen's bed is unmade, the white furs tumbling off and onto the floor. The drapes around it are pushed wide open, and one is hanging partially off. A pillow, embroidered with the same pattern as the door, appears to have been lobbed at a wall and left where it fell. If I were to lie down, place my head on his pillow, would I discover his nightmares? It's hard to believe they'd be possible in such a white and gold bed. His indentation has remained in the mattress. I turn away from it.

There's another table, plainer than the one in the dayroom. Its surface is scarred with knife marks that make letters but not words and show the darker heartwood beneath. I open the drawers and find twigs, a dried rose, a crown made of dead daisies. I take out the crown and let it dangle from my fingers. Crisp petals drop onto the floor. I made this for my prince, my love, my Aelius. He was always so eager for his own crown. Why does Raen have it? My hand closes around the crown. It can't withstand my clutch and the brittle daisies crunch into dust.

Can nothing precious survive in this castle? Opening my fist, I shake out the dust and kick the table. There's a clatter, a thud. A piece of wood almost falls onto my toes. I jump backwards. A louder thud has me crouching. By the gods, have I broken the table? As I pick up the wood, I see the Aegnian book. It's tanned to an autumnal colour, the fire motif stamped in copper on the front. The wood drops from my hand.

I plummet, dive forwards, and grab the book. My skirt bounces up, hits my back. The book's so heavy and large I need both hands to lift it up and into my lap. The cover is rough like the walls in the older part of the castle. Like dry skin. Is it true? My grandmother said the first book was bound in the skin of the first leader. I laugh. Tears come as I pull it to my heart, bend over it, kiss it. The book has a comforting warmth like a well-established hearth fire. The spine smells musty, of sage, of yew berries, of all the hands that have held it. I can feel the impressions of the First Queen, my grandmother, the long line of Aegnian rulers lingering within it. Closing my eyes, I inhale deeply.

A door bangs shut.

My eyelids snap open. My breath catches.

It must be the wind. No, I'd have felt such a strong gust, and I'm sure I didn't leave any doors open. Spirits? Raen? I should put the book back, hide, yet I can't. I pull it closer; I can't give it up now.

'Why do I keep finding you where you shouldn't be?' Raen's voice comes from his dayroom.

I struggle up, searching for a place to stash the book. He can't know I've found it; he'll hide it somewhere better if he knows. He can't. It's mine. I kiss the cover. I kick the fallen panel of wood under his bed and slide the book under with it. As I do so, a tiny square of parchment falls out. I snatch it up and shove it between my breasts, where it sears my skin.

'I wasn't stupid enough to leave the book out where you'd find it.' He sounds amused rather than angry.

Why is he taking so long? Is he giving me enough time to deceive him; does he want to be deceived? I check my reflection in his full-length mirror. My cheeks are flushed with excitement. My eyes are glinting like the flash of a dragonfly's wing in sunlight. I struggle to force my features into a bored expression as I try to invent a reason to be here, but I can't think. The only thing coming to my mind is Vill's salacious suggestion and it's making my skin heat. I rest my palm against my cheek, and the book's perfume is still on me: must, sage. Can I do it for the book? No. I'll say I came to thank him for last night, distract him somehow, and then later, Nessia can get the book.

When he enters the room, I'm standing there steady and composed. He's so vivid in this white room: his skin that honey colour, his hair deep brown and mahogany, the green of his tunic enhancing the dots in his irises. The sight has my lie slipping from my mind, and the smile flitting across my face is genuine. He leans against the door.

'You left this morning before I woke up,' I say.

His gaze lingers over me. I'm as out of my depth as I was in that village river with water above, water below, and no way of knowing which way was up. Nessia isn't here to save me this time. The note digs a sharp corner into my left breast, and I almost press my hand against it.

'I wanted to say thank you,' I say.

'You never say thank you for anything.' He's teasing and his lean becomes more languid as though he's sliding into the river after me.

'I wanted to see you.'

He raises his eyebrows and draws his bottom lip in, implying my smile has hinted at other things. As I watch his lip slide, slowly and smoothly, out, his question echoes in my head: *will you kiss me for it?* And I wonder if he's remembering it, too.

'Did you?' he asks.

My gaze lowers to the floor because I don't want him to see that I lied. Why? I don't know. It's this room. It's being where he sleeps ... where he doesn't sleep, where he's bothered by nightmares he won't share with me.

The sound of him moving draws my attention. His hands have risen to touch the top of the door frame, and his shoulders fill it. He waits, smiling smugly as if he thinks I want to go over there, trace the outline of his body and squeeze those muscles extending out and up. I can't move. His tunic has risen to the waist of his breeches and each breath he takes teases that it might rise higher. Something about my appearance seems to be mesmerising him. What does he see? I glance in the mirror and wish I hadn't because what I see is a face euphoric, eyes blazing green.

My breath catches as he pushes off the door frame like a man giving himself up to a river. Do it because you want to, Nessia said. Do it for power, Vill said. Raen asked, would I kiss him for it, more? Now I've held that book, now he's advancing with such slow grace ... *Do it for the book.* The piece of parchment jabs me and I shiver. I can do it. It's a bargain, nothing more than a bargain, and women have been making such bargains since the beginning of time. Lust is not love.

He holds out his hand, like he's asking me to dance. We're just going to dance, that is all. We've danced before. We've also mated before, but I'll not think about that. Our fingertips touch. Our palms touch. His fingers ease between mine, curl, press my knuckles. He brings them to his lips. 'I'm glad you're here,' he says onto my hand.

His castle scent, his village scent, and the sun from his walk are on his skin. Will the taste be on his lips? His head rises from my hands, gaze lingering on my lips. I can't stop my tongue from moistening them, preparing them. I can't stop them pursing.

His first kiss is hard and closed-mouthed, perhaps punishing me for saying no in the library. More come, their greediness almost sending me staggering backwards but I meet the force of each one and open my mouth to demand more from him. His hands slide through my hair and I grab them, tighter and tighter, as his tongue rouses waves of heat through me. He nips me as if he wants to keep my taste between his teeth and the thought of remaining on him makes my knees weak, makes my hips bob against him. My body remembers, pushing and arching against his, wanting to get through my cage to touch him.

I want to do it, feel him inside me, feel his muscles moving. Almost, I could do it. I can. I don't want to; it's too much like drowning. My hands keep exploring the shape of his features, though: the square jawline, the ridge of his cheekbones, the jut of his nose.

'Niah.'

My name reminds me who I am. His lips lower to my neck. I'm dizzy from his kisses, dizzy from the sun, and this room with its confusing whiteness. A silver glint hits my eyes. My fingers are gritty with the dust of the daisy crown.

'No.' I shove him with all the force I can muster.

'No?'

The glint moves and I see what caused it: Aelius's sword. My neck burns from Raen's lips and I can't help rubbing the skin, making it worse. Last time I saw that sword was in my home, and it had been bloody and muddy. 'Why? Why do you have it? It's not yours.' The hilt had been sticky and dark from Aelius's handprint. 'Why?'

He shrugs.

'You can't have it.' I lunge for the sword, expecting Raen to stop me but he doesn't. It's not as heavy as I remember—no wonder it couldn't save Aelius. I scoop it up, press the hilt against my heart. 'You went to my home.'

'And you are in my rooms, so we're even.'

But it's obvious why that daisy crown was in the drawer, why I was so ... overcome. These are not Raen's rooms. They've been decorated for a sun prince, not this earthy one; they are a sky for Aelius to reign in. How did I not realise this earlier?

'Are you collecting all his things?'

He doesn't answer. He doesn't need to—of course he is. He told me he would. As if he's ashamed, he breaks eye contact. Then he must spot the book or the wood peeking out from under the bed, Aelius's bed, because he bristles. 'That explains it. Did you really think I'd give you the book in payment? That wasn't a serious offer yesterday.' His voice is as stern and flat as it was when we were under the yew. 'I've never paid my women before, and I don't intend to start now.'

'You're disgusting. You're a ... I wouldn't.' I back out of the room where my love slept, where he dreamt of me, us, our future. 'I couldn't ... with you.'

'Yet you were going to.'

'I wasn't. How dare you ... I love Aelius ... you, you don't know what love is.'

'If that is love, then no, I don't.' He slams his bedchamber door behind me and then I hear something hit it.

Chapter Thirty-Three

'WHERE DID YOU GET THAT?' Nessia stops sweeping the floor and rests on the broom.

I've dragged the sword to my rooms, the blade screeching along the floor and drawing the servants' attention. Though it's been cleaned meticulously, I can't help seeing it as it was on the battlefield, covered in blood and mud, dropped beside my love. Why did I bring it here? Death. I toss the sword across the floor. Useless thing, unable to save Aelius. I scowl at it, shining there like it's a thing of beauty and something to be proud of.

'Raen had it.' I wipe the back of my hand across my mouth. My lips feel bruised.

'So that's where you went. I can't see the book, though. You didn't get it?'

'No, but I got something else.' Outwitting him should make me happy, but it doesn't feel like a victory.

'Oh?'

I try to jam my fingers down the bodice of my dress only it's too tight. I wiggle, jump up and down. The note doesn't move.

'What are you doing?' She laughs as I struggle with my cage and dress, yanking and pulling. The material tears.

'Help me.'

She's too slow, and I dance under her hands like a dog desperate to hunt, until I'm finally standing there in my undergarments and the cages are lopsided on the floor. I search around me, lifting my feet.

'That it?' she asks as I pluck up the folded square of parchment.

I hold it between my index finger and thumb. 'Something in the book.'

She locks my door, grinning, and we sneak off to my bedchamber where we sit cross-legged on the floor. The stone is a welcomed chill after the heat of Raen's kisses. We look at the tiny, tight square in my lap, then each other, and in Nessia's expression I find my exhilaration reflected. My heart's beating as fast as a horse galloping into battle.

'It fell out,' I say.

'What is it?'

I shake my head. The parchment's so small, folded in, and in, and in on itself to make sure its secrets are well hidden. I lick my dry lips. 'Do you think she meant this will help me? Not the book itself, but this?'

'You won't know if you don't open it.'

She's right. I pick it up. I peel back one corner, then another, and another until the parchment is open, the creases deep and trying to close in on each other again. Here is my language. The letters my grandmother had me writing in the dirt with a stick. These ones will not be blown away by the wind. These ones will not be drowned by the rain. They're more elegant, more glorious than my scratchings ever were. Nessia puts her weight on my knee as she leans closer. My finger hovers over the Aegnian words, fearful of spoiling them. They flow into each other, and they curve with the same grace as a dandelion seed caught by a breeze. The parchment is thick and rough, and when I bring it closer, it carries the fragrance of sage and lavender with it. My vision is so blurred with happy tears I can barely make out what the letters say.

'I never thought ...' I cough to clear my throat. 'When Onnachild burnt the books, I never thought I'd ever see ... words ... Do you think Grandmother knew about it?'

Nessia rests her chin on my shoulder. She's squinting. 'Possibly. What is it listing? Offerings?'

'I think so. It doesn't say what for.' I sniff back my tears. 'Just to offer these to the gods for the covenant, and that it must be done in the castle.' A familiar charge prickles my finger when I touch the neat writing. 'Maybe Mantona will know.'

Nessia nods. 'What does that say?' She points at a word.

'Wormwood,' I whisper. 'Ivy.' I can't read the last item. 'What?'

Nessia bends nearer. 'Nerium ol ...' She takes it from me, brings it closer to her eyes, then further away. There's writing on the other side:

scrawled, hurried words. 'Oleander?' She passes it back.

I flip the list over to that messy writing. Although the letters are bigger, they are harder to read, and the ink is slightly smudged. There's no mistaking that it's a letter: a love letter. A scrawled signature in one corner: Iansa. The First Queen's name. I drop it.

Nessia picks up the parchment and nudges my shaking hand with it. 'If she didn't want you to read it, she'd have said so.'

We both stare at the First Queen's dressing table as if she's there writing this very letter, her dark hair falling around her as she hunches over the parchment.

'You're right.' There's a tremor in my voice. I cough again before starting to read it out loud so Nessia can shoulder this secret with me. *Beloved, how hard these days and nights are without you here. I only exist until I'm with you again.'* I pause, look at Nessia. She nods to encourage me, though her face has blanched. My eyes trail further down the page, captivated. Surely the First Queen can't have meant for me to see this?

Nessia taps the parchment, and I continue reading to her. *'He knows, and I fear we have so few days and nights left to spend with each other. A friend has given me details for a covenant and all being well, the gods will help us. If you get this letter, it's too late for me. I list the offerings on the other side for you, my darling. You must save yourself. And remember, he hasn't won. He can't win because I have loved you with all my life and you have loved me nobly, bravely, and beautifully. Your Iansa.'*

I stare at Nessia. Her mouth is open but she doesn't speak. Was Onnachild right and his queen was adulterous? All those stillborn children, all those miscarriages ... and then Raen. Is he not Onnachild's? Without taking my eyes off Nessia, I turn over the letter. We must forget what it says despite those words burning through my head. Nessia nods. Her sweaty hand covers mine.

Together we recite the list, again and again, to commit the items to memory. The repetition builds a soothing rhythm. Everything will be fine. I'll create the covenant and somehow ... what did the First Queen say when I called her? Something to help with all of my problems, she said. All my problems: Raen, Ammi, the battle, Onnachild. Nessia and I smile at each other. Giggle.

The sound of footsteps outside makes me jump. It'll be Melody coming so we can pretend to pray before I get ready for the Great Hall. 'I can't go,' I whisper. The loving words from the letter rush into my mind. 'I can't see Raen. What if he realises I have this?'

'You have to or people might think something's wrong. I'll get the things on the list.' Nessia puts her finger to her lips, bidding me to be quiet. She struggles to her feet, groaning.

As she goes to unlock my doors, I refold the parchment, stash it between my breasts. I'll find it a permanent hiding place later. I should probably burn it, but these are the only Aegnian words I have and I'm not ready to give them up yet. They nestle against my skin and I pat them.

'Why is there a sword in your room?' Melody asks.

In the Great Hall, I can't stop fidgeting. My fingers toy with my knife, the stitching around my sleeves, and my heels tap on the floor. I want to see those Aegnian words again. I want to smell the parchment again.

'Quiet,' Beshanie snaps.

I still my feet.

'Is there something you want to tell us?' Nilola asks.

My hand rises towards my chest where the letter digs in, but I manage to stop in time and instead fluff up the feather trim on my bodice. The parchment doesn't feel safe, not when I'm amongst the advisers, Onnachild, and Raen. What would happen if they saw the letter? Would Onnachild banish Raen again? Thank the gods neither of them can read the old language. But I should want Raen banished, shouldn't I?

'Niah.' Beshanie slaps my arm.

'Sorry. I'm ... I'm a little sad,' I say, though I'm anything but this.

'Gavin?' Nilola asks.

I nod.

Beshanie smiles. 'He's unaffected.'

The three of us peer up at the top table where he's sitting talking to Raen. Whatever Gavin thought of Raen appears to have changed as they are laughing together like old friends. He'll be telling his sister good things about Raen now. It doesn't matter. Everything will soon be different. Once I've made the offering, created the covenant, the gods will make it so. They must. These trays full of food will go to the village where they belong, and these rings on my fingers will no longer weigh down my hands.

'When will that princess get here?' Nilola asks Beshanie.

'Soon, Vill said.'

If I shared the letter would it stop the marriage? Eldini? Would she refuse Raen, a man with a question over his parentage? The letter isn't proof enough, though, is it? Not when there are traces of Onnachild in Raen's jaw, his bulk, his nose despite Onnachild's having been broken several times. Even the way Raen carries himself when he's angry is similar. My gaze moves to Onnachild, a conqueror with the evidence of those fights in his battered face and imposing presence.

Did the First Queen ever love him? Maybe when they were younger she'd been enthralled by the exoticness of the foreign invader and the physicality of the noble bear. Perhaps she'd been flattered when his arrogant stare had settled on her. She can't want me to expose her secret, knowing the pain doing so will cause Raen. He'll be reminded of her murder, supposedly justified by Onnachild's accusations of infidelity, and his subsequent banishment and illegitimacy. He'll be that little boy hiding, terrified, and unable to act again. Yet, Raen has things that don't belong to him: my love's rooms, my kisses. I wipe my mouth, and the gesture calls his attention to me. He frowns and then chuckles at something Gavin has said.

'Where are you going?' Beshanie asks, staring up at me as I rise from my seat.

'Mantona,' I say. 'I must speak to her.'

'Sit down,' Nilola hisses. 'It wouldn't look right.'

'We can help,' Beshanie says, slyly.

'Vill advised me to, that she might still have some influence with Onnachild, to help with Gavin,' I lie quickly.

Across the room, Mantona looks forlorn and doesn't realise the man next to her is trying to get her attention. I push out my chest as I walk over to her so the folded parchment stays secure. She seems surprised when I sit beside her, taking in my appearance as if I'm different from how she remembered me. Her eyes are skittish, going from my nose to my cheeks, to the jewels around my neck, everywhere but meeting mine.

I lean closer to her. 'I have it.'

'The book?'

'No, something else. The thing in it. The list. Is that what I was meant to find? What does it do?'

She focuses on the dancers, trying to pretend not to care but her hand has clasped her throat. 'I don't know. I don't remember. A binding ... something about letting out or calling ... Don't do it.'

'Why?'

She picks at a chunk of greasy bread left on the table, ripping it into shreds that settle like webs. 'I shouldn't have told you about it. She had reservations. There must have been a reason.'

'She directed me to it, so that reason can't be valid now.'

'Or maybe she's just angrier? The dead don't always play fair, you know that.' She wipes her fingers on the tablecloth, leaving a translucent stain, and she frowns at it, seemingly puzzled by its appearance.

'The other side—'

'I don't want to hear it.' She's up, gone, chasing after a merchant who has a jolting step and a leaning wig.

She does know. Raen said she wasn't a friend. Is that why Onnachild gifted her the First Queen's ring, for telling him the letter's secret? It's hard to believe such a thing of Mantona, as she dances with the merchant, because she looks so innocuous. Her gaze lingers towards Onnachild, who is arguing with a man almost as large as he is.

Gavin swoops down beside me, asks me to dance with a bashfulness so endearing I can't say no. His dancing is more stilted than normal, his touch a little heavier, and his focus remains over my shoulder. The third time he steps on my toes, he speaks. 'Sorry. I'm sorry.'

For tonight I can be kind; after all, once the battle is prevented he'll leave, not needed, and his sister will be saved from marrying a man who can't love her, can't love anyone. 'Would you tell me what is bothering you?'

'There's just a lot to plan.' He sighs. 'Everyone has an opinion on what we should do once my father's men get here and wants to bend my ear. It's a little ... a lot of responsibility.' He peeps at me. 'Perhaps if I please the King, when we win he'll allow us to ...' He blushes, and the colour makes his eyebrows seem whiter.

'Perhaps.' My smile deepens his blush.

'I shouldn't bore you,' he says. 'Not by talking about battles and ...'

'I'll try and be interested if that is what you wish to talk about,' I say. 'You shouldn't miss out on such a thrilling topic because you've been sweet enough to dance with me.'

I spot Raen moving amongst the tables, heading towards Nilola. Let her have him.

'I'd rather ...' Gavin's voice trails off into a whisper, making it hard to hear him over the music and the Maidens' singing. His hand tentatively presses into the curve of my waist so I presume his speech is affectionate; if I keep smiling, he won't realise I'm not paying attention.

Raen's bending over to talk to Nilola. She's playing with the gems around her neckline, rubbing them between her fingers. She points towards me, and Raen turns. The inflexion of Gavin's voice tells me I should laugh so I do. My breathing speeds in response to the anger in Raen's face. I'm trapped here, not because of Gavin, but because of Raen. The letter stabs my chest with each breath I take, and the words feel like they're branding my skin. The urge to tell him, to share this secret with him is overwhelming and confusing. What would his expression be if I were to read the words to him? *I only exist until I see you again.*

'Please ...' I say. 'I need to ...'

'Of course.' Gavin stops suddenly, and I bang into him. The concern on his face is adorable, and he guides me back to the tables with a gentleness that makes me feel precious. I rather enjoy the feeling so I let myself indulge the fantasy of running away from everything with him, of living a quiet life somewhere else. He pours a glass of wine and holds it up for me.

'I think,' I say, 'that you should leave me. Onnachild wouldn't approve.'

'I ... yes, he ...' His skin pinkens again.

Maybe I shouldn't have reminded him but I need to get away from the Great Hall, from Raen's scrutiny, and from this fake version of myself. I want to hide this note and the potential hurt it could cause. Gavin nods. He casts a wistful glance over his shoulder as he returns to the top table where Onnachild is lively, singing along with the Maidens and gesturing for more wine. Vill is nowhere to be seen, and Raen's giving his full attention to Nilola's hand as it toys with her jewels. Only the advisers seem suspicious, their grey gaze following me as I leave the room.

Nessia is already back from the village and waiting for me in my rooms.

Her face is wind-chapped and smeared with mud as it always used to be. There's a scratch across her cheek and a twinkle in her eyes. At her feet is a full cloth bundle tied in on itself.

'All done,' she says.

'Everything?'

'Everything. Every last thing.'

I sit on the floor, untie the bag, and watch it fall open. With reverence, I lay out each item. 'What if it's the letter, the love letter, or something else, something written in the actual book that is the key and not this?' I gesture at the plants with mud still clinging to their roots. The ivy is a tangled mass of green and white.

'Maybe. But she directed you to the book, and there you found the list.'

'We don't know what this will do.'

'Don't worry, she wouldn't wish you harm.'

I nod but Mantona's warning returns: *the dead don't always play fair.* What other options do I have? I can't share that love letter, and Raen will make sure I don't get the book. I must trust the First Queen and this list. 'And Melody, did she get the hair?'

'Yes.' Nessia skids off into my bedchamber. My fingers stroke the wormwood leaves as I wait. She returns with a small wooden box. Inside is a fluff of Onnachild's hair. She grimaces as she places the tuft beside the ivy.

'I'm impressed,' I say.

Tonight, then. It must be tonight. But I'm not sure if I'm ready. The churning through my stomach could be excitement or fear. I've never tried to create a covenant with the gods before. My grandmother taught me the ritual, making me tell her the steps again and again until I could say them backwards and in both languages, but I never knew what to offer for what desired outcome; she didn't have time to teach me that. And now. Here. I gulp. I have a list, and a chance to prove my place in that long line of powerful women. But, to do so in the castle ... so close to Onnachild ... the advisers. It must be here, though, on that the parchment is clear.

With trepidation, I nod at Nessia to start the preparations. She orders a bath for me. Hopefully, the water will be as purifying as a running river. The servants trundle through my room with the tub and buckets of water. One I'm sure is the hag's son. Is that a good omen or not? He doesn't linger long enough for me to question him or point him out to Nessia.

The perfume of roses fills the room. We chase it away by burning sage and scooping out the petals, which we toss through an open window. As I watch the petals fall, I ask Nessia about the servant. 'Do you remember the hag's boy? Didn't he die?'

'Timmon. He has a grave but I don't think a body was ever found. She said he'd been carried away by a set of grey wolves in the night. Why?'

'No reason.' I shake my head and come away from the window, making sure to close it.

We hide the note under my mattress for want of a better hiding place. My gaze is drawn to the hole in the door, and I drop onto my bed, remembering Raen saying he hid there when they came for the First Queen. Here I am doing what she didn't have time to do. What was it she said? The words won't come. Instead, *these days and nights without you* repeat. I shiver as if her spirit whispered them in my ear. Nessia puts her arm around my shoulder.

'Ready?' she asks.

'I have to be.'

She helps me wash off the day, the castle, this pretend me. Her humming is normally a comfort, but there's an unnerving wobble to it. I draw my knees up, rest my chin on them and stare out at the moon, low tonight and peeking in the window. The colours of fire are in it. A bird is trilling outside, and the sound goes right through me. Must the covenant really be done tonight?

Meeting the gods in one of my expensive and fancy castle dresses seems wrong so I put on one of Nessia's. It's too large for me, but the plain brown fabric is comforting because her scent is in it and it reminds me of the village. She brushes my hair, settling it over my shoulders where it dampens my dress.

'What if I can't do it? What if they don't come?' I grip her hand.

Nessia spurts a brief chortle, shakes her head, and pats my knee. Like me, she was taught all Aegnian women can call the gods, a skill inherited with our green eyes. It's why Onnachild killed them. Perhaps the gods won't recognise me, though? I touch my face, filled out from food and easy living. It doesn't feel like my face anymore.

'What if Vill's right? What if it doesn't stop the battle, help me and Ammi? What if it's better to live in hope than discover—'

'Then we'll have lost nothing.'

'And risked everything. If Onnachild finds out ...'

'He won't.'

I'm not sure how she can guarantee that but I nod and hope she is right. She arranges the chairs into a semi-circle around me and they loom ominously. Nessia leaves, locks the door behind her. She's promised to keep watch outside until I call for her. The fire heats my face as I kneel before it but there's an icy chill trailing down my spine. I'm alone, and the shadows in the room have never been so formidable. I can do this. It's now or never.

Chapter Thirty-Four

I gulp. I take a deep breath. I clear my throat before starting the chant my grandmother taught me. The words ease out the tightness in my chest, settle my stomach, and calm my heart. A faint smile comes to my lips as I imagine my grandmother and the First Queen beside me. I lower my forehead to the stone floor and kiss the ground my ancestors walked on. Then, with a whisper that feeds the flames, I pray to each god—once, twice, three times. Their excitement surges through the red, orange, yellow to fill me. They're remembered; they're needed. They want to know what I've brought for them so I scoop up the plants and feed them one by one into the heart of the fire. It spits, flashes, puffs out acrid-smelling smoke that makes me cough. Onnachild's hair singes up into itself. Its smell is the worst, getting to the back of my throat with a taste that makes me gag.

Flames twist, dart, ebb, spurt onto the stone floor where they fizzle and fade. The heart of the fire is green. The edges of the flames are lilac. It's mesmerising and majestic how the colours dance together. I throw a spider into the centre. There are only my words left to give, words of humility, words of want. I clear my throat before speaking.

'Gods of Adfyr, I make this ... Like those who came before me, I give this offering to request ... a covenant ...' I take a deep breath, try to concentrate, but my grandmother's words won't come back to me. The harder I try the more evasive they are. 'Please. You have to help me. I don't know if this is right ... if these are the right offerings or words or ... There's no one to tell me ... Please, stop Onnachild, the battle. Please, protect the villagers. Help me, please.' My garbled words entice the flames higher, brighter, out.

In the fire's heart, I see history: Onnachild on his black horse trailing death like a miasmic thundercloud, yew trees cut and burnt, starvation-swelled bellies, necks red and raw from the noose, faces dripping maggots from where noses and eyes should be. Charred fingers stretch out from the fire, knuckles glowing like embers. The dead claw at the floor, nails grating. I cover my ears against the piercing sound. They're desperate to be saved, to be returned into the living world, and if not that then they'll take the living for company, for always. I back away, I can't help myself. The tang of shallow graves comes into the room as pungent as shit. I retch. On and on I repeat my plea, louder and louder.

The room blooms into light. I clap like a child to see the gods gathered in the fire. My heart swells. *Help me. Please help me.* I shuffle closer until their impressions are all I see: a goat with the parts of a man, a snake with three hungry heads, a phoenix with feathers aflame, a woman of smoke with features like mine. More and more: feathers, scales, flesh, fur. Bursting out the fire, they come. Dainty feet. Heavy feet. Feet that have more in common with animals than humans. They scurry. They slither. They knock past me.

Fat bees thrum, having been spat out from the fire, and they slam together. Their stingers rain down like burning stars. One lands on my cheek. I swat at the pain. Smoke curls from beneath chairs as the wood ignites under their hot hands. Others thrust their faces at mine, curious to see who has called them. Eyes flash every shade of green: mint, emerald, sage, moss. Pupils slit. Eyelids with a sheen like slugs. Hot, so hot that my body streams with sweat, dampening the stone beneath me. My eyes smart. The gods don't understand, don't want to understand why they're being asked to protect the village when it abandoned them for a new god, killed their chosen people. The gods are jealous.

They swell, taller, wider until they block out the light of the moon and the light of the fire. In the blackness, I feel them tearing at my clothes, leaving searing prints. My skin bubbles and the smell of it burning fills the room. I bite my hand to stop from screaming out. I smack my dress but the flames keep galloping up, up, and up. A god laughs at me, a sound like a mountain falling. I wet myself; the scent's sweet and malty. They drag me across it. They raise me up only to drop me when they're distracted. There's a cracking sound and I don't know if it comes from me or the fire or the walls.

They flash bright green, blinding me. I cover my head as they throw burning furniture from wall to wall. The door rattles, key clattering in the lock. Nessia yells my name, banging on the door. I whisper love to the gods from my parched lips but it doesn't work because there's fear in my voice. I tremble there on the floor, sobbing for my grandmother.

The god of love, a small boy covered in brown fur, sulks in a corner. His body is burning a dark patch into the wood. I pray to him, ask for his help, but he can't control the others. *This is not what I wanted. Not what I meant.* They will eat this room, this castle if they can, me. They bustle against me: sharp fur, moist scales. Cruel words are spat at me from forked tongues, from burning mouths, from mouths that smell of decay, because I forgot them. I didn't. I couldn't. I've been playing, lying. Surely they understand that.

The scent of bluebells wafts into the room, heady and calming. I crawl towards it. There, hidden in the fire, peeping around a white-hot log is the god of peace. He flutters out his orange fur, so soft, so welcoming, and a breeze cavorts across my cheeks. His eyes are the same green as mine. His lashes are thick and red-tipped. He tells me he understands. I sob at his mercy. He says they'll do what I want if I promise ... *Anything. I promise anything.* This land theirs again. Sacrifice. Retribution. *Anything. Anything.* I nod and nod at him. His raspy voice calls the other gods back to the fire, and they go meekly. The temperature drops, colder than winter, colder than ice. I feel a hand on my shoulder before a piece of thick ash falls onto the stone floor and scatters.

The door slamming shut brings me around. I gasp for breath. It hurts my throat. Melody screams. Hearing her has my heart hammering. 'The advisers?' I croak, attempting to rise onto my hands and knees.

'What happened?' Nessia asks. 'By my gods, what happened?' She's down beside me, kissing my cheek, over and over. 'My sweetheart, Niah, I couldn't get in. I tried.' Her tears are cooling my face and seeing them makes me want to cry, too, but there's no moisture left in my sore eyes.

'The Judging Room.' Melody's voice is a trill. 'With Onnachild, telling off Beshanie they were. The advisers. They—'

'Shush,' I blurt out. Something has remained in the room. Something insidious. As I twist to find it, my calves cramp and my toes jerk out of place. I wheeze as I double over against the shooting pain. Melody crosses herself. There's someone by the window casting a dark shadow across the floor that moves as no shadow can. The person has no features. It swings out the window, leaving a trail of mould on the sill. I shriek; I can't help myself. Smoke comes out of my mouth. Am I still on fire? How can I be when I'm so cold my teeth are chattering? I raise my hand to my forehead, stop when I see my fingers are a jutting mess like those that came from the fire. My skin is puckered; I've aged centuries. I hold my hand out to Nessia, shaking. She covers it with her own warm one. Melody looks like she might throw up, but still, she manages to kneel beside me and take my feet in her hands. The heat of her fingers hurts more than her easing my toes back into place.

The furniture is either on its side or broken. Chairs have been smashed, the pieces black and gnawed, and scattered across the room. One leg has been stabbed into the wall. There are muddy prints on the floor: hooves, feet, and paws. There are thick smears where tails were dragged. Are Melody and Nessia pretending not to notice these things to avoid scaring me or scaring themselves?

'They came.' The words make me cough and splutter.

'They came.' Nessia wipes away her tears with the bottom of her dress.

'What happened?' Melody whispers. Her headdress crashes to the floor, making me cry out at Nessia.

'Shush, shush.' Nessia frowns and her wrinkles deepen as she gathers

273

me into her lap.

'I'm scared,' Melody says.

'Stop doing that,' Nessia snaps.

I try to see what Melody is doing but my neck cricks, sending stinging shards down my body. I want Nessia to say it'll be fine but she doesn't. She can't meet my eye, and she's shaking, too.

'I'm fine,' I say in Aegnian, and my voice has more of me in it. I can even manage a deep breath. The pain is ebbing away like snow in sunshine. My blisters have gone without leaving a mark. 'They were angry, but they will help us.'

'Angry? Why would—' Nessia starts.

'Who? Why?' Melody interrupts. 'I don't understand. I don't think I want to understand.'

'Stop your wittering and get Niah some food,' Nessia says, 'some wine.'

Melody sprints from the room, kicking her headdress across the floor in her desperation to be gone from these confusing things. Nessia helps me to my feet, taking all my weight, and waits patiently while my limbs pop into their sockets. All the solid objects in the room become blurs of light and shade as she leads me towards the only remaining chair. I flop into it, my arms and legs splayed.

My hand hovers near my face; I'm too scared to touch it. She tries to smile as she strokes my cheeks like she used to do when the village children upset me. The tenderness in her eyes is as calming as it was then. I want to believe she can make everything all right, that as long as I have her I'm safe, but the gods' viciousness petrified me, still petrifies me when I catch sight of the bruises across my shoulders.

'It is done now,' I say, trying to reassure myself, but I don't know exactly what it is I've done.

Chapter Thirty-Five

I TAKE A MOMENT TO CATCH MY BREATH before heading into the Great Hall. The noise coming through the open door is deafening and disorientating after the quiet of my rooms. It's been five nights since I called the gods and I've still not fully recovered. Just walking here has tired me out and my back is already aching. Perhaps I should have stayed in bed as Nessia recommended, only Vill said any longer would raise suspicion. Truthfully, I'm glad to leave my rooms and be away from whatever is lingering there. I'm also curious to see what the gods have done.

Ascelin comes to the door, almost shuts it before he notices me there. I force myself into my castle pose to hide my nerves. There's nothing in my appearance that should give away what I've done. I've chosen a midnight-blue dress to help me blend into the shadows, and the long sleeves and high neck cover the marks on my body. Nessia has been dabbing an ointment over them to aid the healing but the rub of the dress against my skin still smarts. The gash on my forehead, which cuts across the dent made by the villagers, has been concealed with a mixture of ointment and ground herbs. All I need to do is walk in without limping. Though it pains me, I sail past Ascelin, only gritting my teeth once I'm near my place at the table.

'Careful,' Beshanie snaps when I flop into my seat.

'We've missed you.' Nilola squints at my face. If she spots anything unusual, she doesn't say so.

I don't know what I was expecting the gods to do but everything is the same: the blond wigs, the extravagant clothes, the fat men squashed up against the tables, candlelight glinting off jewels. No one seems to have moved since my last night here. Nilola's dressed in pink, and I can't remember if she was last time I was here or whether that was Beshanie. The man next to her, with cheeks like glazed gammon, is talking loudly to an older man in a tunic that's too tight for him. 'We need to be careful with timing. These foreigners are sneaky bastards. I'm sure the King understands that time is of the essence. Don't you agree?'

I lean across Beshanie to question the men. 'When? How long until the battle?' They don't answer me and continue talking to each other but in quieter voices. I slump back into my seat.

'Seven days after the wedding,' Beshanie says.

'And when is the wedding?' I ask.

'As soon as possible, according to Perkin.'

'If Raen accepts,' Nilola says. 'Nothing has been agreed yet.'

'How long until she gets here?' I ask.

Nilola turns towards the top table, preening. Raen and Onnachild enter together and so we all stand. Has something been decided or smoothed over? It must have been for them to be entering together. Onnachild gestures for everyone to sit. He seems amused. He looks strong and kingly, untouched.

'Poor Vill,' Nilola whispers. 'I've never seen him look less than perfect, and with all these new men coming, well, he must be worried.'

'No one will match Vill for handsomeness,' Beshanie says.

'If they carry on working him like this—'

'No one will match Vill for handsomeness,' Beshanie repeats, firmer this time.

I hadn't even noticed him. To me, he seems the same: perfectly cool and bored as he surveys the room from his seat. His tunic is a little creased around the shoulders, that's all.

As servants appear with their silver trays, Onnachild starts speaking. I can't concentrate on his words. The patterns the servants create as candlelight rebounds off their silver trays makes me dizzy and my eyelids flicker. Beshanie nudges me, and I'm refocusing, listening to Onnachild telling us what is planned for Eldini's arrival: dancers, exotic birds, feasts, poets, and minstrels. Raen sits proudly, a strange smile on his face as Onnachild leads everyone into a high-spirited clap, me included though I don't know why we're clapping. Where are the gods? They said they'd help, yet the battle is still going ahead, Raen and Onnachild seem closer, and Eldini is still on her way. The gods have done nothing. Nothing except hurt me. My forehead itches. I sit on my hands to stop myself from scratching it.

'That princess better appreciate all this effort,' Beshanie moans to me. 'You should be thankful you've been ill and not forced to sit through these tedious displays of talentless morons desperate to be chosen to perform for that mouse.'

'The juggler dropped his club on Aelius's plate the other day—broke it. I don't need to say where he is now,' Nilola says.

There's the clanking of tin on tin and everyone turns towards the noise coming from the gardens. Tall, slender women are entering the room. They're dressed in a translucent material slashed from foot to waist, from wrist to armpit, and black veils weighted down with gold coins cover their faces. There's a faint yellow hue to their skin. Their bare feet patter against the stone floor. A man with a long, black moustache follows behind, banging a steady beat on a copper drum. Nilola laughs at him. A merchant brays from further down the table. The man opposite me falls off his seat, making his companions snigger and spill wine. Beshanie tuts and looks bored.

The dancers remain poised, waiting in the centre of the room, with their arms and hands held in poses of beckoning. The drummer speeds up, gargling and wailing in a tuneful call to the dancers. A foot moves. A hand moves. Flesh peeps out. They pirouette as one. I hear banging, a fist against glass. I spin around too quickly and everything blurs: the reflected candlelight, the moonlight, the coloured dresses, the blond hair, the pale skin. Coming into focus is a village girl, short and darker than me. Her swollen belly presses against the glass. She's not pretty like the dancers, in her stained beige smock, hastily slashed. They don't hear her.

I look around; no one else is acknowledging her. Not Mantona. Not even Raen turns towards her. She joins and copies the dancers, leaving dirty footprints on the floor. Her hips, her knees, and her elbows jut through the rips of her dress while she jerks out of time. Drool shines her chin, dribbling from her slack mouth. Her stringy hair is stuck to her head.

Everyone is clapping along with the music, encouraging the dancers but no one encourages her. Not even the servants who continue winding their way around the tables with trays of food. The girl breathes out puffs of pale smoke, and it twines around the dancers, around the room, and settles down onto the food. I lean closer. The table digs into my waist. My elbow knocks over a goblet. The village girl has no eyes. She has no nose, just gaps. The drummer speeds up, as fast as my heart is pounding. The castle people are trying to keep up with the drum but they can't. Some men are trying to copy the dancers, mocking their hand movements and laughing. Others are trying to reach for the dancers' bare skin. The village girl has vanished.

I look for her, see the glass doors—night, clear, crisp night outside. Up, I bolt. My chair falls over, and Beshanie reprimands me. I rush out of the Great Hall, chasing after the village girl. She's not on the lawn. Her shadow isn't running amongst the ornamental trees. I slump against the wall, try to catch my breath. Nothing is out here. The wind cools my face, bringing with it the perfume of spring. My blood calms, and my heart returns to a steady beat. In the darkness there are no figures, only bright white stars twinkling far away.

Raen leans beside me, his shoulder almost touching mine. 'Is something wrong?'

'Did you see her?' I ask. 'The village girl? The spirit?'

He shakes his head.

'You really didn't see her?'

'There are enough spirits in here,' he taps his chest, 'without me seeing them in there.'

I'm not sure whether to believe him because there's such an odd expression on his face. It's a relief to have him here, though. If we couldn't be seen from the Great Hall, I'd grab his hand.

'Have we stopped arguing now?' he asks.

I can't remember what I was angry about. Something about a sword, Aelius, kisses. My head itches too much and my legs are too weak for me to care about that. The effort needed to stand here has me shaking.

'You're cold?' He touches my arm as if checking but the touch is too lingering. His hand is free of jewels tonight. That's a change. There are none around his neck or on his clothes either. He's dressed in a sombre dark green that's almost black in this light. It makes him look weary, like our argument is weighing on him still. I stumble into him, drawn by the dark smudges underneath his eyes, and the contact startles me.

'Niah?'

'I'll be fine,' I say more to reassure myself as a wave of dizziness hits me.

'You're pale.'

I wish he'd stop staring at my face. If anyone will notice the cut, it'll be him. I touch my hot forehead. It's damp, and I can't tell if it's from Nessia's concoction, my cold sweat or if it's bleeding again. The world is spinning, trees misplacing themselves into sky, and sky mimicking seas. Shadows tumble up, not down, not across but disappearing into themselves.

'You shouldn't be here,' he says.

I don't know where his voice comes from, only that his hand is on my arm and so I cling onto that. When he lifts me off the ground, I hold on tight to his neck. So tight. He's the only non-moving thing in the whole world. I press my head into the curve where his neck meets his shoulder. It fits so well.

He carries me out into the darkness, away from that music and the dancers. 'You've been up to something,' he says. 'And I don't think I'm going to like it, am I?'

I bounce against him with each step he takes, and I feel so light in his arms, not a burden at all. He stops at the servants' door, which must be too small for him to fit through but somehow he does, and then we're in the kitchens, assaulted with noise, wet heat, and food cooking. It's too much. A servant runs in front of us, opens the door to the hallway. Whatever I called from the fire is waiting here for us.

As Raen walks, there are additional footsteps, lighter than his. I check behind us and shush him so I can listen better. The footsteps continue along the floor, up the wall, across the ceiling.

'Can you hear that?' I whisper.

'Hear what?' He's too late, though, and the noise has gone. It doesn't mean that whatever is here has stopped following us, of that I'm certain. We carry on with only his footsteps echoing, and I drift out, resting on him.

Raen knocks on my door with his foot, jolting me back to the present. He can't go inside; he'll know. He'll notice everything that's different: chairs, a missing table, a broken panel, scorch marks we couldn't scrub away. And he'll ask. How much his mother taught him about Adfyrism and the gods, I have no way of knowing. He might guess about the covenant and if he does, maybe I'll be tempted to show him the parchment. I struggle to get out of his arms. 'Thank you. I'll be fine now.'

'I can't come in?'

'Someone might see you. They'd gossip.'

He doesn't seem to believe my reason, but he nods and lowers me to my feet. I don't want him to believe me because Nessia hasn't answered his banging and I can't bear to go in alone; something waits in there with its grave stench, with its awkward shadow that doesn't obey the sunlight or moonlight.

'Why are you scared? What have you done?' he asks.

'Nothing. I've done nothing.'

'I'm far too tired for this,' he mumbles as he squats down so we're eye to eye. He leans closer. His scent is compelling, all tree sap and autumn as though his village part is overcoming his castle part. He brushes a lock of hair from my forehead. I flinch when he touches my cut, stop his hand.

'What is that?' He snatches his finger away. There's a smear of cream and blood on it. 'Tell me.' His voice rises. 'What have you done?'

'If you weren't so scared to oppose your father—'

'Don't push me, Niah. What are you hiding?' His brow lowers, and there's a twitch in his jaw. We stare at each other. Him waiting for an answer and me waiting, just waiting, only I don't know what I'm waiting for. Then the waiting ends and he pushes the door open.

'You wouldn't help,' I say.

Raen ushers me in and shuts the door behind us. He looks around. There's nothing of that presence here. The room is full of a pale light because Nessia has forgotten to draw the curtains. It's warm but not stiflingly so. I sigh with relief; it's gone.

'The room looks different,' he says, pacing around.

This, this is what I was scared of. 'Does it?' My voice is too high.

'You know it does. These are not my mother's chairs.' He kneels in front of the fireplace. 'What is this?' He rolls back a new rug, placed to hide the soot marks on the floor. 'Charred?'

'Melody must have been clumsy.'

'Clumsy enough to have given you that cut, too? Maybe she needs to be taught how to be a better Maiden.'

'It's nothing.' The scabs on my arm itch. I scratch them without thinking, and the motion has him bolting up. He pushes at my sleeves. I grimace as he exposes the red and purple welts around my wrists.

'You can trust me,' he says.

'I can't. I can't trust anyone.'

'Who did this?'

There's a knock at the door. The village girl? That presence? I reach for the walls—they are solid, permanent. Raen's frowning at me but I don't care. My heart's pounding too fast. My head is spinning too much. I can taste smoke in the air.

'Why are you so skittish? It's only a servant. You've not eaten.'

'Yes ... I'm hungry.' My voice wobbles. 'I'll feel better once I've eaten.'

'Open the door,' Raen shouts.

It's the hag's boy, awkward and hesitant about coming in. He knows. He can feel it, the lingering presence of the dead, and if he can then why can't Raen?

'Please, set it down on the table,' Raen says.

'I ... Sir ... there is no table.'

'There. Are you incompetent?' Raen points towards the window where, normally, five days ago, there was a table and now there is nothing. He turns when the hag's boy just stands there. He scowls at the space. 'The floor will do just fine then.'

'Yes. As you say.' The boy glances in my direction before leaving, and he blanches.

I stumble towards the chair and the food. It'll make me feel better. This dizziness is only because I'm hungry and tired. If I'd eaten earlier, this wouldn't be happening. It's hunger, that's all it is. I'll stop shaking if I eat. Perhaps, after, I'll be able to sleep. It has been so long since I've slept. Maybe I can convince Raen to stay in case I have a nightmare again.

He sits at my feet and fills a plate for me. Concern is creating lines in his face. I rest my head against the chair, so soft and comforting.

Everything will be better once I've eaten. No, it will not be. There are footprints across the ceiling, tiny prints from door to window. But four days ago, we cleaned the room. We scrubbed it and the dirty water ran down our arms, and then we washed it again and again. There was nothing left. There was ... nothing. We couldn't rest until ... it was all ... gone.

I stand up. The plate careens to the floor, smashes. Raen shouts my name, but I don't answer. I climb onto the chair, stretch up, trying to reach those footprints. We must have missed them. How did we miss them? All three of us? The chair is swaying beneath me, its feet clattering on the stone. Am I swaying or is someone pushing me? More footprints appear, right before my eyes. Black like tar. A hand, cold, moist, bony, touches me.

'Raen?'

'Come to me.' He's holding out his arms. As I throw myself at him, the chair topples. A scream hurts my throat. It doesn't even sound like me. He keeps me up, gathered close to his chest. The window blows open, bounces off the wall. An angry wind bashes around the room. They're back. I can smell their mould. I can smell burning. They've come for me. I pray in Aegnian, words a jumbled burble that they must, surely, be able to understand. My cut bleeds.

'Niah?'

My throat is hoarse as I keep reciting my prayers to show them I remember. I'm Niah. I'm Aegnian. I'm from the village. *Please don't hurt me. Please don't take me. I want to live.* Their feet patter around the room. They can't find their way out. A tail thuds and drags. I call for my grandmother—she would know what to do.

'Niah, Niah, Niah.' My name over and over again but it's not her voice. It's Raen's.

'Make them go away,' I whimper.

'Who? What's going on?'

I bury my head against him, sob onto his shoulder. I don't want to see. I don't want to smell anything but him. He makes soothing noises and pats my back when I start hiccuping. I think I might vomit all over his back.

'You must ...' I point at the ceiling but it's clean again. 'There were ... You must have seen.'

'I saw nothing.'

I don't believe him; he has those green dots in his irises, he has Aegnian blood in him. 'Whatever happened,' he says, 'it's over now.'

I want to get away from this murdered queen's room, away from the lifeless portrait, away from the sword once drenched in blood. Anything, anywhere, to escape the odour of death that lingers in the corners of this room. Life must assert itself tonight. And I must keep my ear pressed to his chest to hear a heart beating, to feel breath moving in and out, have his warmth thaw this deep-bone chill. 'Please, Raen. Please. I don't want to die.'

'You won't die.' He touches my forehead tenderly with his. He's hazy through my teary lashes and doesn't look real. He's a villager from ancient times, stepped out from one of my grandmother's tales. I can touch him, though; I can feel he's real. His jaw twitches beneath my palm. 'You're not staying here tonight.'

I nod and nestle against him.

Chapter Thirty-Six

HE TAKES ME TO HIS ROOMS, lays me on his bed and then backs away until he bumps into the windowsill. We're both interlopers here, too earthy, too dark amongst this white. His scent surrounds me: it's on the furs, the pillows, the fabric of my dress. It's intoxicating and I take it in with deep breaths. The fragrance of forests, of masculinity. Life. He's too far away. I need to feel a heart, hear breath. His. When I beckon him he obeys, getting to his knees beside the bed. Is he scared of me?

I reach across to trace the thick lines of his eyebrows, expecting him to move, but he stays there. He holds his breath. I think I feel him tremble. The confusion on his face adds a vulnerability that encourages me to continue exploring him, this village man with Aegni flowing through his veins. I'm done with castle things.

'I don't want spirits,' I whisper.

'Neither do I.'

My fingertips sweep along the edge of his jaw, rough with stubble, up to his soft earlobe, across the hard bone of his cheek to his scar. Tingles skip down my arm, to my belly, lower, all the way to my toes. I follow the peaks of his top lip, continue on, press that plump lower one to feel the shape of his teeth beneath. His eyes close. Exploring him is waking up my body, chasing away death as I knew it would. I want to see, learn, and savour everything I missed before. Before. The memory is a familiar song. I know how those lips feel against mine. I know the taste of him, but I must know more, everything. No more pretences. No more secrets.

'Don't hide anything.' My fingertips trail, lightly, along his thick lashes.

They flutter open. The green dots in his irises are luminescent against the brown like rain-washed moss. In them are traces of my ancestors, of the first man. Raen's the only person like me. He's the only person who can understand this need to be me again: Niah from the Aegni, village-raised, and not this thing that Onnachild wants. I shuffle closer to him. My skirt rises, and the cold tickles the back of my thighs as his gaze heats the rest of me. Those stunning, captivating eyes with all those memories, all that history. My hands slide under his tunic, over his warm and solid chest, around to his back, following the hard curves of muscle and bone.

'You don't have to.' His voice rumbles down my ear.

I'm too mesmerised to speak, so I show him he's wrong and I need this, him, by pulling off his tunic and throwing it into the darkness beyond here, the darkness where nothing else exists. He's magnificent. His torso is that of a fighter, an ancient warrior. He'll not succumb to death. His arms are taut, hands pressing into the bed, as he kneels there, struggling to remain steady while my fingers brush through the dark hair fanning out from the centre of his chest, changing the pattern of it. Over the swell of his muscles, my palms slide, following the curve down to the bumps of his ribs. Solid and hard. His breath catches. His heart thuds. Here is life. Here is a heart like mine, under skin like mine. Does his body taste as good as it looks? I open my mouth to it, lap it up. He's woody. He's fresh sweat. My vision blurs with his honey-coloured skin as my teeth test the thickness of his chest, his bicep, the sensitivity of his nipples. He almost keels from my mouth. All this strength in him, reduced to tremors and low moans, is enticing. And me, I too am reduced, just a body humming with anticipation of his touch, ready to give myself up.

'What are you doing to me?' He exhales and his breath shakes. He grabs my hands away from his torso, and we entwine fingers between fingers, palm to palm. His are so large and thick, the knuckles hard peaks. He chuckles, that low belly laugh, and I watch his body move with it.

'Such a divine sound,' I say onto the ridges of his stomach.

His hands wrench from mine, dive into my hair and have me gasping out. The sound is a call for action. I want to kiss his lips, pull that bottom lip between my teeth, nip it. It will lose us both and I so want to be lost, lost in his body, his village body. He stares at my lips. His fingers flare in my hair. I nod. He shakes his head but his eyes are full of teasing and lust. He knows what I want because he wants it, too.

'You can't stop now,' I say.

'I'm not going to.' His words are flames swelling and ebbing from between my thighs, up my belly, up to my chest straining against my dress to be free. My body remembers his, craves the slide of his skin against mine. I want his hair rubbing against the tender places the sun has never shone on. I want to hear him groan with pleasure; will it be gravelly and catch on my skin or will it be so breathy that the hairs on the back of my neck rise?

As he stands, he calls me up from the bed with a curving finger and I follow, palms out towards his shoulders so like smoothed wood. He's the colour of nature, and I can't stop admiring the different hues of him: the faint brown of tiredness under his eyes, the dark dots of his stubble, the mahogany shimmer of his hair, the green in his irises blazing like my core, the hair on his body almost black. In him is something so ancient, so timeless. Does he know this? I untie his breeches and push them over his hips, my hands following them down to his thick thighs, to his bulging calves. And when he steps out of them, I look up to admire him. He stands proud of his nakedness, aware of the effect it has on me, a faint smile softening his features. His body is mine for as long as tonight lasts. The pull of him is like that of a cliff edge and I want to tumble over, experience the thrill of plummeting and not knowing what will catch me, if anything.

I start undoing my dress, yanking at the stitching, tearing it until he bats my hands aside. My knees weaken from the skim of his fingers releasing me from my dress and then the cage. He's quick, but not quick enough, and I ache to have his solid thighs against mine, his weight on me, his arm pressed to my mouth, him inside. He chuckles against my spine and it reverberates through me. I sigh at the contrasting burn of his kisses and the chill of the room on my bare skin. His lips caress my bruises and cuts, transforming the pain to a sharp pleasure that has me wincing and pressing into him as he moves around my shoulders, my arms, my waist, my hips. Naked, I'm more myself, more village, and that excites me as much as his stare sweeping over my skin, which is flushing and ready for him to have all my secrets. He lunges to claim them, burying his face deep between my thighs, licking to taste them, to savour them. I buckle, giving over my weight to his firm hands. Together, we push my hips nearer, closer to his mouth, as hot as my sex, as damp as my sex. It's his name I call out. It's my name whispered into me.

'Not yet,' I moan, struggling against the urge to rush to the peak.

We scrabble onto the bed, yanking each other's arms, legs. My need for him is greater, deeper than hunger. Thigh caressing thigh, sex rubbing sex, lip kissing lip and on his, I taste me. I want to take him with me, together, away from this place with its jewels and gold and fakery. This is real. His skin is more luscious than any material. His scent is headier than any perfume. There's no going back now. I desire him, him as he is now, trusting, vulnerable, and eager—so eager that my name is little more than a pant, a plea, and I answer by raising my hips to beckon him in. I let out a sob as he slides into the place that needs him, this man so like me, so like my ancestors. Home. Safe: we are both safe tonight.

Our eyes remain open, locked. His are so earnest, so unguarded, as he holds himself still. Waiting? Uncertain? His biceps are straining. My body revels in the relief of him there, and for a moment that is enough. Almost. My hips are rocking against his, calling him. He smiles, then he plunges deeper, and I cry out. My thighs grip his waist, demanding more and more. We moan out into the darkness, the uninhibited sound increasing my pleasure. Our bodies match and synchronise, gliding together, gliding almost apart, teasing and tempting. Forcing us to thrust back to each other and this familiar place where only sensations exist. Again and again. On and on. Our breath echoes from mouth to mouth, his to mine, mine to his. My sex throbs for him, squeezes to draw him closer, to bring him along with me. His lips take everything I have as my lust ricochets through me and I buck up to him, around him. My mouth catches his final groan, his final truth, as he follows me and it's gravelly as if it came from the centre of the earth. I grin, knowing I caused it.

Spent, he gives me his weight. A comfort at first, but I can't bear it for long and so I tap his shoulder. He rolls off me, chuckling, and his seed spills out between my trembling legs. His hair's damp, tendrils have stuck to his cheeks and shoulders. There's a shine across his chest from our sweat and the scent fills the room. Aelius's room.

Raen rises onto one elbow, gazes down at me, and he's never looked as handsome as he does now with his cheeks flushed and a half-smile on his lips, and it terrifies me. I turn my back to him, squeeze my eyes shut against the sight. He curls around me, nuzzles close, and places a kiss on the curve of my neck. My heart speeds again, but this time from fear. This is the second time I've betrayed my love. And I think I might want to do it again.

Part III: Fire

Chapter Thirty-Seven

AS I SCURRY DOWN THE HALLS in the murky dawn light, my feet tap out *mistake, mistake.* In my rooms, door locked, the thought keeps going round and round in my head: I made a mistake, another one. Whatever has been lingering here since I called the gods has gone, leaving the room empty and quiet, and too large for one person. The chair has been righted. I open the window despite the chill in the room. It's raining outside, washing the grounds, and it seems fitting considering what I've done. I catch drops in my palm and watch them slide when I tilt my hand. My body tingles and purrs at the cold contact.

I slink towards the fireplace but do not light a fire. The tray is still on the floor, most of the food congealed and unappetising. I pick up a chunk of bread and settle down onto the freezing floor. My fingers pull the bread apart, crumbs dropping onto my lap. When I try to eat, the food sticks in my throat so I give up, throwing it towards the tray and dragging my sore legs up under my chin.

Once was a mistake. Twice was a betrayal. A wilful betrayal this time.

Eyes open this time, to see all, to know all. When I close them, I see Raen as he was when I sneaked out: his hair almost black against the pillow, his lashes a fanned arch, his bare arm like buffed wood over the white fur cover as he slept. My body wants to crawl back to that warmth. I pull my legs closer to my chest. Vill was wrong: I'll not be able to control Raen. But I didn't do it for that reason. That man last night wasn't Raen. He was unreal, a dream in sharp contrast to the nightmares that haunt me. No, not a dream, but a myth made touchable, kissable.

The door to my bedchamber opens and Nessia appears in her nightdress. The candle she brings with her adds golden light and dark shadows to her features, making her look younger, or perhaps that is because castle living has filled out her cheeks. 'Something wrong?' she asks.

'Nothing, I'm just tired.'

She doesn't believe me; she knows me too well. She kneels in front of me, bones creaking, and her candle blinds me. Blinking against the light sends me into my body and the residual pleasure thrumming there. Mistake. Mistake.

'Where have you been?' she asks.

I shake my head.

'Come to bed.'

I nod and follow her even though I know I won't sleep.

As we enter my bedchamber and Aelius's portrait comes into view, I confess, 'I did it again.' My voice must have been too quiet because she says nothing. I sink down at the dressing table and peer into the mirror to see whether I'm different, to see whether I'm what they say I am. My lips are swollen. My chin has a red tinge from the press and rub of Raen's stubble. When I touch it, it's tender. Nessia appears in the mirror, her face round, ruddy, and healthy. Her smile is confusing. 'You've been with Raen?'

'Is it so obvious?'

'I can see it in your eyes.'

I lean closer. They're hooded, a muted green. The contentment in them is such a contrast to how I feel inside that I wonder whether it's someone else I'm seeing, and so I prod the glass to test whether the mirror person will do the same. I open my mouth to tell Nessia everything, but I'm distracted by the memory of it opening to let Raen in. The back of my hand smells of him, making my body purr again. I wipe it on my dress.

'Come to bed,' Nessia says.

I nod but don't move.

'It was this room.' I grimace. 'Whatever was in this room, it made me. I ...' I spin around to face her. 'Death ... and ... Nessia, what have I done?'

'The gods will protect you.'

'I didn't mean that.'

'I know you didn't.'

'I was frightened.' But when I turn back to the mirror, my reflection is as gleeful as any villager who has got away with stealing.

'What is it you're frightened of?' Nessia strokes my hair.

I shake my head. Nothing. Everything. That tenderness in Raen's expression. How handsome he was. How sweet the fall and release had been. His tongue taking my secrets, all of them given to him. Everything. I can't bear to look at myself anymore because my irises remind me of the dots in Raen's.

'There's nothing to be frightened of,' she says.

'Really?'

She nods, slowly.

'It will not happen again,' I say with a determination I don't feel.

'There's nothing wrong with pleasure.' Her eyes twinkle.

I push away from the dressing table, away from her, and climb up onto my bed to face Aelius's portrait. His features are boyish, playing at being

292

regal. My heart aches for the version of him I knew. Would he understand what I've done? I press my lips against his. They don't kiss back. They'll never kiss me back. They're gone; the worms will have taken them now. I place words on those lips: I'm sorry.

Chapter Thirty-Eight

If I had my way, I wouldn't be in the Great Hall tonight, but one thing I'm learning is that I can never have my way in this place and so here I am, cushioned between Beshanie and Nilola, deflecting their questions as they ask me where I vanished to yesterday. With my excuses come forced coughs that I cover with my hand, hoping they'll mask my shame, too.

'Are you trying to put Gavin off you?' Nilola rumples her nose at my black velvet dress, with the high neckline and long arms.

'Something like that,' I mumble.

'Vill must be ashamed to see you in that,' Beshanie says. 'You really must try harder if you want people to keep believing you're cousins.'

I force a smile since there's no malice in her voice or expression. If only she knew the argument we'd had when he'd tried to force me into a red dress, ignoring the marks still on my skin. Was the fight worth it? A modest dress will not undo my actions—surely everyone can see through this facade? I don't want to remember what I did, so I take a sip of wine and focus on the plate of goose before me. At least no one is talking about the battle tonight. Is this the only change the gods have made? No, me, I've changed. Have I? I stare at myself in the goblet. A serene smile is on my stretched golden reflection. I push it away and go to rub my forehead until I remember the cream reapplied by Nessia.

Nilola and Beshanie are gossiping about Perkin but I don't listen because I need to concentrate on not letting my gaze drift to the top table, to Raen. I can feel his stare and it's like his fingertips are playing over my skin again. I fuss with the collar of my dress to stop it prickling my sweaty neck.

'I said,' Beshanie bashes my elbow with hers, 'I hear she wears a veil.'

'Who?'

'Eldini. Pay attention. A full face veil because she's so ugly. Maybe Raen will get the horses to turn around and take her straight back. If she ever gets here, that is.'

'I don't think she can be ugly,' Nilola says. 'Vill said she was as pretty as a fresh pearl and her skin was like snow.'

'He would say that,' Beshanie says.

'And the minstrels, they wouldn't lie.'

Beshanie tuts. 'You know nothing.'

'I know they exaggerate, but they wouldn't lie. They'd praise her ankles if her face wasn't fair. Oh, this wait to meet her is killing me.'

I risk peeping at Raen. He smiles, and I can't help wondering how that movement would feel against my thigh. I reach for my goblet to drink away the thought, but the gold feels strange, as if I've only just learnt what my fingers are for and the sensation of touch is far too exquisite. I put it down.

'You miss out on all the gossip,' Nilola says.

'Gossip? What gossip?' It's hard to keep my voice steady. Has Raen been boasting?

'It's hardly gossip.' Beshanie sways back in her chair to grab one more piece of bread before a servant takes the tray away. 'And it's certainly not interesting. She's delayed. God knows what's keeping her away for so long. They must be searching for a way to make her less ugly.'

'I heard it was a storm,' Nilola says to me, ignoring Beshanie. 'They're waiting for it to pass before taking to the sea. The Princess is too—'

'Who told you that?' Beshanie asks.

'Perkin.'

'Perkin? Rubbish,' Beshanie says, her mouth full of bread. 'Monderinque told me that the Princess' father is having second thoughts. Though how he thinks she could get anyone better—'

'A storm?' I hold my hand up to halt their conversation. Beshanie's eyes narrow. 'When?'

'Two days ago, Perkin said. Onnachild's livid.' Nilola looks pleased to receive my attention.

It's just like him to be angry at the weather, and I picture him in that portrait, challenging the coming thunder clouds with the certainty of a man used to getting his own way. This time he won't, because the storm must be the gods doing; they've given me a reprieve. How I wish I could rush to my rooms and tell Nessia it worked; Eldini isn't coming. No Eldini, no men, no money. I take a congratulatory sip of wine.

'Why are you looking so pleased?' Beshanie asks.

'You know who else looks pleased?' Nilola nods towards the top table, and I forget to stop my gaze drifting that way. Raen's languid against his seat and the sparkle in his eyes is unmistakable even from this distance. 'I might still get my chance with him.'

'Doubt it,' Beshanie says.

Raen's chuckle booms around the room, making everyone look at him and Vill jostling each other like they're great friends. I'm reminded how his stomach moves with that sound. Did I really tell him it was divine? I tug at the neck of my dress.

Beshanie slaps my hand. 'Pulling at it will not make it any less ugly.'

I hide my hands under the table, grip my knees. The advisers must notice my fidgeting but, when I spot them lingering in the corner, they're talking together with serious expressions and their arms folded. Perhaps I can make it through this night.

Raen stands, pushing back his chair with a loud scrape. Is he purposefully trying to get my attention? He has it. He knows this. I watch him smooth his hair behind his ears, and I find myself also touching my hair. Let him dance with Nilola tonight. I don't need to, not now that Eldini isn't coming. No, she's still coming. Delayed, only.

So the gods have given me more time, but what am I meant to do with it? My fingernails tap against the bulb of the goblet in time to Raen's strides, and I can't think of anything but last night. His colours were so vivid, so magnificent in that white room. How is it that the candlelight and the firelight are picking out those same hues and adding further richness to them? He watches me stand, his smile growing as if he expects me to go to him, but I force myself to head towards Mantona.

Her gaze is skittish, and she looks ready to bolt when I sit beside her, so I place my hand over hers. Hers are as cold and as damp as a fish freshly caught. 'I've—'

'You've let them out then,' she says under her breath.

'What? How?'

'Can't you feel them?'

All I can feel is the burn of my shame. A king's former mistress, she must be able to see it radiating from me. There's more: something I don't want to name, humming through my body because Raen's staring at me.

'Debts will be paid soon,' she says. 'I only hope they'll remember my good deeds as well as my bad.'

I focus on the garnet nestled in the dip of her throat, to dull that hum. 'But I only asked them to stop the battle.'

'How do you think they'll do that? Gods with power over life and death?' Her hand slips from mine, and she's rubbing it, frantically, to bring colour to her whitened skin. Skin almost as white as that woman—girl— in the portrait propped against Raen's wall. Not pearly and snowy as Vill said but white like bone. I see that girl, skin blue-tinged, lips purple as she floats down and down into a turbulent sea. 'Do you think ...' I suppress a shudder. 'Mantona, did the gods mean for her to be at sea when the storm hit?'

'A storm is the least they'll do. Still, it's too late now. Go dance with Raen. Put the poor man out of his misery.' She nods towards him trying to escape Nilola.

I leave her, not to do as she says but to escape her face full of dread. Somehow her words have made the room colder, the people into spirits who don't realise they're dead. Their laughter, their words, even the Maidens' music sounds so far away. I glide through the castle people, untouched by them. At the doors leading to the grounds, my fingers skip over the silky curtains, gathered back and pooling daintily. I step into the night, and it's warmer out here. The fragrance of roses is heady in the air. Stars are out tonight and the moon is a bright white, almost low enough for me to grab and bundle into my skirt. The scenery is like a painting, so lush and still, and the trees are too perfect to be real. I can hear the night creatures playing amongst themselves. The men are calmer than they've been for a long time, their chatter little more than a murmur.

I feel Raen's presence. It vibrates through me like a song between lips. I can't move. It's a bird song. It's the hum of a content bee. These things are in me. The moon is in me. The stars are sparking up my spine. I steady myself with a hand to my chest. How have I never noticed how plush velvet is? The skim of my skirt against my arm is like Raen's eyelashes brushing against my cheek. I must have drunk more wine than I thought.

'Niah?' His hesitation adds a breathy quality to my name. I want to sigh in response, but I hold it in. My body turns towards his. He stares down at me, silent. I stare back. The green dots in his irises are the same green as new moss settling on a branch and the black of his pupils is as deep as midnight. His touch makes me jolt despite there being velvet between his hand and my arm. Are we blinking at the same time or not blinking at all? The corners of his eyes crinkle as he smiles. There's a smile coming to my face, too, and I can't stop it. The world is too strange tonight. He leans forwards, his lips pursing. I tip onto the pads of my feet, lift my heels up. He pulls away and chuckles into the night. 'I almost forgot where I was then.'

The world is no longer still. I can hear it turning, the oceans rushing in and out, trees' boughs undulating with the breeze, flowers releasing petals, sleeping creatures twitching in their dreams. Even the stars are noisy above his head. And him here, before me, his breath a faint tune I want to sway to.

'Last night,' he whispers. The words are a low thrum, goosebumping my arms. 'It did happen, didn't it? Say it will happen again.'

'I ... I don't ... it can't ... it won't ...' My voice is full of longing, though, pleading for him to contradict me, but I don't want to feel this alive, this exposed. It hurts how vibrant everything is. How vibrant he is. I shake my head. As he nods, the corners of his eyes lose their crinkle. He steps back to let me walk past, my fingers fluttering towards the edge of his tunic.

Chapter Thirty-Nine

MY ANCESTORS CRAWL INTO MY DREAMS. They show me only death, all the deaths they have suffered through time. They come, worm-worn, and whisper their names into my ear making me carry the burden of each one. Their breath is a damp heat that lingers. It coats my hairline, my neck, my hands, so when I jolt awake I feel greasy. My heart hammers too fast. Dread is heavy in my stomach, like I've been fed stones. Nessia sleeps on beside me, peaceful. My legs fidget and twitch with the need to escape. For a moment, I must have respite.

The stillness in the hallways is unnerving; it's as if death is already settling in. A cold draught gets through my nightdress even though I clutch my cloak tight. The stone floor hurts my feet like it is ice. I should've remembered shoes, but I was too desperate to leave, and I dare not go back. No one is around, but it feels like eyes are watching me, so I hurry on.

Once outside, I can breathe and my heart loses that painful thud. My stomach is lighter, too. The breeze welcomes me by wafting my cloak and my hair, and I turn my face into its freshness. My feet lead me away from the castle, across the damp grass. I sigh at the tickle of it against my soles. Onwards they lead me, towards the crumbled remains of the First Queen's garden where Raen and I sat, fell asleep. Perhaps my feet think that's where I left sleep.

As I settle down, the aroma of lavender drifts over even though there are no tufts of it left here. It's a faint and delicate perfume that reminds me how, after bad dreams, my grandmother would take me out into the night air to cool down and collect lavender to take home with us. She'd rub those nodules between her fingers, purple burs falling onto my bed. Is that memory responsible for bringing me here? My hand runs over the grass, releasing its scent to mix with the lavender. Touching nature connects me to myself and I know who I am. I am Niah. Niah from the Aegni, village-raised, and this is my land. I tug up a blade of grass and stroke it against my cheek.

It doesn't surprise me when Raen appears and kneels down beside me. It would be stranger to be here without him; we belong amongst these scorched things, the wild grass, and the fertile mud. Black and brown and green, we are both made of this place. He looks tired and his clothes are crumpled, suggesting he went to bed in them. His feet, like mine, are bare, and grass has stained the side of his right big toe. He gathers up the length of my cloak and settles it over my knees before sitting beside me, legs out. 'Another nightmare?'

I nod. 'Death.' Though with him here my dream is so far away, so silly. His arm goes around my waist and gently tugs to bring me closer. When I don't tip towards him, he rests his chin on my shoulder.

'There's always death,' he says. 'But before that, there's life.'

I nod. He is life, with his breath tickling my neck, his warmth a pull to my body. All around us is life, nature, continuing while the castle people sleep and it will remain here, unassuming and growing, long after plots have played out.

'What do you dream?' I ask.

He shakes his head. His nightmare has left traces with the lines on his face, the mess of his long hair, and the shadows under his eyes. If I could, I'd smooth away all those worry lines. I take his right hand, settle it in my lap, and follow the lines and dips across his palm. The head line. The heart line. Perhaps the answer lies there. His fingers twitch as I follow a chained line down to his wrist.

'What does it tell you?'

'Nothing.' I close his fingers. Nothing new, I should say, because I discovered it all last night. He shuffles in front of me and holds my upper arms but I can't meet his eyes because they have too much power, too much beauty. 'How did you know I'd be here?'

'I didn't. I couldn't sleep.'

Perhaps his feet led him as my feet led me, our bodies wiser than our minds. As if he can read my thoughts and agrees, he places my palm onto his chest, right by his heart.

'And this?' he asks. 'What does this tell you?'

I feel his chest rising and falling, the muscle filling the curve of my hand, and I picture the dark curls there, my palm tingling with the thought of them brushing against my skin. His heart speeds. Mine too, as though they're competing in a race. His tells me nothing of the past or the future but keeps me pinned to here, to now, to his body, to the night and how it encases us.

He arches down, closer, head tilting, lips pursing, eyelids fluttering closed, and I mirror him. His lips hover on mine, so light, waiting for me to offer more. I part mine, ready to, though there's nothing more to give, nothing he didn't receive before.

'I forgot, you said no.' He leans back, stroking my cheeks instead. I can't control the surge of heat his touch sends throughout me and he must be aware of this. 'What is it I need to learn about you?' His fingertips trace over the dent and cut in my forehead, and I shiver at the mix of pleasure and stinging. 'About Niah from the village?'

'You've learnt everything.'

'Have I? Then why don't I understand what's happening?'

'Neither do I. Perhaps there isn't anything to understand.'

'No?' He taps my chin. I open my eyes to his. Within them are deep forests: the green of shining leaves, the brown of tree trunks, and his pupils are dark clearings. 'You said you didn't know. Do you know now?'

'Yes.'

'And?'

I smile. 'The castle seems so far away.'

'It does.'

'And you're here.'

'I am.'

I don't realise I've shuffled closer until my knees bang into his. He hoists me up onto his lap, and my legs part around his waist, heels digging into the mud to keep me grounded, to remind me. He clutches my ribcage. If he wanted to, he could crush it. The thought has my skin humming, and I tumble against him from the intensity of it.

'What is one more secret?' he asks.

'What is one more secret.' I look up at him, at his square jaw, at the tip of his nose, at the under-curve of his bottom lip. He's gazing over my

301

head, even though his arousal grows against me. I kiss his chin to call his mouth down. He smiles but doesn't answer. His composure is infuriating. His still hands are infuriating.

'Can you keep a secret?' he asks.

'Raen.' I clasp his face, try to tilt it down. His smile widens. His mouth opens. His tongue licks his bottom lip. And, finally, his eyes lock with mine.

'Is it even a secret if we've done it before?' he asks. 'Twice?'

'I don't care.'

'What's changed?'

I don't know, but my hips wiggle closer, pressing and rubbing his arousal to grab his attention, to entice his lips to ease my need for kisses. It's just lust, Nessia said. He can have my body. I can have his. He dips me back, so suddenly I cry out and cling to his biceps. My hair is in the grass. The moonlight is in my eyes.

'No sneaking off,' he warns.

'No sneaking off.'

I'm shocked when his mouth covers my nipple, his tongue dampening my nightdress. What is one more time? When he is here, coaxing my body with pleasure, offering to fill it with the power running through him. He hitches my nightdress up around my hips, yanks off my cloak, and the anticipation of being joined with him again has me shoving him onto his back. He chuckles there amongst the grass, even as I fumble with his clothes, stopping only when I grip him in my hand and tease that sound into a groan.

My tongue will show him I have power, too. He yields to me as I taste the most intimate part of him, and he's digging his fingers into my flank, trying to say my name. Now it's me laughing at seeing him writhing, squirming, and desperate. I mount him, and as soon as I do, I'm no longer in control, our bodies are. They take charge, following something older, timeless, and wiser. Our panting breaks the silence of the night. We own it and we claim it. Triumphant against the castle and all beyond it, we call out together: him low, me high. And our shudders are nothing more than our bodies agreeing.

Spent, we keep clinging to each other, his cheek pressed against my breasts and my chin resting on his head. I look out at the darkness creeping away from the sky—its job has been done. There's nothing scary in the day. He's not scary in the day, at least not like this, with his head bowed to me.

'Imagine if the advisers and Onnachild saw us.' The heat of his words against my damp nightdress makes me judder, again, around him. He lifts his head, leans back, and the movement makes him judder, too. We laugh at each other.

'I think I can sleep.' I rub my palm against his stubble.

He smiles, so unguarded, so relaxed, so handsome. 'Me too.'

He strokes my back, and it's meant to be soothing but it has my sex clenching him again, me sighing again. Will I never have enough of his body? I don't want to. I kiss him, quick and light, to let him know this isn't goodbye as I untangle from him. This is not how it was before. A new night has passed and a new day is approaching, and so I offer my hand and he lets me pull him up.

'How are we going to get you out of here?' Raen asks, his fingers playing down my arm. My nightdress, stained with mud and grass, is on his floor. The midday sun is coming through his bedchamber window. Neither of us moves from the bed or each other. I've slept well, dreamless at last. He seems to have done the same because the lines have gone from his face and his eyes have lost some of the dark smudging from beneath them.

'You could get Nessia?' I'm in no rush to leave, though, because here I'm safe, here nothing exists but his body, warming mine and charging the air with his scent. My fingers curl into his chest hair, give a gentle tug that makes him chuckle and then kiss my forehead.

'If only I didn't have to go.' His toes tickle my shin. 'But Onnachild—'

I stop his words with my index finger on his lips. He takes the tip between his teeth and exerts the slightest pressure.

'Don't go,' I say.

He looks like he's going to agree until there's a knock on his door, then he tenses and lines reappear as he frowns. I dart under the furs to hide, wrapping my arms around his middle and kissing his stomach to tease him and make him shiver. He calls for the person to come in. His elbows answer my teasing by digging into my back, pushing me down so all I can do is rest my cheek against him. I'm tempted to flick my tongue over him but hearing Vill say good morning stops me.

'I thought you might have need of my help.' His voice is full of amusement.

'I think we might.'

I poke Raen's ribs to get him to move his elbows and then flip the furs off my head. Vill's smile is self-congratulatory as if he put me in Raen's bed himself, and just like that, the castle and all its plots return as heavy as a felled yew.

'Get me my nightdress,' I snap.

'I'm better prepared than that,' Vill says, and onto the bed he throws my white dress.

'Seems you've thought of everything.'

He gives the slightest nod as though I've told a joke. A servant girl enters, carrying the cages for me. She dumps them onto the floor like the ugly things they are.

'I will ...' With a flourish of his hand, he pivots on his heels and then draws the servant from the room with him.

Raen's gaze heats me as it travels down my spine, my hips and the curve of my buttocks. 'Are you going to get up then?'

I stare over my shoulder at him. His eyes are mischievous and lusty, probably expecting to watch me dress. Confirming my suspicion, his arms go behind his head as if he's master of all this, of me, as if he's forgotten how subservient his body was last night.

'You could at least try to look less pleased with yourself.'

'I'm happy.' He kisses my right shoulder blade, hands slipping under the fur to caress my breasts.

'No more.' My nipples betray my half-tease by rising, calling for his touch. I grab my dress and use it to cover my front as I slip backwards from the bed.

'Of course.' He rolls onto his side, his stare still fixed on me. I don't understand why it makes me so awkward after all we've done, yet it does and I almost drop my dress.

'Looks like you need help,' he says, sliding out of bed. He's proud in his nakedness and I can't stop following the movement of his thighs as he saunters towards me. My chest heats. My face heats. His chuckle undulates up his torso. 'No more you said.' He positions himself in a patch of sunshine that makes his body glorious with its rays.

'Ever, if you continue being this smug.' But I can't stop admiring the textures the sun highlights: the jut of his hip bone, the light hairs on his thigh, the ridges of his stomach. A lazy smile spreads my lips, a replica of his.

'I'd like to see you try.' His arrogance is annoying because he's right, because my legs are already starting to tremble.

It's not easy to let him dress me when he places kisses and caresses on my skin only to lock them away behind the cage, behind fabric giving the sensation nowhere to go and so it remains there, unsatisfied and throbbing for more.

'You're not being kind,' I say as he kisses my wrist and then pulls my sleeve over it.

'When have I ever been kind?'

Once I'm dressed, I turn and see he's been teasing himself as much as me. Perhaps he won't act so masterful now. When I glance up, he still has that arrogant expression, and it makes me want to force him to his knees, remind him. Only the thought of Vill waiting in the dayroom stops me. It wouldn't surprise me if he was listening at the door.

Raen pulls a blade of grass from my hair. 'Almost respectable.'

'You aren't.' I nod down at his arousal.

He chuckles, and then kisses my nose before quickly dressing.

In our clothes, it seems we've been remade, and with it, the intimacy between us has vanished. He's Onnachild's son again, and I'm a castle woman. He retreats to the window, and I retreat to the table. We do not look at each other. We do not speak to each other, and our poses are formal and stiff. It makes me glad to be leaving and I sense he'd agree. He shouts to Vill that I'm ready to go, his voice more castle than village.

Silently, I follow Vill out into the hallway. As we walk through the castle, I can't shake the worry that I've left something important in Raen's room, something I'll never get back. *It was only mating,* I tell myself, yet everything feels heavier: my dress, my limbs, my heart.

'How did you know to go to Raen's room?' I ask.

'How do you think?' His smirk has me bristling. 'It's obvious Raen's been dallying with someone. Only yesterday Onnachild was remarking on it. He said, as long as Raen still marries Eldini then let him have his fun— his exact words, more or less. Imagine how he'd react if he knew it was you. Why the shock alone would kill him.'

My stomach turns thinking about him finding out. It had seemed funny, a naughty joke, when I'd been wrapped up in Raen's limbs, but it's not so funny now. I should have some retort, something to wipe away Vill's smirk, but there's nothing and so I stay silent all the way to my rooms, stomping ahead to avoid any more of his talk. Luckily, we're only seen by one matron, who beams at him and ignores me.

Vill pushes my door wide open and calls out to Nessia that he has me. She glances around a chair, butter and jam on her chin. Melody kneels up from the floor beside the fire, grinning and showing the gap in her front teeth.

'I knew you could please a prince.' He grabs my face and smacks a kiss on my forehead. 'But two? Well, Niah. Yes, I'm impressed, and I bow to you.' He does despite my scowl.

'What was it like?' Melody jumps up. 'Was it good? What's he like ... you know?'

My blood rushes as I remember the grass around him, the taste of him, the gravelly sound of his final moan. Already my thoughts are rushing ahead to tonight, to Raen dancing, to watching his muscular thighs and imagining them naked.

Nessia reprimanding Melody brings me back into the room, and I swish away the question, using the movement to try to cool my flush.

'If the lady enjoys it, so much the better,' Vill says. 'She's positively blooming.' His hand hovers by my cheek, fingers ready to pinch it. 'As fertile as a summer garden soaked in rain.'

'It's all the blood flowing through her.' Melody's laugh is bawdy and jars so much with her childlike appearance it makes me feel dirty.

'Don't talk about me like I'm not here.' I lurch out of his reach. 'Is this how you talk with the men?'

'With Raen you mean? No,' he says. 'He doesn't gossip. He's told no one about the graveyard or any other time.'

'You said, he told you.'

He shrugs and swaggers over to a tray on the floor laden with steaming jugs, bread, and small clay pots. 'Stop being so serious. Enjoy your triumph.'

I grimace. Triumph? The word taints last night and this morning, turns me into a whore. 'I didn't do it for that.'

'Still peevish, I notice. I hope you aren't like this with Raen.' He pours himself some steaming tea. The clay cup is crude in his elegant hand. 'Although, maybe he enjoys it.' He winks at Melody and sets her off giggling again.

'Come have some bread and jam.' Nessia's beside me, trying to usher me towards the tray.

'See if that will sweeten you up since making the beast with two backs hasn't.' Vill laughs so crudely the sound grates. I twitch as Onnachild's insults are dropping onto my shoulders again. *Filthy, licentious village girl.*

'Behave,' Nessia shouts at them. To me, she whispers, 'If you're happy, then I'm happy.' She cups my jaw.

I was. If only we could have stayed in his bed, naked and our village selves. I slip from Nessia's touch. Turning away from Melody and Vill's continuing laughter, I notice a new table, almost orange in the sunshine, and I'm reminded of the covenant, the gods, Eldini. My body tenses and my stomach is heavy with dread again. 'I heard the Princess is delayed.'

Vill's sniggering comes to a spluttering stop. 'If only a missing captain hadn't delayed the ship she'd have been at sea when the storm hit and ... I don't need to say more.'

'The gods?' Nessia gasps.

I turn to look at her. Awe and fear are in her face. I wince as my fingertips prod the cut on my forehead.

'If it was, then let's pray they're successful this time,' he says.

'She's little more than a child,' I snap. 'It's not her fault.'

Vill shrugs as if it's nothing, as if Eldini is nothing. His eyes are glinting from his tears of laughter. 'You wanted it stopped.'

'Nessia, the gods wouldn't, would they? It was to bind Onnachild. It was to stop the battle.'

'We don't know what it was meant to do.' Her words are measured and slow, suggesting she doesn't want to believe them either. 'Maybe, if that's what is necessary. I don't know.'

'No. Not like this. Don't say that.' I see the Princess, her skin deathly white, her headdress clogged with seaweed, her uneasy expression. My knees buckle and I grab the table to steady myself, the new table with a buffed surface and the scent of varnish still on it. The new table to replace the one broken by the gods. When I picture Eldini's ship, it's destroyed and the shards resemble the remains of the previous table. The gods wouldn't. They can't. I can't have that on my conscience ... No more death.

'They won't,' I assert but there's no conviction in my wobbly voice. I can't control the gods any more than I can control lust. I punch the table. It hurts my fist so I do it again. 'They have to do my bidding. I called them.' It's Nessia I'm appealing to; Vill's too white, too perfect, too much like a memorial. 'I made the covenant.'

She nods, the slightest motion, barely a nod at all, like she's placating a child. Out of the corner of my eye, something dark amongst the sunlight catches my attention. I rush to the window. In the garden is a brown shape, long and thin: a village girl. She dances from foot to foot, arms out to partner the air. The sun shines right through her and she casts no shadow. I lean out, open my mouth to call her but no words come.

'It's simple, use his lust against him, make him refuse his timid virgin,' Vill says. 'Then the gods will have no need to ... harm her.'

I stare down at my dress, expecting to see the white spoilt by mud and mould, because I can smell it in the air. I drag my hand over my face, and when I look out again the girl has vanished. The smell has vanished, and instead, I'm breathing in Raen's scent captured on my skin. Last night was honest, perhaps the only honest thing in this castle where Raen plays at being Onnachild's prince and I play at being whatever Onnachild wants me to be. I shake my head. I will not corrupt that.

'We're getting there, my dear Niah,' Vill says. 'We're truly getting there, but if you aren't able to do what I suggest, I understand, and it's into the lap of the gods we and Eldini go.'

Chapter Forty

I'M STILL BRISTLING FROM VILL'S LAUGHTER as I traipse towards the Sunning Room, scuffing my shoes along the rugs. At least the heat and gossip there might distract me. I scoff at my stupidity: the gossip will be focused on Eldini and Raen. Maybe I'll be lucky and there'll be something to eat because Vill's words had put me off breakfast. Then later, I'll sneak away to call the First Queen and force her to answer my questions.

My shoes tap on a black and white tiled floor, notifying me that I've taken a wrong turn. I've ended up in the hallway for the portrait gallery. An old woman wearing a simple grey dress, loose and long, stands there, rocking back and forth on her heels as she drones on about the people depicted. Her tight bun, piled high, adds to her incredible height. A gurgle cuts through her nasal monotone.

Ammi! There she is, my little Ammi, sitting on the floor. All podge and pink-tinted skin in a white dress, the swaths and layers of material resembling carnation petals. My feet don't know what to do. I want to rush to her, sweep her into my arms, cover those chubby cheeks with kisses and the loving words that are rushing up my chest and catching in my throat. But Onnachild has warned me, twice. And what if she doesn't recognise me? What if I can't let her go again once I hold her?

I stay here, stuck, in the shadows. Tears threaten to fall as I watch her trying to bring her foot to her mouth. Her curls are a paler blonde than

Aelius's, closer in colour to the Second Queen's hair, whose painting the nursemaid has moved in front of.

'Like a gift from God, she came to our noble bear to bless him with a sun child. A child to end the curse placed upon the King and the land by the fire demons. She would become the mother of us all, leading us with her love, to the greater love of God.'

The lies make me grimace. Ammi's more interested in her shoe than the woman's droning. Good girl. I smile and crouch to her level. She pulls off her shoe and hits it against the floor like it's a hammer. The nursemaid grabs Ammi's hand and shakes her arm to force her to release the shoe. 'Pay attention,' she shouts.

I rise, step forwards to reprimand the woman, only Ammi kicks out her shoeless foot and her stubborn act makes me laugh. The nursemaid hoists Ammi up to the level of the paintings, but Ammi's grumbling and pointing at her dropped shoe. My laugh draws the nursemaid's attention. She glares like I'm a child caught poaching. 'Be gone.' She makes a shooing gesture at me.

I should obey and skulk away, think of what Onnachild demands of me, but this is Ammi. My Ammi, and she's struggling against the nursemaid's hold because she wants me. I step closer.

'If you don't go ...' She shields my daughter with a hand on her head, pushing her face down. The force has Ammi wiggling, mithering and kicking out her chubby legs.

'I love you,' I whisper in Aegnian.

'Stop that.' She covers Ammi's ears. 'Go.'

'Ammi,' I whisper her name with each step I take, and it seems to be lulling her because the kicking ceases and she becomes quiet.

The nursemaid stands strong, feet apart and firmly planted, even when I'm close enough to see the silver birds embroidered on Ammi's dress. The woman looks dogged in her determination for them to finish their lesson.

311

'Please.' I hold out my arms to make it easier for her to lower Ammi into them. 'Please. She's my daughter. Do you have children? You must underst—'

'I had good children. I had godly children.'

'She is good. Look at her.'

'Hmm.' The woman rearranges Ammi like my daughter is nothing more than a heavy sack.

'Let me hold her. Just for a moment, please? She is my daughter. Ammi, do you want Mummy?'

'Her name is Grace.'

Ammi's struggling again, baulking against the firm hand of the nursemaid. I reach towards those blonde curls, fine and flat.

'Please, just let me see her.'

'You?' She snatches Ammi away, knocking me with her shoulder. 'Why should you be allowed to see her? You with your immoral village ways? What kind of mother are you? Giving up a child?'

Ammi wails. I lunge for her, desperate to soothe her, to touch her, to show her I'm here. Ducking and weaving as the nursemaid twists and spins to keep my daughter from me, I say, 'The King says I can.'

'And a liar too.' Her free hand bats, swishes at me like I'm a fly. 'The King has given me no such orders, and I take my orders from the King.'

Ammi is like a fish in that woman's arms, slipping, sliding. Her feet are thrashing out, connecting with the nursemaid who doesn't even flinch. Her wail echoes in the hall. My face is hot with suppressed anger, throbbing with it, yet I plead, submissive, straining my voice to keep it from rising. 'Please.' I try to make eye contact with the nursemaid. My hands are out, palms up, begging, ready to drop to my knees if that is what it takes. 'Please.' But she only tosses Ammi higher, up onto her shoulder, and clamps her there.

'You are making the child wild. She doesn't want you. See how she struggles to get away from you. Be gone. I will not tell you again.'

'No, she wants me. She wants her mother.'

'Why would she want someone like you for a mother? Your dirty village blood? She's better off not knowing she's tainted by that. By you.'

I take the insults, hoping the words will wear her out and once she's worn out, she'll be more willing to capitulate to me.

'You prancing around in those ...' Her stern gaze sweeps up and down my dress, settles on my still-bobbing earrings. 'I see you in the Great Hall, dancing away without a care in the world when you should be doing penance, praying for God's forgiveness. If I had my way ... oh, if I had my way.' She makes a move to leave.

I can't let her and so I stretch to grab her elbow.

'Leave the child alone.' Her voice is harsh, and Ammi cries louder as though she's the one being told off. 'Just you wait until I tell the King about this.' The nursemaid gloats when I step back, banging into a portrait.

She pivots, and Ammi manages to lift her head. Her face is bright pink from frustration, and her stubborn expression reminds me of my grandmother. The similarity is reassuring; no one will be able to tell her what to do. Her eyes fix on mine, full of tears but no longer shedding them. They're the colour of an ocean, neither blue nor green but both. Her lashes are golden like sand. She recognises me and feels my love for her, I know she does. We smile. She gurgles and blows a bubble.

'Stop that.' The nursemaid whips Ammi around, hiding her, and then she stomps off, her voice droning again.

I keep watch in case Ammi manages another peep. And as I do, a dash of thick grey, the consistency of smoke, outlines the nursemaid's shadow and stretches up the wall, kinking when they turn a corner and disappear. Out my sob bursts, and in comes a hint of mud and mould. Maybe it's better that I didn't touch Ammi, spoil her. I check my hands, expecting the nails to be dirty but they aren't. They're as clean and neat as any castle woman's. I spot Ammi's white shoe, forgotten by the nursemaid, and bend to pick it up. It's the softest white felt, and the inside is warm from her foot. On the toe is a golden hawk. I rip off the charm, throw it away, and it clatters along the hallway. My fingers trace over the stitching as lightly as they would the lines in her palm.

I give one more glance towards the corner they vanished around, hoping they might reappear but they don't. It's only the portraits here with me and their snobbish blue eyes assessing me, the stupid village girl in a vulgar dress. I want to poke and scratch in those eyes. Snap those frames against my knee and scatter the shards down the hallway. I swipe away my tears. When I'm queen ... By the gods, when I am queen ... And if it doesn't happen soon, I swear I will wring Onnachild's neck with my own hands. And that nursemaid's neck, too. She could have allowed me a hug. A kiss.

The True Queen's portrait catches my eye, her fake pious smile. The symbols of purity, of faithfulness, of motherhood embroidered onto her dress: sieves, pelicans, dogs with fluffy tails. I step to it, glowering and press my dirty village nose to her aquiline one.

'Not named for you,' I hiss.

The dark outside has a moody quality that not even the many candles in the Great Hall can chase away. The doors and windows are open to ease out some of the stuffiness of a coming storm. Perhaps it's the same one that threatened Eldini making its way to the castle.

The nursemaid's words have not left me; they're as sticky as the air and make my skin feel grimy. My tears have left my eyelids sore and swollen. Since Onnachild and the advisers aren't here, I don't bother hiding my emotions. Nilola and Beshanie are too preoccupied with the men to notice.

'All Vill does is sit in that Judging Room with the King. How much can there be to arrange?' Beshanie says, smacking my arm. 'And when I do see him, he doesn't even remember to pay me a compliment.'

Vill's hunched over the top table, nodding as Gavin talks and waves his goblet in the air. They don't seem concerned by Onnachild's absence, no one does. Everyone is noisier, more joyful, more childish. Even Raen as he jokes with the servants. Only I'm antsy tonight, constantly searching the room for the nursemaid. She can't have told Onnachild, can she? If she had, I wouldn't be sitting here.

'I can't even get close to Raen. And what about Gavin?' Nilola elbows me.

'Gavin?'

'Aren't you angry? Him up there going on and on at Vill when Onnachild isn't here and we could be having all kinds of fun.' She crosses her arms and sinks lower into her seat. 'Go interrupt them.'

'Me?'

'Maybe I should give in to Perkin and be done with it.' Nilola pushes away her plate as if it has offended her.

He's chasing a woman, whose blonde wig has slipped, exposing a rim of mousy hair. When he catches her, Beshanie tuts. The woman holds onto her wig as she offers him the dip of her neck.

'None of the men here are worth anything,' Nilola huffs.

'Except Vill.' Beshanie rises from her seat, looking determined to force him to dance with her. I'm almost envious of her bravado. What would I do if I had nothing to lose? Ammi. I tense again and continue searching for her nursemaid.

'Get Raen while you're up there,' Nilola says.

'Get him yourself.'

I finally find the nursemaid: she's way down on Mantona's side of the table, her cheeks bunching with food. She's wearing the same grey dress, and her bun is as high and tight. Despite her recriminations about my behaviour, she's flirting with the portly, old man next to her, brushing something from the sleeve of his tight tunic.

'How did you do it?' Nilola drags her chair closer. 'Get a prince?'

'What?'

She stares at her reflection in her knife. 'I'm as beautiful as you. I'm as charming. Did your people ever tell you ...' Her voice lowers. 'How to get a man ... hard for you.'

'What?'

'I forget we aren't meant to know about that, are we.' Her triumphant expression is unsettling until I realise it isn't directed at me but at Raen, who's sauntering towards us, a goblet dangling between his fingers. The nearer he gets, the wider his smile. He crouches behind us, and Nilola peeps over her bare shoulder at him. His sleeves are rolled up, displaying the width of his wrist, and the sight has my fingers fidgeting to test out its strength.

'At last.' She plays with a long curl resting on her bosom. 'I've hardly seen you. Where have you been?'

'The Judging Room. Seems there are a lot of decisions and agreements to be made.'

'And?' Nilola asks.

'Truth is I've been so tired I've no idea what I've agreed to.' He doesn't look tired now, though, with his eyes full of desire as they skim over the curve of my breasts. 'Can we talk about something else?'

'There are better things than talking,' Nilola says. 'Such as dancing.'

'Exactly why I came over,' Raen says. 'Dance?' It's me he's presenting his hand to though, not her. The nursemaid's insults return and my top lip curls, making Raen frown. I glance quickly, briefly, at the woman, expecting to find her judgemental gaze on me but the portly man is dropping food into her open mouth. And so I take Raen's hand. Part of me is tempted to provoke her. Show her I'm not ashamed, make her think her words aren't still barbed in my skin.

He pulls me tight, palms flat against my back, and my body throbs as if we're naked again. It's thrilling to break protocol and be this close, though it's nothing compared to what these castle people are doing. They're behaving like villagers of old on the last day of summer. Men are chasing after ankles as the women lift their skirts. The woman with Perkin has dropped her wig and two men are kicking it around the room. Nilola is focused on a bare-chested man who must have been attracted by the ping of her curl. Beshanie sits on the top table, blocking Vill and Gavin.

'You look upset,' Raen says.

'Do I?'

'Have you been crying?' His hand hovers near my face. Does he want to soothe the tight skin there? I wish we were alone and he could. 'What's happened?'

If only I could rest my cheek against his chest, close my eyes, and make the castle go away, but as we turn, my attention is drawn to Aelius's empty chair. Would he think the same of me as that nursemaid? From there, my gaze drifts up to the gold stitching in the tapestry, faded and frayed, and I can't help wondering if his hair has done the same in his grave.

'Niah?' Raen stops dancing. His hands run up and down my arms like he's trying to warm me after I've been in the cold too long.

I stand there, gawping at Aelius's seat as though he has returned and is disappointed in me for everything, for believing Raen's touch could ease the pain of being denied Ammi and being insulted. I should shake this off, tell Raen what happened, but I'm not ready to revisit it yet and so I say, 'Nothing.'

A dancing couple bash into us, laughing and groping for each other. Raen looks at me, then the top table. 'Nothing?' His shoulders twitch as if there's a touch he wishes to be rid of. Is Aelius haunting Raen when it should be me he's tormenting?

Raen wipes a hand over his face, and when it's done and settles on my waist, his jaw starts twitching. Peering up at his chin, I tap his neck to get his eyes to meet mine but they remain focused on the distance behind me. They're narrowed. His eyebrows are lowered.

'What the ...?' he mumbles, craning his neck. His long hair brushes across my knuckles as he looks left. I copy him to discover what has caught his attention. It isn't the dancers swaying and nuzzling, nor is it the people sat at the table waving food and threatening to throw it. He tugs me closer. I step on his toe. Then I spot what he has seen, what he's pulling me back from.

A shadow, murky brown like smoke and with eyes the colour of a stagnant pond, is prowling amongst the revellers. Its skull lurches from side to side as it surveys the room. Raen's nose rumples. Can he smell what the shadow brings, an air of decay and the sweetness of rotting grass?

'It's this place,' he says. 'Nothing more.'

The creature halts behind an old woman wearing a simple grey dress and a tight bun piled high. The nursemaid. It's come for her. She keeps eating, oblivious. It doesn't make sense. I called the gods to stop the battle. To stop Onnachild, that's what I asked for. Not the nursemaid and ... Eldini, what of her? I close my eyes, plead to the gods.

'Niah? What are you saying?' Raen squeezes me and the jolt makes my eyes open.

I must have been mouthing the words. There's concern on his face. I peek at the nursemaid; she's still chewing. The shadow has gone.

'Please, can we stop dancing?' I cling to his arm. 'I can't think.'

'We haven't been dancing.' He's trying to make it into a joke so I smile.

Birds are cawing out in warning, but no one else seems to hear them. There's a rumble of thunder no one else notices, so I don't know if these things are real. I peer over Raen's shoulder, out at the night sky where the clouds have swamped the moon, and the sky is turning an inkier purple. Perhaps this isn't the same storm that threatened Eldini but a new one. Is she at sea? Is she at the mercy of the gods? I'd ask Raen, but I'm not sure I want the answer. Instead, I hunt for confirmation in his face that everything is fine, will be fine, that fate is its own master and not my servant.

He's distracted, squinting towards the other side of the hall, and his presence is not calming. It agitates me with my body's want for him, with its desire for Eldini to stay away and for life to triumph: all life. I'm reminded of the nursemaid's insults and pull at the bodice of my dress to prevent my hand doing what it wants: cupping his cheek and bringing his lips to mine.

I follow his gaze beyond the dancers with fingers gripping bottoms, beyond belching merchants, beyond near-naked men letting their bellies out to breathe. To the nursemaid. She's staring at me, judging me, and that disapproval is back. Her hand darts to her throat. Her mouth stretches open. She starts choking. Her face is getting redder, redder, purple. The man next to her shouts out. She plummets from her chair. Raen darts towards her, skidding on the floor. He vanishes into the crowd around her. The music stops. There's a cold hand on my shoulder, and I'm scared to look behind me, scared to look into those pond-coloured eyes.

'Seems the gods are wasting no time in doing your bidding.' It's Vill, and I let out my held breath. 'Don't worry, she hasn't had time to tell Onnachild, and it looks like she won't be saying anything now.'

His words sink in and I freeze, unable to look away from her feet bucking and then easing to a twitch. The blood drains out of my body and I'm forced to grip Vill to remain upright.

'I didn't want this. I didn't ask for this.'

'Truth is you don't know what you asked for.'

Chapter Forty-One

I BLOW TOO HARD and too fast into the flames. They fight back, feeding off the heat of my fury. There's only one person I want to see tonight: the woman whose fault all this is. I chuck the herbs and dried flowers at the fire, some missing it completely and getting lost amongst the dirt and ashes. My incantation rises and dips as I struggle to remain in control of my breath. I'm shouting, demanding: my voice is loud enough to carry from the forgotten graves into village homes and worry dreamers. It should. It should get into the mud, beyond the mud, beyond the horizon to wherever the dead dwell. They killed the nursemaid. They were sent by the gods. I'm as sure of it as I am the ground, hard and cold beneath my knees.

With the First Queen comes the odour of decay. Her mouth hangs open, jaw gnawed at. Her eyes are blank sky.

'What was that covenant for?' I demand, too angry for patience, for reverence.

Her smile is enigmatic, even with her jaw half hanging off. 'Whatever you wanted. Whatever was in your heart.'

'Onnachild stopped, the battle stopped, you know this. No more death.'

'Are you sure?'

'Yes. Yes. You know that's what I wanted.'

Why is she still smiling at me, even as pieces of her jaw keep disintegrating and dissipating into the stormy night? She's becoming as dense as the rain clouds, a green tint coming to her form. Pond green. 'Then that is what they will do.' There is sarcasm in her voice.

'Stop being so evasive. Mantona said something had been let out. What?'

She laughs, crudely, a mimicry of Vill's laughter and puffs of noxious smoke spurt from her mouth. They surge at me, turning into small naked people with grotesque features as they convulse around my face.

'Mating,' she burbles. 'Mating, mating, fucking.' Her face rushes at me. I flail backwards. She's growing denser and bigger, claiming the very edges of the horizon. The smell of burning flesh fills the night. It gets in my eyes, smarting. It gets in my mouth. My cut is bleeding.

'Don't,' I scream. 'Tell me. What will they do? How do I undo the covenant, stop them?'

'He's handsome, is he not? He makes you pant, does he not?'

Then she's gone. My questions unanswered. The fire burns and smoke continues to spiral up to the sky, formless. I scrub in the mud for the herbs that missed earlier and then throw anything and everything onto the fire but it is smothered. I shout for my grandmother, for Aelius, for the gods. I shout at the stormy sky, 'Leave Eldini alone. No more death. No more death. No more.'

My words are not louder than the thunder. The flash of lightning is a mockery of a fire I can't control. Chilling whites, blue, black, a strip of red across the sky is what's left. I tip onto my hands and knees, lower my forehead to the mud, and whisper prayers into where we all must return. The rain batters my head, my neck, and my back. It's so thick that when I look up, it distorts everything and my eyelids struggle against it. It drenches my hair, my clothes, getting down to my bones and making me shiver.

I keep staring out at the storm, at those heavy clouds stretching over the edge of the world, surely touching where Eldini must be. Is she staring out at it, towards me, wondering what has caused this? Will she realise it's a sign to turn back? If only she'd not left her lands ... It's not her fault, though. It's mine: I shouldn't have created that covenant.

'Don't call again,' the First Queen says. The fire is out, drowned by the rain and smothered by my lack of control. She shouldn't be able to speak without the flames. By my gods, have I let her out too? 'You'll find only me. Only me. And I no longer care.'

A crow calls out for a soul to lead away, and I pray it's not already hunting for Eldini's. The rain is making my dress heavier, my hair heavier, and numbing my skin. I struggle to my feet as the mud is glutinous and doesn't want me to go, but I must. I must face whatever I have set in motion.

Raen's in my dayroom, slumped in a chair by the fire as though he's been waiting a long time, but I don't remember arranging to meet him. 'You're soaked,' he says. 'Where have you been? It's almost morning.'

'You could have gone to bed.'

'I would, only it seems I can't sleep without you there. Now come here and tell me what you've been doing.' His arms open for me.

'I should get changed.' I look down at my dress, the velvet ruined by the mud and rain.

'Not until you tell me what's going on.'

'You'll get cold and wet.'

'Then I'll get cold and wet.' He pats the arm of the chair.

I bundle up into his lap where it's clean and warm. He sweeps my drenched hair from my face. 'Your nose is almost blue,' he says, rubbing it. 'Do you want another log added to the fire?'

Staring into it to check, I see those mating figures, leering and groping, tongues licking. *Mating, mating, fucking. He makes you pant, does he not?* I lower a foot to the floor. He jolts me and gathers my leg back up. 'I'm not going to like what you were doing, am I?'

'I wasn't with another man if that's what you mean.'

'I didn't mean that and you know I didn't.' He takes my shoes off, dropping them to the floor. His hands cover my feet, rubbing and kneading warmth into them. I rest my ear against his chest and listen to his heart, which is so much calmer than mine.

'I presume it has something to do with this.' He touches the cut on my forehead and the sting is thrilling.

'What happened to the woman, the one in the Great Hall?'

'Don't change the subject.'

'I'm not. What happened, is she dead?'

I brace myself for his answer.

'She died.'

Did I really need to ask? Avoiding eye contact with Raen, my gaze travels around the room and the damage the gods caused jumps out: the break in the pattern on the wood panelling, the scuff marks on the floor by the replacement table, the new rug. This chair we sit in still contains a hint of the tree it was or is that fragrance coming from Raen? At least I can't feel the dead's presence. Perhaps they've been chased off by Raen or perhaps they've rushed off to Eldini.

'Niah? You haven't answered my question.'

I shiver, and my teeth start chattering as the chill sinks even deeper into my bones and not even Raen's warmth is able to burn it away. That doesn't stop me from burying into his hair and nestling against his neck, savouring him while I can, before he finds out what I've caused. 'I'm tired. Can't we just go to sleep?'

'Not until you answer my question, and if that means I have to keep you awake for days, I'll do it.' He tips me, holds my body at a distance. His jaw is twitching.

I sigh and try arching towards him but he keeps me away. His heat is little more than a candle's. 'Not here.' Not where the gods were, where the First Queen was, where that odious presence finds places to linger.

'Then where? My rooms?'

'But they were—'

'And mine now. You didn't care last night or the night before, so don't pretend it matters now. You'll tell me either here or my rooms. Make your choice.'

Is my lie that obvious? It's not because they were Aelius's that I'm reluctant to go there, though it should be, rather it's because Eldini's portrait is there and her expression is exactly how I imagine it to be as she stares into this storm. I can't tell him this.

Raen nudges me and so I climb off his lap. I warm my hands in front of the fire as he gets to his feet. Not so long ago these flames were spitting and spilling out the gods. How do I explain that? My forehead stings. All I can do is hope he'll understand.

The rain sounds closer in his rooms, smacking against the window and demanding to join us. Raen kneels before the fire, coaxing the flames to take the wood. I rest my cheek against the arch of his back and listen to him breathing, to block out the sound of the storm. Wearing one of his woollen tunics, I'm mostly dry and warm although my wet hair drips onto him.

'Now we talk,' he says once the fire is blazing. He rocks back, twists around and rests his elbows on his knees. The flames are adding enticing tones to him, red tints to his hair and golden ones to his skin. I watch the colours shimmying. He shuffles closer, cupping my bare shin. His stare is intense, and the firelight makes shadows in his face, hardens the plains so he seems impenetrable and unyielding. I reach out to touch an angle but he catches my hand and places it in my lap.

'Don't try and distract me,' he says. 'I shouldn't have been distracted before.' His gaze drifts to my cut. 'Tell me what you've done and I'll undo it.'

How can he be so foolish? There are some things men can't control or wish away. This is no king's army I've dispatched. It's no scrawny group of villagers. I look at him to check whether he'll trust that I didn't mean this.

He frowns. 'I can't undo it?'

I take a deep breath to tell him everything but all I can do is shake my head and stare out at that purple-tinged sky.

'This is ridiculous. Just tell me.'

'It's too late, and you can't change anything, anyway.' My shoulders slump and my wet hair slaps onto them. 'The dead have come.'

'Stop talking nonsense. The truth, Niah.'

'You ask me to speak and now you tell me to stop when you don't like the answer. It's the truth.'

His left eye is twitching, faintly but quickly. The pulse in his jaw has returned.

'I called the gods, and they came and they did this.' I touch my forehead. 'I made a covenant, and they've used the dead to kill the nursemaid, and the storm ... that is the gods' doing, too. They broke those things in my room.'

'Surely, you don't believe that rubbish?'

'You don't?'

'Of course not.'

'Why not? Tonight, in the Great Hall you saw, by the nursemaid, that ... that ...' I gulp. 'That shadow. The dead, I know you did, by the nursemaid and now she is—'

'A trick of the light. A coincidence.'

'No, not a coincidence. Why won't you listen to me? This,' I jab my cut, 'is this not proof enough for you? They're real, and I saw them. And you saw them, and you saw what they can do. Stop denying it.'

He darts up, glares down at me with his arms crossed and his eyebrows lowered. 'I'm denying nothing. I'm sick of all this talk of God and gods. Curses. Blessings. It's nonsense. All of it. Onnachild using his to justify unjustifiable actions. Mother relying ... If your gods were real, then my mother would still be alive. Do you think about that?'

'She believed in them. She knew they were real. She told me what to do, in a—' I catch myself before I blurt out about the parchment. That note can't mean anything, not when he's the image of Onnachild as he looms over me, scowling and rubbing his jaw. 'In the book,' I lie and hope he believes me. 'I read it, before you came in. And I did it. She told me to, that it would help me. She told me she was planning on doing it herself, but she didn't have time, not before—' I stop because his face has blanched and his eyes have shut. His chest is rising and falling rapidly. I get up to comfort him but my hand doesn't make it to his chest because his eyes open and the hatred there weakens my knees, makes me stumble.

'Murdered by Onnachild,' he spits out. 'Before she was murdered by Onnachild.' The scar on his cheek is vivid and deep, set off against the crimson flush of his rage. His irises are almost as dark as his pupils, the green gone from them. 'Do you want that? For yourself? For your daughter to be without a mother? You're a fool. A complete fool.'

'No, I'm not.' I strain up onto my tiptoes. 'She told me to create the covenant ... I did it. The nursemaid is dead, and now they will kill Eldini. Look.' I point at the storm. He doesn't move so I spin him around. 'Look. They did this so she doesn't get here, so she can't fund the battle. And me, I caused it.'

'Nonsense. She's already here.'

'Where? In the castle?'

'No, at the border.'

'Then they still—'

'Stop it.' Raen jerks out of my hold and stomps off, loud as the thunder. I'm not sure whether I'm meant to follow or not so I stay put, staring down at Eldini's portrait. In the storm light her skin has taken on a purple tint. It's death and not womanhood she's facing with that stoic expression; she's braver than I am.

'Here.' Raen's back. He thrusts the book at me. 'There's nothing in it

326

but names, history.'

I struggle with its weight. 'But you can't read it.'

'I know enough,' he says. 'There's nothing. So whatever you've done has nothing to do with the book.' He takes a deep breath and his nostrils flare. 'You know what, I don't care what you've done. Don't tell me if you don't want to.'

I open my mouth to defend myself, and he covers it with his wide palm.

'Just ... just stop plotting against Onnachild. I'm doing everything I can.' His thumb strokes my cheek roughly. 'He'll soon be gone. He's ill. He's not sleeping, and he spends all day in the Judging Room raging at the loss of his perfect son. I can postpone the battle. I'm trying to postpone the battle. And when I'm king, I'll give Ammi back to you.' But he looks too much like a young Onnachild for me to trust him, even with sympathy lining his forehead. He's as stubborn and strong as his father in that portrait, commanding the painted storm. And still the rain hits against the window.

Pushing his hand from my mouth, I mumble, 'I had to do it. You didn't refuse Eldini and with her comes—'

'What would you have me do?'

'Not repeat your father's mistakes.'

'Is that what you think of me? Really?' His hand drops from my face, and he lets out a long sigh that makes his shoulders slump. He shakes his head. I cuddle the book closer, resting my chin on its thick spine as I breathe in the perfume of antiquity and sage. He keeps staring at me, waiting for my answer. A corner of the book digs into my lips.

'Fine,' he mumbles to himself, though his expression doesn't agree. He leads me by my little finger into his bedchamber and together, in silence, we climb onto his bed. I rest the book on my lap, trace the fire emblem on the cover with my finger and then flatten my palm over it. It has the same warmth, the same pull to it as Raen's skin. I look up at him to say sorry, to say I'm wrong. He's drawn, haunted with memories of what his father has done, and I'm ashamed of my accusation. He forces a smile. 'Open it,' he says.

I do. On the first page is a list of the gods, their names written in spiral letters that remind me of sycamore seeds spinning on the wind. At the bottom are scribbled names of newly discovered gods written by different hands. The names are so innocuous on these pages. 'I've seen them,' I tell him.

He nods but I'm sure he doesn't believe me.

I mouth those names, no longer fearful because they are as much a part of me as my grandmother is. Raen's breath tickles my cheek and I realise he's mouthing them, too. 'You know them?' I ask.

'Yes.'

'Did you pray to them?'

'Yes. Me and my mother.' He's frowning and I wonder what memory they're evoking in him. I imagine him as a child, nestled against his mother as she taught him his lessons. A small boy without that scar.

I touch it.

He flinches. 'Don't.'

I drop my hand, and he turns the page.

It shows the first man and woman. Their dark hair streaked with mahogany, the thick strands curving into a shape like a flame. Their naked bodies are the essence of fertility and strength. The man is muscly, broad-shouldered, and erect. The woman is full-breasted, with a rounded belly and eyes the colour of damp moss. With them is the god of the hearth fire, the smallest, most timid god, who gave her name to Adfyrism. The first god the Aegni met. Her tongue is extended. It's orange across the fat, furry part and lined with yellow.

My finger traces over the letters below the image and I pretend it's a quill rewriting the story of the gift giving. This land. The yew. The phoenix. The flames. Green eyes. 'Imagine if I could read this to Ammi,' I say.

'You will in time.'

I imagine Raen as a child tucked up under furs with his honey-coloured face peeping out while his mother read him these stories. Maybe he's remembering it, because there's a longing in his sigh. Our fingers bump as they follow the curves of the letters.

'I thought I might be able to smell my mother's perfume on it,' he says. 'Find a stray hair between the pages. Stupid.'

'It's not stupid.' I, too, want to find everything I've lost in this book. Most of all, I want to find home. 'Come.' I move the book to my other knee.

He understands my action, shifting so his head rests on my lap and he lies there, letting me stroke his hair as I read him a tale a mother might have told a scared little boy.

Chapter Forty-Two

THE STORM HAS BLOWN ITSELF OUT, and the sky is a clear blue. Eldini has survived, as far as I know. Nessia and I are sitting outside, lazing in the heat because the Sunning Room has been shut to prepare it for the Princess. I push the nursemaid from my mind and let myself be lulled by Nessia's humming as she modifies my red dress at Vill's insistence so the neckline is even lower. Birds are singing. Bees are buzzing by. The grass is drying but still glitters in the sunshine, so we've brought out a rug to sit on. Melody bounds over to join us, making so much noise that Nessia stops humming. Melody slumps onto the rug, huffing. Her headdress slips, but she doesn't readjust it.

'What's wrong with you?' Nessia licks the end of her thread into a thin point.

'Lark. Thank God she's being given to Princess Eldini, maybe I'll get some peace without her squawking about in my ear: don't do this, don't do that, yes, do do that. If anyone is as pious as Princess Eldini it'll be Lark.'

'She's here?' I ask. And men and money and ...

'This morning. Early this morning. Very early. Lark woke me up. The moon hadn't even left the sky yet.' She flings her headdress onto the grass. The tinkling sound is too cheerful compared to her dour expression. 'She isn't really as pretty as they say. And she's very boring, very. All she wants to do is pray and pray and sing these little songs in praise to God, all about how He made this world so beautiful and how thankful she is. How can they even think she and Raen ...' Melody frowns at me, hunching her shoulders to brace herself for a telling off.

'You don't think she'll be staying?' I ask.

She shrugs. 'I don't think that Raen can be counted on, not for anything. One minute he's grumpy as sin and then the next minute he has the biggest smile.' She bashes her heels against the grass. 'I have to go to her rooms later. She's to hear us play, but I don't think she'll like what we play. I'm sure it won't be celebratory enough for her. Do you know most of our songs are about death, thanking God for keeping our loved ones for us, about praying for an easy death? I never realised how morbid they were until her women sang some of hers. What were your people's songs about?'

'Life,' I say.

'Love,' Nessia says.

'I like that. She has no eyebrows,' Melody says. 'And no colour at all, not even in her eyes. Well, she has pupils, of course. Is black a colour? Anyway, the servants are saying all her people are the same, that the snow takes their colour. They hide in it and trick the creatures into thinking they're blocks of ice. I'll have to look and see if Gavin has eyebrows.' She picks a blade of grass, puts it between her fingers, and brings it to her lips to try to entice a note from it.

'Have they met yet? Her and Raen?' I prepare myself for an answer I won't like.

She's unable to make the grass sing, so she drops it and picks up another blade. 'I don't think so. The King came to greet her, and he looked at her like she was an angel and, well, I suppose she does have a certain shine about her when she stands in the light. I think it's because her skin is so pale. I thought I could see her blood moving through her veins.' She holds up her right arm and squints at her skin. 'They say she never goes outside because it's too cold in her homeland and she's too delicate, so they keep her inside and teach her. She can play any instrument. She can speak several languages. She likes sewing and sews elaborate religious tapestries with fine threads. They have put some up in her rooms. I haven't seen them, but Lark was telling me about them. She experiments with colours and has created a whole new shade of yellow.'

'Is there anything she can't do?' I moan.

'Oh, I'm sure there are hundreds of things she can't do that you can.' Nessia teases and Melody laughs behind her hand. I should reprimand them but I'm enjoying picturing Raen as he was this morning, pleading for release as my mouth teased him. She'll not know how to do those things, his pale princess.

Melody dives for her headdress and jams it on, her expression becoming pious and blank as the sound of Beshanie and Nilola grumbling drifts over. Nilola waves at us. Behind them are four servants, weighed down with woollen blankets and wide fans that sweep shade across the lawn.

'Should I go?' Nessia puts her sewing down.

'No. Stay,' I say. 'Hopefully, they won't stop.'

331

When Beshanie stands in front of us, she keeps her face shaded with a hand across her forehead. She's sulky and bossy as she tells the servants where to place the blankets. 'I can't believe we've been sent out here, sent out to burn for that princess.' She examines the deep pink sheen on her arm and tuts.

'I don't understand how you do this.' Nilola wipes her hand across her sweaty forehead.

'My village heritage.' I ignore the flash of warning implied by Nessia's raised needle. The women already know, so it doesn't matter, and besides, they have other things to occupy them: hating Eldini.

They struggle down onto the blankets, moaning like old women and fighting their skirts. Beshanie flashes an ankle mottled from the heat. Nilola fluffs out and wafts her skirt, creating a brief and pleasant breeze.

'Aren't you meant to be praying with the Princess?' Nilola asks Melody.

She hangs her head and nods.

'Can't stand her either?' Beshanie asks.

Melody peeps sideways at me, flushed and worried.

'I can't believe the fuss they're making for her.' Beshanie gestures for a fan's shade. 'She better live up to it.'

'They're calling her the snowdrop,' Nilola says.

'They should call her the Ice Princess.' Beshanie laughs at her own joke. 'But you've not seen her, have you?'

Melody lifts her head, eager to please with gossip. 'I have. I can tell you all about her.'

Beshanie ignores her. 'She was half asleep, bumping along. She didn't even notice the flowers and tapestries they'd hung for her. Oh, and she had this awful hood on.' She starts to draw an arch over her head but gives up when the sun touches her fingers. 'It better not become the fashion. What are you doing?' she yells at a servant when the shade veers to the left. 'Here.' She jabs the ground. 'You're useless, stick the fan in there if you can't stand still. The mud will be a better servant than you.'

The servant does as she's told, her glower unnoticed by Beshanie. There's a tint of green in the girl's eyes, the faintest hint, maybe even more hazel than green. I lean forwards. The servant puts a finger to her lips then dips back amongst the others, and I'm distracted by Nilola's shrill voice. 'It's Raen. Raen!' She jumps up, knocking the fan over. She waves at him. He doesn't notice because he's too busy scowling at his feet.

'He must have seen Eldini,' Beshanie says.

Nilola calls him again, and he looks up. A bounce comes to his step when he spots me, giving movement to his long hair, and I'm reminded of the tips tickling my lips when he refused to take any more teasing and pinned me beneath him. My fingers pluck a blade of grass, and I give it my full attention in order to mask my lusty memories.

'What are you doing out here?' he asks.

I glance up, watch his hair swing as he bends to air-kiss Nilola's cheek. She toys with the collar of his tunic. 'We could ask you the same.'

'Escaping.'

His focus is on me as he air-kisses Beshanie. The shade sways towards me but it doesn't cool my skin. It's my turn to receive his kiss, and as he comes close, I focus on the shine around his nose. It doesn't calm me as I'd hoped, rather the woody notes of his sweat return to my tongue. His lips linger too long on my cheek considering the attention Beshanie is paying us so I push him and call out, 'You're crushing me.'

'I forget you're so delicate.' His gaze lowers to my covered shoulder where he left his mark this morning. My fingers travel there, playing with the material. He draws in his bottom lip as if to remind himself of my taste. I start shredding the blade of grass, trying to suppress my smile.

'Have you met the Princess yet?' Beshanie asks.

'Do we have to talk about Eldini?' he says.

Nessia prods me with her needle and nods towards him. His top lip has curled from the feel of her name. Hope flutters in my chest.

'This sun is making you grumpy.' Nilola pats the ground beside her, and when he sits, directs a servant to cover him with a fan's shade.

'It's not the sun making him grumpy,' Nessia says. 'It's marriage.'

His jaw twitches and I think he's going to reprimand her, but instead, calmly, he waves away the shade and says, 'I want to feel the sun.'

The servant retreats and the light glides across Raen's face. He squints up into it, and deep lines appear across his forehead. I can't help wondering how his skin will change over the summer. Will he turn the same shade as me? Will it smell different, taste different? He must feel my lusty thoughts because his head turns my way and he smiles, a lazy smile that shows me his thoughts are lusty, too. I pick another blade of grass.

'Tell me, what have you ladies been doing?' he asks. 'I'm sure it's much more interesting than gossip about me.'

'Hardly,' Melody mumbles, digging at the ground with her heel.

'Nothing. There's no gossip,' Beshanie complains, her attention fixed on me. 'That's the problem. All we've heard is Eldini this and Eldini that and tripped over performers practising their arts for her. I can't turn a corner without some exotic bird squawking in my face.'

'No more Eldini,' he snaps.

If we were alone, I'd ask him what it is about her that's making him scowl: is it her youth, her appearance, or has he realised what she represents?

'Let's discuss Niah then,' Beshanie says.

I flinch and drop the blade of grass. 'Me?'

'Yes. You seem very pleased today.'

'Niah's pleased?' Raen's smile is far too salacious as he leans back on his hands. Even Nessia notices, and she coughs to get his attention and make him stop.

'Are you blushing?' Beshanie asks me, tipping forwards.

334

'I've had too much sun, that's all.'

Nilola sniggers. 'Don't be so shy. With all this talk of marriage, well, everyone's thoughts are turning to ...' she winks at me, 'marriage. Why just yesterday Perkin propositioned me, and I'm sure Gavin will make a similar proposition to you.'

'Proposition?' Melody asks. 'Oh, you mean—'

Nessia lets out a guffaw.

'Yes, I believe that Niah's blushing,' Nilola says. 'Ha.'

'Nothing would make her blush; you're mistaken.' Raen's scowling at the sun again and his shoulders have tensed. Does he believe her? It tempts me to taunt him further, only we're interrupted by a young man as colourless as snow.

'Your Highness.' He bows at Raen who ignores him. 'The King has requested your attendance in the Judging Room.'

Raen sighs and clambers to his feet. 'Now, he wants me.'

Chapter Forty-Three

THE GREAT HALL HAS BEEN TRANSFORMED for Eldini. Tapestries have been removed from the wall and replaced with banners bearing what must be her coat of arms: a scrawny bird with a long neck atop a white tree. Beshanie tells me it's a cormorant and an aspen as she stares at the same emblems woven into the gold material draped across the tables. The room even smells different, heady with the perfume coming from the bundles of flowers strewn throughout the room. At the top table, trailing bouquets of white and yellow flowers have been sprinkled with something that the candlelight picks out and makes sparkle.

'Why does he even need Eldini's wealth?' I mumble as I take in the gaudiness of the castle people with their finery on display. Gold, silver, garnets, emeralds, pearls, sapphires, and a myriad of other jewels I don't know the name of, flash their colours across the walls. Beshanie and Nilola are wearing new dresses, bodices clustered with so many jewels they are more stone than material.

Beshanie glares at the young man behind us, who has ink on his cheek and a long trail of parchment in his hand, as he recites a list of words that almost rhyme with snowdrop. 'I'll be thanking God when this is all over.'

'Where's your sense of country pride?' Nilola says.

'Lost the hundred-millionth time I heard her name.' Beshanie's fingers drum out an incessant and irritating beat on the table.

My stomach churns as I wait to see Eldini. Will she face us with that same stoic expression as in her portrait? I wipe my sweaty palms on the gold cloth, pleased when they leave a mark across a white bird.

Beshanie sits up and stops drumming when Vill appears. The room silences. My stomach groans, and Beshanie tuts at me. I force myself to focus on Vill, magnificent in silver with his skin almost the same colour. His blond hair has been slicked back to show off his sharp features and womanly lips. His eyes glint like the jewels on his fingers and around his neck. He claps Gavin on the back as he sits. Gavin's in white and gold, looking proud and a little abashed, perhaps at the illusion created to deceive his sister.

Just come out. Just show me her face.

Raen is next, though. He's also in silver. It highlights his village heritage and darkens his eyes enough to hide his emotions when I need to see what he's thinking, whether he's thinking of me. I move forwards in my chair. The cut of his tunic has enhanced his broad shoulders and trim waist, showing he's more than strong enough to carry the burdens of castle and village. Nilola sighs lustily. He nods to the crowd as he takes his seat.

We get to our feet when Onnachild appears. Eldini must be next. She must be. My fingers fidget with the heavy bracelet on my arm. His black bulk has been shot through with silver thread resembling a stormy night. He's wearing his crown, a monstrous thing he had made when he first claimed the throne. A bronze hawk is at the front, one wing bent out of shape. I thought Raen said Onnachild was ill, that he wasn't sleeping, but there's nothing troubled in that huge smile. He stands tall and strong with his barrel chest thrust out. I scan the room for traces of the gods, of my ancestors. They're nowhere to be found. Maybe Raen was right: they aren't responsible for the death of the nursemaid. It's clear they weren't able to prevent Eldini's arrival. I think I'm supposed to be pleased about this, yet my stomach still feels heavy.

Onnachild holds his hand out and, from between the curtains behind him, a child's hand extends and then settles in his. Finally, I'm going to see her, this snowdrop, this foreign princess, Raen's potential wife. I'm not sure I'm ready. Her wrist has a glow. It's as thin as the twigs of a winter tree. Her sleeves dangle down in long swaths of material like melting ice. Nilola blocks my view. I squash against the table. The Princess is short even with the arching contraption on her head. Her face is covered by a translucent veil, her lips and nose faint shadows beneath. Multiple layers of white and gold are draped around her, concealing the shape of her body. I was expecting her to tremble, but she isn't.

'Princess Eldini.' Vill's voice is more clipped than normal. He leads a clap to her and as the noise swells she presses her tiny hand to her chest and dips her chin. Onnachild's gaze at her is full of admiration. Is he seeing Eldini or the things she will bring? I dare not look at Raen.

'I thank you.' Her words are precise and her speech measured, giving the impression that she's been practising for days. She peeps up at Onnachild when he pulls out a chair for her, my love's chair, and as she sits a Maiden swishes the veil out of the way and then, once Eldini has settled, arranges the translucent material into even pleats.

'Dear God, the one True God,' the Maidens chant. The whole castle

337

joins in, palms together, heads bowed, and eyes closed. Even Raen. 'We thank you today for the safe arrival of our sister, Princess Eldini. We thank you for blessing us with this food and for making our land one of plenty. Our dear God, we dedicate this feast to you and to your daughter Eldini.'

Is Raen glad she's here? I want to rip his hands apart, yank his head up to meet my eyes and the accusation there; this is the religion that demanded the murder of his mother, our ancestors. Did the words I read to him mean nothing?

When are you going to act and stop this battle? I ask the gods as I stare into a candle's flame. My breath almost extinguishes it.

'Amen,' Eldini says.

'Amen,' Raen says.

People go back to staring at Eldini, their breath held, waiting for her to show herself. No one can be as desperate to see her face as I am; my heart is thudding and when I swallow there's no moisture in my mouth. *Please let her be all the things Beshanie and Melody have said she is so Raen will send her away.* There's a precision to her movements as her tiny hands roll up her veil, turn by turn. Everyone is silent, mesmerised by the dance of those slim fingers. Is she purposefully teasing us? A curved chin is exposed. Short lips, plump and purple-rimmed as if she's freezing, are next. The tip of her nose is rounded and upturned, showing the dark oval of her nostrils which resemble poked holes in the snow. The bridge is slightly flattened, making her pale eyes look too far apart, like a sheep's. The absence of eyelashes or eyebrows makes her forehead vast. How easily Raen could bruise that white skin. She blinks at us as slowly as a child waking up.

'As I said,' Beshanie whispers to me. 'Ugly.'

I'm not sure I agree, but I wouldn't call her beautiful, either. There's an air about her, a serenity, which seems to render such judgements meaningless. She is so spirit-like I pinch myself in case I'm dreaming and the worst has happened. My hand is a farmer's compared to hers. She's fresh winter air, crisp and clean. I am not, and that stings a little. Her veil has become a thick rope which she fastens to her headdress with gold twine and opal-headed pins, her fingers working as if she's playing a harp. Then, once she's done, her hands float down like feathers settling onto her lap. She smiles, smiles as though she's queen already.

Nilola tells me to sit and I do with all the awkwardness I was expecting from Eldini. She's composed, though, with her back rigid and firm against the chair and her chin dipped ever so slightly. Her gaze doesn't move from the flowers on the table before her.

Servants appear, their brownness standing out against this white, silver, and gold. They bring out a cooked swan and place it before her. Onnachild fills her plate. She titters at something he's said, the sound as high and melodious as a tinkle from a Maiden's headdress. She covers her mouth as though embarrassed by the sound. Raen's concentrating on the swan. He doesn't even notice Vill talking to him.

The castle people wait patiently for the servants to bring out all the trays and then they gesture for their neighbour to go first; everyone is on their best behaviour. The chatter is a slight murmur compared to the normal bellowing and hollering, and there is no battle talk, perhaps to avoid reminding the Princess it's bloodshed they want and not her.

'I think she's pretty,' Nilola says.

'There's something about her,' Beshanie concedes, helping herself to slices of boar. 'That hood though.' She snorts. 'When was the last time women wore hoods like that? When the True Queen was alive, that's when.' She scratches her blonde wig. 'It's bad enough that I'm expected to wear this.'

'Don't you think she has a look of the True Queen?' Nilola asks me, ignoring Beshanie.

I nod, unable to speak. The similarities go beyond their appearances: pale, delicate, and blonde. Both are foreign, followers of the new religion, and harbingers of death. I shudder and drop my knife, its clang going right through me.

Eldini doesn't talk to Onnachild, only nodding in response when he addresses her. She pours him water when he pauses, and when his plate is empty, she adds more chunks of meat to it. He keeps beaming at her like she's a god come to offer him forgiveness and benediction. It should be him marrying her. The thought disgusts me. I sip some wine, my appetite gone.

Onnachild stands. His movement hushes the Great Hall. Raen also stands. He's been transformed into a perfect prince with his chin held high, chest thrust out, and arrogance steeling his jaw. I can't find any trace of the emotions he displayed when he lay in my lap: uncertainty, vulnerability, need. Here, now, he needs no one and nothing.

'I raise my glass to welcome Princess Eldini to our land.' Raen's voice doesn't sound like him; there's no village in it. He bows to her. She flushes, and she's cute with that pink added to her cheeks. 'Let's have music and dancing and feasting to celebrate her arrival.'

'Yes. Yes,' the crowd says, clinking their goblets together. Beshanie bashes mine and wine spills onto the cloth, causing her to smirk.

'Bit presumptuous,' she says. 'After all, they haven't agreed to anything yet, and there are so many things that can go wrong, just look at the first one.'

Raen sits. Eldini's eyes follow him as if she's already in love. Their faces are so close as they talk. Hers is white and soft, almost luminescent in the candlelight, his is wooden. I wonder what she smells of. It'd be something light, something relaxing, perhaps chamomile.

When the music starts, it's a village song of celebration, out of place in this ostentatious setting. 'Oh, I love this tune.' Nilola taps out the beat with her knife against her goblet.

'At least there's still dancing,' Beshanie says, rising. 'Vill has no excuse now.'

Raen leans towards Eldini. What can he be saying to her? Is he telling her about this song, his mother, the things he shared with me to make me care whether he smiled or not? She appears to be enthralled by this princely Raen. Will she like the one beneath the façade? The one manly enough to cry? The one who can tease a woman's body with nothing more than the brush of his breath? Even his shouting and sullenness have a beauty to them. That's the real Raen, the one I know. Again my gaze drops to my skin, full of life and shade. There's a faint bruise from his fingers on the bump of my wrist.

Nilola has left, gone to flirt with a man whose forehead is as wide as Eldini's. How easily she's forgotten Raen. I had predicted sourness or sulking from her tonight, but she's as cheerful and as coltish as ever. I need to be like her and so I check my reflection in the goblet to ensure my smile is believable. All I see are my burdens. They're as plain as the embroidery on my sleeves: battles, death, the throne. Did Vill pick such a dark red dress so as to remind me of blood?

I rise so swiftly it makes me dizzy. At least the advisers are too busy directing the Maidens to notice me removing myself to the gardens; watching Raen and Eldini dance to these village songs would be too much. Men are outside, castle men and Eldini's men trying to find common ground. Her men are flustered and curt at the talk of women and wine. They settle on discussing battle tactics. The castle men are boisterous and full of bravado whereas her men are contained and speak quietly. Someone pushes someone, and the crowd becomes a surging yell.

Breath tickles the back of my neck: Raen's breath. He's not forgotten me, and my smile becomes genuine. I can't turn to face him, though; what if Eldini's image is already caught in his eyes?

'Not enjoying the celebrations?' he asks.

'Not especially.'

'I'm glad to hear that.'

'Why?'

'I'm not enjoying it either.'

'You looked like you were.'

He comes to stand before me. 'Is this a convincing smile then?' It's boyish and carefree, suggesting he's never experienced a day of pain. I want to trace the lines it makes either side of his mouth, but instead, I nod and tangle my fingers in my skirt.

'It seems I'm getting better at being a prince,' he mocks. 'Do you think it will have fooled anyone?'

'I'm sure Eldini will like whatever she's told to like.'

'And you?' He closes the distance between us. 'Do you find it appealing?'

'What does it matter what I think? It's Eldini with the riches.'

'Are you calling me a whore now?'

'Take it whatever way you will,' I say as I move to leave.

He steps in my way.

'I'm tired.'

His lips lower, almost touching my cheek. 'If half the castle wasn't out here ...' His gaze lingers on my mouth. The real Raen, the one hidden beneath this pomp and fakery, has returned, and the lust in his eyes tells me he's still mine. The knowledge thrums through me as if his lips are caressing my skin. 'Damn these people.' His fingertips brush mine. His smile drops. 'Will I never be free?' he groans.

I glimpse behind me to discover what's annoyed him. It's Gavin making his way through the men. Raen grips my hand, ducks into a shadow, and gives me such a mischievous smile that I follow his lead.

'Want to see if that silver tree has grown for us?' he asks.

I nod and muffle my laughter against his arm. Together, we shuffle further and further away from the castle, into the gardens, into the darkness. Then we bolt.

His breathy chuckle is such an enticing sound that I chase it across the gardens, weaving and ducking from shadow to shadow. I lose a shoe as I overtake him, at first gloating until I realise he's slowed so he can watch my exposed calves and so I tug my skirt higher. On and on we run, down the dip towards the river, gathering speed. We dart left to run alongside the water, its surface rippling with moonlight. He calls out my name.

I bash into the wall enclosing the castle grounds and manage to spin around moments before he bumps into me. His hands rest either side of my head. His legs part around mine, our feet side by side. There's no need for him to imprison me here. I choose to be trapped by his arms, by his gaze darting from my eyes, my chin, my cheeks, my mouth to the mounds of my breasts swelling as I catch my breath. Under his lusty gaze, I become proud and haughty, luxuriating in its heat and the pleasure it hints at. His face is shining and flushed from the run. His lips hover above mine. Is he teasing or savouring the anticipation? Or getting his own back for my touch tormenting him this morning? Either way, I can't wait, not when his thighs are pressing against mine, not when his fresh sweat imbues the surrounding air. I must kiss him. I must claim him again. That foreign princess can't have him.

My hands, my tongue, my teeth are greedy, are overbearing, grabbing and digging into his muscles, nipping his skin, seizing his mouth. We stagger down, fumbling to get under castle clothing to the real us. He pulls my hair back, stares into my eyes. His arousal tells me he doesn't want a snowdrop princess and he'll send her home.

Chapter Forty-Four

I SEARCH FOR NESSIA throughout the castle grounds, desperate for someone I can be myself with after sitting in the Sunning Room for too long. My steps pound out my frustration as I keep replaying the changes. Material, as translucent as Eldini's veil, hung from the centre of the room creating ceiling swags that made me feel trapped in a spring cloud. Her women were sitting there reading aloud in their language made up of clacks and clicks. The stale smell had gone, and I almost missed it. Instead, the room stunk of the powder castle women had applied to make them as white as the Princess. Clumps had settled around Nilola's nose. The fabric of her dress was thinner than normal, so it bunched and snagged around her cage as the two fashions clashed. What else will this foreign princess change?

Nessia isn't outside so I go inside, searching for a servant who might know where she is. One directs me to the washroom. It's full of dense and fragrant steam, and it's deafening with the sounds of splashing, scrubbing, and slapping of material. Pushing my way through damp dresses hanging from rails and hooks, I find her leaning over a large wooden tub, laughing with a ball of a man. The rim of his steel-coloured hair is damp and flat against his head.

I'm about to step away when she spots me and shouts my name. Her arm darts out around my waist and she brings me closer, dropping suds onto the floor.

'Niah, Llwellyin,' she shouts the introduction.

I nod at the man. He nods and grins, his front teeth protruding. Then he shoos Nessia away with a flutter of his soapy hand and gives his attention back to his washing.

Once outside, Nessia pushes her damp hair off her forehead and rolls her sleeves down over her red skin.

'I wish you wouldn't do my washing,' I say. 'You're not a servant, despite what Onnachild says.' And I am not a castle woman, pale-skinned and delicate.

'I'd just be bored otherwise. There's only so many books I can read.

Besides, I wasn't doing your washing, I was helping Llwellyin. Aren't you meant to be in the Sunning Room?'

'Don't,' I grumble, glaring out the open door at the grounds where Eldini's men are fencing, their swords sending sparks of sunlight onto the white paths.

'Come on, then. Tell me what's wrong.' She turns me around and pushes me towards the exit.

We amble across the grounds as I detail the changes made to the Sunning Room and try to mimic Eldini's language. Nessia laughs, a rasp coming from her throat. I frown at its return. 'Should you be in that room if it's affecting your health?'

She ignores me, lowering onto the grass into a stretch of sunlight. I sit, and she squeezes and pummels my shoulders until they're less tense and tight. Her humming relaxes me further. Men must be playing a game nearby because their cheers and shouts of frustration drift our way.

Melody sidles up to us and bumps down. She has a veil attached to her headdress and it tangles as she yanks and batters it. 'I've been looking for you,' she complains.

'Why is everyone in such a bad mood today?' Nessia asks.

Melody huffs and points at two figures walking our way: one tall and broad, the other short and slight. My heart lurches, and my shoulders tighten again. Is he bringing her over to show her off, his perfect pale princess, or because he can't bear to be alone with her? He's waving as if we should be glad to see them.

'If they ask why I'm not in the Prayer Room, tell them, say that you needed me, that you had a spiritual crisis.' Melody tugs at her veil. 'That's what I told Lark.'

Though I don't want to see them together, I can't tear my eyes away from their forms. The sun is behind them, glowing around their mismatched outlines. He's walking at an odd angle so his ear is nearer to her mouth. She's wearing a pale-blue dress today, all flowing pleats and ripples. It's the same colour as the wall in Raen's rooms. Has she seen them? I hope she smelt me on his pillows.

'Careful or the wind will change and you'll be stuck with that sour expression,' Nessia says.

I grimace at her and then force a brief smile that hurts my cheeks. Melody gets up into a low curtsy which Nessia copies, making her knees creak. 'Oh please.' I almost wish I was back in the Sunning Room.

'Stop sulking and get up,' Nessia says.

I obey her, without question, but with resentment.

Eldini's so slow: a foot rises, leg extends, foot lowers, and then the other slides across to join it giving the impression that she has only just learnt how to walk. Her white veil wafts behind her like the wings of a damselfly. The wait is agonising and my smile is starting to quiver. Raen's fingers are barely on her arm. Does he know he could break her? He's never so careful with me. I scrutinise his face to gauge his feeling towards this girl, seek reassurance from him, but it's blank and princely.

Eldini stops in front of me. Her quizzical expression makes her look even younger.

'Pleasure to meet you,' Nessia says.

The simper in response is ethereal, and Nessia's curtsy drops lower. Raen leans forwards to kiss my cheek in greeting, the same distance between lip and cheek as he uses for Nilola and Beshanie. 'Play fair,' he whispers in my ear.

'As you are?' I hiss in his. Even with Eldini beside him, lust surges through my body in response to his presence. I dig my heels into the soft ground to stop it.

He straightens up and away from me, and then gestures towards the Princess. 'Eldini insisted on meeting you,' he says. Does he think that excuses him?

'I am pleased to meet you.' Her soft speech is measured as she uses words that can't be natural to her. She blinks rapidly at me several times, still with that quizzical expression, and I wonder what she's been told about me and by whom. Up close there's the faintest hint of blue in her irises, the same as in water when it's held up to the sky. Does Raen find them intriguing? Her eyelashes are thick white spikes. I search for a blemish on her pale face, a spot of colour. There's nothing. She isn't even sweating in this heat. I force my smile wider, and she seems satisfied with this response.

'Are you enjoying the castle so far?' Nessia asks.

Eldini turns to Raen as if he should answer for her.

'I hope you are.' His smile is charming.

'People are kind,' she says. 'You, Niah? The eyes, Gavin say.' She points to her own, the large lids resembling the underside of a spoon.

'Oh, did he tell you the sad tale?' Melody asks. 'Sorry, I shouldn't, I should ... I'll be quiet.'

Eldini nods and blinks slowly, solemnly, at me. 'We sit?' she asks Raen.

'If that is what you'd enjoy.'

As soon as her back is turned, he flashes me a warning look. I glare at him, thinking of a million insults I'd enjoy flinging at him. As Eldini floats down he gathers up her veil, draping it over his forearm in a gesture that seems practised. Has he been practising with her? Where? She sits with her legs to the side and beams up at him as he settles the veil around her so it ruffles across the grass resembling sea foam. Her hands nestle together on her lap, a patch of sunburn across one. Her nails are an iridescent pink with the white tips brushed into perfect arcs. The chirping of a bird catches her attention, and she searches for it in the trees above. I force my aching smile higher.

Nessia bumps down with a slight groan. Melody slouches, her veil trapped underneath her crossed legs. I copy Eldini's pose, but it doesn't

347

feel serene as hers appears: it feels tense and my bottom leg twinges. Raen positions himself sideways and slightly behind her so his body is directed at her but his left knee butts against mine. What am I meant to think of that? Her arched hood casts a long shadow over his face, hiding his eyes, but I can sense they're focused on me, assessing my reaction. I relax my jaw and lower my shoulders to hide it from him.

'Gavin asked the King for marriage,' Melody speaks loudly and slowly to Eldini.

'Yes. Gavin say cannot be done.' She glances at Raen, seeming to need his approval before continuing. 'Your guardian not like?'

'There are a few people that wouldn't like it,' Nessia says, a touch of mischievousness in the look she gives me.

'Vill?' A faint frown creases Eldini's vast forehead.

'No, not Vill. Perhaps you could convince her guardian.'

I don't understand what Nessia is doing because she knows I have no interest in Gavin, but then I notice Raen is struggling to keep his princely composure and so my smile becomes a little easier to maintain.

'I not queen yet.' Eldini titters, a trill that has her covering her mouth and widening her eyes. Again, she peeps at Raen. His expression gives nothing away, but it seems to encourage her hand to return to her lap where it drapes over its partner. 'Raen can. You, Raen, talk to guardian. He listen to prince. And say Gavin is prince. Niah be queen. Guardian like that.'

'Imagine that, Niah,' Nessia says. 'A queen.'

Raen's jaw twitches. 'I'm sure Niah has.'

'My brother talk about you.' Eldini's quizzical expression is back. 'He love you. You love him?'

Love! I manage to hide my surprise by pretending there's a loose thread on my sleeve. Thank the gods Nessia answers, 'She talks of him in her sleep.'

When I peer up through my lashes, Eldini is beaming and Raen seems to be fighting a scowl, so I nod. He loses the fight and that pleases me. That will teach him to bring his perfect foreign princess here.

'Unfortunately, we don't have time for more of this tale.' He starts to gather up Eldini's veil.

'We see garden? The garden you say about?'

The material almost slips from his hands. Why? Is it the First Queen's garden she's referring to? He gives the veil his full attention and I suspect he's purposefully ignoring my questioning stare. 'Regretfully, I have to return to my father.'

'Yes. There is much to do.' Eldini's disappointment is evident on her face.

'You should go inside. The sun will ruin your skin.' Melody points to the red patch on Eldini's hand. 'Your skin is beautiful, luminescent, like the moon.'

'I am not moon,' Eldini says. 'Home we go outside. I ride. I walk gardens. We have not much sun but I like when it is come.'

'Niah will walk with you,' Nessia says.

Raen pauses halfway to his feet, panic in his eyes when they meet mine.

'I'd be happy to show you the gardens,' I say to annoy him. I should point out the mud Raen and I disturbed when we mated in his mother's destroyed garden. Or perhaps I'll take her to the wall and tell her how he growled my name when I took charge of him. Either one of those will make her go. And her money. And her men. I want him to worry about everything I could share with her. My smile feels sly and cruel.

He has no choice, but he appears to be searching for one as he chews on his bottom lip and looks longingly at the castle. When Eldini simpers up at him, his charm returns with his lip sliding out and his eyes becoming blank again. It seems he's been observing and learning from Vill. 'If that is what you want.'

She nods, and her fingers flutter in her lap, hinting that she isn't sure how to say goodbye to him. He takes the lead, crouching low and taking up her hand like it's a butterfly. His kiss must be nothing more than a dash across her knuckles but still she flushes.

Her gaze doesn't follow him as he leaves. Mine does, admiring the way his muscles move under his clothes, the way the shadows and light dabble over him as he strides briskly. Is he so eager to be rid of her?

'I not like inside,' she says. 'The air is ... It is old castle.'

'Yes, part of it, and parts of it are new,' Nessia says.

It's me Raen gives a parting glimpse to, over his shoulder, before entering the castle. I rip up a lump of grass, wishing I was following him. Why did I agree to show Eldini anything? It's too late to change my mind, and I can't think of an excuse as she gets to her feet. Melody helps with her veil.

'I have new part. I have room there.' Eldini points to the top of the furthest tower. 'I see long way, over fields. Not all the King's fields?'

'They used to be,' Melody says.

'Yes. That why he want my riches.' Eldini shakes grass from her loose dress.

I will take her to the pleasure gardens where the exotic flowers look too evenly and brightly coloured to be real. The remains of the village-style garden belong to Raen and me.

We walk across the grass to the path, her pace quicker now that Raen isn't with her. Once on the path, we stop so she can wiggle her foot until a stone bounces out from her shoe. I lead us back onto the grass; it'll be softer on her feet, although I'm not sure why I care. Her breaths come as little mews, and the layers of her skirts drift alongside her body like they're floating in water. She must be naturally thin and contained as I can't see the outline of a cage.

'I like here.' Her fingers skip over the purple flowers of a short shrub.

'You like here?'

'It's my home.' My tone is defiant, I can't help it.

If she notices, nothing in her serene expression shows it. She doesn't even acknowledge that I've contradicted my official story. There's something about her that makes it hard to lie and I can't figure out what. It's not those wide-set eyes, seemingly unprotected by the white lashes and white brows. It's not the childlike nose with the nostrils so exposed. When she blinks at me, I'm distracted by an urge to ask whether the sun hurts her pale eyes.

'Before, you not answer question. Now Raen gone, we speak? You love Gavin?'

'With all respects, it is not your concern.'

She blushes and her eyes widen like I've pinched her. 'You could love Gavin.' Her voice rises, implying it's a question but her expression tells me it isn't. She seems so patient and friendly that I open my mouth to explain about Aelius, about love. How it blesses you once and once only, but I can't remember how it felt to have him near, to hear him giggling, to kiss him. She steps closer, her hand hovering over my arm as though she's unsure whether I will permit her touch. Pollen is a golden dust on her fingertips.

'You can't make yourself love someone, it's not that simple,' I say to the bush beside her.

'I dis-a-gr-ee.' She stumbles over the word, separating it out into four separate beats. 'Love can grow. Love can come between man and wife.'

'You mean to make yourself love Raen?' Despite myself, I have sympathy for her, this girl brought here solely for her riches, this girl who will be rejected and returned to her homelands.

'Now it you too friendly.' She titters to herself before moving towards a towering plume of yellow flowers I have no name for.

'This is a nice surprise.' Raen's cheek rests against the open Judging Room door and one hand holds onto the top of the frame.

'You alone?'

He nods, leans out, and after a quick check down the hallway, he's ushering me inside. A fire has recently been lit, and its light makes the room seem smaller, almost homely, though its heat is only dulling the sharp edge of the chill. Onnachild's presence is still here, not quite chased away by the fire. It lingers in the dark corners and scents the room the way a dog marks its territory.

Raen closes the door and leans against it, his eyes bright with mischief. 'Have you come to tell me off?' He bends his right leg and draws up his foot so it rests against the door.

My gaze is attracted to the spread of his thigh muscle. 'You weren't in the Great Hall.'

'I was stuck here.' His voice is a low murmur.

'Why?'

'Why do you think?' He gestures towards the table where there's a single candle flickering yellow light over two goblets, a jug, and a stack of parchments. Eldini. When I look at him, his shoulders have slumped—the weight of those parchments is on them. The front of his tunic is creased, hinting at his shape beneath. He looks tired, and his hair is tousled. I want to smooth these things away but some part of me remembers I'm angry at him, and he has no right to be giving me such a hot stare as he pushes forwards from the door.

'Why did you bring Eldini over?'

'She wanted to meet you.' He strokes my bare arms, making the hairs stand up, and despite my best efforts, I tremble at the touch. His lips hover by my cheek, calling me nearer with the tickle of his breath.

'Why?' The word is little more than a sigh as I savour his slow caress and steady myself with a hand on his thigh.

'You'll have to ask her that.'

'You enjoyed watching me squirm.'

'Maybe.' He hoists me up into his arms, and momentarily I forget I'm annoyed with him. I cling to his neck, breathing in his scent. It complements the hint of burning wood wafting from the fireplace, and the fire's crackles could be the sound of our bodies bouncing together as he strides across the room. The eyes of the phoenix, rising from the throne, seem to wink at me.

'Would you rather it was her sneaking in and away from her maids?' I say. 'Would you like her to show a bit of spirit?'

He chuckles and shakes his head. 'She's a piece of parchment. You are ...' He kisses me quick and hard, and then licks my nose as if to find the answer. The sensation makes me giggle. 'I'm not quite sure what you are.'

He places me onto the table, and I'm torn between sliding my palms over the sleek orange grain or the textures of his face. 'Now shush.' His hands dart under my skirt, around my waist, and he tugs on the ties of the cage. 'No more talk of that.'

I lift my hips to help him yank it down.

'What I want is you, here, now, on this table. Then tomorrow, when Onnachild's going on and on, I can picture you, me.'

I should stop his lips lowering, there are things I need to say, but my mouth parts to let him in. Kisses, light and leisurely, call me nearer and nearer, and I seem to glide across the table to get there. The wood is cool and smooth beneath me as my skirt rides up. The yew charges my skin until I'm all flame, needing more fuel. My hands dive into his hair, luxuriating in the thickness. His kisses make me heady, make me want to forget. Not yet; I must remember why I'm here despite his knuckles brushing my legs as he grapples with my skirt. I must remember my mouth can speak as well as kiss. I pull his head back and come up for air, for sense.

His lips curve into a lazy smile, a shine across that plump bottom one tempting me to return mine. Any moment, I'm going to forget why I'm here. My head is fogging with him, his scent, his hot mouth. 'Stop distracting me,' I say, but my voice doesn't carry any authority.

He slips from my weak hold, and with a quick grab, he's bringing my right leg to his waist, and instantly my left leg joins, curling. My ankles lock around his waist to trap him here. Here against me, when I should be pushing him away so I can think. But his arousal is alluring with the promise that his body can banish my concerns. His eyes are so enchanting in this weak light that I'm rubbing against him, teasing him, teasing myself. I tear my gaze away, towards the throne, and press my palms against the table but the satin-like texture reminds me of his shoulder, and I moan. He chuckles against my collarbone and caresses my hips. 'I think you're distracting yourself.'

I appeal for strength. There are more important things than what my body wants. As I keep staring at the throne, I try to work out how the curves of the phoenixes' wings were made. It helps me tense against Raen's kisses. 'We need to talk.'

'About?'

'Eldini.'

He pauses. His breath is erratic on my neck. 'I thought we had.'

'She means to love you.'

'Then she's stupid.' His hand plunges down the front of my dress, and I'm too dazed to withhold my sigh when he finds my nipple. 'She'll be docile, pliable.' His teeth claim my earlobe adding pleasure and pain to his words. 'This doesn't have to stop.'

And the kisses don't stop, trailing over my cleavage, nipping, licking while his fingers leisurely play with my nipple. He seems to think we've got all the time in the world.

'Raen. No ... I needed to ...' I arch away and tip my head to take a deep breath free of his alluring scent. Staring at the ceiling dotted with cobwebs helps me to collect my thoughts. 'When is she going back?'

'Back?'

I almost topple over when he sweeps up my right leg and rests it on his shoulder. The cold tickles my skin as it whispers under my skirt, and his kisses are hot flickers that set my leg trembling. My eyes close. My fingers splay out, finding the dips and cuts in the table made by my ancestors. 'Yes, back.'

His mouth skims along my calf, higher and higher. 'She's not going back.'

'Not going back?'

'It's a contract, an arrangement, nothing like this.'

'Nothing?'

'Nothing.' He tries to make eye contact with me but I shake my head to bring my hair tumbling over my face, hiding my disappointment from him. 'It's a combining of assets. It's an heir.'

'Then lie with her tonight.' I slide my ankle from his shoulder. 'Let her satisfy you.'

'She's a princess ...'

And not a filthy, licentious village girl, the rest of the sentence is left to linger there. Even when I glare at him, he doesn't apologise for that implication. His jaw twitches, but he stays silent. I pull my legs up onto the table, cross them and cover them with my skirt. 'Yes, a princess,' I say slowly so my pronunciation is all sharp castle accent. 'An innocent, religious little princess. What would she do if she knew ... about this? About us?' I nod at his crotch, still swollen with arousal. He doesn't move away, doesn't even seem ashamed.

'Are you threatening me? Do you think if the castle knew, if Onnachild knew, that it wouldn't reflect badly on you? I'd say you bewitched me with those eyes, with that village blood and he'd believe me, so get that out of your head.' His palms thud onto the table but he doesn't sound angry; he sounds exasperated. 'I've talked to advisers, to Vill, to the King, to half the goddamn castle about this marriage, and I'm not going to talk about it now, with you.'

'You should talk to me. My ancestors made that throne.' I jab my thumb towards it.

He stomps over to the throne, drops down onto it with his legs spread wide and his fingers curling around the arms. 'They're my ancestors, too, but you keep forgetting that.' The green dots in his irises are as bright and small as the phoenixes' eyes.

'Then act like you are part Aegnian.' I spin around to face him, pin him to the throne with my feet on his chest.

'Fine. Then talk, Niah.' His grin is more sneer. 'Here you go.' He shunts the parchments at me. 'Contracts, contracts, and more contracts. If I do this, then that happens and if I do that, then this happens. Since you know everything, since you are so righteous, tell me, what should I do?'

'I don't care about papers.' I swot them from the table. 'Refuse her. You know she doesn't belong here.'

'I need a wife and an heir—'

'And Onnachild needs his battle.'

He sighs and mutters something under his breath before responding to me in a tense and controlled tone. 'And Onnachild needs his battle. She'll make a good queen. A good wife. It's my duty.' His fingers encircle my ankles.

'Duty to who? Onnachild? What about your duty to the village? To your mother?'

His grip tightens, fingers biting into my flesh. 'Don't.' The word is a warning growl, reminding me of Onnachild and so I struggle from his hold, my feet dropping into his lap. I lunge for Raen's face, grabbing it between my hands. My thumbs press into his cheekbones. Staring into his eyes, I try to remember the man who fell asleep in my arms as I read him our myths. My gaze drifts to his scar and it reminds me of the cuts I felt in the table.

'We don't need another foreign queen.' I soften my voice. 'Don't you see the similarities? Raen, she wants to be like the True Queen.'

'Every woman wants to be like that queen.'

'You're not listening. Raen, listen. Like that queen, Eldini will be bringing death. Do you not remember how Onnachild had the Aegni women killed, forced conversions, angered the gods, all so he could marry that woman? How she pushed out your mother. How—'

'You don't need to tell me my history. I know. I lived it.' His top lip curls and his eyes narrow to dark slits.

'Then how can you even consider marrying her? Can you not see how similar to that queen she already is? Pale? Pious? Foreign? We need Adfyrism reinstated. We need to undo Onnachild's wrongs.'

'Who would you rather I marry?' he snaps, slapping my wrists away. 'You?'

'Don't you dare. Don't you dare pretend this is about jealousy.' I scramble off the table, fighting with the extra material of my deflated skirt.

'Isn't it? Shame.' As he watches me, he settles back against the throne and leers. 'Because you know nothing has to change between us.'

'Is that all that matters to you? Is this all you are?'

He shrugs. 'Isn't that what you came for?'

There's some truth to it and seeing him filling the throne, legs wide and knees butting up against its arms heightens his physicality and my lust for it. My cheeks burn.

'You're no better than Onnachild. You're his son through and through. How could anyone doubt that? Look at you there, clutching that throne for dear life. It's not yours and it's not his to give you. You care more about pleasing him than your own mother.' I kick the parchments, slipping on them. 'You ... you disgust me.'

'Then, goodbye, Niah. It's been fun.' He focuses on the parchments as if I'm not here, chest heaving with frustration and words I can't even form. He leans out the throne, gathers them into a neat pile, and then drops it onto the table. He drags the candle over so it illuminates the parchments. His left hand goes into his hair, knuckles showing through as he rests on it. There's a smudge of black ink on one.

'Are you done?' he asks. 'Only I have things to review.'

I yank out a chair, drop into it, and snatch the top parchment. Raen ignores me and focuses on the next one in the pile. The spiky words of Onnachild's language are hard to read, and I silently curse Vill for not letting me continue with my reading. Still, Raen doesn't know that. I recognise the letters of his name at the end of the document. There's a line waiting for his signature. I can stay here all night if it will prevent him signing this thing. Whatever it is. Raen chuckles but I don't dare to look at him. The words start to blur, the slants losing their precision, and the fat full stops dance like impatient children. The fire's warmth has spread to this end of the room, and the light from the candle makes the space strangely cosy. I tuck my feet up under me and rest my chin on my hand. Those words become a black mess.

Chapter Forty-Five

JUST AS WE'RE FINISHING BREAKFAST, there's a knock on my door, one too timid to be Raen or Vill. Melody frowns, flicks back the long veil attached to her headdress and answers the door. Nessia stashes the parchment I stole from the Judging Room under the rug by the fire.

It's Eldini and her calm composure from yesterday has gone; her hands flutter up and down, the fingers twitching. She's frowning, those white eyebrows peaking at the flat bridge of her nose. 'I come ask you walk gardens.' There's a catch in her voice, hinting that she expects a refusal. 'No one walk with me.' She puts a toe over the threshold. 'Gavin with King. My women go Sunning Room, and I want outside.'

Nessia nudges me to respond. Raen's words return: *docile and pliable.* Her pale-blue gown cascades from her skinny shoulders mimicking a waterfall, and her whiteness makes her seem insubstantial against the wood-panelled walls, so I don't have the heart to refuse her. All I can manage is a nod as my mind whirls: can I tell her, can I dissuade her, have the gods brought her to my rooms?

'I'll get your shoes,' Melody says.

Eldini glides forwards into a patch of sunlight that curves around her wide forehead. 'I should not have made request. You look upset. I help?' Her fingers settle on my arm. They're warmer than I was expecting them to be.

'I'm tired, that's all. I couldn't sleep.' I pat them, wanting to make her feel better and that sentiment surprises me.

'No one sleep. Raen tired too.'

'You share his bed?' Nessia asks.

'No ... no ... no.' Smudges of pink colour Eldini's cheeks. 'He almost fall sleep in prayer this morning.' She titters, and the colour disappears. Her pale eyes gleam like the opals on her hood.

So that is where he was. I woke up cold and alone in the Judging Room, mildly irritated that he hadn't thought to take me to my bed. Even the parchments had gone, except for the one under my cheek. The line for his name was smudged from where I must have dribbled on it in my sleep.

'Raen praying?' Melody asks, pausing on her hands and knees by a chair as she hunts for my shoes.

'Raen not pray?'

'No one prays.' Melody sweeps her arm under the chair. 'Well, except for us Maidens.'

'It's a long story.' I step back so Eldini's fingers slip from my arm.

'Then lucky I come and lucky we have all day.' She beams at me.

'Indeed,' I say, hoping she doesn't notice how flat my voice sounds.

She smiles and the sun shines on her white teeth, even and as small as a child's.

'Found them,' Melody shouts, my shoes held high. Village mud is encrusted around the heels, and the jewel has fallen off the toe of one.

'You like walking.' Eldini titters. 'Me too.' She gathers up the hem of her skirts to show the tips of her blue shoes where there is a dark stain. There's a cheekiness to her grin. 'You come too?' she asks Nessia.

'Yes, Nessia, come on. There's nothing that can't wait until tomorrow,' I say.

Nessia races into the bedroom for her shoes, mumbling to herself.

As we walk the hallways, the castle has a calm air to it despite the frantic activity of the servants while they wash the windows. One is humming. He sweeps water across the glass, diffusing the sunlight. It plays across Eldini as she shimmies down the hallways. She pauses at the portraits and grips her fingers tight, but when I ask if something is wrong she shakes her head and glides on. No portrait of Raen has been added. However, the spot left by Aelius's is filled with a portrait of him as a baby. He resembles Ammi so much that my heart hurts. I linger and trace the loose curls trailing over his podgy shoulders. *For you, I'll tell Eldini. I'll make her go so she won't be Queen.*

Was the portrait here when I encountered the nursemaid? I can't remember. I was too overcome by seeing Ammi, but that's no excuse, I should have noticed; I love Aelius. A shudder as if the dead are breathing down my neck makes me run on. Are they here to remind me of my duty?

Nessia squints at me, suspicious, when I catch up with them. I duck my head to avoid her gaze as Eldini continues talking. 'In my land, summers very hot and very cold winters. They say warm here also. They say sun always shines.'

'You must have brought the sunshine,' Nessia says. 'It rains more than it shines.'

Eldini nods as she opens a door to the castle grounds.

Outside, she stands so close to me I can smell her faint scent: lemons and vanilla. 'I do not want talk of weather,' she says. That unease has returned to her fingers and they flutter her long sleeve. 'I have ... how you say? Alt ... Alteret ...' She waves her hand. 'Different reason to walk. You know Raen. Yes?'

'Does anyone really know Raen?' I mumble, remembering last night and how different he was to the man I was becoming friends with. Which one is the real one? The licentious one, obsessed with power, or the one who hoped to find one of his mother's hairs in an old book?

Eldini's forehead lowers, and it brings down her hood. She stamps her foot and Nessia's eyebrows rise in surprise. Eldini pushes her hood back, exposing a fluff of white hair. Nessia goes to help but Eldini moves away with a weak smile. 'I hate it.'

'Then take it off,' I say.

Her eyes widen. 'I not married yet.' She sighs and her narrow shoulders slope in, creating a wave down the front of her dress. 'Please. We walk.'

I nod and we amble off again, walking over the grass which has a dry crackle to it today. Patches have browned from too much sun, and Eldini steps into each one with a childish determination. Nessia and I peer over her at each other and shrug. We follow the path between the rounded trees where the shade mirrors their odd shape. Eldini picks a wilted flower and asks Nessia its name. No one else is around, but she doesn't seem pleased to have the grounds to herself. Her walk, usually a glide, seems heavier today, disturbing the pebbles. She pauses by the fountain and holds out her palm to catch drops of water being dispersed by the gentle breeze.

'What did you want to ask me about?' I sit on the bench and slip off my shoes. 'Raen?'

As she joins me on the bench, her gaze darts around the grounds. She smooths her skirts out, and then she bends forwards and lifts off her hood. The fountain's spray has brightened the opals on it. Her hair is bundled together in a series of plaits, overlapping and tucked in. It's a brilliant white ball, blinding as the sun reflects off it. One fluffy strand rests on her chin. She sighs and tips her head back against the bench, closing her eyes. Where the hood had rested is a sheen of sweat and a red line. The imperfection makes her more earthly and less ethereal. She sighs again, and her frown returns.

Nessia picks Eldini's hood up from the path, drops it again. 'It's heavy.' She shifts its weight evenly between her hands.

'Yes.' Eldini settles into her regal pose. 'Very heavy. Very hot.'

Nessia sits on the side of the fountain, resting the hood on her lap while the water sprinkles onto her grey hair.

'I speak now,' Eldini says.

I nod. She nods back. Nessia dips her fingers into the fountain.

'I ask about what you say about Raen. I must make decision about marriage.' She nods, seemingly pleased with herself for getting out the words. Without her hood on, she's almost beautiful and the plaits make her seem younger. *Docile and pliable.* I stare at my bare toes, remembering how they rested on Raen's buttocks, and they curl, scooping up sharp pebbles. I cross my ankles. The heat on them feels similar to his mouth. My fake smile droops as I fight against the desire to tell her everything: how cruel he is, how he will never love her, how my kisses can bring him to his knees. Why should I not tell her? I peep up at Nessia for help, encouragement, but she's dripping water onto Eldini's hood and making the opals gleam.

'Why me? Didn't you bring someone who could advise you?' I ask.

'Yes. No. My advisers not mine, my father's. My women, they say he handsome. They think only about ... that and not ... not ...'

'Important matters?' Nessia asks.

'Yes, impor ... important.' She nods. 'A lot to think of. We want marriage into this land. It good for us, and good for you.'

'Then you do not have a choice?' Nessia asks.

'I have choice. I can make ... erm ...' She rubs her forehead. 'Objections. Yes, objections if I think, no, not for me. I can have changes if I want. I want to please my father, my people.'

Duty, obligation, an heir, but it's not Raen's words making me uncomfortable, it's the image of his lips pursing, his eyes blazing with lust while he tried to seduce me on the table. How will Eldini respond when she's caught in their sight line? Will she tremble like a sapling? Will her skin brighten like a rose after rain?

'Do you like him?' My voice is so quiet I don't think she heard me but her cheeks flush. Waiting for an answer, I scatter pebbles with my foot. Their sharpness makes me wince but I do it again, once, twice, again until the brown below shows. Nessia puts the hood down on the path and then stops my foot. Eldini's fingers flutter her sleeve again.

'What will make you agree?' Nessia asks.

'If he is good man. If he be good king. You can help me?' She shuffles in her seat, bringing her face closer, and her pale eyes search mine for answers I don't have. If she'd asked me a few days ago, I might still have been fooled by his fake amiability. I want to tell her about the battle, about the death that is coming if she agrees, but I find I can't bear to see the horror such knowledge would bring to her childlike face. That frown is bad enough. I reach for her hands and the contact makes her jump, but she doesn't remove them.

'You must decide based on what you see,' I say, surprising myself by my weakness. 'No one can speak ill of a member of the crowned family.'

'You would?'

'I meant we're not allowed to, that Onnachild would—'

'That why I come to you.' She grips my thumb with unexpected strength. 'Raen say you always say your mind and you do not care to say what Onnachild say.'

'He said that so I can put his case to you.'

'No. No. You say the truth. Nessia?'

We both stare over at her. She looks concerned but I can't tell if it's for me or Eldini. A goldfinch flies above us, and Eldini follows its path through the sky and into the cover of a tree. Her frown deepens into a grimace when our eyes meet again. Then her head lowers, and she lets out a breath so long and forceful it worries the strand of hair by her chin.

'What do you think of Raen?' Nessia asks.

Eldini rests her hands in her lap and straightens her shoulders. There's a determined lift of her chin and it seems she might avoid the question again, but then she starts fidgeting and fiddling with the braiding on her sleeve and peeps at me with an impish grin. 'He is handsome. He make me laugh. He say changes he make to land, to castle. He want to make people godly again. He will make better, fair.'

'He's only saying that so you'll accept,' I moan.

Nessia shakes her head at me. My foot scrabbles for more stones.

'He lie?'

'Do you know his history?' Nessia asks.

'Yes. I hear. Mother was like Niah.'

'Did he tell you that?' I snap.

She squirms under my glare.

'Niah,' Nessia warns.

She's right. I force myself to relax. 'Sorry. Only, no one is meant to know.' My voice sounds so sulky I tense again.

'Onnachild has lie for you,' Eldini says. 'I say to no one. Onnachild is kind. Raen be kind, too.'

I huff at the word kind.

'You not agree?' Eldini asks.

I stare into the sun, let it momentarily blind me and in that blur, the castle disappears. There's the goldfinch's song, the patter of the fountain's spray blown onto the path. Eldini's lemon and vanilla scent. My heavy heart banging away.

'Forgive me,' I say. 'Raen said he wouldn't tell anyone. He said ... he says many things.' I rise to leave but a little gasp from Eldini stops me, and I turn to see what has startled her. It's Raen sauntering across the lawns with Vill beside him, deep in conversation. Their laughter carries over. Behind them are Eldini's men, white blurs like the spots the sun made in my vision.

'Do not be angry at him.' She gestures for Nessia to pass over her hood. Instead, Nessia goes to her and helps settle the contraption back along that line of sweat. 'Do not be angry at me.' Eldini's features are drowned out by the opals and silver of her hood and the material of her veil.

'Who else knows?' I ask.

'Gavin.' She grimaces.

I sink down onto the edge of the fountain, accidentally sitting in a patch of water trapped in a dip of the marble. If Onnachild finds out ... Its coldness seeps through my skirt, causing me to shiver. 'Raen told him?'

She shakes her head, almost getting caught up in her veil as Nessia tries to arrange it. 'King. Gavin say to me. He know I say to no one. I not say.'

'What else do you know?'

She stares at the men and I do too. I can't see Raen but his chuckle still reaches us.

'It's all right.' Nessia pats Eldini's shoulder.

'I fine,' Eldini says. 'Raen not like gossip about ... he hurt when half-brother said about. I not like to hurt him.' She sends a concerned look towards Raen. 'He love half-brother.'

I ignore the lie and repeat my question. 'What else do you know?'

She nods. 'You in love. In love with Aelius. The baby Grace ... his. Yours.' She points at me.

'Onnachild told Gavin this?'

She nods. 'He think it make Gavin not like you. Gavin like you more. Says it show you kind and good-hearted.' She peeps back at Raen. Their chatter is getting louder with her men joining in with the jokes. He will notice us soon and direct them away—he must. My heart is speeding fast for him. My palms are getting sweaty, and the heat of the sun is making me feel faint even with the fountain spraying at me.

'You loved Prince Aelius?' she asks.

I nod and plunge my hand into the chilled water. The coolness does not go far enough. The men are parting, and Raen's turning our way. 'Love has little currency in this castle.'

'Your parents, they help Gavin? They help you?'

'My mother is dead, and I've no idea where my father is.'

'Sorry. I keep saying things make you ... upset.'

'I'm not upset.'

Raen pauses; he's spotted us. I wipe my hand across my hot forehead, startled by the drip of chilled water from my fingers. His shoulders rise. His chuckle drops out from the noise of the men.

'I do not know what I say,' Eldini says. 'I am careless. I want us as friends.'

'It doesn't matter.' I'm unable to move from Raen's scowl. Vill jostles past him, knocking his shoulder. Raen crosses his arms and tilts his head. Thinking I've caused his anger thrills me; let him think I'm telling her. I smile to annoy him further. 'You'll soon learn that Onnachild and Raen don't consider me a suitable friend for you.'

'I decide. Not right to judge. God judge. God see in heart and forgive if heart pure and true.'

Raen pivots on his heels and strides out towards the river, drawing the men after him. Eldini pushes her hood off and into Nessia's waiting hands but her frown remains, even when we talk about more pleasant matters.

Chapter Forty-Six

'WHERE HAVE YOU BEEN TODAY?' Nilola asks me in the Great Hall. She's wearing a white hood similar to Eldini's and it's hard to focus on anything else because it pulls at the corner of her eyes. 'I had some great gossip I wanted to share with you.'

After Eldini left Nessia and me for her afternoon prayers, I returned to my rooms, determined to catch up on my sleep but every time I tried, her face appeared like sun spots blazed into my pupils. I can't tell Nilola that so I distract her by asking about her gossip.

She smiles smugly. 'Vill told me not to tell anyone.'

I shake my head, a little confused. It must be due to tiredness.

'He didn't tell you anything. You didn't even see him today,' Beshanie interjects, pushing herself up against me. She's wearing a pale-orange gown that floats about her broad shoulders and large bosom. It's the same style as Eldini's apart from the cage underneath.

'How do you know?' Nilola says. 'I'm not always with you.'

'Shut up,' Beshanie hisses.

Raen, Eldini, and Onnachild have appeared and everyone stands. Eldini is clutching onto Raen's hand. She's an image of virginity in her white dress with primroses embroidered around the high neck and down the long sleeves. The same yellow is echoed in the jewels dotting her hood. It is more ornate than the one she wore earlier and the arches are more pointed. The highest peak almost reaches Raen's nose. Her frown has gone.

Raen has a simple expression on his face and a contented air about him that implies he managed to sleep, to dream, which is unfair and so it's one more thing to hold against him. His hair has been tied into a low bow at the nape of his neck, same as the other castle men, but he isn't the same as the other men. Does Eldini realise this?

He whispers in her ear, drawing her closer. He doesn't look my way. She titters, covering her mouth and hiding against him so he has to tip his head back to avoid the peak of her hood. He's a master at pretending. Well, he can have that bony thing. Docile and pliable—we'll see how long he enjoys that. Why would any man want that in a wife? These castle men do because they're weak. Aelius wasn't weak. Not like Raen. Not like me, unable to tell Eldini all the truths that would have her running. Even now, my hateful thoughts about her have me feeling ashamed. It's not her fault; it's Raen's. He seems to sense my thoughts, his gaze being drawn to me. It's blank as if I'm not glaring at him, as if we didn't argue last night. I could be a stranger.

Onnachild coughs and Raen's attention darts to his father. A servant subtly passes Onnachild a square of fabric, which he spits into. He looks to Raen, who only shakes his head in response. How can they now understand each other without words? Another thing I've failed in: I was meant to ensure Raen continued displeasing his father. Onnachild squints as though he's searching for something but has forgotten what. There's a waft of mould. I sniff, hunting for the cause amongst the flowers, candlelight, and those banners with Eldini's scrawny bird and Onnachild's hawk.

Music starts: a soft harp and a high-pitched voice singing a lilting tune. Raen whispers in Eldini's ear again, and she nods. Onnachild bumps into his seat, arms splayed. Raen pulls out Aelius's chair for Eldini, and she floats into it. We all sit.

'The little fool.' Beshanie pours wine for me.

'I think it's sweet,' Nilola says.

It's obvious to me now: the decision has been made. It's there in the nervous way Eldini keeps hold of Raen, in the determined tilt of her chin, in the ostentatious hood. When I try to look at Vill, he ignores me and leans over to draw Raen into a conversation, proving how right I am. Both of them seem more relaxed tonight. Even Onnachild is subdued and at peace despite the cough rattling his chest again. I should have dissuaded her. Why didn't I? I drain my goblet and hold it out to Beshanie. She raises her eyebrows but refills it without question.

Please, just get it over and done with.

Onnachild taps Eldini's arm, and she beams up at him. He coughs again, hits his chest. She tugs on Raen's sleeve to get his attention. He looks down at it, not her, and then, as if he's aware I'm watching, he rubs his thumb over her knuckles.

The Maidens circle around the tables, each holding a pale-pink bottle. The flash of it takes me back to the night Raen begged me for a kiss. I've made so many mistakes since then. I should have at least demanded the book from him. My fingers brush my lips. The wine has left some dampness there. I feel Raen's attention on me and so I drop my hand to my lap, stare at the golden birds stitched into the tablecloth. If I had not given in so easily to Raen, to my body, would Aelius's chair still be vacant?

'It doesn't mean anything good,' Melody whispers to me as she pours spirit from the pink bottle into an eggcup-sized glass.

'I guessed as much,' I whisper.

She places the glass in front of Beshanie. Beshanie dips her finger into the liquid and licks it off. 'What's this rubbish?'

'Blessed spirits from Eldini's land.' Melody places one before me. 'To toast with.' She glares up at Raen. He doesn't notice; he's too taken with Eldini's spindly wrist.

'Oh please,' Beshanie moans, dipping her finger in again.

As Melody moves further along the table, I slouch down in my chair. Once everyone has a glass, the Maidens line up behind Eldini, Melody still glaring at Raen. Eldini is rigid in her seat. Onnachild gets to his feet, raises his glass towards her.

'We are pleased to announce negotiations have ended and both sides ...' There's no boom to Onnachild's voice. People at the far end of the table create a rush of whispering asking what he said. Raen rises, places his hand on his father's shoulder. The whispering stops. Onnachild is squinting and searching around the room again. That waft of mould has returned. Are the dead here? *Please, don't hurt Eldini. She's young. She is nothing to do with this.*

'I'm pleased to announce that the beautiful Princess Eldini has formally agreed to be my wife.' Raen's voice is all castle prince.

I peer into the shadowy corners of the room, checking for the dead. Nothing moves. Outside, the blue of the sky is deepening and there's an apricot tinge to the clouds, all calm except for me: my heart is hammering and I can't grab a deep-enough breath.

'It's a great honour she does me and our land. To the blessed future ahead for us, all of us.'

The mixed fragrances of beeswax and roses replace the odour of mould. I dab my sweaty forehead with my sleeve, hoping people are too focused on Raen to notice my bad manners. He raises his glass, small and fragile in his large hand, and slams it back so speedily his pose of princely assurance is ruined. As he wipes his lips, his gaze settles on me. I down my drink, not toasting him, not toasting Eldini. The sound of glasses tapping glasses tinkles around me.

Nilola's coughing.

Raen's attention returns to Eldini, who's sipping at her drink. A clap starts from somewhere and builds in volume as more and more people join in. A woman across from me dabs at her eyes, whether the tears are from emotion or the burn of the drink I can't tell. Maidens are making another lap of the table, refilling glasses. Melody tries to comfort me when she reaches me, but I shake off her touch. I down my drink as soon as it's refilled and shove the glass out for another before she's too far away. The spirit warms me, and my eyelids become heavy.

Others are toasting again, the glasses grating against each other like sword on sword. Eldini's white dress and veil resemble a shroud in the candlelight, and I'm sure her face is paler than normal. Is it regret making her stare, blankly, out into the centre of the room? Her hands are under the table but I'm convinced they'll be fluttering her sleeve. Raen seems distant as he talks to Vill and Gavin. I should have warned Eldini, told her what he said about her.

Still, it's done now. The words are out. It will happen. Beshanie pushes her glass over to me. I dash back the liquid and let myself be reminded of home, home before Onnachild invoked the wrath of the gods and brought famine. I can't remember my grandfather's face, but I remember he smelt of smoke and soot, and when he'd drunk too much, his laugh resembled the rapping of a woodpecker. Reminiscing increases my need for my grandmother, her comfort and wise words, but only Raen's mother will come; did she not threaten me with that? Her face, her recriminations are more than I can bear. *Mating, mating, fucking.*

I didn't even enjoy it with Raen and no, he isn't handsome. Aelius was. Aelius was as beautiful and as precious as the first day of sunshine after winter. Raen's like mud, mud flooded and seeping where it isn't wanted. How could I have thought him attractive? He's too wide, too tall, and it makes him overbearing. And he's always so guarded because he's suspicious of everyone. Nothing like my grinning, trusting Aelius, who didn't have the guile to hide anything. I drink away the sour taste of the First Queen's words. Just thinking about them unsettles my stomach.

'I knew,' Nilola is saying behind me to Beshanie as though I'm not here.

Perhaps I'm not and this is all a dream, only when I pinch my leg it hurts.

'It was so obvious,' she continues. 'Vill was in such a bad mood yesterday. He said he had important business to attend to but couldn't because someone was being ... well, I can't use the word he did. And then today, he's all smiles and compliments again.'

'Of course, you knew. You always know everything.'

'I think she'll be a beautiful bride, such a beautiful bride, and maybe it'll be you next.' Nilola elbows me and that hurts, too. 'Niah, you might get your proposal.'

I fake a smile and nod.

'Yes, maybe now your guardian will release you,' Beshanie mocks.

'Perhaps,' I mumble, too tired to rise to her bait. Maybe I should press for permission and run, run somewhere where I'll not be able to hear about the battle, see Raen. What would it be like to be married to Gavin? He looks attractive sat there amongst his people who are as white as him. Pride is making his chest puff out, and the spirit has added a tint of colour to his cheeks. Perhaps in the marriage bed, at the moment of satisfaction, I could ... He's as slender as Aelius, shorter. I could stare into Gavin's eyes and imagine them a more vibrant blue. A quiet land, Eldini said they came from. A quiet land would be a welcome relief compared to the men getting riled up by the spirit, compared to Beshanie and Nilola arguing about Vill. Maybe quiet is what we need: Nessia, Ammi, and I. Gavin would be a respectable father. *Docile and pliable.* The words make me grimace.

I down another glassful of spirit that has appeared from somewhere. Tears come as it burns the back of my throat. There'd be no peace for me in Gavin's land. No matter how far away from the village I go, the battle echoes will reach me. And my ancestors would never forgive me.

Pushing away from the table, I knock into a servant as they place down a tray. The spirit floods through my body, numbing my legs. I enjoy it blurring and softening me, the room, others, so that nothing matters because it doesn't seem real or permanent. Raen can smile at Eldini, and she can blush as much as she wants. Her little fingers can flutter and worry her sleeves until the fabric disintegrates for all I care.

Onnachild is helped to his feet by the advisers, one under each arm. I halt when his attention settles on me. His smile is disconcerting because it is real. The odour of mould is so strong I lift my arm to check it isn't coming from me. I smell of Raen, Raen and the sweetness of the spirit. The advisers glance my way before vanishing behind the curtain with Onnachild.

A stout merchant barging into me gets me moving again, and I follow him across the room. He forces the doors to the gardens open with one hand and in the other is a lump of bright-red meat that looks like it still needs cooking. 'Whale,' he explains.

'Eldini brought it,' a lithe man from her land says to me. I ignore him, pushing through a group of men shouting over each other.

'No delay.'

'There should be no delay.'

'Those hedge-born bastards.'

'We'll teach them.'

Laughter.

'We don't give up. We will never give up. To King Onnachild.'

Goblets are clanked together. Men. Men and their stupid battles. Their excitement makes me nauseous, and I hide a burp in my palm. My gaze sweeps over the gardens, beyond, into the darkness where the land plunges away to fields, the village, and people who are hungry and worn out. There must be something I can do; I can't have failed.

'Niah, do you need anything? You look a little sickly.' It's Gavin.

I can't smile or pretend to be anyone other than myself tonight. 'Yes, I am a little unwell.' I touch my face. It's hot and clammy.

'Perhaps the excitement is too much?'

'Perhaps.' I hold myself in, arms crossed and hands clutching my elbows.

'I hope you didn't mind me telling my sister about you.' He hangs his head and peeps up through his white lashes like a child caught out.

'No. It's ... relieving that you know the truth and don't think badly of me because of it.'

'I couldn't.' He smiles timidly. 'She wanted to meet you. She told me she looked into your eyes and saw all she needed to.'

'And what was that?'

He steps closer and his arm touches mine, making him retreat and flush. 'She approves. She says she'll talk to Vill. He'll be inclined to talk favourably to your guardian, won't he?'

'Maybe.'

Gavin is almost handsome, same as Eldini is almost beautiful. It's those white eyebrows and lashes. They have similar noses, delicate and petite, though the bridge of his is more defined.

'Why would your guardian not approve? I'm a prince.' His chest puffs out.

'I don't want a prince.' My voice is much harsher than I intended, and my words deflate his chest and have him staring down at my feet. 'Excuse me. I mean, it holds no weight with me. I'm sorry. I've been overexcited today.'

'What's troubling you?' He lifts his face, and the concern on it is so genuine that, for a moment, I think I might cry.

'The battle,' I mumble.

'That is sweet of you to worry but there's no need. We will win.'

'What makes you so sure? Onnachild's not won a battle for twenty years. He lost the sea. He lost—'

'He won the most important battle, though. He won this land for you.'

Eldini was wrong; Gavin knows nothing about me, about this land. It belongs to the Aegni, I want to yell at him. It's not Onnachild's. And it shouldn't be Raen's either, considering the lack of care he's showing it by agreeing to marry this foreign princess. Gavin's as foolish and pompous as Aelius, and I'm urged to ruin his innocence with the truth about death, hatred, battles. When I go to do this, it's an image of Raen that comes to my mind: his head on my lap, jerking, as he spews blood. I reach out, steady myself. Gavin jolts at my fingers touching his arm. His face flushes bright red. Vill's shouting my name, bounding out into the gardens and causing Gavin to shift his weight from foot to foot.

Vill bows graciously to Gavin. 'Pardon me, if I may have a word with Niah?' He doesn't give me the same courtesy, dragging me off into a dark shadow and making enough of a scene for Gavin to skulk away looking chastised.

'Did you not get my instructions? Look stunning, unobtainable, and uninterested, I said. Draw Raen's attention to you, I said.' Vill keeps his voice so low it's almost a hiss. 'It shouldn't be too difficult when Eldini matches the tablecloth, yet he's in there dancing with her and you ... What are you doing sneaking around with Gavin?' He leans closer, closer, backing me up against the castle wall.

'I'm not sneaking around with Gavin.' I rub at the imprint Vill's grip has left on my wrist. 'So now you want me to ignore Gavin? Make up your mind.'

'Oh, please, when have you ever followed my suggestions?' He twists the ring on his thumb around and around. 'Gavin must be made to abandon his pursuit. Are you aware he tried to convince Onnachild again yesterday? He's persistent, I'll give him that, but incredibly foolish if he believes that during the final negotiations for this wedding is the correct time to press for his own.'

'Perhaps I want to marry Gavin.'

'Don't be ridiculous. I'm in no mood for joking today and neither should you be. I take it you heard what was proclaimed in there?'

'Yes. I heard.' I size up to him, straining my neck and tilting up my head. 'You said if I mated with him he wouldn't marry her, that he'd want to please me and not Onnachild. That—' Even as I'm saying the words my cheeks are burning with shame, and I'm not sure whether it's because of what I did or the fact that I didn't use it to my advantage. Either way, it feels good to have anger surging through my veins again.

'Don't blame me. If there's a place where blame should lie ...' He gestures at me.

'Me? Me?'

'I said, as I recall, manipulate him, use your influence, seduce him.' His gaze drops to my fists and his top lip quirks. 'Not lift your skirts and pant after him like some common wench. That didn't work with the last prince so why would it work with this one?'

I lunge for him.

He sidesteps. 'Now, now Niah. Remember where we are.'

'Aelius loved me. He—'

'Yes. Yes, he did.' Vill takes a deep breath and as he exhales, his features settle into his perfect pose of boredom. 'Listen to us. We're behaving worse than Onnachild. It's essential we remain level-headed and not ... My comments, I admit, were uncalled for. I've been in Raen's company for far too long and it's made me forget all my manners. Please, forgive me. Trust me, I'm as frustrated as you are.'

'I doubt it.' I stare over at the groups of men, none of them paying us any mind as they laugh and dance some strange jig together. One man is pretending to be a bull rushing at a tablecloth held out by another. He narrowly misses Raen who's coming out with a pink bottle stuffed under his arm and a crowd of staggering men behind him. His hair is escaping its bow, strands dangling over his face and softening the harsh line of his jaw.

'Niah?' Vill says.

I unfurl my fists. 'Fine. I forgive you.'

'Excellent. Now that is sorted, we need to decide on our next course of action. If we want the wedding stopped, we have only a few days.'

'A few days?' I shake my head. 'Of course, it'd be so soon. Raen doesn't care about the wedding. Neither does Onnachild. They'd be content to see her married in a sack by a drunk priest, just as long as she's married.'

'It's quick because Onnachild's ill, and everyone is keen to see matters finalised in case Onnachild succumbs and can't sign off the contracts. Well, when I say everyone—'

'Raen told me, but Onnachild didn't seem ... he does today. Do you think he'll die?'

'Hard to say, the man has the constitution of a wild pig. Now, where was I? I wish you wouldn't interrupt me; I'm far too tired to keep track of my thoughts. At least with these negotiations over I might actually obtain a moment for myself. I can't wait to sleep again and have my mind back. I swear I'm getting stupider by the day.' His fingers skim over the skin at the corner of his eyes, probably checking for lines. 'Ah yes, the other reason the wedding is being rushed is because the negotiations were so protracted. Onnachild has a specific date for the battle, something about God and auspiciousness and ...' Vill dismisses the notion with a wave of his hand. 'Anyway, Raen's been digging his heels in, finding fault with the contracts, pushing his luck. All a ploy. I suspect he's hoping his father will die or at least be too ill for matters to progress.'

Raen did say he was trying to postpone the battle. Should I trust him? Only last night he showed how little he cares about anything but himself, and as I watch him now, he doesn't seem worried about what follows the wedding. He's clapping the man pretending to be a bull on the back and then he pushes the man towards the cloth. His chuckle resonates across the night and into my body. I slump against the cool wall.

'What this tells me,' Vill says, 'is that he isn't overly keen on this marriage and therefore could still be swayed to cast her aside.'

Raen's actions don't tell me that. All he had to do was say no, yet he cares more for the throne, more for pleasing his father than the people. I hope the dead are here and that they tear the castle apart.

'If we're lucky the excitement of the wedding will see Onnachild in his grave,' Vill says.

'If only.'

Raen's tunic is ripped during a friendly scuffle with the bull-man, exposing a dark triangle of hair on his chest. I press my palm against the rough stone wall behind me and rub it while that exposing triangle moves as he greets well-wishers. Vill's finger taps on my collarbone to get my attention. Raen vanishes amongst the men. His chuckle fades. I shake my head, clearing away his presence, and focus on Vill. 'But there would still be Raen,' I say.

'He has not been declared heir yet nor has the proclamation declaring him a bastard been overturned. A fact that's obviously been kept from Eldini's father. Until Aesc records Raen as heir, we still have everything to play for and there are many other ways that Raen displeases his father. Despite what Raen thinks, this marriage won't necessarily see him claimed and welcomed into the official family. You're not there to witness it but I am. I see it. When Onnachild looks at his son it's like he smells something deeply unpleasant. In fact, I suspect it isn't even Raen he's seeing but the mother. We can work on keeping them apart, and I'll be able to focus on swaying the merchants again without Onnachild getting suspicious. You keep Raen from Eldini. Remember, until he says "I do", nothing is permanent. Actually, even then ... we've all seen how little these men respect the sanctity of marriage.'

Raen tumbles from a group of merchants with his hair a mess and his features slack from drink. That rip in his tunic calls to my fingertips. 'I need to go.' I push off the wall, sidling past Vill's outstretched arms.

Raen's bottle has dropped onto the floor and I step on the shards as I push through the crowd, ducking under sweaty armpits, ignoring crude comments and lecherous hands. I jab my elbow into the hard belly of a merchant to make him move, and he howls at me, but I keep walking. I step on the foot of one of Eldini's men, who apologises. As I turn with surprise at his manners, I bump into Raen. The shock radiates through my body like an errant ember popped from a fire.

'Niah,' he slurs, smiling.

I curtsy as formally, as coldly, as I can. My eyes lock with his, and I hope they remind him of the Aegni women and make him feel guilty for agreeing to this marriage. 'Congratulations,' I say loud enough for his companions to hear.

He bows to me because he should, because it's what he's being trained to do.

'Coward,' I hiss in his ear.

Chapter Forty-Seven

NESSIA'S HAND JUMPS TO HER CHEST when she enters my dayroom mid-afternoon and spots me hunched up in a chair. 'What are you doing here? Aren't you meant to be in the Sunning Room? Have you been here all day?'

'I went there. I came back.' I lob another log into the fire, and glare into the coloured flames.

'Aren't you hot enough already?'

'No.' My face is burning and my palms are sweaty but this seems to be the only way to release this anger from my body.

'Ah, you're sulking.'

'I'm not—' I stop because I do sound sulky.

She laughs, rubbing my head. 'No? Perhaps you're jealous then?'

'Jealous? I'm not jealous. Why would I be jealous?'

'Eldini's only getting the throne, the castle. Raen.'

I lean away from her touch and smooth my hair. A pin gets knocked out onto the floor. I shunt it away with my shoe, the gem shrieking against the stone floor. 'Why does she get to have everything that should be mine?' The childish sentiment disgusts me. I push away from the fire because it's too hot, and it's making me feel grimy.

I stomp to my bedchamber and the mirror there; I want to see my anger. My face is lean and tight, my eyes are florid green. 'I betrayed Aelius for nothing. Nothing.'

'Not for nothing.'

'Vill said if I did, that Raen would send her back ... that ... What does it matter? He's going to marry her. I failed.'

'But you didn't do it for that reason, did you?'

I meet her gaze in the mirror. 'No? Then why did I?'

'You know why.'

I look away. 'It was a mistake. I tricked myself.'

'Don't lie to me or yourself, both will find you out.'

'I—' I wince as the truth of her words hit. The grain of the dressing table mutates, patches become limbs entwined, torsos undulating and joining. I block the sight with my arm. 'My body wanted to.' The words are a whisper. Nessia squeezes my shoulders, reassuring me and encouraging me to speak. 'I wanted to. I wanted to feel something, someone. Sometimes I feel so ... there's nothing left of me, the real me. Niah from the Aegni, the village.' I press along my high cheekbones and around the tilting outline of my eyes. 'Everywhere there's just death and more death. But I ... I felt alive again. When I'm with ... It sounds like an excuse, doesn't it? It does. I don't know what I felt. Perhaps, that I wasn't alone anymore. And I ... I enjoyed it. Him. And now.' I shake my head and close my mouth.

'I forget how young you are sometimes.' She tweaks my chin, drawing my eyes to hers. What I see in the depths of hers makes me want to cry. For within those familiar hazel tones, I see the village, our shared memories and pain. Her half-smile always used to make me believe better times were coming. 'When you're young, the present feels like forever, but it isn't and you have many years ahead of you. As seasons change, so do we, so do our needs. No one is meant to be alone. Raen is lonely, too.'

I shrug and duck from her. Eldini is here and she'll marry Raen and she'll give him children so he won't be alone or lonely. 'Where have you been?' I ask to change the topic; I've moped long enough.

'With Llwellyin.'

'Who's Llwellyin?'

'You met him before, in the washroom. Remember?'

I nod, picturing only a rim of grey hair. Judging by her widening smile and the blue flower poking out of her loose bun, she's had fun. At least one of us is enjoying their time here. My face screws up with annoyance at the self-pitying thought. I rise from the dressing table, and Nessia follows me over to the bed where the parchment I snatched from Raen lies across the furs. The line waiting for his signature is blank, the black ink has faded to purple, and Nessia's thumbprint is sooty in the corner. 'Did you manage to read it?'

'Most of it. It needs him to sign off approval on the villagers joining the wedding feast.'

Nothing that will stop the wedding then. I screw it up. My fists smack against my hips as I march to the fire to throw in the ball of parchment. It unfurls amongst the flames and crackles around the edges, orange and black crinkling them. 'Bastard,' I hiss. 'Bastard.' How he must have laughed when he realised I'd taken that one. 'Bastard.' I throw another log into the fire, dislodging and scattering white ash. 'And saying we could continue like I have no better morals than a ... than—'

'Niah, if you enjoyed it ... why not continue?'

'I don't want him. I don't even like him. It's done. I told him.'

She laughs softly.

'Stop laughing. This isn't him forgetting to pay me a compliment. This isn't him ...' I smear the soot over the dark floor with my foot. 'He doesn't care for anything other than pleasing Onnachild.'

'Are you sure about that?' Her words are hesitant and her voice quiet, but still I scowl at her. She holds out her arms like I'm a child learning to walk. 'Now, come on, come away from the fire. Let's work out how to get that smile back on your face.'

'Why must I pretend with you?' I drag my hand over my face but can't wipe away my emotions. 'I can't always pretend. I'm sick of pretending. All of it. I'm sick of all of it. This place. Raen. Me.' I stare at my dress, the pastel-green skirt smudged with white and black ash. The jewels around my wrist no longer shine. I want out of this dress, this stupid costume that fools no one. No one except me. I kick off my shoes, watching them rebound off the wall. Nessia's palm rests on the small of my back, and I spin away from it.

My attention's drawn to Aelius's portrait, unchanged through these passing seasons when I've changed so much. How many times have I betrayed him? I pace across my room and sink down at the dressing table as I count them on my fingers: the graveyard, his room, the garden, the morning, when we ran to the wall pretending we could be free of this place. My elbows thud onto the wood. My head drops into my hands, and I pull at my hair as I try to stop my body throbbing with those memories.

'I say, I love Aelius. I told him I did. Promised I would forever. How can I believe those words? How can he believe them when I've done what I have with Raen?'

'You can't mean to remain alone for the rest of your life.'

'I should. I said I would.' I whisper Aelius's name onto my skin. The warmth of my breath is quickly replaced by a chill as I inhale, and it sends a shiver down my spine. 'I can't feel him anymore. Aelius was different here, in this castle, and it doesn't seem that he was ever really here, not my Aelius. When I look at the places he was ... Like that portrait, it isn't him. And that sword, I don't understand why I brought it back here. His place in the Great Hall, isn't him. Not even in his rooms ... What am I saying? Raen's rooms now. These things ... they just make him seem so much further away from me.' Tears are falling down my cheek. I can see their reflection but not feel the swell or relief of their release. Nessia goes to wipe them with her sleeve but I stop her, keeping hold of her wrist. 'I don't remember how his skin felt. His laugh. His scent. Instead, all I have is that stupid sword.'

'Let Aelius go, and live again.'

I shake my head and turn back to the mirror. There's a crack across the surface that wasn't there before and a new mottled patch in the left-hand corner. I release Nessia so I can trace over the brown and black pattern.

'Go to bed. Sleep,' she says, tenderly. 'Things will be less overwhelming when you've had a good sleep.'

'I'm scared of dreaming. Anyway, shouldn't I be getting ready for the Great Hall?'

'I think you still have some sulking to do.' She has a faint smile, the one that's meant to make tomorrow seem brighter, and the tease in her voice is an attempt to cheer me up, so I return her smile. 'I'll tell Vill and I'll get us food.' Her calloused hand caresses my cheek. At least that hasn't changed.

I nod and mumble my thanks as she walks away. That mottled patch is seeping across the mirror's surface like blood from a wound. It oozes over my reflection, down to my lips. When I touch them, all I can think of is Raen's mouth on mine. A breeze kisses my cheek. I turn towards it but there's nothing and no one there. The door is closed. I cover the spot with my sweaty palm. It's silent, except for Nessia's feet scuffing across the floor as she crosses the room.

'I'll figure out what to do, I will,' I say over my shoulder to her.

She pauses, her hand on the door. 'You will. I don't doubt it.' Then she's gone, and the door is shut again. I'm left with the sound of the fire and the birds singing outside, their tones carrying the sound of spring. They won't give me the answers I need. I lean closer to the mirror, hoping the answers can be found in my eyes. The green is light near the centre, but darker around the outer ring, almost brown. I've never seen the colour do this before. 'What should I do?' I rise out of my seat to tip closer and closer until I blur into a smudge of browns and greens. My hands hold onto the dressing table, and my fingers caress the wooden surface. The longer I stare at myself the less it is me reflected, and as my eyelids begin to close the image flickers.

Raen comes. A million versions of him that don't look like him but I know they are him because my body tells me so. Tall men with shoulders broad as a bull's. Their gigantic shadows warm everything and cause cabbages, dandelions, and tufty spring greens to sprout from stones. Muddy-looking men with voices so deep and low that the sound vibrates through the earth and forces it to yield to them, same as women's thighs do. A man with a beard dotted red, black, and silver, and a deep sadness in his eyes, the lines beside them are like splits in wood. A plump baby, dark as a hazelnut and with green irises. I jolt awake.

My heart's racing, and my breath's uneven. I search the room for Raen. He's not here. There's a bowl of food on the floor, its meaty scent lingering in the air. The fire is smouldering with only a few red dots within it, and they are losing brightness. Nessia's snoring from the bed. The taste of Raen is in my mouth: wood, autumn, and wine. On my fingertips is the impression of the silky skin beneath his chest hair. I let go of the dressing table.

My neck and back twinge as I rise. The curtains are open, and the sky is a blank black. I must have been asleep for a while. I try not to wake Nessia as I creep across the room to pull the First Queen's letter out from under the mattress and then take it back to the dressing table with me. I can't read it in this light but I don't need to. *Beloved, how hard these days and nights are without you here.* I say the words to my reflection. They hurt my throat and are a weight in my stomach as if I've been force-fed them.

I hold the parchment to my heart and slump in the chair, my bare feet butting up against the chill wall. I tried creating the covenant but the gods have done nothing, except kill the nursemaid and that might not have been their doing. My index finger drifts to the cut they left on my forehead. It's sore, but the pain is welcoming as it slashes through that heaviness in my stomach. I can't see the mark in my reflection. Squinting, I picture the First Queen beside me, her long mahogany-tinted hair against my cheek as she bends to admire her reflection. There's a haughtiness in her pose as she tilts her nose up and beams—it's her right to be in love and no one can tell her otherwise. It makes her green eyes sharper.

'Is the letter what you meant?'

Her lips move but no answer comes. It could stop the wedding, sending Onnachild back to the merchants for funding. Vill said they've already been bled dry, that Onnachild already owes more than they were happy to lend. My heart speeds. I rub my cheek against the parchment. She shakes her hair out and somehow the dark picks out more red tints. The smell of sage tickles my nose.

My gaze drifts to the reflection of the door Raen hid behind. Despite what he is now, he was that child, and inside him is still that young boy. Part Aegni. I can't. I can't hurt him by dredging up those memories of his mother's suspected infidelity and everything that followed, and so I fold the parchment back into the tiniest square with its sharp corners.

At some point, I must have fallen asleep again because when I next glance up, red is stretching across the sky. I watch it turn to bronze to copper to gold. In this magical light, my eyelids look swollen from me crying in my dreams but I don't remember them. Another day has arrived and I'm no nearer to figuring out what to do, only what I can't do. The parchment has dropped from my lap onto the floor. The sun, as it fills the room, chases away the spirits but not my frown. Perhaps Nessia is right and my expression has finally stuck like this.

Chapter Forty-Eight

THE MOON IS STILL OUT, patchy and a thin blue, when I reach the village church. Tomorrow is the wedding. The intervening time has passed in a blur of days spent in the Sunning Room listening to excited chatter detailing the wedding preparations, and nights full of entertainment that does nothing to make me forget my worries. Raen has not sought me out, and I have not sought him out. Our eyes meet only briefly across the Great Hall, each of us challenging the other to give in first. Sleep is sporadic, the tiredness becoming a creature inhabiting me, fighting my every thought and movement, so I'm slow and dazed during the day, but at night, my limbs and mind brim with enough nervous energy for two.

I've forgotten it's so much colder in the village than the castle, and my cloak is no protection against the damp mist hazing the surroundings. It lingers around the yew tree, making it appear further away and in another time. I pull my cloak closer, nestle into its castle scent as I remember my tears beneath the tree, remember Raen's arms around me, comforting, remember the faraway look he had. He must have been staring out to the forgotten graves.

I've not come here for these memories or thoughts, and so I turn away from the yew tree. The path is uneven beneath my feet, and I step over the weeds breaking through it. It's Aelius I've come for. It's his headstone I want to rest against. His body I want beneath mine, even if it's decaying and not what it was. Standing before him, I can't speak. A bouquet of white and yellow flowers has been left for him. I ease one free from the yellow bow tying them together and bring it to my nose. Its perfume is faint and slightly sweet. As I run my fingers through the grave mud, I try not to think of Raen and me here, mating, caught in a fantasy. It smells fertile, of life, and gives away nothing of the decay going on deep beneath it. Will Aelius be nothing but bone now?

'I'm sorry I'm such a disappointment,' I say onto the curve of his headstone. The stone is cold and damp, and leaves a powdery taste on my lips.

A slash of black catches my attention, makes my pulse speed and my breath catch. Turning towards it, I realise it's a female figure. The sounds it makes, skirts swooshing against the ground and a slight cough, proves it's no spirit and so I ease out my breath to avoid drawing the woman's attention. She holds a bundle of roses, red and white. The cloak she wears is too thick, too plush for her to be a villager, and the velvet of her gloves is edged with black fur. She pushes down her hood, exposing her brown and grey hair, long and loose around her shoulders. As she places the flowers on the grave, the woman calls my name. It's Mantona.

'What are you doing here?' she asks, when I reach her.

'Aelius.' His name sounds strange, and I notice how much my village accent has been sharpened by my time in the castle.

'It's hard to let go of the dead, isn't it?'

I nod but she isn't looking my way. Her attention is on the gravestone in front of her, the stone dotted green and dark brown, and the name lost amongst the lichen. 'Who is this?' I ask.

'He doesn't matter. Not anymore.'

'Then why are you here? Why the flowers?'

She shrugs.

'Did you leave the flowers for Aelius?' I ask.

'No.' She picks a snail off the headstone and places it amongst the long grass. 'Maybe it was Onnachild. Despite his many faults, he did love Aelius.'

'But not Raen?'

'He doesn't make it easy to love him, does he?' She turns to me, right hand resting on the headstone. Her face, without the powder she wears, looks younger, the lines less noticeable. There are faint freckles, dark as my skin, across her nose and a mole under her right eye that draws attention to the hazel which is made coppery in this half-light. 'Just like Onnachild in that respect.'

I don't want to talk about Raen or the wedding; my brain is overfull with those topics. Away from the castle, this might be my only chance to get Mantona to talk about the First Queen's letter. 'The note,' I say.

Her hand jumps to her neck, and her gaze darts over my shoulder towards the village square.

'They won't be awake for a while. Please, I need to talk to you about it. You said you hid it. Were you close to her?'

'With everything that is happening, this is what you want to talk to me about?'

I nod.

She peers back at the grave. 'Penitence. That's why I'm here.'

'Penitence?'

'We all do things in moments of crisis we wish, with hindsight, we hadn't. Now, will you tell me why you're really here?'

'Hiding.'

Her laugh has a bitter edge to it. 'From the wedding preparations or Raen?'

'From everyone.'

Birds are singing out the start of a new day. The last day before the wedding. I rub at the creases of my frown, following them down to the tension at my temples.

'If only it was that easy.' She steps closer to the headstone, blows across the top of it and then rubs at the name with her glove. 'So they are to be married.'

'And the battle will go ahead.'

'Is that the only thing that concerns you?' She pauses.

'Not the only thing.'

She nods and goes back to clearing out the indentations of the name, moss dropping onto the grass where it imitates velvet embellishments. I lean forwards to catch one. It's the same colour as the dots in Raen's irises when he's aroused.

'They like to think that we love them as much as we like to believe that they love us.'

'It's not that.' My finger runs over the soft moss.

She smiles and shakes her head. 'No, of course not. I've only been a king's mistress—what would I know?'

'And do you ... now? Would you ...?'

'What are you trying to ask, Niah? Do I love him? Still? Is that what you want to ask? Why? What does it matter? He doesn't love me.'

I can't answer, staring at the moss instead and shrugging.

'You loved once, didn't you? You know what love is, how it lingers.'

I nod despite the emotion seeming as far away as that yew in the mist.

When I bite my lip, it's only my blood I taste.

'The First Queen had love.' She smacks her palms against each other to clear off the moss and dirt, and the sound jars with the quiet of the graveyard. 'Not with Onnachild. Theirs was a marriage of convenience, meant to bind the invaders and us. But you know that already, don't you?' She raises her gaze to me, a grimace bunching up her freckles. 'And you know the rumours surrounding her infidelity and how love brings things, gifts, blessings from gods.' She takes her gloves off and shoves them under her left arm. 'Every woman needs love, queen or not.' She leans forwards and uses her index finger to clean out the last of the mould. 'The note. It was to him.' She beckons me closer. Can she not bear to read out his name?

Dion Candessie it says.

'One of ours. He gave her up for his people, or rather, he tried to.' She clutches her cloak around her but her hand is shaking and the material slides out from those clumsy fingers.

'Why is he buried here then?'

'Perhaps it was Onnachild's last revenge, keeping them apart in the afterlife.'

'But Raen looks so much like Onnachild.'

'Only the gods know the truth.' The last piece of mould falls from the name. 'I never meant for you to find that letter. Truth is, Niah, I forgot the covenant was written on it.' The look she gives me is so full of pain, so full of guilt I drop the moss and stroke her shoulder. She forces a smile and pats my hand. 'I am loyal to you. To Adfyrism, but I don't want to hurt Onnachild or Raen, despite what Raen thinks.'

'I don't either,' I whisper, shocking myself with the sentiment.

She squeezes me. 'Forget it,' she says, forcefully. 'Burn it.'

She bows her head and her lips start moving in what I presume is a prayer. Is it Onnachild's prayer she speaks over the grave or our older one?

I shiver as I think of Dion trapped in that place of Onnachild's god, bereft of love and separated from his people. My actions on the battlefield mean Aelius is waiting for me with my gods, and when I die, we'll be reunited. Yet that thought doesn't bring me the comfort it should; instead, it has me pulling my cloak tighter under my chin. I put it from my mind. 'Does Vill know about it? The note?' I ask.

'No.'

'You haven't told him?'

'I told you, I forgot about it.'

A village man is shouting to hurry the others who are leaving their homes for Onnachild's fields. Another yells back a series of curse words and the familiar sound makes me smile.

'We can't stay hidden here all day.' Mantona sounds sad.

'Why did the First Queen not make the covenant?' I'm scared to ask the real question buzzing in my mind: what does Mantona have to pay penitence for? Is it related to her being gifted the First Queen's ring by Onnachild?

She pulls up the hood of her cloak and stares at the villagers.

'They won't bother us here,' I say. 'The villagers don't come here.' I huff at the truth of the statement; they helped kill my people to assert this religion, culled many yews to build this church, and now they don't care for it. How fickle they are.

'Maybe she just didn't have time,' Mantona says, flipping my hood up over my head.

'That's what she said but I'm not convinced. Maybe she thought it wouldn't work?'

'No, she knew it would work.'

'But the battle, the gods ... they've not done anything I asked.'

'They might not agree with you. The gods do what's best for them and not for us.' She smiles at me. 'Even they have free will.'

'Then why direct me to that covenant? Why give me false hope?'

'You're talking like someone already defeated. You aren't defeated, not yet. Just because Raen marries her it doesn't mean anything has been decided.' She taps my arm to get my attention but I don't give it to her and keep staring at the fabric of my cloak. Raen's cloak. 'Now it begins.'

'Begins? No, now it is over.'

'Vill's still determined,' Mantona says. 'Be patient. You'll be queen and then ... then you can have everything you want.'

'Vill is so often not right.' I flinch at the memory of Raen's naked body and what giving in to it was supposed to achieve. I'd have done it anyway, I realise that from the way just the thought sets off a yearning between my thighs. 'Vill promised me so many things that night he came to the village, and he's delivered none of them. People, he said, in Aralltir, Followers ... yet—'

'Have you not noticed? Niah, how blind you are sometimes. They are here.'

'Here? Who?'

'Just trust Vill.'

I let her lead me to where my horse is tied to one of the church gates. Hers is tied up there, too. They whinny, eager to return to the castle. I'm not quite so keen.

'These feelings,' Mantona says, 'they come and they'll go. Allow them for today, and then tomorrow we'll start over again.'

'I'm done,' I say. 'All I want is Ammi.'

'We'll see.' She mounts her horse, and I watch her gallop away.

I close the church gate, lean against it, and let the metal cool my forehead. A flock of birds squawk and burst out of a tree into the dawn. The moon has left the sky, and the mist has been burnt away. When I look up at the church, I notice the holes in the roof and a brown bird sitting on the golden spire. There's a flash of green in its tail as it preens

392

there. Colours are muted in the village: brown, green, grey are smudged and dusted around. Yet, it's become more beautiful to me than the castle is with those purple-tipped bushes, red roses, and white paths. In the castle nature is cultivated to show off wealth and dominance over it. I wander back into the graveyard and gather up the roses from Dion's grave, whisper one of our prayers and make him a promise, whether he's Raen's father or not, to have him returned to where he should rest.

The perfume of the roses is heady and overpowering as I carry them to the forgotten graves, and I'm so engrossed in their scent and the delicate brush of their petals I don't notice Raen until I'm almost in his eyeline. *No tears, please, no tears today.* If he begs to see his mother again, will I do it? The thought of what she might say heats my cheeks. His back is rigid as he sits on his heels. His chin is up, nose high as he basks in the changing light.

My body wants to go to him, hopes everything can be forgotten while we're here amongst our ancestors, but my pride stops me and so I tiptoe away. Into the bushes I go, sacrificing the roses to the sharp gorse. I settle there, watching his ribs rise and fall. His shoulders bristle and he lowers his head as though he knows I'm here. There's a slight swish of his hair across the swell of his shoulder blades, hinting that he will turn towards my hiding place. He doesn't. Instead, he slides his long legs out and leans back onto his hands. I imagine his eyelids lowering, those long, dark lashes coming together. If only I could tell him what I've heard from Mantona ... what would he do? Would he stop caring about trying to please a man who might not be his father? Would he even believe it? I'm not sure if I do. He looks at peace, the first time I've seen him like this, and so I stay still and silent and keep watch instead. We don't need those answers now.

Chapter Forty-Nine

'HOW WAS IT?' Nessia asks when I return from Eldini's celebration of her last night as a maiden. Tomorrow she'll be married. Tomorrow Raen will have her in his bed. I kick my shoes off.

'As expected.' I pour myself a goblet of wine. 'Poems exalting her beauty, her kindness, her otherworldliness. Some strange coloured birds performing, shitting everywhere. Dancing. Have you any idea how hard it is to dance with castle women, none wanting to lead.' I close the curtains to hide the moon, which Eldini has been likened to far too much tonight.

'Vill left this for you.' Nessia passes me a folded piece of parchment. I don't need to read it to know it will detail where Raen and the men are. Will he be laughing or as apprehensive as Eldini? She tried to hide it well with a half-smile that only occasionally tightened into a grimace. The compliments didn't make her flush as they normally do, so it seemed like she hadn't heard them. I put Vill's note on the table, lift the wine jug and hold it towards Nessia. 'Do you want to commiserate with me?'

She nods so I fill a goblet and pass it over to her.

'Are you going to go?' she asks.

'What good will it do?' I push the parchment around the table, into a patch of spilt wine that seeps into the off-white and across my name.

Nessia snatches it back up and opens it. 'They're in Raen's room.'

'Of course they are.'

'It's worth trying, isn't it? At least, if nothing else, send him off with memories of you.'

'Nessia! He's getting married. Married. Whether I want him or not, whether I ... What the gods bring together let no man split apart ... remember that?'

'He was yours first.'

I scoff. 'He's no ones and he never will be.'

She puts her finger to her mouth. 'Shush.' Her eyebrows rise and her head tilts to the side. There are footsteps, faint little pitter-patters. Raen? Has he come for me? I put down my goblet, wine sploshing over the side. Nessia throws Vill's note at the fire but misses. She shuffles to the door, presses her ear against the wood and holds up her hand to keep me quiet. I tiptoe to the note and drop it in the fire as Nessia opens the door. There's a little sob and then she ushers in Eldini, who has changed her dress since the celebrations and is now in black with a thin cloak around her.

'I come. I come to know.' Her fingers flutter at her cloak's knot. Eldini's steps falter. 'They say your people can do. Can call future.'

It's not the future she should be asking me about, it's the recent past. The thought makes me wince. She startles me by lowering herself to the floor, by kneeling at my feet. There's none of the stoicism shown in her portrait. In her face is the same trepidation that brought so many of the village girls to my home, their fear of the future greater than their fear of me. She isn't a village girl, though, she's a princess, and it isn't a village man she's marrying. I should turn her away. I'm not sure what stops me, what has me joining her on the floor and taking her trembling hands between mine.

I shake my head. She doesn't realise what she asks. The last time the flames showed me the future I saw Aelius dead. I saw carrion birds feasting on flesh. I saw the Aralltirs billowing on the back of their giant horses. And I could do nothing. That day on the battlefield had me swearing I'd never do this calling again.

'I'll get the herbs,' Nessia says. I peep around at her, try to get her attention. Why does she want me to do this? Am I meant to tell Eldini a false future, a true one or the past? But she vanishes into the bedchamber without noticing.

Eldini settles cross-legged and so it appears everything has been decided—at least to her. She pushes back the hood of her cloak. Her hair is in two long plaits, their tightness making her face rounder and with her black clothes, I can't help thinking she does indeed resemble the moon. A pallid and ghostly moon fading out of the sky to make way for day. Colour is coming to her cheeks from the heat of the fire. The flames have almost consumed all of the parchment, only a slight section left curling and turning black.

'I say to no one. I promise.' Her voice wobbles, and her eyes are filling with tears.

'Not even Raen,' Nessia says, handing me my leather bag. 'Onnachild has warned Niah if she's found out—'

'No one. I say to no one.' Eldini clasps my ankles.

'Why do you need to know?' I stare at her tiny, white hands, hands that Raen has held. His presence seems to still be on them. 'Surely it's better not to?'

'No. You would want future, too.'

My fist closes around the bag. The future is not something we should see, my grandmother told me, the visions aren't to be trusted, but she still showed me how to do it. And the only time I did, I saw Aelius. My beautiful Aelius destroyed, and I was powerless to stop it. What will the flames show me now? Eldini and Raen's children with white hair and honey-coloured skin? Her happy? I glimpse at Nessia. She nods at me and mouths, 'Lie'.

Lie. It's easy to lie and deliver false futures. I've done it many times for coin, for food, for the spite of it. The weaver's daughter was told of a future with sickly daughters and a drunken husband for her part in trying to drown me. I open the bag and tip a mixture of dried herbs into my palm. What would a princess want? Sons. Peace. This one wants love. I don't need an elaborate hoax to answer that. All she wants is reassurance. All I want is for her to leave.

'I can't.' I trickle herbs from one hand to another. Pieces drop to the floor, and Eldini gathers them up.

'Please.' Her lip trembles again as she offers the herbs to me.

'You've been lied to. I can't see the future.'

'You show me. I not scared.' Her voice is regal, containing a hint of an order, and that makes my decision to lie easier because she isn't my queen to order me.

I start following the same elaborate ritual Nessia and I invented to fool the village girls. The herbs I throw into the fire are the wrong ones but they give off an impressive smoke and an odour as noxious as old milk. The words I mumble are nonsensical, bastards of my ancestors' language and Onnachild's.

'What you see?' Her question is as unnerving as a spirit's breath on my neck and I hunch up against it.

I hear the whispers of my ancestors and sparks fling themselves out of the fire, trying to get to her. It's not her fault but there's no such thing as fault to the dead. 'Please.' I gesture for her to move back and then shuffle in front of her, blocking her body.

'I cannot see?'

'For your own protection,' Nessia says.

I close my eyes and inhale the sour smoke. It scratches its way into my lungs and I cough. Behind me, Eldini coughs, too. I press my palms to the stone floor, lower my head. The heat radiating from the fire reminds me of Raen lying naked beside me in bed, and the urge to be with him surges within me just like the flames surge now they're filled with herbs and wood.

'Please tell. Bad?' She taps my elbow. Does she think I've forgotten she's there? I glance at her. There's too much trust and hope in her pale, wide-set eyes.

'It's not bad.' My voice is loud so I clear my throat. I shut my eyes to stop them from drifting to hers again. Why is my heart so heavy when the flames have shown me nothing? 'A son. A healthy son who will inherit a prosperous land. Two sons. One who resembles you. One who resembles Raen.'

'I make good wife?' She shuffles closer, adding her scent of lemon and vanilla to the smoke's rancid plume.

'I see you happy. I see him happy.'

'Love?'

Digging my nails into my palm, I answer, 'Yes, love.'

She lets out a sigh of relief, so why do I feel so guilty for lying?

'There's nothing to worry about,' Nessia says.

'Thank you.' Eldini's hug is so unexpected that my eyes dart open. In the fire, flames are forming shapes. But I didn't perform a calling. It was nonsense. There should be nothing. It's not her future forming. It's a message for me. The First Queen's message. The flames twist into those mating figures and her voice echoes through me: *mating, mating, fucking.*

I push Eldini off. I press my thighs together to stop the lust pulsing further but the pressure makes it worse. *He's handsome, is he not? He makes you pant, does he not?* He does, and he is. I don't want him to lie with Eldini, to marry Eldini. Battle or not. I bolt up.

'You must go now,' I say.

And I must go to Raen.

A couple tumble from Raen's room, giggling and trailing clothes. The girl's wearing a hood similar to Eldini's, and it makes her seem taller than the man. Open-mouthed, he lurches for her neck as she playfully swats him. I peer around them into the dimly lit room.

Vill, Gavin, Perkin, Martus, Raen, and a few men I don't recognise are huddled together in a circle of chairs, making them an impenetrable group as they dominate the room and block out the light from the fire. There's raucous laughter, male and female, bursting from his bedchamber. The stale scent of ale, wine, and male sweat makes me cover my nose.

'This is the worst bit.' Nessia adds gentle pressure to my back.

'This is not the worse bit. It'll get a lot worse.'

'Who is that?' Perkin shouts. 'Shut the door. You're letting the cold in.'

'Go in.' Nessia pushes me but I hold my ground. Shunted up against the wall, where Eldini's portrait was, is a long table littered with jugs, candles, and goblets. The curtains rest bunched up on the ends. One is soaking up wine.

'This is not a good idea.' Before I can shut the door, Vill's in front of me. His face is mottled from drink, and his blond hair is loose around his shoulders.

'Excellent.' He stares me up and down, admiring the red dress Nessia altered so the neckline plunged lower.

'Who is it?' Raen's voice is slurred.

'Niah,' Vill calls back.

'Bring her in.'

Nessia leaves me, hurrying away with her head down. I take a deep breath and follow Vill inside. All I can see is the back of Raen's head and his left leg when I need to see his face, gauge his expression and figure out what he's thinking. Is he resigned? Happy? Hopeful? The speed with which servants are pouring drinks means he'll not be thinking anything soon. I want to be drunk too, so I go to the table, grab a goblet and fill it.

'You're not here to enjoy yourself.' Vill covers the bowl of the goblet with his white hand. The silver bands curved around each finger resemble slivers of the moon.

I huff and snatch the goblet out from under his palm. 'Then why am I here? Should I not be pretending to celebrate as everyone else is?'

Raen's chuckling at something one of the men has said. Perkin slaps him on his back creating a hollow-sounding thump. Someone is repeating the riddle about an onion. I drink quickly and then refill my goblet. Vill tuts and fusses with the stray strands of hair framing my face.

'What's taking you so long?' Raen shouts.

Vill drags me away from the table.

'We're not meant to have castle women here,' Perkin moans.

'Would you rather boys?' a voice answers. 'Shall we call for the boys?'

The men laugh.

'Who cares for tradition?' Raen uncurls from his seat, rising unsteadily with a helpful push from Perkin. His face is a patchwork of shadows and candlelight, and it obscures his expression. 'Get a chair, Perkin. Move over, Gavin. Niah wishes to toast my upcoming wedding.'

'I was hoping to have some of those spirits.' I break out of Vill's hold and amble towards Raen.

He drops onto his seat, hidden amongst the men again. From his bedchamber comes a shrill female giggle. Perkin is singing a bawdy song, slapping the arms of his chair with a speeding rhythm that matches my heart. Gavin moves, clattering his chair against the stone floor and now I can see Raen. My steps slow as he turns from watching the fire to watch me. His smile is made luscious by the shine across his bottom lip. His hand sweeps out for my skirt and once he's caught me, it twists and twists into the material to hurry me along. Wine spills from the goblet in his other hand onto the floor and I almost slip in it.

'She should have spirits.' His neck rests on the top rail of the chair, his head lolling back and his dark hair dangling down against the white spindles. In his eyes, I read all his lusty thoughts, and they make me want to put my lips against the extended column of his throat, touch my tongue to his pulse. Will that make him stop this wedding? The sound of Vill putting a chair down next to Raen's is the only thing that stops me. Perkin hits Raen's knee to get his attention.

'What's that riddle about the milk churn?' he asks. 'Remember?'

Raen shakes his head and twists his hand tighter into my skirt, but he doesn't seem to notice he's doing it. The material lifts and brushes my shoes. A servant gives me a tiny glass of spirits, and I clutch it in both hands.

'Do you know the one about the milk churn?' Perkin asks her. She blushes and almost drops the pink bottle she carries. Even Gavin is drunk, sloping in his chair and staring at me unabashed for once while the servant fills his glass.

'To tomorrow.' Martus raises his glass.

'No. No toast to that,' Raen says. 'There'll be enough wedding toasts tomorrow. Let's toast to nights gone by, those nights wives wouldn't approve of.'

'I don't ... Niah,' Gavin says.

'She doesn't care,' Raen says. 'She's not as naïve as she'd like you to think, are you? She knows what I talk about, you know, don't you, Niah? You'll toast to those nights with me, won't you?'

'I'll toast if you wish me to but I don't know what you're talking about.'

He chuckles so hard that he spills wine down his tunic, and the dampness lays the material close to his chest, teasing me with a hint of his shape. He tugs me closer.

'Why are you here?' he asks in a low voice for only me to hear.

'Not for that.'

'No?'

'I wanted to drink.'

'Then why do your eyes tell me something else?' As he talks, I watch his lips move and imagine my tongue tracing up and down the peaks of the top one. My hand rests on the back of his chair, fingers wedging between the spindles.

'I've remembered the milk churn riddle,' he tells Perkin but his stare remains on me. I follow the movement of his swallow. 'Beneath her belt, as she stood, worked his will. They both wiggled. The man—'

'Raen!' Gavin splutters.

'Don't take offence.' Raen strokes my skirt. 'You won't take offence will you, Niah?' He peers up at me, the firelight picking out a twinkle in his blurry irises. 'Don't listen to me. No one listen to me. You'll have to listen to me enough tomorrow. Someone else talk.'

'You've started it wrong,' Perkin shouts, jumping to his feet and knocking over his chair. 'It starts with the man walking ... A man came walking where—'

A woman runs past, chased by a topless man. 'She stood in a corner, stepped out,' she calls, breathless.

'That's it. That's it.' Perkin clears his throat and starts again as the woman laughs and runs towards the table. Raen's hand brushes up against my waist. His cheek is almost flat against my stomach. I'm not sure if he's aware of his actions because he's watching the fire so intensely. It doesn't matter and my body doesn't care because when his gaze returns to me, I feel it as keenly as a trail of hot kisses over my spine. My breasts rise in anticipation. My lips purse. He smiles, all-knowing. I go to touch his stubble-dotted chin, stopped only by the bump of Gavin falling off his chair.

'What do they teach you boys in your lands?' Martus mocks, pointing and laughing at Gavin splayed on the floor.

'Tomorrow, I'm going to rut with as many village girls as I can,' Perkin says. 'The prettiest and the most willing, all and any.'

'Ha, you?' Vill says. 'Not even a blind village girl would slope off with you.'

'Village girls have higher tastes than any of you,' Raen says. 'None of you are rich enough or powerful enough. Isn't that right, Niah?'

'If you continue to talk like this ... in front of her ... I'll take her away.' Gavin tips onto his side as he tries to clamber back onto his chair.

'I'd like to see you try.' Raen smirks. 'Niah, tell me, do you think you'd let him take you away?'

Gavin blushes. He resembles Eldini so much with those pale eyebrows and lashes that I step away from Raen. The distance only intensifies my need for him, trying to fool me into pressing closer, tempting me to believe that doing so will sate my desire when I know it will only make me want more and again. Eldini, she wants to love him. She wants a happy marriage. And I want ... the spirit is working, my body is relaxing, and my thoughts are muddled, so I'm not sure what I want, only what I don't want.

I grab Raen's goblet from him and drink the remaining trickle as he watches. Placing my lips where his have been is as close as I dare go tonight. While the men keep teasing each other, another taking up the forgotten milk churn riddle, Raen scoots forwards in his seat and nestles a leg against my skirt. The realisation that he doesn't care who might notice is thrilling, enticing me to test how far he's willing to go. He stares up at me, the green in his irises murky and a hint of a smile playing across his lips.

'You're drunk.' My tone is more tender than I intended. I brush a lock of his hair from his lips.

'Why are you drinking? Are you really celebrating?'

'What have I got to celebrate?'

He looks away, frowning as he considers my words. I lean down. My cheek is so close to his I feel the points of his stubble. The wine has made him smell sweet but underneath that is his woody scent. I take a deep breath of it. My eyes close to savour it and imprinted on my lids are those mating flames. The vision sends a shimmer through my body. 'Meet me outside.' My lips skim his earlobe.

It's exciting to have him nod and to feel the warmth of his breath when he turns his head and whispers yes. Swiftly, I stand. This has to work: my last chance to convince him. My lust must not overcome me. *Please*, I pray to the gods and my ancestors as I sashay from the room, hoping the swing of my hips is enough to entice him, though I'm not sure what I'll say once we're alone. The truth? But what is the truth? *Charm him. Don't shout as you did before. Don't make demands. More bees are caught with honey than* … I can't remember the saying. All I remember is him naked against me, inside me. I want more of that.

I'm not alone in the hallway for long before the door opens. He lunges to kiss me. He's not as drunk as I thought or I'm weaker than I thought because I melt into him and he takes my weight.

'Did you miss me?' he asks between kisses.

'Yes. Yes.' I sigh as his fingers dance over the bumps and dip of my cleavage, and I breathe in to raise it closer to him.

'You can't stay away. I can't stay away.' He gropes my breast, making the cage and me groan. 'This dress, you are stunning tonight. Almost tempts me to call off the wedding.'

I caress the line of his jaw. 'It isn't too late.'

'I was joking.'

'I know.' My finger runs over his bottom lip, testing the plumpness of it. His tongue touches the tip. 'I'm not. You could say no.'

'Haven't we been here before? I was hoping we could finish the other thing we started in the Judging Room.' His smile is tipsy.

'But, Raen, this … this is different.'

'Is it? How? You've changed your mind?' His bottom lip is casting a shadow, reminding me how plush it feels between mine. How easy it would be to give in, chase those people from his rooms, climb on top of him and … I gulp under his intense stare.

'Send her back.' I slide my hand under his tunic, over the ridges of his stomach, and smile at his sharp intake of breath. Up I go, fingers splaying out to survey the hard plains of his chest. My purpose is heightened by the feel of his body with its quivers and withheld breath. I tug on his chest hair, making him growl. 'You could have me. We could have each other. Raen, I've missed you, this.'

Taking his head between my hands, I pull him down so our eyes meet. I kiss the line between his eyebrows. I kiss his scar. I kiss along his tense jaw and tease that pulsing dip with my tongue. His eyelids flutter, close, and his lips purse. I place mine there, put all my sleepless nights, all my wanting, all my frustration into that kiss. He yanks me closer. His leg pushes between mine and I clasp it there with thighs already beginning to tremble.

'Raen,' I say his name onto his lips. 'I don't want to share you.'

His palm settles on my chest, pressing so hard he must feel my heart beating. 'Yet I must? If you can have my half-brother why can't I have Eldini?' His eyes open and when our gaze meets the magnificence of his takes my breath away. He must feel that too. 'Do you love me?' he whispers. Even the low thrum of his voice is arousing. My heart beats faster, so fast it hurts. The pressure from his hand eases, yet I can't move, can't breathe.

'What, Raen? This isn't ...'

'You should have lied.' He steps back and our hands fall free.

I'm dazed, woozy in the white hall without him to hold onto. 'Do you want me to?'

His lips quirk, almost become a smirk. 'Please, don't insult me. You're nothing but my half-brother's whore.'

The words jolt me, and I slap his cheek. He doesn't flinch or even blink, just sidesteps away from me. The sound keeps ringing. My palm stings.

'And my whore now.'

Then he turns, opens the door to his room, and slams it behind him. Moments later I hear him chuckling.

Chapter Fifty

MORNING HAS COME. Of course it has. It always does. The sun is hitting my sore eyes as I lie in bed. It will be a gorgeous day for their wedding. Why didn't I just lie to him? If I had ... if I had it would've made no difference. I pray to the gods for a sign. *Where are you?* The room is silent. The room is full of sunshine.

'There's still today,' Melody says, but she doesn't sound cheerful. 'He'll realise and it'll be today, I know it. And your dress is lovely. Look. Look, Niah.' She points across the room to where it's draped over a chair. It's the same green as my irises, and silver thread creates flowers and leaves across the material.

'At least my dress will look lovely.' I'm aware that I'm fishing for compliments but I don't care.

Nessia laughs but Melody provides what I need. 'You look lovely, too. A little tired that's all, nothing compared to Raen though. His servant told me he's half dead and his hands are shaking.'

'Good.'

Nessia rolls off the bed, pulling the furs with her. 'No use putting it off.'

She's right, so I get up and make my way into my bath. It's tepid this morning. I sink under the water, welcome the drowning feeling. When Nessia calls my name, I resurface, splashing water onto the floor and wiping it from my face.

'Is this what I think it is?' She's by the dressing table and clutched to her chest is the Aegnian book. My book. Is this Raen's way of apologising? I hold my arms out for it.

'See, he must care.' Melody soaps up my hair, the movement swills around my headache.

'Once he's done his duty he'll come back to you,' Nessia says as she strokes the cover of the book.

'Is that what I should want? Is that what I should be satisfied with? I'd be better off with Gavin,' I moan.

'Stop this nonsense.' Nessia slams the book on the dressing table. 'I'm tired of hearing this self-pity. Raen chooses her because he must and she marries him because she must. There's no love there. There'll be no love there. You'll have the throne for yourself, eventually, so be patient, and when you have it, you can make Raen yours, too, so stop behaving like a spoilt child. You'll go out there today with your head held high. You'll go and laugh and smile and toast, and you will make your grandmother proud.'

She's so stern standing there with her hands on her hips and lips a tense line that I don't answer and, instead, duck under the water to rinse off the soap. I remain silent as Melody dries me, as they both dress me, but I don't smile as Nessia wants and so her scowl remains, too. When I sit at the dressing table, I pull the book onto my lap and flip through the pages, remembering how Raen and I shared these stories. None of this will matter when the battle comes. This day will not matter. Tonight he will lie with Eldini and that will not matter either.

Melody winds my wet hair around her fingers, pins the dark locks into a series of shining spirals. The pinheads catch the light, and the dots of green they reflect across the book's pages resemble my ancestors' irises. Pretending they are with me brings some comfort. The pages near the back contain family names and trees, and I mumble them to myself, stopping only when I reach Candessie. I scan down the page until I find Dion. The name is more faded than the rest—someone has run their finger over it many times. I bat Melody's hands away as I lean closer. A scratched sketch is faint next to the name, so faint I can barely make out the broken lines. I lift the book, bring it closer. Nessia snatches it from me. 'You need to finish getting ready.' She hides it amongst the furs on the bed. 'You can read it when you get back.'

Melody attaches a chunky silver chain with a heavy bird pendant across the bodice of my dress, and I can't help feeling I'm putting on armour as she slides rings onto each of my fingers. When I stand, Nessia pulls a long hair from the back of my dress and holds it up between her thumb and forefinger. There's a red shimmer to it, highlighted by the bright sun. I hold out my palm for it and Nessia coils it there. Raen must have sat at the dressing table last night after bringing over the book. Perhaps he kept watch as I struggled with my dreams. Is this a sign he's changed his mind?

Closing my hand around the hair, I ask, 'Is it too early for wine?'

'It's never too early for wine.' Nessia kisses my cheek, her anger clearly forgotten.

Melody fills a goblet for me, a goblet for Nessia, and one for herself.

'I don't think Eldini would approve,' Nessia says.

'What? It's a wedding. I'm allowed.' Melody takes a sip before anyone can stop her.

'Let her have it,' I say. 'And if it displeases Eldini, so much the better.'

Melody swills it around her mouth, puffing out her cheeks, though her screwed-up nose suggests she's not enamoured of it.

'One last accessory.' Nessia crouches beside me and puts her goblet on the dressing table. 'A smile.' She pokes my cheeks. 'You're Niah and you're worth more than any of them. You will be queen.'

I smile to appease her.

'I knew you could do it.'

'He might still change his mind,' Melody says.

Even though I shake my head, there's a flutter of hope in my chest. What would he have done if I'd lied to him and said yes?

Birds and love knots have been carved onto Eldini's door and the motif continues into her room which is jammed full of women. Her women are in yellow which reflects under their chins like buttercups. The castle women are in either meadow green or peony pink depending on their marital status. The matrons are in green, same as me. I'm not sure what this signifies, whether Eldini is acknowledging my promise to Aelius or that she considers me Gavin's intended.

Wide skirts are crammed against wide skirts, making it difficult for me to squeeze into the room. There's a patch of sunlight brightening the bride as she sits underneath a closed window. Her dress is gold and white making her luminescent in that light. Her hair is loose and kinked from the plaits it was in last night, and that, too, shimmers.

A servant passes me a goblet of white wine. It's too sweet, and the taste turns my stomach. The women chatter amongst themselves, voices quick with excitement and far too loud for my tender head.

'Where did you sneak off to last night?' Beshanie asks. She's in pink and the colour clashes with her auburn hair.

Before I can respond, Eldini's women call on us to toast her beauty. I do as I'm told. They help her to her feet, help her turn to face us so we can admire the artistry of her gown. It swamps her petite frame with its wide skirts and puffed sleeves. As her women rearrange the skirts we're forced back to make space. A sweaty arm squashes against mine. Beshanie snaps at the girl in front of her. The wine swishes in my empty stomach and my head feels too heavy in this claustrophobic room. I force my way into a clear space beside the fireplace, lean against it, and finally get to discard my unfinished drink. The spot gives me a better view of Eldini's dress. There are slits in the top layer so slivers of gold can peep through, and embroidered over the bodice are golden hawks and cormorants. The pattern overwhelms Eldini's petite features, and the vastness of the sleeves makes her wrists appear skinny to the point of emaciation. The bodice is tight and flat. Raen can't want this child, can he?

'Open the window,' someone calls. 'We don't want her getting hot and sweaty.'

'At least not before her wedding night,' Beshanie shouts.

Everyone giggles except Eldini and me. She toys with a strand of her hair, only stopping when one of her women eases it from between her fingers.

'Quick. Come here. You can watch the men leaving,' someone gasps.

'It's bad luck.'

'Step away.'

'Don't let them see us.'

Eldini gets bundled towards the centre of the room. I ignore the women rustling and fussing, and clamber through to the window. It's cooler here. Staring out, I wince from the sting of the sun bouncing off the white courtyard and arch my hand over my eyes. The men below are dressed in white, their sleeves stitched with either golden hawks or cormorants, depending on whether they're Onnachild's men or Eldini's. Where's Raen? I hear him organising the men, a shifting pattern of white, gold, and blond amongst the greenery and black horses. He's at the front, already on his horse. His back is rod straight, shoulders back and chin high. The white tunic he wears has the same design as Eldini's dress. It enhances his broad shoulders and picks out the honey tones of his skin. Why didn't I lie?

If he looks up, it means he's thinking of me. If he looks up, he'll call this wedding off. Please look up. I lean out the window, bashing elbows with the woman next to me. Onnachild rides up beside Raen. He's in gold and black with heavy furs draped around his shoulders despite the heat. From my position up high, I can see where his hair is thinning. His crown is jammed on his head. At his wave, the men start towards the village. Raen doesn't look up.

'He's gone,' someone says.

Turning back into the room, I mask my disappointment with a smile.

There's a warm breeze against the back of my neck, tickling the skin there. The sensation is calming, and I draw in a deep breath of the perfumed air as I lean against the window, hands flat on the sill.

'I go back now?' Eldini's voice comes from within the room.

She gets passed from woman to woman, pushed, yanked between the dresses and hot bodies. Her women follow, diligently rearranging her bulbous skirts. She stretches a quivering hand towards me. I grab it and help her pop out from the mass. She tilts her head to the window, steadies herself against it, and gulps down the fresh air. There's a green tinge to her cheeks. Someone passes her a glass of minted water. Her palms leave sweaty prints on the window when they clasp the cup.

'If you don't want to—' I wish I'd given her a different tale last night, one of unborn babies, of sorrow, of a man who chooses another.

'No,' she says, nodding.

Someone suggests a card game to pass the time, but no one takes up this offer as there's not enough space. Beshanie and Nilola sing bawdy songs until a couple of matrons snap at them, and the green tint comes back to Eldini's cheeks. The room becomes quiet except for an occasional sigh or complaint when someone fidgets. Eldini keeps dunking mint leaves into the water, and they keep floating back up. I pretend the gods have stopped time in this room so the wedding will never happen and instead, as in folk tales, weeds will crawl up the castle walls and trap us forever.

Eventually a woman near the back of the room squeals, announcing the arrival of the servants. A sigh travels around the room. There are a few groans as women start shuffling out. Eldini rests a palm on her chest, closes her eyes, and mumbles to herself. Her jaw is set; she's ready to be married. I wish I had her composure, but my heart is heavy and my headache has returned.

Her women lift the edges of her dress and tiptoe backwards with her. Castle women call out well wishes. I linger until everyone has gone.

411

Eldini's chair is the only item of furniture, and there are a few abandoned goblets knocked over onto the white floor. A servant is picking up broken glass. My attention drifts to the door of her bedchamber. Will Raen come here tonight or will she go to his rooms? I edge nearer. Her initials are entwined with his, and their birds hold a sprig of laurel between them. But it's not his bird, it's Onnachild's hawk. Raen's should be the phoenix, same as me.

'Please.' A servant gestures towards the hallway where everyone else has gone.

I gather up my skirts and rush to catch up with the other women.

Out in the courtyard, servants and white horses are waiting for us. The sun is so hot a few women are complaining and tugging on their sleeves to cover more of their arms. It's so bright I squint and grimace; at least it gives me respite from my forced smile. There's much shouting and pointing as servants and women direct each other with contradictory orders. From a distance, Eldini is an oasis of serenity on top of her horse, its plaited mane tied with gold thread. As I move closer, I notice her fingers are fiddling with the reins. Perhaps it will be her who calls off the wedding. Imagining Raen's shocked expression almost pleases me. I scratch my palm, frowning at the tenderness there.

A servant distracts me by helping me mount a horse and then she takes the reins to lead me to where the matrons are. Beshanie's fake blonde hair is jammed on her head and piled high. The back of her neck has already caught the sun. Her and Nilola gossip together as I pass by. The matrons ignore me when I join them; they are sharing memories of their wedding days, and I'm reminded of the plans Aelius and I made: ribbons and bunting adorning the trees, the silk gown he promised me, and he was going to wear blue to match his eyes. My fake smile droops so I push these things from my mind and whisper a hello to my horse.

Excited cheers from the women at the front set us on our way. The servants rush off, and I wonder whether they'll get to join us in the celebrations later as they did when the First Queen got married. At that wedding, so my grandmother told me, village and castle celebrated together in a raucous feast that lasted for days, with people passing out at odd hours, castle head on village shoulder and vice versa, only to wake up for more eating, drinking, and dancing. Perhaps Eldini will favour the second wedding where the villagers were excluded by the castle wall. I should have paid more attention to the talk in the Sunning Room. I wonder if the hag will be reunited with her boy, even if only for a day. It's too much to hope I'll get my reunion with Ammi.

While we meander towards the village, a woman sings one of Eldini's religious songs. It sounds joyful even with that strange clacking language. Aelius's statue comes into view and, from a distance, it appears to be garlanded by sunshine for Eldini. In its shadow is a scrawny mass of villagers gathered to watch the procession. Once we get closer to the statue, I notice birds have soiled it. He's been neglected, and I've been the worst of them all. I keep my head down to avoid its blank stare but my nightmare returns and I shiver when its shadow touches me.

My parting words to the villagers repeat in my mind: *you wait until I'm riding through this village on my fine horse in the King's procession.* Now I'm here, I don't want them to notice me. It doesn't feel how I thought it would. I thought I'd feel superior to them, that they'd be staring at me in awe. There's no victory for me, only guilt as I stare at hungry and gaunt faces. My shoulders tighten and I swallow hard. I'm Niah from the village, and I should be down there with them, still dreaming of my white horse and love. I guide my horse further in amongst the castle matrons to hide.

As we leave the square, village girls run alongside the procession with their hands out to catch the petals Eldini's women scatter. Will any of them chase after Perkin as I chased after Aelius? I want to tell them not to wish for these things but it wouldn't make a difference. The young women are giddy as they are meant to be, as I was. One of Eldini's women breaks from the procession to gather gifts from the village children: a corn dolly, a plume of weeds, a wooden heart. The children are stunted, with bandy legs and weak ankles. A boy scratches his scalp despite red sores showing through his shorn hair. Thank the gods Ammi won't be like them. I can bear anything as long as Ammi isn't like them.

We pass by the river the villagers tried to drown me in. Boys run through it, kicking up water, as mothers shout at them for ruining their clothes. Again and again, I run my fingers over the dent in my forehead, split with the scar from the gods. Why did I try to save the villagers? Let the men go to their deaths if that's what they want. Ammi and I will remain safe in the castle.

The procession stops in a large field where the men are already congregating. Villagers gather around the edges and hang back. We're helped from our horses, our dresses adding splashes of spring colour to the otherwise barren landscape overlooking what was the battlefield. The valley is now full of activity and life, making it easy to pretend men had never died there. Wooden huts painted blue and green have been built, and the Aralltirs are colourful flecks as they go about their daily life. Onnachild must have chosen this location specifically so our noise will filter down to them, and he can show off.

Raen's standing under a garish arch made of yellow flowers and golden bows. Riding through the village should have convinced him to not marry Eldini, yet his gait shows him ready to fulfil his duty and do it well. Beside him are Vill and Gavin. Onnachild is sitting near, flanked by his advisers. Aesc is clutching a scroll and quill. They are as still as a painting, except for a ball of white and yellow wriggling in Onnachild's lap. Ammi. I step forwards. Mantona rushes towards me, blocking my path and line of vision. As I sidestep past her, Onnachild turns and stares at me, a sly smile on his face.

'We need to find our seats,' Mantona says. I'm grateful for her taking my hand, even with her ring scratching my skin.

Servants usher us towards rows of white chairs neatly arranged before the arch: the men to the left and the women to the right. I sit next to an old woman, whose white hair is dressed with an abundance of flowers. The perfume has my stomach churning. Mantona slides into the seat beside me. A man of Eldini's god walks past and stands under the arch, arms clasped around a gilded book.

I can only see Raen's profile: his straight nose, the press of his lips, his strong jaw. He seems determined, not happy, to be getting married. Would he still be there if I'd lied to him? If I'd said yes? There's no hint of my slap, at least nothing is visible from here. My palm is still tender from it, though, and I press my nails into the skin. The sting calms my stomach. Raen's chest is puffed out as if he's holding his breath. His hands are limp by his side as he watches Ammi.

It is now. If something is to happen, it must be now. My ancestors, the gods, someone must do something. It's their presence I frantically search for in the shade of trees, of tents, under dressed tables. Music starts and it's the song Aelius used to whisper into the dip of my back as we imagined our wedding day. Tears come to my eyes. Women turn in their seats as Eldini appears, so I do the same. A faint wind plays with her veil like a shy lover. Where are the gods to whip up a storm and blow her away? There's not much time left.

She starts her slow glide, toe to heel, towards Raen. Her gaze is down, checking her steps. The matron beside me sighs. My stomach lurches. I press harder into my palm. Eldini stops beside Raen. She's so short next to him, her head not even reaching his heart. The ornate arch and the mass of fabric around her add to the impression she's a child playing at being a bride. She peeks up at him. He doesn't look at her. She passes her bouquet of trailing yellow and white flowers to one of her women. The religious man takes up Eldini's left hand. Raen raises his left hand and places it over hers.

'How in love they seem,' the matron sighs.

Has he ever been in love? Poor Eldini to not have a man who chooses her because he wants her and not the embellishments she comes with. If she had any sense, she'd run. But she doesn't; instead, she stands there, certain that love will come because I told her it would. Why did I do that? I should tell her the truth. I should do it and I should do it now. Tell her about Raen and me. Mantona tugs on my arm as I shuffle forwards in my seat.

'Remember, your daughter,' she whispers.

Is this why Onnachild brought Ammi here, a means of ensuring I behave myself, a means of asserting his power over me? I bump back into my seat, and the woman behind me tuts. Will I get time with Ammi later? Hold her? I squirm in my seat, craning my neck to get a glimpse of her, and it provokes another tut from the woman behind. Ammi's blonde head is resting against Onnachild's fur-covered arm.

A waft of red draws my attention back to the ceremony. The religious man is lacing a red ribbon over and between Eldini and Raen's fingers, tying them together. Eldini lets out a little titter that shakes her shoulders. A Maiden sprinkles water over their joined hands. I can't watch anymore, staring out instead towards the battlefield, hoping and dreading that I might spot Aelius's spirit there. A sapling is growing where he fell. It will be destroyed when the battle starts, and the Aralltir families settled in those huts will be scattered, perhaps irrevocably. The gods have failed me. My ancestors have failed me and so more dead will join my love.

'We have bound you together as our countries will be bound, as your bodies will be bound. We request the blessing of God on this marriage and ask Him, in His wisdom, to bring children and good health to you both.'

There's a dark flash, spotted out the corner of my eye. My heart jumps.

Are the gods here at last? I snatch my hand from Mantona, lean forwards in my seat and grab the chair in front. The matron sitting in it turns around, glares at me. I don't let go. It's not my ancestors or a god; it's the shadow of a raven. I sink back.

'Do you both come free of heart and free of will to this marriage?' the religious man asks.

I hold my breath. *Now. Now, Raen, say it. Say something. The words are so easy to form. Tell them you'll not bring death to the village. Tell them you don't want her.*

'I do.' Eldini answers first. She fidgets and her skirts rustle.

Raen, please say no. We could grab Ammi, run off, run through the battlefield to where Vill says there are other people like us. This is an ugly place. An ugly village.

'I am,' Raen says.

Vill could have spoken up, but he stands there rigid as a silver statue. Mantona could have but she's dabbing at her tears. Me? Ammi's here, stopping me from speaking out. But last night, last night I could have said yes. Why didn't I lie?

Those little words Raen used as excuses before are said again: duty, obey, honour. There's no accent in his voice; he really has given up on the village. Eldini repeats them back to him. Neither promise love. Neither promises anything that has meaning.

I press the back of my hand to my sweaty forehead. The gods must help. My gaze lifts to the sky, praying for rain at least. I want the flowers in that arch to stop being so perky. I want raindrops to drench Eldini's hair so it darkens and loses that gleam of sunlight. I want the field to get muddy and ruin her white dress. My smile is hurting. I must watch, though, know it is done, and so I lower my gaze to the couple.

Raen gently lifts her veil. He's smiling at her. He bends down. His left arm goes around her slender waist. She rises onto her tiptoes. He pecks her lips. Quick. Closed-mouthed. Is this their first kiss? He lets her go. They turn at the same time towards the crowd. Her face is bright red. He takes her hand, and they walk down the aisle, pass by me, eyes only on each other.

The gods did nothing. I did nothing. And so now they are married.

Part IV: Water

Chapter Fifty-One

EVERY MORNING FOR THE LAST THREE DAYS I've come here, stood under Eldini's bedchamber window and watched the bridal-bed linen clap against the wall. The linen is stained with the proof of her virginity, faded to brown. Its display will stop there being any disputes over the wedding night. It proves Raen has done what was needed: duty, obligation, honour. Was he as cold, as impersonal, as those words? Staring up at the window, I wonder what they've been doing shut in that room for three days. Surely, she can't be that entertaining?

Routine has been upended since the wedding with everyone left to entertain themselves however they please. The Sunning Room has been locked. We haven't been called to the Great Hall, although Melody tells me it's been kept open and is full of castle people doing things she couldn't tell me about, but they made her cheeks flush and that bawdy giggle return.

Vill sidles up beside me. 'There you are.' He tries to steer me away.

A group of intoxicated men stumble by, disrupting the quiet with their hollering and guffawing. One has ripped the knee of his breeches, exposing leg hair and the grass-stained skin underneath. Another is wearing a hood similar to Eldini's, the peaks broken and bent. Another is playing with the sore-looking corners of his mouth as he says, 'Skin was like milk, like pure, fresh milk.' He winks at me but his other eye flickers, too. I huff back.

'Who wants milk when he can have wine?' Vill whispers. His comment has me bristling and twitching away. 'Come now, we don't want Raen looking out and seeing you so miserable.' Again, Vill tries to move me.

Is that what I want? A glimpse of Raen? I rub at the tension in my temples. It seems odd to say I miss him but I think I do. Maybe I'm just overtired from sleepless nights, awake and listening to the castle creak and wondering which, if any, of the sounds were made by Eldini and Raen mating.

'I'm intrigued to discover what has happened, changed, between them. If anything has. Are you?'

'No.' Am I lying or not?

A group of young women are lazing on the lawn. They're wearing dresses in the same style as Eldini's, and the flowing fabric is gathered up around ankles, calves, and knees. One woman has her entire left leg on display. I'm still dressed in the old style, glad of the rigid force it exerts on my posture. Without it, I'd probably slouch from my disappointments and worries.

I move: a pivot on my heels. 'Melody tells me the servants are saying how wanton Raen and Eldini are with each other, how they can hear her cries of pleasure. How they've been so passionate they've broken a chair, a table, and even the bed.' I peer over my shoulder, check that linen.

Vill laughs. 'You believe that?'

I shrug.

'Is that how he is with you? Who'd have thought it? But with Eldini?

No, and I would bet my rings on it. In fact, I'd bet every single item of jewellery I own. The only thing likely to be broken is Eldini.'

'You shouldn't talk about her like that.'

'But you can?'

'I wasn't.'

'Of course not.'

Beshanie skips by with her lilac skirts hitched up as Perkin chases behind her, his arms flapping about. 'One rule for castle people another rule for villagers,' I grumble as Perkin tackles her to the grass and she playfully shrieks. 'I thought she had her sights set on you.'

'May the gods bless Perkin.' He laughs as the pair grapple with each other. 'Besides, we don't know if they're going so far as actually mating; thankfully, I'm not in the bedchamber with them.'

'Imagine what Onnachild would do if I was behaving like that.'

'But my dear, you did.'

I glare at him but it's myself I'm annoyed with. These past three nights I've begged for Aelius's forgiveness, confessing I was selfish. I betrayed him. Yet by the time morning began to brighten the curtains, it was Raen's name I whispered, my lips brushing against the fur coverings as I did so.

I shake my head and fan my face to cool the heat coming to it.

'Don't look so peevish,' Vill says. 'What people do is between them, their god, and the poor fools involved.'

Beshanie and Perkin's kisses are a wet-sounding clack that brings the drunken men flocking like scavenging pigeons. My gaze returns to the bed linen, and I remember everyone huddled underneath, cheering and clapping, when it was first slapped out. How humiliated Eldini must have been.

'Don't for a moment think Onnachild will approve of this once he returns. Neither will our little princess.'

'He's just as bad. Melody said he's taken a village woman to his bed.'

Vill laughs.

'I don't see what's funny.'

'Forgive me. It's not that which amuses me; I was thinking how fast false rumours spread in this castle. No, Onnachild is not with a village woman.'

'Then what is he doing? The battle?' My heart drops. Four days left. 'What's happening?'

'The advisers are being very secretive. What I know is I've not been needed and Onnachild hasn't been spotted since the wedding, and I've never been more grateful. It's amazing what a good night's sleep and being bored can accomplish.' He rubs at a faint line between his eyebrows. There's a new ring on his index finger and it has a hawk and a cormorant meeting beak to beak. 'You like?' He holds it out for admiration, and I can't tell if he's intentionally irritating me.

I stomp across the lawn, leaving behind that linen, the sound of Perkin's sloppy kisses, and the women waving their skirts to entice the men. Vill follows me, walking slightly behind, as I make my way to the flower gardens. The bees hurry past me, diving into the marigolds and lilies. I bend down to remove the faded blooms of the marigolds and throw them towards the rounded trees which are starting to lose their shape.

Vill stands in front of me, twisting his new ring round and round his finger. 'We need to decide what to do when Raen and Eldini appear.'

I pause. Will Raen come to me? 'When?'

'Protocol is seven days but with things the way they are, your guess is as good as mine.'

'In time for the battle then.' Battle. The marigolds with their splaying rust-coloured petals remind me too much of blood. I stand and wipe my hands on my dress. Yes, we need to figure out a way to stop the battle. I nod at Vill to continue.

'Once he's out, you must stop him returning to her, keep him from getting a child with her. You're healthy, lusty. You've already carried a child.' He pinches my arm as if I'm a pig at market. 'And Eldini is small-hipped, weak. You understand what I'm implying, don't you?'

'Perfectly. And I will not.' I snatch back my arm. 'It ends now. He's had enough of my body ... I won't give him any more. I certainly won't give him children.'

'That, I believe, is in the hands of the gods. Raen's still hot for you, and Eldini, well, let's be honest and plain-speaking: we both know she won't have been able to satisfy him. She'll have been scared and pious. She'll not have enjoyed it.'

'We're not talking about this.' I walk to where a primrose has escaped the confines of the flower bed and lies across the path. I pick it up and twirl it against my cheek. It's as smooth as the underside of an arm. 'The battle, Vill.'

'There may be good news on that front. I have my suspicions that Onnachild has succumbed to whatever disease he's been suffering from, and I suspect it's something much more serious than the flux, hence the advisers being so secretive. If I'm right then the battle plans become mired in uncertainty. The order hasn't been signed off so, in all probability, it will be postponed which means we have a reprieve and can give our undivided attention to the original goal, getting you the throne. Which is why I suggest you keep Raen from Eldini, a childless union is much easier to go up against.'

Ignoring his comment on Raen, I pull a petal from the primrose and watch it float onto the path. 'Mantona told me the Followers are coming. Is she right?'

Vill nods. 'Some. I managed to get word to them.'

It should make me smile. Vill's staring at me probably expecting one. How can I be so numb? My body feels asleep without Raen's presence, his touch, his lusty stares. I stretch my arms out to the sun but this heat can't wake it.

'What about the merchants?'

'Directly after a wedding is not a good time for me to press our cause. Nothing distracts unhappy subjects more than a wedding, especially if they aren't paying for it. The merchants are currently too drunk on wine, gambling, and whoring, and they would not appreciate me interrupting those pursuits. No. My role has been to remain clear-minded and ensure their debts build up. A man in need of money is a man I can use.' He smiles. 'And drunken men are a lot less able to spot a cheater.' His laugh has a high-pitched trill to it.

'And this bet?' I gesture to myself and my dress with what remains of the primrose. 'When will this be decided, Vill?'

'It seems to have slipped Onnachild's mind with all this planning for weddings and battles. Cantor isn't going to remind him because so far you are doing very nicely at presenting as a loyal castle woman. That doesn't mean you can relax, though. Not yet. Maybe soon.'

'And then I'll be able to see Ammi?'

'Soon.'

It's always soon. Always soon and never now. I drop the primrose and yank out another, roots and mud coming with it. The brown scatters and ruins the white of the path.

'Is nothing going to cheer you today? Let's see if this news will. I've called the dressmaker here. We can look at patterns and embellishments.' He leans back. 'Still no smile?'

'I don't care about dresses.'

'What do you care about, Niah?'

'Ammi. It's been too long since I've seen her.' I rip off a petal. 'Why wasn't I allowed to at the wedding?'

'It would hardly have been proper with Cantor there.' Vill holds out his hand to catch the falling petal.

'And you? What do you care about?'

'Me? You know the answer to that. How can you still doubt me so much?' He throws the petal over his shoulder. 'You wanted me to contact the Followers and I have, at great personal risk to myself, I might add. You need to place your trust in me. There are things in preparation. Things being put in place, even as I meander here with you, my mind is busy, planning.' He taps his temple. 'It's all in here.'

'Am I allowed to know?'

'In good time. You have enough to worry about. Just make sure you look stunning at the celebratory feast when Raen and Eldini make their reappearance. Now come on, give me a smile. Just one.' He smiles at me as if he thinks I've forgotten how to.

There isn't chance for me to check on the bed linen this morning before Melody is marching me towards the Great Hall. The hallways are cluttered with empty goblets and plates, and the light is dank because the dirty windows dull the sunshine. It would seem that the servants have been taking advantage of Onnachild's absence, too.

'Quick. Hurry up,' Melody says. 'Everyone's been called to meet for breakfast. You must be there.' One hand attempts to speed me up while the other keeps hold of her headdress, minus the veil again.

'I don't get what the rush is.' My thoughts drift to the linen, bashing against the wall. How many more days will it stay there? Today is the fourth.

'The cook said that Raen and Eldini are going to be there.'

I stop. There's a flutter in my chest. 'Already? But ... Vill said ...'

'Maybe Raen couldn't bear to be with her any longer, I don't know. The cook didn't say. Please, though, hurry, hurry up. I don't think the King is in a good mood.'

When we turn a corner, we encounter a crowd of castle people stinking of ale, sweat, and pleasure. Their feet are heavy and dragging, creating an ominous bang then swish. The men brush their fingers through their hair and add a lick of spit to stick down errant tufts. Servants hastily rearrange the skirts of castle women, using pins to repair tears.

Something is wrong. I can feel it in the hallway, something as thick and heavy as winter fog is lingering. 'What's going on?' I ask.

'No one's told me, but I hope I get to find out. You'll tell me, won't you? Lark said I've got to go straight to the Prayer Room after I get you to the Great Hall, and I have to stay there the whole day, praying.' She grimaces. 'Haven't I prayed enough already?'

Our pace slows to match the crowd. The trudge jars with the speeding of my heart. I'm not ready to see Raen again, am I? Why am I smiling?

'Are you sure that Raen will be there?' I ask.

'That's what the cook told me and he's very rarely wrong, though he did tell me dogs turn into wolves at full moon so ...' she shrugs, 'maybe he's wrong.'

I hope he is, and I hope he isn't.

Mantona catches up with us, her neat appearance contrasting with the dishevelled state of everyone else. Her freckles are covered, her hair is smoothed into an elaborate series of twists, and her figure is held firm by her cages.

'Can you feel the tension?' She sounds pleased. When I look around the crowd, Mantona seems to be the only gleeful person this morning. A few women are furtively peeping about with red-tinged eyes whereas others hang their heads. A man is slumped against the shoulder of his friend and incoherently shouting. There's sobbing from further back. An old merchant next to me is berating his daughter with a wagging finger but is too drunk to speak.

'Everyone's waiting to be condemned, and wishing they hadn't been quite so reckless now.' Mantona nods towards Beshanie who's glowering at the floor as she joins the shuffle from a side room. 'Better to be an honest mistress than a fake virgin. They always get found out.'

'How? Who'd say?'

'The advisers. Who else? They find out everything. Look at how happy they are.' She nods towards where they're standing either side of the entrance to the Great Hall. 'They know exactly what's on its way.'

As people enter, Aesc scribbles onto his scroll and the noise causes people to flinch. Ascelin rubs the tip of his flat nose, hiding his mouth, but he can't hide the malicious joy in his eyes. They give Mantona a slight bow as we pass them and enter the Great Hall.

The windows and doors have been thrown open, letting in a chill and the perfumes of a summer morning. Unadorned, the room seems bigger, and every little sound is amplified as people shuffle to their places, fidget in their seats, tap nervous feet, yawn. The religious tapestries are back on the walls, faded and patchy in the slate-coloured light.

'Do you think they know about Raen and me?' I whisper.

'I wouldn't be surprised. You're safe, though, because it wouldn't serve them to repeat that gossip. They're loyal to the King but they're even more loyal to themselves, and they realise one day either you or Raen will be in charge.'

'I heard the King has been with a village woman.'

She toys with the bracelets on her wrist, pushing them up and watching them slide down. 'I've been with him,' she says.

What? By the time my shock has subsided enough to formulate questions, she's gone. Was she mating with him or tending to his illness? Was she there to find out information for Vill? I watch her take her seat, as though something in her movements will give me answers, but she settles with her chin high and gives off the impression that she's above reproach.

When I sit, neither Beshanie nor Nilola acknowledges me. Instead, they remain silent with their heads bowed. A man weaves into the Great Hall, singing and then he must notice the anxious faces, whiter than normal, because he's suddenly silent and concentrating on his steps. A few young women, sheepishly, keep their focus on the bare table while their guardians are tense beside them.

'What's happening?' I ask Beshanie.

She shushes me. Nilola lets out a sob, which she tries to muffle behind a hand gloved in white lace. There's slurred gossip coming from men who say Onnachild won't appear, he's not done with his village girl. They demand more wine but the servants stand there, awkward, ignoring them. A man is asleep and snoring, forehead on the table. Aesc goes up to him and smacks him across the shoulders with the rolled-up parchment. The man splutters awake.

'There will be no wine,' Ascelin yells. 'You've had enough wine.'

Once the Great Hall is full and everyone is in their places, Aesc bangs the door shut. The room is silent. Vill, tidy and perfect, is sat at the top table. Gavin is beside him, looking pompous and self-righteous in white. Someone sniffs. Someone coughs. Nilola squirms in her seat and receives a slap from Beshanie. People are trying to compose themselves into postures of modesty and propriety. Their fun is over and regret is all that remains in their faces and poses.

When Onnachild appears, we stand. A man falls over, creating an echoing thump. He gets dragged out by servants.

'Sit,' Onnachild barks.

Everyone drops into their chairs.

Onnachild's swamped by the furs he wears and clutches close. His skin is almost the same colour as the grey in his beard, and his scowl emphasises the weight he's lost. A servant helps him into his seat. It'd be a miracle if Onnachild has been rutting with a woman, so what was

428

Mantona doing with him? I'm about to look at her when Eldini appears and attached to Eldini's hand is Raen. He's clasping her tightly. For her benefit? For his? I don't want to see if he's content, if he's changed. My heart's hammering. My mouth's dry and there's nothing to drink, not even water. His presence has my skin prickling.

With great effort, I force my gaze to remain on Eldini, on her pink dress which is adding colour to her cheeks. Or has that colour come from mating this morning? My stomach lurches at that possibility. She's not broken. She seems stronger and stern, so he must be holding her hand because he wants to. Her white hair is uncovered and tumbling over her slight shoulders. There's a glow to her skin, even in this dim light. Her stern face softens when Raen pulls out a chair for her. She beams up at him and it's full of meanings only they understand. Has she discovered those dips in his body that I first laid claim to: his lower back as it begins the curve up to his buttocks, the indentations that follow his hip bone down and down ...? My gaze drifts over to Raen.

And I wish it hadn't.

By the gods, he's more handsome than I remembered. His focus is on Eldini as he sits beside her, so I can only see his profile. What has changed? His dark hair has been gathered and tied with a bow. Did she tie it for him? His jawline has the same sharp edge. It's freshly shaven. By her? His nose is the same. The pout of his lips is the same. I want to pull his bottom lip between my teeth to test whether its plumpness is also the same. I fidget in my seat. *Please look at me. Turn so I can see your eyes.* They'll show whether he's been able to sleep with her beside him, whether he's forgotten me.

Onnachild whacks the table. Someone gasps. Someone sobs. Eldini turns her stern attention to the castle people. Raen looks ahead, not at me, not at anyone. I can't tell what he's thinking.

'I appreciate you may have become overexcited by the wedding.'

Onnachild's voice is surprisingly loud and steady considering how much he wobbles as he gets to his feet. 'That is no excuse for the wickedness reported to me. Where restitution is due, it will be paid.' Coughing, he gestures to a servant, and she rushes to him with a goblet which he snatches and gulps from. 'I'm disappointed and disgusted.' He smacks the goblet onto the table. 'Fornication, gambling, gluttony.'

Hypocrite, I think, but remain silent. Beshanie swears under her breath. Nilola sobs into her glove.

'These are not the actions of a God-fearing people. How quickly you forgot His lessons, acting no better than ill-bred village girls. You have disrespected me in front of our new princess. And you've disrespected God. No more. I will not have a castle full of peacocks placing their desires above those of God.' He coughs again, bending and waving for a servant to attend to him. Eldini comes to his aid. She stands, puts an arm around him, and passes him his goblet. More women are crying now. Beshanie huffs and tuts.

'We will pray for God's forgiveness.' Eldini's voice has a depth and a maturity that wasn't there before, and it prompts the matrons to holler out 'Amen'. What has Raen said or done to remove her girlish uncertainty and shyness? She's become a woman, and it suits her. I don't want it to. She beams down at Raen. He nods in response and extends his hand out to her again.

'I bet those men that grabbed village girls for their pleasure won't be punished, will they. It's so unfair,' Beshanie moans before copying everyone and pressing her palms together.

Around the room, people hold their hands high, palms together and their elbows resting on the table. Their chins point at the ceiling and their eyes are shut. Eldini leads a prayer. Vill looks bored, lolling in his seat as he prays. Gavin is mouthing the words, and his palms are pressed so tightly together his fingertips have turned red.

Raen. Raen's chin is high, exposing the full thickness of his neck and the tendons there. I wish I was close enough to see the throb of his pulse. Lower my gaze goes, down to the dip at the collar of his tunic which is the perfect shape for my tongue, down to the moving swell of his chest as he breathes, and I picture the brush of dark hair there. His attention is on me, heating my skin even through my dress. My nipples respond, proving I still want him. When I raise my eyes to his face, his lips curve into a teasing smile that tells me he's felt every one of my lusty thoughts. I smile back. He still desires me, too; that hasn't changed.

His praying hands press against his lips. When will I feel the press of them on me again? Never. I focus on his wedding band to remind me. He's married. He's chosen her. Yet my body doesn't seem to care.

Chapter Fifty-Two

ELDINI IS THE LAST PERSON I WANT TO SEE when I'm pacing the grounds and mulling over everything I saw at breakfast. She's sitting alone under a tree, a forlorn figure in a fur that has fallen from her shoulders. Why does she look unhappy? Does she want to be in her room with Raen? More questions. It doesn't matter, and the answers are irrelevant because they won't make a difference. She spots me before I'm able to change direction, calls my name and waves me over to join her.

The pink from her cheeks has gone, replaced by the shadow of the tree. 'I am happy to see you.' Her voice is perky and, along with her words, makes me ashamed of the lusty looks I was giving Raen earlier.

I smile and nod, reluctant to engage in conversation in case my questions start spilling out. She takes the fur from around her waist, shivering in the unseasonable cold, and lays it out on the grass. Her eyes plead with me and so I've no choice but to sit when she pats the fur.

'You look sad?' she says.

'Me?'

She nods. 'No not sad, angry? Someone unkind to you? Men unkind to you?' Her concerned expression seems genuine; I wish it wasn't. I turn my attention to the servants rushing around and neatening up the grounds.

'I've not misbehaved like the rest of the castle. I know my place.'

'Please, I not doubt you. You good woman.'

'Some would not agree.'

'Love is different.' She takes my hand. I can't help picturing hers resting on Raen's chest, her thin fingers lost in his chest hair. Her hold is too tight for me to slip away from. 'God forgives love, not lust, not greed for body. The King is angry, and God is angry.'

'And you?'

'Yes, angry. Things must change.' Her chin juts out, determined.

'And your new life—are you enjoying that?' The question blurts out.

She seems to consider it. I wish I hadn't asked because my mind is filling her silence with all the words she might say: wonderful, amazing, perfect, love. To prepare myself, I search for evidence of the words in her face: her skin tinged blue from the cold, her mouth parted ready to speak, and her eyes showing her struggling over what to share with me. Her thumb taps me in time to her mewing breaths, and I can't help wondering whether this is the same rhythm their mating followed, the same sound she made. The waiting hurts like a thump on my chest.

The servants break the silence, shouting instructions to each other.

I need to know, and so I press again. 'Are we not to be frank with each other? You know everything about me.'

'I do not wish to say.' Her shoulders slouch and her head droops, transforming her from princess to a girl needing a friend. There are goosebumps on her skinny arms and she's shivering again, so I move off the fur, onto the damp grass, and drape it over her shoulders. Her fingers flutter to receive the fur and then clamp shut around it, forming into fists. 'It is cold today,' she says. 'I am cold today. Are you cold today?'

'A little bit.'

She smiles weakly at me, trying to placate me, perhaps, and stop me from probing her further. Without the hood overpowering the whiteness of her skin and her delicate features, she has a modest beauty. Her forehead is less vast and her head is less round. This is the sight Raen has woken up to these last four days. He's been greeted by these serene eyes. And her, what did she find in his? Did those green dots pulse for her as they do for me?

'You looked happy together at breakfast.' I watch for a twitch, a tremble, something to give me a hint of her true emotions, but she's too well trained. Not even her sigh tells me anything.

'I think we away too long.' That determined jut returns to her chin, but her pose is ruined by a blast of wind that makes her shiver.

I move the trailing edges of the fur to cover her knees. My care for her confuses me, but as she stares at me, her irises the very faintest hint of blue, I can't help it. There's a touch of sadness, just a touch, in them that she can't hide.

'I am glad I am back,' she says.

'I'm glad too,' I say to make her smile.

She doesn't. She nods slightly and clutches the fur tighter. 'Walk with me.'

I get up and help her to her feet, taking those little hands that have touched Raen. She brushes grass off my skirt and asks me to check hers. There's a faint mud stain near the hem. The fur trails behind her as we take a stroll down and over the hidden dips of the grounds. She's distracted, her fingers running over and over her collarbone. I lead her to and then around the wall surrounding the grounds, hoping to impress on her how imposing and ugly the structure is. Instead, she runs her palms over its bumps.

'Gavin good too,' she says.

I nod, unsure what I'm expected to say. She's not paying me any attention, though. She's tugging out the weeds growing between the wall's black bricks and letting them drop to our feet. Raen can't have told her its history or she wouldn't be tending to it so carefully. Realising he's not shared this with her gives me a rush of pleasure.

'I am happy outside. I missed outside,' Eldini says.

'Did your time away not please you?'

'It was long. I did not know it would be long. I did my duty.' Her palms press against the wall. 'Niah ...' Her voice wobbles. 'I did not like my duty.'

Her openness startles me, brings a spasm to my gut, and I'm not sure if it's from relief or guilt or sympathy for her. Did she lie beneath him, still as a corpse, wearing that stoic expression from her portrait? Were her eyes clenched shut, her hands away from his skin, and her mind away with her God? It doesn't matter. They're married now. Yet still I ask, 'Was he unkind?' I hold my breath, anticipating what else she might tell me.

'I think I made mistake.' She pats the wall like it's a tame animal. 'I do not please him. I do not know how. It was done. You saw. Every person saw. I did not like that. They came in, hitting and hitting and hitting like this.' She knocks on the wall. 'And they take linen from me. And they do not care. Everyone saw. Everyone saw linen from window.' She gestures towards the castle but doesn't look that way. Her cheeks are a bright crimson. 'Raen did not stop them.' She grabs up the fur and tugs it around her torso. There's grass caught in the pelt. 'I do not go to him. I was scared. He hurt me.'

'I hear it can hurt the first time.'

'It hurt for you?' Her quiet voice draws me nearer. She smells of lemon and vanilla, and not Raen.

434

I shake my head.

Her right cheek bunches up in a fake half-smile.

I should have lied to her. To make up for it, I try to offer some comfort. 'It won't hurt the next time.' The thought makes my stomach lurch.

She dips her chin into the pelt. 'We had a next time.' Her words are muffled.

How many, I want to ask. When? Where? How? I clench my jaw to keep the questions in.

'He not speak to me. He not like me. He not tell me what to do now I am wife. I not know. What I do? No one says.' She looks up at me, tears in her eyes and a smudge from the wall on her nose. 'I want good marriage.'

I should reach out to comfort her, but I can't. My body is stuck as I remember each and every little sign of his pleasure: a hitch of a breath, a tremble, a muscle tensing, a changing hue to his skin, a heartbeat. These hints I discovered by watching and listening, by playing and teasing, and what I found is mine. 'I don't know,' I mumble and hope that will be enough to stop her questions.

'Aelius, you made him happy, yes? How?'

His name is strange in her accent, so it seems to relate to a different person and not him, not the boy I loved and wanted. Wanted in a way that's different to how I want Raen. I repeat Aelius's name to remind myself of what my heart yearns for, and it helps clear my mind. 'I don't know. I was myself, just myself, and that was enough.'

She nods though it's apparent she isn't reassured. 'I do not want to be duty. Some men go to wives only. Choose wives only. I want that. You are friends. You ask him. You ask him what he want, like.' She sniffs.

'I don't think he'd appreciate us speaking about this.'

'Why? He is your friend. I am your friend.' Her bottom lip is quivering.

Her fingers are twisting the fur. 'Niah?'

'These things should stay between a husband and wife. Raen wouldn't like it, and he wouldn't trust you if he heard you'd been talking to me about ... this.'

She starts crying and there's nothing regal in the way her tears make trails over her white cheeks. I dig my nails into my arm and stare up at the sky to stop myself touching her in case that contact gives away something.

'Who else ... say to me about it?' she splutters. Then her head's pressing against my chest and she's clutching my hips. My hands hang limply by my sides while hers paw at me like a kitten and her tears wet my chest. I will not. I can't. I need to get away. Her body is all bones, and it grates against mine. I know what I should do; I don't need Raen's secrets anymore. But they are mine. Surely, someone else can tell her how to please a husband? She has already taken enough from me, must I give her that too? I try to hate her.

Chapter Fifty-Three

I CURSE MYSELF for being so heartless as to march Eldini to her rooms and leave her with her women without even giving a backwards glance. Already she'd forced that stoic expression onto her face. She wasn't going to let them help her. She wanted me to. Why? It's obvious what I should have done but, by the gods, it's too much to ask of me. Every step I take towards my rooms, further and further away from her tear-splotched cheeks, is weighted with her sadness. I can't help her. And I didn't lie, not really, because I don't know how to make Raen happy. If I did, he wouldn't have chosen her. All I want is the solitude of my rooms where I can forget she exists, where I can change my dress and scrub out the black smudges left by her hands.

Melody must have heard my heavy feet because she's opening the door to my rooms before I can grab the handle. 'We found someone looking lost outside.' She grins.

Raen's sitting at a round table with Nessia, his long legs stretched out and his hair loose around his broad shoulders. I'm not sure what I feel at seeing him here, every emotion seems to surge at once. When the door clicks shut, he peers up from the cards in his hands and smirks as if he isn't married. I can't stop myself from returning his smile, from my body responding to his gaze as it lingers over those dark marks left by Eldini.

'Has our time apart cooled your temper?' he teases.

'What are you doing here?' I try to sound angry but it doesn't work.

'Nessia found me wandering the hallways and in need of some company.' He plays a card, causing Nessia to throw hers down and declare she is out.

Melody rushes towards her cards on the floor, screaming, 'Wait, wait.' She kicks her headdress in her haste and sends it flying across the room.

'I've been with Eldini,' I say and wish I hadn't because he goes back to staring at his cards and I'm just ashamed again.

'I'm sure she had much to tell you.'

'She was crying.'

His jaw twitches and I'm not sure if it's from concern or distaste. 'I don't want to talk about Eldini.'

I don't either, I'm too tired, but we must. If for no other reason than to stop me going to him, putting my hands on him. It's bad enough I know the pattern of his leg hair over his thigh and can't stop staring at the spread of the muscle. He's married. I slump against the door, the handle digging into my back. 'You should go comfort her.'

He slaps his cards down and for a moment I think he means to do just that. 'What should I say to her? What can I say that won't be a lie? Or do you want me to lie to her?'

'You don't need to lie to her, say something, I don't know, something to make her think you care.'

'When I don't? Is that not a lie?'

'She's your wife.'

'And I hardly know her and she hardly knows me. Maybe we will grow to care for each other, maybe not. She's not an idiot. She realises this was no love match.'

'How can you be so cold? She's crying.'

He jumps up. His chair falls. Melody snatches up his cards and peeks at them. 'Shall I leave then?' His stare challenges me to say yes. 'Is that what you're saying?'

'No, wait,' Melody shouts. 'I can win this game. I can and you need to let me win back my buttons.' She rights his chair.

'Do you want me to go, Niah?' he asks.

'Why are you even here?' I cross my arms over my chest to stop the rapid rise and fall of it, to hide the proof that I want him to stay, to touch me again.

'Don't be so rude.' Nessia shakes her head, turning to Raen and offering her apologies to him. 'We invited him here.'

'You didn't answer my question.' He shifts his weight to his other foot and crosses his arms.

I uncross mine. 'Do what you want.'

'I'll take that as a no then.' He sits down again, plays another card and looks to Melody, waiting for her to pick one. Chewing the inside of her cheek, she goes to place a card, then she changes her mind and returns it to her hand. She peeps up at him. She peeps at her cards. I want to sigh with relief because he's staying, but I can't let him know that, so I stifle it in my palm. The warmth of my breath reminds me of the warmth of his body, and my head bashes against the door.

'Why was Eldini crying?' His attention is on the messy pile of cards.

Melody places her card, squeals, and quickly swaps it over for another. She shuffles back in her seat, giggling to herself and looking proud.

'It's none of your business,' I say.

'First, you tell me to go comfort my wife and now you won't tell me what she says I've done that has made her cry. I can't win.'

'No, you can't.' Melody wiggles in her seat.

'We had more to talk about than you,' I say.

'I didn't say otherwise but I suspect you had things you wished to find out about me,' he peers over his shoulder at me, 'and her. Am I right?'

'You flatter yourself. I don't care what happened in your locked room.'

Melody huffs at my words, making him and Nessia laugh.

'Have you not missed me then?' He taps his cards against his lips. Is he doing that to purposely draw my attention to that plush bottom one?

'I have found other things to amuse me.'

'Does that mean you'll be called before Onnachild?'

'You'd like that.' I take off my shoes, drop them to the floor. Nessia stares at me like I'm a child having a tantrum. I pull the pins out from my hair, untangle it and shake it loose. It relieves some tension. He pats the chair next to him, his attention remaining on his cards. I'm too tired to fight it anymore and so I slump down next to him, keeping my arms and legs to myself. He draws a card from the deck, smiles as he adds it to his hand. I lean closer to see what it is, pausing when I breathe in his scent. I'd forgotten how good he smells, of forests, of autumn.

'I've heard nothing ill of you.' Raen sounds pleased.

'And you won't,' Nessia says.

'I have had enough of ...' I gesture at him.

He tilts his head to the side and his lips quirk, implying that he doesn't believe me. Melody pulls another card from the deck. 'I've won,' she yells. 'Look, look, Raen. I've won. I'll have the buttons.' She throws her cards on the table and jabs them with her index finger.

439

'You aren't meant to tell them that,' I say to her. 'You're meant to play the card first.'

Raen leans over to check. 'So you have.' He starts sliding the buttons across to her one by one.

She laughs and holds each one up to the light. 'Well, I have still won and we aren't playing for money, anyway, so it doesn't matter. Gambling is sinful. We're playing for buttons and the pride of being the winner and so I have still won. He can't beat me and he knows it. You look.' She jabs her cards again. 'See, whatever card I play I have beaten him and Nessia, too. I am the winner.'

'Now you've lost, you can go,' I tell Raen, my body is beginning to tilt towards his warmth. His arm almost brushes mine as he pushes over the last button.

'Can I see you tonight?' he asks.

'I'll be in the Great Hall with everyone else.'

He scoops the cards up and bows his goodbyes to Melody and Nessia. 'Thank you for an excellent game.' Then he kneels in front of me. His eyes promise all manner of things, and my breath catches, giving me away. His mouth is at the right level to kiss me and I want him to. He must. It must not be me who gives in. He smiles. His tongue darts across his bottom lip. My hands grip the chair.

'Until later.' His smile has turned into a smirk.

I'm only half paying attention to Vill in the Great Hall as he gleefully fills me in on everything that happened in the Judging Room today. Most of my attention is on Raen dancing with Nilola. He's already danced with Beshanie and several other castle women, toying with me. I watch the stretch of his muscular legs, the widening and narrowing of his shoulders, his mouth making words.

The song ends, and I turn to Vill so Raen won't realise I've been scrutinising his movements.

'The schedule will be with everyone tomorrow,' Vill says. 'It's going to cause merry hell.'

'Schedule?'

'Were you not listening?' He glances at the dance floor and must realise what was distracting me because his lips quirk. 'A schedule for praying. The Sunning Room is to be used as a prayer room for the castle people. Morning, afternoon, and night, and that is in addition to the prayers before we eat. People will be furious. They don't want to pray. They want decadence, fornication, as many vices as they can cram into a night, and they want Onnachild to turn a blind eye as he always has. Already they're grumbling at being permitted only two goblets of wine with their meal tonight. A few complain a bit too loudly and there'll be more hanging at traitors' gate. Additional changes have been hinted at but not decided on. The way things are progressing, we'll have people begging to join us.'

'I won't keep funding their excesses.'

'They don't need to know that, though.' Vill lifts the jug and goes to fill his goblet until he realises it's only water in the jug. He frowns and puts it back onto the table. 'A small price to pay.'

My goblet has some wine left in it so I push it over to him. 'Whose idea was this? Eldini's?' I'm impressed. She's sitting at the top table, her earlier sadness gone as she cuts up Onnachild's food for him.

'Partly, but I think this illness might be prompting Onnachild to worry about the afterlife. Now shush, Raen's almost here.'

I don't need Vill to tell me this because I can feel Raen's heat calling me to acknowledge his presence and turn towards him. Even though I try hiding my smile, Vill notices and his lips are quirking again as he pushes away from the table, taking my goblet with him.

Raen thrusts his wide hand at me, the deep lines of it exposed. 'Dance with me.'

I can't think of a reason to refuse except for that mischievous glint in his eye which has my heart racing. New modesty rules impose an awkward distance on the dancing couples and so their arms strain to reach shoulders and waists. Ascelin enforces this by stamping across the dance floor and pushing people apart. Perhaps this will keep me safe.

I rise from my seat, earning an appreciative look from Raen as he takes in the full view of me in my dress. This new style makes me all breasts and hips, with the slinky material cascading from the peaks of my breasts to graze the curve of my hips.

'This new fashion suits you.' His eyes linger on my chest, my nipples tightening in response to his lusty stare.

'Don't.'

As I walk out to the dance space, I feel him watching the rounds of my buttocks moving under the thin material, and so I add a little sway to bring a bounce and a swish to my steps. I hide my pleasure when we face each other, ready to touch. His hand settles on my waist, sliding the silk over my skin as his fingertips search for their place.

'I've missed you, Niah.'

'How can you have missed me when you had a nice, new virgin in your bed?'

'I'm not interested in her. I did my duty.'

'I know. I saw.'

At least he looks ashamed, though he doesn't rise to the bait and his half-smile is soon back. I want to see something real on his face, a hint to show this distance is infuriating him, too. As my feet follow the rhythm of his, my dress slides over me as light as a lover's caress, his caress. The tease has me craving the textures of his naked body: the smoothness of his bicep, the brush of his chest hair, the silkiness of his arousal. I shake my head to dislodge these thoughts. Surely we're too close for this dance? I search for Ascelin, praying he'll come over to reinforce the space, but he's too busying berating Beshanie. I'll try something else to quash this desire.

'Congratulations on making such a good match.' The unsteadiness of my voice must give away how affected I am by his nearness. I clear my throat. 'I wish you both happiness, long life, and many children.'

He chuckles. 'What a good subject you are.'

'To you and your wife. Should you not be more attentive to your wife?' I nod to where she and Vill are twirling together.

'Eldini's fine and happy dancing with the men desperate for her favour and her ear.' His fingertips caress my waist, lifting and sweeping the delicate material between his skin and mine. I hold in my sigh and stare at my hand struggling to remain light on his shoulder. *Don't look into his eyes. Don't look at his lips. Look at Onnachild.*

Onnachild's sitting alone at the top table, little more than a head peeping out of a bulk of black furs. 'What is wrong with Onnachild?' I ask.

Raen's hold loosens. 'Do we have to talk about him? There'll be plenty of time for that later.'

I make the mistake of glancing up at Raen to gauge his expression, my action drawing his eyes to mine. His are so captivating: woody brown, the green of spring grass, and that dark centre. Our hips bump and my breasts press against his chest. And then, we're parting to the required distance, and this time I can't keep my frustrated sigh in. I expect him to be cruel and amused by my weakness but his face reflects back all my hunger. His fingers skip up my side, pause at the swell of my breasts, and then he chuckles, low and quiet. The sound resonates through me as if his fingers hadn't stopped. His hand retreats to where it should be, and he's sweeping me into a twirl as smooth as the silk wafting around my thighs. If I were to relax I'd be adrift in these sensations. This can't happen.

'What should we discuss then?' I say. 'Eldini? The night before your wedding?'

'Come on, Niah, you can't still be angry with me for that. I was drunk.

I was going to be married, and you were there, looking ... I thought ...' He pats his cheek. 'I shouldn't have said what I did, I deserved that. But you said some hateful things, too, not too long before that night, remember? So I'd say we're even, wouldn't you? I've forgiven you.'

'I didn't apologise.'

'I know, you never do,' he teases.

My lips twitch and I shrug, the resulting skim of silk against me tickles like the brush of a finger.

'I have missed you,' he whispers in my ear. 'I must see you tonight, later. Say you'll meet me in my rooms.'

Only once the song ends am I able to find my words again. I push him away with a touch that is far too much like a caress. 'You can wait but I'll not go.'

My resolve is stronger than I anticipated because dawn is almost here and I have not gone to Raen. I'm sitting in front of the fire, dressed, and that little detail isn't lost on me. If I was really determined to not see him I'd be in my nightdress, in bed, asleep. But his earlier touch is echoing through my body—he's got into my bones. My fingers slip my silk dress up and down my belly, and I imagine it's his skin moving against mine. If I was really determined I wouldn't have sent a message to him, turning this into a game of who will give in first.

It pleases me more than it should when he does, knocking on my door and opening it without waiting for my response. 'Well.' He closes the door silently.

'Well.'

He leans against the door and no longer does it feel like I've been triumphant because my heart is hammering and my breathing is so difficult to control. He knows it too, smiling there and running his fingers through his hair so the firelight can pick out the shades. He's waiting for me to stand, move towards him. His eyes sparkle as he catches his lower lip between his teeth and then eases it out.

'You asked me here,' he says.

I try to suppress my smile. 'I did.'

'Well.' He draws out the word.

One of us has to move and close this unbearable space. His arms rise and I think he's going to step away from the door, but he doesn't. He crosses his arms instead, the muscles straining against his sleeves. I laugh at his teasing, and he chuckles. I beckon him with a finger. He shakes his head and copies my gesture. When I don't move, he pivots to leave, his hand going to the door handle. He's calling my bluff, though, looking over his shoulder with his eyebrows raised. I shake my head at him, still laughing at the absurdity of this. His chuckle, rich and earthy, thrums through my body, and I almost stand, but I catch myself in time and rearrange my skirt instead. It doesn't matter; he's not fooled by the gesture and so he saunters over, still chuckling. He sits on his knees before me, looking up. His hands hold the edge of my chair, fingertips almost touching my thighs.

'Kiss me,' he whispers.

I lean closer. Not close enough. Our breath strokes skin. Our lips purse.

'Kiss me.' The demand is harsher this time. But I'm enjoying this moment, this power his lust gives me. He must submit to me; I won't give in. With my feet, I push his torso and he tips back far too easily, too willingly.

'Are you punishing me?' he asks.

'Maybe.'

I stare at him lying there, at his long legs extended, his hair spread around him and the mischievous glint in his eyes. He's planning something. It doesn't take long to discover what. He pulls his tunic off, throws it towards my chair and then lies down, hands behind his neck. The firelight picks out the textures and colours of his torso, flickering across the muscles of his honey-coloured chest, the dark hair there, the bumps of his ribs, the shadowy dip of his belly button. I lean forwards, drawn by a need to run my palm over the ridges of his stomach. I pause.

'There are no excuses here,' he says.

'There are,' I say. 'Eldini.' Evoking her name doesn't stop me from sliding off my chair, onto the floor. His stomach tenses in expectation of my touch but I keep clutching the hard wood of the chair.

'You don't care about her.'

He's right. I don't care that she might be wondering where he is. I don't care that he might go to her after here. My fingers let go of the chair. They hover above him, almost on his stomach, and I can feel the enticing warmth emanating from him.

'So we don't ever do this again?' he whispers. 'Is that what you want?'

When I don't answer, he shuffles out of his breeches. Completely nude, his arousal doesn't make him seem weak but rather more powerful, and I have lost this game. He takes my hand, placing it onto his stomach. Lower my palm glides, fingers splaying out into the hair between his legs.

'Does this mean I'm forgiven?' he asks.

'It means nothing.'

Chapter Fifty-Four

'YOU CALLED ME TO YOUR ROOMS,' I say since it appears Eldini isn't going to speak. She must have found out about last night, me and Raen. That's why she's called me here. My thighs are aching from mating with him, and I'm sure I smell of him despite my bath this morning. She peeps up at me from her cross-legged position on the floor and smiles, so

446

she can't know, not yet anyway.

'Sit.' She hides a titter behind her hand. 'I have surprise.' She calls out to Gavin.

The door to her bedchamber opens, the room where she and Raen consummated their marriage. I fight the urge to peek inside. Gavin exits and in his arms, almost too large to be contained within them, is Ammi. She wiggles to be free. Sinking to the floor, I take a deep breath. Is this real? Has Onnachild permitted this? My gaze flits from Gavin to Eldini. She nods. Why is she doing this for me when I refused to help her yesterday?

Gavin crouches and settles Ammi onto her feet. She sways, unsteady, as she stares at me and holds onto him. Her face is plump but there are still traces of Aelius in the shape of her eyes, in the blonde curls fluffed out, in her pout, in her castle-coloured skin. A blue bow, the same colour as his eyes, is in her hair and it matches the ribbon around her podgy waist. She's the picture of health, with chubby rolls around her elbows and knees. She's adorable. I want to rush at her, gather her back up close to my heart, but I can't seem to move.

'I thought, how I feel if Grace my baby and I not see her,' Eldini says.

I open my mouth to thank her but nothing comes.

'Say hello Niah,' Eldini tells Ammi and then to me, she says, 'please, King not like ... you must be Niah.'

I nod and hold my hand out to Ammi. She stares at it.

'You shy?' Eldini's voice is high-pitched and childlike. 'No need to be shy.'

I'm pleased Ammi's wary. She should be wary in this castle, even of me, especially of me, a mother who gave her away.

'She's a delightful child,' Gavin says.

Ammi grasps the frills on her dress, still uncertain and timid. The door behind me opens, and she grins, claps. Her joy is such a perfect replica of her father it brings the sweetest pain.

'Ra, Ra,' she yells. Her head cranes forwards as she crawls towards Raen. He sweeps her up, twirls her around as she giggles and giggles. She grabs onto the ends of his hair and tries to put them in her mouth.

'Come on, Ammi.' He bounces her up and down. 'Meet your mother.'

'But the King—' Eldini says.

'Her name is Ammi and Niah is her mother,' Raen says it so firmly that Eldini blushes. 'Besides, Onnachild isn't here.'

He lowers my daughter to the floor in front of me. She demands to be lifted again, pulling at his breeches, yet her sea-green eyes remain on me. I don't know what to do, what I'm allowed to do, and it breaks my heart. Here she is and I can't seem to breach this gap between us. This gap I created by abandoning her to Onnachild. I don't deserve to touch her, to hold her, to love her. Onnachild was right: I'm not fit to be her mother. I bite my lip to keep in my tears.

'Sing to her.' Raen sits beside me. Ammi throws herself into his lap, fidgeting and bashing about until she's made a comfortable spot from where she can stare at me some more.

I nod, clear my throat and then start singing an Aegnian song from my childhood. A song about yews that keep your secrets, that cover you with leaves as you sleep beneath them and bless you with dreams of those people you miss. I use my ancestors' language, something no one else can teach her. She's mesmerised, watching my lips move. Hers try to mimic mine. Raen joins in with the chorus, mumbling when I reach a word he doesn't know, and this makes me laugh. Ammi's eyes widen at the sound. Does she recognise my laughter? I start the song again. Raen sings louder, and he bounces her up and down on his knee along with the beat. She giggles and grabs hold of him. Eldini hums the tune, the noise reminding me of her presence. I stumble on the words, uneasy at sharing this with her and Gavin.

When I stop, Ammi struggles from Raen's lap, almost tripping over his foot, and then, to my amazement, she plonks herself onto my lap. She allows me to wrap my arms around her, kiss her soft cheek, and nestle against her curls. Her scent is primrose and castle and babies. Raen reaches across to pull her dress over her dimply knees. He beams at me as I squeeze her closer. Her cheek rests against my chest and I hope my heartbeat reminds her of the time when we were one. If I could, I'd take her back into my body and keep her there where it's safe. Gavin passes a doll to her, a doll with long dark hair, stitched eyes, and a smudged red mouth.

'Niah.' Ammi thrusts it at me.

I kiss the doll's cloth face. Ammi repeats my name, pointing at it.

'Is that your dolly's name?' I ask.

'It is now,' Raen says.

She jams her doll into the crook of my elbow and grins up at me. It is so similar to her father's. How good it feels to have a reminder of him, of our love. I rub my cheek against hers, revelling in the plumpness. She wiggles, giggles.

Ammi grabs my necklace, pulling the gem to her eye. It makes her iris bluer, almost cornflower like Aelius's. How had I forgotten how beautiful that colour is?

'Go on,' Eldini says. 'Say.'

Gavin coughs. 'I wanted ... if I may...'

'Do you like it?' I ask Ammi. 'Do you want it?'

She nods. Raen's fingers tickle my neck as he undoes the chain. It drops into Ammi's palm, and she goes to shove it into her mouth. I stop her and move her hand down. Raen chuckles as she grumbles and tries again.

'No,' he says more firmly. Our eyes lock. How handsome he looks when he's relaxed and content like this. The sight makes me want to bring him into this hug with my daughter, share my happiness with him. Gavin coughs again. I break eye contact with Raen, guilty at what Eldini might have noticed, guilty for even thinking that way about Raen when Ammi's in my lap, and she's such a vivid reminder of Aelius and our love.

'If I may speak plainly ...' Gavin says.

'Please,' I say, though I'm not sure if I want him to talk at all when Ammi is here.

'See,' Eldini says.

Raen leans back, unfolds his legs, and rests there, arms bracing himself as he stares at the floor. His jaw is twitching. I dangle my necklace in front of Ammi and she bashes it from side to side, sending blue flashes over us both.

'I greatly admire you,' Gavin says. 'You are ... You are different from the other castle women. I ...' He gulps and this seems to embolden him. 'I think you're clever and so kind. How you worry about the villagers compared to the other castle women, and you know I don't judge you for the child and your ... her father, and it shows me how brave, how self-sacrificing you are to share her with Onnachild as you do.'

When I look at him, puzzled at where his words are leading, his gaze darts to his knee. 'You've had such a sad life.'

'Niah doesn't need pity,' Raen says.

'No, not pity. Please, don't think ... this isn't because of pity.' Gavin glances at Eldini. She nods at him. 'You must know I ... I think you're amazing.' His face is a vivid red now. 'I would ... we could take your daughter.'

'And leave here?' I ask.

'Niah doesn't want to leave here,' Raen says.

'Whatever you'd like,' Gavin mumbles.

'Really?' His offer is tempting. Leave Onnachild. Leave uncertainty and fear. Who cares about the villagers, about a throne, about anything other than my daughter? I sneak a quick kiss onto her cheek. She squeals and squiggles. Do I not deserve happiness? She climbs off my lap and rushes to Raen, throwing her dolly at him as if frustrated because he's not been paying her enough attention.

'With your permission.' Gavin shuffles closer. 'I'd like to make your guardian change his mind, about me, about us.'

'Raen will make Onnachild allow it,' Eldini says.

'Will I?'

'If not, I can wait,' Gavin says. 'And when the King ...'

'Shush, do not.' Eldini crosses herself.

Gavin apologises to Raen who only shrugs. 'I'll keep trying if I know that I still have your heart. Do I have your heart?'

'It doesn't matter what I feel.' I speak carefully as Raen is watching me, his eyes narrowed.

'Your guardian will want you married eventually,' Gavin says. 'When he knows how we feel and what I can offer you ...' He looks so hopeful. I reach out to touch his hand because I don't know what to say. It's clammy, and he seems embarrassed by this.

'You're so sweet,' I say. There's nothing for me in this castle and yet I can't say yes. What's stopping me from saying yes? Ammi is all I want, and he's promising me her. Would Onnachild let us go? Raen's plaiting the doll's woollen hair while Ammi studies the action intently.

'We be sisters then,' Eldini says.

'Would you want to be my wife?' Gavin is so blunt my mouth opens, closes, without uttering a word. Why shouldn't I say yes? He knows about Ammi and my past and doesn't think badly of me for either. Perhaps Eldini is right and you can grow to love someone. A life of ease, a quiet life is so appealing, and I now understand Raen's attraction to Eldini.

'If you do not, please, say.' Gavin's tensed for the pain of a no.

I look over at Raen, at Ammi, small and safe in his lap as she chatters to him. He's nodding, pretending to understand her nonsensical babble. Nessia's advice returns: *no one is meant to be alone.* But that is what I promised Aelius. And I love Aelius. Besides, Onnachild will never let me take Ammi, and this land is our home. 'I don't think I shall be anyone's wife.'

'Do not give up hope.' Eldini's sympathetic rub of my knee makes me uncomfortable, but I manage to smile, suppressing my shame.

'Have your feelings towards me changed?' Gavin asks.

'No.'

He darts forwards, pecks my cheek so quickly that I'm flustered and unable to speak. I feel like I've lied but my feelings haven't changed: I've never had any feelings for him. When did I say otherwise? Beshanie and Nilola. I'd forgotten the lies they told him. No wonder he's taken my silence as acceptance, kissing my cheek again and clasping my hand. Eldini must do, too, because she's hugging me.

Slowly, Raen lifts up his head, and he glares at me with such disgust. What right does he have to judge me when he married for riches, for war? When he was the one who came begging for my touch last night despite having a wife? And so I decide to allow Gavin and Eldini to continue thinking I've accepted his offer. Perhaps I will.

Chapter Fifty-Five

'TIME FOR PRAYERS,' Eldini's maid tells Ammi, who protests and screams as she's lifted from Raen's lap. 'Now, now, be a good girl.'

Ammi continues to squirm, flailing her legs and arms as the maid struggles to remove her from the room and into the hallway. My daughter's wilfulness, something she has inherited from the Aegni women, has me smiling. Eldini stands, shakes out her dress. Gavin's too pleased to look at me as he gets to his feet. 'Raen?' Eldini asks tentatively, holding open the door.

'I have to meet with my father.' He doesn't move.

I rise, ready to pretend I'm going to join the other castle women for prayers in the Sunning Room while Eldini and Gavin go to the Prayer Room. Raen grabs the hem of my skirt to stop me. Eldini nods and then hurries off with Gavin. I yank free from Raen and rush to the door so I can watch Ammi as she's taken away. Over the maid's shoulder, my daughter peeps at me, smiling and waving goodbye. I wave back, blow her kisses, and try to remain composed.

As soon as she disappears around a corner, my composure breaks and my heart pangs. I press my fist hard against my mouth to prevent my lips curling into a sob. The room is so quiet without her chatter.

Raen slams the door shut. I jolt at the sound.

'You will not marry Gavin.'

I take in a deep breath to push my tears down.

'Niah? Did you hear me? You're not leaving with Gavin.'

He spins me around so forcefully I bump into the door. 'I heard you.' I stare up into his scowl. My tears are so close my lips are quivering. I tense them and cling to my elbows, pulling my arms tight across my chest. Not now.

'I'll give you Ammi back. I told you that. Leave Gavin alone.'

'When will you? Tell me that. How long am I supposed to wait? Or do I only get to see her when ... if ... after I've mated with you?'

His jaw twitches a warning but I can't stop. 'Accepting Gavin's proposal would be no different. At least if I married him I'd be with Ammi all the time.'

'Don't you dare ...' His breath is hot with anger. I don't care. My heart hurts for my daughter. My arms feel empty without her in them. I'm nothing without her, and I don't deserve her because of everything I've done. My eyes are watering and I can't keep in the tears. I want him to hold me, let me cry, lie and tell me it will be all right. Instead, he keeps scowling at me.

'I want Ammi.' My voice breaks. I can't cry here, not in front of him. He doesn't understand. He'll never understand.

I duck further into the room since he's blocking the door. Ammi's doll has been left on the floor, face down and only half her hair plaited. I slump against the fireplace, lower my forehead to the wooden mantelpiece. It doesn't smell of wood. Nothing in this castle is as it should be. Nothing here is natural: daughter not with mother; husbands not loving wives.

'It's not forever,' he says.

'It's long enough.'

'You're not to leave with Gavin.'

'I didn't say I would.'

'And you didn't say you wouldn't. Ammi should be here. You should be here.'

'At Onnachild's bidding. With Onnachild's permission. It's too ... hard ... too much ... I ...' My tears stream down my cheeks, getting into my mouth, smudging across the mantelpiece. My shoulders shake, and my breaths turn to gasps. The only word I can make is his name and I call for him. He's there when I spin around and so I fall into arms already open and waiting for me. My legs buckle as I give in to my sorrow. He holds me up, clasps me close, and the world smells as it should. My arms are full again. I listen to his heart beating as he strokes my back, kisses my head.

'Things will change,' he says.

Things have changed, I want to tell him: Eldini, this praying, fashion, me. He tips my head up with a finger under my chin, and I can't speak. Staring into the brown of his irises with those dots of green, I want to believe him so badly that I nod. He kisses my cheek and my tears leave a shine on his lips.

In the Great Hall, there's no sign of the Raen who let me sleep huddled in his lap once I'd exhausted my sobbing, the Raen whose face had been strained with his inability to take away my sadness but still determined to try. He's sat at the top table with Vill, laughing and joking. His hand is extended across the table and attached to it is Eldini's. Every now and then she tugs gently on it to get his attention, and he smiles affectionately at her as he bends to listen. Is it me or Eldini he's fooling?

'I'm going to starve if this continues,' Beshanie complains. Tonight we've had only one round of trays and there was no meat on it, just summer vegetables.

'You could do with losing some padding,' Nilola says. 'These dresses are not very forgiving.'

Beshanie glares at her and Nilola glares back. Across the table, men are twisting and turning in their seats, seeking out the servants. 'Why don't you tell Niah what happened with Onnachild?' Nilola says.

Beshanie tosses her hair and tuts.

'She's to marry Perkin.'

Beshanie stares straight ahead, still except for a flare of her nostrils.

'I guess that means I get to have Vill then.'

'You will not. I'm hungry,' Beshanie snaps at a servant. 'Get me more bread.'

'There's no more food,' the servant says. 'Princess Eldini's orders. We're observing the saint's day.'

'Which saint?'

The servant shrugs and ambles off, a faint smile on her lips. Beshanie snorts and pushes away her empty plate. Is this one of the changes Raen was referring to and will there be more? None of them will bring me Ammi. Will Gavin? Why is it so much easier to believe him than Raen?

Eldini certainly looks pleased that the castle people are behaving. She must either be ignoring the dour mood and resentful whispers or she hasn't noticed them. It's hard to believe that Onnachild agreed these changes, as Vill suggested yesterday. It's hard to believe Onnachild has the sense to do anything when he's sitting at the table, taunting the candle before him. He keeps lowering his palm and then jerking it away before the flame can burn him. The flame dips when he breathes and coughs at it, only to surge back at him. His skin has a ghostly pallor, exaggerated by the dark furs shaking around him. Is this another one of the changes?

The religious man who presided over the wedding makes his way into the centre space. He's carrying a thick book under his arm.

'Spare me.' Beshanie slouches in her chair. 'Haven't we had to listen to him enough?'

His voice is such a monotonous drone I can't distinguish a single word he reads from the book. I rise despite Nilola hissing at me to stay. Onnachild's too absorbed in his fight with the flame to notice me, and the advisers are arguing with a man in the corner of the room.

Out in the garden, the religious man's words are little more than a wasp's humming. An owl is hooting, competing with him. Amongst the trees are dots of blue and green, giving the impression of a million faces turned towards me. I rub my eyes, swollen and sore from my earlier tears. There's a loud murmur of 'Amen'. There's polite and restrained clapping, followed by strained laughter which sounds like it's coming from the trees rather than the Great Hall. People are filtering out of the room, mumbling and complaining in low voices.

'You had the right idea,' a man with a neck encased in multiple gold chains says to me. 'My arms hurt from all this praying, and if I don't get any more to eat, I might just ...' He stops because Raen has come out. He smiles at Raen, bows, and then shuffles off to continue his moaning with an old man who's cradling his belly. I brace myself for Raen to come over to me but he doesn't. He wanders amongst the men, patting backs, making them laugh and then listening to them so intently lines appear across his forehead. His arms are crossed, and his chin is resting in his hand as he plays at being princely. I shuffle nearer.

'When?' a man asks.

'Why are you in such a hurry?' Raen responds.

'Doesn't the King want that?'

'We must be careful,' Raen says. 'Timing is essential.'

'Are you not bored with waiting?'

'We do what is necessary.'

On he moves to another group of younger men. I can't hear what they're saying but he's animated, mimicking their sense of righteous anger and anticipation. Didn't he tell me he was trying to stop the battle? Was that a lie? He seems as caught up in the excitement as everyone else. His right hand sweeps out across the sky, swoops in like he's gathering up the night, then he chuckles, palm on his chest where my tears had soaked in.

I spot Gavin coming over and force myself to smile at him. Raen is far too changeable for me to trust; at least Gavin is consistent. *Docile, pliable.* My smile turns into a grimace.

'I hope you enjoyed seeing Ammi today.' The hesitation in his voice is touching.

'Thank you,' I say. 'It was kind of you.'

'It was Eldini's idea.' He flushes and stares at his feet. I touch his arm. He lifts up his head but doesn't maintain eye contact, staring over my shoulder and continuing to flush. His eyebrows are vivid white lines across the red of his forehead. 'You look pensive. Did we do the wrong thing?'

I shake my head. 'It's true, I am a little sad, but at the choices I've made, at my mistakes and not anything you've done. They weigh heavily on me.'

Raen's chuckle draws my attention. Our eyes meet; his contain a warning. If he can so easily put aside what passed between us earlier then so can I.

'I'll convince your guardian.' Gavin's persistence and determination are touching, but seeing Ammi today has reminded me why I came to this castle instead of running to Aralltir, and marrying Gavin would be running away, too. Duty, obligation, honour: I understand Raen's words better now. To Aelius, to my gods, to my ancestors and to Ammi I owe these things. I owe them the throne, the land, Adfyrism restored. I've already broken one promise made to Aelius by giving in to lust and mating with Raen. I'm not sure I can bear to break any more.

With a faint smile, I shake my head. 'I can't leave here.'

'We don't have to, not if you'd rather stay. Raen and Eldini will let us stay.'

But I am not her and so I can't marry someone I don't love, hoping and trusting that it will come. And I am not Raen ready to sell myself. 'Don't waste your time on me. I—'

'Gavin,' Raen shouts out, fake joviality in his voice. He waves for Gavin to join him. Gavin glances at me, then Raen, the conflict obvious on his face.

I squeeze his arm. 'Go to him.'

'I suppose I do need to keep him on our side.' Gavin risks pecking my cheek, the touch so light I barely feel it.

Looking out at the grounds, I notice the faces have gone from the trees, chased off by the castle noise, and the branches have stopped dancing. Even the owl is silent; perhaps it was too early for him. Gavin and Raen talk loudly over each other, their voices blending together. Other men slap each other on the back, the arm. They are free of worries, free of fear, and I hate them for it. I step out further away from the crowd, from the noise, to where the grass is spongy under my feet.

The moon's distorted reflection ripples across the surface of the river as the water journeys out of the castle. It makes it look so easy to escape. I trail my fingers in the freezing water, attempting to catch the moon despite it being a pointless task.

'Were you hoping I'd come?' Raen asks. 'Or are you waiting for Gavin?'

I shrug. Over my shoulder, I watch him lean against the tree. A low branch almost hides his face, and he holds onto another one that's the same colour as his irises. His breath blends with the lulling rush of the river. He's like the moon's reflection, ever changing and yet remaining itself.

'You confuse me.' My voice sounds wistful as if I'm longing for a time when he didn't and that causes me to frown because I'm not sure I've ever known who he is.

'Confuse you?' He sounds different out here, slipping into his village accent. Is he doing it on purpose?

'That Raen back there.' I twist around, jab my thumb towards the castle which is nothing more than a slight shadow in the distance. 'Talking war, adoring her ... and then ... Earlier? And now, here. Who are you?'

'Same as I've always been.'

I get to my feet. I step nearer to him, to breathe him in and perhaps find the truth beneath this castle facade. He remains still, steady and strong against the tree trunk, as I hold his face between my hands. I force it towards the moonlight so I can see every faint line, every dot of stubble, and I search for truth in each dip and rise. The branches cast enticing shadows over him as the wind blows through the tree. He belongs here in nature. Life, growth, abundance are him. He's alive with it, a part of it. His scent contains hints of it. This is him, not that man controlled and castle-made who laughs with people who hated him less than a year ago. Other men must cover themselves in jewels to show power and beauty; he doesn't need such adornments. Why can't he remain this man?

'You don't understand about us,' he says.

'I don't want to understand you and her.'

'Us.' He holds my hands away from his face. 'Me and you. Not me and—'

'Then show me.'

He hoists me up, and I gasp as my feet leave the ground, legs wrapping instinctively around his waist. His hands catch my buttocks, keeping me up and our eyes level. His are almost black under the canopy of the tree. He doesn't let me stare at them for long, closing his eyelids as his lips crush mine. My thighs tighten around him, even as we smack into the tree and the bark scratches my shins. I clutch chunks of his hair to trap him against me. His fingers fumble under my loose skirts. Skin on skin has me arching close to feel him, to rush to the place where he can hide nothing from me. My head tilts to coax kisses for my speeding pulse. My gaze fixes on the white moon above. The poets were right: it is so similar to Eldini with its pale roundness. How easy it would be to give in to this moment, to close my eyes and forget everything as I did last night. I'm moaning no, despite my body longing to join with his, the intensity burning to punish me for the word.

'No.' I'm louder this time. 'No. Not this.' I push against his chest until he slides me down his body and onto the ground with such slow control I sigh. The sound seems to confuse him. We stand there, hands clasped, fingers stroking knuckles as our breath settles into a steady rhythm. The river keeps rushing away, its sound filling the night. The tree's shadow sways, hiding his lips, enhancing his eyes, and each time it moves, it gives him a chance to conceal his truth, to change his expression: unease, sadness, confusion are there, are hinted at. I'm not sure which is real.

'Is this all we have?' I ask.

'What more do you want, Niah?'

'I don't know. I want ... Is this what we are? Dishonest? Liars?'

'No.'

'No? Then ...'

'What do you want me to say?'

'What you really think. The truth.'

'This is all I can offer. You know that.'

I tear my hands from his, sit under the tree and slump against its trunk. The sky is a moving patch of navy and grey, the clouds drifting in front of the moon. How things keep changing. Slowly, but changing, nevertheless. I pick up a leaf, stroke the veins. 'I want to trust you, but I can't.'

'Have I done anything to prove you can't?'

'How can I trust a man whose own wife shouldn't trust him?' I peer up at him, wanting to see something like shame, a twitch at my accusation, anything, but he remains still. His chin is jutting out, and the tree is making shadowy patches under his cheekbones.

'What about Ammi?' he asks. 'Us? My mother? The Aegnian book?' His voice is terse and I'm not sure what emotion he's trying to hide. I wish he'd just show me. 'All the secrets I've kept for you, all the times I've stood up to Onnachild for you? Do they tell you nothing?'

'Perhaps they're tricks.'

'Tricks?' His voice rises.

'I don't know you,' I shout, throwing the leaf at the river.

He sits opposite me, fingers tapping my knees until my gaze meets his. 'You know me better than anyone else does, and I know you better than anyone else does. Better than Aelius did. Better than Gavin ever will.'

I lean forwards, touch his scar and for once he doesn't flinch away, though he does take in a quick breath and holds onto it. 'Tell me how you got this.'

He closes his eyes and lets out the breath in a long, juddering sigh. 'Don't you know enough?'

I run my finger over the indentation, over the faint ridge, up to the delicate skin under his eye but he doesn't open it. I brush his eyelashes, remembering them clumped from his tears. Was witnessing them enough? 'I want to be a good person,' I whisper on his cheek.

'So do I.' He's as quiet as the river running away. 'Can't you trust that?'

I want to. This calm man before me, trying so hard to permit my touch as it traces once again over his scar, makes me want to, makes me think I can. But I know how rapidly he'll be gone, replaced by the castle version who is too aware of his power, his position, and is able to perfectly play all the parts demanded of him. 'I want you to be the real you.'

His cheeks twitch. His hold on my knee tightens. 'I am when I'm with you.'

'Then will you tell me how? One day?' I watch the strain come over his face, feel the tension of his jaw against my palm. His eyelashes flutter. He clamps them shut, and his nose rumples. Deep lines are made darker by the tree's shadow. His breath is shallow and ragged but I don't move my finger from his scar. I don't speak, waiting, hoping.

'One day,' he eventually says. 'Maybe.'

Chapter Fifty-Six

'RAEN! NIAH!' Vill's yelling destroys the calmness surrounding us.

Raen pushes my fingers away from his scar and darts up. 'Here,' he shouts back as he helps me to my feet. He keeps hold of my hand, pressing it against his thigh, as we watch Vill sprint towards us, neither of us wanting to move from the safety of the tree's shadow. When he reaches us, his face is sweaty and purple-tinted from the exertion.

'What is it?' Raen asks.

'How did you find us?' I ask.

'It's Onnachild.' Vill pants, bending over and holding his sides. 'He took a turn for the worse. A fall.'

Raen drops my hand.

'Eldini's calling for you.'

Raen nods and then starts running towards the castle. I chase after him, Vill following. The newer, blacker, parts of the castle spike up into the sky, looming as we get nearer, and the windows are lit up bright orange, warning us to stay away but we don't. Raen races to the kitchen door and rests there to catch his breath and wait for us. Perhaps he's noticed the warning, too, and it's made him pause because his eyes are pleading with me. I kiss his cheek and, briefly, he covers the spot before he pushes open the door and creeps inside the castle.

It's quiet. Oddly quiet. There are no servants. Trays have been abandoned, squashed on top of each other in a pile of strange angles. A pot of water is boiling furiously, adding a dense steam to the room which makes it harder to breathe. Raen removes it and places it on the table, knocking off a knife and a bowl which breaks open and spills a thick liquid over the floor. I slip in it as we make our way out into the hallway.

The torches sconced along the walls are blazing, blinding with their ferocity. A gust of wind rushes past, cooling me and thrusting against the flames which push back with noisy bursts of yellow and orange. Rugs waft up and down, riding the gust. Whispers have the presence of rolling fog. A childish giggle has me spinning around. There's no one there. My scar stings, so sharp and deep I wince. Raen stares over his shoulder at me, looking confused. Can he sense them too? I lift my shaking finger to my forehead, expecting to find blood. It comes away with nothing but cold sweat. Raen's name is called, and he's off running towards that voice.

'Seems your covenant might have worked,' Vill says.

My stomach cramps with something like fear, like guilt, like dread. There isn't time to figure it out because Raen has vanished and I can't let him meet this alone. Off I run. The sound of my feet is echoed by heavier steps, a swish, that doesn't come from Vill. There isn't time to worry about that, either. A shadow, thick and black, oozes through a wall. I squeal when it almost touches me. Back it retracts, with a snapping sound that has me flinching. Its stench remains: rotting teeth and stomach bile.

Vill's quick yank keeps me from careening into Raen when he stops outside the Great Hall. There's a mass of castle people gathered in the hallway.

'Where you been?' Eldini shouts at Raen. I've never seen her angry or heard her raise her voice before and judging by Raen's stunned expression neither has he.

'What is it?' His voice is flat.

Eldini shakes her head so fast she seems to be trying to rid herself of the anger but there remains a puce undertone to her skin and a kneading motion of her hands in her sleeves. 'The King ...' She looks up at Raen. The concern on her face makes him shift his weight from one foot to another. 'Someone ... I cannot.' She searches the crowd.

The castle people huddle closer together, skulk against the walls, to avoid answering Eldini's plea. The advisers try to usher them into the Great Hall and away from this scene. Vill's forehead is wrinkled with worry and his lips are down-turned but his eyes expose him, sparkling like the rings on his fingers. Mantona sidles up to me. Her touch is a weightier presence on me than Vill's cold one. 'He got up to dance, only he didn't dance.' She clutches the amethyst at her throat. 'He hasn't danced in years.'

'Dead?' I whisper.

She shakes her head.

He will be soon. I can feel it, death coming. It's a chill whisper on the nape of my neck. Onnachild will see his first queen again, answer her accusations. She's been waiting long enough.

Aesc steps forwards, for once without his scroll or quill. He clears his throat and everyone turns to him. 'The King took a turn.'

Raen nods. His face is blank. A few women start sobbing. Their noise has his jaw twitching.

'The King will be fine ... back ... back ...' Ascelin is shouting, pushing the castle people towards the Great Hall with such panic they easily slip from him. A man stumbles into me. Raen just stands there, staring at the ceiling like he's never noticed the arches before. Why doesn't someone offer him comfort? Why doesn't someone break through that tense hold he has over himself? I move forwards to do so but Mantona and Vill tighten their grips on me.

'Don't,' Vill whispers in my ear.

There's a smudge on Raen's tunic from the tree's dusty bark, I want to brush it off. I want to massage the tension from his shoulders. It'll be fine, I'll tell him. We'll both be free. I realise Beshanie's staring at me. Her arms are crossed as she stands with her feet planted in the entrance to the Great Hall. She looks at my skirt. I follow her gaze and spot stains from Raen's hand on my waist.

'We have phis ... fys ...' Eldini stammers, looking to Aesc for help.

'Physician.'

'Yes, and priest,' Eldini says.

Raen nods, still focusing on the ceiling. 'Has he called for me?'

'No, not ... yet.'

Raen nods. Finally, Eldini reaches out to put an arm around him but he shies from it. 'Well, when he does,' Raen says, 'you can come and get me.' Then he stomps off down the hallway.

There's a shocked silence. Ascelin stops pushing people. Aesc rubs at the ink on his fingers. Should I go after Raen? Vill's tightening grip hurts. Eldini's maids gather around her, shield her from the people staring, and, as one group, they glide down the hallway, whispering. The crowd disperses, some into the Great Hall and others into gossiping huddles.

Crying women dab their eyes as they're led away by husbands or fathers. Servants appear from nowhere, their faces dispassionate as they rush to carry out orders. The advisers slink into the Great Hall.

'What do we think of that then?' Vill asks once we're alone.

'I can't.' I stare off down the hallway where Raen vanished. 'Not now.'

'Leave him,' Vill says. 'We don't need him anymore.'

Numb, I trudge to my rooms, hoping Nessia's awake. I don't know why I obey Vill, perhaps it's shock, perhaps it's the dread of what happens after Onnachild dies: Raen and I competing for the throne. Thankfully Nessia is sat by the fire. She's wrapped in furs despite the sweltering heat of the room. The scent of rot is so overpowering I can almost taste it at the back of my throat.

'So Onnachild's dying,' she says, calmly, as she stares into the flames. 'I dreamt the First Queen was here, looking at me as I slept. She was this close.' Nessia puts her palm to her nose. 'Her breath smelt so bad, meaty. She didn't stay because it wasn't me she wanted.' Nessia shivers.

It must be the First Queen's smell lingering in this room, making my stomach roll. I rush to the window, only just managing to open it in time before I'm throwing up. The cold air dries my sweaty forehead and hurts my streaming eyes as I'm sick again. It splatters red and black over the pale wall outside. It looks so similar to blood that my knees buckle.

Nessia's arm goes around me, and she ushers me to a chair she's brought over. I sink into it, glad for its steadiness beneath me, and keep my head tipped up towards the breeze coming in through the open window. Nessia brushes my hair off my face.

'You need to eat, settle your belly.' She touches the back of her hand to my forehead. 'I've some food left.' She vanishes. When she reappears, she passes me a lump of bread. The crust is the same honey colour as Raen's skin. I hold it between my fingers but I can't eat it. I can't even sit still anymore so I stand, pace over to the panelled wall. First, my palm touches it, then my cheek. A broken section of the feather-and-flame pattern digs in. At least the pain stops me feeling nauseous. Here I can smell the wood, the incense, the herbs from years ago, and it steadies my stomach. My name is whispered, so, so quiet it must be the walls calling to me. I press my ear closer to hear the memories they've kept hold of.

'Raen here?' It's Eldini and slowly I turn towards her. Her eyes are red-rimmed and her fingers are fluttering near her lips as if she's struggling not to bite her nails.

'No,' Nessia says.

'I not find him.' She peeks out my door when we hear a footstep. 'We went every room and ...' She shakes her head. 'You know where he is? I am worried.'

'Maybe he needs to be alone,' I mumble.

'He shouldn't be alone,' Nessia says.

The First Queen's scent is here, not meaty as Nessia said but like rotten eggs. I gag again. Eldini doesn't seem to notice. A shadow crawls past her, so close it disturbs a lock of her loose hair. The odour leaves with the shadow.

'I know they not see eye to eye.' Eldini plays with that lock of hair. 'Father and son too the same.' She forces a little smile. 'There is love there. Raen needs to make peace. Before no time left. How Raen be ... if ...'

'Raen will cope.' But I'm not so sure. How can a son mourn the death of their father when their father is such a man as Onnachild?

'A child always thinks their parents will live forever,' Nessia says.

'Not Raen.' Like me, he'll have thought about this day for years, picturing the moment when Onnachild has to face retribution for what he's done. It'll have sustained Raen through his years of exile and bereavement. Yet, Onnachild is still his father. With Eldini standing before me, chewing the end of her hair, I can't help wondering whether marrying her was more about earning his father's approval than the throne.

'There is not long,' Eldini says. 'Niah, please? You go. You know him. You know where.'

'Do I?' As I say it I realise I do, because he's gone where I would go. When I nod, Eldini forces a smile. 'Get me a horse.'

She nods and darts off with the speed of a field mouse.

Nessia scrubs my face clean with a wet cloth, replacing the smell of vomit with primrose, and then she opens my fist and brushes out the breadcrumbs. They fall like ash to the stone floor. My stomach rumbles, and I think I might be sick again. 'Eat first,' she says. 'You're going to need your strength for what's coming.'

'I'll find Raen. And then ... then I'll worry ... about everything.'

'It'll be all right.'

'Will it?'

She doesn't answer. Instead, she drapes my cloak around my shoulders and ties it under my chin. The brush of her fingers on my windpipe makes me flinch. What help can I be to Raen when I only understand how to hate Onnachild?

I head to the First Queen's resting place, though she's not resting tonight. Raen's bent back is an imperfect curve and even from this distance, I can see he's shaking. The sun is sitting on the horizon but the moon is refusing to leave and so the light has such a strange quality it seems otherworldly. He doesn't move as I approach, despite my steps breaking brittle twigs.

'What are you doing here?' He stares at a pile of wood before him.

'You shouldn't be alone.'

He huffs and I don't know whether it is an invitation or not. In his left hand is a charred stick and his lap is dotted with dried herbs. I settle next to him, almost sitting on a flint he must have dropped in frustration because it still contains a hint of his warmth.

'Make her come,' he says.

I tuck his hair behind his ears, caressing his cheeks as I do so. They are freezing so I undo my cloak, bracing myself against the chill air, and wrap it around his shoulders. He doesn't move. He doesn't stop scowling at the pile of wood, not even when I get a fire started. His eyes must hurt from the light and heat. I'm not sure he's blinked. His fingers are clasped so tightly around the stick I have to prise them off one by one. I place a kiss into his palm, and the dark soot there gets onto my lips. He's still as I gather the herbs from his lap, and he doesn't appear to notice me trickling them onto his palm.

'What have you got there?' I ask.

He doesn't answer, so I bend to smell the herbs: lemon balm, yew berries, rosemary and wormwood. 'Where did you get them?'

Again he doesn't answer. The wind threatens to blow them away so I close his fist, kiss each knuckle, and then guide it towards the fire. Now he does respond, a shuddering sigh escaping through his clenched mouth; perhaps it's the fire's warmth bringing him back.

His hand opens, and he tosses the herbs into the flames. The fragrant smoke billows around us. I mumble words to call his mother into it. His brow lowers. His lips pout. He leans forwards, and his hair flops over his face again. A puff of smoke draws my attention from him.

'Who's that?' he says. 'I don't recognise that woman.'

'My grandmother.'

The deep laughter lines either side of her mouth are lined with the sky. Her hair is the colour of the dust surrounding us. She smiles down at him like he's a child. I put my arm around his waist, and he gives me his weight. 'Please, we need the First Queen,' I say, forcing aside the many questions I have for my grandmother.

'Where's my mother?' Raen demands.

469

'But, my boy, you know where she is.'

'Where?' he shouts.

'The castle of course. She's been let out. But you knew that already, didn't you?'

Then she's gone. We're left with an amber sky and Raen's tears. He doesn't seem to realise he's crying, not until they slide onto my shoulder, and then he scrubs his eyes with his fist. 'Not for that man.' He stares at the dampness on his hand with disgust. It doesn't stop more from coming, coming quicker than he can dash them away. Soot has smeared across his cheek like battle paint.

'Raen?' I say his name as gently, as softly as I can.

He doesn't look at me, but his shoulders twitch. He stares at the colourful horizon as the tears keep falling over his scar. His chin juts as he struggles to stop the wobble there. My touch on his cheek makes him jolt, and then he pivots towards me, diving for my lap as his sobs finally wrench free. He gives in. The sun rises. The moon vanishes. And he sobs until his shoulders stop shaking and his hands stop pummelling my hips.

Chapter Fifty-Seven

RAEN UNFURLS HIMSELF and sits up. I offer him a corner of the cloak to wipe his nose. The mess of his dark hair gives him the air of someone who has been lost amongst privet hedges. I try to brush out the knots, my fingers getting caught. He winces at the first pull and at the fourth he stops me.

'What do we do now?' I ask.

'I don't know.'

His gaze sweeps from my eyes to my lips, back to my eyes and it makes my breath stop. He cups my jaw and caresses my skin like he's never experienced the sight or feel before. He kisses me, closed-mouthed, lingering, and then again. When I go to touch him, he shakes his head. If he needs me to submit and take nothing then I will. Perhaps this is the only comfort I can give him: life to chase away death. A gift he has already given me. I pull off my dress. It's difficult to remain still and let him take his time, let him find whatever he needs to, but I try my best as his fingers trace over the goosebumps on my arms and then my legs. He leaves a trail of heat, which has me trembling more than the chill air.

'I don't think I can stop touching you,' he says, forlornly.

'You don't have to.'

He smiles, but it doesn't replace the sadness in his eyes. I will my kisses to make it better, him better. We both know what the future holds but here, hopefully, we can stave it off, even if pleasure only works momentarily. I'm tender with him, carefully removing his clothes as he watches me. Brief moments might be all we'll have once Onnachild has died. I lie down, bringing Raen with me.

When we come together, he makes no sound. He's light above me, holding off his weight as if I'm breakable. His eyes are open, fixed on mine, searching. If he'd tell me what he's searching for I'd gladly give it to him. His tear-soaked lashes are an enticing frame, drawing me in deeper and deeper as he starts a steady and sleepy rhythm that has me fighting the urge to push for a faster pace, one that matches the frantic pulse of my desire. He pauses to kiss me, to brush my hair from my face. I dig my fingernails into the dust to stop them from sinking into his hips and taking charge. He smiles as though he's enjoying my frustration and the green in his irises seems to brighten. Ever so slowly, suggesting he's savouring the touch, his torso brushes over mine, and ever so slowly he moves within me, again. Again. I bite back his name until I can't fight the urge anymore, can't stay with this gentle rocking. My hips rise. My thighs tighten, squeeze his waist, and I let myself go, juddering and moaning into

471

his open mouth. He follows.

His body relaxes, but he doesn't fall onto me; instead, he scoops me up and we sit together as he keeps me pressed to his beating heart. We're encased in each other, arms and legs around torsos, heads on shoulders, scents merging. 'I don't want to go back.' I place the words into the dip of his collarbone.

'Neither do I. But we have to.'

'I'm scared.'

'You? You aren't scared of anything.'

If only that were true, but there's so much to be scared of. All my life I've waited for Onnachild to die, prayed to the gods it would be soon, and now that he is dying, I want him to live so what must follow is delayed. My tongue darts out, licks up Raen's sweat to bind us closer. It tastes of tears.

'What are you scared of?' Raen asks.

I shake my head because I can't say the words, words he said so many seasons ago. How can I tell him I'm scared we're going to become enemies as we fight for the throne when we're wrapped in each other like this? Raen jolts me when I don't answer. I lean back, safe in his hold, to stare into his face. What I see there shows me I don't need to tell him because he has the same worries. He, too, is pained by the pressure of what we must be, of what we have been. Within the green dots in his irises are traces of our ancestors and here, in this barren place where their ashes have become one with the dust, we're the same. We're made from the same place, the same myths and history. He needs me and I need him.

'We'll do the best we can.' He caresses my cheek.

I nod, but I can't help dreading this will not be good enough. He pats my bottom and so I climb off him. He's slow as he dresses, dazed from mating and lack of sleep. I put my dress on.

'You should go to Eldini.' I kick mud into the fire.

472

'Not yet.'

'She's concerned.'

'I can't care about that ... her.' He shakes out the cloak, settles it around my shoulders and ties it for me. 'We're going to my mother's room.' He strokes the material, smiles at it, and I wonder if he recognises it's his.

Holding hands, we head towards my horse, and he helps me to mount it, before settling behind me. I rest against him, and his chin drops onto my head. His hair skims my cheeks and neck as I nestle into his scent and warmth.

'I wasn't ready before,' he says.

'You are now?'

'No.' At least there's a hint of amusement in his voice and that reassures me.

In my rooms, Raen slumps into a chair. His arms hang on either side of it and his legs are stretched out. The plate of food on his lap is ignored. I send Nessia out for hot water and the tub. His eyes are narrowed, brow lowered as he concentrates on his thoughts. I don't intrude on them but I do point at his plate. When he continues to ignore it, I press a chicken leg into his palm. He smiles at me, so sweet, so adorable I can't resist kissing his cheek. His eyelids flutter, and his hands rise to keep me there. Grease is smeared onto my cheek and he licks it off. The taste seems to remind him how to eat.

As he chews he offers the plate to me. I nod. He makes room for me on the chair's arm, and I sit there beside him, my feet warming underneath him as we share food and watch servants prepare a bath for him. Melody's helping, too. She tries to keep her head ducked but a brief peek up reveals she's been crying. I don't want to ask her about Onnachild, whether he's worse or better. It might be selfish of me to keep Raen here, prolong this intimacy between us, but I'm aware it'll soon be pushed aside for plotting. Forget him, Vill had said. But I know I can't and so for however long this lasts, I'll enjoy the care he shows me when he places bite-sized pieces of cheese into my hand.

As soon as the tub is full and steaming the room with the perfume of roses, we're left alone.

'Come.' I slip off the arm of the chair. 'You'll feel better after a bath.'

'I'm still eating.'

'You can eat in the bath.'

He nods and rises, putting the plate on the floor. Awkward, he stands there holding onto the end of his tunic. 'I've seen it before,' I tease as I tug at his breeches, 'so stop with the false modesty.' I whip them down. He covers himself with his hands to protect his modesty. 'You're beautiful and you know it.'

'Am I?' He smirks. 'As beautiful as Ael—'

'Get in the tub.'

He chuckles as he takes off his tunic, exposing his muscular torso, shyness completely gone, and I realise he was only playing before. I turn away to get the plate and hide my flush as lust starts its tantalising journey through me again. He splashes into the tub, sloshes about.

When I offer him the plate, he refuses it and so I shove a piece of bread into his mouth to stop myself from kissing him and getting distracted. I lather up his back, running my hands over the rises and dips of his ribcage, his shoulder blades, his muscles. The white soap enhances the colour of his skin, and new things reveal themselves to me as I rinse it off. There's a cluster of faint moles under his left shoulder blade, a circular pink scar in the centre of his back, a red crescent from my fingernails. My hands move with his breath as it swells out his chest. He slides down into the tub, legs and feet poking out, the hair there flat and dark against his thighs and calves. On his right knee is a bruise, yellow and brown. He's so large, crammed into that tub, and so trusting with his eyes shut. My sleeves uncurl into the tub and float to his chest, disturbing the pattern of hair there. The touch makes him chuckle and the water laps over and around him.

He sits up, hair darkened to black and straightened by the water. It reaches past his shoulders, almost covering one pink nipple. Yes, he is beautiful, and I stifle the urge to tell him again, tell him more things, everything. Instead of speaking, I'll show him and so I gather up his locks, rub the soap into it and then massage his scalp, finding bumps I've never felt before. He sighs. 'Why are you being so nice to me?' he asks.

'I don't know.'

He opens an eye. There's such a cheeky, tired expression on his face it makes me want him and not just for mating, not just for a night, but like this for always. I'm unable to look away from his strong body which has shown no one else but me how vulnerable it and he can be. He's never felt more mine.

'Why do you look so worried?' he asks.

'You'll be getting cold.' I push at his shoulder to make him sink into the tub.

He does, shaking out his hair so it spreads and dances in the water as if he's a water spirit come to tempt me to my death. I'd go, willingly.

'Sit up,' I say.

He obeys. When I gesture for his arm, he gives me the full weight of it. I rest it on my shoulder so I can lather all the way up into his armpit. My fingers bury themselves in the hair there, wanting to stay trapped, but the tickle has him chuckling and squirming. As I wash his chest, I feel his heartbeat mimicking the speed of mine. He stops my hand and takes the soap from me as if he's not ready to share what's in there. Perhaps he's wise to not do so.

I slink away to the fire and settle on the floor before it, searching within for an answer to a question I haven't fully formed yet, but it has something to do with him, with me, with this fluttering in my stomach that I can't name. I hear him get out of the tub, and the temptation to stare once again at his naked magnificence is too great so I look over my shoulder. A strange contentment comes over me at seeing his skin shining from the care I have given it.

'Let's go to bed,' he says, wrapping himself in a linen. It clings to his form. 'I'm exhausted.'

I nod and rise. I follow him into my bedchamber. We climb into bed together, him naked and me still dressed. 'Whatever happens—'

'Don't.' His finger tilts up my chin so I must look at his tired face. He kisses me to stop me speaking. He's right to do so. Above him is Aelius's portrait, so I close my eyes against both men and settle down into sleep.

Chapter Fifty-Eight

IT'S BEEN FIVE DAYS since Onnachild collapsed, and in that time we've not been called to the Great Hall. When I've walked the hallways, looking for people, I've encountered only servants hurrying with trays from room to room. We've received no news on Onnachild. What I find in the hallways, pungent odours and bronze shadows containing a coldness that chills my bones, tells me everything I need to know. Summer seems to have already ended and we've skipped autumn.

It's been four days since I last saw Raen. My worries and unanswered questions keep me awake at night while his scent fades from my pillow. I wonder whether he's with Eldini, whether he's distancing himself from me in preparation for what is to come. Is it kindness or cruelty he's showing me by staying away? My dreams are brief, visited by the First Queen, and I wake startled and with a pounding heart. She's come for Onnachild. He's going to die, and then what?

Then what? The question follows me as I pace my rooms, throwing an apple from hand to hand. I stare out my window at the deserted grounds. Will this be mine or Raen's? How long will I have to wait until I'm with Ammi?

'Where is everyone? It's too eerie.' A low-level mist has settled, giving everything a strange and sombre light.

'Praying,' Melody says. 'I should ... All night Lark had us praying and today I'm meant to be, too. Why can't she let me sleep?' She blows her nose, still stuffy from her earlier tears. 'I'm not even a real Maiden.'

'Much good that will do him,' Nessia says. 'He has a lot of suffering ahead of him.' She takes a bite of her apple and the crunch goes right through me.

'Nessia, how can you say that?' Melody gasps.

'She's in shock,' I say, trying to end the conversation.

'I am not. It's the truth.'

'He was a good king,' Melody says.

'In his own mind.'

'Leave it,' I say, worried that Melody will start crying again. I can't take more tears. Even the mist outside seems full of them. 'He's an old man, and he's dying.'

'They're the worst because they have more to regret,' Nessia says. 'You can't tell me you feel sorry for him?'

'Sorry? No, not sorry.' If it weren't for Raen I'd be glad and agreeing with Nessia. I dig a nail into the apple's skin and breathe in its crisp scent which fleetingly covers the persisting stench of the First Queen. 'Pity, maybe? Maybe I pity a man who's going to suffer as much as he will.'

'It's no more than he deserves.'

Mantona's words about the covenant return: *debts will be paid soon.* Is Onnachild's illness the gods' doing? My doing? Frowning, I move away from the window and sink into a chair by the tray containing the pile of fruit. The peaches look appealing, and my stomach rumbles. I drop my apple onto the tray. A slow death is what Onnachild deserves, one long enough for him to feel pain for each hanging he ordered. The First Queen will want him to suffer. A quick death might be easier for Raen to bear, perhaps.

'He'll try and wheedle his way out of it.' Nessia lobs her apple core into the fire. 'You mark my words.'

'I don't see how he can.'

'You shouldn't talk like that,' Melody says. 'He's a king and his passing deserves respect.'

'Do you forget what he's done to you?' Nessia picks up two peaches. 'Without him, you'd be in your own lands, with your own name, your own parents.' She passes me a peach. The skin reminds me of the smoothness of Raen's inner thigh.

'I don't even remember them,' Melody says. 'And I might be better off here. I like it here, and he was a great king.'

'He was not a great king,' Nessia snaps.

'Shush.' Their raised voices are making my head pound and with it is a wave of nausea.

'He might not die.' Melody's voice sounds small and distant.

'Hmm.' Nessia stokes the fire, her chin shining with juice. I toss my peach onto the tray, knocking the other fruit and causing a plum to roll off. My stomach growls, but it's easy to ignore when my thoughts are so confusing, so disjointed. What happens next? The throne needs to be sat in. Me or Raen? Raen and I? Raen and Eldini? Ammi? I stare into the flames and rub my temples. I'm not ready for change. What should be excitement is more like boiling mud in my guts. When I close my eyes to try to think, I picture Raen in the tub and the cluster of moles under his shoulder.

'Sorry,' Vill says.

I open my eyes to him knocking on the door even though he's already opened it and entered the room. 'Where have you been?' I moan. 'We need to decide what to do.'

Vill's well rested and pristine in a new tunic with emerald stitching that matches the jewels in his rings. The one with the two birds is missing from his fingers. He looks around the room, avoiding my glare. 'Raen not here?'

'He hasn't been here for several days,' Nessia says.

'Interesting.' He pushes the door shut. 'He's not been with Eldini and he's not with Onnachild. I was sure he'd be here. It's better he isn't. We shouldn't complicate matters further.'

'Complicate?' I splutter the word.

'Surely, you understand you're competing for the same thing? The throne? Anyway, we don't need to talk about him anymore. Let Raen worry about Raen. It's every man, or woman,' he nods at me, 'for themselves now. As for where I've been, well, I've been with Onnachild and, surprisingly, he has asked to see you.'

'Me? Why does he want to see me?' My stomach lurches. I pick up a peach again, hope eating might calm my stomach.

'Does it matter why? Can you not see what a good change of fortune this is?'

'How is he?' Melody asks. 'Is he ...'

'Dying? Yes,' Vill says.

She starts crying.

'Must you be so blunt?' I jump up to get away from the tears. The peach tumbles from my hand and around my feet. I almost squash it.

'Now is not the time for the ambiguity of fancy words.'

I turn to hide my retch from Vill, cover my mouth, and pray for my nausea to pass. My heart feels like it's dropped to my stomach, pulsing too

479

hard and too fast. Vill's tapping his foot, impatient. Nessia's shushing Melody. The sounds make my head throb. I concentrate on my breathing, shut my eyes. Steady, steady, in and out until the nausea has passed.

'It does matter,' I say, once I have control of myself again. 'Why does he want to see me? Answer me that, Vill.'

He stops tapping his foot. 'Because you're a good subject? Because you're the mother of his grandchild? To beg your forgiveness? How could I possibly know? What does it matter? It's immaterial. This is what we know.' Vill pauses until he has our attention. 'One,' he holds up his index finger, 'he has not officially acknowledged Raen as his son. Two,' up pops his middle finger, 'he is dying.'

Melody hides her mouth behind her hands. *Please no more tears*, I silently beg the gods. Of course, they don't answer, they have more pressing business: a king to torment. Vill frowns at her. Nessia brings her into a hug and rocks her.

'And ...' he continues, 'Onnachild realises he's dying and is terrified about the afterlife. But most importantly ...' He creeps closer. 'He has not named his successor. Think of that. And know this, he has not called for Raen. It's you he has asked for. You.' He pokes my arm. 'Niah. The last of the Aegni women. Beautiful Niah who has done everything he asked of her. The mother who was kind enough to ease his grief by gifting him his son's daughter. Niah who is more beautiful than any of the castle women here.'

'You can't think ...' Nessia grimaces.

'Of course not.' Vill laughs. 'Though if he asks.' He shrugs.

'Don't be so foul,' I snap back.

'I'm teasing. Come on, will someone be happy? Anyone.'

'A man is dying,' I whisper.

'And whose fault is that? You called the gods. You can't act coy now.'

My thoughts drift to days after the covenant, to that strange village girl mimicking the dancers. I picture the jerk of her elbows and knees, the drool from her gaping mouth, and her breath coming out as smoke and settling on food, on Onnachild's food. The creak of her bones echoes in my ears, and I shudder. I let her out. And I let out the First Queen when I made that covenant. 'I didn't think—'

'How you deceive yourself, Niah. How else did you think the gods would stop the battle? Remember, Onnachild's not just a man. He's the foreign invader who massacred our people, outlawed our gods, stole our land. The gods haven't forgotten, the dead haven't forgiven, and I don't believe you have, either. He's kept you from your daughter.' Vill presses his face close to mine, that white face too perfect to be real. 'That's better. Get that anger back into your eyes.'

It's not anger, though. I'm not sure what I feel beyond this churning in my stomach, this throbbing head, this tiredness.

'We could get the throne without needing to shed any blood if we play this right,' he says. 'Give him what he wants on the condition he gives you what you want, names you as successor. Dying men are so easy to manipulate.'

It's fear, that's what it is. Fear. But I can't tell Vill I'm fearful of what will be in the room with Onnachild: death, the gods, the First Queen with the froth from hanging oozing out of her mouth. As much as I wanted revenge, dreamt about it as a child, the thought of seeing it enacted in all its gore makes me shake. I should bear witness, as I did that day on the battlefield, so I can record it in my people's book. My fingers run over the scar left by the gods. Neither my heart nor my stomach is strong enough for what I will see. 'Onnachild has Eldini. Let her comfort and tend to him.'

Vill tilts his head and tuts. 'And have her press Raen's case? Are you really that stupid?'

'He's right.' Nessia's voice is quiet and solemn.

Vill's eyes are glinting with expectation as he holds out his hand, the one that had those reasons pointed out on it. Raen not claimed. Raen not called. Raen not named. It's my name in the King's dying mind. Am I not Niah from the Aegni anymore but someone weaker, softer? Did I not surmount that mountain, demand entry to the castle, give up Ammi for this chance? Vill's right: I'd be a fool not to go. I place my hand in his.

Chapter Fifty-Nine

'YOU TOOK YOUR TIME,' Ascelin says, but there's no reprimand in his voice. He seems nervous as he ushers me into Onnachild's bedchamber. The smell hits me like a gust of heat, like a blur of colours: olive-green shit, sweet orange piss, old sweat with a yeasty white film. I cover my nose and mouth, sway as I steady myself against the onslaught. Flies buzz and batter at the closed windows, desperate for escape. Swamped by the vast coverings and ornate headrest of the bed is Onnachild. A small, stinking body. Kingly no more. I step nearer, forcing back a retch.

His eyes are closed, but he's not sleeping easily; his breath is a stuttering groan through slack lips blotched purple. His hair is as thin and brittle as a bad harvest. The pelt of the furs tucked around him has spiked together, and from them comes the acrid stench of bile. A trickle of it has dampened his beard. His cheeks are sunken, skin hanging off as though he's started to melt.

I glance at the advisers, not sure what it is I'm expected to do, but they're staring at the floor. Their faces are ashen and drawn. Aesc cradles his parchment, unwound and trailing by his feet. Vill's by the closed door, surveying everything with his usual bored expression. The flies swarm, flashes of black, as they circle the room, dive towards Onnachild, but not even they can stand the odour and so back to the window they go. Their frustration reverberates around the room. The noise, the heat, and the smell send me staggering to the window to push it open. Still the flies fuss and struggle, unable to feel their way to freedom. One crawls over me as I gasp in the fresh air.

'Why have you opened the window?' Ascelin's voice wobbles.

It's too late, I'm tempted to tell him, the dead have already been let in. Does Onnachild realise this?

'The King needs to be kept warm,' Aesc says.

'The air is diseased. How can you bear it? How can he bear it?' I say.

Onnachild stirs. We turn to him. His arms and legs creak awake. 'She's here?' he asks.

'I have a name and it's Niah.'

'Come here.'

'Do as the King commands.' Ascelin hurries towards me.

I grimace as he drags me closer to that stench. Onnachild notices but isn't ashamed. His stare is steady, challenging me to back away from him, it, as if this odour is his power asserting itself. He sits up, disturbing the furs and the miasma beneath them. 'This is death.' His voice rises but it isn't a question.

'It's the flux,' Aesc says. 'The physician said so ... treatable.'

'Then he is a fool.' Onnachild clutches his chest as he speaks. There's a blue tinge to his knuckles. 'And when he is proved wrong ...' He coughs, splutters, spits out onto his palm whatever was stuck in his throat. Ascelin rushes forwards to clean it but Onnachild batters him away. 'Come closer,' he says to me. 'You are not afraid of your king, are you?'

I lean lower, holding my breath. He snatches my hair. He yanks, and down onto my knees I fall. My breath bursts out. His stench rushes into my mouth. I heave. He smiles, as tight and as spiteful as it was the day he watched his queen die.

'But,' he says, 'I am not your king, am I?'

'I ... I don't know what you mean.'

'Do you take me for a fool?' He winds my hair around his hand, pulling me closer and closer. How does he have such strength? My face is flat against the foul-smelling furs, damp spikes squashed against my cheek. 'That green in your eyes, changes like a fire, like grass. A gem you can never own but must always covet. It's worth making you angry to see them flash like that. They are so like hers, so easy to read.' His free hand rises. His fingers extend. Surely, he can't mean to touch me? He does. I jump, recoil. Strands of my hair rip out. I stifle a yelp—he'll not have that satisfaction from me. I scrabble back, away, bang into the wall. Those strands hang between his fingers, resembling a spider's web. He tries to shake them off but they're stuck to him with phlegm.

'Of course, I know who you are. Your grandmother was a thorn in my foot for many years. Did you really think I would believe your lies?' His lips lift into a sickening smile as his words sink in and I clasp my neck. All this time he's known, playing, toying with me. Why? His laughter rattles. Something stringy drops from his mouth. Was Vill aware of this? I'd check his reaction but I'm too scared to look away from Onnachild, from his protruding eyes with that yellow tint.

'You will read me the rights. You will anoint me back into the old religion.'

'But ...' I shake my head. It's too much. 'You don't even believe. You shed so much blood to assert the new God, forced conversions. You butchered ... to assert that new God. My grandmother ...' I stare at the advisers. They aren't shocked. Vill's nodding at me. Nothing makes sense. If Onnachild's known all this time that I follow Adfyrism then why am I still alive? How am I here in the castle?

'I am king, and I command you.' He thumps the bed, and the sound makes me jump. His face might be hollowing out but it can still show his smug satisfaction at his winning hand. A rush of air flutters my dress and hair. His skin pales. His eyes bulge as he stares to the left of me. And I realise, he hasn't won yet. He's not my king. I straighten my shoulders, lower my hand from my throat, and rise onto my knees.

'She's here again,' he whines. 'Make her leave.'

'I know.' I can feel the First Queen beside me, and I turn towards where she ripples like a shadow cast by a tree. She looks as she must have done on her wedding day: her hair is dark and tinted with mahogany same as Raen's, her eyes are sharp and intelligent, her lips have an arrogant upturn. She doesn't smell of death; she smells of white sage and the sap from yew trees.

The power has shifted. He's dying and I am not. He's scared and I am not. Slowly, I get to my feet. Any pity I had for him has gone. He's not just a dying man, not an ill, old man, dying: he is Onnachild. He's a godless hypocrite. He's a liar, a treaty breaker, a petulant king who believes people must bend to his will simply because it is his. And he's trying to wheedle his way out of his punishment just as Nessia predicted. As he shifts and twists from the vision of his first wife, I purposely position myself so the sunlight hits my irises. Contrary to what he said earlier, the anger in them doesn't please him; it terrifies him. He sucks in a sharp and noisy breath.

'You owe me.' He's frantic. 'You will stop them torturing me. You will. Why do you think I let you live, fed you, gave you my son? I do not care about a bet. I never did.' His face is reddening. His nostrils are flaring. 'I knew about you. I have always known about you. I wanted one of you alive, left in case I had need of you and absolution. Why do you think I let Aelius go to you? You will pay your debt to me.'

'Your battle killed him,' I shout.

The fireplace bursts into life. Light, crackles, flames. Lilacs, greens, reds, blues, yellows the same shade as Onnachild's eyes, pulse, push, surge from the fire's heart. They're here and they won't be kept from their goal any longer. I smile. The advisers are coughing.

'If you ... do not,' Onnachild wheezes. 'I'll see you ... dead.'

I shake my head, and my smile grows. The room is filling with thick smoke and in that smoke are faces he must recognise. 'Stop them. Stop it. I deserve to go peacefully. You owe me. Make them.'

'Please?' Aesc asks.

'I can't.' But as I reach to touch the faces, the smoke clears implying that I could command them. Onnachild settles his horrified eyes on me.

'You can have it, whatever you want.' He's shaking. His mouth is grotesquely misshapen. The edge of his beard is singed. 'Name it. It is yours. The advisers will write it into law. See.' He points at Aesc but doesn't look at him. His gaze is fixed over my shoulder, and I know who is there. Their presence is strengthening me. It's a long line of the dead, maimed in his pointless battles, hanged by his orders, starved by his greed. They whisper in my ear but I can't make out their words over Onnachild's whimpering. 'I repent. I repent. I want to return to the gods.'

'They will not have you.'

'Make them. Make them. You owe me. You owe me your life. I saved you so you could.'

I shake my head, touch my shoulder and a breeze-like breath cools my knuckles.

'The throne,' he cries out. 'That is what you want, is it not? Have it. Have it back. I do not care for it.'

'You do not care for it? You massacred my people for it and now ... now you want to use it to buy your way out of their punishment? The First Queen deserves her revenge and my grandmother ...' I take a deep breath. 'I saw her. I watched her dragged from her home by her feet, clothes torn off her by the villagers, people she'd cared for, saved from death, helped birth their babies, helped birth *them*. And you told them to. You poisoned them against her. She was old. She was weak, and they did

486

your bidding. There was no dignity for her. Why should there be dignity for you?'

'Niah.' It's Vill. He's moved to the fireplace and its flames light up his face. 'Forgive her, Your Highness. She's shocked by your wish to return to the old gods, as we all are.' He holds up his hand to keep me silent. I can't speak anyway, stunned by his words. 'She accepts your offer and will do everything in her power to ease your passing.'

'We will write it. We will,' Aesc says as Onnachild thanks Vill.

Vill bows and offers prayers to Onnachild in the Aegnian language, the one Onnachild tried to wipe out, as he bundles me from the room.

The door banging shut brings me to my senses and I shout out, 'No, No, No.' I push Vill but it doesn't dislodge his sly smile. 'What are you doing?'

'What am I doing? I should ask you what the—'

'Not at the expense of ... not ...' My stomach lurches. My head whirls as if those colours, those tones of Onnachild are in the hallway, seeping from under the door. I double over, heaving to get them out of my body. The floor, I need to be lower, closer to the stones. When I lie on it, it gives up its memories to me: screams of surprise, bones crunching, insides squelching under foot, whispers of gossip and malicious lies, steel scraping. Hot sweat erupts along my body. I can't stop shaking. I vomit.

'What is it?' Vill crouches beside me.

Raen. I want to call for Raen, but I keep his name down. Vill's cool arm goes around me and draws me close. He tries, unsuccessfully, to hide his disgust at the vomit on my dress.

'It's too much,' I whisper. 'He must be punished. The dead must have their revenge.'

'They will, and he will be. Did you misunderstand me? Oh, my poor, poor Niah. No wonder you're so angry. Do you still not trust me?'

'In there you said—'

'Yes, I know what I said and if you trusted me ...' He pats my shoulder. 'I say many, many things to fool that old man, and that's what he is now, nothing more than an old man dying and desperate to hedge his bets. My intention, our intention, is to have him believe you're willing to help. You don't have to do it, just pretend you will, that you are. You're able to do that, aren't you? It's so very easy. Do it and he'll sign over the throne to you. Think on that. Think of how this will all be over in days, maybe less, who can predict how much time he has left, and then you will be Queen Niah.'

The words don't have the same sparkle as they did when I arrived at the castle. They are stones in my belly. Surely even pretending to help will bring Onnachild some peace, take the edge off the sting, when he should have none? The dead, the First Queen, my grandmother deserve better than that. He showed them no compassion, so why should I show him any? My debt is to the Aegni women, to my gods, and not him. They've waited so long for this moment. I can't take it from them. To do so would make me no better than him: traitor, hypocrite, liar. 'I can't.'

'I understand it's been ... a surprise to you. Matters will be clearer once you've rested and you'll thank me then. Let's get you to your rooms or you'll be of no use to anyone. Have you eaten today?'

I let him help me to my feet. I even lean into him as he walks me to my rooms. He keeps whispering in my ear: Ammi, Raen, dresses, jewels, the throne. Everything that can be mine if I pretend to help Onnachild, but nothing comes that easily and Onnachild is not to be trusted. Thinking about it makes me dizzy. I'm just hungry, just tired from everything being so close, and now, now it's almost here ... Why aren't I happy? Hopefully, Vill is right and everything will be clearer once my belly is full.

With food comes Raen, finally. He's clean and neat with his black tunic pressed and his hair brushed so it shines. The facade is ruined by the strain on his face and the dark patches under his eyes. For some reason, seeing me in my nightdress deepens his frown.

'I had to get away from her.' He lingers at my door. 'Crying, praying, and on and on at me to make my peace with him.'

'Come in.' Nessia takes the tray from him and then settles it on my lap.

The food is, thankfully, plain: cheese, bread, and salted pork. Raen closes the door with a light push and sits on the floor beside the fire. It's a calm one, fed with lavender in an attempt to help me relax. Raen seems to be what I needed, though, as at last my shoulders lower and my stomach settles.

'I should be with her.' He picks up a bur of lavender that didn't make it into the fire and scrunches it between his fingers. 'I don't want to be with her.'

'Eldini?'

He grimaces at her name then blows the lavender from his palm into the flames.

'She doesn't know what he's done,' I say.

'No.' He shuffles back so he's sitting against the legs of my chair. I reach down to run my fingers through his hair. 'She's right about one thing, though: he's my father.' He peers up at me, troubled. I slide off my chair, leave the tray there, and settle next to him. Our knees touch. My stomach groans for more food.

'You hate him. He hates you. He killed your mother so he could marry again.'

Raen lets out a big sigh, rests his head back, and knocks the tray. The contact makes him rise, grab it, and bring it onto the floor in front of us. He pulls apart a chunk of bread, adds a piece of cheese, and passes it to me. When I start chewing he speaks again. 'At least you talk plainly. My mother's coming for him, isn't she?'

I nod. He isn't watching for my response; he's drawn instead to the stone floor and the uneven shape of it. His intense concentration and the careful way his fingers follow the indentations remind me of a child learning his letters.

Raen's voice is so quiet I have to lean closer and ask him to repeat himself. 'How is he?' His hand caresses my cheek before handing me more food. 'I know you saw him.'

'Bad.' The bread seems to stick in my throat when I swallow.

He nods and his index finger follows the edge of a scorch mark across the stones. 'What did he want from you?' He stares at me, brow lowered and eyes narrowed. Braced for a lie?

'Comfort. A way to the old gods. Forgiveness.' I keep the rest secret because he looks too tired, already too burdened to be told what Onnachild was bargaining with.

He pushes up and back to sit in the chair. His arms rest on it as if it's the throne, and he scowls at the fire, lips tight and pursed. 'Forgiveness. It's a bit late for that, isn't it?'

'Death makes everyone reassess their life.' Nessia hands him a goblet of wine. He takes it, looking up at her and forcing a smile as she massages his shoulders. 'You need to make your peace with him and leave his punishment to the ancestors and the gods.'

'That's what Eldini says.' He takes a sip of wine. 'It's not as easy as that.'

'What is right is often not easy,' Nessia says.

'No.' He sighs. 'Eat,' he says to me, pointing at the tray. I nod and take up another piece of bread.

Once I'm chewing, he gestures for me to sit on his lap. I do, nestling against his chest, his arms around me and the goblet cold against my thigh. 'He asked for you,' he says. 'He's asked for Eldini. Yet he still hasn't asked for me. If there's anyone's forgiveness he should be begging for it's mine, surely?' He looks to Nessia for an answer.

'Guilt?'

'Guilt?' He doesn't seem convinced.

Nessia and I exchange a glance over his head, and I presume she's remembering that love letter, too, and what it may imply. Would Onnachild's dying be less troubling for Raen if Onnachild wasn't his real father? Nessia mouths 'No' at me and her massaging touch turns into more of a stroke. He reaches up and taps her hand. There's too much of Onnachild in the set of his jaw, in his dark eyes for them to not be related. It's just a love letter, and it doesn't prove anything. I try to soothe the twitch out of his jaw with a caress.

'Guilt,' he says. 'He doesn't know the meaning of the word. He should. He should feel more than guilt ... I hope my mother gives him ...'

'She will,' I say.

'Good.' He shakes off Nessia's touch and wine spills, dripping onto my nightdress.

'You need sleep, both of you are exhausted. And Raen, you need to eat, too,' she says. 'What you've brought isn't enough for two people. Let me.'

He mumbles his thanks to her and, as she leaves the room, he nestles into my hair. 'What did you tell him?' Raen's words tickle my neck. 'Did you agree?'

'No.'

'Good.' He kisses my neck and I lean back for more, but he lifts his head up. His gaze lingers on my face and his scowl starts to soften. The pulse in his jaw slows. 'I've seen my mother.' He taps his temples. 'In here, in my dreams, and she tells me things I can never remember when I wake up but I feel them. They're like a jolt of fear, no, not fear, dread, and the feeling remains all day. It's worse when I'm with her, Eldini.' He rests his chin on my head. 'When I look at her, I can't stop seeing how like the Second Queen she is. All insipid, all that whiteness and ...' He takes a deep breath. 'I should never have married her.'

My heart races at the words. I tense to stop the hope within me from growing, tense so I don't fully experience it because I don't understand what it means.

'You said my mother would be disappointed in me, and,' he whispers as if she is in the other room, 'I think you're right.'

'No.' I hold his face between my hands, but he still can't meet my gaze. 'I shouldn't have said that. You did what you thought was right at the time. Honour, duty, obligation. Remember? She will understand. She loves you; you're her son. Raen.' I tap his chin for his attention. He doesn't give it to me. 'Listen.' I shake him. 'You listen to me. He's dying. He doesn't have long left, we're talking days not weeks, and once he has ... once he's gone, there are no mistakes you can't undo.'

He doesn't respond, and I wonder whether I need to shake him again, repeat myself, but then his eyes flick down briefly to meet mine. There's such sadness in them, no wonder he doesn't want me to see them.

'If I could,' I kiss his cheek, left, right, 'I'd call your mother here, right now...' I kiss his lips, 'into those flames so she could tell you herself. She's busy getting her revenge, but she will come, after.'

'Don't do what he asks.'

I nod. 'I won't. Tomorrow, we'll go together to see him.'

'That isn't going to help.'

'It will, I promise. He needs to see you, needs to face your anger too, and you, you need him to see it. You need your revenge.'

His scowl returns, and he sucks in his lips perhaps to keep in any words of agreement. I kiss his chin, hoping to coax them out. He needs to go there for the little boy abandoned and hurt by his father, for the man who carries the shame of not being able to save his mother.

'What if I'm not able to hate him?' he asks.

'Then I'll hate him enough for the both of us.'

He huffs. It's almost a laugh.

Chapter Sixty

RAEN STANDS BESIDE ME, arms crossed and fingers digging into his bicep, as he stares at his father. There's no hatred in Raen's face. There's no love. The man in the bed could be any one. Raen's shoulders are back and down, feet planted hip-width apart. Everything about his posture emanates power and a terse determination to stay in this room. I want to tell him he can scream, he can shout, he can cry if he needs to; he doesn't have to act the part of a prince. I'd take his hand, but the advisers are here and they're watching him closely like he's a wild animal.

Aesc doesn't have a parchment today, and he appears lost without it. His hands, seemingly unsure of where to place themselves, play with his tunic, his chin, run through his grey hair. The window is closed again, and a fire is burning, bringing a sweaty sheen to the advisers' grey faces. Onnachild is sleeping fitfully, dribbling from his slack mouth.

No one stops me from opening the windows or comments on it. The fresh air blowing in does nothing to ease the tension in the room. Looking around, I take in the faded glory I missed yesterday when I was too overcome by the sight of Onnachild, as overcome as Raen must be now. There's a dark-wood chest of drawers and the sunlight brings out the red tones in it, prompting me to think of Raen's hair, of the First Queen's hair. The gold embossed on the edges has worn away in places, tarnished in others. Beside the window is a portrait of a semi-naked woman who bears some resemblance to a young Mantona. In it, her breasts are bare and a piece of material, now dulled in colour, is draped around her middle. Her feet are surrounded by shells that must have yellowed over time, almost as yellow as the sickness in Onnachild's eyes. Her expression has vanished, lost in the years since it was painted.

Carved into the bed's headboard are two horses with manes of flowing curls. These horses are at play, joyful, unlike the horse in Onnachild's portrait. The sound of Raen dragging a chair over to the bed draws my attention to Onnachild, a sight I've been trying to avoid. The morning light has added an orange hue to the browns and purples of his skin. Red veins make snaking patterns across his cheeks before vanishing under his beard, bushy no more. When Raen sits, Onnachild jolts awake and flails at the furs on his bed like they're bad dreams. Raen leans forwards, elbows on his knees. His skin is the most wonderful shined-walnut colour in the morning light. Onnachild shrinks from the sight. 'What's he doing here?' he rasps.

Raen remains composed and hard-faced.

'Go away.' Onnachild raises his arm across his eyes, blocking out his son. 'Be gone. I do not want him here.'

'I have a right to be.'

The sound of Raen's emotionless voice sets the loose skin under Onnachild's arm wobbling. How small the bone it hangs from is. 'You have no right to anything.'

'I'm not sure my mother would agree.'

'Do not ... do ...' Onnachild splutters and I imagine the words have turned to foul-tasting mulch. He lowers his arm. He frantically checks the room, flinching when he sees the drawers so their colour must remind him, too. He seems to be searching out the remnants of his past, his wealth and glory, until he sees me. Then his eyes widen and his nostrils flare. Raen stiffens.

'Niah, do something,' Ascelin pleads, his hands turning into fists.

'Niah?' Onnachild groans. 'Niah.' He shakes his head. 'I thought it was ... the False Queen—'

'It might help if you didn't call her that,' Raen says.

Onnachild twitches as if he'd forgotten Raen was there, towering over him. What must Onnachild be thinking, seeing this man so full of life and vitality, all the things that are seeping from his own body? But it's not just a man, it's his son. Onnachild's lips quiver and I presume he means to speak a truth, an apology to appease his son. 'This is between her and I.' He tries to wave Raen away but his arm flops with a muffled thud back to the bed.

How could I have been so foolish as to believe there might be anything good or remorseful in that man?

'There are no secrets between me and Niah.' Raen turns towards me and his bitter smile has so much of Onnachild in it that it confuses me and I don't notice, at first, that he's gesturing for me to join him.

As I step nearer, Onnachild's expression slackens from fury to indignation. He must have realised I won't be helping him. The purple fades from his face, and his nostrils stop flaring. When I'm close enough to touch Raen's chair, panic comes to Onnachild's eyes.

Together, Raen and I represent the people he tried to annihilate. They're in the curve of my high cheekbones, the green in our irises, our dark hair, our skin tone. I'm glad I wore white today to enhance my colours, and I smile to exaggerate my cheekbones. Onnachild squirms in his bed, furs falling to the floor. His legs are wasted, have become bruise-dotted. His stained nightdress tangles around his thrashing knees.

'Out,' Ascelin shouts.

Raen pivots towards him, his expression leaving no doubt as to Ascelin's fate should he inherit. 'It's you who doesn't belong here,' he says. 'He's my father.'

'You're a fool,' Onnachild snaps.

'How I wish you weren't.'

'You're more like me than you think. You both are.'

'We'll never be anything like you.'

495

Onnachild laughs so spitefully, so rattily I sense he has something planned, one last twist. My hand slides from the chair to Raen's neck, damp from stress and strain.

'We're not the ones begging for forgiveness,' Raen says.

The words stop Onnachild's laugh. A knock on the door makes Aesc squawk. A Maiden enters, bowing, apologising as she brings in a jug of water. Everyone's silent as she moves across the room.

'Should we return for prayers?' she asks the advisers.

'No,' Raen responds. 'And you,' he shouts to the advisers. 'Out.'

When they don't follow the Maiden, he rises from his chair and they bolt from the room. Onnachild chuckles, sounding so similar to his son that Raen freezes, half up, half down.

'I have nothing to ask forgiveness for,' Onnachild says.

'How can you be so arrogant?' I push past Raen. 'You've destroyed this land, the people and you take, take everything that isn't yours, that's not meant to be yours—'

'Niah.' Raen's voice is firm. 'You won't get what you want, not from him. Leave it to my mother.' He straightens up, strides to the table, and picks up the cup and jug there. I watch him pour water into the cup, swill it around and then tip the water out the window.

While he's refilling the cup, I bend down to Onnachild and whisper in his blue-tinged ear, 'You came begging for my help. Remember that. Remember it when the dead come.'

Something like regret twists his lips but it's impossible to tell what he's regretting: the harm he's done or being unable to escape the punishment coming for him. His eyes widen as the room dims. The shadows deepen in colour and bleed out until they're filling every corner of the room with shades of brown, even the hollows of Onnachild's face are full of them. Within their presence is the anticipation of a breath held. The firelight gives them movement. Onnachild shakes, as he should. Rain starts, and he stares at it being blown in through the windows and onto the floor, where it darkens the stone in messy lines.

When Raen returns with the cup, Onnachild almost grabs him. Their fingers must touch when the cup is passed over because Raen scowls and rubs his palm down the front of his tunic. Water splashes as Onnachild brings the cup to his parched lips. *He's nothing like you*, I think as Raen stands watching.

An uneasy silence fills the room, broken only by the rain and the lap of Onnachild's tongue. Food comes and is placed on the bed for him. Raen sits, brooding and staring at his interlaced fingers. I stand behind him, clutching onto his chair. The fire goes out, plunging the room into the deep blue and brown colours of the storm outside. Onnachild slumps back, cup dropping from his hands, and it rolls over towards Raen's feet. Raen picks it up, holds it between both hands and stares into it. I kneel beside him. 'Come on, we've seen all we need to.'

He shakes his head.

'What more—'

Raen's sudden movement forwards stops me. He picks up a plate, cuts a piece of bacon into small chunks, and then guides a piece into Onnachild's slack and shocked mouth.

'Don't mistake this for kindness,' he says while Onnachild tries to chew. 'I'm only keeping you alive so you suffer longer.'

Raen's care of his father is at odds with the bitterness of his words and the tension in his jaw. I leave them and go to the fireplace. Perhaps without me there they might speak about everything that is between them. They remain silent as I relight the fire. The smoke is thicker than it should be, rolling along the floor in thick greys, tinged black same as Onnachild's beard. He breaks the silence with agitated mumbling that makes no sense. He's squealing, squirming as if flames are licking at his feet. The light from the fire highlights Raen's scar. I hope it reminds

Onnachild of that small boy with unblemished cheeks.

I whisper encouragement to the flames as I think of the wrongs this father has done to his son. There's a crackle from the fire, a spurt. Sparks drop gold and orange along the floor. Within the flames, two green dots are elongating, growing. Onnachild's voice is rising, broken words from the Aegnian language, bastardised in his castle tongue. It won't save him. Raen's silent.

'Come on,' I say to the fire, wishing I had herbs in my pocket that could bring Onnachild's nightmares into the room. The First Queen's already been let out, though; I should have remembered that, and she's taking form amongst the glowing white logs. Her hair licks up the chimney like feathers bristling in the wind. Raen's right: I don't need to do anything to punish Onnachild—she'll do enough for all of us.

Get him out of here, she tells me.

I nod. 'Your mother wants to appear.'

'What did you say?' The strain on Raen's face shows he heard. 'Shut up,' he yells at Onnachild but the stammering only gets louder and louder, as Onnachild mispronounces the gods' names. It'll make them angrier but I don't tell him that; let him learn it for himself. I touch the scar on my forehead, made hot and sweaty by the fire.

'Your mother wants you to go,' I say.

'Why?' Raen gets to his feet, his expression hidden in shadow. 'Why doesn't she want to see me?'

'She will. Not now, though. Leave them.'

He lobs the bowl at the wall. The noise startles Onnachild into muffled mews. He shrinks down under the furs as I cross the room to Raen, my shadow casting itself over the bed. I link my arm with Raen's, expecting him to resist, but he doesn't. Leading him from the room, I risk peeping over my shoulder at the column of smoke moulding into the First Queen. Her head jerks towards me. Her fiery eyes lower. They're hidden by scorched black lashes but there's no mistaking where her gaze settles. My belly. It's the only confirmation I need.

Raen and I sit, pensive, before the fire in my rooms. He's probably trying to forget what he's seen, and I'm trying to remember the last time I bled. As I stroke his arm, I can't help comparing the different shades of our skin, mine the bark and his the heartwood of the same tree. How different our child will look compared to my Ammi, who seems to have all of her father and very little of me. My body has let me and my love down by allowing Raen's seed to take root. Yet, I don't feel angry. I don't know what I feel.

'That's a deep sigh,' Raen says, the first words he has spoken since we left Onnachild's room.

'Is it?'

He strokes my cheek. 'What are you thinking?' he asks. 'Why do you look so worried?'

Should I tell him? The lines in his face are so deep-set they'll be staying. Now is not the time. Once Onnachild is dead, I will. He has enough to worry about. 'So do you.'

He tilts his head and nods. He must sense there are things I can't verbalise yet because he doesn't press me further. 'I feel better here.' He leans forwards to add another log to the fire and holds his hands out for the warmth though the room isn't cold.

'I'm glad.' I curl around his slouched back and rest my cheek against his shoulder blade. He pats my hands when they settle on his chest. I breathe in the scent of him and the burning wood, mixing so well and bringing peace like the best of my grandmother's charms. It chases away the fear of what might come once the First Queen is done with Onnachild. I squeeze Raen so I can always remember how much give and how much resistance there is in his body. I imagine we're somewhere else, a simple home in the village, a time when Onnachild doesn't rule. He gives his weight to me, answering my need to capture all of him.

The fire crackles and pops, the sounds creating a song with his deep and steady breath. Our chests move in unison. He sighs, and it's such a long and slow sound that it seems full of longing and it speaks to my own. Close to him like this, I feel this is where I'm meant to be, hugging him while he stares into the flames and his baby grows in me. Home. My smile hurts and brings tears. Will this continue after Onnachild's dead or will we give each other up and be enemies again? If we ever really were enemies. I wish I could talk about these things with him, make plans, ask for reassurance, but I don't know how to start. I suspect I'm a coward. When my lips open, it's to kiss his neck; I hope he'll sense everything in the way they linger.

My cheek nestles against his warm neck, under his hair where his scent is strong. I didn't mistake his body for Aelius's spirit that night in the graveyard, I couldn't have. Why did I even try pretending? Something else was working its magic, bringing him to me. I needed this solid strength which doesn't dominate but matches mine. Aelius was little more than a boy and I was a girl made delirious from the rush of first love. Did we ever have a future together? Ammi, we had her and so we are forever tied. My poor Ammi without her father, never to have seen him or have his arms around her. Perhaps—probably—she doesn't remember mine.

'Are you crying?' Raen struggles from my tight grasp and shuffles around. I duck my head, dash off the tears.

'It's nothing,' I mutter, clambering away from him and then pacing to the other side of the room. 'Silly tears. Why do I cry for a tyrant?' I try to laugh.

Draped over the door to my bedchamber is my cloak, the cloak Raen gave me. His brother's whore, he called me that day. His whore now, he called me on the eve of his wedding. Does he still believe that? I should tell him there's proof I'm his, and he's mine. Perhaps he won't believe me. Perhaps it won't change anything if he does. I tug the cloak down, press it to my face to soak up my tears. There's none of Raen's scent left in the material.

'Things will be different once he has ...' Raen says.

'Yes.' I want to ask him what will be different, hear him say Eldini will go, that he's choosing me. He said he shouldn't have married her. Once Onnachild has died, there will be no reason to stay married to her. Not when ... my hand settles on my belly. What if this is another fatherless child? I've been so selfish, and yet ... yet I wouldn't change this. Maybe this is one baby I can keep.

'Come back, Niah,' Raen calls out. 'If you won't tell me what's troubling you, at least let me provide some comfort.'

'I should be comforting you.'

'I don't need comfort.'

At least, for tonight, he's mine. Enjoy the moment and let the future worry about itself, Nessia would advise. I sniff back the last of my tears and go to him.

'That's better.' He draws me into his lap. 'Why have you brought that over?' He toys with the end of the cloak. 'Are you cold?'

'It's yours.' I stroke it, too.

'I know.' He settles it around me, ties it under my chin and leans back to admire me. He frowns—is he remembering that meeting? So much has happened since then, but I still remember being held by him, how familiar it seemed. The fire lights only half of his face. I touch the dark side, running a finger over the hidden cheekbone, then down his nose and into the dip above his lips.

'It'll be over soon.' He leans forwards to kiss me. I duck and hide though, tears brimming again because he's wrong. There's still Eldini, there's still the throne, and there's still Aelius. Raen's hand slides around my belly, and I hold my breath wondering if he can feel a hint of our child. He hugs me close. 'I'll make everything right, how it should have been,' he says into my hair.

By the river, the night Onnachild collapsed, Raen told me I could trust him, and so I don't press him further.

Chapter Sixty-One

'YOU MADE YOUR CHOICE,' I say to the Aelius I never knew. 'I must make mine, too.' There's no space left for him in the portrait gallery, so I prop the painting against the wall near to his childhood one. I take a moment to note the features that have remained through generations of Onnachild's line: the square jaw making the women handsome rather than beautiful, the hint of a scowl from a low brow, the dark eyes. Smiling, I imagine adding a portrait of my and Raen's child.

Last night my dreams had been full of us and our children playing in the castle grounds. The trees were no longer forced into strange shapes but wild and alight with the colours of autumn. When he slipped from my bed this morning to go to Onnachild, I wanted to share my dream with him, but he'd been so puffy-eyed from lack of sleep it didn't seem fair to him.

'Go back to sleep,' he told me as he knelt beside my bed and stroked my hair. Then he raised my left hand to his lips and kissed my ring finger, gifting me with the most desirable adornment. 'I'll sleep when everything is sorted out.'

I knew then I had to do this.

Crouching in front of Aelius's portrait, I caress the smooth paint as I did his face while he lay dead on the battlefield. It's a different kind of pain within in me now, more akin to the pricking of a finger with a needle. 'I hope you understand.' I blow the dust off the frame. It tickles my nose and

I sneeze. 'Goodbye, Aelius. You'll always be my first love but ...' I place a kiss on my finger and touch it to his flat lips. 'I have to let go of you to live.'

And then I walk away.

My dreams return to mock me when I turn the corner and see Eldini sat outside Onnachild's room. She's the one who has Raen, not me. She has the wedding ring on her finger; I only have a kiss. Her ring is too big, slipping up and down as she fidgets with the sleeves of her blue dress. She darts up when she notices me. 'How is Raen?' she asks. 'He not say. He not talk to me.'

The door opens, and the Maidens are shoved into the hallway by Raen. 'Didn't I tell you yesterday?' he barks.

Lark looks indignant with her cheeks flushed and mouth opening and closing but no words coming out. Melody's crying. Raen bangs the door shut.

'We have to pray for the King,' Melody wails, her bottom lip wobbling. 'We have to. Tell him, Niah.'

When I don't answer, she pleads with Eldini, whose shoulders only sag in response. I should feel sorry for Eldini but I find I can't.

Raen opens the door again, ignores his wife, and yells my name. I bow at her and the Maidens, hiding the beginnings of my smile because it's me he wants and not her.

'Make sure he is good,' Eldini says and I'm unsure whether she means Raen or Onnachild so I just nod.

It's cooler inside Onnachild's room so the windows must have been left open through the night. The curtains are still closed, though, keeping the room a dull brown. I open them and give them a shake. The light that comes in is grey and muted much like Onnachild's face. He mumbles but nothing more than that. The atmosphere is thick with the remnants of the First Queen: her stench, her sooty footsteps across the stones, Raen.

503

He sits on a chair beside the bed. 'I wish Eldini would go.'

'She's concerned.'

'She wants to make things better. She can't. No one can. No one, except him.' He leans over his father and uses a corner of the fur coverings to wipe crust from Onnachild's mouth. The eyes watching Raen are dulled, emotionless, and full of colours: red-tinged, yellow-stained, purple and brown underneath. 'But you won't do that, will you?' Raen sinks into the chair, stretches out his long legs, and gathers his hair into his hands.

Onnachild wheezes. His chest judders up, drops down as he stares at Raen. I stay with my back to the window, a chill on my neck. The advisers slip in and out, leaving a tray of food. I check the hallway. Eldini has gone although her chair remains and hints she might return. When Onnachild tries to eat, teeth drop out, and one clangs onto the spoon Raen holds. Another bounces off the bed and onto the floor. I pick it up and run a finger over the smoothed edges. There's a brown circle, deepening in shade at its centre. Surreptitiously, I throw it into the fire to give the flames another taste of him. Raen puts the tray onto the floor, kicks it.

Onnachild's stare follows my movements as I walk over and trail my fingers across Raen's shoulder. His eyes widen. *Yes, I have another one of your sons.*

'Let me,' I say.

Raen nods, rises from the chair, running his hands over his face. I pick up the tray and spoon. As I feed Onnachild pottage, Raen lingers by the window, looking on with a furrowed brow. With the sun behind him, he's made more magnificent, the colours of him becoming warmer and glowing. When Onnachild is dead, we'll have Raen's portrait painted and added to the gallery. I'll demand the painter gives him a smile, that lazy one which comes as he's falling asleep in my arms.

'How can you not be proud of him?' I whisper to Onnachild.

He sputters out bobbles of squashed pottage. One drops onto my wrist and I flick it off. Onnachild's mouth gapes open. His eyelids flicker. He knocks the bowl from my hands as he struggles up. Pottage and froth foam from his mouth. His clammy palms slap either side of my face, trying to drag me closer, closer to those coated lips, babbling and babbling. 'You have it. You have it. Aesc wrote it. You have it. The throne, it's yours, make them stop.'

'Get off,' I yell, smacking at Onnachild's stiff hands. 'Get off.'

'Please, make them stop.'

Raen calls my name. I pull back, fall off the bed.

'What is it?' Raen asks. 'Are you all right?'

Thank the gods, he didn't hear Onnachild. I nod, scrubbing the pottage off my cheeks with my sleeve.

'My love ... I did, always,' Onnachild mutters.

I spin around. There's the First Queen. Vivid, domineering, angry. The noose they hanged her by bites into her neck and it thuds alongside her. Thud. Thud. Thud, as she nears the bed. So loud I can hear it even when I cover my ears. Onnachild thrashes, suddenly animated, scrabbling up his bed, clinging to the mane of a horse on his headboard. Raen bolts to me, sweeps me close, and his arms clamp around me, a hand guides my head onto his shoulder. I cling to him, locking my hands around his waist. His breath is erratic. His pulse is hammering. Thud. Thud, she still goes. Raen shuffles backwards, bringing me with him. I call out as my knuckles smack into the wall. My forehead starts bleeding. The copper of my blood adds to the stench of decay.

'What do you want? What do you want from me?' Onnachild's voice is loud, clear, kingly once more.

She laughs, so deep she could make the walls move with it. Onnachild's bowels empty and still she laughs. Raen's shaking. I start singing him a child's song. My blood has stained his tunic. As I lift my head, he tells me, 'Don't watch.'

I have to, though, and so I struggle to turn in his tight hold. He draws my back to his front, arms tensed to keep me close. On and on I sing as the shadows become solid, become things that creep, that slither across the floor to see Onnachild. Red eyes. A claw. The scrape of toenails along stone. A bundle of maggots trailing glistening slime. I stop singing.

The gods are here. Now Raen will surely believe in them. He squeezes me and my breath bursts out. The First Queen stops laughing. She turns towards us. From her eye sockets worms undulate, their skin pink and stretched. Bruises dot her jaw, brown and blue. Her breasts are bare and empty, nipples pointed to the floor. This sight is what I should have protected Raen from—this must be what haunts his dreams. She's fixing her gaze on him, the flaps of her lips tilt into a smile. The worms still.

'My son. My beautiful son.'

I feel Raen's sob catch in his chest but I can't move, can't offer him comfort. Echoes of the battlefield are here. Echoes of Aelius and the others who were slain. All I can think of is him, eaten as she is, coming for me when I'm dying. I should have made him stay with me, away from the battle, away from his death. The guilt threatens to buckle my legs. I clutch onto Raen's arms.

'Take me away,' I whimper.

The First Queen nods, the clicks of her tendons make me shudder. Raen stumbles back, pulling me with him. His hand leaves me, fumbling for the door behind him.

'Don't let go.' I bury my face against his chest.

'Shush, you're safe. She won't hurt you ... shush.' On and on he repeats 'shush', almost drowning out Onnachild's gargles, until he finally has the door open.

'It won't be over for a while yet, husband,' the First Queen says. 'There's a lot of people with a lot of pain to give you.' That deep laugh again. It follows us to my rooms. That stench stays on our clothes. We scramble out of them, chuck them with desperate flicks of our limbs, and bash back together for comfort, for reassurance. We bump into my bedchamber where it's cool. I have to hide in desire with him, away from death, disease, and bodies that show how fragile we really are. I want to see health shining in his sweat, in the blood pulsing through his veins. I need his heart beating strong and incessant beneath my palms. With him, my body can feel life and be life. Our kisses are demanding and salty from tears. The grip of his fingers on my hips hurts. He pauses.

'What?' I try to pull his lips back to mine.

He points to the wall behind me, to the space where Aelius's portrait hung.

'Melody took it down to clean.' I don't know why I lie when I can feel how much he needs and desires me. There's no time to undo my lie, to explain, because he bundles me onto the bed and we escape into each other.

Chapter Sixty-Two

THE FIRST QUEEN KEEPS TOYING WITH ONNACHILD. Weeks pass. The moon gets thinner, disappears, and returns fatter than ever. Over and over again. Onnachild just gets thinner. No trace of the noble bear remains. Instead, he's as timid as a hare under the shadow of an eagle. When I stare into his protruding eyes, I realise his spirit has abandoned him. His hair clings to his skull like pond weed, and his skin is so thin I can see his blue veins beneath and the erratic pace of his blood. When Raen washes him, I expect the body to fall apart like overcooked bacon.

My dress is tight across my middle as I sit beside Raen, despite Nessia having altered it. Although we continue to seek solace in each other, he doesn't notice the changes to my stomach or breasts, or at least he doesn't

507

comment on them. Soon we won't be able to continue ignoring the future.

As we sit in Onnachild's room, Raen's head keeps lowering and then jolting up as he fights against sleep. He crosses his legs, uncrosses them, rests his chin in his hands, and rubs his scar until the skin is red. He says little.

Onnachild murmurs and groans. His eyes are seeping like he's crying, but the consistency resembles phlegm. Raen scowls when he looks at those fake tears. He takes himself off to the window. He extends his arms, pushing back against the glass, and hangs his head in the gap between them. I go to him, stroke his back until his breathing slows to normal. I can feel the bumps of his ribs and spine; he, too, is losing weight. When he lifts his head and the sun hits his cheekbones, I notice how much more pronounced they've become.

'Please,' I say. 'Get some sleep. Have some food. You don't need to keep watch.'

'I do. I need to—'

'You need to take care of yourself.'

'There are more important things than ...' He pushes away from the window.

'Not to me.'

He frowns.

'I'll keep watch,' I say. 'If he gets worse, I'll come and get you.'

He slumps into the chair beside Onnachild's bed. 'I said no.'

'I can't—'

'Then leave.'

'I can't leave you with him.'

'Why? What can he do to me that he hasn't already done? He's dying.'

'And it might take days, weeks, and what will you be like when he's gone? You have to be strong. You have to—'

'I'm fine, and I'll be fine.'

'You aren't, and you won't be if you don't—'

'If you're going to nag me same as Eldini does then just go. I thought you'd understand. I thought you'd get it, what I'm waiting for. He knows.' He jabs his thumb towards Onnachild. 'Don't you, old man? Don't you, Father?'

Onnachild stares up blankly, those seeping eyes unblinking.

'Raen.'

He shrugs off my touch.

I crouch beside him. 'I know what you're waiting for, but he isn't going to give you an apology. He hasn't got it in his heart.'

'An apology? I don't want an apology. I don't expect an apology, and even if I did get one it wouldn't make up for anything, surely you know that?' He twists around to me and although anger and frustration are in his voice, they're not in his face—there's just exhaustion. 'I want more than an apology.'

'I know. I know.' I press my nose flat against Raen's. He caresses my cheek, thumb pressing along the bone, and then his hand lowers, hovers over my stomach. My breath catches. He has realised. How could I think my body could keep a secret from him? He's going to acknowledge it and I won't have to tell him.

But the touch doesn't come. He leans back, fixes me with his eyes. The green dots are muted, and the brown is as dark as charcoal. 'Leave us. You don't have to stay here.'

'I do. For you.'

He forces a smile. We kiss briefly but it's enough to make Onnachild hiss. 'I need you to look after yourself,' Raen says to me.

I nod and leave the room but I lean against the closed door, unable to, unwilling to walk away from him and his pain. The hallway is sombre with the light weakened by the dirty windows. The dead have been given free range in the castle. I can hear them tiptoeing down hallways. Their laughter has the peal of children, though their intentions are anything but childlike. Do I regret calling the gods? I can't decide.

Pregnancy has replaced my dread with something that flutters in my stomach. Nessia said it was happiness, when she helped me dress this morning, yet that isn't it either—although I am content when I wake up in the indentation Raen left in my bed and I inhale his scent from the pillow. Maybe it is hope. But he just compared me to Eldini, and it's odd she's on his mind when he hasn't seen or spoken to her for months. We've not seen anyone apart from Nessia who brings us food, organises a tub and hot water for us, and brings us clean clothes and comforting words. I don't even know where the castle people are; perhaps they're praying.

With my ear pressed against Onnachild's door, I fantasise about Raen and me sitting in the Judging Room with the chairs filled by Followers and villagers as it used to be. Eldini has gone, returned to her homeland, and the kiss Raen gave my ring finger has been replaced by a gold band. I fantasise about us celebrating in the village square with a feast, singing and dancing, and in this last vision Aelius's statue doesn't cast its shadow.

Raen's voice is a rumble through the wood. The odd word I can make out is Aegnian and they're made more musical by Raen's accent: a mix of castle, village, and where he was banished to when his father didn't want him. Has his mother returned? Is he talking to her?

As I'm about to open the door, a servant girl hurries past, her arms loaded with a tray of food. Her clothes are far too fine and clean. Her cheeks are too rounded and her hair's too shiny. She must be a shadow. Are they getting stronger? She stops in front of me. The strange light gives her cheeks a copper tint. I start closing my eyes against the vision but she slams the tray onto the floor and then brushes her hair off her face, displaying a mahogany streak. She's wearing a necklace, a square charm dangling, and on it, there seems to be the Aegnian symbol for fire. I lean closer. Is this what Vill has been doing, gathering more Followers? It

510

would explain why we haven't seen him.

'Is it true?' she whispers. 'Is he really dying?' Her breath smells of sage and wood, like my grandmother. I almost touch her to check she's real.

'Well?' she asks.

'Yes,' I whisper.

'Good.'

Then before I can say another word, ask her where she's from, where she's been, she picks up her tray and scurries off again.

'Wait,' I call out.

'I can't. Beshanie wants me, and you know what she's like about her food.'

I'm left alone again in the castle, the changing castle. Her scent lingers same as a spirit and so I'm not sure whether she was ever there. I open the door to Onnachild's bedchamber, dazed.

Raen's hunched over the bed, holding one of his father's hands between his. He peers up at me. The strain in his face makes him look older. His hair has stuck to his cheeks. His skin is blanched and sweaty. 'Has she come again?' I ask.

He shakes his head and lets out a long, even breath, as if he's trying to show his father how to breathe. My gaze drifts to a nightdress in a crumpled heap on the floor. 'What happened while I was gone?'

'It doesn't matter.'

When Onnachild moans, Raen takes a damp cloth from a bowl on the floor and dabs it across Onnachild's forehead. The skin is tinted yellow, and the veins have turned almost black; the shadows have finally made their way into him.

'Others came,' Raen says. 'I've never ... seen ... I.'

I shouldn't but I can't stop myself bending down and lifting Onnachild's nightdress from the floor. It's stained with blood, with shit, with sweat. The edges are singed. I throw it from me. Raen's shaking.

'I can't do this anymore,' he mumbles, dropping the cloth into the bowl.

Revenge is not pretty. Revenge is not easy. Didn't Nessia say what is right is never easy? I open my mouth to remind him but there's such torment in his eyes I can't.

'You have to help him.' He stares down at Onnachild.

Raen should know not to ask this of me. It's going against my gods, the ancestors, his own mother, and all those who have waited for Onnachild to experience every death he ordered. It would break the covenant I made, and I have no idea what the consequences of doing so would be—my grandmother never told me. Touching my forehead, I feel my scar, a reminder of the gods' anger. I shake my head. 'The dead need their revenge. We can't interfere.'

'Can't you give him some relief? Come on, Niah, he's a man and he's in pain.'

Remember, I tell myself. *Remember to hate Onnachild. Hate him enough for Raen. For both of us. He is not just a man.* As I look at Onnachild, I see the conqueror in his portrait, exaggerated muscles and arrogant expression as he challenges the coming storm. I see the tyrant watching the Aegni women hang, his own wife, his nostrils flaring and a tight smile stretching his lips. And I imagine a father hurting his son, causing that scar on soft and unblemished honey-coloured skin. 'He deserves this.'

'How can you be so heartless?'

'Have you forgiven him?' I ask without recrimination.

'He's my father.'

Onnachild wheezes and it sounds like a laugh. Raen closes his eyes, grimaces. Onnachild jolts in the bed, startling Raen and making him curse. He grabs up the wet cloth, water dripping over his arms and his legs. He dabs his father's eyelids, forehead, and mouth. Onnachild's lips part and his tongue darts out to the cloth. There's no respite for him, though. He's thrashing, wailing. The gods are getting in, cracking him, ripping him. Raen falls into the chair, useless, close to breaking too. His hand fists around the cloth.

'If not for him, then for me? Please, Niah, I can't ...' As he stares at me, his face is unguarded and shows all the suffering he's endured: his father's cruel treatment and abandonment, his mother's death, years banished from his homeland. Can I add more to that suffering by not helping him? He's given me life and moments of happiness in this cold castle. He's stood up for me. In the green dots of his irises, I see who I am, where I came from, and who I could be.

His fingers run through his hair, catch on a knot, and though it makes him wince he tugs against it. 'I've seen enough.'

I have to help Raen. What use are caresses, are kind words, are lullabies if I won't do the one thing he asks of me? 'For you, I will.' I whisper in the hope neither the gods nor my ancestors will hear. Raen can't have heard because his brow remains furrowed, his eyes tortured.

I push down the door handle.

'Where are you going?' he calls out with the desperation of a frightened child.

'To get my herbs.'

'Niah.'

I pause.

He forces a smile. 'Thank you.'

Please, may the gods and my ancestors forgive me.

Chapter Sixty-Three

I'LL FIND NESSIA and send her to the village for what we need so I can

513

return to Raen. It's too much for him to bear alone. I run to my room but she isn't there. Her cloak is draped over a chair, so she can't have gone far. The fire has gone out, and the chill is sharp enough to penetrate my dress—she hasn't been here for a while.

She must be with Llwellyin, so I race to the kitchens. The servants are sitting around a large table doing nothing. They look up at me with guilty expressions.

'Nessia?' I ask. 'Llwellyin?'

A young man shakes his head at me. Everyone seems too scared to speak and just keeps gawping at me.

I leave the servants and sprint down deserted hallways. The laughter of the dead echoes off the walls, ahead of me, always ahead of me, but they leave behind their stench and wisps that could be smoke or shadow. All are drifting towards Onnachild's room to gather for their final moment of glory. There's not much time left. I open doors and thrust my head inside empty rooms, messy and stinking with uneaten food. I run on, leaving them open. I shout Nessia's name until my throat hurts. The faces in the portrait gallery are a blur of brown and white and blue as I dart through. There's nothing in Aelius's for me anymore so I don't slow down.

I run past the Prayer Room. Eldini's voice is loud and desperate. Is she praying for Onnachild's release or for Raen to love her? I can't think about that now. My feet pound along the stone floor, scooting around the rugs. My chest and side hurt, forcing me to pause at the Sunning Room and catch my breath before I vomit. The room is jammed full of castle people praying, their sound a dull dirge. Nilola spots me and taps Beshanie on the shoulder. They smile at me as I tiptoe back, back and straight into Vill.

'What are you doing here?' he asks.

'I didn't hear you.'

'That doesn't surprise me. You're creating enough noise to drown out thunder. What has got into you? Has he died at last?'

'Where's Nessia?'

'Doing something for me.'

'What? Where?'

'Why do you need her?'

'Vill, please stop asking me questions. Where is she?'

'The library ... looking at the accounts so we know which merchants—'

I dart off.

'Don't ...' His words fade as I sprint to that room where I was transformed from Niah into this other person. How long ago that seems now. What would the old me do? Would she feel sympathy for a dying man or would her anger never waiver? It's not Onnachild I do this for, it's Raen; I must remember that. My feet slide across the floor and I smack into a wall. I need to be more careful, but there isn't time to be careful.

'Nessia?' I yell as I push open the library door.

She looks around a chair, her forehead furrowed, and there's ink on her left cheek. A candle picks out the grey in her hair, showing how the colour has spread since we've been in the castle. 'Is he dead?' she asks.

I shake my head as I gulp down air.

'What is it?' she asks. 'What's wrong?'

I rub my temples. It must be done. For Raen. To help him, I must help Onnachild. The request is hard to say, to speak out loud, even to her. 'Please go to the village. I need poppies, lavender, sage.'

Her eyes narrow. 'Why?'

I trip over an open book in my hurry to reach her. 'What is this?'

'The castle accounts. Vill wants a list of who owes Onnachild money so he can—'

'It doesn't matter.'

'Easing his passing does?' She picks up the book and balances it on her knee. I crawl over and cover the page with my hands. My face burns from running and not even my sweat is cooling me.

'Please, I haven't got time to explain. I have to get back to Raen. He's alone with Onnachild. Please, I owe Raen, and he asked me. Don't be angry with me.'

'It's not my anger you have to worry about.'

'Easing Raen's pain is what I'm doing, that's all. He's not sleeping. He's barely eating. He needs us. You care for him, don't you? Please, Nessia. I'd go myself, but he can't deal with this alone. The gods can't punish me for helping Raen, can they? The First Queen would understand, wouldn't she?'

Nessia cups my chin tenderly. The touch makes me want to cry but instead, I hold her calloused hand, pressing it closer, and lean into her, into the faint hint of village that remains in her skin. I push the book off her lap, flinching when it hits the floor. 'Please.'

'What has changed?' she asks.

'Everything.' I feel the weight of that word. The ambiguity of it. How it encompasses so much and yet says very little. It's me, my feelings. I want Raen. With him there's the chance to be me, to stop hiding beneath all these silks and satins that I thought I wanted. I don't, not anymore. The chuckles, the tears. I want all of them and all versions of him. That fluttering in my stomach, I realise, was not happiness nor was it hope: it was love. The vagueness of *everything* hides this and I don't need to hide it from Nessia. Within me, our child waits for a new future, a future within my grasp. 'I love him.'

'I know.' Her smile has a sad quality to it. 'More than the throne, though? More than your ancestors?'

'You can't ask me that. I can't think about that now. I'm having his child.'

'I realised that, too. Has he?'

I shake my head.

'He cares for you, and you—'

'Then, Nessia, how can I refuse to help him? How can I tell him I love him? Why would he believe me? Words are meaningless if I don't do this.'

When Nessia stands, my hands plummet to the chair, the seat still warm from her presence.

'I'll go get them,' she says.

'Thank you. Thank you. Please, don't say anything to Vill about ... this ... Not yet. Please.'

She pats my shoulder and nods. 'If you want something to take the edge off the pain, there's some willow root in Llwellyin's room, in my purse. You'll find him tending the ornamental trees.'

Eldini's sitting outside Onnachild's rooms. She's hiding her face in her hands and her shoulders are shaking. The sound of her women and the Maidens praying comes from the room, and it almost drowns out her sobs. I'm tempted to sneak away but I have Nessia's purse with me and Raen is waiting. There's no one else that can help him so I step forwards on my tiptoes, light as possible, and hope I can slip past her into the room. Her fingers flutter.

I halt. She removes her hands and lifts her head. Her eyes are red-tinged and her nose is red, too; the colour is like blood on a lamb. 'They will not let me in.' Her accent has gone. Has she been practising for when she's queen? Raen can't have told her she'll be leaving. Of course, he hasn't. He's been with me. I clutch Nessia's purse to my stomach. Soon, this will be over. Eldini will be gone, and I won't ever have to lie to her again. I won't have to hear her concerns ever again.

'I tried. My women are in there.' She points towards the door. 'The advisers told them to read the ...' There's determination in her face, and I'm reminded of her portrait, seeing that expression for what it truly was. It wasn't showing someone stoic and fearful of her future, but a princess who will fight for what is hers. 'I should be in there.' She shoots up, faces the door, fist ready to knock, and the look she gives me challenges me to prevent her from doing so. 'I came to read God's words. I will read them. It is my duty. I tried to go in.' She drops her fist. 'But Raen will not let me. He said because I am with child I cannot.'

With child? His child? But when? She looks no different, the same, skinny, bony, straight up and down. She sinks into her chair and even in that position, there's no bulge of either breast or belly. I touch mine. My heart seems to have stopped.

'He said the gods might see my child. Might come for it but he ...' Her vast forehead wrinkles. 'But God is kind. Our God.' Her fingers gather up a lock of her hair, twist it round and round. 'The old gods are not real. He never ...' She lets go of her hair. The loose curl she's made drops out. 'I should be praying over the King's body. Tell him, Niah. He will listen to you.'

I can't look away from her, from that tiny body, the pleat of her dress at her middle, her skin likened to milk by that castle man, her eyes far apart like a sheep's. There's no rosiness in her cheeks as there is in mine. There's no sparkle in her pale eyes like I've seen in mine. I touch my face. My hands are freezing and damp.

'Niah? Tell him.' Her voice is so forceful it startles me from my assessment of her and my gaze darts to outside, out to where the autumn sun is giving everything a copper tinge. She tries to hold my hands in hers but I struggle away.

He's been with me. He told me he shouldn't have married her, said he was going to put things right. At night he comes to me, to my body, not hers. She must be lying. She must be. Or it happened one of those four nights when they were shut in her room, when he did his duty. How many months ago was that? There'd be some sign of it, surely. She must be lying. 'When?'

'They went in ... I do not know.'

'I don't mean that. I mean ...' The words stick in my throat and I can't cough them away. I can't stop my gaze from straying to her middle.

'Oh. I should have said. I wanted to but Raen said to wait as babies can be ...' Again she tries to touch me. Again, I flap her away.

'Do not be upset with me, please, Niah. We can talk after ... after ...' She twists towards the door, her dress creasing around her flat middle.

How long? Will her baby be born before mine? My hand closes around my ring finger, the finger Raen kissed, made me believe. I do believe. He shouldn't have married her, he said that. He would make things right, he said that.

'The King is dying,' Eldini says. 'That is more important. You make him let me in. Tell him I have God's protection.'

She knocks loudly on the door, not waiting for my agreement. Her knock is answered by a scream. She jumps. I drop Nessia's purse and stare at it there at my feet. There's banging, shrieking, a thud resembling rolling thunder.

'You are bleeding,' Eldini gasps.

I touch my forehead. She's right. Blood is smudged over my shaking fingers when I check. Drops fall from them onto the floor, onto Nessia's purse. The door cracks down the middle. Eldini grabs my hand. Hers is warm and the sensation is unsettling, yet I clasp it tight. 'I should ...' I say though I've no idea what I should do.

Her women are shouting, voices breaking as they try to drown out the noises the gods are wrangling from Onnachild. Love, faith, purity: the women shout. What a mockery of me those words are. My hands are dead weights and won't move to my ears no matter how much I want to block out those sounds. Eldini joins in the prayers, her voice steady and loud. She sounds queenly. How can she not be scared? Because she doesn't know. She doesn't believe.

I back away from her, from her boyish frame. I stare at the growing drops of blood on the floor. Somehow the sight calms me even as Onnachild's howls increase. The door rattles. Onnachild yells. There's crying. Eldini tries fussing over me, a length of her sleeve coming up to clean my face. I smack away her care. She attempts to lead me to the chair with her tiny hand that has touched Raen, that has aroused him enough for a baby to be made. She must be lying. I take a deep breath, fill my stomach, and feel it press against my dress.

'Your head,' she says. 'We need to tend to it.'

I duck away from her. Why will she not learn? Wait, I want to tell her, just wait a few months and you'll see Raen never intended to love you. *Duty. Pliable. Honour.* You'll regret offering me this kindness. My words won't come. I wipe the blood from my forehead, lick my palm. It tastes of copper as if I'm made of that and not human at all. Within it is Aelius. Within it is Raen. Maybe Eldini will call me the names he has when she finds out.

'Let me help you.' She nudges the chair against the back of my knees, and I slump into it. I was a fool. She's his wife. Pale as castle perfection should be. I scrub my forehead with my fist. It stings, but at least the bleeding has ceased. Does this mean ...

The door opens, and the scent of death gushes out. Eldini's women are a wailing mass of blue and white. 'Shut up,' Raen growls. 'Shut up.' The Maidens are pushed out, one by one. 'Go. Leave.' His face is crimson. His hair is stuck down with sweat. His eyes are so panicked he doesn't even notice me. I rush to him. Too late. He slams the door shut, the frame bouncing from the force.

Everyone's crying—the sound is so loud, so high-pitched it hurts my ears. Eldini tries to fight her way through the women to the door. One of them grabs her back. Shadows flutter, making butterflies across the floor, and it's too beautiful a sight, too incongruent with the sounds coming from the room. The women crowd Eldini. A torch bursts into flames. I can't blink away the orange dots so like an eye. It doesn't matter. Nothing matters but Raen. Nothing except him not facing this alone. I hate Onnachild enough. I hate him enough for all the Aegni. For Raen. I bang on the door, my knuckles catching the splintered wood. I yell Raen's name, again and again. I yank on the door handle.

There's clattering inside. The sound of glass breaking. Someone is hyperventilating. There's a deep bang as if the floor has fallen away. Raen cursing. I bang again, again, again. It meshes with the sounds beyond the door: the screeching, the cracking, yelping like a dog's being kicked. My head bangs against the door. My palms slap against the door. Surely, it's done now. It has to be done now. I call out Raen's name. The First Queen's name. A boom. A sound like material being ripped apart.

Then silence.

It's worse.

My head has left a bloody smear on the wood. I turn around, trembling, and use the door to stay steady. The women have gone, only Eldini and I remain. She's as regal as a statue. Her chin is tilted up. Her hands are clasped in front of her. Nessia's purse is by her feet, the willow bark spilt and scattered. My blood is on her white shoes. There are no shadows. There are no torches, just a chilling blue light across the hallway and her face. I almost beg her to speak, say anything, to break this silence.

The door opens. Raen slumps against the frame as though he can't bear his own weight any longer. His cheeks are spotted crimson and white. His eyes are dry. His knuckles are red. One hand is swollen. Eldini swoops past me, calling his name and reaching for him.

'Is he?' She sounds so loud in this silent hall.

'Yes.'

She wraps her arms around Raen's waist. Over her head, he scowls at me. 'You were too late.'

'I'm sorry. I tried,' Eldini says, though I know his words are for me.

521

He's right and there's nothing I can say to answer the accusation in his eyes. Trying isn't enough. He hugs her back, kisses her head. Is he trying to hurt me? And all I can do is stare at his damaged hands, wide, strong, on her small frame. His wedding band is almost engulfed by his swollen finger. Bells start ringing, heralding change. Already? So soon.

Part V: Smoke

Chapter Sixty-Four

BELLS HAVE BEEN RINGING INCESSANTLY for a week now. *The King is dead. The King is dead.* Outside a mist has settled, edged in gold by the rising sun and shrouding the distance. A new dawn is coming, that I know, that I feel, only I don't know what it's going to bring. Perhaps the sun will finally burn away this stubborn greyness.

'Come away,' Nessia says from beside the fire where she's altering the black dress I wore when I first met Onnachild and was mourning for Aelius. 'You don't want to catch a chill.'

'Are you sure you left my note somewhere he'd find it?'

'Yes. One on his bed and the other Llwellyin left on the mantelpiece in Eldini's dayroom.'

All my notes, my requests for his company, have been ignored by Raen. I've been to his rooms, to the forgotten graves, Eldini's rooms, everywhere searching for him so I can say I'm sorry. Say I love you and place his hand on my growing belly. I picture his bruised knuckles, the cracked door, and his angry face accusing me.

'And Llwellyin hasn't seen him? You're sure?'

'I'm sure. No one has.'

He must be with Eldini and Ammi. When I went to Eldini's rooms looking for him, I lost my nerve because I could hear her crying and so I didn't knock. I couldn't hear his baritone added to that sound. Creeping away, I wanted her tears to be proof he'd told her they shouldn't have married and she is to go home.

I pace from the window in my dayroom, stop at the fire and bend to watch the flames. They've been so calm since the gods' work has been done. 'Where's Vill?' I throw another log into the fire, where I imagine my notes to Raen have ended up. Has Eldini been reading them, interpreting my meaning, and keeping them from him? Is that why he doesn't come? I rub my tired eyes. It's so hard to sleep with those bells ringing. *The King is dead. The King is dead.* And no answer from Raen. 'What am I supposed to do? Just wait?'

'I suppose so.' Nessia holds up my dress to check the stitching.

This waiting is worse than those three days when he and Eldini were shut away in her bedchamber. I picture that bed sheet banging, its thud adding to the trill of the bells. Did she conceive in those days? She'd be showing by now if she had. How long ago was that? For how long was Onnachild ill? The tension at my temples throbs.

'Waiting. Waiting. This castle has made me weak. I didn't wait before.' I poke at the fire. 'I walked up to the castle. I didn't know what would happen then, did I? But I did it, so why do I do nothing but wait? Wait and write notes and what do I get? Nothing.'

'What do you want to do?'

I shrug. 'Sort this out myself.' I've no idea how to do that, though, when Raen can't be found. I could ask Eldini whether she's leaving, but I'm not sure I can bear any more of her tears. When I close my eyes, I see

Raen's face as it was when he held her, when he kissed her head, and the spite there still stings.

The King is dead. The King is dead. I know, I know. Now what? Now what?

Onnachild offered me the throne if I eased his passing. I didn't. No proclamation has been made declaring Raen heir. The whole castle seems to be asleep, lulled by those infuriating bells.

'Why doesn't Raen come?'

He's with Eldini. He loves Eldini. Even that answer would be better than this silence. His last words to me repeat and repeat in my head when I try to sleep. *You were too late.* And in my head I answer, I'm sorry. I love you. He must give me a chance to tell him these things. He must. I can bear his anger, his hurt, any words he wishes to throw at me as long as he answers my question. What next for us? No more secrets. No more hiding. And I'll get those damn bells to stop.

My fingernails scrape over the grain of the mantelpiece, collect up dirt so deeply ingrained it's become part of the pattern.

'He'll come when he's ready,' Nessia says.

'When?'

'Soon.'

'You're as bad as Vill—"soon".' I flick the dirt from my nails towards the fire. I can't stay here. Waiting and waiting until Raen's ready. At least moving, trying, fools me into thinking I'm doing something productive. It's better than being cooped up in his mother's room.

Just as I'm about to leave, Melody opens the door and skulks past me. Her skin is wan and her back hunched as if she's been in the same position for too long. Her dress is black and grey, and the skirts float around her like smoke. It seems the shadows have returned for me, for my unborn baby, and I cover my belly with my arms.

She sinks down in front of the fire.

'Have you seen Raen?' I ask. 'Do you know where he is?'

She shrugs.

'Where's Vill?'

Again, she shrugs.

'Where have you been?' Nessia asks.

'Praying,' she moans. 'My knees hurt.' She stretches out her legs, flexes her feet.

I shut the door and move to the fire. The light glints across the silver hawk on her grey shoe. 'Was Eldini with you?'

She shakes her head.

'What are the servants saying?'

She's too distressed to answer, sucking her thumb and stroking her nose with her index finger. Nessia wraps a fur around her, tells her to get into bed, but Melody doesn't move from the fire.

Of course, Raen won't come. He's with Eldini, in her rooms. She's holding him, stroking his hair, and it's her lap soaking up his tears. I should have been brave enough to knock on her door, even if it meant finding out I'm the discarded one. Would things have been different if I'd told him about the baby, told him that night when he was ready to offer comfort?

'They told us to stop praying,' Melody says. 'Why did we have to stop? We aren't meant to, not until his soul has gone safely ... and he hasn't gone safely. He hasn't.' She lifts her tear-filled eyes up to me. 'I've never seen anyone dying before.' She tries to shove her fist into her mouth but it's too big and so she gives up, dropping it to her lap. 'It was horrible, and he looked ... he looked like a ... like a normal old man. And it smelt in there. Lark said we couldn't open the window, and it stunk—I think it's on me still.' She sniffs her sleeve. 'Is it on me?' She thrusts it towards me. My stomach turns remembering that odour, but to appease her I bow down and smell it.

'No. Nothing is there.'

'He didn't seem so kingly then. Death doesn't care, does it? Whether you're a king or not, I mean.' She takes off her headdress and pushes the shells backwards and forwards, their tinkling adding to the bells. The sound reminds me too much of Eldini's tittering laugh and so I cover Melody's hand with mine to stop her.

'I was expecting to see God,' she says. 'Or feel God or something but nothing, and I was meant to sing and help ... help him go ... go wherever ... but I couldn't feel God moving through me. I couldn't sing 'cause my throat was so tight like someone was ...' She shudders and the fur slips down off her shoulders. 'So I could only mouth the words. And I couldn't stop staring at him. He twisted, and he screamed, and he twisted and at the end he ... he ...'

I shake my head to rid myself of the vision of him there, cracking, recoiling as the dead claimed him. His veins black and pulsing. It doesn't go.

'He ... soiled himself. It was all my fault. All my fault because I wasn't really singing and it didn't bring him comfort or make his passing easier. Niah, am I a bad person?'

'No, Melody. No, not at all. Death is ugly and scary.' I press my fingers into my temples. *It's over*, I tell myself. Only the vision of Onnachild persists and added to it is Raen beside the bed, exhausted, the cloth dripping water as he said he couldn't take any more, as he pleaded for my help. I let him down. No wonder he doesn't come.

'But Lark ... she didn't ... I heard her singing in my ear. She carried on, and when I looked at her, she had God in her eyes. She looked serene.'

I get Melody some wine. At least one of us should be able to drink away what we've witnessed. She cups the goblet in both hands like it is a bowl of hot soup. She takes a sip and screws her face up at the taste.

'How can you sew?' she asks Nessia. 'How can you carry on like

527

nothing has happened? The King is dead.'

Nessia looks up. 'Because I care nothing for that man and I won't pretend to just because he's dead.'

'I know he has done bad things but ... but—'

'It's all right. It's over.' Kneeling beside Melody, I put my arm around her shoulder, but the touch seems to spook her more.

'I thought he might spit on me and I'd catch what he had. I don't want to die. I don't. Not like that.'

'It will be a while before death comes for you and you don't need to fear it when it does,' I say.

'How do you know? How? I'm not a good person. I don't follow God as I should and God will know. He will.'

'You are a good person and you try so hard,' I say.

She sniffs and nods. 'I did try. And he shouldn't have brought me here, should he? I'm not a Maiden. I am not.' She draws her headdress into a hug and it knocks her goblet. Wine spills onto her dress, making her flinch. 'But I kept thinking of how I had so much to thank him for and all the things you wouldn't understand. He gave me music and I do like that, and without him, I wouldn't have met you, and so I couldn't help but think I owed him this small service. It wasn't much to ask of me, and I realise we don't like him but ... but that is what I was thinking. And I was too busy with that ... perhaps that's why God didn't want to ... and I was listening to Raen. He was strange. He was very strange and not like himself. It scared me and then I could not look at him anymore ... He said ...' She covers her mouth with her fist and spills more wine.

'What?' I whisper.

Melody's gaze flits around the room. 'He said ...' Her voice catches. She coughs. 'That he wanted to watch and make sure that he died. And no one said anything because Raen will be king.'

'Not necessarily,' Nessia says.

I hold up my hand to stop her from saying any more. 'And?' I ask Melody.

She nods. 'And then he started pushing everyone out, yelling, and I was scared, so scared and I didn't ... I ... I ... hid ... under the bed and ...' She gulps at her wine. 'And I heard more ... I ... The King said ... He said he'd give Raen the throne ... if ... if he—' Melody gulps and her lip wobbles.

'The deceitful pig,' Nessia says.

'If he ...' I prompt.

'He said he shouldn't have taken his mother's sins out on him, that he was sorry and he wanted his forgiveness. And he said that Raen was his son and he ... if Raen'd just help him, then ... And Raen said nothing.'

'Go on.'

'The King, he said all these things and ... and I saw Raen just stood there ... no emotion, no tears, nothing. And the King was crying, calling the False Queen all sorts of names, and words I shouldn't repeat.'

'I'm glad we were too late,' Nessia mumbles.

So am I, but then I remember Raen's anger, that kiss on Eldini's head, and his swollen knuckles on her waist. 'And Raen? Did he? Did he forgive him?'

'I don't want to say. It was horrible. I don't want to say.'

'Please,' I say as gently as I can.

Melody nods and blows her nose on her sleeve. 'Well the King, he was crying, wailing like a woman, and I was thinking it odd that a king's screaming should sound so common, so unkingly, and I could hear his stomach moving, and I could smell it ... and I tried to cover my ears but under the bed wasn't big enough and I had to listen and I had to see. He tried to repent and Raen ... he wouldn't accept it. Raen, he asked ... he asked if he could see his mother, the False Queen.'

'The First Queen,' Nessia corrects her.

'Yes that queen, and he asked whether she still had the rope around her neck, and the King cried and begged for forgiveness. Only Raen said he wouldn't forgive him, that the King was not sorry, only scared of death, and Raen cursed him and asked again about his mother. The King said he could see her, that she had come for him … and he cried like a child having a nightmare and begged for Raen to make her go, that he'd make things right if Raen made her go. I peeked out and I couldn't see her. I didn't want to but … she wasn't there but Raen said: "She's come to make sure you spend eternity paying for her murder, and when I die, I'll join her in punishing you." And the King wailed harder about how his son had forsaken him, how he had no sons left and no wives left and … and … no one had really loved him, and he'd picked the wrong god … and … and … A king shouldn't die like that.'

So at the end, Raen didn't need me to hate his father for him, and he doesn't need me now. What about Eldini, does he need her? I hug Melody as she breaks down into sobs.

'Raen finally got his revenge,' Nessia says.

Melody leans away from my embrace and stares up at me while she takes in a juddering breath. 'But … but …' She wheezes on the words. 'You can't reject a dying man's request for forgiveness. God says that we must forgive because only He has the right to pass judgement. The King … the King will be with God, won't he though? We prayed long and hard. I did, at least I tried. Is the trying enough?'

I picture Nessia's purse, open and spilling dried herbs across the stone floor, and Raen's expression. No, trying is not enough, but I can't tell Melody that. 'You couldn't have done anything more,' I manage to say, taking the empty goblet from her and setting it on the floor so I can avoid her stare. 'The First Queen came for him.'

'But what about the other queen? The True Queen? He was meant to return to her when he died. I don't understand. She'll be alone.'

'She should never have seduced another woman's husband.' My words,

530

once I realise what I've said, make me shudder and my face heat with shame.

'Marriage doesn't always make a wife,' Nessia says. 'Not if the man longs for another on his wedding night.'

'But ...?' Melody scratches her nose.

'She's talking nonsense,' I say to end that conversation.

'I think Vill would agree with me,' Nessia says.

I huff. 'If he was here, but he isn't.' I glare at Nessia even though it isn't her fault. The black dress lies limp across her lap, and I remember Onnachild telling me how black didn't suit me. Good. 'I bet Vill's already meeting the dressmaker with patterns for something gaudy to wear to the funeral.'

'No,' Melody says. 'He's in the Judging Room with the advisers. Lark told me she was going to serve them.'

'You said you didn't know where he was.'

'I forgot,' she mumbles.

'The Judging Room?'

She nods.

'Without me? How dare he meet them without me?' And before I've spoken to Raen. The King is dead, as the bells keep reminding me, and so I don't have to be a weak castle woman anymore. I untangle myself from Melody.

I bang on the Judging Room door, like a fool I bang. This room should be mine. It is mine and so I push the door open with as much force as I can muster. Annoyingly, it doesn't bang against the wall to announce my arrival. The four men gathered around the table fall silent and stare at me: Raen, the advisers sat opposite him, and standing by the throne is Vill. They seem frustrated. What right do they have to be frustrated at being interrupted?

'Excuse me,' Vill says to the other men. 'I'll deal with this.'

'Will you?' I stomp over to the table. My table. 'What are you discussing?'

The advisers glance at each other, exchange a smirk. Ascelin opens his mouth to speak until Aesc lays an inky hand on his.

'Niah, shall we ...' Vill makes a sweeping gesture towards the door.

'We shall not.' Parchments are piled up across the table. Old parchments yellowed and with faded ink. 'What are these?' I splay them across the table, hoping to spot Raen's marriage contract amongst them.

No one answers my question or meets my gaze. Raen's jaw, dark with stubble, twitches as he stares straight ahead. His unwashed hair is shiny and limp around his gaunt cheeks. I'd forgotten how much weight he's lost. His tunic is loose and dirty. Where has he been? Judging by his appearance, he's not been with Eldini. What does that mean?

'Raen?'

He tucks his hair behind his ear, and he rests his cheek on his hand. His knuckles are still swollen, and the sight tempts me to kiss them better, to hold him, and confess everything. Sorry. Love. His eyes lower, meet mine. They're tired and bloodshot but the hatred blazes. My fingers slip off the parchments onto the table. I expected anger, had braced myself for that, but not this. Not hate. This can't be because I failed his father, not after what Melody told me. It can't. But then ... what?

'Raen, can we—'

He shakes his head, huffs, and turns his gaze towards the ceiling. I need to say I'm sorry. I need to say so much more. When I take a step closer to him, he closes his eyes.

'Let us deal with this.' Vill catches my arm in a hold that is far too tight. 'It's nothing to concern yourself with.' His smile is tense. 'Excuse us.' He marches me to the door. I keep staring at Raen, willing him to look at me again even when I'm in the hallway.

Vill slams the door behind us. 'Calm yourself. I'm taking care of matters.'

'What have you said? What has been—'

'Niah, my dear, little angry Niah—'

'Don't patronise me.' I step nearer the door.

Vill stops me with a firm grip on my shoulder. 'I understand you're angry, you're frustrated, aren't we all? If you would give me a moment to explain.'

'You're meant to be my man. You're meant to ... And I don't have time.'

'Now you don't have time?' There's mirth in his voice. Is this a game to him when Raen is in there hating me? 'Forgive me, perhaps I should have answered your notes.'

'There is no perhaps. What have you said? Tell me?'

'Let me finish.' He holds his hand up.

I give in and nod, though my foot taps.

'Thank you. As I was going to say, this doesn't require your attendance. We're only deciding how to dispose of Onnachild's body: the old way of burning or the new way of burying. He had to make it so much more complicated by refusing to decide which religion he wished to die in.'

'I'm not so stupid I don't realise the implications of that decision.'

'True, a sign he's returned to Adfyrism will strengthen our claim and I'm doing everything I can to ensure he is burnt, but do you really care what happens to the old tyrant's body as long as it's gone from here? I know I don't but ...' He shrugs. 'I must make a show of it; after all, we have to appear to believe his wish to return to the old gods.'

'I should be in there.'

'You will be, but not today. When you're needed, I promise you'll be called. For now, return to your rooms and gather your strength for what matters.'

'And that is?'

'Whatever you say it is. I am your man, as you like to remind me.'

'And Ammi? I don't understand why she's not with me. Onnachild's dead. It's been a week. When do I get her back? And if you dare say soon ...'

'When this matter is resolved.' He starts opening the door. 'I'll come to you tonight and we'll discuss all of your concerns.'

I catch a glimpse of Raen. 'Stop.'

Vill does and I peer in. Raen's rigid in his seat, spine pushed right up against the back so he's made of tense, hard angles. The golden and orange tones of the throne and table exaggerate the darkness of his hair, stubble, and mourning clothes. I want him to turn towards me, show me the green dots in his irises again, even if they're blazing with that hatred. Surely even that will burn itself out, eventually?

Vill clicks his fingers. 'What?'

'What is happening with Eldini?' I ask.

'Forget her.'

'Do not agree to anything until we've spoken. Wait.'

'Wait? You said you didn't have time.' His eyes narrow, and his assessing gaze sweeps over my face. I thank the gods it doesn't go lower, and I uncross my arms as they've pulled my dress tight across my belly. 'Do you mind telling me what we're waiting for?'

'There are things you don't know.'

'There's nothing I don't know so stop worrying.' He pivots on his heels, and heads into the room. I hear him lock the door behind him.

I should wait here until they come out, but I can't keep waiting. Waiting and waiting and not getting any answers. I've waited too long. The servants gossip, but they don't give Nessia the information I need. Beshanie and Nilola pay well for gossip, Melody told me. They're friends with Perkin, who's Raen's man. If anyone can tell me whether Raen's been with Eldini, it will be them. And then, then, somehow, later, once he's finished in the Judging Room, I'll force Raen to listen and I'll tell him everything. Sorry. Love. Baby. The words throb at my temples.

Chapter Sixty-Five

'TO WHAT DO WE OWE THIS PLEASURE?' Beshanie's eyes are sparkling with spite and her smile is tight as she blocks the way into her rooms.

'Oh, Besh, don't tease her. She's bored like the rest of us.' Nilola pushes Beshanie away.

Both are dressed in black, and their hair is pulled back into severe buns low at their napes. At their necks are brooches bearing a white profile of a young Onnachild before his nose was broken. I frown at the image as Beshanie links her arm with mine and leads me across her room. It's bright despite being in the older part of the castle and despite being cluttered with mismatching furniture. The walls are a pale pink and painted with red roses, the stems thornless. There's the faint perfume of them, too. At least the bells are quieter here.

'Take a seat.' Beshanie gestures to a curved chair containing several pink and red cushions.

I sit opposite a cluster of dolls on top of an ornate chest of drawers. The dolls have the same colour hair as Beshanie, and they scrutinise me as she does. I pull a cushion out from behind me and hide my belly.

'So is Nilola right, are you bored?'

'Terribly.' I fiddle with a loose thread dangling from a heart embroidered on the cushion.

Beshanie crosses her arms over her broad chest, leans back in her seat and squints at me, reminding me of my initial impression of her as a fighter waiting for his opponent to drop their guard. It jars with this girlie room of roses, dolls, lace, and shimmering curtains.

'Really? I wouldn't have thought you'd have time to be bored.' Her eyes sparkle again and I realise it's not with spite. It's excitement. 'What with the King dying.'

I'm not sure what emotion I should show in response to her comment, but thankfully, she's distracted by Nilola dragging over a chair and slapping it down beside me.

'So tell me.' Beshanie leans forwards and our toes almost touch. 'Is it true? Did the King convert? Or should it be revert?'

'How did you find out about that?' I ask.

'I find out everything. So, did he?'

Nilola taps my knee. 'You'll find things very different once you have the throne. There are rules and traditions you'll not be aware of. How could you be?'

Beshanie glares at her for interrupting, but Nilola shrugs, seemingly disinterested in whatever game they intended to play when I knocked on the door. 'You'll have lots to do and decide. Honours and favours.' She tilts her head and peeps up at me through her lashes.

It's on my lips to deny everything, play stupid, but I'm reminded of my first meeting with them, and how they knew so much more about me than they should have and so I remain silent.

'My mother served the First Queen.' Beshanie's podgy hand settles on my knee. 'Back when the castle was fun, before Onnachild married that pious bore. Despite what you think, you can trust us. We're cruel to every new girl to the castle, think of it as a rite of passage. If we hadn't done the same to you, well, it might have given away your little secret.'

'What secret?' I squeeze the cushion closer to my middle even though they can't possibly be referring to that.

'Don't you mean which? You did have so many,' Beshanie says. 'It's obvious you're Aegnian, but the rest? Aelius was always boasting about bedding an Aegni woman. He bored everyone with the banned myths. As for your practising Adfyrism, well, who do you think told us? Vill. We haven't told anyone, though, have we, Nilola?'

Nilola shakes her head.

'It wouldn't matter if you had, Onnachild already knew.'

'Of course, he did. He realised he'd need an Aegni woman if he wanted to be anointed back into Adfyrism. Why else would he keep you around?' Beshanie says.

My fingers run over the scar on my head, and a sly smile slips from my control as I remember how convinced Onnachild was that he could order me to save him from retribution. I won that battle. Beshanie focuses in on my movement and so I return to fiddling with the loose thread on the cushion.

'It's natural you'll want to make changes. What will you change first?' Nilola asks.

'The first thing I'd do is get rid of Eldini,' Beshanie says. 'Miserable little thing she is, like a ghastly shadow you can't shake off. She forgets how important it is to castle morale for us to dance and be well fed.'

'I wouldn't be sad to see her go,' Nilola says.

So Raen hasn't told her to leave. Yet. As far as they're aware. Will he do so after I've spoken to him? Part of me feels I should defend Eldini, but it seems disingenuous when I want her gone, too, so I give a non-committal answer. 'Nothing has been decided.'

'Is that what they are discussing?' Nilola asks Beshanie.

'They are certainly discussing something.' Her smirk draws me in. There's something she isn't telling me. 'For a week now those bells have been ringing. A week now Onnachild has been rotting in his room. He should have been buried days ago so what's holding it up?' She sits back, crosses her arms under her bosom. It seems she knows more but has decided not to tell me. Perhaps if I ask the right question ...

'The sooner it's over the sooner we can get back to normal.' Nilola tugs at her bun and wrinkles her nose.

'What is normal though?' Beshanie asks.

Nilola groans and puts her hand to her forehead, mocking a swoon. 'Praying and praying and starving and ... ugh.' She screws up her face.

'You don't approve of the changes?' I ask.

'Did I not tell you I was bored?' she moans, and then her smile returns.

'Eldini.' Beshanie spits out the name. 'She wants the castle to go back to when the True Queen, Second Queen, whatever you want to call her, was alive. I won't go back to those times.'

'They were dull,' Nilola says. 'I shall die if we have to go back to those times.'

'Indeed.' Beshanie slides off her chair. Her eyes have lost their sparkle. 'And I will not marry Perkin.'

I laugh. I can't help myself. Even though Beshanie flinches, I keep laughing. They are so transparent and shallow, wanting only good times and loose men.

'Don't laugh at me,' Beshanie shouts.

I press my mouth against the cushion but my shoulders still shake. What a shock they'll have when I'm queen. If I'm queen.

'Why are you laughing?' Nilola asks.

'I don't know why you're laughing.' Beshanie thrusts her face at mine. There are pink patches on her cheeks, not quite a flush. 'After what you've been doing with Raen, you're no better. You just haven't been caught.'

I stop laughing and pull the cushion closer. The corner pokes into my chest, hurting my breast. Beshanie rises. She weaves past a beech table, an oak dresser, and steps over a blonde wig on her way to the window. 'I thought that would shut you up. Yes, I know about that.'

'Me too,' Nilola says.

'Why do you think she pretended to be so enamoured with him?' Beshanie shunts over a glass heart so she can perch on the windowsill. Light flashes at me. Blinding. I shield my eyes with my arm so I can see Nilola, check whether Beshanie is telling the truth.

'Vill told me to.' Her chin is up high and she looks pleased with the trick she has played as she fluffs out her sleeves. 'But Raen is rather pleasing to the eye so it was easy, and I'm sure he'd be even more pleasing if that crown was on his head.'

'Where's your loyalty?' Beshanie snaps.

Nilola regards her fingernails.

'It was stupid of him to think he'd ever be king,' Beshanie says. 'The King didn't like him. The King never liked him. Why would he change his mind just because he was dying?'

The sunlight is blinding again and I can't tell if Beshanie is dazzling me on purpose so I can't think. Nothing makes sense, and I'm not sure if it's because I'm too tired to think straight. I wave my hand as if the questions forming are flies in front of me. Beshanie picks up the heart, rests it in her lap, and the sunlight's no longer flashing. She's tapping her fingernail against it in time with that faint clang of the bells. It reminds me. *The King is dead. Take action.* I need to find out about Raen and Eldini, and then go back to the Judging Room. 'It's been a pleasure—'

With the next tap of Beshanie's finger, I notice the solitary ring she's wearing. It's copper and has a phoenix on it. The beak is open, ready to call out. I try to check Nilola's fingers as they poke and prod at her bun. Slimmer than Beshanie's, her hand bears a copper phoenix, too. Are they Followers? Or pretending to be because they think I'll be victorious? Because it's the side Vill is on?

Does this mean the servant wearing the pendant with the Aegnian symbol for fire was not a coincidence? As I look around the room expecting to find her here, I remember another servant. Irises with the faintest green tint in the hazel. Has Vill been gathering them or were they here already? My gaze settles on Beshanie cradling the glass heart. 'I understand it's a lot to take in.' Her voice is full of sympathy which confuses me further.

'Do you need some wine?' Nilola stands.

My mind is too muddled to even answer that simple question. I listen to her skirts swishing against the floor as my focus remains on Beshanie. She poses, expecting to be admired, and the pose is reminiscent of Vill's when he first appeared in the village. There are similarities to him in her face, too: the long and thin nose, her pouting lips, and if she was thinner. But she ... I picture her fingers digging into his thigh, rising higher and higher, stopped only by his hand. Is no one and nothing in the castle what they seem to be?

Nilola nudges my fingers with a goblet. 'So, what is he like?'

'Who? What?' My fingers open to take it.

'Who do you think?'

Beshanie shakes her head at Nilola's question but her stare is as inquisitive and she steps nearer.

'Tell us everything.' Nilola rests her hand on my knee. My gaze darts from her phoenix ring to her brooch with Onnachild's profile, from Nilola to Beshanie, both of them with confusing smiles. 'The mating. What was he like? Raen.'

My cheeks heat despite my mind grappling with my questions. I came here wanting answers, not more questions. Eldini. Raen. Followers.

'There's no need for false modesty now,' Beshanie says.

'Come on.' Nilola squeezes my knee. 'Is it good? Is he good? As good as his half-brother?'

'Good enough to keep now he's served his purpose?' Beshanie asks.

I shake my knee free of Nilola's touch and shift away from their leers.

'Well?' Beshanie takes another step nearer, rests her arms on the top of a chair shaped like a shield. 'Him or Gavin or Vill?'

'You can tell us,' Nilola says.

'If you tell us, we'll tell you what you came here to find out.' Beshanie settles into the chair. 'You didn't come here because you were bored, and it's not a social visit because you've never liked us. It's not hard to guess why you're here.' She takes off her brooch and leans behind her to drop it on a table.

'I ... No one,' I say to give some answer.

Beshanie snorts. Nilola's lips quirk. It's obvious they don't believe me. I take a deep breath, try to call Niah from the Aegni into my spine, into the plains of my face. She feels so far away, though, drowning in my confusion. These women. Raen. Eldini. Her baby.

'If you don't want Raen—well, can I have him?' Nilola purrs.

Her question makes me bristle and scowl. I direct it at a clump of blonde wigs in the corner of the room but not quickly enough and so the women snigger.

'Raen hasn't been with her.' Nilola squirms, seemingly overcome with the pleasure of passing on the gossip. 'Not like that, anyway. He can barely stand to look at her. After the King died, that first night he went to her rooms and just sat there. A servant brought food, wine, and he just sat there as Eldini went on and on in that way she has, and he got more and more tense until he bolted up, almost knocking over the servant trying to give him a goblet of wine, and out he went. Out. I presumed he was going to you. Did he?'

I don't answer.

'Isn't that what you wanted to find out?' Beshanie asks. 'Why you came to visit us?' They both sit there with self-importance keeping their spines straight, their smiles smug, and a haughty tilt to their noses. Despite those phoenix rings, I can't trust these women. Why did I think I could? I want to see the servant, see eyes that bear a trace of the Aegni. Eyes I can trust.

'I want to speak with one of your servants.'

'Why?' Nilola sounds offended.

'I thought you might,' Beshanie says. 'The one with the council seal or the one with the green eyes?'

'The eyes.'

'She's working in the sewing room right now.'

'The sewing room?'

'I forget, you never had your village woman sent there. Third hallway and the fifth door along. There's a carving of a stack of wood on the door.'

'If you need us ...' Nilola says as I rise from my seat.

'Yes, when you need us,' Beshanie says.

A hundred brown faces rise from their sewing to stare at me. A few smile. Others remain blank. The dresses they are working on are either silver or green. The colours make it seem like spring is being held captive in this room. Beshanie's servant gets to her feet, suggesting she was expecting me. Her smile is cheeky, bunching up her face and making her eyes tiny slots. We leave the room together, shut the door, and I guide her towards the long window and the copper sunlight. Her irises are greener than I remember. I clutch her arms tighter than I probably should.

'Who are your family?' I whisper.

'Does it matter? They're dead now.'

'Onnachild?'

'No, he didn't kill them. They died old, in their sleep.'

'Your eyes, though.'

'A distant relative was from the Aegni bloodline.'

I let go of her and bump back into the wall, the old wall built by the Aegni, and run my palm over its rough surface. The floor is uneven and sandy-coloured. I slip a shoe off so I can feel it beneath me. Here the bells are loud but they sound joyous.

'Congratulations.' She bows low, speaking in a whisper.

'It's a little early for that,' I mumble.

She straightens herself, and it's so obvious she isn't a servant. Her bearing is far too confident and her body too well fed. 'How have people not realised you aren't a servant?'

'People see what they want to see. You as a castle woman and me a lowly servant.' She prods her puffed-up chest. 'I'll be happy to be of service to you, though, and tomorrow I will be.'

Tomorrow? There's so much to ask her, so many questions that I can't seem to begin. I press my fingers into my temples and rub at the tension there, hoping to form one but the only one forthcoming is so unimportant compared to the rest. 'Where are you from?'

'Aralltir. There's more of us coming. Didn't Vill tell you?'

I can't remember what Vill has told me. Merchants, Aralltir, Followers. Raen. I shake my head to be free of those words, to focus. 'There's another servant. She has a council seal.' I tap my chest, hitting the onyx pendant hanging there. 'How many are there? More?'

She nods. 'Yes. Vill's put her with the Maidens, and there's another with Eldini. Has been for a while. But there are more than that. You'll see tomorrow.'

'Tomorrow? You mentioned tomorrow already. What's happening tomorrow? Why are you making those dresses?'

'For the Judging. Everyone is desperate to show their allegiances. We've been working on them for days now.'

'Judging? Vill said they were deciding about Onnachild's body.'

'That's part of it, I suppose. But a successor must be decided on. Everyone will be there. Tomorrow both claims will be heard. It's all a formality, a show judging.'

I lunge towards her. 'A show judging? Wait. What does that mean? What will happen?'

'I don't know. I'm not from here.' She stares down at where my hands are gripping her arms again. 'That's what Vill called it.'

I let go, apologise, and lean against the window. The sun heats my face and makes me squint.

'Ask him. He has some nice tricks up those fancy sleeves of his. I'm waiting to find out what my role will be. Whatever it is, I'm sure I'll enjoy it.' She bows, breaking the line of the sun, and then turns towards the sewing room.

Not tomorrow. I need to speak to Raen first. I need to tell him. 'No, wait. Please. I have more questions.'

She looks over her shoulder at me. What was it? I slap my forehead. There are too many, so many. Tomorrow. Tomorrow is too soon. I caress my churning stomach, and I remember. 'Eldini?'

'Why do you want to know about her?'

'That doesn't matter. Tell me, what are the servants saying about their marriage?'

She ushers me into a long shadow where the walls exude a chill that gets into my bones and makes me shiver. The sun is so far away, brightening up the stone floor. 'A more stupid woman I've never met,' she whispers. 'She suspects nothing. Their marriage contract hasn't been discussed, and no one has heard her cry about losing him or being sent away.'

Why does that cause a painful pang in my chest? He's not told her yet. It doesn't mean he won't once I've spoken to him. His dishevelled appearance was proof he hasn't been with her, and Nilola confirmed it. He's not had a chance to tell her he shouldn't have married her, but he will when he's finished in the Judging Room. Then he'll come to me ... but his eyes blazed with hate when they met mine. I grimace but his name still slips from my mouth. 'Raen?'

Her shoulders twitch.

'Why do you care about him? He shouldn't have that throne. He doesn't deserve it. You know that. I know that and the castle knows that. No one likes him; they just pretended to because Vill told them to. Raen will find that out tomorrow.'

Tomorrow. The phoenix jewellery. A Judging. Winter still here; spring doesn't seem to be coming. The sun moving and turning the walls copper. Bells ringing. The King is dead, and nothing is what it seems. I can't form any more questions, nor can I reach out to keep the servant with me while I try to find the words, and so she ducks into the sewing room. I'm left wondering when Eldini conceived, but the reason why that matters has completely left me. Slumping down to the floor, I cradle my belly and let my confusion take over as I shiver in the chill shadow.

Chapter Sixty-Six

VILL ALMOST DROPS THE TORCH he's holding when I step from the dark alcove by his rooms, but he's quick to hide his surprise with a smile. 'I was just about to go and see you.'

'Really? When?'

'What has got you so peevish? You can't still be upset about earlier?'

'I went to the sewing room. I spoke to a servant, a servant with green eyes.'

He shakes his head. His smile doesn't falter.

'Don't play dumb, Vill. Why didn't you tell me?'

'About? Ah ... the Judging.'

'Yes, I've heard about tomorrow, and from a servant. A servant. I told you to wait. What part of waiting don't you understand?'

He tries to step past me but I'm quicker, grabbing his tunic by the collar, and pulling him to me. He'll not evade my questions this time.

He'll look me in the eye and tell me the truth. 'Why didn't you wait? He's grieving.'

'Please. Raen's not grieving. That's what he wants you to think. Now get your hands off me. This is not how a queen behaves.'

'It's just as well I'm not queen, then, isn't it?' I release him.

He yanks down his tunic and smooths out the imprint from my grip. 'This is not the right time to be having disagreements in a hallway.' He leans around me, unlocks his door, and then pushes it open. 'After you.' He gestures for me to enter with an exaggerated bow.

It's a cold room more opulent and sparkly than Onnachild's. Cleaner and less cluttered than Beshanie's. Blue twilight makes the many paintings on his wall ghostly: scenes of wispy maidens and mountains and men who resemble Vill. He shuts the door. 'You should be thanking me, not manhandling me.'

'Thanking you? Thanking you for what?'

He saunters to a silver-topped table where there's a silver tray and a cluster of jewelled goblets gathered around a jug. He takes off his rings, dropping them one by one onto the tray. The clank of them hitting sets my teeth on edge, but I suppress my winces and keep scowling at him.

'You know you look a lot like Raen right now,' he says. 'I always thought his disagreeableness came from Onnachild, perhaps it came from his Aegni side.'

'Vill ... Tomorrow.'

'Yes, yes.' He ambles over to his patterned curtains. 'I tried to waylay the proceedings as per your instructions, but these matters are not solely up to me, despite what you might think.'

'It had to have been you.'

'Why did it have to be me? Why not Raen?' He closes the curtains before lighting a candle which illuminates the golden suns embroidered on the silk material. 'No, it wasn't me. The advisers and Raen are keen to see matters settled as soon as possible, and they can be very persuasive. I found myself agreeing with them. Besides, it's a formality, nothing more. We all know Onnachild promised the throne to you.'

'If I eased his passing. If I anointed him into Adfyrism.'

'I told Aesc you had.' He shakes the curtains, smoothing out the pleats so they match.

'Raen will contest it.'

'He already has, and how the advisers tore him apart for it.' He lifts the single candle and takes it to a free-standing candelabra with vast stems that curve like ivy from the corner of the room. 'Sit.' He gestures at two chairs by a fireplace carved with dancing creatures. 'We shall talk. Wine?'

'No, I don't want any wine.' I sit in the chair made of yew with a green velvet seat and padded back. 'Why didn't you tell me?' I press my cheek against the wood to take strength from the sacred tree and watch as he pours wine into a goblet knobbly with emeralds.

'It was only decided after you left us.'

'Don't lie to me, Vill.'

'I wouldn't lie to you, and I'm hurt you'd think I would.'

'Then why did the servant say they've been preparing for it for days. I saw the dresses.'

'The castle women want to look their best, it's inevitable. You don't need to be a fortune teller to realise there will be a new ruler. Besides, gossip travels fast.' His hand trails over the top of my chair. Without his rings, his fingers are less elegant and his knuckles are bony. 'Perhaps I should have told you the Judging was a possibility, but I didn't want you to worry unnecessarily. I know you aren't sleeping. You do believe me, don't you?'

I shrug.

'When have I ever lied to you?' He sits in the chair beside mine and takes off his fancy shoes. His feet are long and slender, perfectly moulded, and I'm reminded of the first night I saw him and how like a memorial he looked. I didn't trust him fully then, but he helped me into the castle, brought Followers from Aralltir, helped me to see Ammi by distracting the nursemaid. Yes, he's been deceitful. Yes, he wears these masks as he tries to please and play the castle people, and yet, he's always been honest with me about that. With everything that's coming, I have no choice but to trust him. 'Onnachild promised it to Raen. The throne. As he was dying.'

'You know this for certain?' He pivots to face me, his goblet perched on his knee.

I nod.

'Raen didn't mention this. Who told you?'

'Melody.'

'Who else was there?'

'No one.'

'Even at the end.' Vill shakes his head but there's admiration in his voice. 'Well, we'll just have to prove to the castle there's absolutely no way this could possibly be true, won't we? Shouldn't be too difficult. There are things we'll need to say that you might not like, though; please be ready for that.'

'Such as?'

'Raen will be discredited, simple as that.'

'Discredited?'

Vill sips at his wine and rubs the emeralds. 'We might need to remind the castle of some old rumours. The First Queen's infidelity. The edict declaring him a bastard.'

The words of her letter return: *how hard these days and nights are without you here. I only exist until I see you again.* As they do, so does the burn of Raen's hate. How much worse will that be if I hurt him further by reminding him of these things? 'I can't. I do have some principles.'

'It wouldn't please me to raise them either but if we must, then we must.' He swirls his goblet as he stares into it. 'Niah, I know what you're capable of. Raen knows what you're capable of. Please, don't disappoint me. I've worked so hard to get you here. There's no need to discuss Raen anymore. Your feelings towards him have no bearing on what comes next.' He peers at me. 'Isn't that the reason you wanted me to wait? So you could speak to Raen?'

'No,' I lie. As the word lingers, I notice the bells have stopped. The King is still dead, though, and I still don't have my answers. Why am I wasting time here with Vill? I dart out of the chair.

'I do hate being the one to tell you this.' His speech is measured, warning.

I pause. 'What?'

'I didn't think you'd be quite so naïve.' He leans forwards and pats the seat of the chair I vacated. I don't sit but I do wrap my fingers around the smooth, yew back.

'He has played you. Do you really believe he's fallen in love with you? Did he tell you he has? He isn't. He knows how to play this game. Look at how he behaves with Eldini, with Nilola. Ask yourself this, if he loved you, then why has he not already set aside Eldini?'

I flinch from the words I don't want to believe, don't want to hear. My body believes them, though, with my stomach lurching like I've tripped. 'It's not because of him.'

'How strange that you took so much persuading to lie with Raen and now you're besotted with him.'

'I'm hardly besotted.'

'Call it what you want.' He rubs at his fingers as though expecting the rings to still be there. 'You have no reason to be loyal to him.'

My hand goes to my belly to settle the churning there, and it reminds me why I owe him my loyalty. The press of my palm turns into a caress. I remove it before Vill notices the gesture.

'He wants you to feel guilty,' Vill says. 'Because if you do, you'll step aside for him. Because he's a master at manipulation. What do you think he was doing all those years he was banished from the castle? The same as you: planning how he'd get the throne.'

As I sink into the chair, I remember Raen's hair splayed across my lap when I read to him from the Aegnian book, our book. I remember Raen defending me in the Judging Room, and how I felt like bait waived before the noble bear. And then, with the heat of shame, I remember what Vill wanted me to do: seduce Raen so he'd do my bidding. It wasn't a sophisticated plan. It was an obvious one, so why wouldn't Raen do the same? I want to trust him but Vill's right: Eldini is still here. And if he cared for me, really cared for me, then she wouldn't be. He hasn't even been to see me.

'Please don't dwell on it.' There's sympathy on Vill's face and it makes me feel stupid. 'I just don't want there to be any nasty surprises tomorrow. We need you to be strong and proud and remember where you came from.' Then he smiles, a kind one that implies he does understand. 'And after it's settled and you are queen, well if it makes you happy, you can have Raen bound and gagged at your feet.' He laughs.

I force myself to smile in reply.

'Why are you not happy? You are so hard to please,' he teases. 'Onnachild gave the throne to you, I heard and the advisers heard. Don't feel guilty about Raen; after all, don't you think if Onnachild had wanted Raen as his heir he'd have declared it months ago? Everyone knows that father and son were at odds with each other.'

'Easier said than done,' I mumble, staring into the unlit fire. 'Don't discredit the First Queen.'

'If that's what you want.'

'It's what I want.'

'It's decided then. We'll let the advisers take the lead. They've always hated Raen.'

It doesn't make me feel better, only more tired and desperate for tomorrow to be over. I curl my legs up onto the chair, press them against my stomach. As I do, I wonder how Raen has kissed my body and yet not noticed my breasts and belly swelling. He must have realised. He just doesn't care.

There's a knock at Vill's door and when he goes to answer it, I slide off my chair to light the fire. If only I had my herbs with me so I could call the future into the flames. The desire is a dull pang in my chest and I understand Eldini's reasoning now. Love, she wanted me to confirm, and here I am hoping, wanting, the same. I laugh bitterly at my foolishness.

'About time,' Vill says to the person at the door.

Mantona mumbles at him, her sad tone draws my attention. She's dressed in black and her cheeks are mottled from tears.

'Niah,' she calls out as she darts over. She sinks to the floor beside me, taking up my hands into hers. Her rings dig in. She searches my face, but I'm not sure what she's trying to find. In hers, I see only sorrow. There's no guilt and surely there should be because she hid that covenant and without it ...

'Who'd have predicted he'd return to Adfyrism?' she says. 'I always knew in his heart he was sorry.'

'Sorry?' I say. 'He wasn't sorry. He was scared.'

'His end, was it peaceful?' Mantona asks.

'You know how it ended.' Vill bangs the door shut. 'I told you before, and peaceful is not a word I'd use to describe it.'

'I want to hear from Niah.'

A part of me wants to lie to her and let her remember him as the strong, handsome man he was when she first saw him. 'I wasn't there.' I break away from her to poke the fire and avoid her scrutiny. The flames are molten gold tonight. 'In the end, he had the Maidens there, and they prayed to that God. He gave the throne to Raen.'

'People will say anything when they're scared,' Mantona says.

'People will say anything when they're a devious old man,' Vill says.

'If you're going to be rude, then I need wine,' she snaps at him.

While Vill's getting her a drink, she shuffles closer and takes the poker from me. She disturbs the wood, making it crackle, and the sound blocks out her whisper, forcing me to lean closer. 'Raen's in the Judging Room. You love him, don't you? He doesn't know, does he? Tell him. Stop this before it's too late. He wants you, too. He's just hurt.' She peeps over her shoulder to check Vill's still distracted.

How can Raen not know? It was in every caress, every kiss, every lingering glance. My body kept no secrets from him. 'He does know.'

'Did you tell him?'

I shake my head.

She laughs, softly, and it contains a hint of longing. 'Men are clever with some things and as stupid as a newborn baby with others. He won't know. Don't make the same mistake I did.'

Vill returns and is passing her a goblet before I can ask what she'd have done differently. She takes a sip and nods her thanks. As he sits down, she whispers, 'Go to him.'

I can't move though, not even when she rises and nudges my shoulder. What would I have done differently? That long walk with my heels blistering? Mating with Raen? Calling the gods in?

As Mantona and Vill argue about Onnachild, Vill's earlier accusations echo in my mind: Raen doesn't love me, Raen played the game, Raen had no intention of setting Eldini aside. It was a trick to get me to pick him instead of the throne. Already, he's manipulated my feelings for him so I'd agree to ease Onnachild's passing, go against my ancestors. Vill is right. Thank the gods, I haven't humiliated myself by telling Raen.

I poke the logs, ash fluttering out from the fireplace onto my dress. It resembles the dust from the forgotten graves and it reminds me ... has me picturing Raen in the tub. His body giving itself to my care, trusting me. Those moles I found on his shoulder which he probably doesn't even realise are there. Something inside tells me Vill's wrong. My heart? My stomach or is it somewhere even deeper than that?

Mantona calls my name. I turn and smile at her as I remember standing under Eldini's window, watching that linen, missing Raen. Numb. Cold. Asleep. *I only exist until I'm with you again.* Is that what the First Queen meant? Was I in love with Raen then? When did the plot to get him to do my bidding turn into something else? But, it wasn't a plot. Not for me. It never was. It was lust. Need. Does it matter what it was? It's something different now.

Mantona shouts my name. I turn around.

'Aren't you tired?' she asks, surreptitiously gesturing towards the door with her goblet.

'What's distracting you so much tonight?' Vill asks. 'Can I help?'

'I was thinking of the village,' I lie. 'How my grandmother said it used to be ... before Onnachild.'

'You've no idea how much I want those days back, too.' There's a wistfulness to his voice that's never been there before. 'My methods may seem callous but please, believe me, all I want to do is restore this land to those glory days.' He sits beside me on the floor.

Mantona's shaking her head behind him and pointing towards the door.

'It broke my father's heart when Onnachild lost the sea,' he says.

'Did it?' I mumble. 'You never talk about your family.'

'What good would it do?' He stares into the flames, leaning closer to their warmth. 'Now we're so close to achieving our ambitions, though, I find him in my thoughts more and more. He was an odd little man, never happier than when he was setting out to sea.'

'Is that what you intend to do once this over?' I ask. 'Set sail?'

'I intend for us to get it back and never lose it again.' He squeezes and rubs his bare index finger. The fire picks out slight imperfections in his face: faint lines around his eyes, a bump on his chin, how his full lips are not quite symmetrical. 'Do you find yourself thinking more about your grandmother?'

'Yes,' I say, but it's Raen I'm imagining. Him sitting alone in the Judging Room, dreading tomorrow as much as I am. It's not Vill I want to be with tonight, not his memories I want to share, not his intentions I care for. Should I go to Raen? Should I tell him? The words weigh heavy on my shoulders and I want them off, but will they make any difference?

'Shouldn't you be trying to get some rest?' Mantona asks me, nodding towards the door. 'Tomorrow is going to be an exhausting day.'

I told Nessia I wanted Raen and yet here I am doing nothing to get him. My hand strokes the ash off my velvet dress. The material is not as luscious as his skin, and the firelight isn't as captivating as his eyes, even with that hatred in them. I rise onto my knees. Telling him could change tomorrow. It might get rid of that hatred. Has my transformation been so complete that I've truly become a castle woman, unable to tell a man how I feel? No. I am Niah from the Aegni.

I use the excuse Mantona has given me.

Chapter Sixty-Seven

'HAVE YOU COME TO GLOAT?' Raen asks, walking away and leaving the Judging Room door wide open. I'm tempted to turn around and retreat to my rooms, wait out the night there like a coward. He weaves amongst the many chairs crammed into tight lines, knocking several out of their row. Tomorrow is getting nearer and nearer, and those chairs make it more real, so I take a deep breath and close the door behind me.

'I need to talk to you.'

'What can we possibly have left to say to each other?' The coldness in his voice has me wishing for his anger. I chase after him towards the throne, tripping over chair legs.

'Melody told me what happened in Onnachild's chamber and ...' My gaze lowers to his knuckles wrapped around the head of a phoenix. They're covered in scabs and raw skin, suggesting he's been picking at them.

He stretches out his fingers. 'Why didn't you tell me that Onnachild offered you the throne?'

'Who told you that?'

'Does it matter who? What matters is that you didn't.' His brow lowers, trying to hide his emotions from me, only I know him now and he can't hide anything from me anymore. I see hurt and confusion in the way he leans on the throne, in the strain of his fingers over the phoenix, in the twitching of his jaw. And I caused it. I reach towards his jaw, to soothe it, but he bashes my hand away.

'He did, but Raen, that's not important. We need to talk about what we do next ... now he's ... gone.'

'I'd say what we're going to do is pretty obvious, isn't it?' He gestures towards the chairs. 'They're going to delve into everything. All our secrets will be exposed, all our wrongdoings. I hope you're ready for it.'

'Stop ... Raen. This isn't what I wanted to talk about. There are—'

'I always knew it would come to this, the first day I saw you and yet ... yet it still surprises me. Why is that?' He straightens up. 'No, don't bother answering.'

'I told Vill to wait. Wait until—'

'You didn't tell him to stop, though, did you? What difference does it make whether these things are spoken tomorrow or next month or next season? They will still be said.'

I strain across the table to touch the phoenix and place my hand beside his. The corner of the table digs into my hip. He slides his hand forwards encasing the phoenix's emerald eye so there's no space for my hand. 'What were you waiting for?'

'You, Raen.'

'Me?' His knuckles pop out, red and angry. I get a glimpse of the phoenix's eye, as small as the green dots in his irises. 'And what were you hoping I would do? Give up my claim?'

'Please, just let me speak. I don't want to talk about that.'

'No? Then what did you come here to talk about?'

'Us.'

His grip loosens on the throne. For a moment our eyes meet and the coldness leaves his. Does he know what I want to say? What I'm trying to say? My heart speeds, racing towards the uncertain outcome. My mouth dries. I need to touch him, need his skin against mine in order to have the courage to say those three words. I gulp and wrap my hands in my skirts, too fearful of rejection to attempt touching him again. His fingers twitch. Can he sense my urge to hold them, press them to my lips?

'Go on then.' His voice is a low rumble that echoes through the room, through me.

I want to tell him. The words are swelling up from my chest but they catch in my mouth. My face is getting hot with them. My lips want to feel the shape of them. Why can't I say them? He's moving away from me, pulling out the throne. If I could kiss him, that would show him.

'Raen.'

He pauses.

When I don't speak, he sighs. He looks tired. Tired and haunted. I've done this to him, but I can fix it.

'I love you.' It comes out mumbled and flat, not joyous as it should. I duck my head, scared to see his reaction play across his face. He's silent. Has he not heard? Can I take the words back? There's no relief from having said them. The words linger there between us like the curl of smoke coming from the solitary candle on the table.

Then he laughs. It's forced and bitter. 'And all this time I thought it was the throne.'

My gaze jumps up to him. His smile is off, lopsided, and doesn't reach his eyes. 'Don't joke with me, not now.'

'I'm not joking.' He settles into the throne. 'Remember before, the eve of my wedding, I asked you and you said no. Remember that? I was drunk but I remember. So I ask, at what point did you realise you ...' his jaw twitches, 'had these feelings for me? Was it after my father died? Niah, just leave.'

I surge towards him, for one last try. My hands settle on his thighs and although the muscle tenses he doesn't shake me off. 'No, not until, not until you believe me. Raen. I do. I—'

He covers my mouth with his palm. 'Don't. It's too late to try this tactic, so let's not pretend anymore. I think I'd rather face the Judging.'

I push his hand away, try to catch his fingers but they fight free. 'Tactic? No, Raen, I do. Raen, I need—'

He slaps the table. Never has he looked so much like Onnachild as he does at this moment. His jaw is so tight and square, the twitch there pulsing dangerously fast, and his nostrils are flaring, but beyond that anger is hurt. I know. I recognise it because he's shown me this before. The Raen that cries in my arms, that trembles from my touch and lets me care for him, that is the man I need to get through to. I've never wanted that man more than I do now, even as he growls at me. 'I have had to sit here and listen to all my shortcomings as my father saw it. Hear how much he hated me and adored my half-brother. Hear how incompetent he thought me. And, tomorrow, I'll hear all that again and everyone in the castle will, too. That is your doing. So if that is how you show your love ... Love. You throw that word around until it means nothing. If you love me, prove it. Stop tomorrow from happening. Renounce your claim.'

'I can't. Don't ask that of me.'

'Yet you want me to?' He darts up.

'No, Raen. I'm not talking—'

'Here then, try it. If you want the throne so badly.' He catches my wrists, yanks them high above me so I'm on my tiptoes as he swings me towards the throne. He slams me into it, looms over me, legs on either side and arms taut as he clasps the phoenixes. I can't tell what is thrilling my body more, his closeness or the power emanating from the throne. My palms slide over the wood, down the arms to the smooth bulbs at the end. My fingers spread wide. It cradles me, made for my body. The wood is strong and solid behind me, and it gives me the courage I need. I sit up, reach for his cheek. 'You love me too?'

He jolts into the table. His face, unguarded for a moment, says he does. That he wants to, but then it's gone and he's breathing hard and heavy again as if he's trying to call back his anger.

'You said you shouldn't have married Eldini,' I remind him, hoping it prompts other memories of that night, how he came to me, needing me, trusting me.

'Are we back to this?' He speaks calmly. Too calmly. He's acting the prince when I want him to be the man who shares an Aegnian side with me. 'I said many things. You have said many things. Vill has told me many things. About your plan.'

My mouth gapes open. 'No.' He shuts it with a rough touch that hurts my chin, and then grips the phoenixes again, trapping me between his arms. 'My father might have thought me stupid, but I'm not stupid enough to love you. In the graveyard, I saw you for what you were. I've always seen you for what you are. And like you, I am a liar. Now listen carefully because I'm not saying it again. I don't want you. I never wanted you. I want Eldini. I love Eldini.'

Despite how his words smart, I manage to keep staring up at him, at the face I thought I knew as well as my own. Mantona was wrong. I was wrong, and I've made a fool of myself. The humiliation burns as I realise I never knew this castle version. This version? I laugh and the sound makes him bristle but not retreat. This is the real him and I did see it. It's who he was in the graveyard when he tossed those coins at me. It's who he was when he told me I was his whore, when he used me to assert himself against Onnachild. But there's lust in his eyes. He did want me and he wants me still. I'll show him he can't lie about that and I'll leave with some pride at having him still panting after me.

My arms squeeze up between his arms. My fingertips skim over his lips, then his jawline as my knee brushes up his inner thigh, higher and higher, all the way up. He tenses when I press it against his crotch and rub. I can feel how much he wants me. I can see him trying to stifle a moan. 'You are not a good liar.'

When I go to lower my knee, he pins it there with a biting grip. 'And if I'm lying?' The growl of his voice is at odds with his eyes which show something pleading, something vulnerable and tender. They scrutinise me for an answer. His breath is held. His fingers are digging into my thigh. He is a liar. We both are. I realise that now. This pain in my chest is just pretending to be my heart breaking, because there's nothing left of my heart after Aelius died and Ammi was taken. It's really anger and embarrassment and disgust at myself because his words, this pretence, has me realising there's no one I've lied to more than myself. Lust is not love, Nessia said, but I wanted this to be something more noble, more excusable than desire for a quick tumble. It's a wry smile that comes to my lips and it makes Raen back away, slightly, enough that I no longer feel his breath. Yes, he's played a good game, but it isn't over yet.

'You were right,' I say. 'I don't love you.'

He punishes me with a kiss, so sudden, so hard that my head bangs against the throne. Well, I can punish him, too. And so I don't cry out or twist my head away, I grab his hair as if I own it and tug him to me. We fight with kisses and bites, with cruel hands that scratch and grab. We tear clothes. He will not be free of me, and I will not be free of him. We struggle into each other, arms and legs hitting, batting as we entwine with the throne and each other. Tomorrow our bodies will bear bruises and we'll continue this fight with words.

Chapter Sixty-Eight

'DID YOU SEE VILL?' Nessia asks, looking up from her sewing when I burst into my rooms. I kick my shoes off at the wall and slam the door behind me. The cold floor against my soles doesn't cool my anger.

'Yes. And Raen.'

'I take it things didn't go well?'

'What gives you that impression?' I snap, in no mood for her teasing. My dress is ruined, the right sleeve hanging by a single thread, a strong one that refuses to break when I tug on it. 'I told him I loved him.' The words disgust me.

'About time.'

'He didn't believe me.'

She laughs and shakes her head. I yank my sleeve again, satisfied by that final thread breaking. How could I have told him I loved him? 'What are they going to say tomorrow?' I throw my sleeve towards the table, grimacing when it knocks over a goblet. 'Nessia, there are so many secrets.'

'You and Raen?'

The pairing of the words brings back the burn of shame to my face, and the way I limp to the fire doesn't help. I stab the logs with a long poker. Wafts of white ash float out onto my feet, and I shake them off. Nessia levers herself up with the arms of the chair, and I watch as she ambles over to the table, rights the goblet and picks up my sleeve.

'Did you tell him about the baby?'

I stroke my belly, burdened and stretched, and shake my head.

'I think you'll be surprised by his response.' She settles down, my sleeve in her lap.

'Really? Why? What do you think he's going to do? Step aside, offer me the throne with a bow and a kiss as he waves Eldini off?' Exactly what I thought would happen, and not because of the baby, but because he loved me. The bitterness in my voice annoys me more than my stupidity.

'What happened when you said you loved him?'

'I told you, he didn't believe me.'

'How did he react, though?'

'Not how you're hoping.' I shove the ash across the floor, covering my toes in its whiteness.

'Sometimes words are not needed.'

I remember that short, unguarded moment when his expression ... when I thought ... how could I have taken that as a sign? Hope flutters again in my chest, briefly. I thump at it—the emotion is little more than a piece of half-chewed food stuck. That foolishness is what got me in this position, with child, humiliating myself. I glance at Nessia. She smiles and there's a glint in her eyes. 'I should bang your heads together.'

'You say that like we could stop this.'

'You could. Either one of you could say no and let the other have it, but that's not in your nature any more than it's in his.'

'And disappoint my grandmother? Let down Aelius and Ammi?' I grumble. 'I'm too tired for this.'

'You should change before you do anything else.' She smirks and nods at the tear in the bodice of my dress. Damn Raen. I've so few dresses that fit and tomorrow I need to appear queenly, regal, conceal this mound of growing baby. Just as I'm pulling the material flush to my belly to check how much fatter I've grown, Melody comes scooting into the room. She halts. The door slips from her hand. Her frown is replaced by a wide smile that shows the gap in her front teeth.

'Oh, happy days,' Melody says. 'Two babies, Raen must be pleased.'

I let go of my dress and poke the fire again. 'I don't think it works like that.'

'Don't be grumpy. Be happy. A child is a joyous thing, and Grace will have a brother or sister. I always wanted a sister.'

'It'll be another bastard like she's a bastard, and it will have nothing just like she has nothing.'

'Niah!' Nessia snaps.

'But Raen will be so pleased. I've seen how he is with Eldini, so tender and caring, and so loving,' Melody says.

'And sleeping with me.' I glare over my shoulder at her. 'Where have you been, anyway?'

Her smile droops and her eyebrows rise as she glances at Nessia for reassurance.

'Ignore her.' Nessia picks up her sewing. 'She told Raen she loved him.'

Melody's smile returns. 'Ohhhhh.'

'No, not ohh.' I sink down into the chair and as I try to tug my dress around my legs, my foot goes through a tear. Nessia gets up and throws a fur at me. I do not curl it around my shoulders, but bring it to me in a hug and rest my face against the soft pelt.

'What did he say about the baby?' Melody asks Nessia.

'She didn't tell him. It's a secret.'

'And you will keep it secret,' I warn.

'Yes, but—'

'There is no but.' I glare at the flames. 'Now can we talk about something else?'

'What if you're wrong? Does Vill know? Did he say to keep it secret?'

'Not yet,' Nessia says. 'Niah needs to tell Raen first.'

'But when? Niah? When will you tell him?'

'Tomorrow,' I say to shut her up. I'm too tired to think about that. Tomorrow, I can't escape from it. I'll have to sit there before the castle people and face everything I've done. Will I feel guilty? Can I justify myself? The covenant with the gods, mating with Raen, deceiving Eldini. Gavin. I groan and hide in the fur.

'Tomorrow?' Melody's voice wobbles.

'What?' I lift my head. Her skin is pasty and one of her hands is balled up into her mouth. She stares at the floor.

'What?' I repeat. 'I don't have the patience for this.'

She jumps when Nessia chastises me for my tone.

'I'm sorry,' I say; the edge is still in my voice—I can't help that. 'It's been a hard day and tomorrow will be even worse. Please, tell me what's worrying you so I can go to bed.'

She nods but doesn't look up. 'Vill,' she mumbles onto her fist. 'He wants me to ... That's why I came here because I ... I mean, you wouldn't want me to do it, would you?'

I huff, and Nessia slaps the arm of my chair with the torn sleeve to keep me quiet. 'Go on.'

'He made me tell him about what happened, you know, when I was in the King's bedchamber, when he was dying and Vill wants me to say what happened but not what really happened. He told me what to say, and I said nothing but listened and nodded. I ran here and then I got all distracted by ...' She waves her hand my way. 'I shouldn't, should I? Lie, I mean. I have to say what I heard, the truth. And the King did make Raen his heir and is that not the way things should go?'

'Things are not that simple,' Nessia says.

Melody nods. 'I know that. But it's me that will make the castle decide, Vill said. And then everyone will be mad at me.'

'It is not your fault. It's Onnachild's fault,' I say. 'He should never have been king. This is Aegni land. My land.'

'He was king. Lark says he was ordained and chosen by God.'

'That God is not real,' Nessia says.

'He is real. I know He is. They tell me He is,' Melody shouts. Tears trickle down her cheek. 'And I can't lie. God knows, and He'll strike me like He did Onnachild and—'

'Dry your eyes. Say what you saw and heard,' I tell her. 'No lies. I'm done with lies. We fight fair.' I nestle my head into the bundle of fur, try to block out everything, muffle Melody's words but they still get through.

'Raen, what if, what if he thinks I've already lied ... and ... and when they call me to the Judging Room, how can I stand there against you? How can I stand there against Raen? Don't let Vill call me. Please, Niah. Don't let Vill. I can't say all those hateful things about Raen. I can't. I don't hate him. I like him—yes, he scowls a lot and can be grumpy but ... You love Raen and I like him. Oh, does Vill know? He wouldn't make me say those things if he knew, would he?'

'I'll tell Vill not to call you.' My lips brush the fur.

She seems soothed by my words, coming over to join me by the fire. Nessia drops lavender and chamomile into the flames to calm us. My eyelids lower but I fight against the sleepiness because of who I might meet in my dreams: Aelius, Raen. I can't bear to see either tonight. Tomorrow, I must get the throne for my ancestors, then there'll be fewer people I need to beg forgiveness from.

Chapter Sixty-Nine

I WISH NESSIA AND I HADN'T COME to the Judging Room so early. We're the only people here and the room is gloomy and oppressive, exactly as it was the first time I was here. The rows of chairs are still out of place from Raen knocking into them. I need other people to fill this room and chase out the memory of last night. Opening the windows has not helped. At least Onnachild's presence isn't lingering anymore. I smile wryly.

'Don't be anxious. Vill knows what he's doing.' Nessia picks lint off my black dress. 'All this waiting.' She drops the lint to the floor. 'Men always take so long to make a decision. It seems so simple to me.'

My gaze drifts to the throne. It looks smaller with the other chairs crammed into the room, too small to fit two people, yet it did. There's nothing to show what happened last night, only the half-burnt candle remains, but I keep seeing Raen and I struggling into the throne together. How could I have defiled it like that? Afterwards, he dismissed me like I was a servant.

'How are we feeling today?' Vill asks, sauntering into the room. He's flanked by the advisers, their greyness complementing his pale skin like diamonds dangling from a woman's ears. Aesc is carrying a thick, black book under his arm. They're grinning. I don't remember ever seeing them happy before. Ascelin bows at me and I'm not sure what unsettles me more, their grins or that bow. Under the table, Nessia and I clasp hands. Is the clamminess coming from me or her? I sit rigid.

'How about glad, excited, determined? There are some words I'd expect to hear from you this morning,' Vill says.

'I'm glad it'll be over soon,' Nessia says.

'Glad isn't the word I'd use,' I say.

Vill fluffs out his ostentatious sleeves. The gems sewn into the green material seem to draw in every speck of light in order to reflect it over the perfect angles of his face. 'Relieved then?'

'Not even relieved.' My gaze drifts to the throne again, remembering my head bashing against it in time to Raen's thrusts.

'Well, you look divine,' Vill says. 'I was right about the kohl.'

Nessia stops me touching the black lining my eyes, there to make the green stand out. Emerald-topped pins keep my hair back. I stare down at the faint pattern of feathers and flames on my dress, customised by Nessia from one of the First Queen's. These touches are meant to reinforce my link to the Aegni line and therefore the first rulers. Although the dress has been cleaned, I keep catching wafts of her scent: sage and death. Each waft has me wondering what she'd do if she were here. But she isn't. She got what she wanted.

The noise of castle people chattering and gossiping drifts in. I lean across the table towards Vill, my chest squashed against the flat wood. It hurts my breasts, reminding me of the bruise I found on my left one this morning. It's the shape of Raen's mouth. I frown as my gaze drifts once again to the throne. There isn't time to worry about that because castle people are making their way to the chairs.

'Vill.' I beckon for him to come closer. 'You remember what we talked about? What we will not do?'

'Of course. Though why, after last night, you still want to protect him, I'll never understand.'

'How do—'

Nessia tugs my hand, nods behind her. I don't need her to tell me Raen's entered because I feel his presence as surely as if he were breathing on the nape of my neck. His heavy footsteps and the delicate patter of Eldini beside him cause the castle people to hush. I'm grateful for the cage around my torso as it's keeping my spine straight and shoulders back and down. Without it I suspect I might crumple onto the table. Letting go of Nessia, my palms press against my middle to check that the cage is squashing it enough. What am I going to do about this now?

'Breathe,' Nessia whispers.

I take a short and shallow breath. Eldini and Raen ignore me as they take their seats opposite. She nods at the advisers who do her the courtesy of looking embarrassed, although that vanishes when Raen glowers at them. This version of him, banging his elbows on the table, resembles none of the Raens I've known.

Someone, perhaps Eldini, has cut his hair into the style of Onnachild's early years. It falls to his chin, smooth and thick, and curls under his jawline, enhancing the square shape of his face. A blunt fringe stops at his eyebrows, accentuating their thickness. They're drawn low, and his eyes have the determination of a man leading an army. He fixes them on me. I force myself to return his glare and remember my anger from last night. Snatches of our conversation run through my mind and a blush rises as I remember saying it. I love you. The words return to this room, as if they've been carried in on his skin.

I'm glad he didn't believe me. I'd rather that than ... He notices my embarrassment, I'm sure of that, though his expression doesn't change. The black velvet he's wearing gives him an imposing air, calling attention to the width of his chest and shoulders, the angles of his cheekbones, and the line of his jaw. Beneath that tunic are scratches from my nails, bites from my teeth, bruises from my hands. I sit up straighter.

Eldini presses close to him. Her luminescent face has gained weight and her arms are rounder, too; she's seems to have swelled overnight like dough. She tilts her head in response to my stare, giving her a puzzled air. I can't bear her pale, innocent eyes, still so trusting. What is she going to do, think, if it comes out about Raen and me? I direct my gaze beyond her to the blank wall.

The Maidens enter next, shuffling as a group of black and grey. Their headdresses tinkle in different pitches. Melody's face is puffy from crying, reminding me what I need to do. I try to get Vill's attention. His hands are clasped behind his back, making his sleeves stand out, and he sways back and forwards on his heels, smiling at everyone in the room. Nessia coughs and he looks over. I gesture for him. As he bends beside me, Raen scowls at us. I match it with one of my own. Vill keeps his smile.

'Don't call Melody,' I whisper to him. 'She doesn't want to be.'

He nods, but he's watching the door where more castle people are trying to squeeze into the room. They've put aside their mourning clothes and are dressed in either silver or green.

'Well, this is a better turnout than I expected,' Vill whispers. 'Silver for Raen and green for us.'

The flashes of green make the room seem ill and the silver brings a hardness like ice but not its chill to counteract the heat coming from these bodies. There's not enough room for everyone and so they spill into the hallway, jostling and moaning at each other. People are standing, squashed up against the chairs, the walls, even the unlit fireplace. I don't recognise a lot of these people and can't find Mantona amongst them.

I wish I could have worn green, too, and disregard this charade of mourning because it only reminds me of Aelius's death and with that, what I've done. Again, my gaze drifts to the throne. I dry my palms on my skirt. My left leg starts shaking, and no matter how much I tense it will not stop. Raen is unmoving.

'Close the door,' Ascelin barks out.

Aesc opens his book. Grumbles go through the crowd but the door closes. Instantly, the room shrinks and becomes stifling with body odour adding to the clash of flowery scents. No breeze is being blown in through the open windows. The heat is oppressive. I dry my palms on my skirt again and hope I still appear composed despite the sweat I can feel beading around my hairline. Nessia pats her forehead with her sleeve. I slip my shoes off to touch the cold floor and try to ignore the castle people crammed around me, but their gossip is loud and we're meant to hear it.

'Do we want one of those ruling again?'

'I always knew he was no good.'

'Poor Princess.'

What will they say when every secret is exposed? I hold in my stomach and check the bump with a quick sweep. Nessia leans closer, humming low and steady into my ear. It's a song from our village days, meant to remind me of that Niah, the one who was impervious to name-calling, impervious to hate, yet the castle has made me forget her. I can sense the disgust around me. I can see it when Raen's eyes meet mine. The left side of his lips rise, fall. He settles in his chair into a pose of arrogance and bored indifference, another fake princely pose.

'Silence!' Ascelin bellows.

Aesc slams the book onto the table. Eldini flinches. Gavin appears, ruffled and out of breath after having pushed his way through the crowd. She beams at him as he takes a seat beside her, turning it away from me. I will not worry about him or Eldini; after all, I made them no promises, and once I'm queen, they'll be gone. Whether Raen joins her is up to him. The people's chat fades and fades until there's only the sound of breathing, shuffling, and Aesc turning pages.

I focus on the second time I was here, facing Onnachild. How I had traced my fingers over the sturdy wooden table and experienced the thrill at touching something of my ancestors. I do it again, brushing the underside. Before Onnachild, the village had expert craftsmen, a forest of yews, and prosperity. Now it has nothing. These memories are what I'm fighting for, them and my ancestors. The table doesn't give me the same strength as it did that day. Have my ancestors deserted me now they've taken Onnachild?

'We are assembled to hear the claims.' Ascelin's voice is a loud boom around the room and the twang in it reminds me of Onnachild's. His words prompt more shuffling and whispering from the castle people. Vill's gaze sweeps around the room as he saunters to Aesc and the open book. His walk has such grace he could be dancing.

A few rows back, I spot Beshanie and Nilola both in faint-green dresses and with their cheeks flushed and sweaty. Next to Nilola sits Perkin. He's in black, same as Raen. He winks when he realises I'm staring at him. Does he know about Raen and me? Does everyone?

My stomach churns as Vill whispers with Aesc. Am I as nervous as I was when I first met Onnachild? It's hard to say. My leg won't stop trembling despite Nessia's hand on it, and I'm nauseous. It might be the baby, although I should be past the sickness stage. The churning suggests my child isn't happy to be inside me and is fighting against it. I can't blame it. I swallow and pray to the gods the advisers won't call on me to speak as my mouth is so dry. But I don't want Vill to speak for me. His pose seems so affected it makes me think he's enjoying this, the attention, and that this is a chance for him to perform.

When a Maiden brings over a tray with a jug of water and several cups, Nessia pours me a cup of water. I don't take it, worried Raen might see how shaky I am. Gavin is holding Eldini's plump hand, not Raen. He stares ahead like he's not even here. The distance in his eyes is reminiscent of the time we were under the yew, and I wonder if he's dwelling on the people he's lost. It's a glimpse of that Raen, the other him, the one I thought I knew. If only we were alone ...

I tried that. Last night. I blush again. His jaw pulses, the movement enhanced by the frame of his thick hair, but other than that he seems unaffected. I want to press my palm to his chest, discover whether his heart is beating as fast as mine. Instead, I find the faint line of a join under the table and follow it with my nail.

'Niah,' Ascelin says, calling my attention.

As everyone turns towards me, I draw on my training and force a faint smile to my lips and a modest tilt to my head. It feels awkward.

'Is it true that on his death bed the King promised you the throne?' There's a warmth to Ascelin's voice that's never been there before.

Aesc scribbles in his book.

I gulp.

Ascelin nods to encourage me. Vill drifts over, rests his hand on my shoulder. Raen's studying the rings on his fingers. *Look up. You can stop this.* His top lip twitches. Someone in the crowd coughs. I swallow.

'Yes.' My voice is louder and stronger than I expected it to be.

Nessia pats my knee, glances at me proudly. Aesc writes my short word in his book with an exaggerated flourish far too long for a yes. I press my palm against the table to stop myself from rising to check what he's written. My leg finally stops shaking. Raen stares at me with such disdain. I want to shout at him that it's not my fault, but I clamp my lips shut.

'Raen,' Ascelin says.

He turns his head, slowly, towards the adviser.

'You claim the King promised you the throne.'

'I do not claim.' Raen's voice is terse. 'He did.'

'We'll see,' Aesc mumbles.

The castle people are gossiping again. Vill caresses my shoulder. Eldini lifts her chin towards the ceiling as though in a silent prayer. Raen's jaw twitches. My stomach hurts.

'We meet tomorrow to hear the claims,' Ascelin says. 'Both parties must get their lists of witnesses to us by the end of the day.'

'Is that all?' I ask.

'For now.' Aesc slams the book shut.

Already the castle people are struggling out of their chairs. The door opens, and a draught rushes in. Ascelin starts whispering to Vill. Gavin, Raen, and Eldini rise together. Her belly is larger than mine. I never did ask Raen how far along she was. Does it even matter now? The noise of the castle people forcing their way from the room is overwhelming, as loud as a surging sea.

'Why? What was that? I thought?' I turn to Vill. 'Tomorrow? Why not now?'

'It's the way things are done,' Aesc says.

'First the statement, then the examination, then the judgment,' Ascelin says.

'All this worry for nothing.'

'It's the way things are done,' Aesc repeats, sounding exasperated.

Then there'll be another sleepless night for me. Turning in my chair, I watch Eldini, Gavin, and Raen leave in a huddle. There's a swagger to his stride. What does he have to swagger about? What is he going to say in the Judging? I want it to end. I need to sleep. Instead there is more to come.

Chapter Seventy

'I SHOULD NOT COME HERE.' Eldini won't make eye contact with me. She seems preoccupied with staring around my room. I'm glad she won't look at me. 'Raen told me not to come.'

'Then why did you?'

'It is strange, is it not? We were friends and now ...' She opens out her arms. 'You one side of table and us one side of table.' She acts too familiar with my room, gliding across it to pour us both a goblet of wine. Then she's distracted by my curtains, rearranging the pleats. I follow her to the window, step between her and my curtains. If it were anyone else I'd think they were sizing up my rooms for their own acquisition.

'No one is happy,' she says.

'Then let's hope it gets decided quickly.'

'It will not. We know.' She drifts back to my table, picks up a goblet and offers it to me. I shake my head. She frowns and toys with the stem. 'Niah, why you do this?'

'It's mine. I'm Aegnian.'

'It mean more to Raen. You know. You are his friend.'

'There are things you aren't aware of.' I close my curtains so that the darkened room will dull the power of her sad eyes. 'What do you want?'

'Please, do not be angry. All this ... The Judging, Raen says because of you. He says you want to take throne from him, from my child. I come to beg you.' She places her palm over her heart. 'He says I am stupid to trust you but I know you are good. Please, stop. Things will be said in Judging. Things advisers will make us say we not want to say.' She stares at the goblet in her hand. 'They will call you to speak. They will call me to speak.'

'Like what?' I hold onto the curtains, braced for her answer. Me and Raen. Is she flushing? It's hard to tell in this light. A sense of the First Queen standing here, trying to guard her own secrets, comes to me. I think I hear her bitter laugh. My gaze darts around the room. I sniff, nose up in the air, trying to locate her smell.

Eldini sighs, drawing my attention to her. Her body is bent by the weight of her baby, too big for her small frame, and I can't stop staring at it. 'How many cycles?' I blurt out.

'I do not—'

'How many cycles?'

'Four. Five soon.'

Her words are a punch in my gut, but she waves them away and that dismissive flutter makes me want to hurt her. It's not her fault. It's his. I think back, my fingers brushing against the curtains as I count off the days since their wedding.

'Raen will not give up either.'

Her interruption makes me lose count. Why should it make a difference if he's been with her since the wedding? But it does. It does because I thought ... My cheeks burn at my shame, at my stupidity. I turn from her, from the proof he was using us both.

'Niah, please.' The smell of lemon and vanilla grows stronger as she steps nearer. 'Have kindness for him. You have feelings for him? For me? This not need to happen. He is good to you. I am good to you. You can keep Grace.'

'Her name is Ammi, and she's not yours to give to me.'

There are footsteps, heavy and quick in the hallway. We both recognise the sound: Raen. Eldini gasps. I take a deep breath and brace myself for him to burst in.

'Please, Niah. Please.' She grabs my arm and spins me around to face her. 'What can I do to make you stop? Already it gone too far. Your people threaten me, my child. I am scared. Please, Niah.'

Raen yells out her name. Her eyes plead with me. He bangs open the door.

'What are you doing here? I told you to stay away from her,' he bellows. He crosses the floor in five strides and smacks the goblet from her hands. Wine arches then splatters onto the floor. The goblet bangs against the wall. 'There could be anything in that.'

'I had to see. I had to try,' she says.

'Leave her, Raen,' I say.

'As if I'd hurt her—she's my wife.'

There's such fury in his eyes, the green blazing, that I remain silent, but a challenge must be there in my expression because he doesn't look away, not even when she hangs off his arm.

'We stop it. Both of you. Please. Raen. Niah, he is like a brother to you.'

For a moment I feel relief; she knows nothing. He has told her nothing. Then I realise: it doesn't matter because it will all come out tomorrow.

'Do not interfere,' he says, but it's me he's glaring at.

'Raen, I can help,' she says.

'Leave.'

She's a dutiful, docile, pliable wife, and she closes the door gently behind her.

We listen to her steps padding down the hallway. I count the rapid movement of his chest, up and down, waiting for him to explode. One, two, three, four. I start again. I feel my lips curling up in disgust. Four or five cycles. I feel my shoulders rise and my jaw clench. His toes thump against the floor until we can't hear Eldini anymore.

'You know they have threatened her?' He advances on me, trying to back me up against the curtains. I hold my ground.

'Not until just now.'

'And what does she do, but come straight here? She's either very brave or very stupid.'

'I did not threaten her, and I did not ask anyone to threaten her. I don't need to.'

'Doesn't matter whether you did or not, that's what's happened. This is going to run away with you.' He holds the curtains, towering over me, trying to intimidate me.

'No, it's going to run away with you when I tell her. When she realises the kind of man you are.' My chest puffs out, almost touches his as I rise onto my tiptoes. 'Pliable, docile? Aren't those the words you used to describe her? Let's see how docile she is when she hears how you come panting after me, when I tell her what you like and how I found out.'

'You will not hurt her.' He's trying to control himself, trying to keep his voice low and steady.

'You already have. Every time you came to me you hurt her. Every time you went to her after me, you hurt her. And even now, you still want to fuck me, don't you?'

His eyes say yes. The press of his chest against mine says yes. I strain higher, taller, tug on his neck, until our lips are level, until he can feel my breath on his.

'I told you, I wanted what was my brother's. And now I've had it. You. I'm done with it.' He smirks, probably expecting to see me hurt but I show nothing and his smirk vanishes.

'I was happy to be his whore.' I spit the words. 'But I will never be, have never been, yours. You're a fool and you don't deserve a thing of Aelius's. You're too stupid to realise Onnachild was never going to give you the throne. Pretending to was his last joke, his last punishment. He knew you'd never be as good as Aelius, same as I knew.'

He yanks me up. My toes barely graze the floor. I force myself to smile at him though my heart is pounding. His nostrils are flaring and his grip biting, yet I keep poking him. 'And the castle will find that out tomorrow.'

'My father was the fool.' He drops me. My legs buckle and it makes me reach for him to steady myself, but he grabs me first. 'He trusted you, kept you around, and it killed him. How about I tell the castle that?'

'Kept me here as a toy.' I tug against his hold, bash into the windowsill. 'A charm in case they came. Well, they did, and yes, I called them in. He deserved it. Why do you care for Onnachild all of a sudden? Because you're weak, that's why.'

He growls my name but I don't shut up. 'Your mother will have seen how weak, how pathetic you are. You weren't strong enough to fight him in his prime so you had to wait until he was half dead.' I watch as his hands fist and his scabbed knuckles bulge. 'You're not a man. And you're not a son anyone could be proud of.' His fist rises. I duck, twist, and in my speed to get away, misjudge the distance. My temple smacks the windowsill as I fall. He shakes his head, shocked.

576

'Did you think ...?' His punch hasn't been thrown. His fist is still up, arm tense, ready. He yanks me to my feet, steadies me with a grip that presses on bone. Four or five cycles keeps repeating in my mind as he shouts, 'You will listen to me for once.' He jerks me forwards and backwards, fingers digging into my arms as I twist and buck to get free. He thrusts his face at me, the green flashing in his irises. 'This isn't a game. People will get hurt.'

My shoulder smarts from where it must have whacked the wall, but I can't give in. 'I've been hurt,' I shout, trying to slap him off.

'How has anyone hurt you?'

My whole body burns from the memory of those three words. I want him to feel pain, too, even if it is only physical pain I can inflict on him. My hands flail. I kick his leg. He doesn't flinch but his grip gets tighter and tighter. 'Call off your people.'

'I'm sure the advisers will love to hear about this,' Vill says.

Raen curses and throws me from him as if he's been scolded. I smack into the curtains, grappling with them to stay upright. He glowers at me as I lose my footing, winces when I hit the floor and cry out.

'If you dare mention this ...' Raen seethes.

'Oh I will, I'll tell them everything,' Vill says, smiling and gesturing for Raen to leave. Raen slams the door behind him.

'Let's hope there are bruises,' Vill says.

Chapter Seventy-One

THE CASTLE PEOPLE BOO AND CHEER when I enter the Judging Room with Nessia. I want to hold her hand only I can't bear for anyone to see I'm overwhelmed. *Please, don't trip. Please, don't stomp across the floor like the villager you are.* Raen's already sitting at the table with Eldini and Gavin. I hoped seeing him would provoke my anger again, but it doesn't. There's only the sting and shame from the things we said.

'Why are you not wearing a sleeveless dress as I instructed?' Vill whispers to me as he smiles for the benefit of the crowd.

'I'll not play dirty.' I pull at my cuff.

Raen seems confused by my appearance, scrutinising me, perhaps searching for evidence of my head hitting the windowsill. It's been hidden under my hair, curled and pinned by Nessia this morning so a loop lies over it. The bruise throbs under the intensity of his stare. Ascelin pulls a chair out for me. I lower carefully to ensure the lock of hair remains in place and that my belly doesn't protrude too much.

Eldini continues staring at her hands resting on the table. Her nails are bitten and the imperfection has me feeling sorry for her. Gavin has draped his arm around her shoulders. Ascelin coughs to clear his throat and quiet the crowd. He glances over to Aesc who has his quill paused over the open book. Two parchments are beside the book, detailing the witnesses to be called. I crane out of my seat to check Melody's name isn't on one but the table cuts in and hurts so I sit back.

'Good people of the castle,' Ascelin says. 'We're gathered here today to hear the claims that King Onnachild, may he rest in peace, promised this throne to both parties. As the King's trusted ambassadors, advisers, and protectors of his realm we will examine these claims in full and decide the King's true successor. Both parties will be called to present their claims and their witnesses. There will be no doubts and there will be no questions remaining. This Judging will be final.' He peers out at the crowd, challenging anyone to disagree. Chatter rises but no one protests.

Ascelin turns to me. 'You say the King named you as heir.'

'He did.'

'And Raen, you say the King named you heir?'

'You know I did.' He stares ahead, expressionless except for a twitch in his jaw.

The words get written down with frantic scratches.

'I believe there was a Maiden in the room,' Aesc's finger traces over one of the parchments, 'when you claim he made his promise to you.'

'I do not claim. He did.'

'Then first, we will call the Maidens.' Ascelin clicks his fingers.

They line up opposite him. Melody is in the middle, shaking and staring at the floor. Her fingers are crossed. 'You.' Aesc points to her. 'You. Out. Here.' He jabs towards a spot on the floor.

Her head darts up. She holds her headdress. Her gaze flits to me. She's not meant to be called, Vill promised. I hiss his name, trying to attract his attention. Is he ignoring me? Nessia prevents me from waving at him by tugging on my elbow. Melody nods and steps out. Her bottom lip is trembling.

'You are Niah's Maiden?'

She nods.

'Speak.'

'Yes.' She peeps back at Lark who nods at her. Melody frowns. She stares around the room. Her face is turning scarlet. Her gaze settles on Vill standing behind me. I feel his hand drop onto my shoulders. She gulps.

'Vill,' I hiss up at him. He bends down. 'We agreed not to call her. Look at her. Don't make her do this.'

'If the advisers want to call her...'

'No, Vill.'

Nessia's grimacing. Her fingers curl around mine.

'I ...' Melody's blue eyes are filling with tears.

'Speak,' Aesc shouts.

'I don't want to,' she mumbles, uncrossing her fingers. She glances at Raen and then she starts crying.

'It's all right, Melody.' Raen's voice is soft and calm.

'Vill, do something,' I say.

He saunters over to Melody, arms out to comfort her. She peeps up at him, relief on her tearful face. He hugs her and a few castle women sigh. 'She's obviously distressed,' he says to Ascelin. 'Surely there is another Maiden that can be called?'

'We want word from this Maiden. What did you hear the King say?'

Vill smarts at being contradicted, but it only shows briefly before he's replaced his expression with one more sympathetic to Melody's tears.

'I can't,' she says. 'I don't know.'

'You can, you just don't want to,' Ascelin says.

She gulps. Vill whispers something in her ear and she nods. 'I ... he ... He said.' Her gaze flits around the room. The people are hushed and expectant. She wipes away her tears, chews her bottom lip. She closes her eyes. I hold my breath as her mouth opens. 'He said that Raen ... he wanted ...' She screws up her face. 'To have the throne.' Her eyes open. She glances back to Lark, who nods.

I try to mouth to Melody that it's all right but she won't look my way, despite me tapping the table. Her sobs are louder, reverberating around the stunned Judging Room. She's having trouble breathing. Vill draws her against his chest. I push back from the table. Nessia squeezes my arm to try to keep me still.

'And?' Ascelin asks. 'What else?'

I can't bear to watch this. I stand up.

'Sit,' Aesc bellows at me. Melody slumps to the floor, her head in her hands. Vill crouches beside her. Raen looks far too pleased with himself, with his chest thrust out and his chin resting on his clasped hands. He gestures for me to sit and smiles snidely. His knuckles still bear a scattering of scabs from that day so why isn't he worried about what else Melody could say?

'Sirs, sirs.' Another Maiden steps forwards, peeking at Vill. He tries to hide his smile but I've seen it. 'She wasn't there, I was. It was me, hiding under the bed.'

Lark goes to move forwards, perhaps to call out this lie, but Vill prevents her.

'Maidens are not permitted to lie.' Aesc tuts as he scratches through what he has written in his book.

'She doesn't mean any harm, sirs, please. She's scared of that man, and she has reason to be—'

'She's not scared of me.' The harshness of Raen's voice has me bumping down into my seat. Eldini covers his knuckles.

'See, sirs. See. She has reason to be. I've never seen such force, such cruelty as when he pushed everyone from the room, raging he was, and I was scared. I was so scared I dived under the bed. And sirs, she isn't lying, not really. She's saying what I told her and if she weren't so scared she'd say the rest.' There's something in the Maiden's voice. A twang I recognise that's neither castle nor village.

'Fine.' Ascelin huffs.

Melody lets out a loud sob as Vill helps her to her feet and leads her back to the other Maidens.

'Is it as that Maiden said?' Ascelin asks.

'Yes, partly. See the King did say those words, but sir, that isn't the whole story.'

Aesc turns over another page in his book.

'Go on,' Ascelin says.

'The King said those words, but he didn't want to. He was forced. He was made to.'

The crowd gasps. I'm sure Raen's hand burrows further under Eldini's, hiding his knuckles. The pulse in his jaw speeds.

'I saw. I was there, under the bed, trying to say my prayers but I couldn't, so shocked was I, sirs, by what I saw. Like a monster he was, like a wild animal. And I was terrified witless, sirs.' She lets out a little sob and tries to smoother it with her palm. The castle people keep gossiping, despite the advisers clapping and stamping their feet. The gossip gets louder and louder. While everyone is distracted, the Maiden raises her head, smiles at me. Beshanie's servant. She taps her chest where the council pendant rested, providing further confirmation. Back down her head goes. Aesc slams his book against the table and the castle falls silent.

'Can I speak plainly?' she asks.

Ascelin gestures for her to continue.

'Everyone saw that King Onnachild was not fond of Raen,' she says. 'But I've never seen such hatred, and towards a dying man, too.' She crosses herself but the gesture is awkward. 'It made my blood run cold. The things he said to his King. I can't repeat the words he called him but he screamed at him and grabbed him by the neck, screaming at him again and again, "It is my throne, it is mine". Raen said the King had killed his mother and if he didn't give him the throne he would keep away the physician and the priest, see that the King died in torment. And the King promised. And then he ...' She raises her index finger and points at Raen.

Why doesn't he stand up and dispute this? It's as if he's not heard her, as if he's not even in this room because he keeps staring into the distance. Eldini's hand is no longer on his.

'And no physician went in,' the servant says.

'You believe the promise to Raen was made under duress?'

'Yes. Yes, I do.' She nods.

Vill's hiding his mouth, pretending to stroke his lips in contemplation. Why doesn't Melody stand up and say the girl is lying? This is not the scene Melody described to me. Did she lie to make Raen seem more honourable? If she'd told me this earlier, I would never have believed it because I'd seen how gentle he was when feeding and bathing Onnachild—so why am I almost convinced now?

My fingers press into the bruises on my arms as I remember his raised fist. The dull ache from the press eases the one in my heart. Does Eldini believe the servant's story? Her cheek has dropped to rest against his arm, ignored by him. She wouldn't want to believe this story and so she doesn't.

'What say you, Raen?' Ascelin asks.

His jaw twitches but he says nothing.

'He would not harm his father,' Eldini says.

'It's touching that a wife wishes to presume the best of her husband and show such loyalty, but, with respect, that question is not for you to answer. Raen?'

Raen glowers at Ascelin who just smiles back.

'Why isn't he saying anything?' I whisper to Nessia.

She looks as confused as I am, shrugging in response.

'You knew the King was ill,' Ascelin says. 'Had been ill for several months and getting worse, and yet when he collapsed you were nowhere to be found. Where were you? What was more important than your father's health?'

'I don't believe that's any of the castle's business.'

With me. And I remember asking to see the real him. And I remember being convinced I'd seen through to his core as we huddled under the trees. How sure I was that we were good people. Is he remembering it? He will not say anything, the firm set of his jaw shows me this, but the realisation doesn't bring me any relief. There's only disappointment because I wasn't even close to seeing the real him and now I never will.

'You do not think it's any of the Castle's business?' Aesc throws his quill down. 'The man you call Father, the King, was dying. Your wife claims you wouldn't hurt him, yet when he collapsed you were absent. Tell us, how many days did it take for you to visit his deathbed?'

'I do not believe I'm on trial,' Raen says. 'We're here to discuss who my father left the throne to.'

'I wouldn't be too sure of that, after hearing the Maiden's testimony.'

'And this is not the first or only time you've shown your anger,' Vill says, stepping out and spinning to face Raen. The light reflecting off his jewels dances around the room.

'So is this what you mean to do?' Raen leans forwards. 'Discredit me and then have me hanged as a traitor?'

I push my bruises more. I close my eyes.

'Where were you?' Ascelin raises his voice.

Why is Vill not stopping the advisers from pushing this question? I open my eyes, wish I hadn't. Eldini's whispering in Raen's ear, her belly pressed against his side. He shakes his head, dismissing her words with a flick of his hand. Is she trying to get him to confess? Does she know?

'The King called Niah. Niah went. Where were you, Raen?' Vill presses.

I brace myself for his answer but hope he won't.

'This is ridiculous,' Raen says. 'This whole thing is ridiculous. Throne passes from father to son. Why would my father give her the throne? She was just my brother's whore.'

Eldini gasps at the word. The crowd sniggers. I bolt out of my seat. I'm Niah from the Aegni, from a long line of strong women, from a long line of female rulers. I've never been afraid. In the village, I didn't back down from harsh words and I won't be cowed now.

'Advisers,' I shout over the crowd. Castle eyes turn to me, various shades of blue. The servant stares at me, and the admiration in her face gives me strength. I square my shoulders, take a deep breath, and speak slow enough for Aesc to capture everything I say. 'I don't deny that I lay with the True Prince.' I pause to let that title sink in, to let it sting Raen. 'I was young and very much in love. King Onnachild understood that, for did he not make mistakes, too?' I'm going too far; I realise this without Nessia tugging on my skirt to tell me. Vill is right: the First Queen will forgive me if I get that throne back for the Aegni women. Besides, I can't stop. 'He took me in, us in. Grace is my daughter and the daughter of the True Prince. He showed us kindness, and I was happy to return that kindness in his hour of need.' My voice rings out clear and strong, stunning the castle people silent and motionless. Vill nods me on. 'That is why King Onnachild offered me the throne. Grace is the heir of his true son, and he wished it to pass through me to her.' I stare at the advisers, daring them to contradict me.

I feel Raen's fury as I stand there steady and defiant. He'll not call me a whore before the castle and try to humiliate me. That was love. Something he'll never understand. Something I'll never give him. I lower my eyes to meet his, show I'm not afraid of him, that I'm not fooled by him. The green in his is brighter than normal. They threaten me to say more, to say I'm his whore, too, and for a moment the idea of doing so fills me with a spiteful thrill. After all, how can Eldini continue to support him once those words are spoken? I'd like to see Raen truly alone.

'Please sit, Niah,' Vill says. 'Do not distress yourself.'

Everyone around the table can see I'm not distressed and I do not sit.

'I believe Grace gave some comfort to our King,' Vill says wistfully. 'Reminding him of his beloved son.'

'That is true,' says Aesc as though it's written in his book.

Vill joins me, resting an arm around my shoulder and drawing me close. 'Excellent,' he whispers. 'Now cry.'

I can't. I'm too angry. The advisers huddle together. The crowd is whispering again, words I can't make out, just sounds, noises that merge into a single hum that mimics a fly too near my ear. I spot Mantona smiling at me. Can she tell what the crowd is saying? Are they on my side? The advisers are reading over what Aesc has written, nodding and tutting. People in the crowd are fidgeting, the noise adding to their whispers. Eldini is restless in her seat and her fingers are picking at her uneven nails. I steady myself with the side of the table.

'Sit,' Nessia mouths at me. She doesn't seem happy. I can't move.

'Would the King offer his throne to ...' Vill gestures towards Raen. 'A man we shall prove is violent, unpredictable, and unclaimed as his own or—'

'You know he was planning to,' Raen interjects. 'You were in this very room when the papers were being prepared.'

'And yet there are no papers.' Vill smiles at him. 'As I was saying before I was interrupted, would King Onnachild name this man as his successor, a man he didn't even acknowledge as his son, or would he offer his throne to the mother of his beloved grandchild who was as good as married to his true son?'

Raen leans forwards, hisses at me, 'Don't make me do this, Niah.'

Eldini blanches. I do not.

'We shall be careful and considerate,' Aesc says. 'For now, a break is needed.'

Eldini is visibly relieved, drawing Raen's face around to meet hers as his chest heaves and drops.

'Already? What's happening? Vill?' I want the advisers to continue, to keep pushing Raen, let everyone see what a liar he is. The crowd scrambles up. Chairs scrape across the floor. Raen's head drops back against his chair. His breathing is slower. Eldini whispers to Gavin, clutching him. He nods.

'People need to eat,' Vill explains. He bows towards Eldini as Raen helps her from her seat. She keeps her face hidden against him and her palm pressed against her lower back. Raen stares over her head at me. He looks tormented and exhausted, exactly as he did in Onnachild's rooms when he said he needed my help. When he said he couldn't take any more. I can't bear this. His anger I can.

'We will not do it this way.' I turn away from him and listen to his steps as he leads Eldini from the room.

'What was that?' Vill sits beside me. He's so pleased with himself, preening there.

'I don't want to discredit Raen that way, bad-mouth his mother. Play dirty.'

Aesc gathers up his book and looks at me like I'm an idiot.

'But you started it,' Vill says. 'What with that talk of the True Prince. Excellent, subtle touch by the way.'

'I shouldn't have, I was angry.'

'You have every right to be angry,' Nessia says.

'Please, don't humour me,' I say to her. 'I can't use Onnachild's tricks. I won't.'

'He called you a whore,' Nessia says. 'What a hypocrite.'

'We'll talk about my bloodline. We'll remind them how it used to be here and how it should never have been Onnachild's. Remind them the throne passed from Aegni woman to Aegni woman. That's what we're meant to do. That's what my ancestors would want me to do.'

Vill shakes his head. 'Niah, that's very honourable of you, but firstly, the ancestors would want you to do anything as long as you won, and secondly, this castle might not be ready for a return to the old ways. Remember fear was what made it so easy for Onnachild to turn the people against the Aegni, and fearful people are not people who make the best decisions. Besides.' He pats my hand. 'It's too late for that. You better hold on tight, Niah, because I predict things will get much more heated this afternoon. Go put on a sleeveless dress. I intend to make use of those bruises.'

Before I can protest he's off with the advisers. Only Nessia and I remain. I drop my head onto the table, feel the cool wood on my forehead and breathe in its scent.

Chapter Seventy-Two

'WE WILL RECOMMENCE.' Ascelin claps to quieten the room.

'Please, if I may,' Vill says. 'Something has been brought to my attention during the break.'

'Go on.'

Raen's shuffling through the pile of parchments in front of him but his attention is on the Aegnian book I've brought with me. Is he regretting giving it to me?

'Niah, if you would.' Vill distracts me as I strain to read Raen's parchments upside down. 'Please stand.' He holds his hand out to take mine.

'What are you doing? We discussed this.' I tap my book. This will be proof enough to show Onnachild's intention is immaterial. This will show bloodlines and the real history of this land. Prove rule goes from woman to woman and not Onnachild's foreign way of father to son. Not Onnachild to Raen. Vill ignores my tapping but Raen's jaw twitches in time to it.

My stomach churns at the aroma of food brought into the room by the castle people. It torments me for not eating in the break but I was too full of nerves. When I look at the throne for strength, I see me and Raen entwined in it, red-faced, sweating, and panting. That doesn't matter. I'm not that person anymore. This is my chance to prove it, to prove I'm good and not a liar, not deceitful or unnecessarily cruel.

'Up,' Vill insists.

'Why?'

'We understand this is difficult for you,' Aesc says.

'What does he mean?' Nessia whispers.

'The gods only know,' I whisper as I rise.

Roughly, Vill pushes up my sleeves. 'This.' He points at the bruise on my arm before I have the chance to push down my sleeves.

'No, Vill,' I say between clenched teeth.

'If Niah was not so modest we would see more.'

People crane closer. Raen shuffles his papers. Ascelin creeps nearer. Vill gathers back my hair, exposing the bruise on my temple. Ascelin leans in towards me. His breath smells of cloves. I try to free myself, try to roll down my sleeves.

'Stay still,' Ascelin demands.

I hear Aesc clomping across the room. He prods the finger-shaped marks as he counts them. 'The book,' I mumble to Vill. 'We don't need to do this. Please, stop.'

'There are more you say?' Aesc asks.

'There are no more,' I say, despite Vill tilting my head and prodding the one on my shoulder.

'Here and here.' He prods another and I wince.

'Show us. Unpick her sleeves,' Aesc says.

Reluctantly, Nessia rises. Her fingers shake as she works the stitching. 'Sorry,' she whispers. 'It will be worth it.'

Will it, I want to ask, but I'm stunned into submission, exposed in a way I never was in the village, and this is worse, more humiliating, than any of the words anyone has ever called me. I hang my head, unable to meet the many faces staring at me. It takes all my concentration to not tremble. I silently plead for Raen's help, though it's his stare that burns the most. *If you cared. If you ever cared at all.*

My left sleeve comes off. It's placed before me onto the table, beside my book. It's like a flattened eel. This isn't right. This isn't how it should be. Aesc pokes a bruise, one not made during my argument with Raen but during our mating on the throne. Do they recognise the shape of his mouth? Does Eldini? I sway into the table, its edge digging into my stomach. The gossip of the crowd is getting louder and louder. My other sleeve is taken off and I'm suddenly freezing. I can't stop thinking of the village children trying to drown me, standing over me, baying for my death as the carpenter's son held me under. My hands grip the wood. My eyes seek out Raen. He meets mine, looks ashamed, and then he lowers his gaze to the Aegnian book. I see Eldini's fingers fluttering as she counts along with Aesc. I feel Nessia's fingers on the ties at my back. *Please no.* If they loosen my dress, everyone will see I'm with child.

'There's no need,' Ascelin says.

My breath bursts out and I almost collapse onto the table.

'Will you tell us how these came about?' Aesc asks.

I can't speak. Shame is scolding my cheeks, drying my mouth. My palms are slippery.

'She's scared to,' Vill says. 'Who can blame her?'

Not scared—humiliated. I can't lift my gaze from the grain of the table. When I shut my eyes to block out the castle, I see Onnachild's flaring nostrils and tight smile.

'You know how these bruises came about?' Ascelin asks.

'Yes, luckily, I intervened before Niah was hurt any further.' Vill's hand is a dead weight on my shoulder and I dip from the pressure of it. 'Proof again of what a violent temper he has.'

Raen's name goes through the crowd, a whisper that grows and grows, reaching a peak that hurts my ears. I peer through my hair at him, sitting so composed, back straight, and staring at the ceiling as if these bruises had nothing to do with him. *You wanted to claim me. You wanted to own me, well, do it now. Tell them and save me from this humiliation. Let me get dressed.*

'Will you point out who did this?' Ascelin asks. The smell of cloves returns.

Nothing. Raen will do nothing. He'd rather not upset Eldini than come to my aid. I raise my hand. It's shaking and I don't know whether it's from fear, the cold, or anger. I straighten my index finger. Raen lowers his head, stares at me. How dare he look hurt? My hand drops onto the table with a thud. I can't do it. I shake my head.

'See what he has done. See how scared she is. Him. Him there.' Vill points at Raen.

'Why?' Eldini gasps. She covers her mouth, but it's too late, the word is out. Her face flushes. Is she remembering him storming across my room and smashing that goblet from her?

'Why?' Vill shouts. 'Do we need to ask why? He's a bully. He bullied his father and he's trying to bully Niah, force her to relinquish her claim. And what is worse ...' His gaze lowers to my belly. *No. He can't. He doesn't know, does he? How could he? He can't.* I grab his sleeve. Try to plead, but I can't form words. Has Melody told him? Is she punishing me for yesterday? His pause is too long, too quiet, my heart too loud in it. 'He attacks her while she's carrying his child.'

I drop to my seat, rest my forehead on the table, and hide my head with my bare arms. *Not here. Not now.* Not from Vill's mouth. How does he know? Of course, he would; he knows everything. And now the castle does, too. The room is silent. My breath heats my skin, deafens me. My baby kicks against me, coming to its father's defence. It despises its mother.

'Please, don't be angry.' My lips brush the smooth, sweaty wood as I mumble to my baby. 'This is for us, for you.' But my baby knows the truth; I do this for Ammi, for her father, for myself and not this baby. If I cared I'd have tried harder with Raen. I'd have—

Vill's touch makes me jump. 'Don't be scared.'

It's done. The secret is out and so there's nothing left but to be strong. I open my eyes. I raise my head. Smoothing back my hair, I force my features into a haughty expression that I hope resembles one I've seen Beshanie use. Nessia tries to take my hand in hers, but it's not her reassurance I want.

As slow as moving through water, I inspect Raen. First his chin, smooth-shaven and framed by his dark hair, then his mouth, down-turned and slack with shock. His plump bottom lip still tempts me. Then up to his scar, vivid and deep, more so now that the colour has drained from his face. I'm not strong enough to go further and meet his eyes, and so my gaze drops to his shoulders, those shoulders that have taken my tears, my worries. They don't seem broad enough anymore to have done so, collapsed as they are, like a storm-beaten branch, and I find I can't bear to look at them, either.

Shadows and amber-coloured light surround him when Eldini shunts away. She's paled so much her lips are purple. Gavin holds her close. Raen's all alone. Gavin seems to be questioning what it is I am, a puzzled expression on his face. I'm a liar, a deceitful friend. And, same as Onnachild, a promise breaker, too. A strong village accent whispers in my ear: *no, you are Niah from the Aegni.* I ask it, *what should I do?* The crowd is too loud for me to hear the answer.

'Is this true?' Aesc asks.

There's no use denying it for in a matter of weeks it will be obvious. Besides, if I try to, Vill might demand I stand again and then strip me so my belly's on display. Everyone will see what I am, what I've done, and my love for Aelius will seem a falsehood. Maybe it was. Maybe Vill was right and my feelings for Aelius were because he was a prince and offered me a chance to get the throne for my ancestors. People fall in love because the other has something they want, Vill said. Maybe that's why I thought myself in love with Raen, but what was it he had that I wanted? I can't remember. Nothing makes sense anymore, not even me.

Aesc knocks on the table. 'We're waiting.'

'Yes, we're waiting.' Raen's voice is gravelly with suppressed emotion.

I can't remember how I justified my actions. In the graveyard, my body called for life and he responded. It craved not just touch or life but him.

Home. It still craves him. I press the bruise his mouth left on my shoulder. If only he would ... is this my last chance ...? Will this change anything?

I nod. I cough to clear my throat. 'Yes. I'm with child.' My voice slips into my village accent. 'It's Raen's child.'

Will he look at me, called to by the accent he must remember from his childhood, the accent he has a hint of? No, he doesn't. He keeps his breath slow and steady. His chin remains in the air. He licks his teeth. Is his mouth dry, too?

'It could be anyone's. Who knows who she's mated with?' He leans back in his chair, presses his index fingers to his lips. If we were alone would he be denying it?

'The time I talk of here is not the first time he has attacked Niah.' Vill's voice rises so it's louder than the crowd's gossip.

'Quiet. Quiet. Quiet,' both the advisers shout.

'This attack was not the first, for the first time produced this child,' Vill says.

My head snaps up. 'No,' I yell.

'I have witnesses,' Vill says.

'He forced you,' Ascelin says firmly to me.

'Call the witness,' Aesc says.

Vill clicks his fingers, and Beshanie bounds over, pushing her way through the crowd with her elbows. She settles beside Vill, brushing down her skirt and posing meekly.

'What did you see?' Ascelin asks.

'My servant told me and I didn't believe it at first, because like everyone else I presumed Raen was a good man but ...' She sighs and touches her heart.

'This is nonsense,' Raen bellows.

'We will decide that,' Aesc replies.

Beshanie smiles, slyly, at Raen. I'm dumbstruck, too dumbstruck to speak. My arms goosebump in anticipation of her words. *Please don't make it worse, please.* I try to reach for Vill but he slides further away.

'Then we'll talk to the servant,' Ascelin says.

'Here!' The servant jumps up, waving. People turn in their seats to stare at her. Despite the distance, I can make out the hint of green in her eyes.

I push back my chair, shaking my head.

'Don't, Niah.' Nessia holds me in place.

Don't what? She can't approve of this, can she? She likes Raen. She's cared for him and me.

'I can tell you. You don't need to ask her. I didn't just hear it from the servant. May I?' Beshanie bows and simpers at Ascelin.

He nods in response.

She pushes her auburn hair off her shoulders. 'My servant came to fetch me as she knew I was a good friend of Niah's, and we made our way towards the kitchen. It was the night the King, may his soul rest in peace ... succumbed. My servant said she had seen, by the stream, by the trees there ... as I said, I didn't want to believe her but something inside me told me to go with her, and before we made it to the stream ... There was screaming.' She covers her ears with her hands and rumples her nose.

'A lie,' Raen says.

Beshanie shivers and staggers further away from him. She covers her face, and, from between her spread fingers, smirks at me before forcing out a sob. 'He was shouting and Niah was crying and saying, "No, no. It isn't right. I am your brother's." Oh, I'm so ashamed of myself but I was too shocked to go to her aid. When I heard him punching her, I could only stand there. I was so, so scared. Please, Niah, forgive me.' She lifts up her head, brushes away tears that have not fallen.

'Beshanie, no,' I plead.

Aesc keeps scribbling in his book.

'It's true. All true,' the servant calls.

'Only I didn't realise at the time it was Niah. It was after. Once he had gone. I went out to offer assistance, comfort and ... what I saw ...' She sighs and pats at her imaginary tears again.

'You saw nothing.' Raen jumps up from his seat.

'She looked like she might be dead. And he ... he ... he had ravished her.'

'You know for certain it was him?' Aesc asks.

'Yes. Yes, I would recognise his voice anywhere and he—'

Raen thumps the table. Beshanie squeals and makes an exaggerated move for Vill.

'That's not true,' I tell Aesc. 'Don't write it.' No, better to be thought a whore, deceitful, a bad friend. Better to be thought weak for having given in to lust than this. I lunge forwards, try to snatch the quill from him. This lie can't be written where my baby might read it.

'Niah, take care.' Nessia tugs on my skirt.

Aesc slaps away my hands and snatches up his book. Raen warned me about the Judging. He knew how far people would go. Even Eldini warned me. I didn't realise. I was naïve. I thought I knew better. I thought ... How can I stop this? Nessia guides me down into my seat.

'She begged me not to say anything,' Beshanie continues. 'Said no one would believe her, with him being the King's son and what she had done with the True Prince, so I kept my mouth shut, only seeing her now, like that ... Oh, Niah, I'm sorry. I was too scared to save you then, but I will now.'

'Lies. All lies,' Raen says. 'Tell them, Niah. Tell them this is only another one of your lies. There isn't a child, is there. Tell them.' His composure has gone. He's nothing more than a village boy, alone, accused, and terrified by the future. The sun behind him is making the red tones in his hair shimmer, and colour has returned to his skin, honey and wood. The Raen I loved. My hands itch to comfort him, to draw him away from these cruel castle people. 'Tell me,' he mumbles.

Tears are coming and I can't suppress them. It shouldn't have been like this. If only Raen had listened when I tried talking to him in the Judging Room. If only we hadn't argued. I hang my head. If only it were a lie. I shake my head.

'I would not have lain with her.' The power has returned to his voice. 'Why would I choose that when I have my wife? Why would I need to force her?' He's regained control of himself, and he looks as magnificent and powerful as he did when he roused the villagers for another battle. It has my body weakening for him, a thrum ricocheting through me that I can't seem to suppress.

'Because she was Aelius's,' Vill says. 'Just as Eldini was to be Aelius's.'

Eldini? That doesn't make sense, yet the spite in Raen's face shows me it is true ... shows me it's my turn to feel pain. My stomach lurches. I don't believe it. Aelius and I talked about our wedding when we lay before the fire, when we sat in the fields under the moonlight. He promised me a place here, beside him, and he never mentioned her. He would have told me. Aelius was a terrible liar.

'Nessia?' I appeal to her.

She's tearful, and I wonder whether this means she believes Vill. Eldini said there were things she'd have to say—is this it? Do those papers prove it? Is that why they're here? Eldini's flushing as she pushes off Gavin's arm. Aelius can't be a liar, too.

'That has nothing to do with it,' Raen says.

But it does. It does. It explains why he married her. It wasn't honour, duty, or even obligation, but something grubbier. Didn't he warn me under the yew how he intended to have everything that had been his half-brother's? And I gave it to him so willingly. I remember Onnachild's laugh when Vill told him I considered Aelius and me as good as married. He was laughing at me because he knew it couldn't have been true. I sink lower into my chair. That laugh I was going to remember forever, that laugh I was going to prove wrong, how could I not have realised what it hinted at?

Nilola shouts out. 'I saw her bruises, too, another night. Before the wedding, before the King fell ill. She had tried to cover them up. The scar is still there.'

'Me too,' Gavin whispers, but only loud enough for us at the table to hear.

'They were not from me,' Raen says. 'Niah, tell them. Stop lying. I have never forced you. I've never had to force you.'

Eldini's hand touches mine. It's cold and light. Her voice quivers as she asks if it's true. What? I want to ask her. The baby? The mating? The violence? What does she want me to deny? When my eyes meet hers she knows Raen's telling the truth: he never had to force me. Her mouth drops open. She must be replaying those moments when Raen and I danced, touches lingering too intimately, the strain evident in our curled fingers as we fought the desire to sink them into the other's skin. As I think of those moments lust surges through my body like a forest fire. Her eyes keep searching my face, and I have no will to hide anything anymore. Let her find everything she's looking for as I flush with shame at still feeling it.

'I need air,' she mumbles. Only I hear her over the din of the crowd. She shouts it again louder. Gavin shouts it. She pushes back her chair. The crowd parts to let them through, Raen chasing after her.

'Two hours and we will reconvene. This will be sorted out today,' Ascelin says, 'sick woman or no sick woman.'

The castle people grumble and moan as they filter out of the room. People in green jostle the people in silver, and the people in silver jab back with their elbows. Feet step on feet. There are angry words, sharp and short. We've turned the castle against itself. It was meant to be so simple. When I walked up the mountain, I thought it would be. I slide the Aegnian book across the table then tip if off into my lap and gather it close, under my chin. Its smell of the past is comforting.

Mantona squeezes her way through to join us. She stands and toys with the green brooch at the collar of her black dress. Beshanie and Nilola are lingering, talking to Vill and darting sympathetic looks my way. I can't figure out if they're real or not.

'I didn't want Raen to find out like that,' I say to Nessia, letting her hug me to her chest. She smells of village and castle. The fabric of her dress is soft against my forehead. 'I wanted to tell him.'

'What and have him declare his undying love for you?' Vill shouts.

'Shush,' Mantona hisses at him as she strokes my hair.

'I told you it was too late for that. I told you he did not care for you,' Vill says.

'That was cruel,' Nessia snaps.

'It was necessary. Niah, gather up your sleeves and compose yourself. We're almost there.'

I hear him scrabbling through the parchments on Raen's side of the table. 'And don't think I'm not livid with you for not informing me about this development,' he says. 'If you had, maybe all this could have been avoided. How about you let that thought rest with you?'

'So that ... that sham is my fault, now?' I push away from Nessia. 'This is not the way to get me to do what you want. I told you—'

'It is not what I want! This is what you want. Remember.' His eyes are as cold as winter rain.

'Let's put this down to shock and sleepless nights.' Mantona steps between me and Vill. 'Things are moving fast, faster than any of us expected.'

He nods to placate her, and his charming smile returns. 'If you would stop fighting us and stop believing that Raen is ever going to be honourable.'

'That's enough, Vill,' Nessia says.

'She needs to toughen up. He's a prince, playing the game as princes are taught to, as she should be.'

'You can't help who you fall in love with,' Mantona says.

'I'm not.' Then why are new tears falling as each of Vill's words hit?

'No, you aren't. And he isn't in love with you, more's the pity. If you'd have managed to achieve that … but you didn't and if his behaviour today didn't prove his lack of feelings for you, then, here.' He throws a parchment across the table. 'Aelius's marriage contract.'

Nessia snatches it away. I don't need the parchment to prove it … those yellow and white flowers left on Aelius's grave prove it. Left, it's obvious now, by Eldini.

'Vill.' Nessia draws out his name in a warning.

'No, Nessia, it's imperative she hears this. All of it. She needs to focus. He was going to use that. He was going to prove Aelius had no intention of marrying you, that Aelius didn't love you, and if that parchment still fails to sway you, then try to defend his sending Ammi away. Why would he banish her and not inform you? For the same reason he brought that marriage proposal here, to hurt you.'

'What? Wait. What are you saying?' I can't have heard right. Ammi gone?

'Last night Ammi was snatched away from the castle by Raen's men, by his order.'

'You're lying.' He's telling the truth. He is. I can see it in his face, the pleasure that he's right. I look to Mantona. She nods. I look at Nessia. She's shaking her head and frowning. Disbelief?

Raen wouldn't, despite everything … he wouldn't. 'No.'

'Why don't you believe me? You would believe Raen over me, still?

You'd be nothing without me. Who brought you here, made sure you received fine dresses and good food? Who convinced Onnachild to let you stay? Who sang your praises to Raen and tempted him into your bed? I don't expect you to be grateful, but I do expect some recognition and your trust. Think what else he has lied to you about. Did he not say he would get rid of Eldini and yet here she is,' he bangs her chair, 'sat right opposite you. Go and ask him if you don't believe me. Go and ask him where Ammi is.'

'He wouldn't do that to me. Nessia, he wouldn't, would he?'

'Maybe there is some of his father in him,' she says.

I sprint from the Judging Room.

Chapter Seventy-Three

THE FADING SUNLIGHT AND PALE SHADOWS RIPPLE across the floor, making the stones seem alive and shifting under my feet. My shoulders bang into walls and my bare arms collect more scratches. Laughter follows me: the boom of Onnachild's, the trill of a woman, the gleeful giggle of Aelius. My feet pound hard. My calves and shins hurt. My lungs burn with the effort to keep running. And my heart, my heart hurts worst of all. I welcome the pain because it stops me from thinking.

But I must think, same as I must keep running. Where would they be? In Eldini's rooms or Raen's? There isn't time to be wrong. Can I trust Raen? He hasn't mentioned the covenant, he didn't tell the castle about us, and he wasn't the one to mention Aelius, Vill was. Raen's been protecting me. Has he? Maybe he's biding his time as Vill claims. Why would Raen send Ammi away when he promised he'd return her to me? Because he's a liar. He told me he was. Everyone lies in this castle. Even Aelius.

The other stolen children flit through my mind: the hag's boy, presumed dead by the villagers, stolen by wolves according to his mother; Melody a fake Maiden, with a different name she can't remember and parents grieving somewhere; Raen, not stolen but banished. Is Ammi to join this list of motherless children? Is Raen so similar to his father? I cradle my unborn baby as I keep pounding through the hallways. Tears blur my way.

I skid around a corner, into a hallway bright with sunlight and torches. Guards are stationed outside Eldini's door, and they raise their swords, flashes of orange, of gold reflect from the steel. Is this what we've come to? 'Don't you dare,' I scream. 'Out of my way.' I push at the blades. 'I'll kill you if you don't get out of the way.' The blood pouring from my hands shocks them; they can't be used to angry women. It doesn't shock me. 'Move.' I stumble from the force of their push back.

The door opens. The swords drop. Raen is there, stern and tense.

'Let her in,' he says.

The guards move aside.

Into Eldini's rooms I stagger, following Raen. Last time I was here, Ammi was curled up on my lap, showing me her doll with my name. Through the open bedchamber door, I see Eldini sat on her bed, head in her hands. She lifts her head up, peers at me. She looks terrified. Good. I want her to be terrified for did she not promise me Ammi and call us friends? I'm glad I deceived her. 'Out,' I yell at her as I rush inside. 'Out now.'

'These are her rooms.' Gavin moves to stand between me and her.

'Both of you, out, this is between me and Raen.' My chest is heaving with anger. Blood is dripping onto her floor. 'I'll drag you both out if I have to.'

Gavin cups her elbow and starts ushering her from the room. Her eyes, those pale big eyes, too far apart, too full of innocence, keep watch of me until the very last moment. Then the latch clicks, and Raen and I are alone.

We stand there. We're almost mirror images of each other, scowling, jaws clenched. There's shame and guilt in his unblinking stare—he knows why I'm here. Still, I'm aware of how handsome he is, and my body responds to us being alone, aching to end this and make it right the only way it knows how. It's a weakness. I steel myself against it.

'Where's Ammi?' My calves sting as I raise myself up, shove my face at his. I expect him to flinch, want him to, but he keeps staring. His eyes blur into brown and flecks of green. The smell of him makes my heart pang. It can't be true. *Please, Raen, don't let it be true.* My fingers twitch to hold his.

'She's not here.'

'As in these rooms or the castle?'

'Not in the castle. I had to send her away.'

'Where is she?'

'Safe.' One small word. Two slight twitches at the corner of his left eye.

'Safe?' I fall down onto my heels. 'From me? I'm her mother.'

'Yes, safe from you. Safe from all this. Do you think your Followers are the only ones who can threaten innocent children?'

'Threatened?' I reach behind me, and the only steady thing I find is the post of the royal bed. 'Who? What do you mean? Raen, what have you done to her? Don't—'

'Me? Not me. What do you think I am? First a rapist and now a murderer of children?'

'Don't play with me, Raen.' My hands slip on the post. 'Where is my daughter?'

'She's not your daughter anymore. You lost her the second you came into this place. In fact, you didn't lose her. You gave her away. Was it worth it, Niah?'

'Shut up,' I scream. 'She's mine. Tell me where she is.' I grab his tunic.

'So you can tell Vill?'

I push him, and he stumbles from foot to foot. His expression never changes. There's nothing there for me, nothing to let me in. Vill was right. Ammi has gone. All this for nothing. My Ammi. I slap him. Left then right. As hard as I can. He takes the slaps, takes the impact when they turn to punches, and he smiles. Smiles even when I stop and start sobbing. He has won. He has.

'Is that all you've got? Come on, Niah, right here.' He thrusts his jaw at me. 'Go on and then I can tell the castle all about it.'

I fall onto the bed. The same bed he has shared with Eldini. Her imprint is still there. I put my throbbing hand in it. It's warm. My body quivers from spent anger, and I'm suddenly so tired, so hungry. I clutch onto the bedpost, rest my cheek against it. 'Please. Just tell me where she is. Let me see her. Please ... you know how much she means to me.'

'Do I?'

I rock with the motion of him pressing his palms down either side of me. 'You could have had her. Didn't I promise you? I went against Onnachild to take you to her, and what have you done for her? Put her life in danger, but you didn't think of that did you? Same as it never occurred to you that I might actually be a good king. Who do you think stopped the battle? Cut down on the waste here? Started bringing back my mother's people?'

I raise my hand to push him away.

'Vill?' he mocks.

Is that not what I was told? Vill, who has never lied to me. Vill, who tells me things I don't want to hear. I should have believed him. I shouldn't have come here.

'Well, it was me. Not him. Me, and I'd have been good to you.'

'I don't care about that, not now.' My palm rests on his chest. My push is weak. 'Raen. This isn't fair. Tell me, where—'

'And saying I raped you is?'

'I didn't.'

'As good as. Both of us know you were more than willing to lie with me when you thought you might get something out of it, even stooping so low as to say you loved me.'

'I never said that. I never even thought that. You must have dreamt it.'

He chuckles. That sneer is back. The Raen I saw crying over his mother; the Raen who showed me the ruins of her garden; the Raen who tried to protect me from the gods has gone. My blood is smeared across his cheeks. It covers his scar, and a lock of his hair is stuck to it. His eyes are so dark, the green dots almost consumed by it. I force myself to my feet. My head is spinning. Vill lied. No. Raen lied. I lied. Onnachild lied. I imagine him laughing, feel it like pins and needles in my limbs. Raen follows me as I try to escape the room.

His words are cold and calm. 'One day you will have to explain it to Aelius and Ammi, explain how you could be crying over him and fucking me. How many months after he died was it? How many months after you birthed his daughter? Shall we count them?'

'You don't understand love,' I mumble, lurching from side to side while the door seems to be moving further and further away.

Still, Raen goes on and on, at my back like he's my shadow. 'No wonder he didn't want to marry you. He never did. You weren't special to him. You aren't special to me.'

I lunge for the door handle.

'They were to marry that summer. That summer. If he'd lived he would have been her husband. And Ammi would have stayed a bastard.'

'You're just bitter because no one has ever loved you.' I open the door.

He slams it shut.

I fall into it. 'You're lying.'

'Am I? I can get that contract for you, show you clearly where his name appears and where Eldini's appears. Shall I get it? Do you want to see the date? Maybe my little half-brother wasn't so perfect.'

I spin around. If he won't let me leave, then I'll go down fighting. I confront his smug face, so dark and tense. A hard face, a face made sharp by watching his parents die, and nothing like Aelius's soft beauty. 'I pity Eldini, wanting you to love her. No one could love you. At least now she knows who you really are.'

'The only thing I pity are your children, Ammi and that child you carry, if indeed there is anything there. It amazes me that anything good could actually grow inside of you.'

I snatch his wrist, force his hand to my stomach. Pin it there until his fist unfurls. It's my turn to smirk as he's startled, as his eyes widen, as his fingers slide up and down. 'And it will hate you as much as I do,' I say.

Raen shrugs and turns away.

I open the door. This ends now. And I know how.

Chapter Seventy-Four

A PART OF ME CAN'T BELIEVE what I have in my hands, yet I can feel the bumps of the rough parchment and the sharp corners digging into my palms. My hands are so damp with sweat and blood I'm worried the words will be washed away. I wipe them on my skirts. My heart hammers but I'm not afraid anymore, and when Ascelin asks me if I'm ready to continue my yes is so firm and loud that it forces Raen to look at me.

His face has been cleaned; no evidence of my slaps remains. It is as if they never happened. But they did. His words remain, pounding against my temple. He'll regret them. Already, he's lost Eldini's support; she hasn't joined us at the table. Neither has Gavin. I smile. Underneath the table, I unfold the note.

The castle people are poised like animals waiting to steal a kill. There are more green dresses, more green jewels flashing across the room. They're turning against Raen. Good. The sun is fading. Night is coming and in the changing light are the hazy shadows of my ancestors come to witness the final judgment. The First Queen stands by the window, surveying everything that was once hers. No longer is she in her death garb but dressed in furs so lavish they flutter with the breeze coming in through the opened windows. She frowns at me. I'll not protect Raen anymore. By any means, Vill had said. Ammi has gone and so I have nothing left to lose.

'In summary,' Aesc says.

'Not in summary,' I shout. I jump out of my chair, wave the note in the air. 'Raen has no claim to the throne.'

'Just give it up,' he hisses.

Nessia tries to pull me down. 'What are you doing?'

Vill looks smug as he nods at the advisers. The three of them are struggling to hide their smiles. That doesn't matter.

Raen tries to snatch the letter from me. 'What is that?'

'This?' I tease him with it, wafting it so close a strand of his fringe is disturbed. 'Would you like me to read it?' I slap it down onto the table before him. 'Except you can't read the old language, can you?'

Raen leans over the table. He pales as he recognises his mother's writing, her name. Oh, how I enjoy watching Raen's bewilderment as it moves over his features: first his lips falling open, then clamping shut, his eyes narrowing, his brow lowering, and his eyebrows drawing together, deepening the lines between. *Who has won now?* The advisers rush forwards.

'Where? How do you ...?' He peers up at me, hurt creating lines in his face as his finger traces over her name. He won't trick me again with that little-boy-lost expression.

'Written by your mother,' I shout to the castle. 'To her lover.' See, I want to say, I'm not the only unfaithful woman here, and my children are not the only bastards in this castle. 'It proves why he preferred Aelius to you. It proves why he'd never have given you the throne.'

'Lies.' Raen's hand fists around the note.

'If you don't believe me, then ask Mantona.' My voice is as cold as his was in Eldini's room. I cross my arms and glare down at him. 'She'll tell you who your real father is.'

Ascelin calls out Mantona's name.

'Seems the King was right after all,' Aesc says.

'Horse shit.' Raen shoves the table. 'And you know this is horse shit.' His index finger stabs towards Aesc. 'You had your proof. Onnachild had his proof.' He touches his scar. 'You ask Mantona about that letter.' He throws it at me. I don't move; I let it bounce off my shoulder. He'll never forgive me and I'll never forgive him. Now we are even.

'Eldini, Eldini.' The voice is hoarse, implying the woman's been yelling for a long time. Raen turns towards the sound.

'Eldini?' he shouts.

'The baby,' the woman yells.

Nessia grabs my skirt as Raen runs from the room. Aesc picks up the note, smooths it out, and then presses it in between the pages of his book, a sly smile on his face.

'Well done,' Vill says to me. 'I didn't think you would.'

'But Eldini's too early,' I say to Nessia. Her head is down, hidden in her hands. 'Far too early.'

'I knew it,' Vill says. 'I do love it when I'm right.'

Melody is squeezing her way through the castle people, ducking under arms, climbing over chairs. 'Four or five cycles she said,' I tell Nessia. 'She can't be—'

'Niah, did you hear me?' Melody's out of breath. 'Eldini ... asking ... for you.'

'What? Why?'

'She's calling for you. She's in pain. Please, come. We don't know what to do, and she's asking for you. She's in such distress. Please?'

'Don't go.' Vill touches my arm.

'How can you be so cruel?' Nessia raises her head and stares at Vill like he's a stranger.

'It will not do us any favours,' he says.

'I don't know,' I say to Nessia. 'I don't know what to do. Why does she want to see me?'

'What would your grandmother do?' Nessia asks.

None of the things I've done. She'd be ashamed of me. I nod. This is not Eldini's fault. None of this is, and I can't let her suffer for my actions. For Raen's actions. I have to make it up to her. Like me, she's been used. Unlike me, she's remained good.

The three of us speed our way to Eldini's room. At the windows, black shadows peer in with beady green eyes. I'm in too much of a hurry to consider them. We pass the portraits of Onnachild's ancestors and with them is Eldini's portrait. Stoic, uncertain, determined: qualities I've seen in her expression, but none of them are there now. I see only a young woman wanting to be loved. I must get there quicker. I pick up my skirts. Melody's headdress falls off. There is no time to stop for it. Nessia huffs behind us, trying to keep up.

'Get Nessia's purse of herbs,' I shout to Melody. Why did I not think of that sooner? She turns off down a hallway. Nessia and I sprint on. The hallways seem to lengthen, never ending, only turning into another one and another. The same shadows. The same fading sun. And a scent I can't name in my panicked state, but it's familiar, and it has my stomach churning.

We turn left, pause at a yelp from Eldini's room. Nessia looks at me, waits for me to move. I can't, but I must. Nessia nods and opens the door. At least she remembers my grandmother's lessons: compassion, kindness, honesty. I wish I'd remembered them when I entered the castle.

I creep into the room, holding onto the door frame. The stench of blood is strong and meaty. Mine is still on the floor. I follow the splatters, some turned to streaks, into the bedchamber. Nessia's behind me, whispering encouragement for me to continue on.

Eldini is a round and writhing ball on the bed. My blood is on the bedpost. Her women stare at me, eyes pale like hers, pleading.

'The gods help us if we are the last people she sees,' Nessia whispers.

'I'm here.' I force a light tone into my voice pretending Eldini's called me for wine and gossip, but I move towards the bed as tentatively as if I'm in a nightmare.

Her hand floats up, grey as any morning shadow. It trembles as she beckons me over to the bed. She groans, low and guttural. Her arms wrap around her middle. 'Niah,' she calls out once the contraction has passed. Her cold hand clasps mine so tightly, and I don't know how she can bear to touch me after everything I've done to her.

'I didn't know you loved him,' she says.

'It doesn't matter,' I say, unsure whether she means Raen or Aelius.

'It does.' Using me, she tries to pull herself up. The strain brings fresh sweat to her wide forehead.

'Where is Raen?' Nessia asks. 'He ran ahead of us.'

'The midwife wouldn't let him in,' Lark says.

I didn't even realise Lark was here. She's stood with the other Maidens by the closed window, all of them clutching their holy books, which are bright white against their mourning dresses. I look for the midwife but can't find her.

'Get him,' Nessia says. 'It's only right he should be here.'

609

A Maiden nods and skids off into a sprint. Eldini tugs me closer. 'If you said ... I would not ... not married him. Raen. I asked.'

I can't think about what she's saying, can't tell her I don't love him. No, I mustn't think of him as I keep stroking her knuckles. My gods have been here. I see their markings: a brown smudge on her bed sheet, muddy prints on the ceiling, a charred spot on the bed hangings. They are still here.

As my gaze frantically searches the room, one creeps past me, causing shivers up my spine and making my scar sting. It sits down hard on her chest. The god is a mass of worm-coloured flesh, shiny and stretched. He holds the neck of her gown in his long, horny fingers. I try to bash him off with our joined hands. He breathes out thick, brown puffs onto her face.

'Say ... forgive me,' Eldini moans. 'I make peace.'

The god turns its bulbous head towards me. Its eyes are pond green. The thin lips open into a smile. I see into its mouth; the sharp incisors are clogged with traces of raw meat. *No. You are done. You have Onnachild. Leave her.* The god has not been satisfied yet, though. Above it, collecting on the ceiling, are the dead, peering at Eldini as she suffers another contraction.

'Open the windows,' I yell at the Maidens. There's no place for the dead to go otherwise and they must go if we're to save Eldini. Lark fumbles with the latch. The Maidens' black and grey dresses waft and their headdresses tinkle as the wind pushes its way into the room. The god slinks off, its oily skin slipping against my bare arms.

The god's done its job of stealing all Eldini's colour. Her pupils have spread into her irises, covering that pale blue. Her skin is whiter than the pillow she rests on. Her hair has stuck to her face like seaweed, reminding me ... have they really waited this long? Why are the gods so desperate, so vengeful? Have they not had enough death? Onnachild. The nursemaid. Not Eldini too. *Leave her alone. She's done you no harm; she isn't the*

Second Queen. I must focus. 'How long has this been going on?' I ask.

'The bleeding? It started this morning but she ... she insisted on ...' Lark ducks her head. The Judging. All that time she was sat there ...

'Eldini, it's you who must forgive me.' I squeeze her hand.

Her eyelids flutter.

Did Raen know? Did he insist she stay beside him to add to his facade of being a good husband, a good man, while she was bleeding out? She must have known, surely, that she was losing her baby?

'Sing to your god,' I tell the Maidens and her women. Maybe their god is real. Maybe he can undo the damage mine have done. If there's anyone who deserves a god's protection, it's Eldini. The Maidens look at each other, waiting for a decision. Lark takes the lead, her voice wobbling and weak until the others join in. It's a song I recognise from Eldini and Raen's wedding day. Eldini smiles so I don't stop them, even though it makes my own baby fidget. I dare not try to calm it when the gods are so close in case the action draws their attention.

Eldini's hand rips from mine as another contraction takes her over. 'Breathe,' I say. 'Breathe through it.' I glance up at the ceiling. At least the dead have gone. I lean closer to Eldini, feel her breath, a light flutter. It smells of mud and mould.

Nessia comes forwards with a bowl of water and starts mopping Eldini's forehead. The water glides off and into her hair, darkening it.

'Was it ... same for you?' Eldini asks.

'Yes.' My last lie to her, told with the hope it will make her fight to live.

'Don't worry,' Nessia says. 'Melody will be here with my herbs soon. We can ease some of the pain.'

Eldini nods. Her eyes close and she lies there panting, her hand keeping the curve of our clasp as it rests on the bed.

Nessia peels back the furs. Blood, shit, and piss have mingled together, plastering against her thighs where she has bucked and rolled against the pain. It's too late. Raen's child is gone. *Please, can that loss be enough to placate the gods?* Eldini's belly is a bright pink thing, lined and scarred where the skin has been swelled to its limit. She's been broken by Raen's child. Nessia and I look at each other, fearful.

'We must stop the bleeding,' I mumble.

She nods.

'Where is Melody?'

'We should clean her,' Nessia says. 'Before Raen gets here.'

The Maidens rush into action, darting in and out of the room as Lark issues instructions. They bring buckets of water and a block of soap. They clean her. They take away buckets of dirty water. A bath is ordered. Lark rings out a rag and unfurls it. She passes it to me.

'It'll ease your guilt,' she whispers.

Only I'm too scared of Eldini's body, of touching it because it's been loved by Raen, caressed by the same fingers that mine was. 'Where is Raen?' I ask Nessia. 'He must want to check on his wife?' He must know he has little time left to beg for her forgiveness. Perhaps he doesn't care about her. I didn't when I was satisfying my lust. At least I am here now.

Nessia doesn't answer because Eldini moans again and clots pulse out, gloopy and so dark they don't even look like blood.

'We need to get rid of this,' I say.

Between us, we manage to lift Eldini as another Maiden snatches away and balls up the linen containing the last pieces of Raen's child. As gently as possible, we lay Eldini back down. If it were not for the sadness in her eyes, I'd think she was dead. I grab a cloth and start washing her legs. Melody arrives at last. She throws Nessia's purse to me.

'Something for the pain, something for the bleeding,' I say to myself as I tip the contents out over the bed. I caress my belly. *Please, can my baby be stronger than Eldini's?* I want it. I want it so much. As much as Eldini wanted hers. I shouldn't be in here; it's a bad omen. But I have to try to save her from the gods, reverse some of the damage I've done. Nessia starts scrabbling through the herbs, reminding me I need to focus. We sort through them. We scatter dried brown pieces over the bed, onto the floor.

'It'll be all right,' I call over my shoulder to Eldini. She doesn't respond. My hands shake, knock Nessia's as we reach for the same herb. I look again at Eldini, forcing myself to smile to reassure her. Lark shakes her head.

Eldini's face is slack. Her mouth is open. Her chest isn't moving. Her belly is still swollen for a baby that decided not to wait, and she's never been more moonlike than she is now with her face so round, with her skin tinged blue. The musicians will write the most beautiful songs for her.

I'm useless. Here, once again, to be a witness only, just as I was on the battlefield. Is this something else I should write in the Aegnian book? We caused this, Raen and I, by being unable to stand up to Onnachild, by squabbling like children over something that wasn't important. He was right: we are like him. Neither of us has won. Onnachild has. He's corrupted us both.

'What is she doing here?' Raen shouts.

I jump and the herbs trickle from my hand as Raen and I watch them.

'We tried,' Nessia says.

The women are crying.

'Tried? What do you mean you tried?' He doesn't move from the door. He doesn't let go of the door frame as he surveys the scene. 'What's happened?'

Surely, he can see. He must know. His nostrils are flared, taking in the odour of death and blood. He doesn't move to be with her. His brow lowers. His hand drops from the door.

Behind him, helping to carry a tub with other servants, is the hag's boy. His face is ashen; he realises what's happened, even if Raen's too shocked to. The tub thumps onto the floor.

'She did it! Her and them fire-beasts.'

'What have you done?' Raen's voice is little more than a whisper.

'The baby ...' Lark says.

He grimaces. 'And Eldini?'

'At peace.'

'Peace?' Raen's voice booms above the sobbing women.

'Dead,' the hag's boy shouts. 'Dead. And she did it. That hedge-born heathen. Evil.'

Raen's eyes lock onto mine. 'Shut up!' he yells. The colour drains from him and he's as pale as a castle man. His jaw pulses. His nostrils flare.

'Killed her, she did. That fire-fucker. Oh, protect us! Protect us from them fire-beasts. Get her.'

'What did you put in that wine?' Raen shoots across the room. No one can stop him. I can't step away.

'Get her.'

He pins me to the wall. My toes dangle in the air. Nessia calls his name.

'Get her. Get the evil bitch.'

Raen smacks me against the wall, knocks the air from my lungs. 'You destroy everything. My half-brother. My father—' His hands fasten around my throat. I should fight him but I can't, because it was me. He's right but not the wine. It's my fault for calling in things I don't understand.

'Raen! Raen!' Nessia sounds so distant.

'Get her. Get her.' Glee tinges the boy's voice as it did when the children watched me struggle in the river. Raen's grip tightens. But it's his fault, too. As his fingers bite into my neck, my body fights of its own accord. *Let me give up, please.* I bite my tongue, taste my own blood.

'Stop it.' Nessia tries to prise off Raen's hands. 'You've already lost one child.'

Women are shouting, are running.

'Find Vill.'

'Get her. Get her.'

There's too much in my head, too many thoughts, memories, images that are mine and images that are not mine: Onnachild as a young man, more handsome than Raen, riding through our lands, his sword slashing through my people; a child staring up in wonder at his mother and in his dark eyes, three green dots; villagers, hateful and hungry, ripping bricks out of a wall to find secrets, so many secrets; my grandmother's feet swinging; and love as a magnificent yellow light like the first spark of the first fire. Then black fills me, my eyes, my head, my body; the shadows are coming for me. *Is it me you have wanted all along?*

Part VI: Soot

Chapter Seventy-Five

IN MY DREAMS, he comes for me, my unknown and unnamed child. His face is unfeatured, little more than mud. A dark fuzz of mahogany-coloured hair covers his head. He totters towards me with unsteady steps, his stumpy legs wobbly from weakness, and it takes all his concentration to walk towards my open arms. I call him, but no sound comes from my mouth. He gurgles with pleasure at his achievement, and chuckles when I sweep him up and swing him around. The colours of the garden blur together as we spin: browns, greens, yellows, gold, white. He's soft in my arms. He smells of mushrooms and the damp forests he's been playing in. When he kicks his legs out in excitement, brown smudges are left on my white dress. Our laughter mixes into a single sound, one similar to the song of the trees surrounding us. Yews, laburnums, shaking aspens. He clings to me while I lavish his podgy cheeks with kisses. Birds appear around us, flying up into thick branches which keep the bright sun from his hazelnut-coloured skin.

The clouds darken and thicken. All the colours become smudges of grey, bleeding together into one mess of night. Thunder booms. Lightning cuts through the darkness. A golden hawk flies overhead. My son screams. The sound judders through my body, making my ears sting. Shadows rise from the earth, climbing around the silver trees with their long limbs and disjointed fingers. Even the birds are shrieking. Goldfinches, phoenixes, cormorants. They try to fly away but they're stuck to the tarry shadows and the more they fight the more their wings are coated.

I try to hide my son in the folds of my cloak but he's already gone, turned to a purse of ash. The ash trickles out, as steady as one long, exhaled breath until there's only an empty purse in my arms. My feet are grey and buried in the ash. The smell of the dead is creeping over the perfumed flowers, smothering them and turning them to black shrivelled stumps. Leaves flutter down like dead moths. The ground is puckering and sucking at my feet. I try to pull free, try to cling onto the branches above me but they break in my hand. Milk oozes from my breasts, congealed and yellow. The stench makes me gag. I scream. I scream and the sound is black smoke from my mouth.

My eyes snap open. I'm in my bed, not home but the castle. I lie there hot and sweating under the furs, scared of what might have seeped from my dreams. 'Nessia,' I whisper. 'Nessia.'

She jolts awake, lifts her head from the pillow beside me. 'Yes?'

I feel my belly, running my palm over it with the hope that my dream lied to me. 'Gone?' My throat scratches with the word. She leans closer. *Please, don't make me say it again.*

'Hush now. Hush.' The sadness in her eyes gives me my answer. 'Don't trouble yourself. You need to sleep. Go back to sleep.'

'I can't.' I cough. 'I'm scared to. My dreams ...'

'Niah, you're exhausted.' She strokes my forehead. Does my skin feel as hot to touch as it does to be in? 'You must let your dreams take you where

617

they want to. Don't fight them. They'll heal you.'

'I can't. You don't understand. They don't come to help. They come to take me. I don't want to die. I don't.' I push off the furs. 'I must leave this room. They linger here. They were in my breath, in my eyes. They came back with me. They did. There.' Hiding underneath a chair by the fire, I see one of them pretending to mix with the normal shadow. They can't fool me. 'I must get out. I need the sun. I need air.' I force myself off the bed, coughing, spluttering from the roughness of words. Nessia fusses around me as if I'm a baby she's waiting to catch.

'Come to bed. Wait. I'll open the curtains—will that be better?' She rushes to let the sun in and it bursts in like a golden army. I remember other things that were gold which I've tarnished.

The bells are ringing, ding, dong, ding, dong, ringing incessantly for another death. Is it mine? Yet I stand here, breathing, trembling. It can't be me.

'Who? The bells?'

'Vill. They hanged him.'

It can't be true. Perfectly sculptured Vill isn't human enough to die. I stumble, half fall, to the windows and struggle to open them wide. My hands cling to the frame as I lean out into the wind. It's so cool and refreshing, as cold as Vill's eyes, and the sky is as white as his skin. Some people have gone into the sky. Some have gone into the fire. Some will remain in the castle, haunting it with their scent of vanilla and lemon. I'm next, and where will I go? My feet lift from the floor. I could let go. I could let the wind take my body.

'Niah. Come away from the window.'

'Mantona?'

'Dead too.'

'Then I'm next. Onnachild was right.'

'About what?'

The trees outside are magnificent, each leaf a small fire: reds, ambers, yellows. Robins are ready for winter. Their little red breasts are patches of colour against the white sky. The trees are talking to each other; they'll have much to gossip about. I laugh at how stupid they must think us.

Raen's walking alone, weaving amongst the trees. He's a dark stain disappearing into shadows, reappearing. His shoulders are so broad. I remember the curve of them, the taste of them. He runs his fingers through his hair, and I see the different colours, just like the leaves. He's a wood nymph, blending with the trees and the earthy colours of autumn. Is that why his children are taken? They go back into the forest to feed up the soil, return to the trees that made them.

I shout out to him.

He looks up. His eyes are mottled like bark. Nessia tries to drag me into the room. I let go of the windowsill, give myself up to what will be.

'I know where your children are,' I shout.

Losing my footing, I land on her and laugh. How ridiculous this is. Everything: my empty stomach, Vill hanged, my numb heart. 'I know where they were taken,' I tell Nessia. 'They aren't real children. They aren't real at all. We were carriers of nothing like life, me, Eldini.'

'Hush.' She strokes my face, again and again. Why does she seem so panicked? 'The physician will be here soon. Let us get you ready for him. Come on back to bed.'

'It's too late for a physician. My baby has gone. They took him back. Look. Feel. I'm empty.'

She tries to lead me to the bed, but I will not return to those dreams. Does she not understand? Where are the dead? 'They were there, underneath the chair. Have they left? Check for me, please.'

'Then you will go to bed?'

They've had enough now; they must leave. I'll tell them. They won't listen to me. She gets onto her hands and knees. The shadow under the

619

chair moves, darkens her hand as she sweeps it back and forth. 'There's nothing there. See.'

They'll return but I don't tell her that. 'What happened to the fire?'

'Would you like one?'

I nod.

She works quickly and skilfully to coax out the flames. They dance together, sliding, jumping, lifting each other. Within the smoke, I look for my child's features. Nessia rubs wet, cold linen across my face. Her rough touch makes my head wobble. Melody's at the door with a stranger. He has a long grey beard and his hair is tied back. There are bumps across his scalp. He seems in need of a wife.

'This is the Royal Physician,' Nessia says.

'Hello, Niah.' He moves towards me. Melody hides behind him.

'You're too late. Eldini doesn't need you anymore.' I turn my attention to the flames' beauty. If I could catch one I'd make it talk to me, tell me about fate, about pain. When I reach the land of the dead, I must remember to ask Mantona about her mistakes and what she wanted to do differently. Perhaps someone there will tell me what I should have done.

'What is it that ails you?' His voice is as croaky as a frog's and the resemblance makes me laugh.

'Nothing. Frogs can't help me.'

'You're sick. Let him help you,' Nessia pleads.

He kneels before me. His eyes are hazel—green and brown have merged and faded. I don't like them. He puts his freezing hands to my throat.

I flinch. 'Stop touching me.'

Then to my head.

'I don't want anyone touching me.' I slap him off, scrabble away.

'She's not been herself since ... since ...' Nessia says. 'She sleeps little and has these imaginings.'

'Imaginings?' he croaks.

'Not imaginings,' I say, but he's in the new religion, Onnachild's religion. He wouldn't understand these things. 'Nessia, tell him.'

'I will.'

'She mutters to herself,' Melody says. 'She sees things, everywhere on the ceiling, in the water, in the fire. Horrible things. I don't ... it's scary.'

'And her wounds?'

I laugh to hear it called that. Wounds? They never heal. They are scar tissue now, hard and ridged, but still so easy to tear again and again and again.

'Healing well. There was no fever, no pus. I thought at first this was poison on her brain, but there are no signs,' Nessia says.

'Let me see.'

Nessia and Melody take my weight between them. I'm too little of nothing to fight them as they strip me for the physician, but I have a voice, raspy as it is.

'Don't let him look at me. I don't know him. Leave me some dignity.' Though I'm aware, truly, I lost that a long time ago, when I was someone else. When I was wrapped in rags and someone else's cloak, believing I had a right and a place here. It makes me laugh. They allow him to prod and poke me, move my limbs, peer at my flesh.

The door opens, and I cry out at seeing Raen there. I break free of Nessia and Melody, manage to pull furs around my naked body. 'I don't want him here. I don't want any more of his disappearing children. My body is broken.'

His mother is by his side. She wears the dress Nessia altered for me. I can't read the First Queen's expression. She must be angry. Has she come to punish me? You've done enough, I want to tell her, but I hide under the furs. They smell of sweat, of fear. They smell of the wall. Oh, if only I had not passed through it but stayed in the village, staring up at it, dreaming. Dreams should not come true; they are only nightmares when they do. Still, I can hear his voice. Still, I can see her ambiguous expression. She looks too much like him when he's trying to hide something from me.

'She's completely mad. I can see no physical reason for these outbursts,' the physician says.

'She isn't. She's choosing to play mad.' Raen pulls the fur from my head. 'Is this another of your tricks?'

'You are the biggest trickster. You should wear a fool's hat and dance in the moonlight for all the things you don't understand.' I grin at him, as wide as I can.

'She's doing it to punish me. Aren't you, Niah? Tell them you are.'

'I forgot all about you weeks ago. You can no longer hurt me. I know where the children are. I know where you put them.'

Melody's crying, but it sounds like my voice. When I touch my face, there are no tears.

'What are you talking about?'

'I won't tell you. If you've forgotten where they are then that is better for them.'

'There are places overseas where she might find respite,' the physician says. 'Perhaps I may suggest Saddle House.'

'She isn't going,' Raen says.

'Yes. Take me there. Take me away.' I stare into his dark eyes that have no end. I narrow mine that resemble his mother's; he'll not have those, either. Which face of his is this one supposed to be: gaunt, deep lines, and that fuzz over his jaw and cheeks? Not castle. Not village. His hair has lost the careful shape it was cut into for the Judgment. Who are you pretending to be now, Raen?

'You are not mad.'

I enjoy the quiver of uncertainty in his voice. 'But you'd like me to be.'

'No. Niah. No.' He crushes me to his chest, pinning my breath between us. My chest shrivels against him.

'Get him off me,' I shout as loud as I can. 'I won't let him touch me again.'

He drops away. 'We'll talk.' He leads the physician from my room.

'Dress me,' I snap at Melody and Nessia. 'I'm not mad. I'm not. There's nothing mad about me. Why am I mad? The gods visited me. If he had faith, he'd see.' I drag a dress from the floor and pull it on as they stand still as statues. The thought makes me laugh. The gold of my love. The silver of Vill. Emeralds of my eyes. My fingers shake too much for me to fasten my dress. Nessia starts weeping. I turn my back to them for their help.

'Don't cry for me. I don't need tears. They can't give me anything I want.'

I smile at myself in the mirror but I don't recognise the person there, even though my hair is the same dark shade as always and my irises the same green. My fingers reach for the mirror, to trace the line of my jaw, the puffs around my eyes. My skin is paler than I remember and my cheeks are thinner. The imprint of Raen's fingers is around my neck, purple like lavender, brown like bark, and yellow like sickness. New bones have appeared across my chest, resembling the fingers of corpses, and my breasts are lumps added as an afterthought to make me appear womanly.

'Appearances are not important.' I turn away from the mirror.

'Where are you going?' Melody asks.

'The garden. Alone.'

'Can we let her? Should she?'

'I'll not kill myself.' I know what punishment is waiting for me after death and who is waiting for me. It's worse than this. This childlessness. Two I had. One I gave away. One was taken away.

I walk proudly through the hallways, ignoring the people who stop

623

their conversations to watch me pass. They bunch together, whispering behind my back. They'll see the disappearance of my children as a fitting punishment from their God. Let them. Let them learn a lesson from me. I walk by the Judging Room where, in my grandmother's youth, women shouted loudest. Playing out is my judgment. There's Raen's voice, spiteful. I run my palm over the carvings in the door as I go by: eyes and ears. How blind, deaf, and uncaring I found this place to be. Just like me.

Out in the garden, it's both bright and cold; even the season has lost its consistency. The wind and sun will try to lodge themselves into my bones so they can be brought back to bed. My soles slide over the grass and I realise I've forgotten my shoes. I giggle as I point my toes as daintily as possible. My steps are light—they're stroking a lover's skin just like Vill instructed. There will be no more lovers, only the grass and the ground, and they'll welcome my return one day. My feet take me down dips, run away from me until I fall over and roll the rest of the way to the river.

It's peaceful and still, with only the river bubbling to itself. It has its work to do, running constantly through the land, past boundaries and out to the sea where it begins its journey anew. The water numbs my hands. I let the current brace their limpness but it has too much to do to take me with it. My sleeves fall into the water. The ends billow and darken in colour. It's pretty, the way they move with the current, enticing it to play. My toes dip into the water. Blades of grass float from them and are away, out of the castle. The water twinkles in the fading sunshine, carrying away a queen's jewels. It'll beat them back down to sand, and in some village, a woman will walk them into her home only to sweep them away later.

What would I ask the First Queen if she were here with me? What did she love more, her son or her religion? What did she cry for with her last breath? The river has an easy duty, not like a queen's; it only needs to run and hurry to the sea. As long as it makes its gentle sound we're happy. I tear my sleeves off to let them be free, and I chase them to where the water dives under the wall. Can I make myself small enough to fit through?

I climb into the river, gasping at the coldness, but I carry on walking. It comes up to my shoulders. I let it nudge my legs away, drag my skirt down, lift my arms. It cushions me. I'm giggling like I never did when I was a girl. Giggling like Ammi should be. No one has ever held me with such tenderness as the river holds me. I let it bob me. Here is some peace. Here is some life. I'd rather have had a water baby. The tears I cry are calm and quiet. They are taken into the river and away from the castle.

Night comes, and the stars shine in their bright spots. They are consistent, happy to remain and be. The smallest, most timid, god sits on my wet shoulder. She sings me a sweet song in her high voice. She licks at my tears with her furry tongue. It tickles my cheek. She tells me what I must do. Things just are, her song says. Fate just is. She settles down in my collarbone and purrs like a kitten. It's not easy for me to learn submission, but I become a stone, washed and smoothed over time by the river.

We wait together for the sun to come up, to prove that day continues to overpower night. As dawn colours sweep across the sky she leaves me. In payment for the peace she gifts, I let her take my youth. The last part of me I abandon in the water with my reflection. No more will my irises flash such a vivid green. I step out of the river, dragging my heavy dress with me, and head to my rooms, not caring who sees or slips in the watery trail behind me.

Melody rushes at me as soon as I enter my dayroom, squashing my arms in her desperation to hug me. 'We thought you'd gone.'

I feel a warm kiss on my cheek. She staggers with me through the room, towards my bedchamber. 'She's back.'

Nessia squints at me through tear-swollen eyes. 'Are you cold?'

'Where have you been?' Melody asks.

'Melody, go and get a tub of hot water,' Nessia says.

Melody nods and runs off, leaving me and Nessia alone. I sit on my bed. My dress clings, cold and wet, but I don't take it off. It reminds me. 'Don't worry. I'm more than myself now.'

Nessia sinks down beside me.

'The smallest god came for me and left something precious in my heart. Replaced my grief.' I touch my chest to show her where it lodges.

'What did she take? Grief is not a pretty payment for a god.'

'She took my ability to care. She flew away with it in the morning and it sparkled in her little claws, and I was glad she took it away. I don't need it.'

'You made a hard bargain.'

'No, I haven't. You don't understand. Nessia, love has no place in this world. It brings no joy. It brings no compassion, no consideration, so I have let it go. I have let them all go. There's nothing anyone can take from me nor threaten me with. In that moment with her, I realised how unimportant I am. I accept my fate. Raen will not let me be happy and it's better our child has gone. What life would it have had? Raen will remarry; he understands his duty better than anyone. I'll not cry for what isn't meant to be mine.'

'But, Niah, he is yours. The final judgment was passed and written. You're to marry, rule together so there'll be no more disputes over the throne, and there can be other children. He can give you more children.'

My laugh is sour and hard. Like the phoenix, it seems I must rise up from the ashes. Well, I don't want to try flying anymore. 'It doesn't matter. I don't want anything. There'll be no more children with him or anyone else.'

'Another child is what you need. You were so happy. That's what you need, a family.'

'Not now. I don't want anything anymore. That's what the god gave me, that's what I'm trying to describe. If you wish to leave that can't hurt me. If Melody leaves that can't hurt me. Ammi not being mine no longer hurts. I've been touched by the stars and they left little pieces of coldness in my heart. It has saved me. It has released me.'

'I won't leave you.' Nessia's rough hands rub warmth into my skin as they did that day she rescued me from the village children.

'That's your choice, but it's my gift to you. If you wish for a husband, your own children.'

'It's flattering you think I'm young enough,' Nessia says with forced joviality and a tweak of my chin. 'Besides, you've always been like my own child.'

The door opens. It's Melody struggling with a huge pail of hot water. The steam almost obstructs her face. A brown-eyed servant drags in the tub and behind her is Raen. He's drunk and dishevelled.

'I did not ask for him,' I say.

'But I've come.'

Nessia rises, turns away from me, and directs Melody and the servant into the dayroom. She shuts the door. I rise, dragging my water-heavy dress, and start to add more wood to the fire. Raen crouches next to me on the floor. He takes the wood from me as if I can't be trusted with such a simple task. Let him do it if that's what he wants. The peace I felt in my veins becomes heavy like he's poured molten steel into me.

'Where were you, Niah?' He twists around on the floor, takes my hands in his. My fingers don't curl. The drink has enhanced his village accent, but the castle one is still there, and so I'll concentrate on that sharpness instead. 'I thought you'd done something stupid.'

'I'm done with doing stupid things.'

'You weren't yourself. You seemed ...' He brings my hands to his lips. I look away and breathe in air as cold as the stars that shone last night.

'Mad? You can say it. The word will not make it so. There's no

627

freedom for me in madness.'

'I knew it.' He pulls me into his lap, my legs scraping against the stone floor. The chill of my dress combats his warmth and I remain limp in his arms. 'Whatever you want, I'll give you. Whatever, but not leaving.' He rocks me as he did under that yew, only now, it's him crying. We should have stayed there rather than chasing after thrones or hoping for silver trees to grow. He takes a deep breath. 'We need to talk. Please?'

Let him speak his words. The sooner it's done, the sooner he'll leave. I do not have to listen. He tries to make eye contact, but I keep watch of the flames, dull because they've better things to do.

'Where should I start? The day of the funeral? Before then? Shall I start with Onnachild and make that my first confession?' He guides my head onto his shoulder. He'll be as cold and damp as me soon. The odour of stale sweat, ale, and smoky rooms clings to him. I won't inhale deeper. 'Or the eve of my wedding? Do you remember what I asked? I asked if you loved me. Remember? Truth now. I did want a yes. I told myself it would've changed everything. It was weak of me to need that yes. Was it pride? Maybe. Maybe even if you had said yes ... who knows? I'm as stubborn as you. Do I need to confess I was jealous of Aelius?'

Aelius, another liar. Another love. That doesn't hurt either anymore. Someone told me I was blinded by too much gold and they were right: the gold of his hair, the goldfinches embroidered on his clothes, the heart of the daisies in the crown I made him, his smile which lit up the room like a sun shining off a goblet.

'Bringing the marriage contract to the Judging, that was ... You didn't need that. I did it to hurt you, but you wanted to hurt me, too. Seems we both succeeded in that.' His laugh is bitter and short. 'My next confession is ... the hardest, and maybe it took you ...' He kisses my cheek. The touch reminds me that I can speak.

'I don't want you to confess anything.'

'Niah, please don't be spiteful. I'm trying. I need to. I've been waiting while you've been ... it's been going round and round in my head; I've got to get it out. If I say it, say it and nothing changes then so be it, but at least let me try. I've been a fool ... worse than a fool, I've been a coward. That night in the Judging Room, when you said you loved me, I'd let Vill get in my ear ... and he told me it was all a scheme, a plot and ... and it was easier to ... to believe him than believe you, than risk ... I wanted it to be true, what you said. As soon as you left, I was kicking myself for not saying it back because I did. I do. I love you, Niah.'

Though my heart leaps the sensation isn't as strong or as incessant as it has been; it's just habit. He gathers my wet hair off my face, perhaps to check I'm me but I'm not me. I'm not Niah village-raised, not Niah from the Aegni, and nor am I the Niah castle-made and moulded by Onnachild. 'It doesn't matter.'

'Doesn't matter?'

'What does any of it matter now? Eldini is dead.'

'And I'll be atoning for my mistakes forever. I shouldn't have married her. You were right. Part of me did want Onnachild's approval; you were right about that, too. Does it please you to know you were? He knew it. Of course, he did. And did I get it at the end? No. His final punishment, but I don't want to talk about him. He's had enough out of us. Niah, I thought you were going to ... that I'd ... I'm so sorry for ...' His hand is a shake of honey, edging towards the colours he left on my neck. They'll be gone soon. 'I know you wouldn't hurt her. There are no excuses. I never thought I'd be capable of ...' His hand stops before I have to tell him no. It's returned to my hip, pressing my river-chilled dress to me, but I don't shiver and I don't tremble. 'Maybe I don't understand love, but I want to try to. I always wanted to try to with you.'

The words slide off me like the water dripping from my hair. They're too late. He no longer feels like home, though his lap is warm and

629

comfortable, though the beat of his heart is familiar. Home was destroyed by the villagers when I went after my dreams. Well, I don't believe in dreams anymore. All I can believe in is death.

'Vill can't be brought back to life. Mantona can't be brought back to life.' And neither can I. I was stupid to think I could be.

'There's no excuse, but I thought it'd make me feel ... better, punishing them. It didn't and ... You need to know, Niah, she wrote that letter. Mantona, and she started those rumours about my mother, both at Onnachild's request. He wanted proof so he could ... so he could justify what he did and Mantona willingly gave it to him. I never thought I'd see it, that letter. It's not Mother's handwriting; I'd recognise hers anywhere ... Mantona confessed but I've always known it was her. Mother told me. And for years, I wanted to ... planned ... Revenge, it's all I've known for so long, you understand that, I know you do. I never thought I'd get the chance ... And I certainly never thought I'd meet you. If I could, of course, I'd do things differently. So differently. There's so much I'd do differently.'

'Some things can't be undone; have you not learnt that?' Only babies can be undone. And love, too; I forgot that, that can be undone. 'You're like Onnachild, thinking they can.'

'Don't. I'm nothing like him, and you know that.' He tucks my hair behind my ear. A drop of water gets under the neck of my dress, tickles down my spine. 'I realise I can't just say I'm sorry and all my mistakes will be corrected, forgiven.'

'I learnt my lessons, though it took me long enough, and I'll not be anyone's whore again.'

'I shouldn't have said that, and Niah, I'm not asking for that. Didn't you hear me? I love you. Ammi's returned. Niah, you have the throne. You won.'

'I didn't win. Onnachild won. He's ruined both of us.'

'No, he hasn't. I'm going to fix things. I'm going to create something good out of the mess. For days, I've been convincing the advisers it'd be in the castle's best interest for us to marry, to share the throne and the land.'

'I don't want your charity.'

'By all the gods, by all the stars, by my mother, and whatever else you want me to swear by, it's not charity. I love you. And you love me. Niah, I need you, and this land needs an Aegni woman on that throne, ruling.' He presses his cheek against my forehead. His skin is too hot, like a pan I got burnt by, and yet all I can do is tense against it and let it hurt.

'I don't want the throne; it's poisonous.'

'Of course you do.'

'No. I want to make things. Things that last.'

'That won't be enough. You'll change your mind, I know you will. If you need me to prove myself to you, then I will. We can wait until then before getting married, before trying for more children if that's what you need. We can wait until I've restored the village to its former glory if that's what it takes for me to prove myself, but let me try. Say you'll let me try and say we'll at least be friends again. Do you not miss that? What if I tell you how I got my scar? You always wanted to know, remember?' He presses my palm to that scar, keeps it pinned there. His tears are as cold and wet as river water on my fingertips.

'I lied,' he says. 'Onnachild didn't do it. He wouldn't do it himself, of course he wouldn't, but he ordered for it to be done, and watched to make sure it was. Ascelin pinned me down and Aesc sliced out a chunk of my skin. I was three. I screamed and screamed for my father to help me but he just stood watching, arms crossed. That was the day I realised ...' His swallow is loud. 'He didn't care about me.' His jaw pulses against my palm, calling for my body to respond. My dress may be drying but I can recall the river, the littlest god and everything she held in her claws. I am empty. I am tired. I have no tears left, no, not even for a small boy.

'Later, once I'd been sent away, I learnt it was meant to prove I wasn't

631

his son, make it much easier for him to get rid of my mother and me. Mantona told him your grandmother would somehow ... I don't know, there'd be some charm or herb or something ... the how disappeared with her. What I do know is that it proved I was his.'

He leans back. His watery eyes plead with me to give him no lies, no secrets but they also plead for me to make it better. Something I can't do. 'I'm sorry for that boy but you aren't him anymore. I loved who he could have been before—'

'Inside, I'm still that boy. You know I am. You know me.'

'I understand you perfectly. You've been a cruel lover just as I've been. And now, I find I've no love left for you.'

'But you're holding onto me. You're nestling close.'

'That's your imagination. You hold me.'

His arms loosen, lower, and I shuffle off him, closer to the fire. The flames are leaping, angry and scarlet, as if demanding an offering. I'll not play with them again. 'You tell me I can't leave—well, I shan't physically leave but I'm gone here.' I tap my head, my nails scratch. 'And here.' I rest my hand over my heart. 'I have no need for you.'

He stares at me blankly.

'I have no need for you,' I shout.

'I think you should leave,' Nessia's voice comes from the doorway.

He nods. I keep my eyes from him as he walks out. With him gone, I can take a long, deep breath. And now my heart is racing. My arms are empty. Somewhere, inside me, still, a trace of my old self wants to chase, to run after him, take his body back, listen to his chuckle. My belly aches for his babies. I remain by the fire.

NOTE FROM THE AUTHOR

Thank you for reading The Waiting Usurper. I hope you enjoyed spending time with my characters. (Is it wrong to hope you had a little cry at the end?) If you have a moment, please leave a review. Reviews enable readers and writers to find each other so your help would be much appreciated.

Want more? You can copy and paste the link below into your Internet browser to access an exclusive story featuring Niah and Aelius.

https://mailchi.mp/e1a7a7012fa7/spark

A.M. VIVIAN

A.M. Vivian is a poet, novelist, beta reader, and blogger. She has wanted to be a writer since she was 11 years old and started writing her first novel. She still has it somewhere. Since then she has studied Creative Writing at Bath Spa University, Cardiff University, and Sussex University. Drawn to the dark and tragic, she's interested in telling stories that explore why we do the things we do, how we lie to ourselves and whether truth really exists. In her spare time she can found soaking up the wails of a guitar at the front row of a gig or stumbling through dark city streets singing to herself and pretending she owns the night.

To stay in contact

You can read her blog at publishordietrying.wordpress.com
Sign up for updates, access exclusive content, and see more information on her books at www.amvivian.com
Connect with her on Twitter and Instagram @A_M_Vivian

Also by A.M. Vivian

The Family Care

Asphodel Meadows

The Waiting Usurper

Sign up at www.amvivian.com for updates

I wasn't always like this. I was different and kind. A good sister. I didn't have bitten nails or scabs on my arms. And I was naive and stupid and someone else. Someone with no secrets worth keeping. I've chosen to be this.

Life used to be simple. Cameron was her brother. Milton knew who she was and she wanted nothing more than to travel and become a film director. Then she discovers the family secret.

She's not Milton Jones and Cameron isn't her brother.

The truth doesn't set you free, especially when the family motto is don't say anything—ever. Don't rock the boat. Don't be anything other than okay, all right, fine. But it isn't as easy as it used to be. Soon her secrets are multiplying out of control. And she's unravelling.

She always could rely on Cameron. Her prince. Her best friend. But he's pulling away and things between them are getting messy. Will he abandon her, too?

The Family Care is a heartbreaking story of forbidden love that explores complex issues of self-esteem, identity, and the darker side of family life.

Asphodel Meadows

I'm that presence following you home. That presence you can feel just behind your right shoulder but can never see. I'm the one who knows everything about you. Everything. Don't believe me? You'll soon see.

My name's Jamie Scott and I'm your narrator, guide, whatever. Time is nothing in Asphodel Meadows: day is day is day and nothing changes— ever. Except for tonight. Tonight is not the same as every other night.

It's seven o'clock, 6 September, and they're here. Finally.

Jamie's a precocious teen with a messiah complex. And he wants vengeance. Skulk along the walkway with him as he spies on his neighbours and he'll show you why he's called four malevolent strangers to the tower block.

You'll meet Kath, recently divorced and sacked after an affair with a student; Paul, a writer who can't write; Jamie's abusive mother, the Fat Beast; Char, a sex worker and her clients; the strangely perfect Lott family; and Sam, the resident drug addict as they struggle with forgiveness, missed connections, and loneliness.

If you're lucky, Jamie'll give you the best seat for the final act.

Inspired by the Biblical story of Sodom, **Asphodel Meadows** is surreal and confronting. It explores the gaps and ambiguities in the original story while questioning notions of sin and redemption.

Made in United States
Orlando, FL
26 October 2022

23869987R00352